The yellowbacks... classics of popular fiction

The yellowjackets or yellowbacks were a great series of bestselling adventure and crime thrillers that had its origins in the mid to late 19th century following on from the 'penny dreadfuls'. They virtually began the mass market revolution of the early 20th century with a clear standard format and imprint/series livery (what would today be called branding). Hodder & Stoughton published the yellowjackets in two main series with series run dates of: 1923-1939 and later 1949-1957.

As the tagline ('where thrillers really began') on the back cover implies, the imprint and series focused on thrillers that were the bestsellers of their time. This current reissue or retro revival if you will, brings back many of these masterpieces, now classics in their own way and extends it further by including key titles from that period that were either great crime or thriller or even general commercial fiction (including sub-genres of noir, horror, gothic, romance, westerns, etc.) influences of their time. There are some perennial favourites and many rarities either lost or not easily available being revived in the current series. Writers and characters ranged from adventure heroes like Bulldog Drummond, Allan Quatermain, Richard Hannay or the Saint through thriller grandmasters Edgar Wallace and E. Phillips Oppenheim, crime and mystery maestros like Patricia Wentworth, G.K. Chesterton, Agatha Christie and the Detection club, to western and swashbucklers like Zane Grey, Max Brand, Captain Blood and even romance or general fiction classics like Hermina Black, Denise Robins, Marie Corelli or Stella Morton. These were books that had storytelling at their heart and always entertained.

The yellowbacks had both hardback (with varying design elements) and paperback (which built the series look) versions with the latter still carrying the imprint 'yellowjacket'. The current reissues pay tribute to both and use an amalgam of elements from both editions while retaining the complete yellow (or 'mustard-plaster') livery with the author's name in blue beveled type with a 'simulated emboss' effect and a white outer 'outline', and the book title in black. These reissues retain the distinctive size of the original mass market paperback and follow the three main category variations—the thrillers (crime, westerns, mystery, adventure) had blue lettering for the author's name, while Romance and softer general fiction had red; and other categories like humour had green.

For more details and a full list of titles visit https://www.hachetteindia.com/home/yellowbacks

THE COMPLETE CONTINENTAL OP

VOLUME II

THE COMPLETE CONTINENTAL OP

Dashiell Hammett, (1894-1961), was an American writer who created the hard-boiled school of detective fiction. Hammett left school at 13 and worked at a variety of low-paying jobs before working eight years as a detective for the Pinkerton agency. He served in World War I, contracted tuberculosis, and spent the immediate postwar years in army hospitals. He began to publish short stories and novelettes in pulp magazines and wrote two novels—*Red Harvest* and *The Dain Curse* (both published in 1929)—before writing *The Maltese Falcon* (1930), generally considered his finest work. It introduced Sam Spade, Hammett's fictional detective creation, played by Humphrey Bogart in the film version directed by John Huston (1941), which became a classic of its genre. He also wrote *The Glass Key* (1931) and *The Thin Man* (1934), which initiated a motion picture and later a television series built around his detecting couple, Nick and Nora Charles. Nora was based on the playwright Lillian Hellman, with whom he formed a romantic alliance in 1930 that lasted until his death. Her *Pentimento* (1973) has an account of their life together.

After 1934, Hammett devoted his time to left-wing political activities and to the defense of civil liberties. He served in World War II as an enlisted man. In 1951, he went to jail for six months because he refused to reveal the names of the contributors to the bail bond fund of the Civil Rights Congress, of which he was a trustee.

THE COMPLETE CONTINENTAL OP

Dashiell Hammett

VOLUME II

Section Three: The Shaw Years

Bonus: The Unfinished Op

Section Four: The Continental Op Novels

hachette

The Complete Continental Op
The Continental Op's first appearance was in 1923. This collection across 2 volumes includes all 37 stories featuring the Op - comprising the 28 short stories, the unfinished story and the eight parts of the two serialized novels, *The Cleansing of Poisonville (Red Harvest)* and *The Dain Curse* as they first appeared in the pulp magazines. See contents pages for detailed publishing history.

1

The texts in these editions in most cases have been reprinted as is, with minimal editorial changes and by and large no bowdlerizing for political correctness; though in some editions, a few words and phrases considered archaic, or those considered offensive now, along with archaic punctuation may have been modified in places to make the text more accessible to today's readers. The narratives, language, beliefs, social mores and/or cultural depictions in these volumes are a reflection of their times and must be viewed as such. They may also contain certain cultural, racial and gender prejudices and stereotypes that may be outdated or clearly wrong then and wrong today; but their removal would be tantamount to claiming these prejudices never existed. The Publisher does not endorse or support those depictions or stereotypes; and these books have been made available for a discerning audience that will read it for entertainment value and a chronicle/record of popular fiction of past times.

Cover design by Priya Singh adapted from the original classic yellowjacket by Hodder & Stoughton.

Cover illustration by Ishan Trivedi.

Series note: Some of the books in the series (unless otherwise credited) may have cover or inside illustrations from the original yellowbacks or early editions, and while full restoration has been attempted, some images may be grainy or faded due to the condition of the original material. The endnotes or bonus material or blurb details may have been sourced from the public domain or free use publications such as Wikipedia and attribution is hereby made also allowing similar free use reproduction from here. Sources requiring further specific attribution may write in and further detailing and/or corrections shall be made in subsequent printings/editions.

Reprint specifications may be subject to change including but not limited to finishes, paper, colour sections.

ISBN: 978-93-5731-235-6

Hachette Book Publishing India Pvt. Ltd.
4th & 5th Floors, Corporate Centre,
Plot No. 94, Sector 44, Gurugram - 122 003, India

Typeset in Electra LT STD 10/12.5 pt by Manipal Technologies Limited, Manipal

Printed and bound in India by Manipal Technologies Limited, Manipal

CONTENTS

1. Section Three: The Shaw Years 1
2. Bonus: The Unfinished Op 311
3. Section Four: The Continental Op Novels 319

Sections One and Two (the Sutton and Cody years) are in Vol 1. Section Three (the Shaw years), the unfinished story and the Novels *Red Harvest* and *The Dain Curse* are in Vol 2.

Section Three: The Shaw years (stories in the Black mask)

(The Shaw years refers to the stewardship of Joseph T. Shaw who was the editor of *Black Mask* from 1926 to 1936)

Publication history

22. 'The Big Knock-Over' (Black Mask, February 1927)
23. '$106,000 Blood Money' (Black Mask, May 1927) (BK) (CS).
24. 'The Main Death' (Black Mask, June 1927)
25. 'This King Business' (Mystery Stories, January 1928)
26. 'Fly Paper' (Black Mask, August 1929)
27. 'The Farewell Murder' (Black Mask, February 1930)
28. 'Death and Company' (Black Mask, November 1930)

Bonus Story: The Unfinished Op

Publication history

'Three Dimes' (Unpublished - posthumously published. Unfinished story that existed only as a partial draft and a set of notes.)

Section Four: The Continental Op Novels: *Red Harvest* and *The Dain Curse*

Publication history

Red Harvest was originally serialized in four installments in *Black Mask*:

Part 1: 'The Cleansing of Poisonville' (Black Mask, November 1927).
Part 2: 'Crime Wanted - Male or Female' (Black Mask, December 1927).
Part 3: 'Dynamite' (Black Mask, January 1928).
Part 4: 'The 19th Murder' (Black Mask, February 1928).

The Dain Curse was originally serialized in four installments in *Black Mask* as below. (The novel of the same title based on the Black Mask serial is composed of three parts, each concerning different mysteries — Part One, The Dains; Part Two, The Temple; and Part Three, Quesada)

Part 1: 'Black Lives' (Black Mask, November 1928)
Part 2: 'The Hollow Temple' (Black Mask, December 1928)
Part 3: 'Black Honeymoon' (Black Mask, January 1929)
Part 4: 'Black Riddle' (Black Mask, February 1929)

Section Three: The Shaw Years

CONTENTS

1. The Big Knock-Over 5
2. $106,000 Blood Money 69
3. The Main Death 121
4. This King Business 148
5. Fly Paper 213
6. The Farewell Murder 253
7. Death and Company 298

1

THE BIG KNOCK-OVER

BLACK MASK, FEBRUARY 1927

Before they actually do it, one is inclined to say it isn't done. But the gang warfare in Illinois, the big mail-truck holdup in Jersey found bandits using airplanes, bombs and machine guns. And now Mr Hammett pictures a daring action that is almost stunning in its scope and effectiveness—yet can anyone be sure that it isn't likely to occur?

I found paddy the Mex in Jean Larrouy's dive.

Paddy—an amiable con man who looked like the King of Spain—showed me his big white teeth in a smile, pushed a chair out for me with one foot, and told the girl who shared his table:

"Nellie, meet the biggest-hearted dick in San Francisco. This little fat guy will do anything for anybody, if only he can send 'em over for life in the end." He turned to me, waving his cigar at the girl: "Nellie Wade, and you can't get anything on her. She don't have to work—her old man's a bootlegger."

She was a slim girl in blue—white skin, long green eyes, short chestnut hair. Her sullen face livened into beauty when she put a hand across the table to me, and we both laughed at Paddy.

"Five years'" she asked.

"Six," I corrected.

"Damn!" said Paddy, grinning and hailing a waiter. "Some day I'm going to fool a sleuth."

So far he had fooled all of them—he had never slept in a hoosegow.

I looked at the girl again. Six years before, this Angel Grace Cardigan had buncoed half a dozen Philadelphia boys out of plenty. Dan Morey and I had nailed her, but none of her victims would go to the bat against her, so she had been turned loose. She was a kid of nineteen then, but already a smooth grifter.

In the middle of the floor one of Larrouy's girls began to sing "Tell Me What You Want and I'll Tell You What You Get." Paddy the Mex tipped a gin bottle over the glasses of gingerale the waiter had brought. We drank and I gave Paddy a piece of paper with a name and address penciled on it.

"Itchy Maker asked me to slip you that," I explained. "I saw him in the Folsom big house yesterday. It's his mother, he says, and he wants you to look her up and see if she wants anything. What he means, I suppose, is that you're to give her his cut from the last trick you and he turned."

"You hurt my feelings," Paddy said, pocketing the paper and bringing out the gin again.

I downed the second gin-gingerale and gathered in my feet, preparing to rise and trot along home. At that moment four of Larrouy's clients came in from the street. Recognition of one of them kept me in my chair. He was tall and slender and all dolled up in what the well-dressed man should wear. Sharp-eyed, sharp-faced, with lips thin as knife-edges under a small pointed mustache—Bluepoint Vance. I wondered what he was doing three thousand miles away from his New York hunting-grounds.

While I wondered I put the back of my head to him, pretending interest in the singer, who was now giving the customers "I Want to Be a Bum." Beyond her, back in a corner, I spotted another familiar face that belonged in another city—Happy Jim Hacker, round and rosy Detroit gunman, twice sentenced to death and twice pardoned.

When I faced front again, Bluepoint Vance and his three companions had come to rest two tables away. His back was to us. I sized up his playmates.

Facing Vance sat a wide-shouldered young giant with red hair, blue eyes and a ruddy face that was good-looking in a tough, savage way. On his left was a shifty-eyed dark girl in a floppy hat. She was talking to Vance. The red-haired giant's attention was all taken by the fourth member of the party, on his right. She deserved it.

She was neither tall nor short, thin nor plump. She wore a black Russian tunic affair, green-trimmed and hung with silver dinguses. A black fur coat was spread over the chair behind her. She was probably twenty. Her eyes were blue, her mouth red, her teeth white, the hairends showing under her black-green-and-silver turban were brown, and she had a nose. Without getting steamed up over the details, she was nice. I said so. Paddy the Mex agreed with a "That's what," and Angel Grace suggested that I go over and tell Red O'Leary I thought her nice.

"Red O'Leary the big bird?" I asked, sliding down in my seat so I could stretch a foot under the table between Paddy and Angel Grace. "Who's his nice girl friend?"

"Nancy Regan, and the other one's Sylvia Yount."

"And the slicker with his back to us?" I probed.

Paddy's foot, hunting the girl's under the table, bumped mine.

"Don't kick me, Paddy," I pleaded. "I'll be good. Anyway, I'm not going to stay here to be bruised. I'm going home."

I swapped so-longs with them and moved toward the street, keeping my back to Bluepoint Vance.

At the door I had to step aside to let two men come in. Both knew me, but neither gave me a tumble—Sheeny Holmes (not the old-timer who staged the Moose Jaw looting back in the buggyriding days) and Denny Burke, Baltimore's King of Frog Island. A good pair—neither of them would think of taking a life unless assured of profit and political protection.

Outside, I turned down toward Kearny Street, strolling along, thinking that Larrouy's joint had been full of crooks this one night, and that there seemed to be more than a sprinkling of prominent visitors in our midst. A shadow in a doorway interrupted my brain-work.

The shadow said, "Ps-s-s-s! Ps-s-s-s!"

Stopping, I examined the shadow until I saw it was Beno, a hophead newsie who had given me a tip now and then in the past—some good, some phoney.

"I'm sleepy," I growled as I joined Beno and his arm-load of newspapers in the doorway, "and I've heard the story about the Mormon who stuttered, so if that's what's on your mind, say so, and I'll keep going."

"I don't know nothin' about no Mormons," he protested, "but I know somethin' else."

"Well?"

"'S all right for you to say 'Well,' but what I want to know is, what am I gonna get out of it?"

"Flop in the nice doorway and go shut-eye," I advised him, moving toward the street again. "You'll be all right when you wake up."

"Hey! Listen, I got somethin' for you. Hones' to Gawd!"

"Well?"

"Listen!" He came close, whispering. "There's a caper rigged for the Seaman's National. I don't know what's the racket, but it's real. Hones' to Gawd! I ain't stringin' you. I can't give you no monickers. You know I would if I knowed 'em. Hones' to Gawd! Gimme ten bucks. It's worth that to you, ain't it? This is straight dope—hones' to Gawd!"

"Yeah, straight from the nose-candy!"

"No! Hones' to Gawd! I—"

"What *is* the caper, then?"

"I don't know. All I got was that the Seaman's is gonna be nicked. Hones' to—"

"Where'd you get it?"

Beno shook his head. I put a silver dollar in his hand.

"Get another shot and think up the rest of it," I told him, "and if it's amusing enough I'll give you the other nine bucks."

I walked on down to the corner, screwing up my forehead over Beno's tale. By itself, it sounded like what it probably was—a yarn designed to get a dollar out of a trusting gumshoe. But it wasn't altogether by itself. Larrouy's—just one drum in a city that had a number—had been heavy with grifters who were threats against life and property. It was worth a look-see, especially since the insurance company covering the Seaman's National Bank was a Continental Detective Agency client.

Around the corner, twenty feet or so along Kearny Street, I stopped.

From the street I had just quit came two bangs—the reports of a heavy pistol. I went back the way I had come. As I rounded the corner I saw men gathering in a group up the street. A young Armenian—a dapper boy of nineteen or twenty—passed me, going the other way, sauntering along, hands in pockets, softly whistling "Broken-hearted Sue."

I joined the group—now becoming a crowd—around Beno. Beno was dead, blood from two holes in his chest staining the crumpled newspapers under him.

I went up to Larrouy's and looked in. Red O'Leary, Bluepoint Vance, Nancy Regan, Sylvia Yount, Paddy the Mex, Angel Grace, Denny Burke, Sheeny Holmes, Happy Jim Hacker—not one of them was there.

Returning to Beno's vicinity, I loitered with my back to a wall while the police arrived, asked questions, learned nothing, found no witnesses, and departed, taking what was left of the newsie with them.

I went home and to bed.

II

In the morning I spent an hour in the agency fileroom, digging through the gallery and records. We didn't have anything on Red O'Leary, Denny Burke, Nancy Regan, Sylvia Yount, and only some guesses on Paddy the Mex. Nor were there any open jobs definitely chalked against Angel Grace, Bluepoint Vance, Sheeny Holmes and Happy Jim Hacker, but their photos were there. At ten o'clock—bank opening time—I set out for the Seaman's National, carrying these photos and Beno's tip.

The Continental Detective Agency's San Francisco office is located in a Market Street office building. The Seaman's National Bank occupies the ground floor of a tall gray building in Montgomery Street, San Francisco's financial center. Ordinarily, since I don't like even seven blocks of unnecessary walking, I would have taken a street car. But there was some sort of traffic jam on Market Street, so I set out afoot, turning off along Grant Avenue.

A few blocks of walking, and I began to see that something was wrong with the part of town I was heading for. Noises for one thing—roaring, rattling, explosive noises. At Sutter Street a man passed me, holding his face with both hands and groaning as he tried to push a dislocated jaw back in place. His cheek was scraped red.

I went down Sutter Street. Traffic was in a tangle that reached to Montgomery Street. Excited, bare-headed men were running around. The explosive noises were clearer. An automobile full of policemen went down past me, going as fast as traffic would let it. An ambulance came up the street, clanging its gong, taking to the sidewalks where the traffic tangle was worst.

I crossed Kearny Street on the trot. Down the other side of the street two patrolmen were running. One had his gun out. The explosive noises were a drumming chorus ahead.

Rounding into Montgomery Street, I found few sightseers ahead of me. The middle of the street was filled with trucks, touring cars, taxis—deserted there. Up in the next block—between Bush and Pine Streets—hell was on a holiday.

The holiday spirit was gayest in the middle of the block, where the Seaman's National Bank and the Golden Gate Trust Company faced each other across the street.

For the next six hours I was busier than a flea on a fat woman.

III

Late that afternoon I took a recess from blood-hounding and went up to the office for a pow-wow with the Old Alan. He was leaning back in his chair, staring out the window, tapping on his desk with the customary long yellow pencil.

A tall, plump man in his seventies, this boss of mine, with a white-mustached, baby-pink grandfatherly face, mild blue eyes behind rimless spectacles, and no more warmth in him than a hangman's rope. Fifty years of crook-hunting for the Continental had emptied him of everything except brains and a soft-spoken, gently smiling shell of politeness that was the same whether things went good or bad—and meant as little at one time as another. We who worked under him were proud of his cold-bloodedness. We used to boast that he could spit icicles in July, and we called him Pontius Pilate among ourselves, because he smiled politely when he sent us out to be crucified on suicidal jobs.

He turned from the window as I came in, nodded me to a chair, and smoothed his mustache with the pencil. On his desk the afternoon papers screamed the news of the Seaman's National Bank and Golden Gate Trust Company double-looting in five colors.

"What is the situation?" he asked, as one would ask about the weather.

"The situation is a pip," I told him. "There were a hundred and fifty crooks in the push if there was one. I saw a hundred myself—or think I did—and there were slews of them that I didn't see—planted where they could jump out and bite when fresh teeth were needed. They bit, too. They bushwacked the police and made a merry wreck out of 'em—going and coming. They hit the two banks at ten sharp—took over the whole block—chased away the reasonable people—dropped the others. The actual looting was duck soup to a mob of that size. Twenty or thirty of 'em to each of the banks while the others held the street. Nothing to it but wrap up the spoils and take 'em home.

"There's a highly indignant business men's meeting down there now—wild-eyed stockbrokers up on their hind legs yelling for the chief of police's heart's blood. The police didn't do any miracles, that's a cinch, but no police department is equipped to handle a trick of that size—no matter how well they think they are. The whole thing lasted less than twenty minutes. There were, say, a hundred and fifty thugs in *on it*, loaded for bear, every play mapped to the inch. How are you going to get enough coppers down there, size up the racket, plan your battle, and put it over in that little time? It's easy enough to say the police should look ahead—should have a dose for every emergency—but these same birds who are yelling, 'Rotten,' down there now would be the first to squawk, 'Robbery,' if their taxes were boosted a couple of cents to buy more policemen and equipment.

"But the police fell down—there's no question about that—and there will be a lot of beefy necks feel the ax. The armored cars were no good, the grenading was about fifty-fifty, since the bandits knew how to play that game, too. But the real disgrace of the party was the police machine-guns. The bankers and brokers are saying they were fixed. Whether they were deliberately tampered with, or were only carelessly taken care of, is anybody's guess, but only one of the damned things would shoot, and it not very well.

"The getaway was north on Montgomery to Columbus. Along Columbus the parade melted, a few cars at a time, into side streets. The police ran into an ambush between Washington and Jackson, and by the time they had shot their way through it the bandit cars had scattered all over the city. A lot of 'em have been picked up since then—empty.

"All the returns aren't in yet, but right now the score stands something like this: The haul will run God only knows how far into the millions—easily the richest pickings ever got with civilian guns. Sixteen coppers were knocked off, and three times that many wounded. Twelve innocent spectators, bank clerks, and the like, were killed and about as many banged around. There are two dead and five shot-ups who might be either thugs or spectators that got too close. The bandits lost seven dead that we know of, and thirty-one prisoners, most of them bleeding somewhere.

"One of the dead was Eat Boy Clarke. Remember him? He shot his way out of a Des Moines courtroom three or four years ago. Well, in his pocket we found a piece of paper, a map of Montgomery Street between Pine and Bush, the block of the looting. On the back of the map were typed instructions, telling him exactly what to do and when to do it. An X on the map showed him where he was to park the car in which he arrived with his seven men, and there was a circle where he was to stand with them, keeping an eye on things in general and on the windows and roofs of the buildings across the street in particular. Figures 1, 2, 3, 4, 5, 6, 7, 8 on the map marked doorways, steps, a deep window, and so on, that were to be used for shelter if shots had to be traded with those windows and roofs. Clarke was to pay no attention to the Bush Street end of the block, but if the police charged the Pine Street end he was to move his men up there, distributing them among points marked a, b, c, d, e, f, g, and h. (His body was found on the spot marked a.) Every five minutes during the looting he was to send a man to an automobile standing in the street at a point marked on the map with a star, to see if there were any new instructions. He was to tell his men that if he were shot down one of them must report to the car, and a new leader would be given them. When the signal for the getaway was given, he was to send one of his men to the car in which he had come. If it was still in commission, this man was to drive it, not passing the car ahead of him. If it was out of whack, the man was to report to the star-marked car for instructions how to get a new one. I suppose they counted on finding enough parked cars to take care of this end. While Clarke waited for his car he and his men were to throw as much lead as possible at every target in their district, and none of them was to board the car until it came abreast of them. Then they were to drive out Montgomery to Columbus to—blank.

"Get that?" I asked. "Here are a hundred and fifty gunmen, split into groups under group-leaders, with maps and schedules showing what each man is to do, showing the fire-plug he's to kneel behind, the brick he's to stand on, where he's to spit—

everything but the name and address of the policeman he's to shoot! It's just as well Beno couldn't give me the details—I'd have written it off as a hop-head's dream!"

"Very interesting," the Old Man said, smiling blandly.

"The Fat Boy's was the only timetable we found," I went on with my history. "I saw a few friends among the killed and caught, and the police are still identifying others. Some are local talent, but most of 'em seem to be imported stock. Detroit, Chi, New York, St. Louis, Denver, Portland, L.A., Philly, Baltimore—all seem to have sent delegates. As soon as the police get through identifying them I'll make out a list.

"Of those who weren't caught, Bluepoint Vance seems to be the main squeeze. He was in the car that directed operations. I don't know who else was there with him. The Shivering Kid was in on the festivities, and I think Alphabet Shorty McCoy, though I didn't get a good look at him. Sergeant Bender told me he spotted Toots Saida and Darby M'Laughlin in the push, and Morgan saw the Did-and-Dat Kid. That's a good cross-section of the layout—gunmen, swindlers, hijackers from all over Rand-McNally.

"The Hall of Justice has been a slaughterhouse all afternoon. The police haven't killed any of their guests—none that I know of—but they're sure-God making believers out of them. Newspaper writers who like to sob over what they call the third degree should be down there now. After being knocked around a bit, some of the guests have talked. But the hell of it is they don't know a whole lot. They know some names—Denny Burke, Toby the Lugs, Old Pete Best, Fat Boy Clarke and Paddy the Mex were named—and that helps some, but all the smacking power in the police force arm can't bring out anything else.

"The racket seems to have been organized like this: Denny Burke, for instance, is known as a shifty worker in Baltimore. Well, Denny talks to eight or ten likely boys, one at a time.

'How'd you like to pick up a piece of change out on the Coast?' he asks them. 'Doing what?' the candidate wants to know. 'Doing what you're told,' the King of Frog Island says. 'You know me. I'm telling you this is the fattest picking ever rigged, a kick in the pants to go through—air-tight. Everybody in on it will come home lousy with cush—and they'll all come home if they don't dog it. That's all I'm spilling. If you don't like it—forget it.'

"And these birds did know Denny, and if he said the job was good that was enough for them. So they put in with him. He told them nothing. He saw that they had guns, gave 'em each a ticket to San Francisco and twenty bucks, and told them where to meet him here. Last night he collected them and told them they went to work this morning. By that time they had moved around the town enough to see that it was bubbling over with visiting talent, including such moguls as Toots Saida, Bluepoint Vance and the Shivering Kid. So this morning they went forth eagerly with the King of Frog Island at their head to do their stuff.

"The other talkers tell varieties of the same tale. The police found room in their crowded jail to stick in a few stool-pigeons. Since few of the bandits knew very many of the others, the stools had an easy time of it, but the only thing they could add to what we've got is that the prisoners are looking for a wholesale delivery tonight. They seem to think their mob will crash the prison and turn 'em loose. That's probably a lot of chewing-gum, but anyway this time the police will be ready.

"That's the situation as it stands now. The police are sweeping the streets, picking up everybody who needs a shave or can't show a certificate of attendance signed by his parson, with special attention to outward bound trains, boats and automobiles. I sent Jack Counihan and Dick Foley down North Beach way to play the joints and see if they can pick up anything."

"Do you think Bluepoint Vance was the actual directing intelligence in this robbery?" the Old Man asked.

"I hope so—we know him."

The Old Man turned his chair so his mild eyes could stare out the window again, and he tapped his desk reflectively with the pencil.

"I'm afraid not," he said in a gently apologetic tone. "Vance is a shrewd, resourceful and determined criminal, but his weakness is one common to his type. His abilities are all for present action and not for planning ahead. He has executed some large operations, but I've always thought I saw in them some other mind at work behind him."

I couldn't quarrel with that. If the Old Man said something was so, then it probably was, because he was one of these cautious babies who'll look out of the window at a cloudburst and say, "It seems to be raining," on the off-chance that somebody's pouring water off the roof.

"And who is this arch-gonif?" I asked.

"You'll probably know that before I do," he said, smiling benignantly.

IV

I went back to the Hall and helped boil more prisoners in oil until around eight o'clock, when my appetite reminded me I hadn't eaten since breakfast. I attended to that, and then turned down toward Larrouy's, ambling along leisurely, so the exercise wouldn't interfere with my digestion. I spent three-quarters of an hour in Larrouy's, and didn't see anybody who interested me especially. A few gents I knew were present, but they weren't anxious to associate with me—it's not always healthy in criminal circles to be seen wagging your chin with a sleuth right after a job has been turned.

Not getting anything there, I moved up the street to Wop Healy's—another hole. My reception was the same here—I was given a table and let alone. Healy's orchestra was giving "Don't You Cheat" all they had, while those customers who felt athletic were romping it out on the dance-floor. One of the dancers was Jack Counihan, his arms full of a big olive-skinned girl with a pleasant, thick-featured, stupid face.

Jack was a tall, slender lad of twenty-three or four who had drifted into the Continental's employ a few months before. It was the first job he'd ever had, and he wouldn't have had it if his father hadn't insisted that if sonny wanted to keep his fingers in the family till he'd have to get over the notion that squeezing through a college graduation was enough work for one lifetime. So Jack came to the agency. He thought gumshoeing would be fun. In spite of the fact that he'd rather catch the wrong man than wear the wrong necktie, he was a promising young thief catcher A likable youngster, well-muscled for all his slimness, smooth-haired, with a gentleman's face and a gentleman's manner, nervy, quick with head and hands, full of the don't-give-a-damn gaiety that belonged to his youthfulness. He was jingle-brained, of course, and needed holding, but I would rather work with him than with a lot of old-timers I knew.

Half an hour passed with nothing to interest me.

Then a boy came into Healy's from the street—a small kid, gaudily dressed, very pressed in the pants-legs, very shiny in the shoes, with an impudent sallow face of pronounced cast. This was the boy I had seen sauntering down Broadway a moment after Beno had been rubbed out.

Leaning back in my chair so that a woman's wide-hatted head was between us, I watched the young Armenian wind between tables to one in a far corner, where three men sat. He spoke to them—off-hand—perhaps a dozen words—and moved away to another table where a snub-nosed, black-haired man sat alone. The boy dropped into the chair facing snub-nose, spoke a few words, sneered at snub-nose's questions, and ordered a drink. When his glass was empty he crossed the room to speak to a lean, buzzard-faced man, and then went out of Healy's.

I followed him out, passing the table where Jack sat with the girl, catching his eye. Outside, I saw the young Armenian half a block away. Jack Counihan caught up with me, passed me. With a Fatima in my mouth I called to him:

"Got a match, brother?"

While I lighted my cigarette with a match from the box he gave me I spoke behind my hands:

"The goose in the glad rags—tail him. I'll string behind you. I don't know him, but if he blipped Beno off for talking to me last night, he knows me. On his heels!"

Jack pocketed his matches and went after the boy. I gave Jack a lead and then followed him. And then an interesting thing happened.

The street was fairly well filled with people, mostly men, some walking, some loafing on corners and in front of soft-drink parlors. As the young Armenian reached the corner of an alley where there was a light, two men came up and spoke to him, moving a little apart so that he was between them. The boy would have kept walking apparently paying no attention to them, but one checked him by stretching an arm out in front of him. The other man took his right hand out of his pocket and flourished it in the boy's face so that the nickel-plated knuckles on it twinkled in the light. The boy ducked swiftly under threatening hand and outstretched arm, and went on across the alley, walking, and not even looking over his shoulder at the two men who were now closing on his back.

Just before they reached him another reached them—a broad-backed, long-armed, ape-built man I had not seen before. His gorilla's paws went out together. Each caught a man. By the napes of their necks he yanked them away from the boy's back, shook them till their hats fell off, smacked their skulls together with a crack that was like a broom-handle breaking, and dragged their rag-limp bodies out of sight up the alley. While this was happening the boy walked jauntily down the street, without a backward glance.

When the skull-cracker came out of the alley I saw his face in the light—a dark-skinned, heavily-lined face, broad and flat, with jaw muscles bulging like abscesses under his ears. He spit, hitched his pants, and swaggered down the street after the boy.

The boy went into Larrouy's. The skull-cracker followed him in. The boy came out, and in his rear—perhaps twenty feet behind—the skull-cracker rolled. Jack had tailed them into Larrouy's while I had held up the outside.

"Still carrying messages?" I asked.

"Yes. He spoke to five men in there. He's got plenty of body-guard, hasn't he?"

"Yeah," I agreed. "And you be damned careful you don't get between them. If they split, I'll shadow the skull-cracker, you keep the goose."

We separated and moved after our game. They took us to all the hangouts in San Francisco, to cabarets, grease-joints, pool-rooms, saloons, flop-houses, hook-shops,gambling-joints and what have you. Everywhere the kid found men to speak his dozen words to, and between calls, he found them on street-corners.

I would have liked to get behind some of these birds, but I didn't want to leave Jack alone with the boy and his bodyguard—they seemed to mean too much. And I couldn't stick Jack on one of the others, because it wasn't safe for me to hang too close to the Armenian boy. So we played the game as we had started it, shadowing our pair from hole to hole, while night got on toward morning.

It was a few minutes past midnight when they came out of a small hotel up on Kearny Street, and for the first time since we had seen them they walked together, side by side, up to Green

Street, where they turned east along the side of Telegraph Hill. Half a block of this, and they climbed the front steps of a ramshackle furnished-room house and disappeared inside. I joined Jack Counihan on the corner where he had stopped.

"The greetings have all been delivered," I guessed, "or he wouldn't have called in his bodyguard. If there's nothing stirring within the next half hour I'm going to beat it. You'll have to take a plant on the joint till morning."

Twenty minutes later the skull-cracker came out of the house and walked down the street.

"I'll take him," I said. "You stick to the other baby."

The skull-cracker took ten or twelve steps from the house and stopped. He looked back at the house, raising his face to look at the upper storeys. Then Jack and I could hear what had stopped him. Up in the house a man was screaming. It wasn't much of a scream in volume. Even now; when it had increased in strength, it barely reached our ears. But in it—in that one wailing voice—everything that fears death seemed to cry out its fear. I heard Jack's teeth click. I've got horny skin all over what's left of my soul, but just the same my forehead twitched. The scream was so damned weak for what it said.

The skull-cracker moved. Five gliding strides carried him back to the house. He didn't touch one of the six or seven front steps. He went from pavement to vestibule in a spring no monkey could have beaten for swiftness, ease or silence. One minute, two minutes, three minutes, and the screaming stopped. Three more minutes and the skull-cracker was leaving the house again. He paused on the sidewalk to spit and hitch his pants. Then he swaggered off down the street.

"He's your meat, Jack," I said. "I'm going to call on the boy. He won't recognize me now."

V

The street-door of the rooming-house was not only unlocked but wide open. I went through it into a hallway, where a dim light burning upstairs outlined a flight of steps. I climbed them and turned toward the front of the house. The scream had come from the front—either this floor or the third. There was a fair likelihood of the skull-cracker having left the room-door unlocked, just as he had not paused to close the street-door.

I had no luck on the second floor, but the third knob I cautiously tried on the third floor turned in my hand and let its door edge back from the frame. In front of this crack I waited a moment, listening to nothing but a throbbing snore somewhere far down the hallway. I put a palm against the door and eased it open another foot. No sound. The room was black as an honest politician's prospects. I slid my hand across the frame, across a few inches of wallpaper, found a light button, pressed it. Two globes in the center of the room threw their weak yellow light on the shabby room and on the young Armenian who lay dead across the bed.

I went into the room, closed the door and stepped over to the bed. The boy's eyes were wide and bulging. One of his temples was bruised. His throat gaped with a red slit that ran actually from ear to ear. Around the slit, in the few spots not washed red, his thin neck showed dark bruises. The skull-cracker had dropped the boy with a poke in the temple and had choked him until he thought him dead. But the kid had revived enough to scream—not enough to keep from screaming. The skull-cracker had returned to finish the job with a knife. Three streaks on the bed-clothes showed where the knife had been cleaned.

The lining of the boy's pockets stuck out. The skull-cracker had turned them out. I went through his clothes, but with no better luck than I expected—the killer had taken everything.

The room gave me nothing—a few clothes, but not a thing out of which information could be squeezed.

My prying done, I stood in the center of the floor scratching my chin and considering. In the hall a floor-board creaked. Three backward steps on my rubber heels put me in the musty closet, dragging the door all but half an inch shut behind me.

Knuckles rattled on the room door as I slid my gun off my hip. The knuckles rattled again and a feminine voice said, "Kid, oh, Kid!" Neither knuckles nor voice was loud. The lock clicked as the knob was turned. The door opened and framed the shifty-eyed girl who had been called Sylvia Yount by Angel Grace.

Her eyes lost their shiftiness for surprise when they settled on the boy.

"Holy hell!" she gasped, and was gone.

I was half out of the closet when I heard her tip-toeing back. In my hole again, I waited, my eye to the crack. She came in swiftly, closed the door silently, and went to lean over the dead boy. Her hands moved over him, exploring the pockets whose linings I had put back in place.

"Damn such luck!" she said aloud when the unprofitable frisking was over, and went out of the house.

I gave her time to reach the sidewalk. She was headed toward Kearny Street when I left the house. I shadowed her down Kearny to Broadway, up Broadway to Larrouy's. Larrouy's was busy, especially near the door, with customers going and coming. I was within five feet of the girl when she stopped a waiter and asked, in a whisper that was excited enough to carry, "Is Red here?"

The waiter shook his head.

"Ain't been in tonight."

The girl went out of the dive, hurrying along on clicking heels to a hotel in Stockton Street.

While I looked through the glass front, she went to the desk and spoke to the clerk. He shook his head. She spoke again and he gave her paper and envelope, on which she scribbled with the pen beside the register. Before I had to leave for a safer position from which to cover her exit, I saw which pigeon-hole the note went into.

From the hotel the girl went by street-car to Market and Powell Streets, and then walked up Powell to O'Farrell, where a fat-faced young man in gray overcoat and gray hat left the curb to link arms with her and lead her to a taxi stand up O'Farrell Street. I let them go, making a note of the taxi number—the fat-faced man looked more like a customer than a pal.

It was a little shy of two in the morning when I turned back into Market Street and went up to the office. Fiske, who holds down the agency at night, said Jack Counihan had not reported, nothing else had come in. I told him to rouse me an operative, and in ten or fifteen minutes he succeeded in getting Mickey Linehan out of bed and on the wire.

"Listen, Mickey," I said, "I've got the nicest corner picked out for you to stand on the rest of the night. So pin on your diapers and toddle down there, will you?"

In between his grumbling and cursing I gave him the name and number of the Stockton Street hotel, described Red O'Leary, and told him which pigeon-hole the note had been put in.

"It mightn't be Red's home, but the chance is worth covering," I wound up. "If you pick him up, try not to lose him before I can get somebody down there to take him off your hands."

I hung up during the outburst of profanity this insult brought.

The Hall of Justice was busy when I reached it, though nobody had tried to shake the upstairs prison loose yet. Fresh lots of suspicious characters were being brought in every few minutes. Policemen in and out of uniform were everywhere. The detective bureau was a bee-hive.

Trading information with the police detectives, I told them about the Armenian boy. We were making up a party to visit the remains when the captain's door opened and Lieutenant Duff came into the assembly room.

"*Allez! Oop!*' he said, pointing a thick finger at O'Gar, Tully, Reeder, Hunt and me. "There's a thing worth looking at in Fillmore."

We followed him out to an automobile.

VI

A gray frame house in Fillmore Street was our destination. A lot of people stood in the street looking at the house. A police-wagon stood in front of it, and police uniforms were indoors and out.

A red-mustached corporal saluted Duff and led us into the house, explaining as we went, "'Twas the neighbors give us the rumble, complaining of the fighting, and when we got here, faith, there weren't no fight left in nobody."

All the house held was fourteen dead men.

Eleven of them had been poisoned—overdoses of knockout drops in their booze, the doctors said. The other three had been shot, at intervals along the hall. From the looks of the remains, they had drunk a toast—a loaded one—and those who hadn't drunk, whether because of temperance or suspicious natures, had been gunned as they tried to get away.

The identity of the bodies gave us an idea of what their toast had been. They were all thieves—they had drunk their poison to the day's looting.

We didn't know all the dead men then, but all of us knew some of them, and the records told us who the others were later. The completed list read like *Who's Who in Crookdom.*

There was the Dis-and-Dat Kid, who had crushed out of Leavenworth only two months before; Sheeny Holmes; Snohomish Whitey, supposed to have died a hero in France in 1919; L. A. Slim, from Denver, sockless and underwearless as usual, with a thousand-dollar bill sewed in each shoulder of his coat; Spider Girrucci wearing a steel-mesh vest under his shirt and a scar from crown to chin where his brother had carved him years ago; Old Pete Best, once a congressman; Nigger Vojan, who once won $75,000 in a Chicago crap-game—*Abacadbra* tattooed on him in three places; Alphabet Shorty McCoy; Tom Brooks, Alphabet Shorty's brother-in-law, who invented the Richmond *razzle-dazzle*, and bought three hotels with the profits; Red Cudahy, who stuck up a Union Pacific train in 1924; Denny Burke; Bull McGonickle, still pale from fifteen years in Joliet; Toby the Lugs, Bull's running-mate, who used to brag about picking President Wilson's pocket in a Washington vaudeville theater; and Paddy the Mex.

Duff looked them over and whistled.

"A few more tricks like this," he said, "and we'll all be out of jobs. There won't be any grifters left to protect the taxpayers from."

"I'm glad you like it," I told him. "Me—I'd hate like hell to be a San Francisco copper the next few days."

"Why especially?"

"Look at this—one grand piece of double-crossing. This village of ours is full of mean lads who are waiting right now for these stiffs to bring 'em their cut of the stick-up. What do you think's going to happen when the word gets out that there's not going to be any gravy for the mob? There are going to be a hundred and more stranded thugs busy raising getaway dough. There'll be three burglaries to a block and a stick-up to every corner until the carfare's raised. God bless you, my son, you're going to sweat for your wages!"

Duff shrugged his thick shoulders and stepped over bodies to get to the telephone. When he was through I called the agency.

"Jack Counihan called a couple of minutes ago," Fiske told me, and gave me an Army Street address. "He says he put his man in there, with company."

I phoned for a taxi, and then told Duff, "I'm going to run out for a while. I'll give you a ring here if there's anything to the angle, or if there isn't. You'll wait?"

"If you're not too long."

I got rid of my taxicab two blocks from the address Fiske had given me, and walked down Army Street to find Jack Counihan planted on a dark corner.

"I got a bad break," was what he welcomed me with. "While I was phoning from the lunch-room up the street some of my people ran out on me."

"Yeah? What's the dope?"

"Well, after that apey chap left the Green Street house he trolleyed to a house in Fillmore Street, and—"

"What number?"

The number Jack gave was that of the death-house I had just left.

"In the next ten or fifteen minutes just about that many other chaps went into the same house. Most of them came afoot, singly or in pairs. Then two cars came up together, with nine men in them—I counted them. They went into the house, leaving their machines in front. A taxi came past a little later, and I stopped it, in case my chap should motor away.

"Nothing happened for at least half an hour after the nine chaps went in. Then everybody in the house seemed to become demonstrative—there was a quantity of yelling and shooting. It lasted long enough to awaken the whole neighborhood. When it stopped, ten men—I counted them—ran out of the house, got into the two cars, and drove away. My man was one of them.

"My faithful taxi and I cried *Yoicks* after them, and they brought us here, going into that house down the street in front of which one of their motors still stands. After half an hour or so I thought I'd better report, so, leaving my taxi around the corner—where it's still running up expenses—I went up to yon all-night caravansary and phoned Fiske. And when I came back, one of the cars was gone—and I, woe is me!—don't know who went with it. Am I rotten?"

"Sure! You should have taken their cars along to the phone with you. Watch the one that's left while I collect a strong-arm squad."

I went up to the lunch-room and phoned Duff, telling him where I was, and:

"If you bring your gang along maybe there'll be profit in it. A couple of carloads of folks who were in Fillmore Street and didn't stay there came here, and part of 'em may still be here, if you make it sudden."

Duff brought his four detectives and a dozen uniformed men with him. We hit the house front and back. No time was wasted ringing the bell. We simply tore down the doors and went in. Everything inside was black until flashlights lit it up. There was no resistance. Ordinarily the six men we found in there would have damned near ruined us in spite of our outnumbering them. But they were too dead for that.

We looked at one another sort of open-mouthed.

"This is getting monotonous," Duff complained, biting off a hunk of tobacco. "Everybody's work is pretty much the same thing over and over, but I'm tired of walking into roomfuls of butchered crooks."

The catalog here had fewer names than the other, but they were bigger names. The Shivering Kid was here—nobody would collect all the reward money piled up on him now; Darby M'Laughlin, his horn-rimmed glasses crooked on his nose, ten thousand dollars' worth of diamonds on fingers and tie; Happy Jim Hacker; Donkey Marr, the last of the bow-legged Marrs, killers all, father and five sons; Toots Saida, the strongest man in crookdom, who had once picked up and run away with two Savannah coppers to whom he was handcuffed; and Rumdum Smith, who killed Lefty Read in Chi in 1916—a rosary wrapped around his left wrist.

No gentlemanly poisoning here—these boys had been mowed down with a .30-30 rifle fitted with a clumsy but effective home-made silencer. The rifle lay on the kitchen table. A door connected the kitchen with the dining-room. Directly opposite that door, double doors—wide open—opened into the room in which the dead thieves lay. They were all close to the front wall, lying as if they had been lined up against the wall to be knocked off.

The gray-papered wall was spattered with blood, punctured with holes where a couple of bullets had gone all the way through. Jack Counihan's young eyes picked out a stain on the paper that wasn't accidental. It was close to the floor, beside the Shivering Kid, and the Kid's right hand was stained with blood. He had written on the wall before he died—with fingers dipped in his own and Toots Saida's blood. The letters in the words showed breaks and gaps where his fingers had run dry, and the letters were crooked and straggly, because he must have written them in the dark.

By filling in the gaps, allowing for the kinks, and guessing where there weren't any indications to guide us, we got two words: *Big Flora*.

"They don't mean anything to me," Duff said, "but it's a name and most of the names we have belong to dead men now, so it's time we were adding to our list."

"What do you make of it?" asked bullet-headed O'Gar, detective-sergeant in the Homicide Detail, looking at the bodies. "Their pals got the drop on them, lined them against the wall, and the sharpshooter in the kitchen shot 'em down—bing-bing-bing-bing-bing-bing?"

"It reads that way," the rest of us agreed.

"Ten of 'em came here from Fillmore Street," I said. "Six stayed here. Four went to another house—where part of 'em are now cutting down the other part. All that's necessary is to trail the corpses from house to house until there's only one man left—and he's bound to play it through by croaking himself, leaving the loot to be recovered in the original packages. I hope you folks don't have to stay up all night to find the remains of that last thug. Come on, Jack, let's go home for some sleep."

VII

It was exactly 5 A.M. when I separated the sheets and crawled into my bed. I was asleep before the last draw of smoke from my good-night Fatima was out of my lungs. The telephone woke me at 5:15.

Fiske was talking: "Mickey Linehan just phoned that your Red O'Leary came home to roost half an hour ago."

"Have him booked," I said, and was asleep again by 5:17.

With the help of the alarm clock I rolled out of bed at nine, breakfasted, and went down to the detective bureau to see how the police had made out with the redhead. Not so good.

"He's got us stopped," the captain told me. "He's got alibis for the time of the looting and for last night's doings. And we can't even vag the son-of-a-gun. He's got means of support. He's salesman for Humperdickel's Universal Encyclopaediac Dictionary of Useful and Valuable Knowledge, or something like it. He started peddling these pamphlets the day before the knock-over, and at the time it was happening he was ringing doorbells and asking folks to buy his durned books. Anyway, he's got three witnesses that say so. Last night, he was in a hotel from eleven to four-thirty this morning, playing cards, and he's got witnesses. We didn't find a durned thing on him or in his room."

I borrowed the captain's phone to call Jack Counihan's house.

"Could you identify any of the men you saw in the cars last night?" I asked when he had been stirred out of bed.

"No. It was dark and they moved too fast. I could barely make sure of my chap."

"Can't, huh?" the captain said. "Well, I can hold him twenty-four hours without laying charges, and I'll do that, but I'll have to spring him then unless you can dig up something."

"Suppose you turn him loose now," I suggested after thinking through my cigarette for a few minutes. "He's got himself all alibied up, so there's no reason why he should hide out on us. We'll let him alone all day—give him time to make sure he isn't being tailed—and then we'll get behind him tonight and stay behind him. Any dope on Big Flora?"

"No. That kid that was killed in Green Street was Bernie Bernheimer, alias the Motsa Kid. I guess he was a dip—he ran with dips—but he wasn't very—"

The buzz of the phone interrupted him. He said, "Hello, yes," and "Just a minute," into the instrument, and slid it across the desk to me.

A feminine voice: "This is Grace Cardigan. I called your agency and they told me where to get you. I've got to see you. Can you meet me now?"

"Where are you?"

"In the telephone station on Powell Street."

"I'll be there in fifteen minutes," I said.

Calling the agency, I got hold of Dick Foley and asked him to meet me at Ellis and Market right away. Then I gave the captain back his phone, said "See you later," and went uptown to keep my dates.

Dick Foley was on his corner when I got there. He was a swarthy little Canadian who stood nearly five feet in his high-heeled shoes, weighed a hundred pounds minus, talked like a Scotchman's telegram, and could have shadowed a drop of salt water from the Golden Gate to Hong Kong without ever losing sight of it.

"You know Angel Grace Cardigan?" I asked him.

He saved a word by shaking his head, no.

"I'm going to meet her in the telephone station. When I'm through, stay behind her. She's smart, and she'll be looking for you, so it won't be duck soup, but do what you can."

Dick's mouth went down at the corners and one of his rare long-winded streaks hit him.

"Harder they look, easier they are," he said.

He trailed along behind me while I went up to the station. Angel Grace was standing in the doorway. Her face was more sullen than I had ever seen it, and therefore less beautiful—except her green eyes, which held too much fire for sullenness. A rolled newspaper was in one of her hands. She neither spoke, smiled nor nodded.

"We'll go to Charley's, where we can talk," I said, guiding her down past Dick Foley.

Not a murmur did I get out of her until we were seated cross-table in the restaurant booth, and the waiter had gone off with our orders. Then she spread the newspaper out on the table with shaking hands.

"Is this on the level?" she demanded.

I looked at the story her shaking finger tapped—an account of the Fillmore and Army Street findings, but a cagey account. A glance showed that no names had been given, that the police had censored the story quite a bit. While I pretended to read I wondered whether it would be to my advantage to tell the girl the story was a fake. But I couldn't see any clear profit in that, so I saved my soul a lie.

"Practically straight," I admitted.

"You were there?"

She had pushed the paper aside to the floor and was leaning over the table.

"With the police."

"Was—?" Her voice broke huskily. Her white fingers wadded the tablecloth in two little bunches half-way between us. She cleared her throat. "Who was—?" was as far as she got this time.

A pause. I waited. Her eyes went down, but not before I had seen water dulling the fire in them. During the pause the waiter came in, put our food down, went away.

"You know what I want to ask," she said presently, her voice low, choked. "Was he? Was he? For God's sake tell me!"

I weighed them—truth against lie, lie against truth. Once more truth triumphed.

"Paddy the Mex was shot—killed—in the Fillmore Street house," I said.

The pupils of her eyes shrank to pinpoints—spread again until they almost covered the green irises. She made no sound. Her face was empty. She picked up a fork and lifted a forkful of salad to her mouth—another. Reaching across the table, I took the fork out of her hand.

"You're only spilling it on your clothes," I growled. "You can't eat without opening your mouth to put the food in."

She put her hands across the table, reaching for mine, trembling, holding my hand with fingers that twitched so that the nails scratched me.

"You're not lying to me?" she half sobbed, half chattered. "You're on the square! You were white to me that time in Philly! Paddy always said you were one white dick! You're not tricking me?"

"Straight up," I assured her. "Paddy meant a lot to you?"

She nodded dully, pulling herself together, sinking back in a sort of stupor.

"The way's open to even up for him," I suggested.

"You mean—?"

"Talk."

She stared at me blankly for a long while, as if she was trying to get some meaning out of what I had said. I read the answer in her eyes before she put it in words.

"I wish to God I could! But I'm Paper-box-John Cardigan's daughter. It isn't in me to turn anybody up. You're on the wrong side. I can't go over. I wish I could. But there's too much Cardigan in me. I'll be hoping every minute that you nail them, and nail them dead right, but—"

"Your sentiments are noble, or words to that effect," I sneered at her. "Who do you think you are—Joan of Arc? Would your brother Frank be in stir now if his partner, Johnny the Plumber, hadn't put the finger on him for the Great Falls bulls? Come to life, dearie! You're a thief among thieves, and those who don't double-cross get crossed. Who rubbed your Paddy the Mex out? Pals! But you mustn't slap back at 'em because it wouldn't be clubby. My God!"

My speech only thickened the sullenness in her face.

"I'm going to slap back," she said, "but I can't, can't split. I can't, I tell you. If you were a gun, I'd—Anyway, what help I get will be on my side of the game. Let it go at that, won't you? I know how you feel about it, but—Will you tell me who besides—who else was—was found in those houses?"

"Oh, sure!" I snarled. "I'll tell you everything. I'll let you pump me dry. But you mustn't give me any hints, because it might not be in keeping with the ethics of your highly honorable profession!"

Being a woman, she ignored all this, repeating, "Who else?"

"Nothing stirring. But I will do this—I'll tell you a couple who weren't there—Big Flora and Red O'Leary."

Her dopiness was gone. She studied my face with green eyes that were dark and savage.

"Was Bluepoint Vance?" she demanded.

"What do you guess?" I replied.

She studied my face for a moment longer and then stood up.

"Thanks for what you've told me," she said, "and for meeting me like this. I do hope you win."

She went out to be shadowed by Dick Foley. I ate my lunch.

VIII

At four o'clock that afternoon Jack Counihan and I brought our hired automobile to rest within sight of the front door of the Stockton Street hotel.

"He cleared himself with the police, so there's no reason why he should have moved, maybe," I told Jack, "and I'd rather not monkey with the hotel people, not knowing them. If he doesn't show by late we'll have to go up against them then."

We settled down to cigarettes, guesses on who'd be the next heavyweight champion and when, the possibilities of Prohibition being either abolished or practiced, where to get good gin and what to do with it, the injustice of the new agency ruling that for purposes of expense accounts Oakland was not to be considered out of town, and similar exciting topics, which carried us from four o'clock to ten minutes past nine.

At 9:10 Red O'Leary came out of the hotel.

"God is good," said Jack as he jumped out of the machine to do the footwork while I stirred the motor.

The fire-topped giant didn't take us far. Larrouy's front door gobbled him. By the time I had parked the car and gone into the dive, both O'Leary and Jack had found seats. Jack's table was on the edge of the dance-floor. O'Leary's was on the other side of the establishment, against the wall, near a corner. A fat blond couple were leaving the table back in that corner when

I came in, so I persuaded the waiter who was guiding me to a table to make it that one.

O'Leary's face was three-quarters turned away from me. He was watching the front door, watching it with an earnestness that turned suddenly to happiness when a girl appeared there. She was the girl Angel Grace had called Nancy Regan. I have already said she was nice. Well, she was. And the cocky little blue hat that hid all her hair didn't handicap her niceness any tonight.

The redhead scrambled to his feet and pushed a waiter and a couple of customers out of his way as he went to meet her. As reward for his eagerness he got some profanity that he didn't seem to hear and a blue-eyed, white-toothed smile that was—well—nice. He brought her back to his table and put her in a chair facing me, while he sat very much facing her.

His voice was a baritone rumble out of which my snooping ears could pick no words. He seemed to be telling her a lot, and she listened as if she liked it.

"But, Reddy, dear, you shouldn't," she said once. Her voice—I know other words, but we'll stick to this one—was nice. Outside of the music in it, it had quality. Whoever this gunman's moll was, she either had had a good start in life or had learned her stuff well. Now and then, when the orchestra came up for air, I would catch a few words, but they didn't tell me anything except that neither she nor her rowdy playmate had anything against the other.

The joint had been nearly empty when she came in. By ten o'clock it was fairly crowded, and ten o'clock is early for Larrouy's customers. I began to pay less attention to Red's girl—even if she was nice—and more to my other neighbors. It struck me that there weren't many women in sight. Checking up on that, I found damned few women in proportion to the men. Men—rat-faced men, hatchet-faced men, square-jawed men, slack-chinned men, pale men, ruddy men, dark men, bull-necked men, scrawny men, funny-looking men, tough-looking men, ordinary men—sitting two to a table, four to a table, more coming in—and damned few women.

These men talked to one another, as if they weren't much interested in what they were saying. They looked casually around the joint, with eyes that were blankest when they came to O'Leary. And always those casual—bored—glances did rest on O'Leary for a second or two.

I returned my attention to O'Leary and Nancy Regan. He was sitting a little more erect in his chair than he had been, but it was an easy, supple erectness, and though his shoulders had hunched a bit, there was no stiffness in them. She said something to him. He laughed, turning his face toward the center of the room, so that he seemed to be laughing not only at what she had said, but also at these men who sat around him, waiting. It was a hearty laugh, young and careless.

The girl looked surprised for a moment, as if something in the laugh puzzled her, then she went on with whatever she was telling him. She didn't know she was sitting on dynamite, I decided. O'Leary knew. Every inch of him, every gesture, said, "I'm big, strong, young, tough and redheaded. When you boys want to do your stuff I'll be here."

Time slid by. Few couples danced. Jean Larrouy went around with dark worry in his round face. His joint was full of customers, but he would rather have had it empty.

By eleven o'clock I stood up and beckoned to Jack Counihan. He came over, we shook hands, exchanged *How's every things* and *Getting muches*, and he sat at my table.

"What is happening?" he asked under cover of the orchestra's din. "I can't see anything, but there is something in the air. Or am I being hysterical?"

"You will be presently. The wolves are gathering, and Red O'Leary's the lamb. You could pick a tenderer one if you had a free hand, maybe. But these bimbos once helped pluck a bank, and when pay-day came there wasn't anything in their envelopes, not even any envelopes. The word got out that maybe Red knew how-come. Hence this. They're waiting now—maybe for somebody—maybe till they get enough hooch in them."

"And we sit here because it's the nearest table to the target for all these fellows' bullets when the blooming lid blows off?" Jack inquired. "Let's move over to Red's table. It's still nearer, and I rather like the appearance of the girl with him."

"Don't be impatient, you'll have your fun," I promised him. "There's no sense in having this O'Leary killed. If they bargain with him in a gentlemanly way, we'll lay off. But if they start heaving things at him, you and I are going to pry him and his girl friend loose."

"Well spoken, my hearty!" He grinned, whitening around the mouth. "Are there any details, or do we just simply and unostentatiously pry 'em loose?"

"See the door behind me, to the right? When the pop-off comes, I'm going back there and open it up. You hold the line midway between. When I yelp, you give Red whatever help he needs to get back there."

"Aye, aye!" He looked around the room at the assembled plug-uglies, moistened his lips, and looked at the hand holding his cigarette, a quivering hand. "I hope you won't think I'm in a funk," he said. "But I'm not an antique murderer like you. I get a reaction out of this prospective slaughtering."

"Reaction, my eye," I said. "You're scared stiff. But no nonsense, mind! If you try to make a vaudeville act out of it I'll ruin whatever these guerrillas leave of you. You do what you're told, and nothing else. If you get any bright ideas, save 'em to tell me about afterward."

"Oh, my conduct will be most exemplary!" he assured me.

IX

It was nearly midnight when what the wolves waited for came. The last pretense of indifference went out of faces that had been gradually taking on tenseness. Chairs and feet scraped as men pushed themselves back a little from their tables. Muscles flexed bodies into readiness for action. Tongues licked lips and eyes looked eagerly at the front door.

Bluepoint Vance was coming into the room. He came alone, nodding to acquaintances on this side and that, carrying his tall body gracefully, easily, in its well-cut clothing. His sharp-featured face was smilingly self-confident. He came without haste and without delay to Red O'Leary's table. I couldn't see Red's face, but muscles thickened the back of his neck. The girl smiled cordially at Vance and gave him her hand. It was naturally done. She didn't know anything.

Vance turned his smile from Nancy Regan to the red-haired giant—a smile that was a trifle cat-to-mousey.

"How's everything, Red?" he asked.

"Everything suits me," bluntly.

The orchestra had stopped playing. Larrouy, standing by the street door, was mopping his forehead with a handkerchief. At the table to my right, a barrel-chested, broken-nosed bruiser in a widely striped suit was breathing heavily between his gold teeth, his watery gray eyes bulging at O'Leary, Vance and Nancy. He was in no way conspicuous—there were too many others holding the same pose.

Bluepoint Vance turned his head, called to a waiter: "Bring me a chair."

The chair was brought and put at the unoccupied side of the table, facing the wall. Vance sat down, slumping back in the chair, leaning indolently toward Red, his left arm hooked over the chair-back, his right hand holding a cigarette.

"Well, Red," he said when he was thus installed, "have you got any news for me?"

His voice was suave, but loud enough for those at nearby tables to hear.

"Not a word." O'Leary's voice made no pretense of friendliness, nor of caution.

"What, no spinach?" Vance's thin-lipped smile spread, and his dark eyes had a mirthful but not pleasant glitter. "Nobody gave you anything to give me?"

"No," said O'Leary, emphatically.

"My goodness!" said Vance, the smile in his eyes and mouth deepening, and getting still less pleasant. "That's ingratitude! Will you help me collect, Red?"

"No."

I was disgusted with this redhead—half-minded to let him go under when the storm broke. Why couldn't he have stalled his way out—fixed up a fancy tale that Bluepoint would have had to half-way accept? But no—this O'Leary boy was so damned childishly proud of his toughness that he had to make a show of it when he should have been using his bean. If it had been only his own carcass that was due for a beating, it would have been all right. But it wasn't all right that Jack and I should have to suffer. This big chump was too valuable to lose. We'd have to get ourselves all battered up saving him from the rewards of his own pigheadedness. There was no justice in it.

"I've got a lot of money coming to me, Red." Vance spoke lazily, tauntingly. "And I need that money." He drew on his cigarette, casually blew the smoke into the redhead's face, and drawled, "Why, do you know the laundry charges twenty-six cents just for doing a pair of pajamas? I need money."

"Sleep in your underclothes," said O'Leary.

Vance laughed. Nancy Regan smiled, but in a bewildered way. She didn't seem to know what it was all about, but she couldn't help knowing that it was about something.

O'Leary leaned forward and spoke deliberately, loud enough for any to hear:

"Bluepoint, I've got nothing to give you—now or ever. And that goes for anybody else that's interested. If you or them think I owe you something—try and get it. To hell with you, Bluepoint Vance! If you don't like it—you've got friends here. Call 'em on!"

What a prime young idiot! Nothing would suit him but an ambulance—and I must be dragged along with him.

Vance grinned evilly, his eyes glittering into O'Leary's face.

"You'd like that, Red?"

O'Leary hunched his big shoulders and let them drop.

"I don't mind a fight," he said. "But I'd like to get Nancy out of it." He turned to her. "Better run along, honey, I'm going to be busy."

She started to say something, but Vance was talking to her. His words were lightly spoken, and he made no objection to her going. The substance of what he told her was that she was going to be lonely without Red. But he went intimately into the details of that loneliness.

Red O'Leary's right hand rested on the table. It went up to Vance's mouth. The hand was a fist when it got there. A wallop of that sort is awkward to deliver. The body can't give it much. It has to depend on the arm muscles, and not on the best of those. Yet Bluepoint Vance was driven out of his chair and across to the next table.

Larrouy's chairs went empty. The shindig was on.

"On your toes," I growled at Jack Counihan, and, doing my best to look like the nervous little fat man I was, I ran toward the back door, passing men who were moving not yet swiftly toward O'Leary. I must have looked the part of a scared trouble-dodger, because nobody stopped me, and I reached the door before the pack had closed on Red. The door was closed, but not locked. I wheeled with my back to it, black-jack in right hand, gun in left. Men were in front of me, but their backs were to me.

O'Leary was towering in front of his table, his tough red face full of bring-on-your-hell, his big body balanced on the balls of his feet. Between us, Jack Counihan stood, his face turned to me, his mouth twitching in a nervous grin, his eyes dancing with delight. Bluepoint Vance was on his feet again. Blood trickled from his thin lips, down his chin. His eyes were cool. They looked at Red O'Leary with the business-like look of a logger sizing up the tree he's going to bring down. Vance's mob watched Vance.

"Red!" I bawled into the silence. "This way, Red!"

Faces spun to me—every face in the joint—millions of them.

"Come on, Red!" Jack Counihan yelped, taking a step forward, his gun out.

Bluepoint Vance's hand flashed to they of his coat. Jack's gun snapped at him. Bluepoint had thrown himself down before the boy's trigger was yanked. The bullet went wide, but Vance's draw was gummed.

Red scooped the girl up with his left arm. A big automatic blossomed in his right fist. I didn't pay much attention to him after that. I was busy.

Larrouy's home was pregnant with weapons—guns, knives, saps, knucks, club-swung chairs and bottles, miscellaneous implements of destruction. Men brought their weapons over to mingle with me. The game was to nudge me away from my door. O'Leary would have liked it. But I was no fire-haired young rowdy. I was pushing forty, and I was twenty pounds overweight. I had the liking for ease that goes with that age and weight. Little ease I got.

A squint-eyed Portuguese slashed at my neck with a knife that spoiled my necktie. I caught him over the ear with the side of my gun before he could get away, saw the ear tear loose. A grinning kid of twenty went down for my legs—football stuff.

I felt his teeth in the knee I pumped up, and felt them break. A pock-marked mulatto pushed a gun-barrel over the shoulder of the man in front of him. My blackjack crunched the arm of the man in front. He winced sidewise as the mulatto pulled the trigger—and had the side of his face blown away.

I fired twice—once when a gun was leveled within a foot of my middle, once when I discovered a man standing on a table not far off taking careful aim at my head. For the rest I trusted to my arms and legs, and saved bullets. The night was young and I had only a dozen pills—six in the gun, six my pocket.

It was a swell bag of nails. Swing right, swing left, kick, swing right, swing left, kick. Don't hesitate, don't look for targets. God will see that there's always a mug there for your gun or blackjack to sock, a belly for your foot.

A bottle came through and found my forehead. My hat saved me some, but the crack didn't do me any good. I swayed and broke a nose where I should have smashed a skull. The room seemed stuffy, poorly ventilated. Somebody ought to tell Larrouy about it. How do you like that lead-and-leather pat on the temple, blondy? This rat on my left is getting too close. I'll draw him in by bending to the right to poke the mulatto, and then I'll lean back into him and let him have it. Not bad! But I can't keep this up all night. Where are Red and Jack? Standing off watching me?

Somebody socked me in the shoulder with something—a piano from the feel of it. A bleary-eyed Greek put his face where I couldn't miss it. Another thrown bottle took my hat and part of my scalp. Red O'Leary and Jack Counihan smashed through, dragging the girl between them.

X

While Jack put the girl through the door, Red and I cleared a little space in front of us. He was good at that. When he chucked them back they went back. I didn't dog it on him, but I did let him get all the exercise he wanted.

"All right!" Jack called.

Red and I went through the door, slammed it shut. It wouldn't hold even if locked. O'Leary sent three slugs through it to give the boys something to think about, and our retreat got under way.

We were in a narrow passageway lighted by a fairly bright light. At the other end was a closed door. Halfway down, to the right, steps led up.

"Straight ahead?" asked Jack, who was in front.

O'Leary said, "Yes." And I said, "No. Vance will have that blocked by now if the bulls haven't. Upstairs—the roof."

We reached the stairs. The door behind us burst open. The light went out. The door at the other end of the passage slammed open. No light came through either door. Vance would want light. Larrouy must have pulled the switch, trying to keep his dump from being torn to toothpicks.

Tumult boiled in the dark passage as we climbed the stairs by the touch system. Whoever had come through the back door was mixing it with those who had followed us—mixing it with blows, curses and an occasional shot. More power to them! We climbed, Jack leading, the girl next, then me, and last of all, O'Leary.

Jack was gallantly reading road-signs to the girl: "Careful of the landing, half a turn to the left now, put your right hand on the wall and—"

"Shut up!" I growled at him. "It's better to have her falling down than to have everybody in the drum fall on us."

We reached the second floor. It was black as black. There were three storeys to the building.

"I've mislaid the blooming stairs," Jack complained.

We poked around in the dark, hunting for the flight that should lead up toward our roof. We didn't find it. The riot downstairs was quieting. Vance's voice was telling his push that they were mixing it with each other, asking where we had gone. Nobody seemed to know. We didn't know, either.

"Come on," I grumbled, leading the way down the dark hall toward the back of the building. "We've got to go somewhere."

There was still noise downstairs, but no more fighting. Men were talking about getting lights. I stumbled into a door at the end of the hall, pushed it open. A room with two windows through which came a pale glow from the street lights. It seemed brilliant after the hall. My little flock followed me in and we closed the door.

Red O'Leary was across the room, his noodle to an open window.

"Back street," he whispered. "No way down unless we drop."

"Anybody in sight?" I asked.

"Don't see any."

I looked around the room—bed, couple of chairs, chest of drawers, and a table.

"The table will go through the window," I said. "We'll chuck it as far as we can and hope the racket will lead 'em out there before they decide to look up here."

Red and the girl were assuring each other that each was still all in one piece. He broke away from her to help me with the table. We balanced it, swung it, let it go. It did nicely, crashing into the wall of the building opposite, dropping down into a backyard to clang and clatter on a pile of tin, or a collection of garbage cans, or something beautifully noisy. You couldn't have heard it more than a block and a half away.

We got away from the window as men bubbled out of Larrouy's back door.

The girl, unable to find any wounds on O'Leary, had turned to Jack Counihan. He had a cut cheek. She was monkeying with it and a handkerchief.

"When you finish that," Jack was telling her, "I'm going out and get one on the other side."

"I'll never finish if you keep talking—you jiggle your cheek."

"That's a swell idea," he exclaimed. "San Francisco is the second largest city in California. Sacramento is the state capital. Do you like geography? Shall I tell you about Java? I've never been there, but I drink their coffee. If—"

"Silly!" she said, laughing. "If you don't hold still I'll stop now."

"Not so good," he said. "I'll be still."

She wasn't doing anything except wiping blood off his cheek, blood that had better been let dry there. When she finished this perfectly useless surgery, she took her hand away slowly, surveying the hardly noticeable results with pride. As her hand came on a level with his mouth, Jack jerked his head forward to kiss the tip of one passing finger.

"Silly!" she said again, snatching her hand away.

"Lay off that," said Red O'Leary, "or I'll knock you off."

"Pull in your neck," said Jack Counihan.

"Reddy!" the girl cried, too late.

The O'Leary right looped out. Jack took the punch on the button, and went to sleep on the floor. The big redhead spun on the balls of his feet to loom over me.

"Got anything to say?" he asked.

I grinned down at Jack, up at Red.

"I'm ashamed of him," I said. "Letting himself be stopped by a palooka who leads with his right."

"You want to try it?"

"Reddy! Reddy!" the girl pleaded, but nobody was listening to her.

"If you'll lead with your right," I said.

"I will," he promised, and did.

I grandstanded, slipping my head out of the way, laying a forefinger on his chin.

"That could have been a knuckle," I said.

"Yes? This one is."

I managed to get under his left, taking the forearm across the back of my neck. But that about played out the acrobatics. It looked as if I would have to see what I could do to him, if any. The girl grabbed his arm and hung on.

"Reddy, darling, haven't you had enough fighting for one night? Can't you be sensible, even if you are Irish?"

I was tempted to paste the big chaw while his playmate had him tied up.

He laughed down at her, ducked his head to kiss her mouth, and grinned at me.

"There's always some other time," he said good-naturedly.

XI

"We'd better get out of here if we can," I said. "You've made too much rumpus for it to be safe."

"Don't get it up in your neck, little man," he told me. "Hold on to my coat-tails and I'll pull you out."

The big tramp. If it hadn't been for Jack and me he wouldn't have had any coat-tail by now.

We moved to the door, listened there, heard nothing.

"The stairs to the third floor must be up front," I whispered. "We'll try for them now."

We opened the door carefully. Enough light went past us into the hall to show a promise of emptiness. We crept down the hall, Red and I each holding one of the girl's hands. I hoped

Jack would come out all right, but he had put himself to sleep, and I had troubles of my own.

I hadn't known that Larrouy's was large enough to have two miles of hallway. It did. It was an even mile in the darkness to the head of the stairs we had come up. We didn't pause there to listen to the voices below. At the end of the next mile O'Leary's foot found the bottom step of the flight leading up.

Just then a yell broke out at the head of the other flight.

"All up—they're up here!"

A white light beamed up on the yeller, and a brogue addressed him from below: "Come on down, ye windbag."

"The police," Nancy Regan whispered, and we hustled up our new-found steps to the third floor.

More darkness, just like that we'd left. We stood still at the top of the stairs. We didn't seem to have any company.

"The roof," I said. "We'll risk matches."

Back in a corner our feeble match-light found us a ladder nailed to the wall, leading to a trap in the ceiling. As little later as possible we were on Larrouy's roof, the trap closed behind us.

"All silk so far," said O'Leary, "and if Vance's rats and the bulls will play a couple of seconds longer—bingavast."

I led the way across the roofs. We dropped ten feet to the next building, climbed a bit to the next, and found on the other side of it a fire-escape that ran down to a narrow court with an opening into the back street.

"This ought to do it," I said, and went down.

The girl came behind me, and then Red. The court into which we dropped was empty—a narrow cement passage between buildings. The bottom of the fire-escape creaked as it hinged down under my weight, but the noise didn't stir anything. It was dark in the court, but not black.

"When we hit the street, we split," O'Leary told me, without a word of gratitude for my help—the help he didn't seem to know he had needed. "You roll your hoop, we'll roll ours."

"Uh-huh," I agreed, chasing my brains around in my skull. "I'll scout the alley first."

Carefully I picked my way down to the end of the court and risked the top of my hatless head to peep into the back street. It was quiet, but up at the corner, a quarter of a block above, two loafers seemed to be loafing attentively. They weren't coppers. I stepped out into the back street and beckoned them down. They couldn't recognize me at that distance, in that light, and there was no reason why they shouldn't think me one of Vance's crew, if they belonged to him.

As they came toward me I stepped back into the court and hissed for Red. He wasn't a boy you had to call twice to a row. He got to me just as they arrived. I took one. He took the other.

Because I wanted a disturbance, I had to work like a mule to get it. These bimbos were a couple of lollipops for fair. There wouldn't have been an ounce of fight in a ton of them. The one I had didn't know what to make of my roughing him around. He had a gun, but he managed to drop it first thing, and in the wrestling it got kicked out of reach. He hung on while I sweated ink jockeying him around into position. The darkness helped, but even at that it was no cinch to pretend he was putting up a battle while I worked him around behind O'Leary, who wasn't having any trouble at all with his man.

Finally I made it. I was behind O'Leary, who had his man pinned against the wall with one hand, preparing to sock him again with the other. I clamped my left hand on my playmate's wrist, twisted him to his knees, got my gun out, and shot O'Leary in the back, just below the right shoulder.

Red swayed, jamming his man into the wall. I beaned mine with the gun-butt.

"Did he get you, Red?" I asked, steadying him with an arm, knocking his prisoner across the noodle.

"Yeah."

"Nancy," I called.

She ran to us.

"Take his other side," I told her. "Keep on your feet, Red, and we'll make the sneak O.K."

The bullet was too freshly in him to slow him up yet, though his right arm was out of commission. We ran down the back street to the corner.

We had pursuers before we made it. Curious faces looked at us in the street. A policeman a block away began to move our way. The girl helping O'Leary on one side, me on the other, we ran half a block away from the copper, to where I had left the automobile Jack and I had used. The street was active by the time I got the machinery grinding and the girl had Red stowed safely in the back seat. The copper sent a yell and a high bullet after us. We left the neighborhood.

I didn't have any special destination yet, so, after the necessary first burst of speed, I slowed up a little, went around lots of corners, and brought the bus to rest in a dark street beyond Van Ness Avenue.

Red was drooping in one corner of the back, the girl holding him up, when I screwed around in my seat to look at them.

"Where to?" I asked.

"A hospital, a doctor, something!" the girl cried. "He's dying!"

I didn't believe that. If he was, it was his own fault. If he had had enough gratitude to take me along with him as a friend I wouldn't have had to shoot him so I could go along as nurse.

"Where to, Red?" I asked him, prodding his knee with a finger.

He spoke thickly, giving me the address of the Stockton Street hotel.

"That's no good," I objected. "Everybody in town knows you bunk there, and if you go back, it's lights out for yours. Where to?"

"Hotel," he repeated.

I got up, knelt on the seat, and leaned back to work on him. He was weak. He couldn't have much resistance left. Bulldozing a man who might after all be dying wasn't gentlemanly, but I had invested a lot of trouble in this egg, trying to get him to lead me to his friends, and I wasn't going to quit in the stretch. For a while it looked as if he wasn't weak enough yet, as if I'd have to shoot him again. But the girl sided with me, and between us we finally convinced him that his only safe bet was to go somewhere where he could hide while he got the right kind of care. We didn't actually convince him—we wore him out and he gave in because he was too weak to argue longer. He gave me an address out by Holly Park.

Hoping for the best, I pointed the machine thither.

XII

The house was a small one in a row of small houses. We took the big boy out of the car and between us to the door. He could just about make it with our help. The street was dark. No light showed from the house. I rang the bell.

Nothing happened. I rang again, and then once more.

"Who is it?" a harsh voice demanded from the inside.

"Red's been hurt," I said.

Silence for a while. Then the door opened half a foot. Through the opening a light came from the interior, enough light to show the flat face and bulging jaw-muscles of the skull-cracker who had been the Motsa Kid's guardian and executioner.

"What the hell?" he asked.

"Red was jumped. They got him," I explained, pushing the limp giant forward.

We didn't crash the gate that way. The skull-cracker held the door as it was.

"You'll wait," he said, and shut the door in our faces. His voice sounded from within, "Flora." That was all right—Red had brought us to the right place.

When he opened the door again he opened it all the way, and Nancy Regan and I took our burden into the hall. Beside the skull-cracker stood a woman in a low-cut black silk gown—Big Flora, I supposed.

She stood at least five feet ten in her high-heeled slippers. They were small slippers, and I noticed that her ringless hands were small. The rest of her wasn't. She was broad-shouldered, deep-bosomed, thick-armed, with a pink throat which, for all its smoothness, was muscled like a wrestler's. She was about my age—close to forty—with very curly and very yellow bobbed hair, very pink skin, and a handsome, brutal face. Her deep-set eyes were gray, her thick lips were well-shaped, her nose was just broad enough and curved enough to give her a look of strength, and she had chin enough to support it. From forehead to throat her pink skin was underlaid with smooth, thick, strong muscles.

This Big Flora was no toy. She had the look and the poise of a woman who could have managed the looting and the double-crossing afterward. Unless her face and body lied, she had all the strength of physique, mind and will that would be needed, and some to spare. She was made of stronger stuff than either the ape-built bruiser at her side or the red-haired giant I was holding.

"Well?" she asked, when the door had been closed behind us. Her voice was deep but not masculine—a voice that went well with her looks.

"Vance ganged him in Larrouy's. He took one in the back," I said.

"Who are you?"

"Get him to bed," I stalled. "We've got all night to talk."

She turned, snapping her fingers. A shabby little old man darted out of a door toward the rear. His brown eyes were very scary.

"Get to hell upstairs," she ordered. "Fix the bed, get hot water and towels."

The little old man scrambled up the stairs like a rheumatic rabbit.

The skull-cracker took the girl's side of Red, and he and I carried the giant up to a room where the little man was scurrying around with basins and cloth. Flora and Nancy Regan followed us. We spread the wounded man face-down on the bed and stripped him. Blood still ran from the bullet-hole. He was unconscious.

Nancy Regan went to pieces.

"He's dying! He's dying! Get a doctor! Oh, Reddy, dearest—"

"Shut up!" said Big Flora. "The damned fool ought to croak—going to Larrouy's tonight!" She caught the little man by the shoulder and threw him at the door. "Zonite and more water," she called after him. "Give me your knife, Pogy."

The ape-built man took from his pocket a spring-knife with a long blade that had been sharpened until it was narrow and thin. This is the knife, I thought, that cut the Motsa Kid's throat.

With it, Big Flora cut the bullet out of Red O'Leary's back.

The ape-built Pogy kept Nancy Regan over in a corner of the room while the operating was done. The little scared man knelt beside the bed, handing the woman what she asked for, mopping up Red's blood as it ran from the wound.

I stood beside Flora, smoking cigarettes from the pack she had given me. When she raised her head, I would transfer the cigarette from my mouth to hers. She would fill her lungs with a draw that ate half the cigarette and nod. I would take the cigarette from her mouth. She would blow out the smoke and bend to her work again. I would light another cigarette from what was left of that one, and be ready for her next smoke.

Her bare arms were blood to the elbows. Her face was damp with sweat. It was a gory mess, and it took time. But when she straightened up for the last smoke, the bullet was out of Red, the bleeding had stopped, and he was bandaged.

"Thank God that's over," I said, lighting one of my own cigarettes. "Those pills you smoke are terrible."

The little scared man was cleaning up. Nancy Regan had fainted in a chair across the room, and nobody was paying any attention to her.

"Keep your eye on this gent, Pogy," Big Flora told the skull-cracker, nodding at me, "while I wash up."

I went over to the girl, rubbed her hands, put some water on her face, and got her awake.

"The bullet's out. Red's sleeping. He'll be picking fights again within a week," I told her.

She jumped up and ran over to the bed.

Flora came in. She had washed and had changed her blood-stained black gown for a green kimono affair, which gaped here and there to show a lot of orchid-colored underthings.

"Talk," she commanded, standing in front of me. "Who, what and why?"

"I'm Percy Maguire," I said, as if this name, which I had just thought up, explained everything.

"That's the who," she said, as if my phoney alias explained nothing. "Now what's the what and why?"

The ape-built Pogy, standing on one side, looked me up and down. I'm short and lumpy. My face doesn't scare children, but it's a more or less truthful witness to a life that hasn't been overburdened with refinement and gentility. The evening's entertainment had decorated me with bruises and scratches, and had done things to what was left of my clothes.

"Percy," he echoed, showing wide-spaced yellow teeth in a grin. "My Gawd, brother, your folks must of been color-blind!"

"That's the what and why," I insisted to the woman, paying no attention to the wheeze from the zoo. "I'm Percy Maguire, and I want my hundred and fifty thousand dollars."

The muscles in her brows came down over her eyes.

"You've got a hundred and fifty thousand dollars, have you?"

I nodded up into her handsome brutal face.

"Yeah," I said. "That's what I came for."

"Oh, you haven't got them? You want them?"

"Listen, sister, I want my dough." I had to get tough if this play was to go over. "This swapping *Oh-have-yous* and *Yes-I-haves* don't get me anything but a thirst. We were in the big knock-over, see? And after that, when we find the payoff's a bust, I said to the kid I was training with, 'Never mind, Kid, we'll get our whack. Just follow Percy.' And then Bluepoint comes to me and asks me to throw in with him, and I said, 'Sure!' and me and the kid throw in with him until we all come across Red in the dump tonight. Then I told the kid, 'These coffee-and-doughnut guns are going to rub Red out, and that won't get us anything. We'll take him away from 'em and make him steer us to where Big Flora's sitting on the jack. We ought to be good for a hundred and fifty grand apiece, now that there's damned few in on it. After we get that, if we want to bump Red off, all right. But business before pleasure, and a hundred and fifty thou is business.' So we did. We opened an out for the big boy when he didn't have any. The kid got mushy with the broad along the road and got knocked for a loop. That was all right with me. If she was worth a hundred and fifty grand to him—fair enough. I came on with Red. I pulled the big tramp out after he stopped the slug. By rights I ought to collect the kid's dib, too—making three hundred thou for me—but give me the hundred and fifty I started out for and we'll call it even-steven."

I thought this hocus ought to stick. Of course I wasn't counting on her ever giving me any money, but if the rank and file of the mob hadn't known these people, why should these people know everybody in the mob?

Flora spoke to Pogy:

"Get that damned heap away from the front door."

I felt better when he went out. She wouldn't have sent him out to move the car if she had meant to do anything to me right away.

"Got any food in the joint?" I asked, making myself at home.

She went to the head of the steps and yelled down, "Get something for us to eat."

Red was still unconscious. Nancy Regan sat beside him, holding one of his hands. Her face was drained white. Big Flora came into the room again, looked at the invalid, put a hand on his forehead, felt his pulse.

"Come on downstairs," she said.

"I—I'd rather stay here, if I may," Nancy Regan said. Voice and eyes showed utter terror of Flora.

The big woman, saying nothing, went downstairs. I followed her to the kitchen, where the little man was working on ham and eggs at the range. The window and back door, I saw, were reinforced with heavy planking and braced with timbers nailed to the floor. The clock over the sink said 2:50 A.M.

Flora brought out a quart of liquor and poured drinks for herself and me. We sat at the table and while we waited for our food she cursed Red O'Leary and Nancy Regan, because he had got himself disabled keeping a date with her at a time when Flora needed his strength most. She cursed them individually, as a pair, and was making it a racial matter by cursing all the Irish when the little man gave us our ham and eggs.

We had finished the solids and were stirring hooch in our second cups of coffee when Pogy came back. He had news.

"There's a couple of mugs hanging around the corner that I don't much like."

"Bulls or—?" Flora asked.

"Or," he said.

Flora began to curse Red and Nancy again. But she had pretty well played that line out already. She turned to me.

"What the hell did you bring them here for?" she demanded. "Leaving a mile-wide trail behind you! Why didn't you let the lousy bum die where he got his dose?"

"I brought him here for my hundred and fifty grand. Slip it to me and I'll be on my way. You don't owe me anything else. I don't owe you anything. Give me my rhino instead of lip and I'll pull my freight."

"Like hell you will," said Pogy.

The woman looked at me under lowered brows and drank her coffee.

XIII

Fifteen minutes later the shabby little old man came running into the kitchen, saying he had heard feet on the roof. His faded brown eyes were dull as an ox's with fright, and his withered lips writhed under his straggly yellow-white mustache.

Flora profanely called him a this-and-that kind of old one-thing-and-another and chased him upstairs again. She got up from the table and pulled the green kimono tight around her big body.

"You're here," she told me, "and you'll put in with us. There's no other way. Got a rod?"

I admitted I had a gun but shook my head at the rest of it.

"This is not my wake—yet," I said. "It'll take one hundred and fifty thousand berries, spot cash, paid in the hand, to buy Percy in on it."

I wanted to know if the loot was on the premises.

Nancy Regan's tearful voice came from the stairs:

"No, no, darling! Please, please, go back to bed! You'll kill yourself, Reddy, dear!"

Red O'Leary strode into the kitchen. He was naked except for a pair of gray pants and his bandage. His eyes were feverish and happy. His dry lips were stretched in a grin. He had a gun in his left hand. His right arm hung useless. Behind him trotted Nancy. She stopped pleading and shrank behind him when she saw Big Flora.

"Ring the gong, and let's go," the half-naked redhead laughed. "Vance is in our street."

Flora went over to him, put her fingers on his wrist, held them there a couple of seconds, and nodded:

"You crazy son-of-a-gun," she said in a tone that was more like maternal pride than anything else. "You're good for a fight right now. And a damned good thing, too, because you're going to get it."

Red laughed—a triumphant laugh that boasted of his toughness—then his eyes turned to me. Laughter went out of them and a puzzled look drew them narrow.

"Hello," he said. "I dreamed about you, but I can't remember what it was. It was—Wait. I'll get it in a minute. It was—By God! I dreamed it was you that plugged me!"

Flora smiled at me, the first time I had seen her smile, and she spoke quickly:

"Take him, Pogy!"

I twisted obliquely out of my chair.

Pogy's fist took me in the temple. Staggering across the room, struggling to keep my feet, I thought of the bruise on the dead Motsa Kid's temple.

Pogy was on me when the wall bumped me upright.

I put a fist—spat!—in his flat nose. Blood squirted, but his hairy paws gripped me. I tucked my chin in, ground the top of my head into his face. The scent Big Flora used came strong to me. Her silk clothes brushed against me. With both hands full of my hair she pulled my head back, stretching my neck for Pogy. He took hold of it with his paws. I quit. He didn't throttle me any more than was necessary, but it was bad enough.

Flora frisked me for gun and blackjack.

".38 special," she named the caliber of the gun. "I dug a .38 special bullet out of you, Red." The words came faintly to me through the roaring in my ears.

The little old man's voice was chattering in the kitchen. I couldn't make out anything he said. Pogy's hands went away from me. I put my own hands to my throat. It was hell not to have any pressure at all there. The blackness went slowly away from my eyes, leaving a lot of little purple clouds that floated around and around. Presently I could sit up on the floor. I knew by that I had been lying down on it.

The purple clouds shrank until I could see past them enough to know there were only three of us in the room now. Cringing in a chair, back in a corner, was Nancy Regan. On another chair, beside the door, a black pistol in his hand, sat the scared little old man. His eyes were desperately frightened. Gun and hand shook at me. I tried to ask him to either stop shaking or move his gun away from me, but I couldn't get any words out yet.

Upstairs, guns boomed, their reports exaggerated by the smallness of the house.

The little man winced.

"Let me get out," he whispered with unexpected abruptness, "and I will give you everything. I will! Everything—if you will let me get out of this house!"

This feeble ray of light where there hadn't been a dot gave me back the use of my vocal apparatus.

"Talk turkey," I managed to say.

"I will give you those upstairs—that she-devil. I will give you the money. I will give you all—if you will let me go out. I am old. I am sick. I cannot live in prison. What have I to do with robberies? Nothing. Is it my fault that she-devil—? You have seen it here. I am a slave—I who am near the end of my life. Abuse, cursings, beatings—and those are not enough. Now I must go to prison because that she-devil is a she-devil. I am an old man who cannot live in prisons. You let me go out. You do me that kindness. I will give you that she-devil—those other devils—the money they stole. That I will do!"

Thus this panic-stricken little old man, squirming and fidgeting on his chair.

"How can I get you out?" I asked, getting up from the floor, my eye on his gun. If I could get to him while we talked....

"How not? You are a friend of the police—that I know. The police are here now—waiting for daylight before they come into this house. I myself with my old eyes saw them take that Bluepoint Vance. You can take me out past your friends, the police. You do what I ask, and I will give you those devils and their moneys."

"Sounds good," I said, taking a careless step toward him. "But can I just stroll out of here when I want to?"

"No! No!" he said, paying no attention to the second step I took toward him. "But first I will give you those three devils. I will give them to you alive but without power. And their money. That I will do, and then you will take me out—and this girl here." He nodded suddenly at Nancy, whose white face, still nice in spite of its terror, was mostly wide eyes just now; "She, too, has nothing to do with those devils' crimes. She must go with me."

I wondered what this old rabbit thought he could do. I frowned exceedingly thoughtful while I took still another step toward him.

"Make no mistake," he whispered earnestly. "When that she-devil comes back into this room you will die—she will kill you certainly."

Three more steps and I would be close enough to take hold of him and his gun.

Footsteps were in the hall. Too late for a jump.

"Yes?" he hissed desperately.

I nodded a split-second before Big Flora came through the door.

XIV

She was dressed for action in a pair of blue pants that were probably Pogy's, beaded moccasins, a silk waist. A ribbon held her curly yellow hair back from her face. She had a gun in one hand, one in each hip pocket.

The one in her hand swung up.

"You're done," she told me, quite matter-of-fact.

My newly acquired confederate whined, "Wait, wait, Flora! Not here like this, please! Let me take him into the cellar."

She scowled at him, shrugging her silken shoulders.

"Make it quick," she said. "It'll be light in another half-hour."

I felt too much like crying to laugh at them. Was I supposed to think this woman would let the rabbit change her plans? I suppose I must have put some value on the old gink's help, or I wouldn't have been so disappointed when this little comedy told me it was a frame-up. But any hole they worked me into couldn't be any worse than the one I was in.

So I went ahead of the old man into the hall, opened the door he indicated, switched on the basement light, and went down the rough steps.

Close behind me he was whispering, "I'll first show you the moneys, and then I will give to you those devils. And you will not forget your promise? I and that girl shall go out through the police?"

"Oh, yes," I assured the old joker.

He came up beside me, sticking a gun-butt in my hand.

"Hide it," he hissed, and, when I had pocketed that one, gave me another, producing them with his free hand from under his coat.

Then he actually showed me the loot. It was still in the boxes and bags in which it had been carried from the banks. He insisted on opening some of them to show me the money—green bundles belted with the bank's yellow wrappers. The boxes and bags were stacked in a small brick cell that was fitted with a padlocked door, to which he had the key.

He closed the door when we were through looking, but he did not lock it, and he led me back part of the way we had come.

"That, as you see, is the money," he said. "Now for those. You will stand here, hiding behind these boxes."

A partition divided the cellar in half. It was pierced by a doorway that had no door. The place the old man told me to hide was close beside this doorway, between the partition and four packing-cases. Hiding there, I would be to the right of, and a little behind, anyone who came downstairs and walked through the cellar toward the cell that held the money. That is, I would be in that position when they went to go through the doorway in the partition.

The old man was fumbling beneath one of the boxes. He brought out an eighteen-inch length of lead pipe stuffed in a similar length of black garden hose. He gave this to me as he explained everything.

"They will come down here one at a time. When they are about to go through this door, you will know what to do with this. And then you will have them, and I will have your promise. Is it not so?"

"Oh, yes," I said, all up in the air.

He went upstairs. I crouched behind the boxes, examining the guns he had given me—and I'm damned if I could find anything wrong with them. They were loaded and they seemed to be in working order. That finishing touch completely balled me up. I didn't know whether I was in a cellar or a balloon.

When Red O'Leary, still naked except for pants and bandage, came into the cellar, I had to shake my head violently to clear it in time to bat him across the back of the noodle as his first bare foot stepped through the doorway. He sprawled down on his face.

The old man scurried down the steps, full of grins.

"Hurry! Hurry!" he panted, helping me drag the redhead back into the money cell. Then he produced two pieces of cord and tied the giant hand and foot.

"Hurry!" he panted again as he left me to run upstairs, while I went back to my hiding-place and hefted the lead-pipe, wondering if Flora had shot me and I was now enjoying the rewards of my virtue—in a heaven where I could enjoy myself forever and ever socking folks who had been rough with me down below.

The ape-built skull-cracker came down, reached the door. I cracked his skull. The little man came scurrying. We dragged Pogy to the cell, tied him up.

"Hurry!" panted the old gink, dancing up and down in his excitement. "That she-devil next—and strike hard!"

He scrambled upstairs and I could hear his feet pattering overhead.

I got rid of some of my bewilderment, making room for a little intelligence in my skull. This foolishness we were up to wasn't so. It couldn't be happening. Nothing ever worked out just that way. You didn't stand in corners and knock down people one after the other like a machine, while a scrawny little bozo up at the other end fed them to you. It was too damned silly! I had enough!

I passed up my hiding place, put down the pipe and found another spot to crouch in, under some shelves, near the steps.

I hunkered down there with a gun in each fist. This game I was playing in was—it had to be—gummy around the edges. I wasn't going to stay put any longer.

Flora came down the steps. Two steps behind her the little man trotted.

Flora had a gun in each hand. Her gray eyes were everywhere. Her head was down like an animal's coming to a fight. Her nostrils quivered. Her body, coming down neither slowly nor swiftly, was balanced like a dancer's. If I live to a million I'll never forget the picture this handsome brutal woman made coming down those unplaned cellar stairs. She was a beautiful fight-bred animal going to a fight.

She saw me as I straightened.

"Drop 'em!" I said, but I knew she wouldn't.

The little man flicked a limp brown blackjack out of his sleeve and knocked her behind the ear just as she swung her left gun on me.

I jumped over and caught her before she hit the cement.

"Now, you see!" the old man said gleefully. "You have the money and you have them. And now you will get me and that girl out."

"First we'll stow this with the others," I said.

After he had helped me do that I told him to lock the cell door. He did, and I took the key with one hand, his neck with the other. He squirmed like a snake while I ran my other hand over his clothes, removing the blackjack and a gun, and finding a money-belt around his waist.

"Take it off," I ordered. "You don't carry anything out with you."

His fingers worked with the buckle, dragged the belt from under his clothes, let it fall on the floor. It was padded fat.

Still holding his neck, I took him upstairs, where the girl still sat frozen on the kitchen chair. It took a stiff hooker of whisky and a lot of words to thaw her into understanding that she was going out with the old man and that she wasn't to say a word to anybody, especially not to the police.

"Where's Reddy?" she asked when color had come back into her face—which had even at the worst never lost its niceness—and thoughts to her head.

I told her he was all right, and promised her he would be in a hospital before the morning was over. She didn't ask anything else. I shooed her upstairs for her hat and coat, went with the old man while he got his hat, and then put the pair of them in the front ground-floor room.

"Stay here till I come for you," I said, and I locked the door and pocketed the key when I went out.

XV

The front door and the front window on the ground floor had been planked and braced like the rear ones. I didn't like to risk opening them, even though it was fairly light by now. So I went upstairs, fashioned a flag of truce out of a pillowslip and a bed-slat, hung it out a window, waited until a heavy voice said, "All right, speak your piece," and then

I showed myself and told the police I'd let them in.

It took five minutes' work with a hatchet to pry the front door loose. The chief of police, the captain of detectives, and half the force were waiting on the front steps and pavement when I got the door open. I took them to the cellar and turned Big Flora, Pogy and Red O'Leary over to them, with the money. Flora and Pogy were awake, but not talking.

While the dignitaries were crowded around the spoils I went upstairs. The house was full of police sleuths. I swapped greetings with them as I went through to the room where I had left Nancy Regan and the old gink. Lieutenant Duff was trying the locked door, while O'Gar and Hunt stood behind him.

I grinned at Duff and gave him the key.

He opened the door, looked at the old man and the girl—mostly at her—and then at me. They were standing in the center of the room. The old man's faded eyes were miserably worried, the girl's blue ones darkly anxious. Anxiety didn't ruin her looks a bit.

"If that's yours I don't blame you for locking it up," O'Gar muttered in my ear.

"You can run along now," I told the two in the room. "Get all the sleep you need before you report for duty again."

They nodded and went out of the house.

"That's how your agency evens up?" Duff said. "The she-employees make up in looks for the ugliness of the he's."

Dick Foley came into the hall.

"How's your end?" I asked.

"Finis. The Angel led me to Vance. He led here. I led the bulls here. They got him—got her."

Two shots crashed in the street.

We went to the door and saw excitement in a police car down the street. We went down there. Bluepoint Vance, handcuffs on his wrists, was writhing half on the seat, half on the floor.

"We were holding him here in the car, Houston and me," a hard-mouthed plainclothes man explained to Duff. "He made a break, grabbed Houston's gat with both hands. I had to drill him—twice. The cap'll raise hell! He specially wanted him kept here to put up against the others. But God knows I wouldn't of shot him if it hadn't been him or Houston!"

Duff called the plainclothes man a damned clumsy mick as they lifted Vance up on the seat. Bluepoint's tortured eyes focused on me.

"I—know—you?" he asked painfully. "Continental—New—York?"

"Yes," I said.

"Couldn't—place—you—Larrouy's—with—Red."

He stopped to cough blood.

"Got—Red?"

"Yeah," I told him. "Got Red, Flora, Pogy and the cush."

"But—not—Papa—dop—oul—os."

"Papa does what?" I asked impatiently, a shiver along my spine.

He pulled himself up on the seat.

"Papadopoulos," he repeated, with an agonizing summoning of the little strength left in him. "I tried—shoot him—saw him—walk 'way—with girl—bull—too damn quick—wish..."

His words ran out. He shuddered. Death wasn't a sixteenth of an inch behind his eyes. A white-coated intern tried to get past me into the car. I pushed him out of the way and leaned in, taking Vance by the shoulders. The back of my neck was ice. My stomach was empty.

"Listen, Bluepoint," I yelled in his face, "Papadopoulos? Little old man? Brains of the push?"

"Yes," Vance said, and the last live blood in him came out with the word.

I let him drop back on the seat and walked away.

Of course! How had I missed it? The little old scoundrel—if he hadn't, for all his scariness, been the works, how could he have so neatly-turned the others over to me one at a time? They had been absolutely cornered. It was be killed fighting, or surrender and be hanged. They had no other way out. The police had Vance, who could and would tell them that the little buzzard was the headman—there wasn't even a chance for him beating the courts with his age, his weakness and his mask of being driven around by the others.

And there I had been—with no choice but to accept his offer. Otherwise lights out for me. I had been putty in his hands, his accomplices had been putty. He had slipped the cross over on them as they had helped him slip it over on the others—and I had sent him safely away.

Now I could turn the city upside down for him—my promise had been only to get him out of the house—but...

What a life!

2

$106,000 BLOOD MONEY

BLACK MASK, MAY 1927

The big knock-over told of the looting of two banks by a large band of crooks gathered from all parts of the country for that purpose. Following the successful getaway with the plunder, a number of well-known members of the underworld of various cities are found murdered. These men were seen before the holdup and were suspected leaders of small groups participating in it. It becomes evident that the division of spoils is to be made among a few rather than between many. Murder succeeds murder, as the Continental detective narrows his search for the unknown head of the huge plot. In the end he finds him, only to let him escape, as the price of his own life, without knowing him to be the man he was after. $106,000 BLOOD MONEY *is a sequel to* THE BIG KNOCK-OVER.

"I'm Tom-Tom Carey," he said, drawling the words.

I nodded at the chair beside my desk and weighed him in while he moved to it. Tall, wide-shouldered, thick-chested, thin-bellied, he would add up to say a hundred and ninety pounds. His swarthy face was hard as a fist, but there was nothing ill-humored in it. It was the face of a man of forty-something who lived life raw and thrived on it. His blue clothes were good and he wore them well.

In the chair, he twisted brown paper around a charge of Bull Durham and finished introducing himself:

"I'm Paddy the Mex's brother."

I thought maybe he was telling the truth. Paddy had been like this fellow in coloring and manner.

"That would make your real name Carrera," I suggested.

"Yes," he was lighting his cigarette. "Alfredo Estanislao Cristobal Carrera, if you want all the details."

I asked him how to spell Estanislao, wrote the name down on a slip of paper, adding alias *Tom-Tom Carey,* rang for Tommy Howd, and told him to have the file clerk see if we had anything on it.

"While your people are opening graves I'll tell you why I'm here," the swarthy man drawled through smoke when Tommy had gone away with the paper.

"Tough—Paddy being knocked off like that," I said.

"He was too damned trusting to live long," his brother explained. "This is the kind of hombre he was—the last time I saw him was four years ago, here in San Francisco. I'd come in from an expedition down to—never mind where. Anyway I was flat. Instead of pearls all I'd got out of the trip was a bullet-crease over my hip. Paddy was dirty with fifteen thousand or so he'd just nicked somebody for. The afternoon I saw him he had a date that he was leery of toting so much money to. So he gives me the fifteen thousand to hold for him till that night."

Tom-Tom Carey blew out smoke and smiled softly past me at a memory.

"That's the kind of hombre he was," he went on. "He'd trust even his own brother. I went to Sacramento that afternoon and caught a train east. A girl in Pittsburgh helped me spend the fifteen thousand. Her name was Laurel. She liked rye whisky with milk for a chaser. I used to drink it with her till I was all curdled inside, and I've never had any appetite for *schmierkiise* since. So there's a hundred thousand dollars reward on this Papadopoulos, is there?"

"And six. The insurance companies put up a hundred thousand, the bankers' association five, and the city a thousand."

Tom-Tom Carey chucked the remains of his cigarette in the cuspidor and began to assemble another one.

"Suppose I hand him to you?" he asked. "How many ways will the money have to go?"

"None of it will stop here," I assured him. "The Continental Detective Agency doesn't touch reward money—and won't let its hired men. If any of the police are in on the pinch they'll want a share."

"But if they aren't, it's all mine?"

"If you turn him in without help, or without any help except ours."

"I'll do that." The words were casual. "So much for the arrest. Now for the conviction part. If you get him, are you sure you can nail him to the cross?"

"I ought to be, but he'll have to go up against a jury—and that means anything can happen."

The muscular brown hand holding the brown cigarette made a careless gesture.

"Then maybe I'd better get a confession out of him before I drag him in," he said off-hand.

"It would be safer that way," I agreed. "You ought to let that holster down an inch or two. It brings the gunbutt too high. The bulge shows when you sit down."

"Uh-huh. You mean the one on the left shoulder. I took it away from a fellow after I lost mine. Strap's too short. I'll get another one this afternoon."

Tommy came in with a folder labeled, *Carey, Tom-Tom, 1361-C*. It held some newspaper clippings, the oldest dated ten years back, the youngest eight months. I read them through, passing each one to the swarthy man as I finished it. Tom-Tom Carey was written down in them as soldier of fortune, gun-runner, seal poacher, smuggler and pirate. But it was all alleged, supposed and suspected. He had been captured variously but never convicted of anything.

"They don't treat me right," he complained placidly when we were through reading. "For instance, stealing that Chinese gunboat wasn't my fault. I was forced to do it—I was the one that was double-crossed. After they'd got the stuff aboard they wouldn't pay for it. I couldn't unload it. I couldn't do anything but take gunboat and all. The insurance companies must want this Papadopoulos plenty to hang a hundred thousand on him."

"Cheap enough if it lands him," I said. "Maybe he's not all the newspapers picture him as, but he's more than a handful. He gathered a whole damned army of strong-arm men here, took over a block in the center of the financial district, looted the two biggest banks in the city, fought off the whole police department, made his getaway, ditched the army, used some of his lieutenants to bump off some more of them,—that's where your brother Paddy got his,—then, with the help of Pogy Reeve, Big Flora Brace and Red O'Leary, wiped out the rest of his lieutenants. And remember, these lieutenants weren't schoolboys—they were slick grifters like Bluepoint Vance and the Shivering Kid and Darby M'Laughlin—birds who knew their what's what."

"Uh-huh." Carey was unimpressed. "But it was a bust just the same. You got all the loot back, and he just managed to get away himself."

"A bad break for him," I explained. "Red O'Leary broke out with a complication of love and vanity. You can't chalk that against Papadopoulos. Don't get the idea he's half-smart. He's dangerous, and I don't blame the insurance companies for thinking they'll sleep better if they're sure he's not out where he can frame some more tricks against their policy-holding banks."

"Don't know much about this Papadopoulos, do you?"

"No." I told the truth. "And nobody does. The hundred thousand offer made rats out of half the crooks in the country. They're as hot after him as we—not only because of the reward but because of his wholesale double-crossing. And they know just as little about him as we do—that he's had his fingers in a dozen or more jobs, that he was the brains behind Bluepoint Vance's bond tricks, and that his enemies have a habit of dying young. But nobody knows where he came from, or where he lives when he's home. Don't think I'm touting him as a Napoleon or a Sunday-supplement master mind—but he's a shifty, tricky old boy. As you say, I don't know much about him—but there are lots of people I don't know much about."

Tom-Tom Carey nodded to show he understood the last part and began making his third cigarette.

"I was in Nogales when Angel Grace Cardigan got word to me that Paddy had been done in," he said. "That was nearly a month ago. She seemed to think I'd romp up here pronto—but it was no skin off my face. I let it sleep. But last week I read in a newspaper about all this reward money being posted on the hombre she blamed for Paddy's rub-out. That made it different—a hundred thousand dollars different. So I shipped up here, talked to her, and then came in to make sure there'll be nothing between me and the blood money when I put the loop on this Papa-doodle."

"Angel Grace sent you to me?" I inquired.

"Uh-huh—only she don't know it. She dragged you into the story—said you were a friend of Paddy's, a good guy for a sleuth, and hungry as hell for this Papadoodle. So I thought you'd be the gent for me to see."

"When did you leave Nogales?"

"Tuesday—last week."

"That," I said, prodding my memory, "was the day after Newhall was killed across the border."

The swarthy man nodded. Nothing changed in his face.

"How far from Nogales was that?" I asked.

"He was gunned down near Oquitoa—that's somewhere around sixty miles southwest of Nogales. You interested?"

"No—except I was wondering about your leaving the place where he was killed the day after he was killed, and coming up where he had lived. Did you know him?"

"He was pointed out to me in Nogales as a San Francisco millionaire going with a party to look at some mining property in Mexico. I was figuring on maybe selling him something later, but the Mexican patriots got him before I did."

"And so you came north?"

"Uh-huh. The hubbub kind of spoiled things for me. I had a nice little business in—call it supplies—to and fro across the line. This Newhall killing turned the spotlight on that part of the country. So I thought I'd come up and collect that hundred thousand and give things a chance to settle down there. Honest, brother, I haven't killed a millionaire in weeks, if that's what's worrying you."

"That's good. Now, as I get it, you're counting on landing Papadopoulos. Angel Grace sent for you, thinking you'd run him down just to even up for Paddy's killing, but it's the money you want, so you figure on playing with me as well as the Angel. That right?"

"Check."

"You know what'll happen if she learns you're stringing along with me?"

"Uh-huh. She'll chuck a convulsion—kind of balmy on the subject of keeping clear of the police, isn't she?"

"She is—somebody told her something about honor among thieves once and she's never got over it. Her brother's doing a hitch up north now—Johnny the Plumber sold him out. Her man Paddy was mowed down by his pals. Did either of those things wake her up? Not a chance. She'd rather have Papadopoulos go free than join forces with us."

"That's all right," Tom-Tom Carey assured me. "She thinks I'm the loyal brother—Paddy couldn't have told her much about me—and I'll handle her. You having her shadowed?"

I said: "Yes—ever since she was turned loose. She was picked up the same day Flora and Pogy and Red were grabbed, but we hadn't anything on her except that she had been Paddy's ladylove, so I had her sprung. How much dope did you get out of her?"

"Descriptions of Papadoodle and Nancy Regan, and that's all. She don't know any more about them than I do. Where does this Regan girl fit in?"

"Hardly any, except that she might lead us to Papadopoulos. She was Red's girl. It was keeping a date with her that he upset the game. When Papadopoulos wriggled out he took the girl with him. I don't know why. She wasn't in on the stick-ups."

Tom-Tom Carey finished making and lighting his fifth cigarette and stood up.

"Are we teamed?" he asked as he picked up his hat.

"If you turn in Papadopoulos I'll see that you get every nickel you're entitled to," I replied. "And I'll give you a clear field—I won't handicap you with too much of an attempt to keep my eyes on your actions."

He said that was fair enough, told me he was stopping at a hotel in Ellis Street, and went away.

II

Calling the late Taylor Newhall's office on the phone, I was told that if I wanted any information about his affairs I should try his country residence, some miles south of San Francisco. I tried it. A ministerial voice that said it belonged to the butler told me that Newhall's attorney, Franklin Ellert, was the person I should see. I went over to Ellert's office.

He was a nervous, irritable old man with a lisp and eyes that stuck out with blood pressure.

"Is there any reason," I asked point-blank, "for supposing that Newhall's murder was anything more than a Mexican bandit outburst? Is it likely that he was killed purposely, and not resisting capture?"

Lawyers don't like to be questioned. This one sputtered and made faces at me and let his eyes stick out still further and, of course, didn't give me an answer.

"How? How?" he snapped disagreeably. "Exthplain your meaning, thir!"

He glared at me and then at the desk, pushing papers around with excited hands, as if he were hunting for a police whistle. I told my story—told him about Tom-Tom Carey.

Ellert sputtered some more, demanded, "What the devil do you mean?" and made a complete jumble of the papers on his desk.

"I don't mean anything," I growled back. "I'm just telling you what was said."

"Yeth! Yeth! I know!" He stopped glaring at me and his voice was less peevish. "But there ith abtholutely no reathon for thuthpecting anything of the thort. None at all, thir, none at all!"

"Maybe you're right." I turned to the door. "But I'll poke into it a little anyway."

"Wait! Wait!" He scrambled out of his chair and ran around the desk to me. "I think you are mithtaken, but if you are going to invethtigate it I would like to know what you dithcover. Perhapth you'd better charge me with your regular fee for whatever ith done, and keep me informed of your progreth. Thatithfactory?"

I said it was, came back to his desk and began to question him. There was, as the lawyer had said, nothing in Newhall's affairs to stir us up. The dead man was several times a millionaire, with most of his money in mines. He had inherited nearly half his money. There was no shady practice, no claim-jumping, no trickery in his past, no enemies. He was a widower with one daughter. She had everything she wanted while he lived, and she and her father had been very fond of one another. He had gone to Mexico with a party of mining men from New York who expected to sell him some property there. They had been attacked by bandits, had driven them off, but Newhall and a geologist named Parker had been killed during the fight.

Back in the office, I wrote a telegram to our Los Angeles branch, asking that an operative be sent to Nogales to pry into Newhall's killing and Tom-Tom Carey's affairs. The clerk to whom I gave it to be coded and sent told me the Old Man wanted to see me. I went into his office and was introduced to a short, rolly-polly man named Hook.

"Mr Hook," the Old Man said, "is the proprietor of a restaurant in Sausalito. Last Monday he employed a waitress named Nelly Riley. She told him she had come from Los Angeles. Her description, as Mr Hook gives it, is quite similar to the description you and Counihan have given of Nancy Regan. Isn't it?" he asked the fat man.

"Absolutely. It's exactly what I read in the papers. She's five feet five inches tall, about, and medium in size, and she's got blue eyes and brown hair, and she's around twenty-one or two, and she's got looks, and the thing that counts most is she's high-hat as the devil—she don't think nothin's good enough for her. Why, when I tried to be a little sociable she told me to keep my 'dirty paws' to myself. And then I found out she didn't know hardly nothing about Los Angeles, though she claimed to have lived there two or three years. I bet you she's the girl, all right," and he went on talking about how much reward money he ought to get.

"Are you going back there now?" I asked him.

"Pretty soon. I got to stop and see about some dishes. Then I'm going back."

"This girl will be working?"

"Yes."

"Then we'll send a man over with you—one who knows Nancy Regan."

I called Jack Counihan in from the operatives' room and introduced him to Hook. They arranged to meet in half an hour at the ferry and Hook waddled out.

"This Nelly Riley won't be Nancy Regan," I said. "But we can't afford to pass up even a hundred to one chance."

I told Jack and the Old Man about Tom-Tom Carey and my visit to Ellert's office. The Old Man listened with his usual polite attentiveness. Young Counihan—only four months in the man-hunting business—listened with wide eyes.

"You'd better run along now and meet Hook," I said when I had finished, leaving the Old Man's office with Jack. "And if she should be Nancy Regan—grab her and hang on." We were out of the Old Man's hearing, so I added, "And for God's sake don't let your youthful gallantry lead you to a poke in the jaw this time. Pretend you're grown up."

The boy blushed, said, "Go to hell!" adjusted his necktie, and set off to meet Hook.

I had some reports to write. After I had finished them I put my feet on my desk, made cavities in a package of Fatimas, and thought about Tom-Tom Carey until six o'clock. Then I went down to the States for my abalone chowder and minute steak and home to change clothes before going out Sea Cliff way to sit in a poker game.

The telephone interrupted my dressing. Jack Counihan was on the other end.

"I'm in Sausalito. The girl wasn't Nancy, but I've got hold of something else. I'm not sure how to handle it. Can you come over?"

"Is it important enough to cut a poker game for?"

"Yes, it's—I think it's big." He was excited. "I wish you would come over. I really think it's a lead."

"Where are you?"

"At the ferry there. Not the Golden Gate, the other."

"All right. I'll catch the first boat."

III

An hour later I walked off the boat in Sausalito. Jack Counihan pushed through the crowd and began talking:

"Coming down here on my way back—"

"Hold it till we get out of the mob," I advised him. "It must be tremendous—the eastern point of your collar is bent."

He mechanically repaired this defect in his otherwise immaculate costuming while we walked to the street, but he was too intent on whatever was on his mind to smile.

"Up this way," he said, guiding me around a corner. "Hook's lunch-room is on the corner. You can take a look at the girl if you like. She's of the same size and complexion as Nancy Regan, but that is all. She's a tough little job who probably was fired for dropping her chewing gum in the soup the last place she worked."

"All right. That lets her out. Now what's on your mind?"

"After I saw her I started back to the ferry. A boat came in while I was still a couple of blocks away. Two men who must have come in on it came up the street. They were Greeks, rather young, tough, though ordinarily I shouldn't have paid much attention to them. But, since Papadopoulos is a Greek, we have been interested in them, of course, so I looked at these chaps. They were arguing about something as they walked, not talking loud, but scowling at one another. As they passed me the chap on the gutter side said to the other, 'I tell him it's been twenty-nine days.'

"Twenty-nine days. I counted back and it's just twenty-nine days since we started hunting for Papadopoulos. He is a Greek and these chaps were Greeks. When I had finished counting I turned around and began to follow them. They took me all the way through the town and up a hill on the fringe. They went to a little cottage—it couldn't have more than three rooms—set back in a clearing in the woods by itself. There was a 'For Sale' sign on it, and no curtains in the windows, no sign of occupancy—but on the ground behind the back door there was a wet place, as if a bucket or pan of water had been thrown out.

"I stayed in the bushes until it got a little darker. Then I went closer. I could hear people inside, but I couldn't see anything through the windows. They're boarded up. After a while the two chaps I had followed came out, saying something in a language I couldn't understand to whoever was in the cottage. The cottage door stayed open until the two men had gone out of sight down the path—so I couldn't have followed them without being seen by whoever was at the door.

"Then the door was closed and I could hear people moving around inside—or perhaps only one person—and could smell cooking, and some smoke came out of the chimney. I waited and waited and nothing more happened and I thought I had better get in touch with you."

"Sounds interesting," I agreed.

We were passing under a street light. Jack stopped me with a hand on my arm and fished something out of his overcoat pocket.

"Look!" He held it out to me. A charred piece of blue cloth. It could have been the remains of a woman's hat that had been three-quarters burned. I looked at it under the street light and then used my flashlight to examine it more closely.

"I picked it up behind the cottage while I was nosing around," Jack said, "and—"

"And Nancy Regan wore a hat of that shade the night she and Papadopoulos vanished," I finished for him. "On to the cottage."

We left the street lights behind, climbed the hill, dipped down into a little valley, turned into a winding sandy path, left that to cut across sod between trees to a dirt road, trod half a mile of that, and then Jack led the way along a narrow path that wound through a black tangle of bushes and small trees. I hoped he knew where he was going.

"Almost there," he whispered to me.

A man jumped out of the bushes and took me by the neck.

My hands were in my overcoat pockets—one holding the flashlight, the other my gun.

I pushed the muzzle of the pocketed gun toward the man—pulled the trigger.

The shot ruined seventy-five dollars' worth of overcoat for me. But it took the man away from my neck.

That was lucky. Another man was on my back.

I tried to twist away from him—didn't altogether make it—felt the edge of a knife along my spine.

That wasn't so lucky—but it was better than getting the point.

I butted back at his face—missed—kept twisting and squirming while I brought my hands out of my pockets and clawed at him.

The blade of his knife came flat against my cheek. I caught the hand that held it and let myself go—down backward—him under.

He said: "Uh!"

I rolled over, got hands and knees on the ground, was grazed by a fist, scrambled up.

Fingers dragged at my ankle.

My behavior was ungentlemanly. I kicked the fingers away—found the man's body—kicked it twice—hard.

Jack's voice whispered my name. I couldn't see him in the blackness, nor could I see the man I had shot.

"All right here," I told Jack. "How did you come out?"

"Top-hole. Is that all of it?"

"Don't know, but I'm going to risk a peek at what I've got."

Tilting my flashlight down at the man under my foot, I snapped it on. A thin blond man, his face blood-smeared, his pink-rimmed eyes jerking as he tried to play 'possum in the glare.

"Come out of it!" I ordered.

A heavy gun went off back in the bush—another, lighter one. The bullets ripped through the foliage.

I switched off the light, bent to the man on the ground, knocked him on the top of the head with my gun.

"Crouch down low," I whispered to Jack.

The smaller gun snapped again, twice. It was ahead, to the left.

I put my mouth to Jack's ear.

"We're going to that damned cottage whether anybody likes it or no. Keep low and don't do any shooting unless you can see what you're shooting at. Go ahead."

Bending as close to the ground as I could, I followed Jack up the path. The position stretched the slash in my back—a scalding pain from between my shoulders almost to my waist.

I could feel blood trickling down over my hips—or thought I could.

The going was too dark for stealthiness. Things crackled under our feet, rustled against our shoulders. Our friends in the bush used their guns. Luckily, the sound of twigs breaking and leaves rustling in pitch blackness isn't the best of targets. Bullets zipped here and there, but we didn't stop any of them. Neither did we shoot back.

We halted where the end of the bush left the night a weaker gray.

"That's it," Jack said about a square shape ahead.

"On the jump," I grunted and lit out for the dark cottage.

Jack's long slim legs kept him easily at my side as we raced across the clearing.

A man-shape oozed from behind the blot of the building and his gun began to blink at us. The shots came so close together that they sounded like one long stuttering bang.

Pulling the youngster with me, I flopped, flat to the ground except where a ragged-edged empty tin-can held my face up.

From the other side of the building another gun coughed. From a tree-stem to the right, a third.

Jack and I began to burn powder back at them.

A bullet kicked my mouth full of dirt and pebbles. I spit mud and cautioned Jack:

"You're shooting too high. Hold it low and pull easy."

A hump showed in the house's dark profile. I sent a bullet at it.

A man's voice yelled: "Ow—ooh!" and then, lower but very bitter, "Oh, damn you—damn you!"

For a warm couple of seconds bullets spattered all around us. Then there was not a sound to spoil the night's quietness.

When the silence had lasted five minutes, I got myself up on hands and knees and began to move forward, Jack following. The ground wasn't made for that sort of work. Ten feet of it was enough. We stood up and walked the rest of the way to the building.

"Wait," I whispered, and leaving Jack at one corner of the building, I circled it, seeing nobody, hearing nothing but the sounds I made.

We tried the front door. It was locked but rickety.

Bumping it open with my shoulder, I went indoors—flashlight and gun in my fists.

The shack was empty.

Nobody—no furnishings—no traces of either in the two bare rooms—nothing but bare wooden walls, bare floor, bare ceiling, with a stove-pipe connected to nothing sticking through it.

Jack and I stood in the middle of the floor, looked at the emptiness, and cursed the dump from back door to front for being empty. We hadn't quite finished when feet sounded outside, a white light beamed on the open doorway, and a cracked voice said:

"Hey! You can come out one at a time—kind of easy like!"

"Who says so?" I asked, snapping off the flashlight, moving over close to a side wall.

"A whole goldurned flock of deputy sheriffs," the voice answered.

"Couldn't you push one of 'em in and let us get a look at him?" I asked. "I've been choked and carved and shot at tonight until I haven't got much faith left in anybody's word."

A lanky, knock-kneed man with a thin leathery face appeared in the doorway. He showed me a buzzer, I fished out my credentials, and the other deputies came in. There were three of them in all.

"We were driving down the road bound for a little job near the point when we heard the shooting," the lanky one explained. "What's up?"

I told him.

"This shack's been empty a long while," he said when I had finished. "Anybody could have camped in it easy enough. Think it was that Papadopoulos, huh? We'll kind of look around for him and his friends—especial since there's that nice reward money."

We searched the woods and found nobody. The man I had knocked down and the man I had shot were both gone.

Jack and I rode back to Sausalito with the deputies. I hunted up a doctor there and had my back bandaged. He said the cut was long but shallow. Then we returned to San Francisco and separated in the direction of our homes.

And thus ended the day's doings.

IV

Here is something that happened next morning. I didn't see it. I heard about it a little before noon and read about it in the papers that afternoon. I didn't know then that I had any personal interest in it, but later I did—so I'll put it in here where it happened.

At ten o'clock that morning, into busy Market Street, staggered a man who was naked from the top of his battered head to the soles of his bloodstained feet. From his bare chest and sides and back, little ribbons of flesh hung down, dripping blood. His left arm was broken in two places. The left side of his bald head was smashed in. An hour later he died in the emergency hospital—without having said a word to anyone, with the same vacant, distant look in his eyes.

The police easily ran back the trail of blood drops. They ended with a red smear in an alley beside a small hotel just off Market Street. In the hotel, the police found the room from which the man had jumped, fallen, or been thrown. The bed was soggy with blood. On it were torn and twisted sheets that had been knotted and used rope-wise. There was also a towel that had been used as a gag.

The evidence read that the naked man had been gagged, trussed up and worked on with a knife. The doctors said the ribbons of flesh had been cut loose, not torn or clawed. After the knife-user had gone away, the naked man had worked free of his bonds, and, probably crazed by pain, had either jumped or fallen out of the window. The fall had crushed his skull and broken his arm, but he had managed to walk a block and a half in that condition.

The hotel management said the man had been there two days. He was registered as H. F. Barrows, City. He had a black Gladstone bag in which, besides clothes, shaving implements and so on, the police found a box of .38 cartridges, a black handkerchief with eye-holes cut in it, four skeleton keys, a small jimmy, and a quantity of morphine, with a needle and the rest of the kit. Elsewhere in the room they found the rest of his clothes, a .38 revolver and two quarts of liquor. They didn't find a cent.

The supposition was that Barrows had been a burglar, and that he had been tied up, tortured and robbed, probably by pals, between eight and nine that morning. Nobody knew anything about him. Nobody had seen his visitor or visitors. The room next to his on the left was unoccupied. The occupant of the room on the other side had left for his work in a furniture factory before seven o'clock.

While this was happening I was at the office, sitting forward in my chair to spare my back, reading reports, all of which told how operatives attached to various Continental Detective Agency branches had continued to fail to turn up any indications of the past, present, or future whereabouts of Papadopoulos and Nancy Regan. There was nothing novel about these reports—I had been reading similar ones for three weeks.

The Old Man and I went out to luncheon together, and I told him about the previous night's adventures in Sausalito while we ate. His grandfatherly face was as attentive as always, and his smile as politely interested, but when I was half through my story he turned his mild blue eyes from my face to his salad and he stared at his salad until I had finished talking. Then, still not looking up, he said he was sorry I had been cut. I thanked him and we ate a while.

Finally he looked at me. The mildness and courtesy he habitually wore over his cold-bloodedness were in face and eyes and voice as he said:

"This first indication that Papadopoulos is still alive came immediately after Tom-Tom Carey's arrival."

It was my turn to shift my eyes.

I looked at the roll I was breaking while I said: "Yes."

That afternoon a phone call came in from a woman out in the Mission who had seen some highly mysterious happenings and was sure they had something to do with the well-advertised bank robberies. So I went out to see her and spent most of the afternoon learning that half of her happenings were imaginary and the other half were the efforts of a jealous wife to get the low-down on her husband.

It was nearly six o'clock when I returned to the agency. A few minutes later Dick Foley called me on the phone. His teeth were chattering until I could hardly get the words.

"C-c-canyoug-g-get-t-townt-t-tooth-ar-r-rbr-r-spittle?"

"What?" I asked, and he said the same thing again, or worse. But by this time I had guessed that he was asking me if I could get down to the Harbor Hospital.

I told him I could in ten minutes, and with the help of a taxi I did.

V

The little Canadian operative met me at the hospital door. His clothes and hair were dripping wet, but he had had a shot of whisky and his teeth had stopped chattering.

"Damned fool jumped in bay!" he barked as if it were my fault.

"Angel Grace?"

"Who else was I shadowing? Got on Oakland ferry. Moved off by self by rail. Thought she was going to throw something over. Kept eye on her. Bingo! She jumps." Dick sneezed. "I was goofy enough to jump after her. Held her up. Were fished out. In there," nodding his wet head toward the interior of the hospital.

"What happened before she took the ferry?"

"Nothing. Been in joint all day. Straight out to ferry."

"How about yesterday?"

"Apartment all day. Out at night with man. Roadhouse. Home at four. Bad break. Couldn't tail him off."

"What did he look like?"

The man Dick described was Tom-Tom Carey.

"Good," I said. "You'd better beat it home for a hot bath and some dry rags."

I went in to see the near-suicide.

She was lying on her back on a cot, staring at the ceiling. Her face was pale, but it always was, and her green eyes were no more sullen than usual. Except that her short hair was dark with dampness she didn't look as if anything out of the ordinary had happened.

"You think of the funniest things to do," I said when I was beside the bed.

She jumped and her face jerked around to me, startled. Then she recognized me and smiled—a smile that brought into her face the attractiveness that habitual sullenness kept out.

"You have to keep in practice—sneaking up on people?" she asked. "Who told you I was here?"

"Everybody knows it. Your pictures are all over the front pages of the newspapers, with your life history and what you said to the Prince of Wales."

She stopped smiling and looked steadily at me.

"I got it!" she exclaimed after a few seconds. "That runt who came in after me was one of your ops—tailing me. Wasn't he?"

"I didn't know anybody had to go in after you," I answered. "I thought you came ashore after you had finished your swim. Didn't you want to land?"

She wouldn't smile. Her eyes began to look at something horrible.

"Oh! Why didn't they let me alone?" she wailed, shuddering. "It's a rotten thing, living."

I sat down on a small chair beside the white bed and patted the lump her shoulder made in the sheets.

"What was it?" I was surprised at the fatherly tone I achieved. "What did you want to die for, Angel?"

Words that wanted to be said were shiny in her eyes, tugged at muscles in her face, shaped her lips—but that was all. The words she said came out listlessly, but with a reluctant sort of finality. They were:

"No. You're law. I'm thief. I'm staying on my side of the fence. Nobody can say—"

"All right! All right!" I surrendered. "But for God's sake don't make me listen to another of those ethical arguments. Is there anything I can do for you?"

"Thanks, no."

"There's nothing you want to tell me?"

She shook her head.

"You're all right now?"

"Yes. I was being shadowed, wasn't I? Or you wouldn't have known about it so soon."

"I'm a detective—I know everything. Be a good girl."

From the hospital I went up to the Hall of Justice, to the police detective bureau. Lieutenant Duff was holding down the captain's desk. I told him about the Angel's dive.

"Got any idea what she was up to?" he wanted to know when I had finished.

"She's too far off center to figure. I want her vagged."

"Yeah? I thought you wanted her loose so you could catch her."

"That's about played out now; I'd like to try throwing her in the can for thirty days. Big Flora is in waiting trial. The Angel knows Flora was one of the troupe that rubbed out her Paddy. Maybe Flora don't know the Angel. Let's see what will come of mixing the two babies for a month."

"Can do," Duff agreed. "This Angel's got no visible means of support, and it's a cinch she's got no business running around jumping in people's bays. I'll put the word through."

From the Hall of Justice I went up to the Ellis Street hotel at which Tom-Tom Carey had told me he was registered. He was out. I left word that I would be back in an hour, and used that hour to eat. When I returned to the hotel the tall swarthy man was sitting in the lobby. He took me up to his room and set out gin, orange juice and cigars.

"Seen Angel Grace?" I asked.

"Yes, last night. We did the dumps."

"Seen her today?"

"No."

"She jumped in the bay this afternoon."

"The hell she did." He seemed moderately surprised. "And then?"

"She was fished out. She's O.K."

The shadow in his eyes could have been some slight disappointment.

"She's a funny sort of kid," he remarked. "I wouldn't say Paddy didn't show good taste when he picked her, but she's a queer one!"

"How's the Papadopoulos hunt progressing?"

"It is. But you oughtn't have split on your word. You half-way promised you wouldn't have me shadowed."

"I'm not the big boss," I apologized. "Sometimes what I want don't fit in with what the headman wants. This shouldn't bother you much—you can shake him, can't you?"

"Uh-huh. That's what I've been doing. But it's a damned nuisance jumping in and out of taxis and back doors."

We talked and drank a few minutes longer, and then I left Carey's room and hotel, and went to a drug-store telephone booth, where I called Dick Foley's home, and gave Dick the swarthy man's description and address.

"I don't want you to tail Carey, Dick. I want you to find out who is trying to tail him—and that shadower is the bird you're to stick to. The morning will be time enough to start—get yourself dried out."

And that was the end of that day.

VI

I woke to a disagreeable rainy morning. Maybe it was the weather, maybe I'd been too frisky the day before, anyway the slit in my back was like a foot-long boil. I phoned Dr Canova, who lived on the floor below me, and had him look at the cut before he left for his downtown office. He rebandaged it and told me to take life easy for a couple of days. It felt better after he had fooled with it, but I phoned the agency and told the Old Man that unless something exciting broke I was going to stay on sick-call all day.

I spent the day propped up in front of the gas-log, reading, and smoking cigarettes that wouldn't burn right on account of the weather. That night I used the phone to organize a poker game, in which I got very little action one way or the other. In the end I was fifteen dollars ahead, which was just about five dollars less than enough to pay for the booze my guests had drunk on me.

My back was better the following day, and so was the day. I went down to the agency. There was a memorandum on my desk saying Duff had phoned that Angel Grace Cardigan had been vagged—thirty days in the city prison. There was a familiar pile of reports from various branches on their operatives' inability to pick up anything on Papadopoulos and Nancy Regan. I was running through these when Dick Foley came in.

"Made him," he reported. "Thirty or thirty-two. Five, six. Hundred, thirty. Sandy hair, complexion. Blue eye. Thin face, some skin off. Rat. Lives dump in Seventh Street."

"What did he do?"

"Tailed Carey one block. Carey shook him. Hunted for Carey till two in morning. Didn't find him. Went home. Take him again?"

"Go up to his flophouse and find out who he is."

The little Canadian was gone half an hour.

"Sam Arlie," he said when he returned. "Been there six months. Supposed to be barber—when he's working—if ever."

"I've got two guesses about this Arlie," I told Dick. "The first is that he's the gink who carved me in Sausalito the other night. The second is that something's going to happen to him."

It was against Dick's rules to waste words, so he said nothing.

I called Tom-Tom Carey's hotel and got the swarthy man on the wire.

"Come over," I invited him. "I've got some news for you."

"As soon as I'm dressed and breakfasted," he promised.

"When Carey leaves here you're to go along behind him," I told Dick after I had hung up. "If Arlie connects with him now, maybe there'll be something doing. Try to see it."

Then I phoned the detective bureau and made a date with Sergeant Hunt to visit Angel Grace Cardigan's apartment. After that I busied myself with paper work until Tommy came in to announce the swarthy man from Nogales.

"The jobbie who's tailing you," I informed him when he had sat down and begun work on a cigarette, "is a barber named Arlie," and I told him where Arlie lived.

"Yes. A slim-faced, sandy lad?"

I gave him the description Dick had given me.

"That's the hombre," Tom-Tom Carey said. "Know anything else about him?"

"No."

"You had Angel Grace vagged."

It was neither an accusation nor a question, so I didn't answer it.

"It's just as well," the tall man went on. "I'd have had to send her away. She was bound to gum things with her foolishness when I got ready to swing the loop."

"That'll be soon?"

"That all depends on how it happens." He stood up, yawned and shook his wide shoulders. "But nobody would starve to death if they decided not to eat any more till I'd got him. I oughtn't have accused you of having me shadowed."

"It didn't spoil my day."

Tom-Tom Carey said, "So long," and sauntered out.

I rode down to the Hall of Justice, picked up Hunt, and we went to the Bush Street apartment house in which Angel Grace Cardigan had lived. The manager—a highly scented fat woman with a hard mouth and soft eyes—already knew her tenant was in the cooler. She willingly took us up to the girl's rooms.

The Angel wasn't a good housekeeper. Things were clean enough, but upset. The kitchen sink was full of dirty dishes. The folding bed was worse than loosely made up. Clothes and odds and ends of feminine equipment hung over everything from bathroom to kitchen.

We got rid of the landlady and raked the place over thoroughly. We came away knowing all there was to know about the girl's wardrobe, and a lot about her personal habits. But we didn't find anything pointing Papadopoulos-ward.

No report came in on the Carey-Arlie combination that afternoon or evening, though I expected to hear from Dick every minute.

At three o'clock in the morning my bedside phone took my ear out of the pillows. The voice that came over the wire was the Canadian op's.

"Exit Arlie," he said.

"R.I.P.?"

"Yep."

"How?"

"Lead."

"Our lad's?"

"Yep."

"Keep till morning?"

"Yep."

"See you at the office," and I went back to sleep.

VII

When I arrived at the agency at nine o'clock, one of the clerks had just finished decoding a night letter from the Los Angeles operative who had been sent over to Nogales. It was a long telegram, and meaty.

It said that Tom-Tom Carey was well known along the border. For some six months he had been engaged in over-the-line traffic—guns going south, booze, and probably dope and immigrants, coming north. Just before leaving there the previous week he had made inquiries concerning one Hank Barrows. This Hank Barrows' description fit the H. F. Barrows who had been cut into ribbons, who had fallen out the hotel window and died.

The Los Angeles operative hadn't been able to get much of a line on Barrows, except that he hailed from San Francisco, had been on the border only a few days, and had apparently returned to San Francisco. The operative had turned up nothing new on the Newhall killing—the signs still read that he had been killed resisting capture by Mexican patriots.

Dick Foley came into my office while I was reading this news. When I had finished he gave me his contribution to the history of Tom-Tom Carey.

"Tailed him out of here. To hotel. Arlie on corner. Eight o'clock, Carey out. Garage. Hire car without driver. Back hotel. Checked out. Two bags. Out through park. Arlie after him in flivver. My boat after Arlie. Down boulevard. Oft cross-road. Dark. Lonely. Arlie steps on gas. Closes in. Bang! Carey stops. Two guns going. Exit Arlie. Carey back to city. Hotel Marquis. Registers George F Danby, San Diego. Room 622."

"Did Tom-Tom frisk Arlie after he dropped him?"

"No. Didn't touch him."

"So? Take Mickey Linehan with you. Don't let Carey get out of your sight. I'll get somebody up to relieve you and Mickey late tonight, if I can, but he's got to be shadowed twenty-four hours a day until—" I didn't know what came after that so I stopped talking.

I took Dick's story into the Old Man's office and told it to him, winding up:

"Arlie shot first, according to Foley, so Carey gets a self-defense on it, but we're getting action at last and I don't want to do anything to slow it up. So I'd like to keep what we know about this shooting quiet for a couple of days. It won't increase our friendship any with the county sheriff if he finds out what we're doing, but I think it's worth it."

"If you wish," the Old Man agreed, reaching for his ringing phone.

He spoke into the instrument and passed it on to me.

Detective-sergeant Hunt was talking:

"Flora Brace and Grace Cardigan crushed out just before daylight. The chances are they—"

I wasn't in a humor for details.

"A clean sneak?" I asked.

"Not a lead on 'em so far, but—"

"I'll get the details when I see you. Thanks," and I hung up.

"Angel Grace and Big Flora have escaped from the city prison," I passed the news on to the Old Man.

He smiled courteously, as if at something that didn't especially concern him.

"You were congratulating yourself on getting action," he murmured.

I turned my scowl to a grin, mumbled, "Well, maybe," went back to my office and telephoned Franklin Ellert. The lisping attorney said he would be glad to see me, so I went over to his office.

"And now, what progreth have you made?" he asked eagerly when I was seated beside his desk.

"Some. A man named Barrows was also in Nogales when Newhall was killed, and also came to San Francisco right after. Carey followed Barrows up here. Did you read about the man found walking the streets naked, all cut up?"

"Yeth."

"That was Barrows. Then another man comes into the game—a barber named Arlie. He was spying on Carey. Last night, in a lonely road south of here, Arlie shot at Carey. Carey killed him."

The old lawyer's eyes came out another inch.

"What road?" he gasped.

"You want the exact location?"

"Yeth!"

I pulled his phone over, called the agency, had Dick's report read to me, gave the attorney the information he wanted.

It had an effect on him. He hopped out of his chair. Sweat was shiny along the ridges wrinkles made in his face.

"Mith Newhall ith down there alone! That plath ith only half a mile from her houth!"

I frowned and beat my brains together, but I couldn't make anything out of it.

"Suppose I put a man down there to look after her?" I suggested.

"Exthellent!" His worried face cleared until there weren't more than fifty or sixty wrinkles in it. "The would prefer to thay there during her firth grief over her fatherth death. You will thend a capable man?"

"The Rock of Gibraltar is a leaf in the breeze beside him. Give me a note for him to take down. Andrew MacElroy is his name."

While the lawyer scribbled the note I used his phone again to call the agency, to tell the operator to get hold of Andy and tell him I wanted him. I ate lunch before I returned to the agency. Andy was waiting when I got there.

Andy MacElroy was a big boulder of a man—not very tall, but thick and hard of head and body. A glum, grim man with no more imagination than an adding machine. I'm not even sure he could read. But I was sure that when Andy was told to do something, he did it and nothing else. He didn't know enough not to.

I gave him the lawyer's note to Miss Newhall, told him where to go and what to do, and Miss Newhall's troubles were off my mind.

Three times that afternoon I heard from Dick Foley and Mickey Linehan. Tom-Tom Carey wasn't doing anything very exciting, though he had bought two boxes of .44 cartridges in a Market Street sporting goods establishment.

The afternoon papers carried photographs of Big Flora Brace and Angel Grace Cardigan, with a story of their escape. The story was as far from the probable facts as newspaper stories generally are. On another page was an account of the discovery of the dead barber in the lonely road. He had been shot in the head and in the chest, four times in all. The county officials' opinion was that he had been killed resisting a stick-up, and that the bandits had fled without robbing him.

At five o'clock Tommy Howd came to my door.

"That guy Carey wants to see you again," the freckle-faced boy said.

"Shoot him in."

The swarthy man sauntered in, said "Howdy," sat down, and made a brown cigarette.

"Got anything special on for tonight?" he asked when he was smoking.

"Nothing I can't put aside for something better. Giving a party?"

"Uh-huh. I had thought of it. A kind of surprise party for Papadoodle. Want to go along?"

It was my turn to say, "Uh-huh."

"I'll pick you up at eleven—Van Ness and Geary," he drawled. "But this has got to be a kind of tight party—just you and me—and him."

"No. There's one more who'll have to be in on it. I'll bring him along."

"I don't like that." Tom-Tom Carey shook his head slowly, frowning amiably over his cigarette. "You sleuths oughtn't outnumber me. It ought to be one and one."

"You won't be out-numbered," I explained. "This jobbie I'm bringing won't be on my side more than yours. And it'll pay you to keep as sharp an eye on him as I do—and to see he don't get behind either of us if we can help it."

"Then what do you want to lug him along for?"

"Wheels within wheels," I grinned.

The swarthy man frowned again, less amiably now.

"The hundred and six thousand reward money—I'm not figuring on sharing that with anybody."

"Right enough," I agreed. "Nobody I bring along will declare themselves in on it."

"I'll take your word for it." He stood up. "And we've got to watch this hombre, huh?"

"If we want everything to go all right."

"Suppose he gets in the way—cuts up on us. Can we put it to him, or do we just say, 'Naughty! Naughty!'?"

"He'll have to take his own chances."

"Fair enough." His hard face was good-natured again as he moved toward the door. "Eleven o'clock at Van Ness and Geary."

VIII

I went back into the operatives' room, where Jack Counihan was slumped down in a chair reading a magazine.

"I hope you've thought up something for me to do," he greeted me. "I'm getting bed-sores from sitting around."

"Patience, son, patience—that's what you've got to learn if you're ever going to be a detective. Why when I was a child of your age, just starting in with the agency, I was lucky—"

"Don't start that," he begged. Then his good-looking young face got earnest. "I don't see why you keep me cooped up here. I'm the only one besides you who really got a good look at Nancy Regan. I should think you would have me out hunting for her."

"I told the Old Man the same thing," I sympathized. "But he is afraid to risk something happening to you. He says in all his fifty years of gumshoeing he's never seen such a handsome op, besides being a fashion plate and a social butterfly and the heir to millions. His idea is we ought to keep you as a sort of show piece, and not let you—"

"Go to hell!" Jack said, all red in the face.

"But I persuaded him to let me take the cotton packing off you tonight," I continued. "So meet me at Van Ness and Geary before eleven o'clock."

"Action?" He was all eagerness.

"Maybe."

"What are we going to do?"

"Bring your little pop-gun along." An idea came into my head and I worded it. "You'd better be all dressed up—evening duds."

"Dinner coat?"

"No—the limit—everything but the high hat. Now for your behavior: you're not supposed to be an op. I'm not sure just what you're supposed to be, but it doesn't make any difference. Tom-Tom Carey will be along. You act as if you were neither my friend nor his—as if you didn't trust either of us. We'll be cagey with you. If anything is asked that you don't know the answer to—you fall back on hostility. But don't crowd Carey too far. Got it?"

"I—I think so." He spoke slowly, screwing up his forehead. "I'm to act as if I was going along on the same business as you, but that outside of that we weren't friends. As if I wasn't willing to trust you. That it?"

"Very much. Watch yourself. You'll be swimming in nitroglycerine all the way."

"What is up? Be a good chap and give me some idea."

I grinned up at him. He was a lot taller than I.

"I could," I admitted, "but I'm afraid it would scare you off. So I'd better tell you nothing. Be happy while you can. Eat a good dinner. Lots of condemned folks seem to eat hearty breakfasts of ham and eggs just before they parade out to the rope. Maybe you wouldn't want 'em for dinner, but—"

At five minutes to eleven that night, Tom-Tom Carey brought a black touring car to the corner where Jack and I stood waiting in a fog that was like a damp fur coat.

"Climb in," he ordered as we came to the curb.

I opened the front door and motioned Jack in. He rang up the curtain on his little act, looking coldly at me and opening the rear door.

"I'm going to sit back here," he said bluntly.

"Not a bad idea," and I climbed in beside him.

Carey twisted around in his seat and he and Jack stared at each other for a while. I said nothing, did not introduce them. When the swarthy man had finished sizing the youngster up, he looked from the boy's collar and tie—all of his evening clothes not hidden by his overcoat—to me, grinned, and drawled:

"Your friend's a waiter, huh?"

I laughed, because the indignation that darkened the boy's face and popped his mouth open was natural, not part of his acting. I pushed my foot against his. He closed his mouth, said nothing, looked at Tom-Tom Carey and me as if we were specimens of some lower form of animal life.

I grinned back at Carey and asked, "Are we waiting for anything?"

He said we weren't, left off staring at Jack, and put the machine in motion. He drove us out through the park, down the boulevard. Traffic going our way and the other loomed out of and faded into the fog-thick night. Presently we left the city behind, and ran out of the fog into clear moonlight. I didn't look at any of the machines running behind us, but I knew that in one of them Dick Foley and Mickey Linehan should be riding.

Tom-Tom Carey swung our car off the boulevard, into a road that was smooth and well made, but not much traveled.

"Wasn't a man killed down along here somewhere last night?" I asked.

Carey nodded his head without turning it, and, when we had gone another quarter-mile, said: "Right here."

We rode a little slower now, and Carey turned off his lights. In the road that was half moon-silver, half shadow-gray, the machine barely crept along for perhaps a mile. We stopped in the shade of tall shrubs that darkened a spot of the road.

"All ashore that's going ashore," Tom-Tom Carey said, and got out of the car.

Jack and I followed him. Carey took off his overcoat and threw it into the machine.

"The place is just around the bend, back from the road," he told us. "Damn this moon! I was counting on fog."

I said nothing, nor did Jack. The boy's face was white and excited.

"We'll bee-line it," Carey said, leading the way across the road to a high wire fence.

He went over the fence first, then Jack, then—the sound of someone coming along the road from ahead stopped me. Signalling silence to the two men on the other side of the fence, I made myself small beside a bush. The coming steps were light, quick, feminine.

A girl came into the moonlight just ahead. She was a girl of twenty-something, neither tall nor short, thin nor plump. She was short-skirted, bare-haired, sweatered. Terror was in her white face, in the carriage of her hurrying figure—but something else was there too—more beauty than a middle-aged sleuth was used to seeing.

When she saw Carey's automobile bulking in the shadow, she stopped abruptly, with a gasp that was almost a cry.

I walked forward, saying:

"Hello, Nancy Regan."

This time the gasp was a cry.

"Oh! Oh!" Then, unless the moonlight was playing tricks, she recognized me and terror began to go away from her. She put both hands out to me, with relief in the gesture.

"Well?" A bearish grumble came from the big boulder of a man who had appeared out of the darkness behind her. "What's all this?"

"Hello, Andy," I greeted the boulder.

"Hullo," MacElroy echoed and stood still.

Andy always did what he was told to do. He had been told to take care of Miss Newhall. I looked at the girl and then at him again.

"Is this Miss Newhall?" I asked.

"Yeah," he rumbled. "I came down like you said, but she told me she didn't want me—wouldn't let me in the house. But you hadn't said anything about coming back. So I just camped outside, moseying around, keeping my eyes on things. And when I seen her shinnying out a window a little while ago, I just went on along behind her to take care of her, like you said I was to do."

Tom-Tom Carey and Jack Counihan came back into the road, crossed it to us. The swarthy man had an automatic in one hand. The girl's eyes were glued on mine. She paid no attention to the others.

"What is it all about?" I asked her.

"I don't know," she babbled, her hands holding on to mine, her face close to mine. "Yes, I'm Ann Newhall. I didn't know. I thought it was fun. And then when I found out it wasn't I couldn't get out of it."

Tom-Tom Carey grunted and stirred impatiently. Jack Counihan was staring down the road. Andy MacElroy stood stolid in the road, waiting to be told what to do next. The girl never once looked from me to any of these others.

"How did you get in with them?" I demanded. "Talk fast."

IX

I had told the girl to talk fast. She did. For twenty minutes she stood there and turned out words in a chattering stream that had no breaks except where I cut in to keep her from straying from the path I wanted her to follow. It was jumbled, almost incoherent in spots, and not always plausible, but the notion stayed with me throughout that she was trying to tell the truth—most of the time.

And not for a fraction of a second did she turn her gaze from my eyes. It was as if she was afraid to look anywhere else.

This millionaire's daughter had, two months before, been one of a party of four young people returning late at night from some sort of social affair down the coast. Somebody suggested that they stop at a roadhouse along their way—a particularly tough joint. Its toughness was its attraction, of course—toughness was more or less of a novelty to them. They got a first-hand view of it that night, for, nobody knew just how, they found themselves taking part in a row before they had been ten minutes in the dump.

The girl's escort had shamed her by showing an unreasonable amount of cowardice. He had let Red O'Leary turn him over his knee and spank him—and had done nothing about it afterward. The other youth in the party had been not much braver. The girl, insulted by this meekness, had walked across to the red-haired giant who had wrecked her escort, and she had spoken to him loud enough for everybody to hear:

"Will you please take me home?"

Red O'Leary was glad to do it. She left him a block or two from her city house. She told him her name was Nancy Regan. He probably doubted it, but he never asked her any questions, pried into her affairs. In spite of the difference in their worlds, a genuine companionship had grown up between them. She liked him. He was so gloriously a roughneck that she saw him as a romantic figure. He was in love with her, knew she was miles above him, and so she had no trouble making him behave so far as she was concerned.

They met often. He took her to all the rowdy holes in the bay district, introduced her to yeggs, gunmen, swindlers, told her wild tales of criminal adventuring. She knew he was a crook, knew he was tied up in the Seamen's National and Golden Gate Trust jobs when they broke. But she saw it all as a sort of theatrical spectacle. She didn't see it as it was.

She woke up the night they were in Larrouy's and were jumped by the crooks that Red had helped Papadopoulos and the others doublecross. But it was too late then for her to wriggle clear. She was blown along with Red to Papadopoulos' hangout after I had shot the big lad. She saw then what her romantic figures really were—what she had mixed herself with.

When Papadopoulos escaped, taking her with him, she was wide awake, cured, through forever with her dangerous trifling with outlaws. So she thought. She thought Papadopoulos was the little, scary old man he seemed to be—Flora's slave, a harmless old duffer too near the grave to have any evil in him. He had been whining and terrified. He begged her not to forsake him, pleaded with her while tears ran down his withered cheeks, begging her to hide him from Flora. She took him to her country house and let him fool around in the garden, safe from prying eyes. She had no idea that he had known who she was all along, had guided her into suggesting this arrangement.

Even when the newspapers said he had been the commander-in-chief of the thug army, when the hundred and six thousand dollar reward was offered for his arrest, she believed in his innocence. He convinced her that Flora and Red had simply put the blame for the whole thing on him so they could get off with lighter sentences. He was such a frightened old gink—who wouldn't have believed him?

Then her father's death in Mexico had come and grief had occupied her mind to the exclusion of most other things until this day, when Big Flora and another girl—probably Angel Grace Cardigan—had come to the house. She had been deathly afraid of Big Flora when she had seen her before. She was more afraid now; and she soon learned that Papadopoulos was not Flora's slave but her master. She saw the old buzzard as he really was. But that wasn't the end of her awakening.

Angel Grace had suddenly tried to kill Papadopoulos. Flora had overpowered her. Grace, defiant, had told them she was Paddy's girl. Then she had screamed at Ann Newhall:

"And you, you damned fool, don't you know they killed your father? Don't you know—?"

Big Flora's fingers, around Angel Grace's throat, stopped her words. Flora tied up the Angel and turned to the Newhall girl.

"You're in it," she said brusquely. "You're in it up to your neck. You'll play along with us, or else—Here's how it stands, dearie. The old man and I are both due to step off if we're caught. And you'll do the dance with us. I'll see to that. Do what you're told, and we'll all come through all right. Get funny, and I'll beat holy hell out of you."

The girl didn't remember much after that. She had a dim recollection of going to the door and telling Andy she didn't want his services. She did this mechanically, not even needing to be prompted by the big blonde woman who stood close behind her. Later, in the same fearful daze, she had gone out her bedroom window, down the vine-covered side of the porch, and away from the house, running along the road, not going anywhere, just escaping.

That was what I learned from the girl. She didn't tell me all of it. She told me very little of it in those words. But that is the story I got by combining her words, her manner of telling them, her facial expressions, with what I already knew, and what I could guess.

And not once while she talked had her eyes turned from mine. Not once had she shown that she knew there were other men standing in the road with us. She stared into my face with a desperate fixity, as if she was afraid not to, and her hands held mine as if she might sink through the ground if she let go.

"How about your servants?" I asked.

"There aren't any there now."

"Papadopoulos persuaded you to get rid of them?"

"Yes—several days ago."

"Then Papadopoulos, Flora and Angel Grace are alone in the house now?"

"Yes."

"They know you ducked?"

"I don't know: I don't think they do. I had been in my room some time. I don't think they suspected I'd dare do anything but what they told me."

It annoyed me to find I was staring into the girl's eyes as fixedly as she into mine, and that when I wanted to take my gaze away it wasn't easily done. I jerked my eyes away from her, took my hands away.

"The rest of it you can tell me later," I growled, and turned to give Andy MacElroy his orders. "You stay here with Miss Newhall until we get back from the house. Make yourselves comfortable in the car."

The girl put a hand on my arm.

"Am I—? Are you—?"

"We're going to turn you over to the police, yes," I assured her.

"No! No!"

"Don't be childish," I begged. "You can't run around with a mob of cut-throats, get yourself tied up in a flock of crimes, and then when you're tripped say, 'Excuse it, please,' and go free. If you tell the whole story in court—including the parts you haven't told me—the chances are you'll get off. But there's no way in God's world for you to escape arrest. Come on," I told Jack and Tom-Tom Carey. "We've got to shake it up if we want to find our folks at home."

Looking back as I climbed the fence, I saw that Andy had put the girl in the car and was getting in himself.

"Just a moment," I called to Jack and Carey, who were already starting across the field.

"Thought of something else to kill time," the swarthy man complained.

I went back across the road to the car and spoke quickly and softly to Andy:

"Dick Foley and Mickey Linehan should be hanging around the neighborhood. As soon as we're out of sight, hunt 'em up. Turn Miss Newhall over to Dick. Tell him to take her with him and beat it for a phone—rouse the sheriff. Tell Dick he's to turn the girl over to the sheriff, to hold for the San Francisco police. Tell him he's not to give her up to anybody else—not even to me. Got it?"

"Got it."

"All right. After you've told him that and have given him the girl, then you bring Mickey Linehan to the Newhall house as fast as you can make it. We'll likely need all the help we can get as soon as we can get it."

"Got you," Andy said.

X

"What are you up to?" Tom-Tom Carey asked suspiciously when I rejoined Jack and him.

"Detective business."

"I ought to have come down and turned the trick all by myself," he grumbled. "You haven't done a damned thing but waste time since we started."

"I'm not the one that's wasting it now."

He snorted and set out across the field again, Jack and I following him. At the end of the field there was another fence to be climbed. Then we came over a little wooded ridge and the Newhall house lay before us—a large white house, glistening in the moonlight, with yellow rectangulars where blinds were down over the windows of lighted rooms. The lighted rooms were on the ground floor. The upper floor was dark. Everything was quiet.

"Damn the moonlight!" Tom-Tom Carey repeated, bringing another automatic out of his clothes, so that he now had one in each hand.

Jack started to take his gun out, looked at me, saw I was letting mine rest, let his slide back in his pocket.

Tom-Tom Carey's face was a dark stone mask—slits for eyes, slit for mouth—the grim mask of a manhunter, a mankiller. He was breathing softly, his big chest moving gently. Beside him, Jack Counihan looked like an excited school-boy. His face was ghastly, his eyes all stretched out of shape, and he was breathing like a tire-pump. But his grin was genuine, for all the nervousness in it.

"We'll cross to the house on this side," I whispered. "Then one of us can take the front, one the back, and the other can wait till he sees where he's needed most. Right?"

"Right," the swarthy one agreed.

"Wait!" Jack exclaimed. "The girl came down the vines from an upper window. What's the matter with my going up that way? I'm lighter than either of you. If they haven't missed her, the window would still be open. Give me ten minutes to find the window, get through it, and get myself placed. Then when you attack I'll be there behind them. How's that?" he demanded applause.

"And what if they grab you as soon as you light?" I objected.

"Suppose they do. I can make enough racket for you to hear. You can gallop to the attack while they're busy with me. That'll be just as good."

"Blue hell!" Tom-Tom Carey barked. "What good's all that? The other way's best. One of us at the front door, one at the back, kick 'em in and go in shooting."

"If this new one works, it'll be better," I gave my opinion. "If you want to jump in the furnace, Jack, I won't stop you. I won't cheat you out of your heroics."

"No!" the swarthy man snarled. "Nothing doing!"

"Yes," I contradicted him. "We'll try it. Better take twenty minutes, Jack. That won't give you any time to waste."

He looked at his watch and I at mine, and he turned toward the house.

Tom-Tom Carey, scowling darkly, stood in his way. I cursed and got between the swarthy man and the boy. Jack went around my back and hurried away across the too-bright space between us and the house.

"Keep your feet on the ground," I told Carey. "There are a lot of things to this game you don't know anything about."

"Too damned many!" he snarled, but he let the boy go.

There was no open second-storey window on our side of the building. Jack rounded the rear of the house and went out of sight.

A faint rustling sounded behind us. Carey and I spun together. His guns went up. I stretched out an arm across them, pushing them down.

"Don't have a hemorrhage," I cautioned him. "This is just another of the things you don't know about."

The rustling had stopped.

"All right," I called softly.

Mickey Linehan and Andy MacElroy came out of the tree-shadows.

Tom-Tom Carey stuck his face so close to mine that I'd have been scratched if he had forgotten to shave that day.

"You double-crossing—"

"Behave! Behave! A man of your age!" I admonished him. "None of these boys want any of your blood money."

"I don't like this gang stuff," he snarled. "We—"

"We're going to need all the help we can get," I interrupted, looking at my watch. I told the two operatives: "We're going to close in on the house now. Four of us ought to be able to wrap it up snug. You know Papadopoulos, Big Flora and Angel Grace by description. They're in there. Don't take any chances with them—Flora and Papadopoulos are dynamite. Jack Counihan is trying to ease inside now. You two look after the back of the joint. Carey and I will take the front. We'll make the play. You see that nobody leaks out on us. Forward march!"

The swarthy man and I headed for the front porch—a wide porch, grown over with vines on the side, yellowly illuminated now by the light that came through four curtained French windows.

We hadn't taken our first steps across the porch when one of these tall windows moved—opened.

The first thing I saw was Jack Counihan's back.

He was pushing the casement open with a hand and foot, not turning his head.

Beyond the boy—facing him across the brightly lighted room—stood a man and a woman. The man was old, small, scrawny, wrinkled, pitifully frightened—Papadopoulos. I saw he had shaved off' his straggly white mustache. The woman was tall, full-bodied, pink-fleshed and yellow-haired—a she-athlete of forty with clear gray eyes set deep in a handsome brutal face—Big Flora Brace. They stood very still, side by side, watching the muzzle of Jack Counihan's gun.

While I stood in front of the window looking at this scene, Tom-Tom Carey, his two guns up, stepped past me, going through the tall window to the boy's side. I did not follow him into the room.

Papadopoulos' scary brown eyes darted to the swarthy man's face. Flora's gray ones moved there deliberately, and then looked past him to me.

"Hold it, everybody!" I ordered, and moved away from the window, to the side of the porch where the vines were thinnest.

Leaning out between the vines, so my face was clear in the moonlight, I looked down the side of the building. A shadow in the shadow of the garage could have been a man. I put an arm out in the moonlight and beckoned. The shadow came toward me—Mickey Linehan. Andy MacElroy's head peeped around the back of the house. I beckoned again and he followed Mickey.

I returned to the open window.

Papadopoulos and Flora—a rabbit and a lioness—stood looking at the guns of Carey and Jack. They looked again at me when I appeared, and a smile began to curve the woman's full lips.

Mickey and Andy came up and stood beside me. The woman's smile died grimly.

"Carey," I said, "you and Jack stay as is. Mickey, Andy, go in and take hold of our gifts from God."

When the two operatives stepped through the window—things happened.

Papadopoulos screamed.

Big Flora lunged against him, knocking him at the back door.

"Go! Go!" she roared.

Stumbling, staggering, he scrambled across the room.

Flora had a pair of guns—sprung suddenly into her hands. Her big body seemed to fill the room, as if by willpower she had become a giantess. She charged—straight at the guns Jack and Carey held—blotting the back door and the fleeing man from their fire.

A blur to one side was Andy MacElroy moving.

I had a hand on Jack's gun-arm.

"Don't shoot," I muttered in his ear.

Flora's guns thundered together. But she was tumbling. Andy had crashed into her. Had thrown himself at her legs as a man would throw a boulder.

When Flora tumbled, Tom-Tom Carey stopped waiting.

His first bullet was sent so close past her that it clipped her curled yellow hair. But it went past—caught Papadopoulos just as he went through the door. The bullet took him low in the back—smeared him out on the floor.

Carey fired again—again—again—into the prone body.

"It's no use," I growled. "You can't make him any deader."

He chuckled and lowered his guns.

"Four into a hundred and six." All his ill-humor, his grimness was gone. "That's twenty-six thousand, five hundred dollars each of those slugs was worth to me."

Andy and Mickey had wrestled Flora into submission and were hauling her up off the floor.

I looked from them back to the swarthy man, muttering, "It's not all over yet."

"No?" He seemed surprised. "What next?"

"Stay awake and let your conscience guide you," I replied, and turned to the Counihan youngster. "Come along Jack."

I led the way out through the window and across the porch, where I leaned against the railing. Jack followed and stood in front of me, his gun still in his hand, his face white and tired from nervous tension. Looking over his shoulder, I could see the room we had just quit. Andy and Mickey had Flora sitting between them on a sofa. Carey stood a little to one side, looking curiously at Jack and me. We were in the middle of the band of light that came through the open window. We could see inside—except that Jack's back was that way—and could be seen from there, but our talk couldn't be overheard unless we made it loud.

All that was as I wanted it.

"Now tell me about it," I ordered Jack.

XI

"Well, I found the open window," the boy began.

"I know all that part," I cut in. "You came in and told your friends—Papadopoulos and Flora—about the girl's escape, and that Carey and I were coming. You advised them to make out you had captured them single-handed. That would draw Carey and me in. With you unsuspected behind us, it would be easy for the three of you to grab the two of us. After that you could stroll down the road and tell Andy I had sent you for the girl. That was a good scheme—except that you didn't know I had Dick and Mickey up my sleeve, didn't know I wouldn't let you get behind me. But all that isn't what I want to know. I want to know why you sold us out—and what you think you're going to do now."

"Are you crazy?" His young face was bewildered, his young eyes horrified. "Or is this some—?"

"Sure, I'm crazy," I confessed. "Wasn't I crazy enough to let you lead me into that trap in Sausalito? But I wasn't too crazy to figure it out afterward. I wasn't too crazy to see that Ann Newhall was afraid to look at you. I'm not crazy enough to think you could have captured Papadopoulos and Flora unless they wanted you to. I'm crazy—but in moderation."

Jack laughed—a reckless young laugh, but too shrill. His eyes didn't laugh with mouth and voice. While he was laughing his eyes looked from me to the gun in his hand and back to me.

"Talk, Jack," I pleaded huskily, putting a hand on his shoulder. "For God's sake why did you do it?"

The boy shut his eyes, gulped, and his shoulders twitched. When his eyes opened they were hard and glittering and full of merry hell.

"The worst part of it," he said harshly, moving his shoulder from under my hand, "is that I wasn't a very good crook, was I? I didn't succeed in deluding you."

I said nothing.

"I suppose you've earned your right to the story," he went on after a little pause. His voice was consciously monotonous, as if he was deliberately keeping out of it every tone or accent that might seem to express emotion. He was too young to talk naturally. "I met Ann Newhall three weeks ago, in my own home. She had gone to school with my sisters, though I had never met her before. We knew each other at once, of course—I knew she was Nancy Regan, she knew I was a Continental operative.

"So we went off by ourselves and talked things over. Then she took me to see Papadopoulos. I liked the old boy and he liked me. He showed me how we together could accumulate unheard-of piles of wealth. So there you are. The prospect of all that money completely devastated my morals. I told him about Carey as soon as I had heard from you, and I led you into that trap, as you say. He thought it would be better if you stopped bothering us before you found the connection between Newhall and Papadopoulos.

"After that failure, he wanted me to try again, but I refused to have a hand in any more fiascos. There's nothing sillier than a murder that doesn't come off. Ann Newhall is quite innocent of everything except folly. I don't think she has the slightest suspicion that I have had any part in the dirty work beyond refraining from having everybody arrested. That, my dear Sherlock, about concludes the confession."

I had listened to the boy's story with a great show of sympathetic attentiveness. Now I scowled at him and spoke accusingly, but still not without friendliness.

"Stop spoofing! The money Papadopoulos showed you didn't buy you. You met the girl and were too soft to turn her in. But your vanity—your pride in looking at yourself as a pretty cold proposition—wouldn't let you admit it even to yourself. You had to have a hard-boiled front. So you were meat to Papadopoulos' grinder. He gave you a part you could play to yourself—a super-gentleman-crook, a master-mind, a desperate suave villain, and all that kind of romantic garbage. That's the way you went, my son. You went as far as possible beyond what was needed to save the girl from the hoosegow—just to show the world, but chiefly yourself, that you were not acting through sentimentality, but according to your own reckless desires. There you are. Look at yourself."

Whatever he saw in himself—what I had seen or something else—his face slowly reddened, and he wouldn't look at me. He looked past me at the distant road.

I looked into the lighted room beyond him. Tom-Tom Carey had advanced to the center of the floor, where he stood watching us. I jerked a corner of my mouth at him—a warning.

"Well," the boy began again, but he didn't know what to say after that. He shuffled his feet and kept his eyes from my face.

I stood up straight and got rid of the last trace of my hypocritical sympathy.

"Give me your gun, you lousy rat!" I snarled at him.

He jumped back as if I had hit him. Craziness writhed in his face. He jerked his gun chest-high.

Tom-Tom Carey saw the gun go up. The swarthy man fired twice. Jack Counihan was dead at my feet.

Mickey Linehan fired once. Carey was down on the floor, bleeding from the temple.

I stepped over Jack's body, went into the room, knelt beside the swarthy man. He squirmed, tried to say something, died before he could get it out. I waited until my face was straight before I stood up.

Big Flora was studying me with narrowed gray eyes. I stared back at her.

"I don't get it all yet," she said slowly, "but if you—"

"Where's Angel Grace?" I interrupted.

"Tied to the kitchen table," she informed me, and went on with her thinking aloud. "You've dealt a hand that—"

"Yeah," I said sourly, "I'm another Papadopoulos."

Her big body suddenly quivered. Pain clouded her handsome brutal face. Two tears came out of her lower eye-lids.

I'm damned if she hadn't loved the old scoundrel!

XII

It was after eight in the morning when I got back to the city. I ate breakfast and then went up to the agency, where I found the Old Man going through his morning mail.

"It's all over," I told him. "Papadopoulos knew Nancy Regan was Taylor Newhall's heiress. When he needed a hiding-place after the bank jobs flopped, he got her to take him down to the Newhall country place. He had two holds on her. She pitied him as a misused old duffer, and she was—even if innocently—an accomplice after the fact in the stick-ups.

"Pretty soon Papa Newhall had to go to Mexico on business. Papadopoulos saw a chance to make something. If Newhall was knocked off, the girl would have millions—and the old thief knew he could take them away from her. He sent Barrows down to the border to buy the murder from some Mexican bandits. Barrows put it over, but talked too much. He told a girl in Nogales that he had to go back 'to Frisco to collect plenty from an old Greek,' and then he'd return and buy her the world. The girl passed the news on to Tom-Tom Carey. Carey put a lot of twos together and got at least a dozen for an answer. He followed Barrows up here.

"Angel Grace was with him the morning he called on Barrows here—to find out if his 'old Greek' really was Papadopoulos, and where he could be found. Barrows was too full of morphine to listen to reason. He was so dope-deadened that even after the dark man began to reason with a knife-blade he had to whittle Barrows all up before he began to feel hurt. The carving sickened Angel Grace. She left, after vainly trying to stop Carey. And when she read in the afternoon papers what a finished job he had made of it, she tried to commit suicide, to stop the images from crawling around in her head.

"Carey got all the information Barrows had, but Barrows didn't know where Papadopoulos was hiding. Papadopoulos learned of Carey's arrival—you know how he learned. He sent Arlie to stop Carey. Carey wouldn't give the barber a chance—until the swarthy man began to suspect Papadopoulos might be at the Newhall place. He drove down there, letting Arlie follow. As soon as Arlie discovered his destination, Arlie closed in, hell-bent on stopping Carey at any cost. That was what Carey wanted. He gunned Arlie, came back to town, got hold of me, and took me down to help wind things up.

"Meanwhile, Angel Grace, in the cooler, had made friends with Big Flora. She knew Flora but Flora didn't know her. Papadopoulos had arranged a crush-out for Flora. It's always easier for two to escape than one. Flora took the Angel along, took her to Papadopoulos. The Angel went for him, but Flora knocked her for a loop.

"Flora, Angel Grace and Ann Newhall, alias Nancy Regan, are in the county jail," I wound up. "Papadopoulos, Tom-Tom Carey and Jack Counihan are dead."

I stopped talking and lighted a cigarette, taking my time, watching cigarette and match carefully throughout the operation. The Old Man picked up a letter, put it down without reading it, picked up another.

"They were killed in course of making the arrests?" His mild voice held nothing but its usual unfathomable politeness.

"Yes. Carey killed Papadopoulos. A little later he shot Jack. Mickey—not knowing—not knowing anything except that the dark man was shooting at Jack and me—we were standing apart talking—shot and killed Carey." The words twisted around my tongue, wouldn't come out straight. "Neither Mickey nor Andy know that Jack—Nobody but you and I know exactly what the thing—exactly what Jack was doing. Flora Brace and Ann Newhall did know, but if we say he was acting on orders all the time, nobody can deny it."

The Old Man nodded his grandfatherly face and smiled, but for the first time in the years I had known him I knew what he was thinking. He was thinking that if Jack had come through alive we would have had the nasty choice between letting him go free or giving the agency a black-eye by advertising the fact that one of our operatives was a crook.

I threw away my cigarette and stood up. The Old Man stood also, and held out a hand to me.

"Thank you," he said.

I took his hand, and I understood him, but I didn't have anything I wanted to confess—even by silence.

"It happened that way," I said deliberately. "I played the cards so we would get the benefit of the breaks—but it just happened that way."

He nodded, smiling benignantly.

"I'm going to take a couple of weeks off," I said from the door.

I felt tired, washed out.

This story is a sequel to THE BIG KNOCK-OVER which appeared in February BLACK MASK. If you missed reading it, send a request to the Editor for a free copy of that issue.

THE MAIN DEATH

In the JUNE issue of BLACK MASK

After an enforced absence from literary work, Mr Hammett is once more in the lineup of BLACK MASK regular contributors, and, judging from the many enthusiastic comments on The Big Knock-Over, his popularity is greater than ever. In The Main Death—which, by the way, is a short story—he is at his cleverest and best. By its surprise development, its subtleties, its wonderfully clear picturization, its easy, swift movement to the climax, this tale will delight every lover of the short story. It is a gem—a model of what the short story can be.

3

THE MAIN DEATH

BLACK MASK, JUNE 1927

A curious tangle of a robbery, a mysterious killing and jealousy.

The captain told me Hacken and Begg were handling the job.

I caught them leaving the detectives' assembly room. Begg was a freckled heavyweight, as friendly as a Saint Bernard puppy, but less intelligent. Lanky detective-sergeant Hacken, not so playful, carried the team's brains behind his worried hatchet face.

"In a hurry?" I inquired.

"Always in a hurry when we're quitting for the day," Begg said, his freckles climbing up his face to make room for his grin.

"What do you want?" Hacken asked.

"I want the low-down on the Main doings—if any."

"You going to work on it?"

"Yes," I said, "for Main's boss—Gungen."

"Then you can tell us something. Why'd he have the twenty thou in cash?"

"Tell you in the morning," I promised. "I haven't seen Gungen yet. Got a date with him tonight."

While we talked we had gone into the assembly room, with its school-room arrangement of desks and benches. Half a dozen police detectives were scattered among them, doing reports. We three sat around Hacken's desk and the lanky detective-sergeant talked:

"Main got home from Los Angeles at eight, Sunday night, with twenty thousand in his wallet. He'd gone down there to sell something for Gungen. You find out why he had that much in cash. He told his wife he had driven up from L.A. with a friend—no name. She went to bed around ten-thirty, leaving him reading. He had the money—two hundred hundred-dollar bills—in a brown wallet.

"So far, so good. He's in the living-room reading. She's in the bedroom sleeping. Just the two of them in the apartment. A racket wakes her. She jumps out of bed, runs into the living-room. There's Main wrestling with a couple of men. One's tall and husky. The other's little—kind of girlish built. Both have got black handkerchiefs over their mugs and caps pulled down.

"When Mrs Main shows, the little one breaks away from Main and sticks her up. Puts a gun in Mrs Main's face and tells her to behave. Main and the other guy are still scuffling. Main has got his gun in his hand, but the thug has him by the wrist, trying to twist it. He makes it pretty soon—Main drops the rod. The thug flashes his own, holding Main off while he bends down to pick up the one that fell.

"When the man stoops, Main piles on him. He manages to knock the fellow's gun out of his hand, but by that time the fellow had got the one on the floor—the one Main had dropped. They're heaped up there for a couple of seconds. Mrs Main can't see what's happening. Then bang! Main's falling away, his vest burning where the shot had set fire to it, a bullet in his heart, his gun smoking in the masked guy's fist. Mrs Main passes out.

"When she comes to there's nobody in the apartment but herself and her dead husband. His wallet's gone, and so is his gun. She was unconscious for about half an hour. We know that, because other people heard the shot and could give us the time—even if they didn't know where it come from.

"The Mains' apartment is on the sixth floor. It's an eight-storey building. Next door to it, on the corner of Eighteenth Avenue, is a two-storey building—grocery downstairs, grocer's flat upstairs. Behind these buildings runs a narrow back street—an alley. All right.

"Kinney—the patrolman on that beat—was walking down Eighteenth Avenue. He heard the shot. It was clear to him, because the Mains' apartment is on that side of the building—the side overlooking the grocer's—but Kinney couldn't place it right away. He wasted time scouting around up the street. By the time he got down as far as the alley in his hunting, the birds had flown. Kinney found signs of 'em though—they had dropped a gun in the alley—the gun they'd taken from Alain and shot him with. But Kinney didn't see 'em—didn't see anybody who might have been them.

"Now, from a hall window of the apartment house's third floor to the roof of the grocer's building is easy going. Anybody but a cripple could make it—in or out—and the window's never locked. From the grocer's roof to the back street is almost as easy. There's a cast iron pipe, a deep window, a door with heavy hinges sticking out—a regular ladder up and down that back wall. Begg and I did it without working up a sweat. The pair could have gone in that way. We know they left that way. On the grocer's roof we found Alain's wallet—empty, of course—and a handkerchief. The wallet had metal corners. The handkerchief had caught on one of 'em, and went with it when the crooks tossed it away."

"Main's handkerchief?"

"A woman's—with an E in one corner."

"Mrs Main's?"

"Her name is Agnes," Hacken said. "We showed her the wallet, the gun, and the handkerchief. She identified the first two as her husband's, but the handkerchief was a new one on her. However, she could give us the name of the perfume on it—*Desir du Coeur.* And—with it for a guide—she said the smaller of the masked pair could have been a woman. She had already described him as kind of girlish built."

"Any finger-prints, or the like?" I asked.

"No. Phels went over the apartment, the window, the roof, the wallet and the gun. Not a smear."

"Mrs Alain identify 'em?"

"She says she'd know the little one. Maybe she would."

"Got anything on the who?"

"Not yet," the lanky detective-sergeant said as we moved toward the door.

In the street I left the police sleuths and set out for Bruno Gungen's home in Westwood Park.

The dealer in rare and antique jewelry was a little bit of a man and a fancy one. His dinner jacket was corset-tight around his waist, padded high and sharp at the shoulders. Hair, mustache and spade-shaped goatee were dyed black and greased until they were as shiny as his pointed pink finger-nails. I wouldn't bet a cent that the color in his fifty-year-old cheeks wasn't rouge.

He came out of the depths of a leather library chair to give me a soft, warm hand that was no larger than a child's, bowing and smiling at me with his head tilted to one side.

Then he introduced me to his wife, who bowed without getting up from her seat at the table. Apparently she was a little more than a third of his age. She couldn't have been a day over nineteen, and she looked more like sixteen. She was as small as he, with a dimpled olive-skinned face, round brown eyes, a plump painted mouth and the general air of an expensive doll in a toy-store window.

Bruno Gungen explained to her at some length that I was connected with the Continental Detective Agency, and that he had employed me to help the police find Jeffrey Main's murderers and recover the stolen twenty thousand dollars.

She murmured, "Oh, yes!" in a tone that said she was not the least bit interested, and stood up, saying, "Then I'll leave you to—"

"No, no, my dear!" Her husband was waving his pink fingers at her. "I would have no secrets from you."

His ridiculous little face jerked around to me, cocked itself sidewise, and he asked, with a little giggle:

"Is not that so? That between husband and wife there should be no secrets?"

I pretended I agreed with him.

"You, I know, my dear," he addressed his wife, who had sat down again, "are as much interested in this as I, for did we not have an equal affection for dear Jeffrey? Is it not so?"

She repeated, "Oh, yes!" with the same lack of interest.

Her husband turned to me and said, "Now?" encouragingly.

"I've seen the police," I told him. "Is there anything you can add to their story? Anything new? Anything you didn't tell them?"

He whisked his face around toward his wife.

"Is there, Enid, dear?"

"I know of nothing," she replied.

He giggled and made a delighted face at me.

"That is it," he said. "We know of nothing."

"He came back to San Francisco eight o'clock Sunday night—three hours before he was killed and robbed—with twenty thousand dollars in hundred-dollar bills. What was he doing with it?"

"It was the proceeds of a sale to a customer," Bruno Gungen explained. "Mr Nathaniel Ogilvie, of Los Angeles."

"But why cash?"

The little man's painted face screwed itself up into a shrewd leer.

"A bit of hanky-panky," he confessed complacently, "a trick of the trade, as one says. You know the genus collector? Ah, there is a study for you! Observe. I obtain a golden tiara of early Grecian workmanship, or let me be correct—purporting to be of early Grecian workmanship, purporting also to have been found in Southern Russia, near Odessa. Whether there is any truth in either of these suppositions I do not know, but certainly the tiara is a thing of beauty."

He giggled.

"Now I have a client, a Mr Nathaniel Ogilvie, of Los Angeles, who has an appetite for curios of the sort—a very devil of a *cacoethes carpendi.* The value of these items, you will comprehend, is exactly what one can get for them—no more, little less. This tiara—now ten thousand dollars is the least I could have expected for it, if sold as one sells an ordinary article of the sort. But can one call a golden cap made long ago for some forgotten Scythian king an ordinary article of any sort? No! No! So, swaddled in cotton, intricately packed, Jeffrey carries this tiara to Los Angeles to show our Mr Ogilvie.

"In what manner the tiara came into our hands Jeffrey will not say. But he will hint at devious intrigues, smuggling, a little of violence and lawlessness here and there, the necessity for secrecy. For your true collector, there is the bait! Nothing is anything to him except as it is difficultly come by. Jeffrey will not lie. No! *Mon Dieu,* that would be dishonest, despicable! But he will suggest much, and he will refuse, oh, so emphatically! to take a check for the tiara. No check, my dear sir! Nothing which may be traced! Cash moneys!

"Hanky-panky, as you see. But where is the harm? Mr Ogilvie is certainly going to buy the tiara, and our little deceit simply heightens his pleasure in his purchase. He will enjoy its possession so much the more. Besides, who is to say that this tiara is not authentic? If it is, then these things Jeffrey suggests are indubitably true. Mr Ogilvie does buy it, for twenty thousand dollars, and that is why poor Jeffrey had in his possession so much cash money."

He flourished a pink hand at me, nodded his dyed head vigorously, and finished with:

"*Voilà!* That is it!"

"Did you hear from Main after he got back?" I asked.

The dealer smiled as if my question tickled him, turning his head so that the smile was directed at his wife.

"Did we, Enid, darling?" he passed on the question.

She pouted and shrugged her shoulders indifferently.

"The first we knew he had returned," Gungen interpreted these gestures to me, "was Monday morning, when we heard of his death. Is it not so, my dove?"

His dove murmured, "Yes," and left her chair, saying, "You'll excuse me? I have a letter to write."

"Certainly, my dear," Gungen told her as he and I stood up.

She passed close to him on her way to the door. His small nose twitched over his dyed mustache and he rolled his eyes in a caricature of ecstasy.

"What a delightful scent, my precious!" he exclaimed. "What a heavenly odor! What a song to the nostrils! Has it a name, my love?"

"Yes," she said, pausing in the doorway, not looking back.

"And it is?"

"*Dèsir du Coeur,*" she replied over her shoulder as she left us.

Bruno Gungen looked at me and giggled.

I sat down again and asked him what he knew about Jeffrey Main.

"Everything, no less," he assured me. "For a dozen years, since he was a boy of eighteen he has been my right eye, my right hand."

"Well, what sort of man was he?"

Bruno Gungen showed me his pink palms side by side.

"What sort is any man?" he asked over them.

That didn't mean anything to me, so I kept quiet, waiting.

"I shall tell you," the little man began presently. "Jeffrey had the eye and the taste for this traffic of mine. No man living save myself alone has a judgment in these matters which I would prefer to Jeffrey's. And, honest, mind you! Let nothing I say mislead you on that point. Never a lock have I to which Jeffrey had not also the key, and might have it forever, if he had lived so long.

"But there is a but. In his private life, rascal is a word that only does him justice. He drank, he gambled, he loved, he spent—dear God, how he spent! He was, in this drinking and gaming and loving and spending, a most promiscuous fellow, beyond doubt. With moderation he had nothing to do. Of the moneys he got by inheritance, of the fifty thousand dollars or more his wife had when they were married, there is no remainder. Fortunately, he was well insured—else his wife would have been left penniless. Oh, he was a true Heliogabalus, that fellow!"

Bruno Gungen went down to the front door with me when I left. I said, "Good night," and walked down the gravel path to where I had left my car. The night was clear, dark, moonless. High hedges were black walls on both sides of the Gungen place. To the left there was a barely noticeable hole in the blackness—a dark-gray hole—oval—the size of a face.

I got into my car, stirred up the engine and drove away. Into the first cross-street I turned, parked the machine, and started back toward Gungen's afoot. I was curious about that face-size oval.

When I reached the corner, I saw a woman coming toward me from the direction of Gungen's. I was in the shadow of a wall. Cautiously, I backed away from the corner until I came to a gate with brick buttresses sticking out. I made myself flat between them.

The woman crossed the street, went on up the driveway, toward the car line. I couldn't make out anything about her, except that she was a woman. Maybe she was coming from Gungen's grounds, maybe not. Maybe it was her face I had seen against the hedge, maybe not. It was a heads or tails proposition. I guessed yes and tailed her up the drive.

Her destination was a drug store on the car line. Her business there was with the telephone. She spent ten minutes at it. I didn't go into the store to try for an earful, but stayed on the other side of the street, contenting myself with a good look at her.

She was a girl of about twenty-five, medium in height, chunky in build, with pale gray eyes that had little pouches under them, a thick nose and a prominent lower lip. She had no hat over her brown hair. Her body was wrapped in a long blue cape.

From the drug store I shadowed her back to the Gungen house. She went in the back door. A servant, probably, but not the maid who had opened the door for me earlier in the evening.

I returned to my car, drove back to town, to the office.

"Is Dick Foley working on anything?" I asked Fiske, who sits on the Continental Detective Agency's affairs at night.

"No. Did you ever hear the story about the fellow who had his neck operated on?"

With the slightest encouragement, Fiske is good for a dozen stories without a stop, so I said:

"Yes. Get hold of Dick and tell him I've got a shadow-job out Westwood Park way for him to start on in the morning."

I gave Fiske—to be passed on to Dick—Gungen's address and a description of the girl who had done the phoning from the drug store. Then I assured the night man that I had also heard the story about the pickaninny named Opium, and likewise the one about what the old man said to his wife on their golden wedding anniversary. Before he could try me with another, I escaped to my own office, where I composed and coded a telegram to our Los Angeles branch, asking that Main's recent visit to that city be dug into.

The next morning Hacken and Begg dropped in to see me and I gave them Gungen's version of why the twenty thousand had been in cash. The police detectives told me a stool-pigeon had brought them word that Bunky Dahl—a local guerrilla who did a moderate business in hijacking—had been flashing a roll since about the time of Main's death.

"We haven't picked him up yet," Hacken said. "Haven't been able to place him, but we've got a line on his girl. Course, he might have got his dough somewhere else."

At ten o'clock that morning I had to go over to Oakland to testify against a couple of flimflammers who had sold bushels of stock in a sleight-of-hand rubber manufacturing business. When I got back to the agency, at six that evening, I found a wire from Los Angeles on my desk.

Jeffrey Main, the wire told me, had finished his business with Ogilvie Saturday afternoon, had checked out of his hotel immediately, and had left on the Owl that evening, which would have put him in San Francisco early Sunday morning. The hundred-dollar bills with which Ogilvie had paid for the tiara had been new ones, consecutively numbered, and Ogilvie's bank had given the Los Angeles operative the numbers.

Before I quit for the day, I phoned Hacken, gave him these numbers, as well as the other dope in the telegram.

"Haven't found Dahl yet," he told me.

Dick Foley's report came in the next morning. The girl had left the Gungen house at 9:15 the previous night, had gone to the corner of Miramar Avenue and Southwood Drive, where a man was waiting for her in a Buick coupé. Dick described him: Age about 30; height about five feet ten; slender, weight about 140; medium complexion; brown hair and eyes; long, thin face with pointed chin; brown hat, suit and shoes and gray overcoat.

The girl got into the car with him and they drove out to the beach, along the Great Highway for a little while, and then back to Miramar and Southwood, where the girl got out. She seemed to be going back to the house, so Dick let her go and tailed the man in the Buick down to the Futurity Apartments in Mason Street.

The man stayed in there for half an hour or so and then came out with another man and two women. This second man was of about the same age as the first, about five feet eight inches tall, would weigh about a hundred and seventy pounds, had brown hair and eyes, a dark complexion, a flat, broad face with high cheek bones, and wore a blue suit, gray hat, tan overcoat, black shoes, and a pear-shaped pearl tie-pin.

One of the women was about twenty-two years old, small, slender and blonde. The other was probably three or four years older, red-haired, medium in height and build, with a turned-up nose.

The quartet had got in the car and gone to the Algerian Cafe, where they had stayed until a little after one in the morning. Then they had returned to the Futurity Apartments. At half-past three the two men had left, driving the Buick to a garage in Post Street, and then walking to the Mars Hotel.

When I had finished reading this I called Mickey Linehan in from the operatives' room, gave him the report and instructions:

"Find out who these folks are."

Mickey went out. My phone rang.

Bruno Gungen: "Good morning. May you have something to tell me today?"

"Maybe," I said. "You're downtown?"

"Yes, in my shop. I shall be here until four."

"Right. I'll be in to see you this afternoon."

At noon Mickey Linehan returned. "The first bloke," he reported, "the one Dick saw with the girl, is named Benjamin Weel. He owns the Buick and lives in the Mars—room 410. He's a salesman, though it's not known what of. The other man is a friend of his who has been staying with him for a couple of days. I couldn't get anything on him. He's not registered. The two women in the Futurity are a couple of hustlers. They live in apartment 303. The larger one goes by the name of Mrs Effie Roberts. The little blonde is Violet Evarts."

"Wait," I told Mickey, and went back into the file room, to the index-card drawers.

I ran through the W's—*Weel, Benjamin, alias Coughing Ben*, 36,312W.

The contents of folder No. 36,312W told me that Coughing Ben Weel had been arrested in Amador County in 1916 on a high grading charge and had been sent to San Quentin for three years. In 1922 he had been picked up again in Los Angeles and charged with trying to blackmail a movie actress, but the case had fallen through. His description fit the one Dick had given of the man in the Buick. His photograph—a copy of the one taken by the Los Angeles police in '22—showed a sharp-featured young man with a chin like a wedge.

I took the photo back to my office and showed it to Mickey.

"This is Weel five years ago. Follow him around a while."

When the operative had gone I called the police detective bureau. Neither Hacken nor Begg was in. I got hold of Lewis, in the identification department.

"What does Bunky Dahl look like?" I asked him.

"Wait a minute," Lewis said, and then: "32, 67'72, 174, medium, brown, brown, broad flat face with prominent cheek-bones, gold bridge work in lower left jaw, brown mole under right ear, deformed little toe on right foot."

"Have you a picture of him to spare?"

"Sure."

"Thanks, I'll send a boy down for it."

I told Tommy Howd to go down and get it, and then went out for some food. After luncheon I went up to Gungen's establishment in Post Street. The little dealer was gaudier than ever this afternoon in a black coat that was even more padded in the shoulders and tighter in the waist than his dinner coat had been the other night, striped gray pants, a vest that leaned toward magenta, and a billowy satin tie wonderfully embroidered with gold thread.

We went back through his store, up a narrow flight of stairs to a small cube of an office on the mezzanine floor.

"And now you have to tell me?" he asked when we were seated, with the door closed.

"I've got more to ask than tell. First, who is the girl with the thick nose, the thick lower lip, and the pouches under gray eyes, who lives in your house?"

"That is one Rose Rubury." His little painted face was wrinkled in a satisfied smile. "She is my dear wife's maid."

"She goes riding with an ex-convict."

"She does?" He stroked his dyed goatee with a pink hand, highly pleased. "Well, she is my dear wife's maid, that she is."

"Main didn't drive up from Los Angeles with a friend, as he told his wife. He came up on the train Saturday night—so he was in town twelve hours before he showed up at home."

Bruno Gungen giggled, cocking his delighted face to one side.

"Ah!" he tittered. "We progress! We progress! Is it not so?"

"Maybe. Do you remember if this Rose Rubury was in the house on Sunday night—say from eleven to twelve?"

"I do remember. She was. I know it certainly. My dear wife was not feeling well that night. My darling had gone out early that Sunday morning, saying she was going to drive out into the country with some friends—what friends I do not know. But she came home at eight o'clock that night complaining of a distressing headache. I was quite frightened by her appearance, so that I went often to see how she was, and thus it happens that I know her maid was in the house all of that night, until one o'clock, at least."

"Did the police show you the handkerchief they found with Main's wallet?"

"Yes." He squirmed on the edge of his chair, his face like the face of a kid looking at a Christmas tree.

"You're sure it's your wife's?"

His giggle interfered with his speech, so he said, "Yes," by shaking his head up and down until the goatee seemed to be a black whiskbroom brushing his tie.

"She could have left it at the Mains' some time when she was visiting Mrs Main," I suggested.

"That is not possible," he corrected me eagerly. "My darling and Mrs Main are not acquainted."

"But your wife and Main were acquainted?"

He giggled and brushed his tie with his whisker again.

"How well acquainted?"

He shrugged his padded shoulders up to his ears.

"I know not," he said merrily. "I employ a detective."

"Yeah?" I scowled at him. "You employ this one to find out who killed and robbed Alain—and for nothing else. If you think you're employing him to dig up your family secrets, you're as wrong as Prohibition."

"But why? But why?" He was flustered. "Have I not the right to know? There will be no trouble over it, no scandal, no divorce suing, of that be assured. Even Jeffrey is dead, so it is what one calls ancient history. While he lived I knew nothing, was blind. After he died I saw certain things. For my own satisfaction—that is all, I beg you to believe—I should like to know with certainty."

"You won't get it out of me," I said bluntly. "I don't know anything about it except what you've told me, and you can't hire me to go further into it. Besides, if you're not going to do anything about it, why don't you keep your hands off—let it sleep?"

"No, no, my friend." He had recovered his bright-eyed cheerfulness. "I am not an old man, but I am fifty-two. My dear wife is eighteen, and a truly lovely person." He giggled. "This thing happened. May it not happen again? And would it not be the part of husbandly wisdom to have—shall I say—a hold on her? A rein? A check? Or if it never happen again, still might not one's dear wife be the more docile for certain information which her husband possesses?"

"It's your business." I stood up, laughing. "But I don't want any part of it."

"Ah, do not let us quarrel!" He jumped up and took one of my hands in his. "If you will not, you will not. But there remains the criminal aspect of the situation—the aspect that has engaged you thus far. You will not forsake that? You will fulfil your engagement there? Surely?"

"Suppose—just suppose—it should turn out that your wife had a hand in Main's death. What then?"

"That"—he shrugged, holding his hands out, palms up—"would be a matter for the law."

"Good enough. I'll stick—if you understand that you're entitled to no information except what touches your 'criminal aspect.' "

"Excellent! And if it so happens you cannot separate my darling from that—"

I nodded. He grabbed my hand again, patting it. I took it away from him and returned to the agency.

A memorandum on my desk asked me to phone detective-sergeant Hacken. I did.

"Bunky Dahl wasn't in on the Main job," the hatchet-faced man told me. "He and a pal named Coughing Ben Weed were putting on a party in a roadhouse near Vallejo that night. They were there from around ten until they were thrown out after two in the morning for starting a row. It's on the up-and-up. The guy that gave it to me is right—and I got a check-up on it from two others."

I thanked Hacken and phoned Gungen's residence, asking for Mrs Gungen, asking her if she would see me if I came out there.

"Oh, yes," she said. It seemed to be her favorite expression, though the way she said it didn't express anything.

Putting the photos of Dahl and Weel in my pocket, I got a taxi and set out for Westwood Park. Using Fatima-smoke on my brains while I rode, I concocted a wonderful series of lies to be told my client's wife—a series that I thought would get me the information I wanted.

A hundred and fifty yards or so up the drive from the house I saw Dick Foley's car standing.

A thin, pasty-faced maid opened the Gungens' door and took me into a sitting room on the second floor, where Mrs Gungen put down a copy of *The Sun Also Rises* and waved a cigarette at a nearby chair. She was very much the expensive doll this afternoon in a Persian orange dress, sitting with one foot tucked under her in a brocaded chair.

Looking at her while I lighted a cigarette, remembering my first interview with her and her husband, and my second one with him, I decided to chuck the tale-of-woe I had spent my ride building.

"You've a maid—Rose Rubury," I began. "I don't want her to hear what's said."

She said, "Very well," without the least sign of surprise, added, "Excuse me a moment," and left her chair and the room.

Presently she was back, sitting down with both feet tucked under her now.

"She will be away for at least half an hour."

"That will be long enough. This Rose is friendly with an ex-convict named Weel."

The doll face frowned, and the plump painted lips pressed themselves together. I waited, giving her time to say something. She didn't say it. I took Weel's and Dahl's pictures out and held them out to her.

"The thin-faced one is your Rose's friend. The other's a pal of his—also a crook."

She took the photographs with a tiny hand that was as steady as mine, and looked at them carefully. Her mouth became smaller and tighter, her brown eyes darker. Then, slowly, her face cleared, she murmured, "Oh, yes," and returned the pictures to me.

"When I told your husband about it"—I spoke deliberately—"he said, 'She's my wife's maid,' and laughed."

Enid Gungen said nothing.

"Well?" I asked. "What did he mean by that?"

"How should I know?" she sighed.

"You know your handkerchief was found with Main's empty wallet." I dropped this in a by-the-way tone, pretending to be chiefly occupied putting cigarette ash in a jasper tray that was carved in the form of a lidless coffin.

"Oh, yes," she said wearily, "I've been told that."

"How do you think it happened?"

"I can't imagine."

"I can," I said, "but I'd rather know positively. Mrs Gungen, it would save a lot of time if we could talk plain language."

"Why not?" she asked listlessly. "You are in my husband's confidence, have his permission to question me. If it happens to be humiliating to me—well, after all, I am only his wife. And it is hardly likely that any new indignities either of you can devise will be worse than those to which I have already submitted."

I grunted at this theatrical speech and went ahead.

"Mrs Gungen, I'm only interested in learning who robbed and killed Main. Anything that points in that direction is valuable to me, but only in so far as it points in that direction. Do you understand what I mean?"

"Certainly," she said. "I understand you are in my husband's employ."

That got us nowhere. I tried again:

"What impression do you suppose I got the other evening, when I was here?"

"I can't imagine."

"Please try."

"Doubtless"—she smiled faintly—"you got the impression that my husband thought I had been Jeffrey's mistress."

"Well?"

"Are you"—her dimples showed; she seemed amused—"asking me if I really was his mistress?"

"No—though of course I'd like to know."

"Naturally you would," she said pleasantly.

"What impression did you get that evening?" I asked.

"I?" She wrinkled her forehead. "Oh, that my husband had hired you to prove that I had been Jeffrey's mistress." She repeated the word mistress as if she liked the shape of it in her mouth.

"You were wrong."

"Knowing my husband, I find that hard to believe."

"Knowing myself, I'm sure of it," I insisted. "There's no uncertainty about it between your husband and me, Mrs Gungen. It is understood that my job is to find who stole and killed—nothing else."

"Really?" It was a polite ending of an argument of which she had grown tired.

"You're tying my hands," I complained, standing up, pretending I wasn't watching her carefully. "I can't do anything now but grab this Rose Rubury and the two men and see what I can squeeze out of them. You said the girl would be back in half an hour?"

She looked at me steadily with her round brown eyes.

"She should be back in a few minutes. You're going to question her?"

"But not here," I informed her. "I'll take her down to the Hall of Justice and have the men picked up. Can I use your phone?"

"Certainly. It's in the next room." She crossed to open the door for me.

I called Davenport 20 and asked for the detective bureau.

Mrs Gungen, standing in the sitting room, said, so softly I could barely hear it:

"Wait."

Holding the phone, I turned to look through the door at her. She was pinching her red mouth between thumb and finger, frowning. I didn't put down the phone until she took the hand from her mouth and held it out toward me. Then I went back into the sitting-room.

I was on top. I kept my mouth shut. It was up to her to make the plunge. She studied my face for a minute or more before she began:

"I won't pretend I trust you." She spoke hesitantly, half as if to herself. "You're working for my husband, and even the money would not interest him so much as whatever I had done. It's a choice of evils—certain on the one hand, more than probable on the other."

She stopped talking and rubbed her hands together. Her round eyes were becoming indecisive. If she wasn't helped along she was going to balk.

"There's only the two of us," I urged her. "You can deny everything afterward. It's my word against yours. If you don't tell me—I know now I can get it from the others. Your calling me from the phone lets me know that. You think I'll tell your husband everything. Well, if I have to fry it out of the others, he'll probably read it all in the papers. Your one chance is to trust me. It's not as slim a chance as you think. Anyway, it's up to you."

A half-minute of silence.

"Suppose," she whispered, "I should pay you to—"

"What for? If I'm going to tell your husband, I could take your money and still tell him, couldn't I?"

Her red mouth curved, her dimples appeared and her eyes brightened.

"That is reassuring," she said. "I shall tell you. Jeffrey came back from Los Angeles early so we could have the day together in a little apartment we kept. In the afternoon two men came in—with a key. They had revolvers. They robbed Jeffrey of the money. That was what they had come for. They seemed to know all about it and about us. They called us by name, and taunted us with threats of the story they would tell if we had them arrested.

"We couldn't do anything after they had gone. It was a ridiculously hopeless plight they had put us in. There wasn't anything we could do—since we couldn't possibly replace the money. Jeffrey couldn't even pretend he had lost it or had been robbed of it while he was alone. His secret early return to San Francisco would have been sure to throw suspicion on him. Jeffrey lost his head. He wanted me to run away with him. Then he wanted to go to my husband and tell him the truth. I wouldn't permit either course—they were equally foolish.

"We left the apartment, separating, a little after seven. We weren't, the truth is, on the best of terms by then. He wasn't—now that we were in trouble—as—No, I shouldn't say that."

She stopped and stood looking at me with a placid doll's face that seemed to have got rid of all its troubles by simply passing them to me.

"The pictures I showed you are the two men?" I asked.

"Yes."

"This maid of yours knew about you and Main? Knew about the apartment? Knew about his trip to Los Angeles and his plan to return early with the cash?"

"I can't say she did. But she certainly could have learned most of it by spying and eavesdropping and looking through my—I had a note from Jeffrey telling me about the Los Angeles trip, making the appointment for Sunday morning. Perhaps she could have seen it. I'm careless."

"I'm going now," I said. "Sit tight till you hear from me. And don't scare up the maid."

"Remember, I've told you nothing," she reminded me as she followed me to the sitting-room door.

From the Gungen house I went direct to the Mars Hotel. Mickey Linehan was sitting behind a newspaper in a corner of the lobby.

"They in?" I asked him.

"Yep."

"Let's go up and see them."

Mickey rattled his knuckles on door number 410. A metallic voice asked: "Who's there?"

"Package," Mickey replied in what was meant for a boy's voice.

A slender man with a pointed chin opened the door. I gave him a card. He didn't invite us into the room, but he didn't try to keep us out when we walked in.

"You're Weel?" I addressed him while Mickey closed the door behind us, and then, not waiting for him to say yes, I turned to the broad-faced man sitting on the bed. "And you're Dahl?"

Weel spoke to Dahl, in a casual, metallic voice:

"A couple of gumshoes."

The man on the bed looked at us and grinned.

I was in a hurry.

"I want the dough you took from Main," I announced.

They sneered together, as if they had been practicing.

I brought out my gun.

Weel laughed harshly.

"Get your hat, Bunky," he chuckled. "We're being taken into custody."

"You've got the wrong idea," I explained. "This isn't a pinch. It's a stick-up. Up go the hands!"

Dahl's hands went up quick. Weel hesitated until Mickey prodded him in the ribs with the nose of a .38-special.

"Frisk 'em," I ordered Mickey.

He went through Weel's clothes, taking a gun, some papers, some loose money, and a moneybelt that was fat. Then he did the same for Dahl.

"Count it," I told him.

Mickey emptied the belts, spit on his fingers and went to work.

"Nineteen thousand, one hundred and twenty-six dollars and sixty-two cents," he reported when he was through.

With the hand that didn't hold my gun, I felt in my pocket for the slip on which I had written the numbers of the hundred-dollar bills Main had got from Ogilvie. I held the slip out to Mickey.

"See if the hundreds check against this."

He took the slip, looked, said, "They do."

"Good—pouch the money and the guns and see if you can turn up any more in the room."

Coughing Ben Weel had got his breath by now.

"Look here!" he protested. "You can't pull this, fellow! Where do you think you are? You can't get away with this!"

"I can try," I assured him. "I suppose you're going to yell, *Police*! Like hell you are! The only squawk you've got coming is at your own dumbness in thinking because your squeeze on the woman was tight enough to keep her from having you copped, you didn't have to worry about anything. I'm playing the same game you played with her and Main—only mine's better, because you can't get tough afterward without facing stir. Now shut up!"

"No more jack," Mickey said. "Nothing but four postage stamps."

"Take 'em along," I told him. "That's practically eight cents. Now we'll go."

"Hey, leave us a couple of bucks," Weel begged.

"Didn't I tell you to shut up?" I snarled at him, backing to the door, which Mickey was opening.

The hall was empty. Mickey stood in it, holding his gun on Weel and Dahl while I backed out of the room and switched the key from the inside to the outside. Then I slammed the door, twisted the key, pocketed it, and we went downstairs and out of the hotel.

Mickey's car was around the corner. In it, we transferred our spoils—except the guns—from his pockets to mine. Then he got out and went back to the agency. I turned the car toward the building in which Jeffrey Main had been killed.

Mrs Main was a tall girl of less than twenty-five, with curled brown hair, heavily-lashed gray-blue eyes, and a warm, full-featured face. Her ample body was dressed in black from throat to feet.

She read my card, nodded at my explanation that Gungen had employed me to look into her husband's death, and took me into a gray and white living room.

"This is the room?" I asked.

"Yes." She had a pleasant, slightly husky voice.

I crossed to the window and looked down on the grocer's roof, and on the half of the back street that was visible. I was still in a hurry.

"Mrs Main," I said as I turned, trying to soften the abruptness of my words by keeping my voice low, "after your husband was dead, you threw the gun out the window. Then you stuck the handkerchief to the corner of the wallet and threw that. Being lighter than the gun, it didn't go all the way to the alley, but fell on the roof. Why did you put the handkerchief—?"

Without a sound she fainted.

I caught her before she reached the floor, carried her to a sofa, found Cologne and smelling salts, applied them.

"Do you know whose handkerchief it was?" I asked when she was awake and sitting up.

She shook her head from left to right.

"Then why did you take that trouble?"

"It was in his pocket. I didn't know what else to do with it. I thought the police would ask about it. I didn't want anything to start them asking questions."

"Why did you tell the robbery story?"

No answer.

"The insurance?" I suggested.

She jerked up her head, cried defiantly:

"Yes! He had gone through his own money and mine. And then he had to—to do a thing like that. He—"

I interrupted her complaint:

"He left a note, I hope—something that will be evidence." Evidence that she hadn't killed him, I meant.

"Yes." She fumbled in the bosom of her black dress.

"Good," I said, standing. "The first thing in the morning, take that note down to your lawyer and tell him the whole story."

I mumbled something sympathetic and made my escape.

Night was coming down when I rang the Gungens' bell for the second time that day. The pasty-faced maid who opened the door told me Mr Gungen was at home. She led me upstairs.

Rose Rubury was coming down the stairs. She stopped on the landing to let us pass. I halted in front of her while my guide went on toward the library.

"You're done, Rose," I told the girl on the landing. "I'll give you ten minutes to clear out. No word to anybody. If you don't like that—you'll get a chance to see if you like the inside of the can."

"Well—the idea!"

"The racket's flopped." I put a hand into a pocket and showed her one wad of the money I had got at the Mars Hotel. "I've just come from visiting Coughing Ben and Bunky."

That impressed her. She turned and scurried up the stairs.

Bruno Gungen came to the library door, searching for me. He looked curiously from the girl—now running up the steps to the third storey—to me. A question was twisting the little man's lips, but I headed it off with a statement:

"It's done."

"Bravo!" he exclaimed as we went into the library. "You hear that, my darling? It is done!"

His darling, sitting by the table, where she had sat the other night, smiled with no expression in her doll's face, and murmured, "Oh, yes," with no expression in her words.

I went to the table and emptied my pockets of money.

"Nineteen thousand, one hundred and twenty-six dollars and seventy cents, including the stamps," I announced. "The other eight hundred and seventy-three dollars and thirty cents is gone."

"Ah!" Bruno Gungen stroked his spade-shaped black beard with a trembling pink hand and pried into my face with hard bright eyes. "And where did you find it? By all means sit down and tell us the tale. We are famished with eagerness for it, eh, my love?"

His love yawned, "Oh, yes!"

"There isn't much story," I said. "To recover the money I had to make a bargain, promising silence. Main was robbed Sunday afternoon. But it happens that we couldn't convict the robbers if we had them. The only person who could identify them—won't."

"But who killed Jeffrey?" The little man was pawing my chest with both pink hands. "Who killed him that night?"

"Suicide. Despair at being robbed under circumstances he couldn't explain."

"Preposterous!" My client didn't like the suicide.

"Mrs Main was awakened by the shot. Suicide would have canceled his insurance—would have left her penniless. She threw the gun and wallet out the window, hid the note he left, and framed the robber story."

"But the handkerchief!" Gungen screamed. He was all worked up.

"That doesn't mean anything," I assured him solemnly, "except that Main—you said he was promiscuous—had probably been fooling with your wife's maid, and that she—like a lot of maids—helped herself to your wife's belongings."

He puffed up his rouged cheeks, and stamped his feet, fairly dancing. His indignation was as funny as the statement that caused it.

"We shall see!" He spun on his heel and ran out of the room, repeating over and over, "We shall see!"

Enid Gungen held a hand out to me. Her doll face was all curves and dimples.

"I thank you," she whispered.

"I don't know what for," I growled, not taking the hand. "I've got it jumbled so anything like proof is out of the question. But he can't help knowing—didn't I practically tell him?"

"Oh, that!" She put it behind her with a toss of her small head. "I'm quite able to look out for myself so long as he has no definite proof."

I believed her.

Bruno Gungen came fluttering back into the library, frothing at the mouth, tearing his dyed goatee, raging that Rose Rubury was not to be found in the house.

The next morning Dick Foley told me the maid had joined Weel and Dahl and had left for Portland with them.

4

THIS KING BUSINESS

A COMPLETE NOVELETTE

MYSTERY STORIES, JANUARY 1928

The desire to rule is inherent in the breasts of most of us, notwithstanding the number of thrones that have toppled in the past decade. Mr Hammett tells us of the strange series of events which led an American youth to seek kingship in "the Powder Magazine of Europe"—the Balkans. The consequences were—to put it mildly—exciting.

I

"YES"—AND "NO"

The train from Belgrade set me down in Stefania, capital of Muravia, in early afternoon—a rotten afternoon. Cold wind blew cold rain in my face and down my neck as I left the square granite barn of a railroad station to climb into a taxicab.

English meant nothing to the chauffeur, nor French. Good German might have failed. Mine wasn't good. It was a hodgepodge of grunts and gargles. This chauffeur was the first person who had ever pretended to understand it. I suspected him of guessing, and I expected to be taken to some distant suburban point. Maybe he was a good guesser. Anyhow, he took me to the Hotel of the Republic.

The hotel was a new six-storey affair, very proud of its elevators, American plumbing, private baths, and other modern tricks. After I had washed and changed clothes I went down to the cafe for luncheon. Then, supplied with minute instructions in English, French, and sign-language by a highly uniformed head porter, I turned up my raincoat collar and crossed the muddy plaza to call on Roy Scanlan, United States *charge d'affaires* in this youngest and smallest of the Balkan States.

He was a pudgy man of thirty, with smooth hair already far along the gray route, a nervous, flabby face, plump white hands that twitched, and very nice clothes. He shook hands with me, patted me into a chair, barely glanced at my letter of introduction, and stared at my necktie while saying:

"So you're a private detective from San Francisco?"

"Yes."

"And?"

"Lionel Grantham."

"Surely not!"

"Yes."

"But he's—" The diplomat realized he was looking into my eyes, hurriedly switched his gaze to my hair, and forgot what he had started to say.

"But he's what?" I prodded him.

"Oh!"—with a vague upward motion of head and eyebrows—"not that sort."

"How long has he been here?" I asked.

"Two months. Possibly three or three and a half or more."

"You know him well?"

"Oh, no! By sight, of course, and to talk to. He and I are the only Americans here, so we're fairly well acquainted."

"Know what he's doing here?"

"No, I don't. He just happened to stop here in his travels, I imagine, unless, of course, he's here for some special reason. No doubt there's a girl in it—she is General Radnjak's daughter—though I don't think so."

"How does he spend his time?"

"I really haven't any idea. He lives at the Hotel of the Republic, is quite a favorite among our foreign colony, rides a bit, lives the usual life of a young man of family and wealth."

"Mixed up with anybody who isn't all he ought to be?"

"Not that I know of, except that I've seen him with Mahmoud and Einarson. They are certainly scoundrels, though they may not be."

"Who are they?"

"Nubar Mahmoud is private secretary to Doctor Semich, the President. Colonel Einarson is an Icelander, just now virtually the head of the army. I know nothing about either of them."

"Except that they are scoundrels?"

The *chargé d'affaires* wrinkled his round white forehead in pain and gave me a reproachful glance.

"Not at all," he said. "Now, may I ask, of what is Grantham suspected?"

"Nothing."

"Then?"

"Seven months ago, on his twenty-first birthday, this Lionel Grantham got hold of the money his father had left him—a nice wad. Till then the boy had had a tough time of it. His mother had, and has, highly developed middle-class notions of refinement. His father had been a genuine aristocrat in the old manner—a hard-souled, soft-spoken individual who got what he wanted by simply taking it; with a liking for old wine and young women, and plenty of both, and for cards and dice and running horses—and fights, whether he was in them or watching them.

"While he lived the boy had a he-raising. Mrs Grantham thought her husband's tastes low, but he was a man who had things his own way. Besides, the Grantham blood was the best in America. She was a woman to be impressed by that. Eleven years ago—when Lionel was a kid of ten—the old man died. Mrs Grantham swapped the family roulette wheel for a box of dominoes and began to convert the kid into a patent leather Galahad.

"I've never seen him, but I'm told the job wasn't a success. However, she kept him bundled up for eleven years, not even letting him escape to college. So it went until the day when he was legally of age and in possession of his share of his father's estate. That morning he kisses Mamma and tells her casually that he's off for a little run around the world—alone. Mamma does and says all that might be expected of her, but it's no good. The Grantham blood is up. Lionel promises to drop her a post-card now and then, and departs.

"He seems to have behaved fairly well during his wandering. I suppose just being free gave him all the excitement he needed. But a few weeks ago the trust company that handles his affairs got instructions from him to turn some railroad bonds into cash and ship the money to him in care of a Belgrade bank. The amount was large—over the three million mark—so the trust company told Mrs Grantham about it. She chucked a fit. She had been getting letters from him—from Paris, without a word said about Belgrade.

"Mamma was all for dashing over to Europe at once. Her brother, Senator Walbourn, talked her out of it. He did some cabling, and learned that Lionel was neither in Paris nor in Belgrade, unless he was hiding. Mrs Grantham packed her trunks and made reservations. The Senator headed her off again, convincing her that the lad would resent her interference, telling her the best thing was to investigate on the quiet. He brought the job to the agency. I went to Paris, learned that a friend of Lionel's there was relaying his mail, and that Lionel was here in Stefania. On the way down I stopped off in Belgrade and learned that the money was being sent here to him—most of it already has been. So here I am."

Scanlan smiled happily.

"There's nothing I can do," he said. "Grantham is of age, and it's his money."

"Right," I agreed, "and I'm in the same fix. All I can do is poke around, find out what he's up to, try to save his dough if he's being gypped. Can't you give me even a guess at the answer? Three million dollars—what could he put it into?"

"I don't know." The *charge d'affaires* fidgeted uncomfortably. "There's no business here that amounts to anything. It's purely an agricultural country, split up among small land-owners—ten, fifteen, twenty acre farms. There's his association with Einarson and Mahmoud, though. They'd certainly rob him if they got the chance. I'm positive they're robbing him. But I don't think they would. Perhaps he isn't acquainted with them. It's probably a woman."

"Well, whom should I see? I'm handicapped by not knowing the country, not knowing the language. To whom can I take my story and get help?"

"I don't know," he said gloomily. Then his face brightened. "Go to Vasilije Djudakovich. He is Minister of Police. He is the man for you! He can help you, and you may trust him. He has a digestion instead of a brain. He'll not understand a thing you tell him. Yes, Djudakovich is your man!"

"Thanks," I said, and staggered out into the muddy street.

II

ROMAINE

I found the Minister of Police's offices in the Administration Building, a gloomy concrete pile next to the Executive Residence at the head of the plaza. In French that was even worse than my German, a thin, white-whiskered clerk, who looked like a consumptive Santa Claus, told me His Excellency was not in. Looking solemn, lowering my voice to a whisper, I repeated that I had come from the United States *chargé d'affaires.* This hocus-pocus seemed to impress Saint Nicholas. He nodded understandingly and shuffled out of the room. Presently he was back, bowing at the door, asking me to follow him.

I tailed him along a dim corridor to a wide door marked "15." He opened it, bowed me through it, wheezed, "*Asseyez-vous, s'il vans plait*" closed the door and left me. I was in an office, a large, square one. Everything in it was large. The four windows were double-size. The chairs were young benches, except the leather one at the desk, which could have been the rear half of a touring car. A couple of men could have slept on the desk. Twenty could have eaten at the table.

A door opposite the one through which I had come opened, and a girl came in, closing the door behind her, shutting out a throbbing purr, as of some heavy machine, that had sounded through.

"I'm Romaine Frankl," she said in English, "His Excellency's secretary. Will you tell me what you wish?"

She might have been any age from twenty to thirty, something less than five feet in height, slim without boniness, with curly hair as near black as brown can get, black-lashed eyes whose gray irises had black rims, a small, delicate-featured face, and a voice that seemed too soft and faint to carry as well as it did.

She wore a red woolen dress that had no shape except that which her body gave it, and when she moved—to walk or raise a hand—it was as if it cost her no energy—as if some one else were moving her.

"I'd like to see him," I said while I was accumulating this data.

"Later, certainly," she promised, "but it's impossible now." She turned, with her peculiar effortless grace, back to the door, opening it so that the throbbing purr sounded in the room again. "Hear?" she said. "He's taking his nap."

She shut the door against His Excellency's snoring and floated across the room to climb up in the immense leather chair at the desk.

"Do sit down," she said, wriggling a tiny forefinger at a chair beside the desk. "It will save time if you will tell me your business, because, unless you speak our tongue, I'll have to interpret your message to His Excellency."

I told her about Lionel Grantham and my interest in him, in practically the same words I had used on Scanlan, winding up:

"You see, there's nothing I can do except try to learn what the boy's up to and give him a hand if he needs it. I can't go to him—he's too much Grantham, I'm afraid, to take kindly to what he'd think was nurse-maid stuff. Mr Scanlan advised me to come to the Minister of Police."

"You were fortunate." She looked as if she wanted to make a joke about my country's representative but weren't sure how I'd take it. "Your *chargé d'affaires* is not always easy to understand."

"Once you get the hang of it, it's not hard," I said. "You just throw out all his statements that have *no's* or *not's* or *nothing's* or *don't's* in them."

"That's it! That's it, exactly!" She leaned toward me, laughing. "I've always known there was some key to it, but nobody's been able to find it before. You've solved our national problem."

"For reward, then, I should be given all the information you have about Grantham."

"You should, but I'll have to speak to His Excellency first. He'll wake presently."

"You can tell me unofficially what you think of Grantham. You know him?"

"Yes. He's charming. A nice boy, delightfully naif, inexperienced, but really charming."

"Who are his friends here?"

She shook her head and said:

"No more of that until His Excellency wakes. You're from San Francisco? I remember the funny little street cars, and the fog, and the salad right after the soup, and Coffee Dan's."

"You've been there?"

"Twice. I was in the United States for a year and half, in vaudeville, bringing rabbits out of hats."

We were still talking about that half an hour later when the door opened and the Minister of Police came in.

The over-size furniture immediately shrank to normal, the girl became a midget, and I felt like somebody's little boy.

This Vasilije Djudakovich stood nearly seven feet tall, and that was nothing to his girth. Maybe he wouldn't weigh more than five hundred pounds, but, looking at him, it was hard to think except in terms of tons. He was a blondhaired, blond-bearded mountain of meat in a black frock coat. He wore a necktie, so I suppose he had a collar, but it was hidden all the way around by the red rolls of his neck. His white vest was the size and shape of a hoop-skirt, and in spite of that it strained at the buttons. His eyes were almost invisible between the cushions of flesh around them, and were shaded into a colorless darkness, like water in a deep well. His mouth was a fat red oval among the yellow hairs of his whiskers and mustache. He came into the room slowly, ponderously, and I was surprised that the floor didn't creak nor the room tremble.

Romaine Frankl was watching me attentively as she slid out of the big leather chair and introduced me to the Minister. He gave me a fat, sleepy smile and a hand that had the general appearance of a naked baby, and let himself down slowly into the chair the girl had quit. Planted there, he lowered his head until it rested on the pillows of his several chins, and then he seemed to go to sleep.

I drew up another chair for the girl. She took another sharp look at me—she seemed to be hunting for something in my face—and began to talk to him in what I suppose was the native lingo. She talked rapidly for about twenty minutes, while he gave no sign that he was listening or that he was even awake.

When she was through, he said: "*Da.*" He spoke dreamily, but there was a volume to the syllable that could have come from no place smaller than his gigantic belly.

The girl turned to me, smiling.

"His Excellency will be glad to give you every possible assistance. Officially, of course, he does not care to interfere in the affairs of a visitor from another country, but he realizes the importance of keeping Mr Grantham from being victimized while here. If you will return tomorrow afternoon, at, say, three o'clock..."

I promised to do that, thanked her, shook hands with the mountain again, and went out into the rain.

III

SHADOWING

Back at the hotel, I had no trouble learning that Lionel Grantham occupied a suite on the sixth floor and was in it at that time. I had his photograph in my pocket and his description in my head. I spent what was left of the afternoon and the early evening waiting for a look at him. At a little after seven I got it.

He stepped out of the elevator, a tall, flat-backed boy with a supple body that tapered from broad shoulders to narrow hips, carried erectly on long, muscular legs—the sort of frame that tailors like. His pink, regular-featured, really handsome face wore an expression of aloof superiority that was too marked to be anything else than a cover for youthful self-consciousness.

Lighting a cigarette, he passed into the street. The rain had stopped, though clouds overhead promised more shortly. He turned down the street afoot. So did I.

We went to a much gilded restaurant two blocks from the hotel, where a gypsy orchestra played on a little balcony stuck insecurely high on one wall. All the waiters and half the diners seemed to know the boy. He bowed and smiled to this side and that as he walked down to a table near the far end, where two men were waiting for him.

One of them was tall and thick-bodied, with bushy dark hair and a flowing dark mustache. His florid, short-nosed face wore the expression of a man who doesn't mind a fight now and then. This one was dressed in a green and gold military uniform, with high boots of the shiniest black leather. His companion was in evening clothes, a plump, swarthy man of medium height, with oily black hair and a suave, oval face.

While young Grantham joined this pair I found a table some distance from them for myself. I ordered dinner and looked around at my neighbors. There was a sprinkling of uniforms in the room, some dress coats and evening gowns, but most of the diners were in ordinary daytime clothes. I saw a couple of faces that were probably British, a Greek or two, a few Turks. The food was good and so was my appetite. I was smoking a cigarette over a tiny cup of syrupy coffee when Grantham and the big florid officer got up and went away.

I couldn't have got my bill and paid it in time to follow them, without raising a disturbance, so I let them go. Then I settled for my meal and waited until the dark, plump man they had left behind called for his check. I was in the street a minute or more ahead of him, standing, looking up toward the dimly electric-lighted plaza with what was meant for the expression of a tourist who didn't quite know where to go next.

He passed me, going up the muddy street with the soft, careful-where-you-put-your-foot tread of a cat.

A soldier—a bony man in sheepskin coat and cap, with a gray mustache bristling over gray, sneering lips—stepped out of a dark doorway and stopped the swarthy man with whining words.

The swarthy man lifted hands and shoulders in a gesture that held both anger and surprise.

The soldier whined again, but the sneer on his gray mouth became more pronounced. The plump man's voice was low, sharp, angry, but he moved a hand from pocket to soldier, and the brown of Muravian paper money showed in the hand. The soldier pocketed the money, raised a hand in a salute, and went across the street.

When the swarthy man had stopped staring after the soldier, I moved toward the corner around which sheepskin coat and cap had vanished. My soldier was a block and a half down the street, striding along with bowed head. He was in a hurry. I got plenty of exercise keeping up with him. Presently the city began to thin out. The thinner it got, the less I liked this expedition. Shadowing is at its best in daytime, downtown in a familiar large city. This was shadowing at its worst.

He led me out of the city along a cement road bordered by few houses. I stayed as far back as I could, so he was a faint, blurred shadow ahead. He turned a sharp bend in the road. I hustled toward the bend, intending to drop back again as soon as I had rounded it. Speeding, I nearly gummed the works.

The soldier suddenly appeared around the curve, coming toward me.

A little behind me, a small pile of lumber on the roadside was the only cover within a hundred feet. I stretched my short legs thither.

Irregularly piled boards made a shallow cavity in one end of the pile, almost large enough to hold me. On my knees in the mud, I huddled into that cavity.

The soldier came into sight through a chink between boards. Bright metal gleamed in one of his hands. A knife, I thought. But when he halted in front of my shelter I saw it was a revolver of the old-style nickel-plated sort.

He stood still, looking at my shelter, looking up the road and down the road. He grunted, came toward me. Slivers stung my cheek as I rubbed myself flatter against the timber-ends. My gun was with my blackjack—in my Gladstone bag, in my room in my hotel. A fine place to have them now! The soldier's gun was bright in his hand.

Rain began to patter on boards and ground. The soldier turned up the collar of his coat as he came. Nobody ever did anything I liked more. A man stalking another wouldn't have done that. He didn't know I was there. He was hunting a hiding place for himself. The game was even! If he found me, he had the gun, but I had seen him first.

His sheepskin coat rasped against the wood as he went by me, bending low as he passed my corner for the back of the pile, so close to me that the same raindrops seemed to be hitting both of us. I undid my fists after that. I couldn't see him, but I could hear him breathing, scratching himself, even humming.

A couple of weeks went by.

The mud I was kneeling in soaked through my pants-legs, wetting my knees and shins. The rough wood filed skin off my face every time I breathed. My mouth was as dry as my knees were wet, because I was breathing through it for silence.

An automobile came around the bend, headed for the city. I heard the soldier grunt softly, heard the click of his gun as he cocked it. The car came abreast, went on. The soldier blew out his breath and started scratching himself and humming again.

Another couple of weeks passed.

Men's voices came through the rain, barely audible, louder, quite clear. Four soldiers in sheepskin coats and hats walked down the road the way we had come, their voices presently shrinking into silence as they disappeared around the curve.

In the distance an automobile horn barked two ugly notes. The soldier grunted—a grunt that said clearly: "Here it is." His feet slopped in the mud, and the lumber pile creaked under his weight. I couldn't see what he was up to.

White light danced around the bend in the road, and an automobile came into view—a high-powered car going cityward with a speed that paid no attention to the wet slipperiness of the road. Rain and night and speed blurred its two occupants, who were in the front seat.

Over my head a heavy revolver roared. The soldier was working. The speeding car swayed crazily along the wet cement, its brakes screaming.

When the sixth shot told me the nickel-plated gun was probably empty, I jumped out of my hollow.

The soldier was leaning over the lumber pile, his gun still pointing at the skidding car while he peered through the rain.

He turned as I saw him, swung the gun around to me, snarled an order I couldn't understand. I was betting the gun was empty. I raised both hands high over my head, made an astonished face, and kicked him in the belly.

He folded over on me, wrapping himself around my leg. We both went down. I was underneath, but his head was against my thigh. His cap fell off. I caught his hair with both hands and yanked myself into a sitting position. His teeth went into my leg. I called him disagreeable things and put my thumbs in the hollows under his ears. It didn't take much pressure to teach him that he oughtn't to bite people. When he lifted his face to howl, I put my right fist in it, pulling him into the punch with my left hand in his hair. It was a nice solid sock.

I pushed him off my leg, got up, took a handful of his coat collar, and dragged him out into the road.

IV

INTRODUCTIONS

White light poured over us. Squinting into it, I saw the automobile standing down the road, its spotlight turned on me and my sparring partner. A big man in green and gold came into the light—the florid officer who had been one of Grantham's companions in the restaurant. An automatic was in one of his hands.

He strode over to us, stiff-legged in his high boots, ignored the soldier on the ground, and examined me carefully with sharp little dark eyes.

"British?" he asked.

"American."

He bit a corner of his mustache and said meaninglessly:

"Yes, that is better."

His English was guttural, with a German accent.

Lionel Grantham came from the car to us. His face wasn't as pink as it had been.

"What is it?" he asked the officer, but he looked at me.

"I don't know," I said. "I took a stroll after dinner and got mixed up on my directions. Finding myself out here, I decided

I was headed the wrong way. When I turned around to go back I saw this fellow duck behind the lumber pile. He had a gun in his hand. I took him for a stick-up, so I played Indian on him. Just as I got to him he jumped up and began spraying you people. I reached him in time to spoil his aim. Friend of yours?"

"You're an American," the boy said. "I'm Lionel Grantham. This is Colonel Einarson. We're very grateful to you." He screwed up his forehead and looked at Einarson. "What do you think of it?"

The officer shrugged his shoulders, growled, "One of my children—we'll see," and kicked the ribs of the man on the ground.

The kick brought the soldier to life. He sat up, rolled over on hands and knees, and began a broken, long-winded entreaty, plucking at the Colonel's tunic with dirty hands.

"Ach!" Einarson knocked the hands down with a tap of pistol barrel across knuckles, looked with disgust at the muddy marks on his tunic, and growled an order.

The soldier jumped to his feet, stood at attention, got another order, did an about-face, and marched to the automobile. Colonel Einarson strode stiff-legged behind him, holding his automatic to the man's back. Grantham put a hand on my arm.

"Come along," he said. "We'll thank you properly and get better acquainted after we've taken care of this fellow."

Colonel Einarson got into the driver's seat, with the soldier beside him. Grantham waited while I found the soldier's revolver. Then we got into the rear seat. The officer looked doubtfully at me out of his eye-corners, but said nothing. He drove the car back the way it had come. He liked speed, and we hadn't far to go. By the time we were settled in our seats the car was whisking us through a gateway in a high stone wall, with a sentry on each side presenting arms. We did a sliding half-circle into a branching driveway and jerked to a stand-still in front of a square whitewashed building.

Einarson prodded the soldier out ahead of him. Grantham and I got out. To the left, a row of long, low buildings showed pale gray in the rain—barracks. The door of the square, white building was opened by a bearded orderly in green. We went in. Einarson pushed his prisoner across the small reception hall and through the open door of a bedroom. Grantham and I followed them in. The orderly stopped in the doorway, traded some words with Einarson, and went away, closing the door.

The room we were in looked like a cell, except that there were no bars over the one small window. It was a narrow room, with bare, whitewashed walls and ceiling. The wooden floor, scrubbed with lye until it was almost as white as the walls, was bare. For furniture there was a black iron cot, three folding chairs of wood and canvas, and an unpainted chest of drawers, with comb, brush, and a few papers on top. That was all.

"Be seated, gentlemen," Einarson said, indicating the camp chairs. "We'll get at this thing now."

The boy and I sat down. The officer laid his pistol on the top of the chest of drawers, rested one elbow beside the pistol, took a corner of his mustache in one big red hand, and addressed the soldier. His voice was kindly, paternal. The soldier, standing rigidly upright in the middle of the floor, replied, whining, his eyes focused on the officer's with a blank, in-turned look.

They talked for five minutes or more. Impatience grew in the Colonel's voice and manner. The soldier kept his blank abjectness. Einarson ground his teeth together and looked angrily at the boy and me.

"This pig!" he exclaimed, and began to bellow at the soldier.

Sweat sprang out on the soldier's gray face, and he cringed out of his military stiffness. Einarson stopped bellowing at him and yelled two words at the door. It opened and the bearded orderly came in with a short, thick, leather whip. At a nod from

Einarson, he put the whip beside the automatic on the top of the chest of drawers and went out.

The soldier whimpered. Einarson spoke curtly to him. The soldier shuddered, began to unfasten his coat with shaking fingers, pleading all the while with whining, stuttering words. He took off his coat, his green blouse, his gray undershirt, letting them fall on the floor, and stood there, his hairy, not exactly clean body naked from the waist up. He worked his fingers together and cried.

Einarson grunted a word. The soldier stiffened at attention, hands at sides, facing us, his left side to Einarson.

Slowly Colonel Einarson removed his own belt, unbuttoned his tunic, took it off, folded it carefully, and laid it on the cot. Beneath it he wore a white cotton shirt. He rolled the sleeves up above his elbows and picked up the whip.

"This pig!" he said again.

Lionel Grantham stirred uneasily on his chair. His face was white, his eyes dark.

V

A FLOGGING

Leaning his left elbow on the chest of drawers again, playing with his mustache-end with his left hand, standing indolently cross-legged, Einarson began to flog the soldier. His right arm raised the whip, brought the lash whistling down to the soldier's back, raised it again, brought it down again. It was especially nasty because he was not hurrying himself, not exerting himself. He meant to flog the man until he got what he wanted, and he was saving his strength so that he could keep it up as long as necessary.

With the first blow the terror went out of the soldier's eyes. They dulled sullenly and his lips stopped twitching. He stood woodenly under the beating, staring over Grantham's head. The officer's face had also become expressionless. Anger was gone. He showed no pleasure in his work, not even that of relieving his feelings. His air was the air of a stoker shoveling coal, of a carpenter sawing a board, of a stenographer typing a letter. Here was a job to be done in a workman-like manner, without haste or excitement or wasted effort, without either enthusiasm or repulsion. It was nasty, but it taught me respect for this Colonel Einarson.

Lionel Grantham sat on the edge of his folding chair, staring at the soldier with white-ringed eyes. I offered the boy a cigarette, making an unnecessarily complicated operation out of lighting it and my own—to break up his score-keeping. He had been counting the strokes, and that wasn't good for him.

The whip curved up, swished down, cracked on the naked back—up, down, up, down. Einarson's florid face took on the damp glow of moderate exercise. The soldier's gray face was a lump of putty. He was facing Grantham and me. We couldn't see the marks of the whip.

Grantham said something to himself in a whisper. Then he gasped:

"I can't stand this!"

Einarson didn't look around from his work.

"Don't stop it now," I muttered. "We've gone this far."

The boy got up unsteadily and went to the window, opened it and stood looking out into the rainy night. Einarson paid no attention to him. He was putting more weight into the whipping now, standing with his feet far apart, leaning forward a little, his left hand on his hip, his right carrying the whip up and down with increasing swiftness.

The soldier swayed and a sob shook his hairy chest. The whip cut—cut—cut. I looked at my watch. Einarson had been at it for forty minutes, and looked good for the rest of the night.

The soldier moaned and turned toward the officer. Einarson did not break the rhythm of his stroke. The lash cut the man's shoulder. I caught a glimpse of his back—raw meat. Einarson spoke sharply. The soldier jerked himself to attention again, his left side to the officer. The whip went on with its work—up, down, up, down, up, down.

The soldier flung himself on hands and knees at Einarson's feet and began to pour out sob-broken words. Einarson looked down at him, listening carefully, holding the lash of the whip in his left hand, the butt still in his right. When the man had finished, Einarson asked questions, got answers, nodded, and the soldier stood up. Einarson put a friendly hand on the man's shoulder, turned him around, looked at his mangled red back, and said something in a sympathetic tone. Then he called the orderly in and gave him some orders. The soldier, moaning as he bent, picked up his discarded clothes and followed the orderly out of the bedroom.

Einarson tossed the whip up on top of the chest of drawers and crossed to the bed to pick up his tunic. A leather pocketbook slid from an inside pocket to the floor. When he recovered it, a soiled newspaper clipping slipped out and floated across to my feet. I picked it up and gave it back to him—a photograph of a man, the Shah of Persia, according to the French caption under it.

"That pig!" he said—meaning the soldier, not the Shah—as he put on his tunic and buttoned it. "He has a son, also until last week of my troops. This son drinks too much of wine. I reprimand him. He is insolent. What kind of army is it without discipline? Pigs! I knock this pig down, and he produces a knife. Ach! What kind of army is it where a soldier may attack his officers with knives? After I—personally, you comprehend—have finished with this swine, I have him court-martialed and sentenced to twenty years in the prison. This elder pig, his father, does not like that. So he will shoot me tonight. Ach! What kind of army is that?"

Lionel Grantham came away from his window. His young face was haggard. His young eyes were ashamed of the haggardness of his face.

Colonel Einarson made me a stiff bow and a formal speech of thanks for spoiling the soldier's aim—which I hadn't—and saving his life. Then the conversation turned to my presence in Muravia. I told them briefly that I had held a captain's commission in the military intelligence department during the war. That much was the truth, and that was all the truth I gave them. After the war—so my fairy tale went—I had decided to stay in Europe, had taken my discharge there and had drifted around, doing odd jobs at one place and another. I was vague, trying to give them the impression that those odd jobs had not always, or usually, been lady-like. I gave them more definite—though still highly imaginary—details of my recent employment with a French syndicate, admitting that I had come to this corner of the world because I thought it better not to be seen in Western Europe for a year or so.

"Nothing I could be jailed for," I said, "but things could be made uncomfortable for me. So I roamed over into *Mitteleuropa*, learned that I might find a connection in Belgrade, got there to find it a false alarm, and came on down here. I may pick up something here. I've got a date with the Minister of Police tomorrow. I think I can show him where he can use me."

"The gross Djudakovich!" Einarson said with frank contempt. "You find him to your liking?"

"No work, no eat," I said.

"Einarson," Grantham began quickly, hesitated, said: "Couldn't we—don't you think—" and didn't finish.

The Colonel frowned at him, saw I had noticed the frown, cleared his throat, and addressed me in a gruffly hearty tone:

"Perhaps it would be well if you did not too speedily engage yourself to this fat minister. It may be—there is a possibility that we know of another field where your talents might find employment more to your taste—and profit."

I let the matter stand there, saying neither yes nor no.

VI

CARDS ON THE TABLE

We returned to the city in the officer's car. He and Grantham sat in the rear. I sat beside the soldier who drove. The boy and I got out at our hotel. Einarson said good night and was driven away as if he were in a hurry.

"It's early," Grantham said as we went indoors. "Come up to my room."

I stopped at my own room to wash off the mud I'd gathered around the lumber stack and to change my clothes, and then went up with him. He had three rooms on the top floor, overlooking the plaza.

He set out a bottle of whisky, a syphon, lemons, cigars and cigarettes, and we drank, smoked, and talked. Fifteen or twenty minutes of the talk came from no deeper than the mouth on either side—comments on the night's excitement, our opinions of Stefania, and so on. Each of us had something to say to the other. Each was weighing the other in before he said it.

I decided to put mine over first.

"Colonel Einarson was spoofing us tonight," I said.

"Spoofing?" The boy sat up straight, blinking.

"His soldier shot for money, not revenge."

"You mean—?" His mouth stayed open.

"I mean the little dark man you ate with gave the soldier money."

"Mahmoud! Why, that's—You are sure?"

"I saw it."

He looked at his feet, yanking his gaze away from mine as if he didn't want me to see that he thought I was lying.

"The soldier may have lied to Einarson," he said presently, still trying to keep me from knowing he thought me the liar. "I can understand some of the language, as spoken by the educated Muravians, but not the country dialect the soldier talked, so I don't know what he said, but he may have lied, you know."

"Not a chance," I said. "I'd bet my pants he told the truth."

He continued to stare at his outstretched feet, fighting to hold his face cool and calm. Part of what he was thinking slipped out in words:

"Of course, I owe you a tremendous debt for saving us from—"

"You don't. You owe that to the soldier's bad aim. I didn't jump him till his gun was empty."

"But—" His young eyes were wide before mine, and if I had pulled a machine gun out of my cuff he wouldn't have been surprised. He suspected me of everything on the blotter. I cursed myself for overplaying my hand. There was nothing to do now but spread the cards.

"Listen, Grantham. Most of what I told you and Einarson about myself is the bunk. Your uncle, Senator Walbourn, sent me down here. You were supposed to be in Paris. A lot of your dough was being shipped to Belgrade. The Senator was leery of the racket, didn't know whether you were playing a game or somebody was putting over a fast one. I went to Belgrade, traced you here, and came here, to run into what I ran into. I've traced the money to you, have talked to you. That's all I was hired to do. My job's done—unless there's anything I can do for you now."

"Not a thing," he said very calmly. "Thanks, just the same." He stood up, yawning. "Perhaps I'll see you again before you leave for the United States."

"Yeah." It was easy for me to make my voice match his in indifference: I hadn't a cargo of rage to hide. "Good night."

I went down to my room, got into bed, and, not having anything to think about, went to sleep.

VII

LIONEL'S PLANS

I slept till late the next morning and then had breakfast in my room. I was in the middle of it when knuckles tapped my door. A stocky man in a wrinkled gray uniform, set off with a short, thick sword, came in, saluted, gave me a square white envelope, looked hungrily at the American cigarettes on my table, smiled and took one when I offered them, saluted again, and went out.

The square envelope had my name written on it in a small, very plain and round, but not childish, handwriting. Inside was a note from the same pen:

> *The Minister of Police regrets that departmental affairs prevent his receiving you this afternoon.*

It was signed "Romaine Frankl," and had a postscript:

> "If it's convenient for you to call on me after nine this evening, perhaps I can save you some time.
>
> R. F."

Below this an address was written.

I put the note in my pocket and called: "Come in," to another set of knocking knuckles.

Lionel Grantham entered.

His face was pale and set.

"Good morning," I said, making it cheerfully casual, as if I attached no importance to last night's rumpus. "Had breakfast yet? Sit down, and—"

"Oh, yes, thanks. I've eaten." His handsome red face was reddening. "About last night—I was—"

"Forget it! Nobody likes to have his business pried into."

"That's good of you," he said, twisting his hat in his hands. He cleared his throat. "You said you'd—ah—do—ah—help me if I wished."

"Yeah. I will. Sit down."

He sat down, coughed, ran his tongue over his lips.

"You haven't said anything to any one about last night's affair with the soldier?"

"No," I said.

"Will you not say anything about it?"

"Why?"

He looked at the remains of my breakfast and didn't answer. I lit a cigarette to go with my coffee and waited. He stirred uneasily in his chair and, without looking up, asked:

"You know Mahmoud was killed last night?"

"The man in the restaurant with you and Einarson?"

"Yes. He was shot down in front of his house a little after midnight."

"Einarson?"

The boy jumped.

"No!" he cried. "Why do you say that?"

"Einarson knew Mahmoud had paid the soldier to wipe him out, so he plugged Mahmoud, or had him plugged. Did you tell him what I told you last night?"

"No." He blushed. "It's embarrassing to have one's family sending guardians after one."

I made a guess:

"He told you to offer me the job he spoke of last night, and to caution me against talking about the soldier. Didn't he?"

"Y-e-s."

"Well, go ahead and offer."

"But he doesn't know you're— "

"What are you going to do, then?" I asked. "If you don't make me the offer, you'll have to tell him why."

"Oh, Lord, what a mess!" he said wearily, putting elbows on knees, face between palms, looking at me with the harried eyes of a boy finding life too complicated.

He was ripe for talk. I grinned at him, finished my coffee, and waited.

"You know I'm not going to be led home by an ear," he said with a sudden burst of rather childish defiance.

"You know I'm not going to try to take you," I soothed him.

We had some more silence after that. I smoked while he held his head and worried. After a while he squirmed in his chair, sat stiffly upright, and his face turned perfectly crimson from hair to collar.

"I'm going to ask for your help," he said, pretending he didn't know he was blushing. "I'm going to tell you the whole foolish thing. If you laugh, I'll—You won't laugh, will you?"

"If it's funny I probably will, but that needn't keep me from helping you."

"Yes, do laugh! It's silly! You ought to laugh!" He took a deep breath. "Did you ever—did you ever think you'd like to be a"—he stopped, looked at me with a desperate sort of shyness, pulled himself together, and almost shouted the last word—"king?"

"Maybe. I've thought of a lot of things I'd like to be, and that might be one of 'em."

"I met Mahmoud at an embassy ball in Constantinople," he dashed into the story, dropping his words quickly as if glad to get rid of them. "He was President Semich's secretary. We got quite friendly, though I wasn't especially fond of him. He persuaded me to come here with him, and introduced me to Colonel Einarson. Then they—there's really no doubt that the country is wretchedly governed. I wouldn't have gone into it if that hadn't been so.

"A revolution was being prepared. The man who was to lead it had just died. It was handicapped, too, by a lack of money. Believe this—it wasn't all vanity that made me go into it. I believed—I still believe—that it would have been—will be—for the good of the country. The offer they made me was that if I would finance the revolution I could be—could be king.

"Now wait! The Lord knows it's bad enough, but don't think it sillier than it is. The money I have would go a long way in this small, impoverished country. Then, with an American ruler, it would be easier—it ought to be—for the country to borrow in America or England. Then there's the political angle. Muravia is surrounded by four countries, any one of which is strong enough to annex it if it wants. Even Albania, now that it is a protege of Italy's. Muravia has stayed independent so far only because of the jealousy among its stronger neighbors and because it hasn't a seaport. But with the balance shifting—with Greece, Italy, and Albania allied against Jugoslavia for control of the Balkans—it's only a matter of time before something will happen here, as it now stands.

"But with an American ruler—and if loans in America and England were arranged, so we had their capital invested here—there would be a change in the situation. Muravia would be in a stronger position, would have at least some slight claim on the friendship of stronger powers. That would be enough to make the neighbors cautious.

"Albania, shortly after the war, thought of the same thing, and offered its crown to one of the wealthy American Bonapartes. He didn't want it. He was an older man and had already made his career. I did want my chance when it came. There were"—some of the embarrassment that had left him during his talking returned—"there were kings back in the Grantham lines. We trace our descent from James the Fourth, of Scotland. I wanted—it was nice to think of carrying the line back to a crown.

"We weren't planning a violent revolution. Einarson holds the army. We simply had to use the army to force the Deputies—those who were not already with us—to change the form of government and elect me king. My descent would make it easier than if the candidate were one who hadn't royal blood in him. It would give me a certain standing in spite—in spite of my being young, and—and the people really want a king, especially the peasants. They don't think they're really entitled to call themselves a nation without one. A president means nothing to them—he's simply an ordinary man like themselves. So, you see, I—It was—Go ahead, laugh! You've heard enough to know how silly it is!" His voice was high-pitched, screechy. "Laugh! Why don't you laugh?"

"What for?" I asked. "It's crazy, God knows, but not silly. Your judgment was gummy, but your nerve's all right. You've been talking as if this were all dead and buried. Has it flopped?"

"No, it hasn't," he said slowly, frowning, "but I keep thinking it has. Mahmoud's death shouldn't change the situation, yet I've a feeling it's all over."

"Much of your money sunk?"

"I don't mind that. But—well—suppose the American newspapers get hold of the story, and they probably will. You know how ridiculous they could make it. And then the others who'll know about it—my mother and uncle and the trust company. I won't pretend I'm not ashamed to face them. And then—" His face got red and shiny. "And then Valeska—Miss Radnjak—her father was to have led the revolution. He did lead it—until he was murdered. She is—I never could be good enough for her." He said this in a peculiarly idiotic tone of awe. "But I've hoped that perhaps by carrying on her father's work, and if I had something besides mere money to offer her—if I had done something—made a place for myself—perhaps she'd—you know."

I said: "Uh-huh."

"What shall I do?" he asked earnestly. "I can't run away. I've got to see it through for her, and to keep my own self-respect. But I've got that feeling that it's all over. You offered to help me. Help me. Tell me what I ought to do!"

"You'll do what I tell you—if I promise to bring you through with a clean face?" I asked, just as if steering millionaire descendants of Scotch kings through Balkan plots were an old story to me, merely part of the day's work.

"Yes!"

"What's the next thing on the revolutionary program?"

"There's a meeting tonight. I'm to bring you."

"What time?"

"Midnight."

"I'll meet you here at eleven-thirty. How much am I supposed to know?"

"I was to tell you about the plot, and to offer you whatever inducements were necessary to bring you in. There was no definite arrangement as to how much or how little I was to tell you."

VIII

AN ENLIGHTENING INTERVIEW

At nine-thirty that night a cab set me down in front of the address the Minister of Police's secretary had given in her note. It was a small two-storey house in a badly paved street on the city's eastern edge. A middle-aged woman in very clean, stiffly starched, ill-fitting clothes opened the door for me. Before I could speak, Romaine Frankl, in a sleeveless pink satin gown, floated into sight behind the woman, smiling, holding out a small hand to me.

"I didn't know you'd come," she said.

"Why?" I asked, with a great show of surprise at the notion that any man would ignore an invitation from her, while the servant closed the door and took my coat and hat.

We were standing in a dull-rose-papered room, finished and carpeted with oriental richness. There was one discordant note in the room—an immense leather chair.

"We'll go upstairs," the girl said, and addressed the servant with words that meant nothing to me, except the name Marya. "Or would you"—she turned to me and English again—"prefer beer to wine?"

I said I wouldn't, and we went upstairs, the girl climbing ahead of me with her effortless appearance of being carried. She took me into a black, white, and gray room that was very daintily furnished with as few pieces as possible, its otherwise perfect feminine atmosphere spoiled by the presence of another of the big padded chairs.

The girl sat on a gray divan, pushing away a stack of French and Austrian magazines to make a place for me beside her. Through an open door I could see the painted foot of a Spanish bed, a short stretch of purple counterpane, and half of a purple-curtained window.

"His Excellency was very sorry," the girl began, and stopped.

I was looking—not staring—at the big leather chair. I knew she had stopped because I was looking at it, so I wouldn't take my eyes away.

"Vasilije," she said, more distinctly than was really necessary, "was very sorry he had to postpone this afternoon's appointment. The assassination of the President's secretary—you heard of it?—made us put everything else aside for the moment."

"Oh, yes, that fellow Mahmoud—" slowly shifting my eyes from the leather ehair to her. "Found out who killed him?"

Her black-ringed, black-centered eyes seemed to study me from a distance while she shook her head, jiggling the nearly black curls.

"Probably Einarson," I said.

"You haven't been idle." Her lower lids lifted when she smiled, giving her eyes a twinkling effect.

The servant Marya came in with wine and fruit, put them on a small table beside the divan, and went away. The girl poured wine and offered me cigarettes in a silver box. I passed them up for one of my own. She smoked a king-size Egyptian cigarette—big as a cigar. It accentuated the smallness of her face and hand—which is probably why she favored that size.

"What sort of revolution is this they've sold my boy?" I asked.

"It was a very nice one until it died."

"How come it died?"

"It—do you know anything about our history?"

"No."

"Well, Muravia came into existence after the war as a result of the fear and jealousy of four countries. The nine or ten thousand square miles that make this country aren't very valuable land. There's little here that any of those four countries especially wanted, but no three of them would agree to let the fourth have it. The only way to settle the thing was to make a separate country out of it. That was done in 1923.

"Doctor Semich was elected the first president, for a ten-year term. He is not a statesman, not a politician, and never will be. But since he was the only Muravian who had ever been heard of outside his own town, it was thought that his election would give the new country some prestige. Besides, it was a fitting honor for Muravia's only great man. He was not meant to be anything but a figure-head. The real governing was to be done by General Danilo Radnjak, who was elected vice-president, which, here, is more than equivalent to Prime Minister. General Radnjak was a capable man. The army worshiped him, the peasants trusted him, and our *bourgeoisie* knew him to be honest, conservative, intelligent, and as good a business administrator as a military one.

"Doctor Semich is a very mild, elderly scholar with no knowledge whatever of worldly affairs. You can understand him from this—he is easily the greatest of living bacteriologists, but he'll tell you, if you are on intimate terms with him, that he doesn't believe in the value of bacteriology at all. 'Mankind must learn to live with bacteria as with friends,' he'll say. 'Our bodies must adapt themselves to diseases, so there will be little difference between having tuberculosis, for example, or not having it. That way lies victory. This making war on bacteria is a futile business. Futile but interesting. So we do it. Our poking around in laboratories is perfectly useless—but it amuses us.'

"Now when this delightful old dreamer was honored by his countrymen with the presidency, he took it in the worst possible way. He determined to show his appreciation by locking up his laboratory and applying himself heart and soul to running the government. Nobody expected or wanted that. Radnjak was to have been the government. For a while he did control the situation, and everything went well enough.

"But Mahmoud had designs of his own. He was Doctor Semich's secretary, and he was trusted. He began calling the President's attentions to various trespasses of Radnjak's on the presidential powers. Radnjak, in an attempt to keep Mahmoud from control, made a terrible mistake. He went to Doctor Semich and told him frankly and honestly that no one expected him, the President, to give all his time to executive business, and that it had been the intention of his countrymen to give him the honor of being the first president rather than the duties.

"Radnjak had played into Mahmoud's hands—the secretary became the actual government. Doctor Semich was now thoroughly convinced that Radnjak was trying to steal his authority, and from that day on Radnjak's hands were tied. Doctor Semich insisted on handling every governmental detail himself, which meant that Mahmoud handled it, because the President knows as little about statesmanship today as he did when he took office. Complaints—no matter who made them—did no good. Doctor Semich considered every dissatisfied citizen a fellow conspirator of Radnjak's. The more Mahmoud was criticized in the Chamber of Deputies, the more faith Doctor Semich had in him. Last year the situation became intolerable, and the revolution began to form.

"Radnjak headed it, of course, and at least ninety percent of the influential men in Muravia were in it. The attitude of people as a whole, it is difficult to judge. They are mostly peasants, small land-owners, who ask only to be let alone. But there's no doubt they'd rather have a king than a president, so the form was to be changed to please them. The army, which worshiped Radnjak, was in it. The revolution matured slowly. General Radnjak was a cautious, careful man, and, as this is not a wealthy country, there was not much money available.

"Two months before the date set for the outbreak, Radnjak was assassinated. And the revolution went to pieces, split up into half a dozen factions. There was no other man strong enough to hold them together. Some of these groups still meet and conspire, but they are without general influence, without real purpose. And this is the revolution that has been sold Lionel Grantham. We'll have more information in a day or two, but what we've learned so far is that Mahmoud, who spent a month's vacation in Constantinople, brought Grantham back here with him and joined forces with Einarson to swindle the boy.

"Mahmoud was very much out of the revolution, of course, since it was aimed at him. But Einarson had been in it with his superior, Radnjak. Since Radnjak's death Einarson has succeeded in transferring to himself much of the allegiance that the soldiers gave the dead general. They do not love the Icelander as they did Radnjak, but Einarson is spectacular, theatrical—has all the qualities that simple men like to see in their leaders. So Einarson had the army and could get enough of the late revolution's machinery in his hands to impress Grantham. For money he'd do it. So he and Mahmoud put on a show for your boy. They used Valeska Radnjak, the general's daughter, too. She, I think, was also a dupe. I've heard that the boy and she are planning to be king and queen. How much did he invest in this little farce?"

"Maybe as much as three million American dollars."

Romaine Frankl whistled softly and poured more wine.

IX

CONJECTURES

"How did the Minister of Police stand, when the revolution was alive?" I asked.

"Vasilije," she told me, sipping wine between phrases, "is a peculiar man, an original. He is interested in nothing except his comfort. Comfort to him means enormous amounts of food and drink and at least sixteen hours of sleep each day, and not having to move around much during his eight waking hours. Outside of that he cares for nothing. To guard his comfort he has made the police department a model one. They've got to do their work smoothly and neatly. If they don't, crimes will go unpunished, people will complain, and those complaints might disturb His Excellency. He might even have to shorten his afternoon nap to attend a conference or meeting. That wouldn't do. So he insists on an organization that will keep crime down to a minimum, and catch the perpetrators of that minimum. And he gets it."

"Catch Radnjak's assassin?"

"Killed resisting arrest ten minutes after the murder."

"One of Mahmoud's men?"

The girl emptied her glass, frowning at me, her lifted lower lids putting a twinkle in the frown.

"You're not so bad," she said slowly, "but now it's my turn to ask: Why did you say Einarson killed Mahmoud?"

"Einarson knew Mahmoud had tried to have him and Grantham shot earlier in the evening."

"Really?"

"I saw a soldier take money from Mahmoud, ambush Einarson and Grantham, and miss 'em with six shots."

She clicked a finger-nail against her teeth.

"That's not like Mahmoud," she objected, "to be seen paying for his murders."

"Probably not," I agreed. "But suppose his hired man decided he wanted more pay, or maybe he'd only been paid part of his wages. What better way to collect than to pop out and ask for it in the street a few minutes before he was scheduled to turn the trick?"

She nodded, and spoke as if thinking aloud:

"Then they've got all they expect to get from Grantham, and each was trying to hog it by removing the other."

"Where you go wrong," I told her, "is in thinking that the revolution is dead."

"But Mahmoud wouldn't, for three million dollars, conspire to remove himself from power."

"Right! Mahmoud thought he was putting on a show for the boy. When he learned it wasn't a show—learned Einarson was in earnest—he tried to have him knocked off."

"Perhaps." She shrugged her smooth bare shoulders. "But now you're guessing."

"Yes? Einarson carries a picture of the Shah of Persia. It's worn, as if he handled it a lot. The Shah of Persia is a Russian soldier who went in there after the war, worked himself up until he had the army in his hands, became dictator, then Shah. Correct me if I'm wrong. Einarson is an Icelandic soldier who came in here after the war and has worked himself up until he's got the army in his hands. If he carries the Shah's picture and looks at it often enough to have it shabby from handling, does it mean he hopes to follow his example? Or doesn't it?"

Romaine Frankl got up and roamed around the room, moving a chair two inches here, adjusting an ornament there, shaking out the folds of a window-curtain, pretending a picture wasn't quite straight on the wall, moving from place to place with the appearance of being carried—a graceful small girl in pink satin.

She stopped in front of a mirror, moved a little to one side so she could see my reflection in it, and fluffed her curls while saying:

"Very well, Einarson wants a revolution. What will your boy do?"

"What I tell him."

"What will you tell him?"

"Whatever pays best. I want to take him home with all his money."

She left the mirror and came over to me, rumpled my hair, kissed my mouth, and sat on my knees, holding my face between small warm hands.

"Give me a revolution, nice man!" Her eyes were black with excitement, her voice throaty, her mouth laughing, her body trembling. "I detest Einarson. Use him and break him for me. But give me a revolution!"

I laughed, kissed her, and turned her around on my lap so her head would fit against my shoulder.

"We'll see," I promised. "I'm to meet the folks at midnight. Maybe I'll know then."

"You'll come back after the meeting?"

"Try to keep me away!"

X

EINARSON IN CONTROL

I got back to the hotel at eleven-thirty, loaded my hips with gun and blackjack, and went upstairs to Grantham's suite. He was alone, but said he expected Einarson. He seemed glad to see me.

"Tell me, did Mahmoud go to any of the meetings?" I asked.

"No. His part in the revolution was hidden even from most of those in it. There were reasons why he couldn't appear."

"There were. The chief one was that everybody knew he didn't want any revolts, didn't want anything but money."

Grantham chewed his lower lip and said: "Oh, Lord, what a mess!"

Colonel Einarson arrived, in a dinner coat, but very much the soldier, the man of action. His hand-clasp was stronger than it needed to be. His little dark eyes were hard and bright.

"You are ready, gentlemen?" he addressed the boy and me as if we were a multitude. "Excellent! We shall go now. There will be difficulties tonight. Mahmoud is dead. There will be those of our friends who will ask: 'Why now revolt?' Ach!" He yanked a corner of his flowing dark mustache. "I will answer that. Good souls, our confreres, but given to timidity. There is no timidity under capable leadership. You shall see!" And he yanked his mustache again. This military gent seemed to be feeling Napoleonic this evening. But I didn't write him off as a musical-comedy revolutionist—I remembered what he had done to the soldier.

We left the hotel, got into a machine, rode seven blocks, and went into a small hotel on a side street. The porter bowed to the belt when he opened the door for Einarson. Grantham and I followed the officer up a flight of stairs, down a dim hall. A fat, greasy man in his fifties came bowing and clucking to meet us. Einarson introduced him to me—the proprietor of the hotel. He took us into a low-ceilinged room where thirty or forty men got up from chairs and looked at us through tobacco smoke.

Einarson made a short, very formal speech which I couldn't understand, introducing me to the gang. I ducked my head at them and found a seat beside Grantham. Einarson sat on his other side. Everybody else sat down again, in no especial order.

Colonel Einarson smoothed his mustache and began to talk to this one and that, shouting over the clamor of other voices when necessary. In an undertone, Lionel Grantham pointed out the more important conspirators to me—a dozen or more members of the Chamber of Deputies, a banker, a brother of the Minister of Finance (supposed to represent that official), half a dozen officers (all in civilian clothes tonight), three professors from the university, the president of a labor union, a newspaper publisher and his editor, the secretary of a students' club, a politician from out in the country, and a handful of small business men.

The banker, a white-bearded fat man of sixty, stood up and began a speech, staring intently at Einarson. He spoke deliberately, softly, but with a faintly defiant air. The Colonel didn't let him get far.

"Ach!" Einarson barked and reared up on his feet. None of the words he said meant anything to me, but they took the pinkness out of the banker's cheeks and brought uneasiness into the eyes around us.

"They want to call it off," Grantham whispered in my ear. "They won't go through with it now. I know they won't."

The meeting became rough. A lot of people were yelping at once, but nobody talked down Einarson's bellow. Everybody was standing up, either very red or very white in the face. Fists, fingers, and heads were shaking. The Minister of Finance's brother—a slender, elegantly dressed man with a long, intelligent face—took off his nose glasses so savagely that they broke in half, screamed words at Einarson, spun on his heel, and walked to the door.

He pulled it open and stopped.

The hall was full of green uniforms. Soldiers leaned against the wall, sat on their heels, stood in little groups. They hadn't guns—only bayonets in scabbards at their sides. The Minister of Finance's brother stood very still at the door, looking at the soldiers.

A brown-whiskered, dark-skinned, big man, in coarse clothes and heavy boots, glared with red-rimmed eyes from the soldiers to Einarson, and took two heavy steps toward the Colonel. This was the country politician. Einarson blew out his lips and stepped forward to meet him. Those who were between them got out of the way.

Einarson roared and the countryman roared. Einarson made the most noise, but the countryman wouldn't stop on that account.

Colonel Einarson said: "Ach!" and spat in the countryman's face.

The countryman staggered back a step and one of his paws went under his brown coat. I stepped around Einarson and shoved the muzzle of my gun in the countryman's ribs.

Einarson laughed, called two soldiers into the room. They took the countryman by the arms and led him out. Somebody closed the door. Everybody sat down. Einarson made another speech. Nobody interrupted him. The white-whiskered banker made another speech. The Minister of Finance's brother rose to say half a dozen polite words, staring near-sightedly at Einarson, holding half of his broken glasses in each slender hand. Grantham, at a word from Einarson, got up and talked. Everybody listened very respectfully.

Einarson spoke again. Everybody got excited. Everybody talked at once. It went on for a long time. Grantham explained to me that the revolution would start early Thursday morning—it was now early Wednesday morning—and that the details were now being arranged for the last time. I doubted that anybody was going to know anything about the details, with all this hubbub going on. They kept it up until half-past three. The last couple of hours I spent dozing in a chair, tilted back against the wall in a corner.

Grantham and I walked back to our hotel after the meeting. He told me we were to gather in the plaza at four o'clock the next morning. It would be daylight by six, and by then the government buildings, the President, most of the officials and Deputies who were not on our side, would be in our hands. A meeting of the Chamber of Deputies would be held under the eyes of Einarson's troops, and everything would be done as swiftly and regularly as possible.

I was to accompany Grantham as a sort of bodyguard, which meant, I imagined, that both of us were to be kept out of the way as much as possible. That was all right with me.

I left Grantham at the fifth floor, went to my room, ran cold water over my face and hands, and then left the hotel again.

There was no chance of getting a cab at this hour, so I set out afoot for Romaine Frankl's house.

I had a little excitement on the way.

A wind was blowing in my face as I walked. I stopped and put my back to it to light a cigarette. A shadow down the street slid over into a building's shadow. I was being tailed, and not very skillfully. I finished lighting my cigarette and went on my way until I came to a sufficiently dark side street. Turning into it, I stopped in a street-level dark doorway.

A man came puffing around the corner. My first crack at him went wrong—the blackjack took him too far forward, on the cheek. The second one got him fairly behind the ear. I left him sleeping there and went on to Romaine Frankl's house.

XI

A ROMANTIC INTERLUDE

The servant Marya, in a woolly gray bathrobe, opened the door and sent me up to the black, white, and gray room, where the Minister's secretary, still in the pink gown, was propped up among cushions on the divan. A tray full of cigarette butts showed how she'd been spending her time.

"Well?" she asked as I moved her over to make a seat for myself beside her.

"Thursday morning at four we revolute."

"I knew you'd do it," she said, patting my hand.

"It did itself, though there were a few minutes when I could have stopped it by simply knocking our Colonel behind the ear and letting the rest of them tear him apart. That reminds me—somebody's hired man tried to follow me here tonight."

"What sort of a man?"

"Short, beefy, forty—just about my size and age."

"But he didn't succeed?"

"I slapped him flat and left him sleeping there."

She laughed and pulled my ear.

"That was Gopchek, our very best detective. He'll be furious."

"Well, don't sic any more of 'em on me. You can tell him I'm sorry I had to hit him twice, but it was his own fault. He shouldn't have jerked his head back the first time."

She laughed, then frowned, finally settling on an expression that held half of each.

"Tell me about the meeting," she commanded.

I told her what I knew. When I had finished she pulled my head down to kiss me, and held it down to whisper:

"You do trust me, don't you, dear?"

"Yeah. Just as much as you trust me."

"That's far from being enough," she said, pushing my face away with a hand flat against my nose.

Marya came in with a tray of food. We pulled the table around in front of the divan and ate.

"I don't quite understand you," Romaine said over a stalk of asparagus. "If you don't trust me why do you tell me things? As far as I know, you haven't done much lying to me. Why should you tell me the truth if you've no faith in me?"

"My susceptible nature," I explained. "I'm so overwhelmed by your beauty and charm and one thing and another that I can't refuse you anything."

"Don't!" she exclaimed, suddenly serious. "I've capitalized that beauty and charm in half the countries in the world. Don't say things like that to me ever again. It hurts, because—because—" She pushed her plate back, started to reach for a cigarette, stopped her hand in midair, and looked at me with disagreeable eyes. "I love you," she said.

I took the hand that was hanging in the air, kissed the palm of it, and asked:

"You love me more than any one else in the world?"

She pulled the hand away from me.

"Are you a book-keeper?" she demanded. "Must you have amounts, weights, and measurements for everything?"

I grinned at her and tried to go on with my meal. I had been hungry. Now, though I had eaten only a couple of mouthfuls, my appetite was gone. I tried to pretend I still had the hunger I had lost, but it was no go. The food didn't want to be swallowed. I gave up the attempt and lighted a cigarette.

She used her left hand to fan away the smoke between us.

"You don't trust me," she insisted. "Then why do you put yourself in my hands?"

"Why not? You can make a flop of the revolution. That's nothing to me. It's not my party, and its failure needn't mean that I can't get the boy out of the country with his money."

"You don't mind a prison, an execution, perhaps?"

"I'll take my chances," I said. But what I was thinking was: if, after twenty years of scheming and slickering in big-time cities, I let myself get trapped in this hill village, I'd deserve all I got.

"And you've no feeling at all for me?"

"Don't be foolish." I waved my cigarette at my uneaten meal. "I haven't had anything to eat since eight o'clock last night."

She laughed, put a hand over my mouth, and said:

"I understand. You love me, but not enough to let me interfere with your plans. I don't like that. It's effeminate."

"You going to turn out for the revolution?" I asked.

"I'm not going to run through the streets throwing bombs, if that's what you mean."

"And Djudakovich?"

"He sleeps till eleven in the morning. If you start at four, you'll have seven hours before he's up." She said all this perfectly seriously. "Get it done in that time. Or he might decide to stop it."

"Yeah? I had a notion he wanted it."

"Vasilije wants nothing but peace and comfort."

"But listen, sweetheart," I protested. "If your Vasilije is any good at all, he can't help finding out about it ahead of time. Einarson and his army are the revolution. These bankers and deputies and the like that he's carrying with him to give the party a responsible look are a lot of movie conspirators. Look at 'em! They hold their meetings at midnight, and all that kind of foolishness. Now that they're actually signed up to something, they won't be able to keep from spreading the news. All day they'll be going around trembling and whispering together in odd corners."

"They've been doing that for months," she said. "Nobody pays any attention to them. And I promise you Vasilije shan't hear anything new. I won't tell him, and he never listens to anything any one else says."

"All right." I wasn't sure it was all right, but it might be. "Now this row is going through—if the army follows Einarson?"

"Yes, and the army will follow him."

"Then, after it's over, our real job begins?"

She rubbed a flake of cigarette ash into the table cloth with a small pointed finger, and said nothing.

"Einarson's got to be dumped," I continued.

"We'll have to kill him," she said thoughtfully. "You'd better do it yourself."

XII

THE NIGHT BEFORE

I saw Einarson and Grantham that evening, and spent several hours with them. The boy was fidgety, nervous, without confidence in the revolution's success, though he tried to pretend he was taking things as a matter of course. Einarson was full of words. He gave us every detail of the next day's plans. I was more interested in him than in what he was saying. He could put the revolution over, I thought, and I was willing to leave it to him. So while he talked I studied him, combing him over for weak spots.

I took him physically first—a tall, thick-bodied man in his prime, not as quick as he might have been, but strong and tough. He had an amply jawed, short-nosed, florid face that a fist wouldn't bother much. He wasn't fat, but he ate and drank too much to be hard-boiled, and your florid man can seldom stand much poking around the belt. So much for the gent's body.

Mentally, he wasn't a heavy-weight. His revolution was crude stuff. It would get over chiefly because there wasn't much opposition. He had plenty of will-power, I imagined, but I didn't put a big number on that. People who haven't much brains have to develop will-power to get anywhere. I didn't know whether he had guts or not, but before an audience I guessed he'd make a grand showing, and most of this act would be before an audience. Off in a dark corner I had an idea he would go watery. He believed in himself—absolutely. That's ninety percent of leadership, so there was no flaw in him there. He didn't trust me. He had taken me in because as things turned out it was easier to do so than to shut the door against me.

He kept on talking about his plans. There was nothing to talk about. He was going to bring his soldiers in town in the early morning and take over the government. That was all the plan that was needed. The rest of it was the lettuce around the dish, but this lettuce part was the only part we could discuss. It was dull.

At eleven o'clock Einarson stopped talking and left us, making this sort of speech:

"Until four o'clock, gentlemen, when Muravia's history begins." He put a hand on my shoulder and commanded me: "Guard His Majesty!"

I said, "Uh-huh," and immediately sent His Majesty to bed. He wasn't going to sleep, but he was too young to confess it, so he went off willingly enough. I got a taxi and went out to Romaine's.

She was like a child the night before a picnic. She kissed me and she kissed the servant Marya. She sat on my knees, beside me, on the floor, on all the chairs, changing her location every half minute. She laughed and talked incessantly, about the revolution, about me, about herself, about anything at all. She nearly strangled herself trying to talk while swallowing wine. She lit her big cigarettes and forgot to smoke them, or forgot to stop smoking them until they scorched her lips. She sang lines from songs in half a dozen languages. She made puns and jokes and goofy rhymes.

I left at three o'clock. She went down to the door with me, pulled my head down to kiss my eyes and mouth.

"If anything goes wrong," she said, "come to the prison. We'll hold that until—"

"If it goes wrong enough I'll be brought there," I promised.

She wouldn't joke now.

"I'm going there now," she said. "I'm afraid Einarson's got my house on his list."

"Good idea," I said. "If you hit a bad spot get word to me."

I walked back to the hotel through the dark streets—the lights were turned off at midnight—without seeing a single other person, not even one of the gray-uniformed policemen. By the time I reached home rain was falling steadily.

In my room, I changed into heavier clothes and shoes, dug an extra gun—an automatic—out of my bag and hung it in a shoulder holster. Then I filled my pocket with enough ammunition to make me bow-legged, picked up hat and raincoat, and went upstairs to Lionel Grantham's suite.

"It's ten to four," I told him. "We might as well go down to the plaza. Better put a gun in your pocket."

He hadn't slept. His handsome young face was as cool and pink and composed as it had been the first time I saw him, though his eyes were brighter now.

He got into an overcoat, and we went downstairs.

XIII

PROGRESS GOES "BETUNE"

Rain drove into our faces as we went toward the center of the dark plaza. Other figures moved around us, though none came near. We halted at the foot of an iron statue of somebody on a horse.

A pale young man of extraordinary thinness came up and began to talk rapidly, gesturing with both hands, sniffing every now and then, as if he had a cold in his head. I couldn't understand a word he said.

The rumble of other voices began to compete with the patter of rain. The fat, white-whiskered face of the banker who had been at the meeting appeared suddenly out of the darkness and went back into it just as suddenly, as if he didn't want to be recognized. Men I hadn't seen before gathered around us, saluting Grantham with a sheepish sort of respect. A little man in a too big cape ran up and began to tell us something in a cracked, jerky voice. A thin, stooped man with glasses freckled by raindrops translated the little man's story into English for us:

"He says the artillery has betrayed us, and guns are being mounted in the government buildings to sweep the plaza at daybreak." There was an odd sort of hopefulness in his voice, and he added: "In that event, we can, naturally, do nothing."

"We can die," Lionel Grantham said gently.

There wasn't the least bit of sense to that crack. Nobody was here to die. They were all here because it was so unlikely that anybody would have to die, except perhaps a few of Einarson's soldiers. That's the sensible view of the boy's speech. But it's God's own truth that even I—a middle-aged detective who had forgotten what it was like to believe in fairies—felt suddenly warm inside my wet clothes. And if anybody had said to me: "This boy is a real king," I wouldn't have argued the point.

An abrupt hush came in the murmuring around us, leaving only the rustle of rain, and the tramp, tramp, tramp of orderly marching up the street—Einarson's men. Everybody commenced to talk at once, happily, expectantly, cheered by the approach of those whose part it was to do the heavy work.

An officer in a glistening slicker pushed through the crowd—a small, dapper boy with a too large sword. He saluted Grantham elaborately, and said in English, of which he seemed proud:

"Colonel Einarson's respects, Mister, and this progress goes betune."

I wondered what the last word meant.

Grantham smiled and said: "Convey my thanks to Colonel Einarson."

The banker appeared again, bold enough now to join us. Others who had been at the meeting appeared. We made an inner group around the statue, with the mob around us—more easily seen now in the gray of early morning. I didn't see the countryman into whose face Einarson had spat.

The rain soaked us. We shifted our feet, shivered, and talked. Daylight came slowly, showing more and more who stood around us wet and curious-eyed. On the edge of the crowd men burst into cheers. The rest of them took it up. They forgot their wet misery, laughed and danced, hugged and kissed one another. A bearded man in a leather coat came to us, bowed to Grantham, and explained that Einarson's own regiment could be seen occupying the Administration Building and the Executive Residence.

Day came fully. The mob around us opened to make way for an automobile that was surrounded by a squad of cavalrymen. It stopped in front of us. Colonel Einarson, holding a bare sword in his hand, stepped out of the car, saluted, and held the door open for Grantham and me. He followed us in, smelling of victory like a chorus girl of Coty? The cavalrymen closed around the car again, and we were driven to the Administration Building, through a crowd that yelled and ran red-faced and happy after us. It was all quite theatrical.

XIV

CORONATION

"The city is ours," said Einarson, leaning forward in his seat, his sword's point on the car floor, his hands on its hilt. "The President, the Deputies, nearly every official of importance, is taken. Not a single shot fired, not a window broken!"

He was proud of his revolution, and I didn't blame him. I wasn't sure that he might not have brains, after all. He had had sense enough to park his civilian adherents in the plaza until his soldiers had done their work.

We got out at the Administration Building, walking up the steps between rows of infantrymen at present-arms, rain sparkling on their fixed bayonets. More green-uniformed soldiers presented arms along the corridors. We went into an elaborately furnished dining-room, where fifteen or twenty officers stood up to receive us. There were lots of speeches made. Everybody was triumphant. All through breakfast there was much talking. I didn't understand any of it. I attended to my eating.

After the meal we went to the Deputies' Chamber, a large, oval room with curved rows of benches and desks facing a raised platform. Besides three desks on the platform, some twenty chairs had been put there, facing the curved seats. Our breakfast party occupied these chairs. I noticed that Grantham and I were the only civilians on the platform. None of our fellow conspirators were there, except those who were in Einarson's army. I wasn't so fond of that.

Grantham sat in the first row of chairs, between Einarson and me. We looked down on the Deputies. There were perhaps a hundred of them distributed among the curved benches, split sharply in two groups. Half of them, on the right side of the room, were revolutionists. They stood up and hurrahed at us. The other half, on the left, were prisoners. Most of them seemed to have dressed hurriedly. They looked at us with uneasy eyes.

Around the room, shoulder to shoulder against the wall except on the platform and where the doors were, stood Einarson's soldiers.

An old man came in between two soldiers—a mild-eyed old gentleman, bald, stooped, with a wrinkled, clean-shaven, scholarly face.

"Doctor Semich," Grantham whispered.

The President's guards took him to the center one of the three desks on the platform. He paid no attention to us who were sitting on the platform, and he did not sit down.

A red-haired Deputy—one of the revolutionary party—got up and talked. His fellows cheered when he had finished. The President spoke—three words in a very dry, very calm voice, and left the platform to walk back the way he had come, the two soldiers accompanying him.

"Refused to resign," Grantham informed me.

The red-haired Deputy came up on the platform and took the center desk. The legislative machinery began to grind. Men talked briefly, apparently to the point—revolutionists. None of the prisoner Deputies rose. A vote was taken. A few of the in-wrongs didn't vote. Most of them seemed to vote with the ins.

"They've revoked the constitution," Grantham whispered.

The Deputies were hurrahing again—those who were there voluntarily. Einarson leaned over and mumbled to Grantham and me:

"That is as far as we may safely go today. It leaves all in our hands."

"Time to listen to a suggestion?" I asked.

"Yes."

"Will you excuse us a moment?" I said to Grantham, and got up and walked to one of the rear corners of the platform.

Einarson followed me, frowning suspiciously.

"Why not give Grantham his crown now?" I asked when we were standing in the corner, my right shoulder touching his left, half facing each other, half facing the corner, our backs to the officers who sat on the platform, the nearest less than ten feet away. "Push it through. You can do it. There'll be a howl, of course. Tomorrow, as a concession to that howl, you'll make him abdicate. You'll get credit for that. You'll be fifty percent stronger with the people. Then you will be in a position to make it look as if the revolution was his party, and that you were the patriot who kept this newcomer from grabbing the throne. Meanwhile you'll be dictator, and whatever else you want to be when the time comes. See what I mean? Let him bear the brunt. You catch yours on the rebound."

He liked the idea, but he didn't like it to come from me. His little dark eyes pried into mine.

"Why should you suggest this?" he asked.

"What do you care? I promise you he'll abdicate within twenty-four hours."

He smiled under his mustache and raised his head. I knew a major in the A.E.F. who always raised his head like that when he was going to issue an unpleasant order. I spoke quickly:

"My raincoat—do you see it's folded over my left arm?"

He said nothing, but his eyelids crept together.

"You can't see my left hand," I went on.

His eyes were slits, but he said nothing. "There's an automatic in it," I wound up. "Well?" he asked contemptuously.

"Nothing—only—get funny, and I'll let your guts out."

"Ach!"—he didn't take me seriously—"And after that?"

"I don't know. Think it over carefully, Einarson. I've deliberately put myself in a position where I've got to go ahead if you don't give in. I can kill you before you do anything. I'm going to do it if you don't give Grantham his crown now. Understand? I've got to. Maybe—most likely—your boys would get me afterward, but you'd be dead. If I back down now, you'll certainly have me shot. So I can't back down. If neither of us backs down, we'll both take the leap. *I've* gone too far to weaken now. *You'll* have to give in. Think it over. I can't possibly be bluffing."

He thought it over. Some of the color washed out of his face, and a little rippling movement appeared in the flesh of his chin. I crowded him along by moving the raincoat enough to show him the muzzle of the gun that actually was there in my left hand. I had the big heaver—he hadn't nerve enough to take a chance on dying in his hour of victory. A little earlier, a little later, I might have had to gun him. Now I had him.

He strode across the platform to the desk at which the redhead sat, drove the redhead away with a snarl and a gesture, leaned over the desk, and bellowed down into the chamber. I stood a little to one side of him, a little behind, close enough so no one could get between us.

No Deputy made a sound for a long minute after the Colonel's bellow had stopped. Then one of the anti-revolutionists jumped to his feet and yelped bitterly. Einarson pointed a long brown finger at him. Two soldiers left their places by the wall, took the Deputy roughly by neck and arms, and dragged him out.

Another Deputy stood up, talked, and was removed. After the fifth drag-out everything was peaceful.

Einarson put a question and got a unanimous answer.

He turned to me, his gaze darting from my face to my raincoat and back, and said: "That is done."

"We'll have the coronation now," I commanded. "Any kind of ceremony, so it's short."

I missed most of the ceremony. I was busy keeping my hold on the florid officer, but finally Lionel Grantham was officially installed as Lionel the First, King of Muravia. Einarson and I congratulated him, or whatever it was, together. Then I took the officer aside.

"We're going to take a walk," I said. "No foolishness. Take me out a side door."

I had him now, almost without needing the gun. He would have to deal quietly with Grantham and me—kill us without any publicity—if he were to avoid being laughed at—this man who had let himself be stuck up and robbed of a throne in the middle of his army.

We went roundabout from the Administration Building to the Hotel of the Republic without meeting any one who knew us. The population was all in the plaza. We found the hotel deserted. I made him run the elevator to my floor, and herded him down the corridor to my room.

I tried the door, found it unlocked, let go the knob, and told him to go in. He pushed the door open and stopped.

Romaine Frankl was sitting cross-legged in the middle of my bed, sewing a button on one of my union suits.

XV

BARGAIN HUNTERS

I prodded Einarson into the room and closed the door. Romaine looked at him and at the automatic that was now uncovered in my hand. With burlesque disappointment she said:

"Oh, you haven't killed him yet!"

Colonel Einarson stiffened. He had an audience now—one that saw his humiliation. He was likely to do something. I'd have to handle him with gloves, or—maybe the other way was better. I kicked him on the ankle and snarled:

"Get over in the corner and sit down!"

He spun around to me. I jabbed the muzzle of the pistol in his face, grinding his lip between it and his teeth. When his head jerked back I slammed him in the belly with my other fist. He grabbed for air with a wide mouth. I pushed him over to a chair in one corner of the room.

Romaine laughed and shook a finger at me, saying:

"You're a rowdy!"

"What else can I do?" I protested, chiefly for my prisoner's benefit. "When somebody's watching him he gets notions that he's a hero. I stuck him up and made him crown the boy king. But this bird has still got the army, which is the government. I can't let go of him, or both Lionel the Once and I will gather lead. It hurts me more than it does him to have to knock him around, but I can't help myself. I've got to keep him sensible."

"You're doing wrong by him," she replied. "You've got no right to mistreat him. The only polite thing for you to do is to cut his throat in a gentlemanly manner."

"Ach!" Einarson's lungs were working again.

"Shut up," I yelled at him, "or I'll come over there and knock you double-jointed."

He glared at me, and I asked the girl: "What'll we do with him? I'd be glad to cut his throat, but the trouble is, his army might avenge him, and I'm not a fellow who likes to have anybody's army avenging on him."

"We'll give him to Vasilije," she said, swinging her feet over the side of the bed and standing up. "He'll know what to do."

"Where is he?"

"Upstairs in Grantham's suite, finishing his morning nap, I suppose."

Then she said lightly, casually, as if she hadn't been thinking seriously about it: "So you had the boy crowned?"

"I did. You want it for your Vasilije? Good! We want five million American dollars for our abdication. Grantham put in three to finance the doings, and he deserves a profit. He's been regularly elected by the Deputies. He's got no real backing here, but he can get support from the neighbors. Don't overlook that. There are a couple of countries not a million miles away that would gladly send in an army to support a legitimate king in exchange for whatever concessions they liked. But Lionel the First isn't unreasonable. He thinks it would be better for you to have a native ruler. All he asks is a decent provision from the government. Five million is low enough, and he'll abdicate tomorrow. Tell that to your Vasilije."

She went around me to avoid passing between my gun and its target, stood on tiptoe to kiss my ear, and said:

"You and your king are a couple of brigands. I'll be back in a few minutes."

She went out.

"Ten millions," Colonel Einarson said.

"I can't trust you now," I said. "You'd pay us off in front of a firing squad."

"You can trust this pig Djudakovich?"

"He's got no reason to hate us."

"He will when he's told of you and his Romaine."

I laughed.

"Besides, how can he be king? Ach! What is his promise to pay if he cannot become in a position to pay? Suppose even I am dead. What will he do with my army? Ach! You have seen the pig! What kind of king is he?"

"I don't know," I said truthfully. "I'm told he was a good Minister of Police because inefficiency would spoil his comfort. Maybe he'd be a good dictator or king for the same reason. I've seen him once. He's a bloated mountain, but there's nothing ridiculous about him. He weighs a ton, and moves without shaking the floor. I'd be afraid to try on him what I did to you."

This insult brought the soldier up on his feet, very tall and straight. His eyes burned at me while his mouth hardened in a thin line. He was going to make trouble for me before I was rid of him. I scowled at him and wondered what I should do next.

The door opened and Vasilije Djudakovich came in, followed by the girl. I grinned at the fat Minister. He nodded without smiling. His little dark eyes moved coldly from me to Einarson.

The girl said:

"The government will give Lionel the First a draft for four million dollars, American, on either a Vienna or Athens bank, in exchange for his abdication." She dropped her official tone and added: "That's every nickel I could get out of him."

"You and your Vasilije are a couple of rotten bargain hunters," I complained. "But we'll take it. We've got to have a special train to Saloniki—one that will put us across the border before the abdication goes into effect."

"That will be arranged," she promised.

"Good! Now to do all this your Vasilije has got to take the army away from Einarson. Can he do it?"

"Ach!" Colonel Einarson reared up his head, swelled his thick chest. "That is precisely what he has got to do!"

The fat man grumbled sleepily through his yellow beard. Romaine came over and put a hand on my arm.

"Vasilije wants a private talk with Einarson. Leave it to him. We'll go upstairs."

I agreed and offered Djudakovich my automatic. He paid no attention to the gun or to me. He was looking with a clammy sort of patience at the officer. I went out with the girl and closed the door. At the foot of the stairs I took her by the shoulders and turned her around.

"Can I trust your Vasilije?" I asked.

"Oh my dear, he could handle half a dozen Einarsons."

"I don't mean that. He won't try to gyp me?"

She frowned at me, asking: "Why should you start worrying about that now?"

"He doesn't seem to be exactly all broken out with friendliness."

She laughed, and twisted her face around to bite at one of my hands on her shoulders.

"He's got ideals," she explained. "He despises you and your king for a pair of adventurers who are making a profit out of his country's troubles. That's why he's so sniffy. But he'll keep his word."

Maybe he would, I thought, but he hadn't given me his word—the girl had.

"I'm going over to see His Majesty," I said. "I won't be long—then I'll join you up in his suite. What was the idea of the sewing act? I had no buttons off."

"You did," she contradicted me, rummaging in my pocket for cigarettes. "I pulled one off when one of our men told me you and Einarson were headed this way. I thought it would look domestic."

XVI

LIONEL REX

I found my king in a wine and gold drawing-room in the Executive Residence, surrounded by Muravia's socially and politically ambitious. Uniforms were still in the majority, but a sprinkling of civilians had finally got to him, along with their wives and daughters. He was too occupied to see me for a few minutes, so I stood around, looking the folks over. Particularly one—a tall girl in black, who stood apart from the others, at a window.

I noticed her first because she was beautiful in face and body, and then I studied her more closely because of the expression in the brown eyes with which she watched the new king. If ever anybody looked proud of anybody else, this girl did of Grantham. The way she stood there, alone, by the window, and looked at him—he would have had to be at least a combination of Apollo, Socrates, and Alexander to deserve half of it. Valeska Radnjak, I supposed.

I looked at the boy. His face was proud and flushed, and every two seconds turned toward the girl at the window while he listened to the jabbering of the worshipful group around him. I knew he wasn't any Apollo-Socrates-Alexander, but he managed to look the part. He had found a spot in the world that he liked. I was half sorry he couldn't hang on to it, but my regrets didn't keep me from deciding that I had wasted enough time.

I pushed through the crowd toward him. He recognized me with the eyes of a park sleeper being awakened from sweet dreams by a nightstick on his shoe-soles. He excused himself to the others and took me down a corridor to a room with stained glass windows and richly carved office furniture.

"This was Doctor Semich's office," he told me. "I shall—" He broke off and looked away from me.

"You'll be in Greece by tomorrow," I said bluntly.

He frowned at his feet, a stubborn frown.

"You ought to know you can't hold on," I argued. "You may think everything is going smoothly. If you do, you're deaf, dumb, and blind. I put you in with the muzzle of a gun against Einarson's liver. I've kept you in this long by kidnapping him. I've made a deal with Djudakovich—the only strong man I've seen here. It's up to him to handle Einarson. I can't hold him any longer. Djudakovich will make a good dictator, and a good king later, if he wants it. He promises you four million dollars and a special train and safe-conduct to Saloniki. You go out with your head up. You've been a king. You've taken a country out of bad hands and put it into good—this fat guy is real. And you've made yourself a million profit."

Grantham looked at me and said:

"No. You go. I shall see it through. These people have trusted me, and I shall—"

"My God, that's old Doc Semich's line! These people haven't trusted you—not a bit of it. I'm the people who trusted you. I made you king, understand? I made you king so you could go home with your chin up—not so you could stay here and make an ass of yourself! I bought help with promises. One of them was that you'd get out within twenty-four hours. You've got to keep the promises I made in your name. The people trusted you, huh? You were crammed down their throats, my son! And I did the cramming! Now I'm going to uncram you. If it happens to be tough on your romance—if your Valeska won't take any price less than this lousy country's throne—that's—"

"That's enough." His voice came from some point at least fifty feet above me. "You shall have your abdication. I don't want the money. You will send word to me when the train is ready."

"Write the get-out now," I ordered.

He went over to the desk, found a sheet of paper, and with a steady hand wrote that in leaving Muravia he renounced his throne and all rights to it. He signed the paper *Lionel Rex* and gave it to me. I pocketed it and began sympathetically:

"I can understand your feelings, and I'm sorry that—"

He put his back to me and walked out of the room. I returned to the hotel.

At the fifth floor I left the elevator and walked softly to the door of my room. No sound came through. I tried the door, found it unlocked, and went in. Emptiness. Even my clothes and bags were gone. I went up to Grantham's suite.

Djudakovich, Romaine, Einarson, and half the police force were there.

XVII

MOB LAW

Colonel Einarson sat very erect in an armchair in the middle of the room. Dark hair and mustache bristled. His chin was out, muscles bulged everywhere in his florid face, his eyes were hot—he was in one of his finest scrapping moods. That came of giving him an audience.

I scowled at Djudakovich, who stood on wide-spread giant's legs with his back to a window. Why hadn't the fat fool known enough to keep Einarson off in a lonely corner, where he could be handled? Djudakovich looked sleepily at my scowl.

Romaine floated around and past the policeman who stood or sat everywhere in the room, and came to where I stood, just inside the door.

"Are your arrangements all made?" she asked.

"Got the abdication in my pocket."

"Give it to me."

"Not yet," I said. "First I've got to know that your Vasilije is as big as he looks. Einarson doesn't look squelched to me. Your fat boy ought to have known he'd blossom out in front of an audience."

"There's no telling what Vasilije is up to," she said lightly, "except that it will be adequate."

I wasn't as sure of that as she was. Djudakovich rumbled a question at her, and she gave him a quick answer. He rumbled some more—at the policemen. They began to go away from us, singly, in pairs, in groups. When the last one had gone the fat man pushed words out between his yellow whiskers at Einarson. Einarson stood up, chest out, shoulders back, grinning confidently under his flowing dark mustache.

"What now?" I asked the girl.

"Come along and you'll see," she said. Her breath came and went quickly, and the gray of her eyes was almost as dark as the black.

The four of us went downstairs and out the hotel's front door. The rain had stopped. In the plaza was gathered most of Stefania's population, thickest in front of the Administration Building and Executive Residence. Over their heads we could see the sheepskin caps of Einarson's regiment, still around those buildings as he had left them.

We—or at least Einarson—were recognized and cheered as we crossed the plaza. Einarson and Djudakovich went side by side in front, the soldier marching, the fat giant waddling. Romaine and I went close behind them. We headed straight for the Administration Building.

"What is he up to?" I asked irritably.

She patted my arm, smiled excitedly, and said:

"Wait and see."

There didn't seem to be anything else to do—except worry while I waited.

We arrived at the foot of the Administration Building's stone steps. Bayonets had an uncomfortably cold gleam in the early evening light as Einarson's troops presented arms. We climbed the steps. On the broad top step Einarson and Djudakovich turned to face soldiers and citizens below. The girl and I moved around behind the pair. Her teeth were chattering, her fingers were digging into my arm, but her lips and eyes were smiling recklessly.

The soldiers who were around the Executive Residence came to join those already before us, pushing back the citizens to make room. Another detachment came up. Einarson raised his hand, bawled a dozen words, growled at Djudakovich, and stepped back, giving the blond giant the center of the stage.

Djudakovich spoke, a drowsy, effortless roar that could have been heard as far as the hotel. As he spoke, he took a paper out of his pocket and held it before him. There was nothing theatrical in his voice or manner. He might have been talking about anything not too important. But—looking at his audience, you'd have known it was important.

The soldiers had broken ranks to crowd nearer, faces were reddening, a bayoneted gun was shaken aloft here and there. Behind them the citizens were looking at one another with frightened faces, jostling each other, some trying to get nearer, some trying to get away.

Djudakovich talked on. The turmoil grew. A soldier pushed through his fellows and started up the steps, others at his heels. Angry voices raised cries.

Einarson cut in on the fat man's speech, stepping to the edge of the top step, bawling down at the upturned faces, with the voice of a man accustomed to being obeyed.

The soldiers on the steps tumbled down. Einarson bawled again. The broken ranks were slowly straightened, flourished guns were grounded. Einarson stood silent a moment, glowering at his troops, and then began an address. I couldn't understand his words any more than I had the fat man's, but there was no question about his impressiveness. And there was no doubt that the anger was going out of the faces below.

I looked at Romaine. She shivered and was no longer smiling. I looked at Djudakovich. He was as still and as emotionless as the mountain he resembled.

I wished I knew what it was all about, so I'd know whether it was wisest to shoot Einarson and duck through the apparently empty building behind us or not. I could guess that the paper in Djudakovich's hand had been evidence of some sort against the Colonel, evidence that would have stirred the soldiers to the point of attacking him if they hadn't been too accustomed to obeying him.

While I was wishing and guessing Einarson finished his address, stepped to one side, clicked his heels together, pointed a finger at Djudakovich, barked an order.

Down below, soldiers' faces were indecisive, shifty-eyed, but four of them stepped briskly out at their colonel's order and came up the steps. "So," I thought, "my fat candidate has lost! Well, he can have the firing squad. The back door for mine." My hand had been holding the gun in my coat pocket for a long time. I kept it there while I took a slow step back, drawing the girl with me.

"Move when I tell you," I muttered.

"Wait!" she gasped. "Look!"

The fat giant, sleepy-eyed as ever, put out an enormous paw and caught the wrist of Einarson's pointing hand. Pulled Einarson down. Let go the wrist and caught the Colonel's shoulder. Lifted him off his feet with that one hand that held his shoulder. Shook him at the soldiers below. Shook Einarson at them with one hand. Shook his piece of paper—whatever it was—at them with the other. And I'm damned if one seemed any more strain on his monstrous arms than the other!

While he shook them—man and paper—he roared sleepily, and when he had finished roaring he flung his two handfuls down to the wild-eyed ranks. Flung them with a gesture that said, *"Here is the man and here is the evidence against him. Do what you like."*

And the soldiers who had cringed back into ranks at Einarson's command when he stood tall and domineering above them, did what could have been expected when he was tossed down to them.

They tore him apart—actually—piece by piece. They dropped their guns and fought to get at him. Those farther away climbed over those nearer, smothering them, trampling them. They surged back and forth in front of the steps, an insane pack of men turned wolves, savagely struggling to destroy a man who must have died before he had been down half a minute.

I put the girl's hand off my arm and went to face Djudakovich.

"Muravia's yours," I said. "I don't want anything but our draft and train. Here's the abdication."

Romaine swiftly translated my words and then Djudakovich's:

"The train is ready now. The draft will be delivered there. Do you wish to go over for Grantham?"

"No. Send him down. How do I find the train?"

"I'll take you," she said. "We'll go through the building and out a side door."

One of Djudakovich's detectives sat at the wheel of a car in front of the hotel. Romaine and I got in it. Across the plaza tumult was still boiling. Neither of us said anything while the car whisked us through darkening streets. She sat as far from me as the width of the rear seat would let her.

Presently she asked very softly:

"And now you despise me?"

"No." I reached for her. "But I hate mobs, lynchings—they sicken me. No matter how wrong the man is, if a mob's against him, I'm for him. The only thing I ever pray to God for is a chance some day to squat down behind a machine gun with a lynching party in front of me. I had no use for Einarson, but I wouldn't have given him that! Well, what's done is done. What was the document?"

"A letter from Mahmoud. He had left it with a friend to be given to Vasilije if anything ever happened to him. He knew Einarson, it seems, and prepared his revenge. The letter confessed his—Mahmoud's—part in the assassination of General Radnjak, and said that Einarson was also implicated. The army worshiped Radnjak, and Einarson wanted the army."

"Your Vasilije could have used that to chase Einarson out—without feeding him to those wolves," I complained.

She shook her head and said:

"Vasilije was right. Bad as it was, that was the way to do it. It's over and settled forever, with Vasilije in power. An Einarson alive, an army not knowing he had killed their idol—too risky. Up to the end Einarson thought he had power enough to hold his troops, no matter what they knew. He—"

"All right—it's done. And I'm glad to be through with this king business. Kiss me."

She did, and whispered:

"When Vasilije dies—and he can't live long, the way he eats—I'm coming to San Francisco."

"You're a cold-blooded hussy," I said.

Lionel Grantham, ex-king of Muravia, was only five minutes behind us in reaching our train. He wasn't alone. Valeska Radnjak, looking as much like the queen of something as if she had been, was with him. She didn't seem to be all broken up over the loss of her throne.

The boy was pleasant and polite enough to me during our rattling trip to Saloniki, but obviously not very comfortable in my company. His bride-to-be didn't know anybody but the boy existed, unless she happened to find some one else directly in front of her. So I didn't wait for their wedding, but left Saloniki on a boat that pulled out a couple of hours after we arrived.

I left the draft with them, of course. They decided to take out Lionel's three millions and return the fourth to Muravia. And I went back to San Francisco to quarrel with my boss over what he thought were unnecessary five-and ten-dollar items in my expense account.

5

FLY PAPER

Black Mask, AUGUST 1929

The "Continental" detective tackles a killer.

I

It was a wandering daughter job.

The Hambletons had been for several generations a wealthy and decently prominent New York family. There was nothing in the Hambleton history to account for Sue, the youngest member of the clan. She grew out of childhood with a kink that made her dislike the polished side of life, like the rough. By the time she was twenty-one, in 1926, she definitely preferred Tenth Avenue to Fifth, grifters to bankers, and Hymie the Riveter to the Honorable Cecil Win-down, who had asked her to marry him.

The Hambletons tried to make Sue behave, but it was too late for that. She was legally of age. When she finally told them to go to hell and walked out on them there wasn't much they could do about it. Her father, Major Waldo Hambleton, had given up all the hopes he ever had of salvaging her, but he didn't want her to run into any grief that could be avoided. So he came into the Continental Detective Agency's New York office and asked to have an eye kept on her.

Hymie the Riveter was a Philadelphia racketeer who had moved north to the big city, carrying a Thompson submachine-gun wrapped in blue-checkered oil cloth, after a disagreement with his partners. New York wasn't so good a field as Philadelphia for machine-gun work. The Thompson lay idle for a year or so while Hymie made expenses with an automatic, preying on small-time crap games in Harlem.

Three or four months after Sue went to live with Hymie he made what looked like a promising connection with the first of the crew that came into New York from Chicago to organize the city on the western scale. But the boys from Chi didn't want Hymie; they wanted the Thompson. When he showed it to them, as the big item in his application for employment, they shot holes in the top of Hymie's head and went away with the gun.

Sue Hambleton buried Hymie, had a couple of lonely weeks in which she hocked a ring to eat, and then got a job as hostess in a speakeasy run by a Greek named Vassos.

One of Vassos' customers was Babe McCloor, two hundred and fifty pounds of hard Scotch-Irish-Indian bone and muscle, a black-haired, blue-eyed, swarthy giant who was resting up after doing a fifteen-year hitch in Leavenworth for ruining most of the smaller post offices between New Orleans and Omaha. Babe was keeping himself in drinking money while he rested by playing with pedestrians in dark streets.

Babe liked Sue. Vassos liked Sue. Sue liked Babe. Vassos didn't like that. Jealousy spoiled the Greek's judgment. He kept the speakeasy door locked one night when Babe wanted to come in. Babe came in, bringing pieces of the door with him. Vassos got his gun out, but couldn't shake Sue off his arm. He stopped trying when Babe hit him with the part of the door that had the brass knob on it. Babe and Sue went away from Vassos' together.

Up to that time the New York office had managed to keep in touch with Sue. She hadn't been kept under constant surveillance. Her father hadn't wanted that. It was simply a matter of sending a man around every week or so to see that she was still alive, to pick up whatever information he could from her friends and neighbors, without, of course, letting her know she was being tabbed. All that had been easy enough, but when she and Babe went away after wrecking the gin mill, they dropped completely out of sight.

After turning the city upside-down, the New York office sent a journal on the job to the other Continental branches throughout the country, giving the information above and enclosing photographs and descriptions of Sue and her new playmate. That was late in 1927.

We had enough copies of the photographs to go around, and for the next month or so whoever had a little idle time on his hands spent it looking through San Francisco and Oakland for the missing pair. We didn't find them. Operatives in other cities, doing the same thing, had the same luck.

Then, nearly a year later, a telegram came to us from the New York office. Decoded, it read:

Major Hambleton today received telegram from daughter in San Francisco quote Please wire me thousand dollars care apartment two hundred six number six hundred one Eddis Street stop I will come home if you will let me stop Please tell me if I can come but please please wire money anyway unquote Hambleton authorizes payment of money to her immediately stop Detail competent operative to call on her with money and to arrange for her return home stop If possible have man and woman operative accompany her here stop Hambleton wiring her stop Report immediately by wire.

II

The Old Man gave me the telegram and a check, saying:

"You know the situation. You'll know how to handle it."

I pretended I agreed with him, went down to the bank, swapped the check for a bundle of bills of several sizes, caught a street car, and went up to 601 Eddis Street, a fairly large apartment building on the corner of Larkin.

The name on Apartment 206's vestibule mail box was J. M. Wales.

I pushed 206's button. When the locked door buzzed off I went into the building, past the elevator to the stairs, and up a flight. 206 was just around the corner from the stairs.

The apartment door was opened by a tall, slim man of thirty-something in neat dark clothes. He had narrow dark eyes set in a long pale face. There was some gray in the dark hair brushed flat to his scalp.

"Miss Hambleton," I said.

"Uh—what about her?" His voice was smooth, but not too smooth to be agreeable.

"I'd like to see her."

His upper eyelids came down a little and the brows over them came a little closer together. He asked, "Is it—?" and stopped, watching me steadily.

I didn't say anything. Presently he finished his question:

"Something to do with a telegram?"

"Yeah."

His long face brightened immediately. He asked:

"You're from her father?"

"Yeah."

He stepped back and swung the door wide open, saying:

"Come in. Major Hambleton's wire came to her only a few minutes ago. He said someone would call."

We went through a small passageway into a sunny living-room that was cheaply furnished, but neat and clean enough.

"Sit down," the man said, pointing at a brown rocking chair.

I sat down. He sat on the burlap-covered sofa facing me. I looked around the room. I didn't see anything to show that a woman was living there.

He rubbed the long bridge of his nose with a longer forefinger and asked slowly:

"You brought the money?"

I said I'd feel more like talking with her there.

He looked at the finger with which he had been rubbing his nose, and then up at me, saying softly:

"But I'm her friend."

I said, "Yeah?" to that.

"Yes," he repeated. He frowned slightly, drawing back the corners of his thin-lipped mouth. "I've only asked whether you've brought the money."

I didn't say anything.

"The point is," he said quite reasonably, "that if you brought the money she doesn't expect you to hand it over to anybody except her. If you didn't bring it she doesn't want to see you. I don't think her mind can be changed about that. That's why I asked if you had brought it."

"I brought it."

He looked doubtfully at me. I showed him the money I had got from the bank. He jumped up briskly from the sofa.

"I'll have her here in a minute or two," he said over his shoulder as his long legs moved him toward the door. At the door he stopped to ask: "Do you know her? Or shall I have her bring means of identifying herself?"

"That would be best," I told him.

He went out, leaving the corridor door open.

III

In five minutes he was back with a slender blonde girl of twenty-three in pale green silk. The looseness of her small mouth and the puffiness around her blue eyes weren't yet pronounced enough to spoil her prettiness.

I stood up.

"This is Miss Hambleton," he said.

She gave me a swift glance and then lowered her eyes again, nervously playing with the strap of a handbag she held.

"You can identify yourself?" I asked.

"Sure," the man said. "Show them to him, Sue."

She opened the bag, brought out some papers and things, and held them up for me to take.

"Sit down, sit down," the man said as I took them.

They sat on the sofa. I sat in the rocking chair again and examined the things she had given me. There were two letters addressed to Sue Hambleton here, her father's telegram welcoming her home, a couple of receipted department store bills, an automobile driver's license, and a savings account pass book that showed a balance of less than ten dollars.

By the time I had finished my examination the girl's embarrassment was gone. She looked levelly at me, as did the man beside her. I felt in my pocket, found my copy of the photograph New York had sent us at the beginning of the hunt, and *looked* from it to her.

"Your mouth could have shrunk, maybe," I said, "but how could your nose have got that much longer?"

"If you don't like my nose," she said, "how'd you like to go to hell?" Her face had turned red.

"That's not the point. It's a swell nose, but it's not Sue's." I held the photograph out to her. "See for yourself."

She glared at the photograph and then at the man.

"What a smart guy you are," she told him.

He was watching me with dark eyes that had a brittle shine to them between narrow-drawn eyelids. He kept on watching me while he spoke to her out the side of his mouth, crisply:

"Pipe down."

She piped down. He sat and watched me. I sat and watched him. A clock ticked seconds away behind me. His eyes began shifting their focus from one of my eyes to the other. The girl sighed.

He said in a low voice: "Well?"

I said: "You're in a hole."

"What can you make out of it?" he asked casually.

"Conspiracy to defraud."

The girl jumped up and hit one of his shoulders angrily with the back of a hand, crying:

"What a smart guy you are, to get me in a jam like this. It was going to be duck soup—yeh! Eggs in the coffee—yeh! Now look at you. You haven't even got guts enough to tell this guy to go chase himself." She spun around to face me, pushing her red face down at me—I was still sitting in the rocker—snarling: "Well, what are you waiting for? Waiting to be kissed goodbye? We don't owe you anything, do we? We didn't get any of your lousy money, did we? Outside, then. Take the air. Dangle."

"Stop it, sister," I growled. "You'll bust something."

The man said:

"For God's sake stop that bawling, Peggy, and give somebody else a chance." He addressed me: "Well, what do you want?"

"How'd you get into this?" I asked.

He spoke quickly, eagerly:

"A fellow named Kenny gave me that stuff and told me about this Sue Hambleton, and her old man having plenty. I thought I'd give it a whirl. I figured the old man would either wire the dough right off the reel or wouldn't send it at all. I didn't figure on this send-a-man stuff. Then when his wire came, saying he was sending a man to see her, I ought to have dropped it.

"But hell! Here was a man coming with a grand in cash. That was too good to let go of without a try. It looked like there still might be a chance of copping, so I got Peggy to do Sue for me. If the man was coming today, it was a cinch he belonged out here on the Coast, and it was an even bet he wouldn't know Sue, would only have a description of her. From what Kenny had told me about her, I knew Peggy would come pretty close to fitting her description. I still don't see how you got that photograph. Television? I only wired the old man yesterday. I mailed a couple of letters to Sue, here, yesterday, so we'd have them with the other identification stuff to get the money from the telegraph company on."

"Kenny gave you the old man's address?"

"Sure he did."

"Did he give you Sue's?"

"No."

"How'd Kenny get hold of the stuff?"

"He didn't say."

"Where's Kenny now?"

"I don't know. He was on his way east, with something else on the fire, and couldn't fool with this. That's why he passed it on to me."

"Big-hearted Kenny," I said. "You know Sue Hambleton?"

"No," emphatically. "I'd never even heard of her till Kenny told me."

"I don't like this Kenny," I said, "though without him your story's got some good points. Could you tell it leaving him out?"

He shook his head slowly from side to side, saying:

"It wouldn't be the way it happened."

"That's too bad. Conspiracies to defraud don't mean as much to me as finding Sue. I might have made a deal with you."

He shook his head again, but his eyes were thoughtful, and his lower lip moved up to overlap the upper a little.

The girl had stepped back so she could see both of us as we talked, turning her face, which showed she didn't like us, from one to the other as we spoke our pieces. Now she fastened her gaze on the man, and her eyes were growing angry again.

I got up on my feet, telling him:

"Suit yourself. But if you want to play it that way I'll have to take you both in."

He smiled with indrawn lips and stood up.

The girl thrust herself in between us, facing him.

"This is a swell time to be dummying up," she spit at him. "Pop off, you lightweight, or I will. You're crazy if you think I'm going to take the fall with you."

"Shut up," he said in his throat.

"Shut me up," she cried.

He tried to, with both hands. I reached over her shoulders and caught one of his wrists, knocked the other hand up.

She slid out from between us and ran around behind me, screaming:

"Joe does know her. He got the things from her. She's at the St. Martin on O'Farrell Street—her and Babe McCloor."

While I listened to this I had to pull my head aside to let Joe's right hook miss me, had got his left arm twisted behind him, had turned my hip to catch his knee, and had got the palm of my left hand under his chin. I was ready to give his chin the Japanese tilt when he stopped wrestling and grunted:

"Let me tell it."

"Hop to it," I consented, taking my hands away from him and stepping back.

He rubbed the wrist I had wrenched, scowling past me at the girl. He called her four unlovely names, the mildest of which was "a dumb twist," and told her:

"He was bluffing about throwing us in the can. You don't think old man Hambleton's hunting for newspaper space, do you?" That wasn't a bad guess.

He sat on the sofa again, still rubbing his wrist. The girl stayed on the other side of the room, laughing at him through her teeth.

I said: "All right, roll it out, one of you."

"You've got it all," he muttered. "I glaumed that stuff last week when I was visiting Babe, knowing the story and hating to see a promising layout like that go to waste."

"What's Babe doing now?" I asked.

"I don't know."

"Is he still puffing them?"

"I don't know."

"Like hell you don't."

"I don't," he insisted. "If you know Babe you know you can't get anything out of him about what he's doing."

"How long have he and Sue been here?"

"About six months that I know of."

"Who's he mobbed up with?"

"I don't know. Any time Babe works with a mob he picks them up on the road and leaves them on the road."

"How's he fixed?"

"I don't know. There's always enough grub and liquor in the joint."

Refers to a joke postcard with faux Japanese characters and the caption: "If you can't understand Japanese, tilt your head to the right." Read from the right are English letters that spell out: "You look really silly, asshole."

Half an hour of this convinced me that I wasn't going to get much information about my people here.

I went to the phone in the passageway and called the agency. The boy on the switchboard told me MacMan was in the operatives' room. I asked to have him sent up to me, and went back to the living-room. Joe and Peggy took their heads apart when I came in.

MacMan arrived in less than ten minutes. I let him in and told him:

"This fellow says his name's Joe Wales, and the girl's supposed to be Peggy Carroll who lives upstairs in 421. We've got them cold for conspiracy to defraud, but I've made a deal with them. I'm going out to look at it now. Stay here with them, in this room. Nobody goes in or out, and nobody but you gets to the phone. There's a fire-escape in front of the window. The window's locked now. I'd keep it that way. If the deal turns out O.K. we'll let them go, but if they cut up on you while I'm gone there's no reason why you can't knock them around as much as you want."

MacMan nodded his hard round head and pulled a chair out between them and the door. I picked up my hat.

Joe Wales called:

"Hey, you're not going to uncover me to Babe, are you? That's got to be part of the deal."

"Not unless I have to."

"I'd just as leave stand the rap," he said. "I'd be safer in jail."

"I'll give you the best break I can," I promised, "but you'll have to take what's dealt you."

IV

Walking over to the St. Martin—only half a dozen blocks from Wales's place—I decided to go up against McCloor and the girl as a Continental op who suspected Babe of being in on a branch bank stick-up in Alameda the previous week. He hadn't been in on it—if the bank people had described half-correctly the men who had robbed them—so it wasn't likely my supposed suspicions would frighten him much. Clearing himself, he might give me some information I could use. The chief thing I wanted, of course, was a look at the girl, so I could report to her father that I had seen her. There was no reason for supposing that she and Babe knew her father was trying to keep an eye on her. Babe had a record. It was natural enough for sleuths to drop in now and then and try to hang something on him.

The St. Martin was a small three-storey apartment house of red brick between two taller hotels. The vestibule register showed, *R. K. McCloor*, 313, as Wales and Peggy had told me.

I pushed the bell button. Nothing happened. Nothing happened any of the four times I pushed it. I pushed the button labeled *Manager.*

The door clicked open. I went indoors. A beefy woman in a pink-striped cotton dress that needed pressing stood in an apartment doorway just inside the street door.

"Some people named McCloor live here?" I asked.

"Three-thirteen," she said.

"Been living here long?"

She pursed her fat mouth, looked intently at me, hesitated, but finally said: "Since last June."

"What do you know about them?"

She balked at that, raising her chin and her eyebrows.

I gave her my card. That was safe enough; it fit in with the pretext I intended using upstairs.

Her face, when she raised it from reading the card, was oily with curiosity.

"Come in here," she said in a husky whisper, backing through the doorway.

I followed her into her apartment. We sat on a Chesterfield and she whispered:

"What is it?"

"Maybe nothing." I kept my voice low, playing up to her theatricals. "He's done time for safe-burglary. I'm trying to get a line on him now; on the off chance that he might have been tied up in a recent job. I don't know that he was. He may be going straight for all I know." I took his photograph—front and profile, taken at Leavenworth—out of my pocket. "This him?"

She seized it eagerly, nodded, said, "Yes, that's him, all right," turned it over to read the description on the back, and repeated, "Yes, that's him, all right."

"His wife is here with him?" I asked.

She nodded vigorously.

"I don't know her," I said. "What sort of looking girl is she?"

She described a girl who could have been Sue Hambleton. I couldn't show Sue's picture; that would have uncovered me if she and Babe heard about it.

I asked the woman what she knew about the McCloors. What she knew wasn't a great deal: paid their rent on time, kept irregular hours, had occasional drinking parties, quarreled a lot.

"Think they're in now?" I asked. "I got no answer on the bell."

"I don't know," she whispered. "I haven't seen either of them since night before last, when they had a fight."

"Much of a fight?"

"Not much worse than usual."

"Could you find out if they're in?" I asked.

She looked at me out of the ends of her eyes.

"I'm not going to make any trouble for you," I assured her. "But if they've blown I'd like to know it, and I reckon you would too."

"All right, I'll find out." She got up, patting a pocket in which keys jingled. "You wait here."

"I'll go as far as the third floor with you," I said, "and wait out of sight there."

"All right," she said reluctantly.

On the third floor, I remained by the elevator. She disappeared around a corner of the dim corridor, and presently a muffled electric bell rang. It rang three times. I heard her keys jingle and one of them grate in a lock. The lock clicked. I heard the doorknob rattle as she turned it.

Then a long moment of silence was ended by a scream that filled the corridor from wall to wall.

I jumped for the corner, swung around it, saw an open door ahead, went through it, and slammed the door shut behind me.

The scream had stopped.

I was in a small dark vestibule with three doors besides the one I had come through. One door was shut. One opened into a bathroom. I went to the other.

The fat manager stood just inside it, her round back to me. I pushed past her and saw what she was looking at.

Sue Hambleton, in pale yellow pajamas trimmed with black lace, was lying across a bed. She lay on her back. Her arms were stretched out over her head. One leg was bent under her, one stretched out so that its bare foot rested on the floor. That bare foot was whiter than a live foot could be. Her face was white as her foot, except for a mottled swollen area from the right eyebrow to the right cheek-bone and dark bruises on her throat.

"Phone the police," I told the woman, and began poking into corners, closets and drawers.

It was late afternoon when I returned to the agency. I asked the file clerk to see if we had anything on Joe Wales and Peggy Carroll, and then went into the Old Man's office.

He put down some reports he had been reading, gave me a nodded invitation to sit down, and asked:

"You've seen her?"

"Yeah. She's dead."

The Old Man said, "Indeed," as if I had said it was raining, and smiled with polite attentiveness while I told him about it—from the time I had rung Wales's bell until I had joined the fat manager in the dead girl's apartment.

"She had been knocked around some, was bruised on the face and neck," I wound up. "But that didn't kill her."

"You think she was murdered?" he asked, still smiling gently.

"I don't know. Doc Jordan says he thinks it could have been arsenic. He's hunting for it in her now. We found a funny thing in the joint. Some thick sheets of dark gray paper were stuck in a book—*The Count of Monte Cristo*—wrapped in a month-old newspaper and wedged into a dark corner between the stove and the kitchen wall."

"Ah, arsenical fly paper," the Old Man murmured. "The Maybrick-Seddons trick. Mashed in water, four to six grains of arsenic can be soaked out of a sheet—enough to kill two people."

I nodded, saying:

"I worked on one in Louisville in 1916. The mulatto janitor saw McCloor leaving at half-past nine yesterday morning. She was probably dead before that. Nobody's seen him since. Earlier in the morning the people in the next apartment had heard them talking, her groaning. But they had too many fights for the neighbors to pay much attention to that. The landlady told me they had a fight the night before that. The police are hunting for him."

"Did you tell the police who she was?"

"No. What do we do on that angle? We can't tell them about Wales without telling them all."

"I dare say the whole thing will have to come out," he said thoughtfully. "I'll wire New York."

I went out of his office. The file clerk gave me a couple of newspaper clippings. The first told me that, fifteen months ago, Joseph Wales, alias Holy Joe, had been arrested on the complaint of a farmer named Toomey that he had been taken for twenty-five hundred dollars on a phoney "Business Opportunity" by Wales and three other men. The second clipping said the case had been dropped when Toomey failed to appear against Wales in court—bought off in the customary manner by the return of part or all of his money. That was all our files held on Wales, and they had nothing on Peggy Carroll.

V

MacMan opened the door for me when I returned to Wales's apartment.

"Anything doing?" I asked him.

"Nothing—except they've been bellyaching a lot."

Wales came forward, asking eagerly:

"Satisfied now?"

The girl stood by the window, looking at me with anxious eyes.

I didn't say anything.

"Did you find her?" Wales asked, frowning. "She was where I told you?"

"Yeah," I said.

"Well, then." Part of his frown went away. "That lets Peggy and me out, doesn't—" He broke off, ran his tongue over his lower lip, put a hand to his chin, asked sharply: "You didn't give them the tip-off on me, did you?"

I shook my head, no.

He took his hand from his chin and asked irritably:

"What's the matter with you, then? What are you looking like that for?"

Behind him the girl spoke bitterly.

"I knew damned well it would be like this," she said. "I knew damned well we weren't going to get out of it. Oh, what a smart guy you are!"

"Take Peggy into the kitchen, and shut both doors," I told MacMan. "Holy Joe and I are going to have a real heart-to-heart talk."

The girl went out willingly, but when Mac-Man was closing the door she put her head in again to tell Wales:

"I hope he busts you in the nose if you try to hold out on him."

MacMan shut the door.

"Your playmate seems to think you know something," I said.

Wales scowled at the door and grumbled: "She's more help to me than a broken leg." He turned his face to me, trying to make it look frank and friendly. "What do you want? I came clean with you before. What's the matter now?"

"What do you guess?"

He pulled his lips in between his teeth.

"What do you want to make me guess for?" he demanded. "I'm willing to play ball with you. But what can I do if you won't tell me what you want? I can't see inside your head."

"You'd get a kick out of it if you could."

He shook his head wearily and walked back to the sofa, sitting down bent forward, his hands together between his knees.

"All right," he sighed. "Take your time about asking me. I'll wait for you."

I went over and stood in front of him. I took his chin between my left thumb and fingers, raising his head and bending my own down until our noses were almost touching. I said:

"Where you stumbled, Joe, was in sending the telegram right after the murder."

"He's dead?" It popped out before his eyes had even had time to grow round and wide.

The question threw me off balance. I had to wrestle with my forehead to keep it from wrinkling, and I put too much calmness in my voice when I asked:

"Is who dead?"

"Who? How do I know? Who do you mean?"

"Who did you think I meant?" I insisted.

"How do I know? Oh, all right! Old man Hambleton, Sue's father."

"That's right," I said, and took my hand away from his chin.

"And he was murdered, you say?" He hadn't moved his face an inch from the position into which I had lifted it. "How?"

"Arsenic—fly paper."

"Arsenic fly paper." He looked thoughtful. "That's a funny one."

"Yeah, very funny. Where'd you go about buying some if you wanted it?"

"Buying it? I don't know. I haven't seen any since I was a kid. Nobody uses fly paper here in San Francisco anyway. There aren't enough flies."

"Somebody used some here," I said, "on Sue."

"Sue?" He jumped so that the sofa squeaked under him.

"Yeah. Murdered yesterday morning—arsenical fly paper."

"Both of them?" he asked incredulously.

"Both of who?"

"Her and her father."

"Yeah."

He put his chin far down on his chest and rubbed the back of one hand with the palm of the other.

"Then I am in a hole," he said slowly.

"That's what," I cheerfully agreed. "Want to try talking yourself out of it?"

"Let me think."

I let him think, listening to the tick of the clock while he thought. Thinking brought drops of sweat out on his gray-white face. Presently he sat up straight, wiping his face with a fancily colored handkerchief.

"I'll talk," he said. "I've got to talk now. Sue was getting ready to ditch Babe. She and I were going away. She—Here, I'll show you."

He put his hand in his pocket and held out a folded sheet of thick notepaper to me. I took it and read:

"Dear Joe:

I can't stand this much longer—we've simply got to go soon. Babe beat me again tonight. Please, if you really love me, let's make it soon.

Sue"

The handwriting was a nervous woman's, tall, angular, and piled up.

"That's why I made the play for Hambleton's grand," he said. "I've been shatting on my uppers for a couple of months, and when that letter came yesterday I just had to raise dough somehow to get her away. She wouldn't have stood for tapping her father though, so I tried to swing it without her knowing."

"When did you see her last?"

"Day before yesterday, the day she mailed that letter. Only I saw her in the afternoon—she was here—and she wrote it that night."

"Babe suspect what you were up to?"

"We didn't think he did. I don't know. He was jealous as hell all the time, whether he had any reason to be or not."

"How much reason did he have?"

Wales looked me straight in the eye and said:

"Sue was a good kid."

I said: "Well, she's been murdered."

He didn't say anything.

Day was darkening into evening. I went to the door and pressed the light button. I didn't lose sight of Holy Joe Wales while I was doing it.

As I took my finger away from the button, something clicked at the window: The click was loud and sharp.

I looked at the window:

A man crouched there on the fire-escape, looking in through glass and lace curtain. He was a thick-featured dark man whose size identified him as Babe McCloor. The muzzle of a big black automatic was touching the glass in front of him. He had tapped the glass with it to catch our attention.

He had our attention.

There wasn't anything for me to do just then. I stood there and looked at him. I couldn't tell whether he was looking at me or at Wales. I could see him clearly enough, but the lace curtain spoiled my view of details like that. I imagined he wasn't neglecting either of us, and I didn't imagine the lace curtain hid much from him. He was closer to the curtain than we, and I had turned on the room's lights.

Wales, sitting dead still on the sofa, was looking at McCloor. Wales's face wore a peculiar, stiffly sullen expression. His eyes were sullen. He wasn't breathing.

McCloor flicked the nose of his pistol against the pane, and a triangular piece of glass fell out, tinkling apart on the floor. It didn't, I was afraid, make enough noise to alarm MacMan in the kitchen. There were two closed doors between here and there.

Wales looked at the broken pane and closed his eyes. He closed them slowly, little by little, exactly as if he were falling asleep. He kept his stiffly sullen blank face turned straight to the window:

McCloor shot him three times.

The bullets knocked Wales down on the sofa, back against the wall. Wales's eyes popped open, bulging. His lips crawled back over his teeth, leaving them naked to the gums. His tongue came out. Then his head fell down and he didn't move any more.

When McCloor jumped away from the window I jumped to it. While I was pushing the curtain aside, unlocking the window and raising it, I heard his feet land on the cement paving below.

MacMan flung the door open and came in, the girl at his heels.

"Take care of this," I ordered as I scrambled over the sill. "McCloor shot him."

VI

Wales's apartment was on the second floor. The fire-escape ended there with a counter-weighted iron ladder that a man's weight would swing down into a cement-paved court.

I went down as Babe McCloor had gone, swinging down on the ladder till within dropping distance of the court, and then letting go.

There was only one street exit to the court. I took it.

A startled looking, smallish man was standing in the middle of the sidewalk close to the court, gaping at me as I dashed out.

I caught his arm, shook it.

"A big guy running." Maybe I yelled. "Where?"

He tried to say something, couldn't, and waved his arm at billboards standing across the front of a vacant lot on the other side of the street.

I forgot to say, "Thank you," in my hurry to get over there.

I got behind the billboards by crawling under them instead of going to either end, where there were openings. The lot was large enough and weedy enough to give cover to anybody who wanted to lie down and bushwhack a pursuer—even anybody as large as Babe McCloor.

While I considered that, I heard a dog barking at one corner of the lot. He could have been barking at a man who had run by. I ran to that corner of the lot. The dog was in a board-fenced backyard, at the corner of a narrow alley that ran from the lot to a street.

I chinned myself on the board fence, saw a wire-haired terrier alone in the yard, and ran down the alley while he was charging my part of the fence.

I put my gun back into my pocket before I left the alley for the street.

A small touring car was parked at the curb in front of a cigar store some fifteen feet from the alley. A policeman was talking to a slim dark-faced man in the cigar store doorway.

"The big fellow that come out of the alley a minute ago," I said. "Which way did he go?"

The policeman looked dumb. The slim man nodded his head down the street, said, "Down that way," and went on with his conversation.

I said, "Thanks," and went on down to the corner. There was a taxi phone there and two idle taxis. A block and a half below, a street car was going away.

"Did the big fellow who came down here a minute ago take a taxi or the street car?" I asked the two taxi chauffeurs who were leaning against one of the taxis.

The rattier looking one said:

"He didn't take a taxi."

I said:

"I'll take one. Catch that street car for me."

The street car was three blocks away before we got going. The street wasn't clear enough for me to see who got on and off it. We caught it when it stopped at Market Street.

"Follow along," I told the driver as I jumped out.

On the rear platform of the street car I looked through the glass. There were only eight or ten people aboard.

"There was a great big fellow got on at Hyde Street," I said to the conductor. "Where'd he get off?"

The conductor looked at the silver dollar I was turning over in my fingers and remembered that the big man got off at Taylor Street. That won the silver dollar.

I dropped off as the street car turned into Market Street. The taxi, close behind, slowed down, and its door swung open.

"Sixth and Mission," I said as I hopped in.

McCloor could have gone in any direction from Taylor Street. I had to guess. The best guess seemed to be that he would make for the other side of Market Street.

It was fairly dark by now. We had to go down to Fifth Street to get off Market, then over to Mission, and back up to Sixth. We got to Sixth Street without seeing McCloor. I couldn't see him on Sixth Street—either way from the crossing.

"On up to Ninth," I ordered, and while we rode told the driver what kind of man I was looking for.

We arrived at Ninth Street. No McCloor. I cursed and pushed my brains around.

The big man was a yegg. San Francisco was on fire for him. The yegg instinct would be to use a rattler to get away from trouble. The freight yards were in this end of town. Maybe he would be shifty enough to lie low instead of trying to powder. In that case, he probably hadn't crossed Market Street at all. If he stuck, there would still be a chance of picking him up tomorrow. If he was high-tailing, it was catch him now or not at all.

"Down to Harrison," I told the driver.

We went down to Harrison Street, and down Harrison to Third, up Bryant to Eighth, down Brannan to Third again, and over to Townsend—and we didn't see Babe McCloor.

"That's tough, that is," the driver sympathized as we stopped across the street from the Southern Pacific passenger station.

"I'm going over and look around in the station," I said. "Keep your eyes open while I'm gone."

When I told the copper in the station my trouble he introduced me to a couple of plainclothes men who had been planted there to watch for McCloor. That had been done after Sue Hambleton's body was found. The shooting of Holy Joe Wales was news to them.

I went outside again and found my taxi in front of the door, its horn working over-time, but too asthmatically to be heard indoors. The ratty driver was excited.

"A guy like you said come up out of King Street just now and swung on a No. 16 car as it pulled away," he said.

"Going which way?"

"That away" pointing southeast.

"Catch him," I said, jumping in.

The street car was out of sight around a bend in Third Street two blocks below. When we rounded the bend, the street car was slowing up, four blocks ahead. It hadn't slowed up very much when a man leaned far out and stepped off. He was a tall man, but didn't look tall on account of his shoulder spread. He didn't check his momentum, but used it to carry him across the sidewalk and out of sight.

We stopped where the man had left the car.

I gave the driver too much money and told him:

"Go back to Townsend Street and tell the copper in the station that I've chased Babe McCloor into the S. P. yards."

VII

I thought I was moving silently down between two strings of box cars, but I had gone less than twenty feet when a light flashed in my face and a sharp voice ordered:

"Stand still, you."

I stood still. Men came from between cars. One of them spoke my name, adding: "What are you doing here? Lost?" It was Harry Pebble, a police detective.

I stopped holding my breath and said:

"Hello, Harry. Looking for Babe?"

"Yes. We've been going over the rattlers."

"He's here. I just tailed him in from the street."

Pebble swore and snapped the light off.

"Watch, Harry," I advised. "Don't play with him. He's packing plenty of gun and he's cut down one boy tonight."

"I'll play with him," Pebble promised, and told one of the men with him to go over and warn those on the other side of the yard that McCloor was in, and then to ring for reinforcements.

"We'll just sit on the edge and hold him in till they come," he said.

That seemed a sensible way to play it. We spread out and waited. Once Pebble and I turned back a lanky bum who tried to slip into the yard between us, and one of the men below us picked up a shivering kid who was trying to slip out. Otherwise nothing happened until Lieutenant Duff arrived with a couple of carloads of coppers.

Most of our force went into a cordon around the yard. The rest of us went through the yard in small groups, working it over car by car. We picked up a few hoboes that Pebble and his men had missed earlier, but we didn't find McCloor.

We didn't find any trace of him until somebody stumbled over a railroad bull huddled in the shadow of a gondola. It took a couple of minutes to bring him to, and he couldn't talk then. His jaw was broken. But when we asked if McCloor had slugged him, he nodded, and when we asked in which direction McCloor had been headed, he moved a feeble hand to the east.

We went over and searched the Santa Fe yards.

We didn't find McCloor.

VIII

I rode up to the Hall of Justice with Duff. MacMan was in the captain of detectives' office with three or four police sleuths.

"Wales die?" I asked.

"Yep."

"Say anything before he went?"

"He was gone before you were through the window."

"You held on to the girl?"

"She's here."

"She say anything?"

"We were waiting for you before we tapped her," detective-sergeant O'Gar said, "not knowing the angle on her."

"Let's have her in. I haven't had any dinner yet. How about the autopsy on Sue Hambleton?"

"Chronic arsenic poisoning."

"Chronic? That means it was fed to her little by little, and not in a lump?"

"Uh-huh. From what he found in her kidney, intestines, liver, stomach and blood, Jordan figures there was less than a grain of it in her. That wouldn't be enough to knock her off. But he says he found arsenic in the tips of her hair, and she'd have to be given some at least a month ago for it to have worked out that far."

"Any chance that it wasn't arsenic that killed her?"

"Not unless Jordan's a bum doctor."

A policewoman came in with Peggy Carroll.

The blonde girl was tired. Her eyelids, mouth corners and body drooped, and when I pushed a chair out toward her she sagged down in it.

O'Gar ducked his grizzled bullet head at me.

"Now, Peggy," I said, "tell us where you fit into this mess."

"I don't fit into it." She didn't look up. Her voice was tired. "Joe dragged me into it. He told you."

"You his girl?"

"If you want to call it that," she admitted.

"You jealous?"

"What," she asked, looking up at me, her face puzzled, "has that got to do with it?"

"Sue Hambleton was getting ready to go away with him when she was murdered."

The girl sat up straight in the chair and said deliberately:

"I swear to God I didn't know she was murdered."

"But you did know she was dead," I said positively.

"I didn't," she replied just as positively.

I nudged O'Gar with my elbow. He pushed his undershot jaw at her and barked:

"What are you trying to give us? You knew she was dead. How could you kill her without knowing it?"

While she looked at him I waved the others in. They crowded close around her and took up the chorus of the sergeant's song. She was barked, roared, and snarled at plenty in the next few minutes.

The instant she stopped trying to talk back to them I cut in again.

"Wait," I said, very earnestly. "Maybe she didn't kill her."

"The hell she didn't," O'Gar stormed, holding the center of the stage so the others could move away from the girl without their retreat seeming too artificial. "Do you mean to tell me this baby—"

"I didn't say she didn't," I remonstrated. "I said maybe she didn't."

"Then who did?"

I passed the question to the girl: "Who did?"

"Babe," she said immediately.

O'Gar snorted to make her think he didn't believe her.

I asked, as if I were honestly perplexed:

"How do you know that if you didn't know she was dead?"

"It stands to reason he did," she said. "Anybody can see that. He found out she was going away with Joe, so he killed her and then came to Joe's and killed him. That's just exactly what Babe would do when he found it out."

"Yeah? How long have *you* known they were going away together?"

"Since they decided to. Joe told me a month or two ago."

"And you didn't mind?"

"You've got this all wrong," she said. "Of course I didn't mind. I was being cut in on it. You know her father had the bees. That's what Joe was after. She didn't mean anything to him but an in to the old man's pockets. And I was to get my dib. And you needn't think I was crazy enough about Joe or anybody else to step off in the air for them. Babe got next and fixed the pair of them. That's a cinch."

"Yeah? How do you figure Babe would kill her?"

"That guy? You don't think he'd—"

"I mean, how would he go about killing her?"

"Oh!" She shrugged. "With his hands, likely as not."

"Once he'd made up his mind to do it, he'd do it quick and violent?" I suggested.

"That would be Babe," she agreed.

"But you can't see him slow-poisoning her—spreading it out over a month?"

Worry came into the girl's blue eyes. She put her lower lip between her teeth, then said slowly:

"No, I can't see him doing it that way. Not Babe."

"Who can you see doing it that way?"

She opened her eyes wide, asking:

"You mean Joe?"

I didn't say anything.

"Joe might have," she said persuasively. "God only knows what he'd want to do it for, why he'd want to get rid of the kind of meal ticket she was going to be. But you couldn't always guess what he was getting at. He pulled plenty of dumb ones. He was too slick without being smart. If he was going to kill her, though, that would be about the way he'd go about it."

"Were he and Babe friendly?"

"No."

"Did he go to Babe's much?"

"Not at all that I know about. He was too leary of Babe to take a chance on being caught there. That's why I moved upstairs, so Sue could come over to our place to see him."

"Then how could Joe have hidden the fly paper he poisoned her with in her apartment?"

"Fly paper!" Her bewilderment seemed honest enough.

"Show it to her," I told O'Gar.

He got a sheet from the desk and held it close to the girl's face.

She stared at it for a moment and then jumped up and grabbed my arm with both hands.

"I didn't know what it was," she said excitedly. "Joe had some a couple of months ago. He was looking at it when I came in. I asked him what it was for, and he smiled that wisenheimer smile of his and said, 'You make angels out of it,' and wrapped it up again and put it in his pocket. I didn't pay much attention to him: he was always fooling with some kind of tricks that were supposed to make him wealthy, but never did."

"Ever see it again?"

"No."

"Did you know Sue very well?"

"I didn't know her at all. I never even saw her. I used to keep out of the way so I wouldn't gum Joe's play with her."

"But you know Babe?"

"Yes, I've been on a couple of parties where he was. That's all I know him."

"Who killed Sue?"

"Joe," she said. "Didn't he have that paper you say she was killed with?"

"Why did he kill her?"

"I don't know. He pulled some awful dumb tricks sometimes."

"You didn't kill her?"

"No, no, no!"

I jerked the corner of my mouth at O'Gar.

"You're a liar," he bawled, shaking the fly paper in her face. "You killed her." The rest of the team closed in, throwing accusations at her. They kept it up until she was groggy and the policewoman beginning to look worried.

Then I said angrily:

"All right. Throw her in a cell and let her think it over." To her: "You know what you told Joe this afternoon: this is no time to dummy up. Do a lot of thinking tonight."

"Honest to God I didn't kill her," she said.

I turned my back to her. The policewoman took her away.

"Ho-hum," O'Gar yawned. "We gave her a pretty good ride at that, for a short one."

"Not bad," I agreed. "If anybody else looked likely, I'd say she didn't kill Sue. But if she's telling the truth, then Holy Joe did it. And why should he poison the goose that was going to lay nice yellow eggs for him? And how and why did he cache the poison in their apartment? Babe had the motive, but damned if he looks like a slow-poisoner to me. You can't tell, though; he and Holy Joe could even have been working together on it."

"Could," Duff said. "But it takes a lot of imagination to get that one down. Anyway you twist it, Peggy's our best bet so far. Go up against her again, hard, in the morning?"

"Yeah," I said. "And we've got to find Babe."

The others had had dinner. MacMan and I went out and got ours. When we returned to the detective bureau an hour later it was practically deserted of the regular operatives.

"All gone to Pier 42 on a tip that McCloor's there," Steve Ward told us.

"How long ago?"

"Ten minutes."

MacMan and I got a taxi and set out for Pier 42. We didn't get to Pier 42.

On First Street, half a block from the Embar-cadero, the taxi suddenly shrieked and slid to a halt.

"What—?" I began, and saw a man standing in front of the machine. He was a big man with a big gun. "Babe," I grunted, and put my hand on MacMan's arm to keep him from getting his gun out.

"Take me to—" McCloor was saying to the frightened driver when he saw us. He came around to my side and pulled the door open, holding the gun on us.

He had no hat. His hair was wet, plastered to his head. Little streams of water trickled down from it. His clothes were dripping wet.

He looked surprised at us and ordered:

"Get out."

As we got out he growled at the driver:

"What the hell you got your flag up for if you had fares?"

The driver wasn't there. He had hopped out the other side and was scooting away down the street. McCloor cursed him and poked his gun at me, growling:

"Go on, beat it."

Apparently he hadn't recognized me. The light here wasn't good, and I had a hat on now; he had seen me for only a few seconds in Wales's room.

I stepped aside. MacMan moved to the other side.

McCloor took a backward step to keep us from getting him between us and started an angry word.

MacMan threw himself on McCloor's gun arm.

I socked McCloor's jaw with my fist. I might just as well have hit somebody else for all it seemed to bother him.

He swept me out of his way and pasted MacMan in the mouth. MacMan fell back till the taxi stopped him, spit out a tooth, and came back for more.

I was trying to climb up McCloor's left side.

MacMan came in on his right, failed to dodge a chop of the gun, caught it square on the top of the noodle, and went down hard. He stayed down.

I kicked McCloor's ankle, but couldn't get his foot from under him. I rammed my right fist into the small of his back and got a left-handful of his wet hair, swinging on it. He shook his head, dragging me off my feet.

He punched me in the side and I could feel my ribs and guts flattening together like leaves in a book.

I swung my fist against the back of his neck. That bothered him. He made a rumbling noise down in his chest, crunched my shoulder in his left hand, and chopped at me with the gun in his right.

I kicked him somewhere and punched his neck again.

Down the street, at the Embarcadero, a police whistle was blowing. Men were running up First Street toward us.

McCloor snorted like a locomotive and threw me away from him. I didn't want to go. I tried to hang on. He threw me away from him and ran up the street.

I scrambled up and ran after him, dragging my gun out.

At the first corner he stopped to squirt metal at me—three shots. I squirted one at him. None of the four connected.

He disappeared around the corner. I swung wide around it, to make him miss if he were flattened to the wall waiting for me. He wasn't. He was a hundred feet ahead, going into a space between two warehouses. I went in after him, and out after him at the other end, making better time with my hundred and ninety pounds than he was making with his two-fifty.

He crossed a street, turning up, away from the waterfront. There was a light on the corner. When I came into its glare he wheeled and leveled his gun at me. I didn't hear it click, but I knew it had when he threw it at me. The gun went past with a couple of feet to spare and raised hell against a door behind me.

McCloor turned and ran up the street. I ran up the street after him.

I put a bullet past him to let the others know where we were. At the next corner he started to turn to the left, changed his mind, and went straight on.

I sprinted, cutting the distance between us to forty or fifty feet, and yelped:

"Stop or I'll drop you."

He jumped sidewise into a narrow alley.

I passed it on the jump, saw he wasn't waiting for me, and went in. Enough light came in from the street to let us see each other and our surroundings. The alley was blind—walled on each side and at the other end by tall concrete buildings with steel-shuttered windows and doors.

McCloor faced me, less than twenty feet away. His jaw stuck out. His arms curved down free of his sides. His shoulders were bunched.

"Put them up," I ordered, holding my gun level.

"Get out of my way, little man," he grumbled, taking a stiff-legged step toward me. "I'll eat you up."

"Keep coming," I said, "and I'll put you down."

"Try it." He took another step, crouching a little. "I can still get to you with slugs in me."

"Not where I'll put them." I was wordy, trying to talk him into waiting till the others came up. I didn't want to have to kill him. We could have done that from the taxi. "I'm no Annie Oakley, but if I can't pop your kneecaps with two shots at this distance, you're welcome to me. And if you think smashed kneecaps are a lot of fun, give it a whirl."

"Hell with that," he said and charged.

I shot his right knee.

He lurched toward me.

I shot his left knee.

He tumbled down.

"You would have it," I complained.

He twisted around, and with his arms pushed himself into a sitting position facing me.

"I didn't think you had sense enough to do it," he said through his teeth.

IX

I talked to McCloor in the hospital. He lay on his back in bed with a couple of pillows slanting his head up. The skin was pale and tight around his mouth and eyes, but there was nothing else to show he was in pain.

"You sure devastated me, bo," he said when I came in.

"Sorry," I said, "but—"

"I ain't beefing. I asked for it."

"Why'd you kill Holy Joe?" I asked, off-hand, as I pulled a chair up beside the bed.

"Uh-uh—you're tooting the wrong ringer."

I laughed and told him I was the man in the room with Joe when it happened.

McCloor grinned and said:

"I thought I'd seen you somewheres before. So that's where it was. I didn't pay no attention to your mug, just so your hands didn't move."

"Why'd you kill him?"

He pursed his lips, screwed up his eyes at me, thought something over, and said:

"He killed a broad I knew."

"He killed Sue Hambleton?" I asked.

He studied my face a while before he replied: "Yep."

"How do you figure that out?"

"Hell," he said, "I don't have to. Sue told me. Give me a butt."

I gave him a cigarette, held a lighter under it, and objected:

"That doesn't exactly fit in with other things I know. Just what happened and what did she say? You might start back with the night you gave her the goog."

He looked thoughtful, letting smoke sneak slowly out of his nose, then said:

"I hadn't ought to hit her in the eye, that's a fact. But, see, she had been out all afternoon and wouldn't tell me where she'd been, and we had a row over it. What's this—Thursday morning? That was Monday, then. After the row I went out and spent the night in a dump over on Army Street. I got home about seven the next morning. Sue was sick as hell, but she wouldn't let me get a croaker for her. That was kind of funny, because she was scared stiff."

McCloor scratched his head meditatively and suddenly drew in a great lungful of smoke, practically eating up the rest of the cigarette. He let the smoke leak out of mouth and nose together, looking dully through the cloud at me. Then he said bruskly:

"Well, she went under. But before she went she told me she'd been poisoned by Holy Joe."

"She say how he'd given it to her?"

McCloor shook his head.

"I'd been asking her what was the matter, and not getting anything out of her. Then she starts whining that she's poisoned. 'I'm poisoned, Babe,' she whines. 'Arsenic. That damned Holy

Joe,' she says. Then she won't say anything else, and it's not a hell of a while after that that she kicks off."

"Yeah? Then what'd you do?"

"I went gunning for Holy Joe. I knew him but didn't know where he jungled up, and didn't find out till yesterday. You was there when I came. You know about that. I had picked up a boiler and parked it over on Turk Street, for the getaway. When I got back to it, there was a copper standing close to it. I figured he might have spotted it as a hot one and was waiting to see who came for it, so I let it alone, and caught a street car instead, and cut for the yards. Down there I ran into a whole flock of hammer and saws and had to go overboard in China Basin, swimming up to a pier, being ranked again by a watchman there, swimming off to another, and finally getting through the line only to run into another bad break. I wouldn't of flagged that taxi if the *For Hire* flag hadn't been up."

"You knew Sue was planning to take a run-out on you with Joe?"

"I don't know it yet," he said. "I knew damned well she was cheating on me, but I didn't know who with."

"What would you have done if you had known that?" I asked.

"Me?" He grinned wolfishly. "Just what I did."

"Killed the pair of them," I said.

He rubbed his lower lip with a thumb and asked calmly:

"You think I killed Sue?"

"You did."

"Serves me right," he said. "I must be getting simple in my old age. What the hell am I doing barbering with a lousy dick? That never got nobody nothing but grief. Well, you might just as well take it on the heel and toe now, my lad. I'm through spitting."

And he was. I couldn't get another word out of him.

X

The Old Man sat listening to me, tapping his desk lightly with the point of a long yellow pencil, staring past me with mild blue, rimless-spectacled, eyes. When I had brought my story up to date, he asked pleasantly:

"How is MacMan?"

"He lost two teeth, but his skull wasn't cracked. He'll be out in a couple of days."

The Old Man nodded and asked:

"What remains to be done?"

"Nothing. We can put Peggy Carroll on the mat again, but it's not likely we'll squeeze much more out of her. Outside of that, the returns are pretty well all in."

"And what do you make of it?"

I squirmed in my chair and said: "Suicide."

The Old Man smiled at me, politely but skeptically.

"I don't like it either," I grumbled. "And I'm not ready to write it in a report yet. But that's the only total that what we've got will add up to. That fly paper was hidden behind the kitchen stove. Nobody would be crazy enough to try to hide something from a woman in her own kitchen like that. But the woman might hide it there.

"According to Peggy, Holy Joe had the fly paper. If Sue hid it, she got it from him. For what? They were planning to go away together, and were only waiting till Joe, who was on the nut, raised enough dough. Maybe they were afraid of Babe, and had the poison there to slip him if he tumbled to their plan before they went. Maybe they meant to slip it to him before they went anyway.

"When I started talking to Holy Joe about murder, he thought Babe was the one who had been bumped off. He was surprised, maybe, but as if he was surprised that it had happened so soon. He was more surprised when he heard that Sue had died too, but even then he wasn't so surprised as when he saw McCloor alive at the window.

"She died cursing Holy Joe, and she knew she was poisoned, and she wouldn't let McCloor get a doctor. Can't that mean that she had turned against Joe, and had taken the poison herself instead of feeding it to Babe? The poison was hidden from Babe. But even if he found it, I can't figure him as a poisoner. He's too rough. Unless he caught her trying to poison him and made her swallow the stuff. But that doesn't account for the month-old arsenic in her hair."

"Does your suicide hypothesis take care of that?" the Old Man asked.

"It could," I said. "Don't be kicking holes in my theory. It's got enough as it stands. But, if she committed suicide this time, there's no reason why she couldn't have tried it once before—say after a quarrel with Joe a month ago—and failed to bring it off. That would have put the arsenic in her. There's no real proof that she took any between a month ago and day before yesterday."

"No real proof," the Old Man protested mildly, "except the autopsy's finding—chronic poisoning."

I was never one to let experts' guesses stand in my way. I said:

"They base that on the small amount of arsenic they found in her remains—less than a fatal dose. And the amount they find in your stomach after you're dead depends on how much you vomit before you die."

The Old Man smiled benevolently at me and asked:

"But you're not, you say, ready to write this theory into a report? Meanwhile what do you propose doing?"

"If there's nothing else on tap, I'm going home, fumigate my brains with Fatimas, and try to get this thing straightened out in my head. I think I'll get a copy of *The Count of Monte Cristo* and run through it. I haven't read it since I was a kid. It looks like the book was wrapped up with the fly paper to make a bundle large enough to wedge tightly between the wall and stove, so it wouldn't fall down. But there might be something in the book. I'll see anyway."

"I did that last night," the Old Man murmured.

I asked: "And?"

He took a book from his desk drawer, opened it where a slip of paper marked a place, and held it out to me, one pink finger marking a paragraph.

"Suppose you were to take a millegramme of this poison the first day, two millegrammes the second day, and so on. Well, at the end of ten days you would have taken a centigramme: at the end of twenty days, increasing another millegramme, you would have taken three hundred centigrammes; that is to say, a dose you would support without inconvenience, and which would be very dangerous for any other person who had not taken the same precautions as yourself. Well, then, at the end of the month, when drinking water from the same carafe, you would kill the person who had drunk this water, without your perceiving otherwise than from slight inconvenience that there was any poisonous substance mingled with the water."

"That does it," I said. "That does it. They were afraid to go away without killing Babe, too certain he'd come after them. She tried to make herself immune from arsenic poisoning by getting her body accustomed to it, taking steadily increasing doses, so when she slipped the big shot in Babe's food she could eat it with him without danger. She'd be taken sick, but wouldn't die, and the police couldn't hang his death on her because she too had eaten the poisoned food.

"That clicks. After the row Monday night, when she wrote Joe the note urging him to make the getaway soon, she tried to hurry up her immunity, and increased her preparatory doses too quickly, took too large a shot. That's why she cursed Joe at the end: it was his plan."

"Possibly she overdosed herself in an attempt to speed it along," the Old Man agreed, "but not necessarily. There are people who can cultivate an ability to take large doses of arsenic without trouble, but it seems to be a sort of natural gift with them, a matter of some constitutional peculiarity. Ordinarily, any one who tried it would do what Sue Hambleton did—slowly poison themselves until the cumulative effect was strong enough to cause death."

Babe McCloor was hanged, for killing Holy Joe Wales, six months later.

THE MALTESE FALCON

Begins in the next issue—the September issue—of Black Mask, and we enthusiastically recommend it to all lovers of detective fiction and particularly those who are, as Mr Herbert Asbury, the nationally known critic, says, tired of conventional plots.

As all Black Mask Readers know, this magazine has been developing a new kind of detective story more in keeping with the times, more true to life than the wild, imaginative plot of earlier days and, therefore, of far more gripping interest to its readers.

Dashiell Hammett has been the leader in this development, and with publication of his Black Mask stories in book form, by a publisher of highest standing, is becoming recognized as the foremost writer of detective fiction of the present time.

THE MALTESE FALCON is too big a story to allow an adequate description of it—we can merely assure you that it is the best story of its kind we have ever seen in print and we only hope that you may have as much enjoyment from it as we, who are obliged to read so many millions of words a year, have had in our examination of it.

6

THE FAREWELL MURDER

BLACK MASK, FEBRUARY 1930

The Continental Op is called in to protect a man and runs into plenty grief.

I

I was the only one who left the train at Farewell.

A man came through the rain from the passenger shed. He was a small man. His face was dark and flat. He wore a gray waterproof cap and a gray coat cut in military style.

He didn't look at me. He looked at the valise and Gladstone bag in my hands. He came forward quickly, walking with short, choppy steps.

He didn't say anything when he took the bags from me. I asked:

"Kavalov's?"

He had already turned his back to me and was carrying my bags towards a tan Stutz coach that stood in the roadway beside the gravel station platform. In answer to my question he bowed twice at the Stutz without looking around or checking his jerky half-trot.

I followed him to the car.

Three minutes of riding carried us through the village. We took a road that climbed westward into the hills. The road looked like a seal's back in the rain.

The flat-faced man was in a hurry. We purred over the road at a speed that soon carried us past the last of the cottages sprinkled up the hillside.

Presently we left the shiny black road for a paler one curving south to run along a hill's wooded crest. Now and then this road, for a hundred feet or more at a stretch, was turned into a tunnel by tall trees heavily leafed boughs interlocking overhead.

Rain accumulated in fat drops on the boughs and came down to thump the Stutz's roof. The dullness of rainy early evening became almost the blackness of night inside these tunnels.

The flat-faced man switched on the lights, and increased our speed.

He sat rigidly erect at the wheel. I sat behind him. Above his military collar, among the hairs that were clipped short on the nape of his neck, globules of moisture made tiny shining points. The moisture could have been rain. It could hate been sweat.

We were in the middle of one of the tunnels.

The flat-faced man's head jerked to the left, and he screamed:

"A-a-a-a-a!"

It was a long, quivering, high-pitched bleat, thin with terror.

I jumped up, bending forward to see what was the matter with him.

The car swerved and plunged ahead, throwing me back on the seat again.

Through the side window I caught a one-eyed glimpse of something dark lying in the road.

I twisted around to try the back window, less rain-bleared.

I saw a black man lying on his back in the road, near the left edge. His body was arched, as if its weight rested on his heels and the back of his head. A knife handle that couldn't have been less than six inches long stood straight up in the air from the left side of his chest.

By the time I had seen this much we had taken a curve and were out of the tunnel.

"Stop," I called to the flat-faced man.

He pretended he didn't hear me. The Stutz was a tan streak under us. I put a hand on the driver's shoulder.

His shoulder squirmed under my hand, and he screamed "A-a-a-a!" again as if the dead black man had him.

I reached past him and shut off the engine.

He took his hands from the wheel and clawed up at me. Noises came from his mouth, but they didn't make any words that I knew.

I got a hand on the wheel. I got my other forearm under his chin. I leaned over the back of his seat so that the weight of my upper body was on his head, mashing it down against the wheel.

Between this and that and the help of God, the Stutz hadn't left the road when it stopped moving.

I got up off the flat-faced man's head and asked:

"What the hell's the matter with you?"

He looked at me with white eyes, shivered, and didn't say anything.

"Turn it around," I said. "We'll go back there."

He shook his head from side to side, desperately, and made some more of the mouth-noises that might have been words if I could have understood them.

"You know who that was?" I asked.

He shook his head.

"You do," I growled.

He shook his head.

By then I was beginning to suspect that no matter what I said to this fellow I'd get only head-shakes out of him.

I said:

"Get away from the wheel, then. I'm going to drive back there."

He opened the door and scrambled out.

"Come back here," I called.

He backed away, shaking his head.

I cursed him, slid in behind the wheel, said, "All right, wait here for me," and slammed the door.

He retreated backwards slowly, watching me with scared, whitish eyes while I backed and turned the coach.

I had to drive back farther than I had expected, something like a mile.

I didn't find the black man.

The tunnel was empty.

If I had known the exact spot in which he had been lying, I might have been able to find something to show how he had been removed. But I hadn't had time to pick out a landmark, and now any one of four or five places looked like the spot.

With the help of the coach's lamps I went over the left side of the road from one end of the tunnel to the other.

I didn't find any blood. I didn't find any footprints. I didn't find anything to show that any body had been lying in the road. I didn't find anything.

It was too dark by now for me to try searching the woods.

I returned to where I had left the flat-faced man.

He was gone.

It looked, I thought, as if Mr Kavalov might be right in thinking he needed a detective.

II

Half a mile beyond the place where the flat-faced man had deserted me, I stopped the Stutz in front of a grilled steel gate that blocked the road. The gate was padlocked on the inside. From either side of it tall hedging ran off into the woods. The upper part of a brown-roofed small house was visible over the hedge-top to the left.

I worked the Stutz's horn.

The racket brought a gawky boy of fifteen or sixteen to the other side of the gate. He had on bleached whipcord pants and a wildly striped sweater. He didn't come out to the middle of the road, but stood at one side, with one arm out of sight as if holding something that was hidden from me by the hedge.

"This Kavalov's?" I asked.

"Yes, sir," he said uneasily.

I waited for him to unlock the gate. He didn't unlock it. He stood there looking uneasily at the car and at me.

"Please, mister," I said, "can I come in?"

"What—who are you?"

"I'm the guy that Kavalov sent for. If I'm not going to be let in, tell me, so I can catch the six-fifty back to San Francisco."

The boy chewed his lip, said, "Wait till I see if I can find the key," and went out of sight behind the hedge.

He was gone long enough to have had a talk with somebody.

When he came back he unlocked the gate, swung it open, and said:

"It's all right, sir. They're expecting you."

When I had driven through the gate I could see lights on a hilltop a mile or so ahead and to the left.

"Is that the house?" I asked.

"Yes, sir. They're expecting you."

Close to where the boy had stood while talking to me through the gate, a double-barrel shotgun was propped up against the hedge.

I thanked the boy and drove on. The road wound gently uphill through farm land. Tall, slim trees had been planted at regular intervals on both sides of the road.

The road brought me at last to the front of a building that looked like a cross between a fort and a factory in the dusk. It was built of concrete. Take a flock of squat cones of various sizes, round off the points bluntly, mash them together with the largest one somewhere near the center, the others grouped around it in not too strict accordance with their sizes, adjust the whole collection to agree with the slopes of a hilltop, and you would have a model of the Kavalov house. The windows were steel-sashed. There weren't very many of them. No two were in line either vertically or horizontally. Some were lighted.

As I got out of the car, the narrow front door of this house opened.

A short, red-faced woman of fifty or so, with faded blonde hair wound around and around her head, came out. She wore a high-necked, tight-sleeved, gray woolen dress. When she smiled her mouth seemed wide as her hips.

She said:

"You're the gentleman from the city?"

"Yeah. I lost your chauffeur somewhere back on the road."

"Lord bless you," she said amiably, "that's all right."

A thin man with thin dark hair plastered down above a thin, worried face came past her to take my bags when I had lifted them out of the car. He carried them indoors.

The woman stood aside for me to enter, saying:

"Now I suppose you'll want to wash up a little bit before you go in to dinner, and they won't mind waiting for you the few minutes you'll take if you hurry."

I said, "Yeah, thanks," waited for her to get ahead of me again, and followed her up a curving flight of stairs that climbed along the inside of one of the cones that made up the building.

She took me to a second-storey bedroom where the thin man was unpacking my bags.

"Martin will get you anything you need," she assured me from the doorway, "and when you're ready, just come on downstairs."

I said I would, and she went away. The thin man had finished unpacking by the time I had got out of coat, vest, collar and shirt. I told him there wasn't anything else I needed, washed up in the adjoining bathroom, put on a fresh shirt and collar, my vest and coat, and went downstairs.

The wide hall was empty. Voices came through an open doorway to the left.

One voice was a nasal whine. It complained:

"I will not have it. I will not put up with it. I am not a child, and I will not have it."

This voice's t's were a little too thick for t's, but not thick enough to bed's.

Another voice was a lively, but slightly harsh, barytone. It said cheerfully:

"What's the good of saying we won't put up with it, when we are putting up with it?"

The third voice was feminine, a soft voice, but flat and spiritless. It said:

"But perhaps he did kill him."

The whining voice said: "I do not care. I will not have it."

The barytone voice said, cheerfully as before: "Oh, won't you?"

A doorknob turned farther down the hall. I didn't want to be caught standing there listening. I advanced to the open doorway.

III

I was in the doorway of a low-ceilinged oval room furnished and decorated in gray, white and silver. Two men and a woman were there.

The older man—he was somewhere in his fifties—got up from a deep gray chair and bowed ceremoniously at me. He was a plump man of medium height, completely bald, dark-skinned and pale-eyed. He wore a wax-pointed gray mustache and a straggly gray imperial.

"Mr Kavalov?" I asked.

"Yes, sir." His was the whining voice.

I told him who I was. He shook my hand and then introduced me to the others.

The woman was his daughter. She was probably thirty. She had her father's narrow, full-lipped mouth, but her eyes were dark, her nose was short and straight, and her skin was almost colorless. Her face had Asia in it. It was pretty, passive, unintelligent.

The man with the barytone voice was her husband. His name was Ringgo. He was six or seven years older than his wife, neither tall nor heavy, but well set up. His left arm was in splints and a sling. The knuckles of his right hand were darkly bruised. He had a lean, bony, quick-witted face, bright dark eyes with plenty of lines around them, and a good-natured hard mouth.

He gave me his bruised hand, wriggled his bandaged arm at me, grinned, and said:

"I'm sorry you missed this, but the future injuries are yours."

"How did it happen?" I asked.

Kavalov raised a plump hand.

"Time enough it is to go into that when we have eaten," he said. "Let us have our dinner first."

We went into a small green and brown dining-room where a small square table was set. I sat facing Ringgo across a silver basket of orchids that stood between tall silver candlesticks in the center of the table. Mrs Ringgo sat to my right, Kavalov to my left. When Kavalov sat down I saw the shape of an automatic pistol in his hip pocket.

Two men servants waited on us. There was a lot of food and all of it was well turned out. We ate caviar, some sort of consomme, sand dabs, potatoes and cucumber jelly, roast lamb, corn and string beans, asparagus, wild duck and hominy cakes, artichoke-and-tomato salad, and orange ice. We drank white wine, claret, Burgundy, coffee and *creme de menthe.*

Kavalov ate and drank enormously. None of us skimped.

Kavalov was the first to disregard his own order that nothing be said about his troubles until after we had eaten. When he had finished his soup he put down his spoon and said:

"I am not a child. I will not be frightened."

He blinked pale, worried eyes defiantly at me, his lips pouting between mustache and imperial.

Ringgo grinned pleasantly at him. Mrs Ringgo's face was as serene and inattentive as if nothing had been said.

"What is there to be frightened of?" I asked.

"Nothing," Kavalov said. "Nothing excepting a lot of idiotic and very pointless trickery and play-acting."

"You can call it anything you want to call it," a voice grumbled over my shoulder, "but I seen what I seen."

The voice belonged to one of the men who was waiting on the table, a sallow, youngish man with a narrow, slack-lipped face. He spoke with a subdued sort of stubbornness, and without looking up from the dish he was putting before me.

Since nobody else paid any attention to the servant's clearly audible remark, I turned my face to Kavalov again. He was trimming the edge of a sand dab with the side of his fork.

"What kind of trickery and play-acting?" I asked.

Kavalov put down his fork and rested his wrists on the edge of the table. He rubbed his lips together and leaned over his plate towards me.

"Supposing"—he wrinkled his forehead so that his bald scalp twitched forward—"you have done injury to a man ten years ago." He turned his wrists quickly, laying his hands palms-up on the white cloth. "You have done this injury in the ordinary business manner—you understand?—for profit. There is not anything personal concerned. You do not hardly know him. And then supposing he came to you after all those ten years and said to you: 'I have come to watch you die.'" He turned his hands over, palms down. "Well, what would you think?"

"I wouldn't," I replied, "think I ought to hurry up my dying on his account."

The earnestness went out of his face, leaving it blank. He blinked at me for a moment and then began eating his fish. When he had chewed and swallowed the last piece of sand dab he looked up at me again. He shook his head slowly, drawing down the corners of his mouth.

"That was not a good answer," he said. He shrugged, and spread his fingers. "However, you will have to deal with this Captain Cat-and-mouse. It is for that I engaged you."

I nodded.

Ringgo smiled and patted his bandaged arm, saying:

"I wish you more luck with him than I had."

Mrs Ringgo put out a hand and let the pointed fingertips touch her husband's wrist for a moment.

I asked Kavalov:

"This injury I was to suppose I had done: how serious was it?"

He pursed his lips, made little wavy motions with the fingers of his right hand, and said:

"Oh—ah—ruin."

"We can take it for granted, then, that your captain's really up to something?"

"Good God!" said Ringgo, dropping his fork. "I wouldn't like to think he'd broken my arm just in fun."

Behind me the sallow servant spoke to his mate:

"He wants to know if we think the captain's really up to something."

"I heard him," the other said gloomily. "A lot of help he's going to be to us."

Kavalov tapped his plate with a fork and made angry faces at the servants.

"Shut up," he said. "Where is the roast?" He pointed the fork at Mrs Ringgo. "Her glass is empty." He looked at the fork. "See what care they take of my silver," he complained, holding it out to me. "It has not been cleaned decently in a month."

He put the fork down. He pushed back his plate to make room for his forearms on the table. He leaned over them, hunching his shoulders. He sighed. He frowned. He stared at me with pleading pale eyes.

"Listen," he whined. "Am I a fool? Would I send to San Francisco for a detective if I did not need a detective? Would I pay you what you are charging me, when I could get plenty good enough detectives for half of that, if I did not require the best detective I could secure? Would I require so expensive a one if I did not know this captain for a completely dangerous fellow?"

I didn't say anything. I sat still and looked attentive.

"Listen," he whined. "This is not April-foolery. This captain means to murder me. He came here to murder me. He will certainly murder me if somebody does not stop him from it."

"Just what has he done so far?" I asked.

"That is not it." Kavalov shook his bald head impatiently. "I do not ask you to undo anything that he has done. I ask you to keep him from killing me. What has he done so far? Well, he has terrorized my people most completely. He has broken Dolph's arm. He has done these things so far, if you must know."

"How long has this been going on? How long has he been here?"

"A week and two days."

"Did your chauffeur tell you about the black man we saw in the road?"

Kavalov pushed his lips together and nodded slowly.

"He wasn't there when I went back," I said.

He blew out his lips with a little puff and cried excitedly:

"I do not care anything about your black men and your roads. I care about not being murdered."

"Have you said anything to the sheriff's office?" I asked, trying to pretend I wasn't getting peevish.

"That I have done. But to what good? Has he threatened me? Well, he has told me he has come to watch me die. From him, the way he said it, that is a threat. But to your sheriff it is not a threat. He has terrorized my people. Have I proof that he has done that? The sheriff says I have not. What absurdity! Do I need proof? Don't I know? Must he leave finger-prints on the fright he causes? So it comes to this: the sheriff will keep an eye on him. 'An eye,' he said, mind you. Here I have twenty people, servants and farm hands, with forty eyes. And he comes and goes as he likes. An eye!"

"How about Ringgo's arm?" I asked.

Kavalov shook his head impatiently and began to cut up his lamb.

Ringgo said:

"There's nothing we can do about that. I hit him first." He looked at his bruised knuckles. "I didn't think he was that tough. Maybe I'm not as good as I used to be. Anyway, a dozen people saw me punch his jaw before he touched me. We performed at high noon in front of the post office."

"Who is this captain?"

"It's not him," the sallow servant said. "It's that black devil."

Ringgo said:

"Sherry's his name, Hugh Sherry. He was a captain in the British army when we knew him before—quartermasters' department in Cairo. That was in 1917, all of twelve years ago. The commodore"—he nodded his head at his father-in-law—"was speculating in military supplies. Sherry should have been a line officer. He had no head for desk work. He wasn't timid enough. Somebody decided the commodore wouldn't have made so much money if Sherry hadn't been so careless. They knew Sherry hadn't made any money for himself. They cashiered Sherry at the same time they asked the commodore please to go away."

Kavalov looked up from his plate to explain:

"Business is like that in wartime. They wouldn't let me go away if I had done anything they could keep me there for."

"And now, twelve years after you had him kicked out of the army in disgrace," I said, "he comes here, threatens to kill you, so you believe, and sets out to spread panic among your people. Is that it?"

"That is not it," Kavalov whined. "That is not it at all. I did not have him kicked out of any armies. I am a man of business. I take my profits where I find them. If somebody lets me take a profit that angers his employers, what is their anger to me? Second, I do not believe he means to kill me. I know that."

"I'm trying to get it straight in my mind."

"There is nothing to get straight. A man is going to murder me. I ask you not to let him do it. Is not that simple enough?"

"Simple enough," I agreed, and stopped trying to talk to him.

Kavalov and Ringgo were smoking cigars, Mrs Ringgo and I cigarettes over *crème de menthe* when the red-faced blonde woman in gray wool came in.

She came in hurriedly. Her eyes were wide open and dark. She said:

"Anthony says there's a fire in the upper field."

Kavalov crunched his cigar between his teeth and looked pointedly at me.

I stood up, asking:

"How do I get there?"

"I'll show you the way," Ringgo said, leaving his chair.

"Dolph," his wife protested, "your arm."

He smiled gently at her and said:

"I'm not going to interfere. I'm only going along to see how an expert handles these things."

IV

I ran up to my room for hat, coat, flashlight and gun.

The Ringgos were standing at the front door when I started downstairs again.

He had put on a dark raincoat, buttoned tight over his injured arm, its left sleeve hanging empty. His right arm was around his wife.

Both of her bare arms were around his neck. She was bent far back, he far forward over her. Their mouths were together.

Retreating a little, I made more noise with my feet when I came into sight again. They were standing apart at the door, waiting for me. Ringgo was breathing heavily, as if he had been running. He opened the door.

Mrs Ringgo addressed me:

"Please don't let my foolish husband be too reckless."

I said I wouldn't, and asked him:

"Worth while taking any of the servants or farm hands along?"

He shook his head.

"Those that aren't hiding would be as useless as those that are," he said. "They've all had it taken out of them."

He and I went out, leaving Mrs Ringgo looking after us from the doorway. The rain had stopped for the time, but a black muddle overhead promised more presently.

Ringgo led me around the side of the house, along a narrow path that went downhill through shrubbery, past a group of small buildings in a shallow valley, and diagonally up another, lower, hill.

The path was soggy. At the top of the hill we left the path, going through a wire gate and across a stubbly field that was both gummy and slimy under our feet. We moved along swiftly. The gumminess of the ground, the sultriness of the night air, and our coats, made the going warm work.

When we had crossed this field we could see the fire, a spot of flickering orange beyond intervening trees. We climbed a low wire fence and wound through the trees.

A violent rustling broke out among the leaves overhead, starting at the left, ending with a solid thud against a tree trunk just to our right. Then something *plopped* on the soft ground under the tree.

Off to the left a voice laughed, a savage, hooting laugh.

The laughing voice couldn't have been far away. I went after it.

The fire was too small and too far away to be of much use to me: blackness was nearly perfect among the trees.

I stumbled over roots, bumped into trees, and found nothing. The flashlight would have helped the laugher more than me, so I kept it idle in my hand.

When I got tired of playing peekaboo with myself, I cut through the woods to the field on the other side, and went down to the fire.

The fire had been built in one end of the field, a dozen feet or less from the nearest tree. It had been built of dead twigs and broken branches that the rain had missed, and had nearly burnt itself out by the time I reached it.

Two small forked branches were stuck in the ground on opposite sides of the fire. Their forks held the ends of a length of green sapling. Spitted on the sapling, hanging over the fire, was an eighteen-inch-long carcass, headless, tailless, footless, skinless, and split down the front.

On the ground a few feet away lay an Airedale puppy's head, pelt, feet, tail, insides, and a lot of blood.

There were some dry sticks, broken in convenient lengths, beside the fire. I put them on as Ringgo came out of the woods to join me. He carried a stone the size of a grapefruit in his hand.

"Get a look at him?" he asked.

"No. He laughed and went."

He held out the stone to me, saying:

"This is what was chucked at us."

Drawn on the smooth gray stone, in red, were round blank eyes, a triangular nose, and a grinning, toothy mouth—a crude skull.

I scratched one of the red eyes with a fingernail, and said:

"Crayon."

Ringgo was staring at the carcass sizzling over the fire and at the trimmings on the ground.

"What do you make of that?" I asked.

He swallowed and said:

"Mickey was a damned good little dog."

"Yours?"

He nodded.

I went around with my flashlight on the ground. I found some footprints, such as they were.

"Anything?" Ringgo asked.

"Yeah." I showed him one of the prints. "Made with rags tied around his shoes. They're no good."

We turned to the fire again.

"This is another show," I said. "Whoever killed and cleaned the pup knew his stuff; knew it too well to think he could cook him decently like that. The outside will be burnt before the inside's even warm, and the way he's put on the spit he'd fall off if you tried to turn him."

Ringgo's scowl lightened a bit.

"That's a little better," he said. "Having him killed is rotten enough, but I'd hate to think of anybody eating Mickey, or even meaning to."

"They didn't," I assured him. "They were putting on a show. This the sort of thing that's been happening?"

"Yes."

"What's the sense of it?"

He glumly quoted Kavalov:

"Captain Cat-and-mouse."

I gave him a cigarette, took one myself, and lighted them with a stick from the fire.

He raised his face to the sky, said, "Raining again; let's go back to the house," but remained by the fire, staring at the cooking carcass. The stink of scorched meat hung thick around us.

"You don't take this very seriously yet, do you?" he asked presently, in a low, matter-of-fact voice.

"It's a funny layout."

"He's cracked," he said in the same low voice. "Try to see this. Honor meant something to him. That's why we had to trick him instead of bribing him, back in Cairo. Less than ten years of dishonor can crack a man like that. He'd go off and hide and brood. It would be either shoot himself when the blow fell—or that. I was like you at first." He kicked at the fire. "This is silly. But I can't laugh at it now; except when I'm around Miriam and the commodore. When he first showed up I didn't have the slightest idea that I couldn't handle him. I had handled him all right in Cairo. When I discovered I couldn't handle him I lost my head a little. I went down and picked a row with him. Well, that was no good either. It's the silliness of this that makes it bad. In Cairo he was the kind of man who combs his hair before he shaves, so his mirror will show an orderly picture. Can you understand some of this?"

"I'll have to talk to him first," I said. "He's staying in the village?"

"He has a cottage on the hill above. It's the first one on the left after you turn into the main road." Ringgo dropped his cigarette into the fire and looked thoughtfully at me, biting his lower lip. "I don't know how you and the commodore are going to get along. You can't make jokes with him. He doesn't understand them, and he'll distrust you on that account."

"I'll try to be careful," I promised. "No good offering this Sherry money?"

"Hell, no," he said softly. "He's too cracked for that."

We took down the dog's carcass, kicked the fire apart, and trod it out in the mud before we returned to the house.

V

The country was fresh and bright under clear sunlight the next morning. A warm breeze was drying the ground and chasing raw-cotton clouds across the sky.

At ten o'clock I set out afoot for Captain Sherry's. I didn't have any trouble finding his house, a pinkish stuccoed bungalow with a terracotta roof, reached from the road by a cobbled walk.

A white-clothed table with two places set stood on the tiled veranda that stretched across the front of the bungalow.

Before I could knock, the door was opened by a slim black man, not much more than a boy, in a white jacket. His features were thinner than most American negroes', aquiline, pleasantly intelligent.

"You're going to catch colds lying around in wet roads," I said, "if you don't get run over."

His mouth-ends ran towards his ears in a grin that showed me a lot of strong yellow teeth.

"Yes, sir," he said, buzzing his s's, rolling the r, bowing. "The *capitaine* have waited breakfast that you be with him. You do sit down, sir. I will call him."

"Not dog meat?"

His mouth-ends ran back and up again and he shook his head vigorously.

"No, sir." He held up his black hands and counted the fingers. "There is orange and kippers and kidneys grilled and eggs and marmalade and toast and tea or coffee. There is not dog meat."

"Fine," I said, and sat down in one of the wicker armchairs on the veranda.

I had time to light a cigarette before Captain Sherry came out.

He was a gaunt tall man of forty. Sandy hair, parted in the middle, was brushed flat to his small head, above a sunburned face. His eyes were gray, with lower lids as straight as ruler-edges. His mouth was another hard straight line under a close-clipped sandy mustache. Grooves like gashes ran from his nostrils past his mouth-corners. Other grooves, just as deep, ran down his cheeks to the sharp ridge of his jaw. He wore a gaily striped flannel bathrobe over sand-colored pajamas.

"Good morning," he said pleasantly, and gave me a semi-salute. He didn't offer to shake hands. "Don't get up. It will be some minutes before Marcus has breakfast ready. I slept late. I had a most abominable dream." His voice was a deliberately languid drawl. "I dreamed that Theodore Kavalov's throat had been cut from here to here." He put bony fingers under his ears. "It was an atrociously gory business. He bled and screamed horribly, the swine."

I grinned up at him, asking:

"And you didn't like that?"

"Oh, getting his throat cut was all to the good, but he bled and screamed so filthily." He raised his nose and sniffed. "That's honeysuckle somewhere, isn't it?"

"Smells like it. Was it throat-cutting that you had in mind when you threatened him?"

"When I threatened him," he drawled. "My dear fellow, I did nothing of the sort. I was in Udja, a stinking Moroccan town close to the Algerian frontier, and one morning a voice spoke to me from an orange tree. It said: 'Go to Farewell, in California, in the States, and there you will see Theodore Kavalov die.' I thought that a capital idea. I thanked the voice, told Marcus to pack, and came here. As soon as I arrived I told Kavalov about it, thinking perhaps he would die then and I wouldn't be hung up here waiting. He didn't, though, and too late I regretted not having asked the voice for a definite date. I should hate having to waste months here."

"That's why you've been trying to hurry it up?" I asked.

"I beg your pardon?"

"*Schreckltchkeit*," I said, "rocky skulls, dog barbecues, vanishing corpses."

"I've been fifteen years in Africa," he said. "I've too much faith in voices that come from orange trees where no one is to try to give them a hand. You needn't fancy I've had anything to do with whatever has happened."

"Marcus?"

Sherry stroked his freshly shaven cheeks and replied:

"That's possible. He has an incorrigible bent for the ruder sort of African horse-play. I'll gladly cane him for any misbehavior of which you've reasonably definite proof."

"Let me catch him at it," I said, "and I'll do my own caning."

Sherry leaned forward and spoke in a cautious undertone:

"Be sure he suspects nothing till you've a firm grip on him. He's remarkably effective with either of his knives."

"I'll try to remember that. The voice didn't say anything about Ringgo?"

"There was no need. When the body dies, the hand is dead."

Black Marcus came out carrying food. We moved to the table and I started on my second breakfast.

Sherry wondered whether the voice that had spoken to him from the orange tree had also spoken to Kavalov. He had asked Kavalov, he said, but hadn't received a very satisfactory answer. He believed that voices which announced deaths to people's enemies usually also warned the one who was to die. "That is," he said, "the conventional way of doing it, I believe."

"I don't know," I said. "I'll try to find out for you. Maybe I ought to ask him what he dreamed last night, too."

"Did he look nightmarish this morning?"

"I don't know. I left before he was up."

Sherry's eyes became hot gray points.

"Do you mean," he asked, "that you've no idea what shape he's in this morning, whether he's alive or not, whether my dream was a true one or not?"

"Yeah."

The hard line of his mouth loosened into a slow delighted smile.

"By Jove," he said, "That's capital! I thought—you gave me the impression of knowing positively that there was nothing to my dream, that it was only a meaningless dream."

He clapped his hands sharply.

Black Marcus popped out of the door.

"Pack," Sherry ordered. "The bald one is finished. We're off."

Marcus bowed and backed grinning into the house.

"Hadn't you better wait to make sure?" I asked.

"But I am sure," he drawled, "as sure as when the voice spoke from the orange tree. There is nothing to wait for now: I have seen him die."

"In a dream."

"Was it a dream?" he asked carelessly.

When I left, ten or fifteen minutes later, Marcus was making noises indoors that sounded as if he actually was packing.

Sherry shook hands with me, saying:

"Awfully glad to have had you for breakfast. Perhaps we'll meet again if your work ever brings you to northern Africa. Remember me to Miriam and Dolph. I can't sincerely send condolences."

Out of sight of the bungalow, I left the road for a path along the hillside above, and explored the country for a higher spot from which Sherry's place could be spied on. I found a pip, a vacant ramshackle house on a jutting ridge off to the northeast. The whole of the bungalow's front, part of one side, and a good stretch of the cobbled walk, including its juncture with the road, could be seen from the vacant house's front porch. It was a rather long shot for naked eyes, but with field glasses it would be just about perfect, even to a screen of over-grown bushes in front.

When I got back to the Kavalov house Ringgo was propped up on gay cushions in a reed chair under a tree, with a book in his hand.

"What do you think of him?" he asked. "Is he cracked?"

"Not very. He wanted to be remembered to you and Mrs Ringgo. How's the arm this morning?"

"Rotten. I must have let it get too damp last night. It gave me hell all night."

"Did you see Captain Cat-and-mouse?" Kavalov's whining voice came from behind me. "And did you find any satisfaction in that?"

I turned around. He was coming down the walk from the house. His face was more gray than brown this morning, but what I could see of his throat, above the v of a wing collar, was uncut enough.

"He was packing when I left," I said. "Going back to Africa."

VI

That day was Thursday. Nothing else happened that day.

Friday morning I was awakened by the noise of my bedroom door being opened violently.

Martin, the thin-faced valet, came dashing into my room and began shaking me by the shoulder, though I was sitting up by the time he reached my bedside.

His thin face was lemon-yellow and ugly with fear.

"It's happened," he babbled. "Oh, my God, it's happened!"

"What's happened?"

"It's happened. It's happened."

I pushed him aside and got out of bed. He turned suddenly and ran into my bathroom. I could hear him vomiting as I pushed my feet into slippers.

Kavalov's bedroom was three doors below mine, on the same side of the building.

The house was full of noises, excited voices, doors opening and shutting, though I couldn't see anybody.

I ran down to Kavalov's door. It was open.

Kavalov was in there, lying on a low Spanish bed. The bedclothes were thrown down across the foot.

Kavalov was lying on his back. His throat had been cut, a curving cut that paralleled the line of his jaw between points an inch under his ear lobes.

Where his blood had soaked into the blue pillow case and blue sheet it was purple as grapejuice. It was thick and sticky, already clotting.

Ringgo came in wearing a bathrobe like a cape.

"It's happened," I growled, using the valet's words.

Ringgo looked dully, miserably, at the bed and began cursing in a choked, muffled, voice.

The red-faced blonde woman—Louella Qually, the housekeeper—came in, screamed, pushed past us, and ran to the bed, still screaming. I caught her arm when she reached for the covers.

"Let things alone," I said.

"Cover him up. Cover him up, the poor man!" she cried.

I took her away from the bed. Four or five servants were in the room by now. I gave the housekeeper to a couple of them, telling them to take her out and quiet her down. She went away laughing and crying.

Ringgo was still staring at the bed.

"Where's Mrs Ringgo?" I asked.

He didn't hear me. I tapped his good arm and repeated the question.

"She's in her room. She—she didn't have to see it to know what had happened."

"Hadn't you better look after her?"

He nodded, turned slowly, and went out.

The valet, still lemon-yellow, came in.

"I want everybody on the place, servants, farm hands, everybody downstairs in the front room," I told him. "Get them all there right away, and they're to stay there till the sheriff comes."

"Yes, sir," he said and went downstairs, the others following him.

I closed Kavalov's door and went across to the library, where I phoned the sheriff's office in the county seat. I talked to a deputy named Hilden. When I had told him my story he said the sheriff would be at the house within half an hour.

I went to my room and dressed. By the time I had finished, the valet came up to tell me that everybody was assembled in the front room—everybody except the Ringgos and Mrs Ringgo's maid.

I was examining Kavalov's bedroom when the sheriff arrived. He was a white-haired man with mild blue eyes and a mild voice that came out indistinctly under a white mustache. He had brought three deputies, a doctor and a coroner with him.

"Ringgo and the valet can tell you more than I can," I said when we had shaken hands all around. "I'll be back as soon as I can make it. I'm going to Sherry's. Ringgo will tell you where he fits in."

In the garage I selected a muddy Chevrolet and drove to the bungalow. Its doors and windows were tight, and my knocking brought no answer.

I went back along the cobbled walk to the car, and rode down into Farewell. There I had no trouble learning that Sherry and Marcus had taken the two-ten train for Los Angeles the afternoon before, with three trunks and half a dozen bags that the village expressman had checked for them.

After sending a telegram to the agency's Los Angeles branch, I hunted up the man from whom Sherry had rented the bungalow.

He could tell me nothing about his tenants except that he was disappointed in their not staying even a full two weeks. Sherry had returned the keys with a brief note saying he had been called away unexpectedly.

I pocketed the note. Handwriting specimens are always convenient to have. Then I borrowed the keys to the bungalow and went back to it.

I didn't find anything of value there, except a lot of fingerprints that might possibly come in handy later. There was nothing there to tell me where my men had gone.

I returned to Kavalov's.

The sheriff had finished running the staff through the mill.

"Can't get a thing out of them," he said. "Nobody heard anything and nobody saw anything, from bedtime last night, till the valet opened the door to call him at eight o'clock this morning, and saw him dead like that. You know any more than that?"

"No. They tell you about Sherry?"

"Oh, yes. That's our meat, I guess, huh?"

"Yeah. He's supposed to have cleared out yesterday afternoon, with his black man, for Los Angeles. We ought to be able to find the work in that. What does the doctor say?"

"Says he was killed between three and four this morning, with a heavyish knife—one clean slash from left to right, like a left-handed man would do it."

"Maybe one clean cut," I agreed, "but not exactly a slash. Slower than that. A slash, if it curved, ought to curve up, away from the slasher, in the middle, and down towards him at the ends—just the opposite of what this does."

"Oh, all right. Is this Sherry a southpaw?"

"I don't know," I wondered if Marcus was. "Find the knife?"

"Nary hide nor hair of it. And what's more, we didn't find anything else, inside or out. Funny a fellow as scared as Kavalov was, from all accounts, didn't keep himself locked up tighter. His windows were open. Anybody could of got in them with a ladder. His door wasn't locked."

"There could be half a dozen reasons for that. He—"

One of the deputies, a big-shouldered blond man, came to the door and said:

"We found the knife."

The sheriff and I followed the deputy out of the house, around to the side on which Kavalov's room was situated. The knife's blade was buried in the ground, among some shrubs that bordered a path leading down to the farm hands' quarters.

The knife's wooden handle—painted red—slanted a little toward the house. A little blood was smeared on the blade, but the soft earth had cleaned off most. There was no blood on the painted handle, and nothing like a finger-print.

There were no footprints in the soft ground near the knife. Apparently it had been tossed into the shrubbery.

"I guess that's all there is here for us," the sheriff said. "There's nothing much to show that anybody here had anything to do with it, or didn't. Now we'll look after this here Captain Sherry."

I went down to the village with him. At the post office we learned that Sherry had left a forwarding address: General Delivery, St. Louis, Mo. The postmaster said Sherry had received no mail during his stay in Farewell.

We went to the telegraph office, and were told that Sherry had neither received nor sent any telegrams. I sent one to the agency's St. Louis branch.

The rest of our poking around in the village brought us nothing—except we learned that most of the idlers in Farewell had seen Sherry and Marcus board the southbound two-ten train.

Before we returned to the Kavalov house a telegram came from the Los Angeles branch for me:

Sherry's trunks and bags in baggage room here not yet called for are keeping them under surveillance.

When we got back to the house I met Ringgo in the hall, and asked him:

"Is Sherry left-handed?"

He thought, and then shook his head. "I can't remember," he said. "He might be. I'll ask Miriam. Perhaps she'll know—women remember things like that."

When he came downstairs again he was nodding:

"He's very nearly ambidextrous, but uses his left hand more than his right. Why?"

"The doctor thinks it was done with a left hand. How is Mrs Ringgo now?"

"I think the worst of the shock is over, thanks."

VII

Sherry's baggage remained uncalled for in the Los Angeles passenger station all day Saturday. Late that afternoon the sheriff made public the news that Sherry and the black were wanted for murder, and that night the sheriff and I took a train south.

Sunday morning, with a couple of men from the Los Angeles police department, we opened the baggage. We didn't find anything except legitimate clothing and personal belongings that told us nothing.

That trip paid no dividends.

I returned to San Francisco and had bales of circulars printed and distributed.

Two weeks went by, two weeks in which the circulars brought us nothing but the usual lot of false alarms.

Then the Spokane police picked up Sherry and Marcus in a Stevens Street rooming house.

Some unknown person had phoned the police that one Fred Williams living there had a mysterious black visitor nearly every day, and that their actions were very suspicious. The Spokane police had copies of our circular. They hardly needed the H. S. monograms on Fred Williams' cuff links and handkerchiefs to assure them that he was our man.

After a couple of hours of being grilled, Sherry admitted his identity, but denied having murdered Kavalov.

Two of the sheriff's men went north and brought the prisoners down to the county seat.

Sherry had shaved off his mustache. There was nothing in his face or voice to show that he was the least bit worried.

"I knew there was nothing more to wait for after my dream," he drawled, "so I went away. Then, when I heard the dream had come true, I knew you johnnies would be hot after me—as if one can help his dreams—and I—ah—sought seclusion."

He solemnly repeated his orange-tree-voice story to the sheriff and district attorney. The newspapers liked it.

He refused to map his route for us, to tell us how he had spent his time.

"No, no," he said. "Sorry, but I shouldn't do it. It may be I shall have to do it again some time, and it wouldn't do to reveal my methods."

He wouldn't tell us where he had spent the night of the murder. We were fairly certain that he had left the train before it reached Los Angeles, though the train crew had been able to tell us nothing.

"Sorry," he draw led. "But if you chaps don't know where I was, how do you know that I was where the murder was?"

We had even less luck with Marcus. His formula was:

"Not understand the English very good. Ask the *capitaine.* I don't know."

The district attorney spent a lot of time walking his office floor, biting his finger nails, and telling us fiercely that the case was going to fall apart if we couldn't prove that either Sherry or Marcus was within reach of the Kavalov house at, or shortly before or after, the time of the murder.

The sheriff was the only one of us who hadn't a sneaky feeling that Sherry's sleeves were loaded with assorted aces. The sheriff saw him already hanged.

Sherry got a lawyer, a slick looking pale man with horn-rim glasses and a thin twitching mouth. His name was Schaeffer. He went around smiling to himself and at us.

When the district attorney had only thumb nails left and was starting to work on them, I borrowed a car from Ringgo and started following the railroad south, trying to learn where Sherry had left the train. We had mugged the pair, of course, so I carried their photographs with me.

I displayed those damned photographs at every railroad stop between Farewell and Los Angeles, at every village within twenty miles of the tracks on either side, and at most of the houses in between. And it got me nothing.

There was no evidence that Sherry and Marcus hadn't gone through to Los Angeles.

Their train would have put them there at ten-thirty that night. There was no train out of Los Angeles that would have carried them back to Farewell in time to kill Kavalov. There were two possibilities: an airplane could have carried them back in plenty of time; and an automobile might have been able to do it, though that didn't look reasonable.

I tried the airplane angle first, and couldn't find a flyer who had had a passenger that night. With the help of the Los Angeles police and some operatives from the Continental's Los Angeles branch, I had everybody who owned a plane—public or private—interviewed. All the answers were no.

We tried the less promising automobile angle. The larger taxicab and hire-car companies said, "No." Four privately owned cars had been reported stolen between ten and twelve o'clock that night. Two of them had been found in the city the next morning: they couldn't have made the trip to Farewell and back. One of the others had been picked up in San Diego the next day. That let that one out. The other was still loose, a Packard sedan. We got a printer working on postcard descriptions of it.

To reach all the small-fry taxi and hire-car owners was quite a job, and then there were the private car owners who might have hired out for one night. We went into the newspapers to cover these fields.

We didn't get any automobile information, but this new line of inquiry—trying to find traces of our men here a few hours before the murder—brought results of another kind.

At San Pedro (Los Angeles's seaport, twenty-five miles away) a negro had been arrested at one o'clock on the morning of the murder. The negro spoke English poorly, but had papers to prove that he was Pierre Tisano, a French sailor. He had been arrested on a drunk and disorderly charge.

The San Pedro police said that the photograph and description of the man we knew as Marcus fit the drunken sailor exactly.

That wasn't all the San Pedro police said.

Tisano had been arrested at one o'clock. At a little after two o'clock, a white man who gave his name as Henry Somerton had appeared and had tried to bail the negro out. The desk sergeant had told Somerton that nothing could be done till morning, and that, anyway, it would be better to let Tisano sleep off his jag before removing him. Somerton had readily agreed to that, had remained talking to the desk sergeant for more than half an hour, and had left at about three. At ten o'clock that morning he had reappeared to pay the black man's fine. They had gone away together.

The San Pedro police said that Sherry's photograph—without the mustache—and description were Henry Somerton's.

Henry Somerton's signature on the register of the hotel to which he had gone between his two visits to the police matched the handwriting in Sherry's note to the bungalow's owner.

It was pretty clear that Sherry and Marcus had been in San Pedro—a nine-hour train ride from Farewell—at the time that Kavalov was murdered.

Pretty clear isn't quite clear enough in a murder job: I carried the San Pedro desk sergeant north with me for a look at the two men.

"Them's them, all righty," he said.

VIII

The district attorney ate up the rest of his thumb nails.

The sheriff had the bewildered look of a child who had held a balloon in his hand, had heard a pop, and couldn't understand where the balloon had gone.

I pretended I was perfectly satisfied.

"Now we're back where we started," the district attorney wailed disagreeably, as if it was everybody's fault but his, "and with all those weeks wasted."

The sheriff didn't look at the district attorney, and didn't say anything.

I said:

"Oh, I wouldn't say that. We've made some progress."

"What?"

"We know that Sherry and the dinged have alibis."

The district attorney seemed to think I was trying to kid him. I didn't pay any attention to the faces he made at me, and asked:

"What are you going to do with them?"

"What can I do with them but turn them loose? This shoots the case to hell."

"It doesn't cost the county much to feed them," I suggested. "Why not hang on to them as long as you can, while we think it over? Something new may turn up, and you can always drop the case if nothing does. You don't think they're innocent, do you?"

He gave me a look that was heavy and sour with pity for my stupidity.

"They're guilty as hell, but what good's that to me if I can't get a conviction? And what's the good of saying I'll hold them? Damn it, man, you know as well as I do that all they've got to do now is ask for their release and any judge will hand it to them."

"Yeah," I agreed. "I'll bet you the best hat in San Francisco that they don't ask for it."

"What do you mean?"

"They want to stand trial," I said, "or they'd have sprung that alibi before we dug it up. I've an idea that they tipped off the Spokane police themselves. And I'll bet you that hat that you get no *habeas corpus* motions out of Schaeffer."

The district attorney peered suspiciously into my eyes.

"Do you know something that you're holding back?" he demanded.

"No, but you'll see I'm right."

I was right. Schaeffer went around smiling to himself and making no attempt to get his clients out of the county prison.

Three days later something new turned up.

A man named Archibald Weeks, who had a small chicken farm some ten miles south of the Kavalov place, came to see the district attorney. Weeks said he had seen Sherry on his—Weeks's—place early on the morning of the murder.

Weeks had been leaving for Iowa that morning to visit his parents. He had got up early to see that everything was in order before driving twenty miles to catch an early morning train.

At somewhere between half-past five and six o'clock he had gone to the shed where he kept his car, to see if it held enough gasoline for the trip.

A man ran out of the shed, vaulted the fence, and dashed away down the road. Weeks chased him for a short distance, but the other was too speedy for him. The man was too well-dressed for a hobo: Weeks supposed he had been trying to steal the car.

Since Weeks's trip east was a necessary one, and during his absence his wife would have only their two sons—one seventeen, one fifteen—there with her, he had thought it wisest not to frighten her by saying anything about the man he had surprised in the shed.

He had returned from Iowa the day before his appearance in the district attorney's office, and after hearing the details of the Kavalov murder, and seeing Sherry's picture in the papers, had recognized him as the man he had chased.

We showed him Sherry in person. He said Sherry was the man. Sherry said nothing.

With Weeks's evidence to refute the San Pedro police's, the district attorney let the case against Sherry come to trial. Marcus was held as a material witness, but there was nothing to weaken his San Pedro alibi, so he was not tried.

Weeks told his story straight and simply on the witness stand, and then, under cross-examination, blew up with a loud bang. He went to pieces completely.

He wasn't, he admitted in answer to Schaeffer's questions, quite as sure that Sherry was the man as he had been before. The man had certainly, the little he had seen of him, looked something like Sherry, but perhaps he had been a little hasty in saying positively that it was Sherry. He wasn't, now that he had had time to think it over, really sure that he had actually got a good look at the man's face in the dim morning light. Finally, all that Weeks would swear to was that he had seen a man who had seemed to look a little bit like Sherry.

It was funny as hell.

The district attorney, having no nails left, nibbled his finger-bones.

The jury said, "Not guilty."

Sherry was freed, forever in the clear so far as the Kavalov murder was concerned, no matter what might come to light later.

Marcus was released.

The district attorney wouldn't say goodbye to me when I left for San Francisco.

IX

Four days after Sherry's acquittal, Mrs Ringgo was shown into my office.

She was in black. Her pretty, unintelligent, Oriental face was not placid. Worry was in it.

"Please, you won't tell Dolph I have come here?" were the first words she spoke.

"Of course not, if you say not," I promised and pulled a chair over for her.

She sat down and looked big-eyed at me, fidgeting with her gloves in her lap.

"He's so reckless," she said.

I nodded sympathetically, wondering what she was up to.

"And I'm so afraid," she added, twisting her gloves. Her chin trembled. Her lips formed words jerkily: "They've come back to the bungalow."

"Yeah?" I sat up straight. I knew who *they* were.

"They can't," she cried, "have come back for any reason except that they mean to murder Dolph as they did father. And he won't listen to me. He's so sure of himself. He laughs and calls me a foolish child, and tells me he can take care of himself. But he can't. Not, at least, with a broken arm. And they'll kill him as they killed father. I know it. I know it."

"Sherry hates your husband as much as he hated your father?"

"Yes. That's it. He does. Dolph was working for father, but Dolph's part in the—the business that led up to Hugh's trouble was more—more active than father's. Will you—will you keep them from killing Dolph? Will you?"

"Surely."

"And you mustn't let Dolph know," she insisted, "and if he does find out you're watching them, you mustn't tell him I got you to. He'd be angry with me. I asked him to send for you, but he—" She broke off, looking embarrassed: I supposed her husband had mentioned my lack of success in keeping Kavalov alive. "But he wouldn't."

"How long have they been back?"

"Since the day before yesterday."

"Any demonstrations?"

"You mean things like happened before? I don't know. Dolph would hide them from me."

"I'll be down tomorrow," I promised. "If you'll take my advice you'll tell your husband that you've employed me, but I won't tell him if you don't."

"And you won't let them harm Dolph?"

I promised to do my best, took some money away from her, gave her a receipt, and bowed her out.

Shortly after dark that evening I reached Farewell.

X

The bungalow's windows were lighted when I passed it on my way uphill. I was tempted to get out of my coupé and do some snooping, but was afraid that I couldn't out-Indian Marcus on his own grounds, and so went on.

When I turned into the dirt road leading to the vacant house I had spotted on my first trip to Farewell, I switched off the coupé's lights and crept along by the light of a very white moon overhead.

Close to the vacant house I got the coupé off the path and at least partly hidden by bushes.

Then I went up on the rickety porch, located the bungalow, and began to adjust my field glasses to it.

I had them partly adjusted when the bungalow's front door opened, letting out a slice of yellow light and two people.

One of the people was a woman.

Another least turn of the set-screw and her face came clear in my eyes—Mrs Ringgo.

She raised her coat collar around her face and hurried away down the cobbled walk. Sherry stood on the veranda looking after her.

When she reached the road she began running uphill, towards her house.

Sherry went indoors and shut the door.

I took the glasses away from my eyes and looked around for a place where I could sit. The only spot I could find where sitting wouldn't interfere with my view of the bungalow was the porch-rail. I made myself as comfortable as possible there, with a shoulder against the corner post, and prepared for an evening of watchful waiting.

Two hours and a half later a man turned into the cobbled walk from the road. He walked swiftly to the bungalow, with a cautious sort of swiftness, and he looked from side to side as he walked.

I suppose he knocked on the door.

The door opened, throwing a yellow glow on his face, Dolph Ringgo's face.

He went indoors. The door shut.

My watch-tower's fault was that the bungalow could only be reached from it roundabout by the path and road. There was no way of cutting cross-country.

I put away the field glasses, left the porch, and set out for the bungalow; I wasn't sure that I could find another good spot for the coupé, so I left it where it was and walked.

I was afraid to take a chance on the cobbled walk.

Twenty feet above it, I left the road and moved as silently as I could over sod and among trees, bushes and flowers. I knew the sort of folks I was playing with: I carried my gun in my hand.

All of the bungalow's windows on my side showed lights, but all the windows were closed and their blinds drawn. I didn't like the way the light that came through the blinds helped the moon illuminate the surrounding ground. That had been swell when I was up on the ridge getting cock-eyed squinting through glasses. It was sour now that I was trying to get close enough to do some profitable listening.

I stopped in the closest dark spot I could find—fifteen feet from the building—to think the situation over.

Crouching there, I heard something.

It wasn't in the right place. It wasn't what I wanted to hear. It was the sound of somebody coming down the walk towards the house.

I wasn't sure that I couldn't be seen from the path. I turned my head to make sure. And by turning my head I gave myself away.

Mrs Ringgo jumped, stopped dead still in the path, and then cried:

"Is Dolph in there? Is he? Is he?"

I was trying to tell her that he was by nodding, but she made so much noise with her *Is he's* that I had to say "Yeah" out loud to make her hear.

I don't know whether the noise we made hurried things up indoors or not, but guns had started going off inside the bungalow.

You don't stop to count shots in circumstances like those, and anyway these were too blurred together for accurate score-keeping, but my impression was that at least fifty of them had been fired by the time I was bruising my shoulder on the front door.

Luckily, it was a California door. It went in the second time I hit it.

Inside was a reception hall opening through a wide arched doorway into a living-room. The air was hazy and the stink of burnt powder was sharp.

Sherry was on the polished floor by the arch, wriggling sidewise on one elbow and one knee, trying to reach a Luger that lay on an amber rug some four feet away. His upper teeth were sunk deep into his lower lip, and he was coughing little stomach coughs as he wriggled.

At the other end of the room, Ringgo was upright on his knees, steadily working the trigger of a black revolver in his good hand. The pistol was empty. It went snap, snap, snap, snap foolishly, but he kept on working the trigger. His broken arm was still in the splints, but had fallen out of the sling and was hanging down. His face was puffy and florid with blood. His eyes were wide and dull. The white bone handle of a knife stuck out of his back, just over one hip, its blade all the way in. He was clicking the empty pistol at Marcus.

The black boy was on his feet, feet far apart under bent knees. His left hand was spread wide over his chest, and the black fingers were shiny with blood. In his right hand he held a white bone-handled knife—its blade a foot long—held it, knife-fighter fashion, as you'd hold a sword. He was moving toward Ringgo, not directly, but from side to side, obliquely, closing in with shuffling steps, crouching, his hand turning the knife restlessly, but holding the point always towards Ringgo. Marcus's eyes were bulging and red-veined. His mouth was a wide grinning crescent. His tongue, far out, ran slowly around and around the outside of his lips. Saliva trickled down his chin.

He didn't see us. He didn't hear us. All of his world just then was the man on his knees, the man in whose back a knife—brother of the one in the black hand—was wedged.

Ringgo didn't see us. I don't suppose he even saw the black. He knelt there and persistently worked the trigger of his empty gun.

I jumped over Sherry and swung the barrel of my gun at the base of Marcus's skull. It hit. Marcus dropped.

Ringgo stopped working the gun and looked surprised at me.

"That's the idea; you've got to put bullets in them or they're no good," I told him, pulled the knife out of Marcus's hand, and went back to pick up the Luger that Sherry had stopped trying to get.

Mrs Ringgo ran past me to her husband.

Sherry was lying on his back now. His eyes were closed.

He looked dead, and he had enough bullet holes in him to make death a good guess.

Hoping he wasn't dead, I knelt beside him—going around him so I could kneel facing Ringgo—and lifted his head up a little from the floor.

Sherry stirred then, but I couldn't tell whether he stirred because he was still alive or because he had just died.

"Sherry," I said sharply. "Sherry."

He didn't move. His eyelids didn't even twitch.

I raised the fingers of the hand that was holding up his head, making his head move just a trifle.

"Did Ringgo kill Kavalov?" I asked the dead or dying man.

Even if I hadn't known Ringgo was looking at me I could have felt his eyes on me.

"Did he, Sherry?" I barked into the still face. The dead or dying man didn't move.

I cautiously moved my fingers again so that his dead or dying head nodded, twice.

Then I made his head jerk back, and let it gently down on the floor again.

"Well," I said, standing up and facing Ringgo, "I've got you at last."

XI

I've never been able to decide whether I would actually have gone on the witness stand and sworn that Sherry was alive when he nodded, and nodded voluntarily, if it had been necessary for me to do so to convict Ringgo.

I don't like perjury, but I knew Ringgo was guilty, and there I had him.

Fortunately, I didn't have to decide.

Ringgo believed Sherry had nodded, and then, when Marcus gave the show away, there was nothing much for Ringgo to do but try his luck with a plea of guilty.

We didn't have much trouble getting the story out of Marcus. Ringgo had killed his beloved *capitaine*. The black boy was easily persuaded that the law would give him his best revenge.

After Marcus had talked, Ringgo was willing to talk.

He stayed in the hospital until the day before his trial opened. The knife Marcus had planted in his back had permanently paralyzed one of his legs, though aside from that he recovered from the stabbing.

Marcus had three of Ringgo's bullets in him. The doctors fished two of them out, but were afraid to touch the third. It didn't seem to worry him. By the time he was shipped north to begin an indeterminate sentence in San Quentin for his part in the Kavalov murder he was apparently as sound as ever.

Ringgo was never completely convinced that I had ever suspected him before the last minute when I had come charging into the bungalow.

"Of course I had, right along," I defended my skill as a sleuth. That was while he was still in the hospital. "I didn't believe Sherry was cracked. He was one hard, sane-looking scoundrel. And I didn't believe he was the sort of man who'd be worried much over any disgrace that came his way. I was willing enough to believe that he was out for Kavalov's scalp, but only if there was some profit in it. That's why I went to sleep and let the old man's throat get cut. I figured Sherry was scaring him up—nothing more—to get him in shape for a big-money shake-down. Well, when I found out I had been wrong there I began to look around.

"So far as I knew, your wife was Kavalov's heir. From what I had seen, I imagined your wife was enough in love with you to be completely in your hands. All right, you, as the husband of his heir, seemed the one to profit most directly by Kavalov's death. You were the one who'd have control of his fortune when he died. Sherry could only profit by the murder if he was working with you."

"But didn't his breaking my arm puzzle you?"

"Sure. I could understand a phoney injury, but that seemed carrying it a little too far. But you made a mistake there that helped me. You were too careful to imitate a left-hand cut on Kavalov's throat; did it by standing by his head, facing his body when you cut him, instead of by his body, facing his head, and the curve of the slash gave you away. Throwing the knife out the window wasn't so good, either. How'd he happen to break your arm? An accident?"

"You can call it that. We had that supposed fight arranged to fit in with the rest of the play, and I thought it would be fun to really sock him. So I did. And he was tougher than I thought, tough enough to even up by snapping my arm. I suppose that's why he killed Mickey too. That wasn't on the schedule. On the level, did you suspect us of being in cahoots?"

I nodded.

"Sherry had worked the game up for you, had done everything possible to draw suspicion on himself, and then, the day before the murder, had run off to build himself an alibi. There couldn't be any other answer to it: he had to be working with you. There it was, but I couldn't prove it. I couldn't prove it till you were trapped by the thing that made the whole game possible—your wife's love for you sent her to hire me to protect you. Isn't that one of the things they call ironies of life?"

Ringgo smiled ruefully and said:

"They should call it that. You know what Sherry was trying on me, don't you?"

"I can guess. That's why he insisted on standing trial."

"Exactly. The scheme was for him to dig out and keep going, with his alibi ready in case he was picked up, but staying uncaught as long as possible. The more time they wasted hunting him, the less likely they were to look elsewhere, and the colder the trail would be when they found he wasn't their man. He tricked me there. He had himself picked up, and his lawyer hired that Weeks fellow to egg the district attorney into not dropping the case. Sherry wanted to be tried and acquitted, so he'd be in the clear. Then he had me by the neck. He was legally cleared forever. I wasn't. He had me. He was supposed to get a hundred thousand dollars for his part. Kavalov had left Miriam something more than three million dollars. Sherry demanded one-half of it. Otherwise, he said, he'd go to the district attorney and make a complete confession. They couldn't do anything to him. He'd been acquitted. They'd hang me. That was sweet."

"You'd have been wise at that to have given it to him," I said.

"Maybe. Anyway I suppose I would have given it to him if Miriam hadn't upset things. There'd have been nothing else to do. But after she came back from hiring you she went to see Sherry, thinking she could talk him into going away. And he lets something drop that made her suspect I had a hand in her father's death, though she doesn't even now actually believe that I cut his throat.

"She said you were coming down the next day. There was nothing for me to do but go down to Sherry's for a showdown that night, and have the whole thing settled before you came poking around. Well, that's what I did, though I didn't tell Miriam I was going. The showdown wasn't going along very well, too much tension, and when Sherry heard you outside he thought I had brought friends, and—fireworks."

"Whatever got you into a game like that in the first place?" I asked. "You were sitting pretty enough as Kavalov's son-in-law, weren't you?"

"Yes, but it was tiresome being cooped up in that hole with him. He was young enough to live a long time. And he wasn't always easy to get along with. I'd no guarantee that he wouldn't get up on his ear and kick me out, or change his will, or anything of the sort.

"Then I ran across Sherry in San Francisco, and we got to talking it over, and this plan came out of it. Sherry had brains. On the deal back in Cairo that you know about, both he and I made plenty that Kavalov didn't know about. Well, I was a chump. But don't think I'm sorry that I killed Kavalov. I'm sorry I got caught. I'd done his dirty work since he picked me up as a kid of twenty, and all I'd got out of it was damned little except the hopes that since I'd married his daughter I'd probably get his money when he died—if he didn't do something else with it."

They hanged him.

IN MARCH *BLACK MASK*

...Ned Beaumont was clipping the end of a pale spotted cigar. The shakiness of his hands was incongruous with the steadiness of his voice asking: "Was Taylor there?" He looked at Madvig without raising his head.

"Not for dinner. Why?"

Ned Beaumont stretched out crossed legs, leaned back in his chair, moved the hand holding his cigar in a careless arc, and said: "He's dead in a gutter up the street."

Madvig, unruffled, asked: "Is that so?"

Ned Beaumont leaned forward. Muscles tightened in his lean face.

The wrapper of his cigar broke between his fingers with a thin cracking sound. He asked irritably: "Did you understand what I said?"

Madvig nodded slowly.

"Well?"

"Well what?"

"He was killed."

"All right," Madvig said. "Do you want me to get hysterical about it?"

Ned Beaumont sat up straight in his chair and asked: "Shall I call the police?"

Madvig raised his eyebrows a little. "Don't they know it?"

Ned Beaumont, looking steadily at the blond man, replied: "There was nobody around when I saw him. I wanted to see you before I did anything. Is it all right for me to say I found him?"

Madvig's eyebrows came down over blank eyes. "Why not?"

Ned Beaumont rose, took two steps towards the telephone, halted and faced the blond man again. He spoke with slow emphasis: "His hat wasn't there."

"He won't need it now." Then Madvig drew his brows together and said: "You're a—damned fool, Ned."

Ned Beaumont said, "One of us is," and went to the telephone....

7

DEATH AND COMPANY

BLACK MASK, NOVEMBER 1930

The Continental Op turns in a Case.

The old man introduced me to the other man in his office—his name was Chappell—and said: "Sit down."

I sat down.

Chappell was a man of forty-five or so, solidly built and dark-complexioned, but shaky and washed out by worry or grief or fear. His eyes were red-rimmed and their lower lids sagged, as did his lower lip. His hand, when I shook it, had been flabby and damp.

The Old Man picked up a piece of paper from his desk and held it out to me. I took it. It was a letter crudely printed in ink, all capital letters.

> MARTIN CHAPPELL
> *DEAR SIR—*
> *IF YOU EVER WANT TO SEE YOUR WIFE ALIVE AGAIN YOU WILL DO JUST WHAT YOU ARE TOLD AND THAT IS GO TO THE LOT ON*

THE CORNER OF TURK AND LARKIN ST. AT EXACTLY 12 TONIGHT AND PUT $3000 IN $100 BILLS UNDER THE PILE OF BRICKS BEHIND THE BILL BOARD. IF YOU DO NOT DO THIS OR IF YOU GO TO THE POLICE OR IF YOU TRY ANY TRICKS YOU WILL GET A LETTER TOMORROW TELLING YOU WHERE TO FIND HER CORPSE. WE MEAN BUSINESS.

DEATH & CO.

I put the letter back on the Old Man's desk.

He said: "Mrs Chappell went to a matinee yesterday afternoon. She never returned home. Mr Chappell received this in the mail this morning."

"She go alone?" I asked.

"I don't know," Chappell said. His voice was very tired. "She told me she was going when I left for the office in the morning, but she didn't say which show she was going to or if she was going with anybody."

"Who'd she usually go with?"

He shook his head hopelessly. "I can give you the names and addresses of all her closest friends, but I'm afraid that won't help. When she hadn't come home late last night I telephoned all of them—everybody I could think of—and none of them had seen her."

"Any idea who could have done this?" I asked.

Again he shook his head hopelessly.

"Any enemies? Anybody with a grudge against you, or against her? Think, even if it's an old grudge or seems pretty slight. There's something like that behind most kidnappings."

"I know of none," he said wearily. "I've tried to think of anybody I know or ever knew who might have done it, but I can't."

"What business are you in?"

He looked puzzled, but replied: "I've an advertising agency."

"How about discharged employees?"

"No, the only one I've ever discharged was John Hacker and he has a better job now with one of my competitors and we're on perfectly good terms."

I looked at the Old Man. He was listening attentively, but in his usual aloof manner, as if he had no personal interest in the job. I cleared my throat and said to Chappell: "Look here. I want to ask some questions that you'll probably think—well—brutal, but they're necessary. Right?"

He winced as if he knew what was coming, but nodded and said: "Right."

"Has Mrs Chappell ever stayed away over night before?"

"No, not without my knowing where she was." His lips jerked a little. "I think I know what you are going to ask. I'd like—I'd rather not hear. I mean I know it's necessary, but, if I can, I think I'd rather try to tell you without your asking."

"I'd like that better too," I agreed. "I hope you don't think I'm getting any fun out of this."

"I know," he said. He took a deep breath and spoke rapidly, hurrying to get it over: "I've never had any reason to believe that she went anywhere that she didn't tell me about or had any friends she didn't tell me about. Is that"—his voice was pleading—"what you wanted to know?"

"Yes, thanks." I turned to the Old Man again. The only way to get anything out of him was to ask for it, so I said: "Well?"

He smiled courteously, like a well-satisfied blank wall, and murmured: "You have the essential facts now, I think. What do you advise?"

"Pay the money of course—first," I replied, and then complained: "It's a damned shame that's the only way to handle a kidnapping. These Death and Co. birds are pretty dumb, picking that spot for the pay-off. It would be duck soup to nab them there." I stopped complaining and asked Chappell: "You can manage the money all right?"

"Yes.'"

I addressed the Old Man: "Now about the police?"

Chappell began: "No, not the police! Won't they—?"

I interrupted him: "We've got to tell them, in case something goes wrong and to have them all set for action as soon as Mrs Chappell is safely home again. We can persuade them to keep their hands off till then." I asked the Old Man: "Don't you think so?"

He nodded and reached for his telephone. "I think so. I'll have Lieutenant Fielding and perhaps someone from the District Attorney's office come up here and we'll lay the whole thing before them."

Fielding and an Assistant District Attorney named McPhee came up. At first they were all for making the Turk-and-Larkin-Street-brick-pile a midnight target for half the San Francisco police force, but we finally persuaded them to listen to reason. We dug up the history of kidnapping from Ross to Parker and waved it in their faces and showed them that the statistics were on our side: more success and less grief had come from paying what was asked and going hunting afterwards than from trying to nail the kidnappers before the kidnapped were released.

At half past eleven o'clock that night Chappell left his house, alone, with five thousand dollars wrapped in a sheet of brown paper in his pocket. At twenty minutes past twelve he returned.

His face was yellowish and wet with perspiration and he was trembling.

"I put it there," he said difficultly. "I didn't see anybody."

I poured out a glass of his whiskey and gave it to him.

He walked the floor most of the night. I dozed in a sofa. Half a dozen times at least I heard him go to the street door to open it and look out. Detective-sergeants Muir and Callahan went to bed. They and I had planted ourselves there to get any information Mrs Chappell could give us as soon as possible.

She did not come home.

At nine in the morning Callahan was called to the telephone. He came away from it scowling.

"Nobody's come for the dough yet," he told us.

Chappell's drawn face became wide-eyed and open-mouthed with horror. "You had the place watched?" he cried.

"Sure," Callahan said, "but in an all right way. We just had a couple of men stuck up in an apartment down the block with field-glasses. Nobody could tumble to that."

Chappell turned to me, horror deepening in his face. "What—?"

The door-bell rang.

Chappell ran to the door and presently came back excitedly tearing a special-delivery-stamped envelope open. Inside was another of the crudely printed letters.

> MARTIN CHAPPELL
> *DEAR SIR—*
> *WE GOT THE MONEY ALL RIGHT BUT HATE GOT TO HAVE MORE TONIGHT THE SAME AMOUNT AT THE SAME TIME AND EVERYTHING ELSE THE SAME. THIS TIME WE WILL HONESTLY SEND YOUR WIFE HOME ALIVE IF YOU DO AS YOU ARE TOLD. IF YOU DO NOT OR SAY A WORD TO THE POLICE YOU KNOW WHAT TO EXPECT AND YOU BET YOU WILL GET I T.*
> *DEATH & CO.*

Callahan said: "What the hell?"

Muir growled: "Them—at the window must be blind."

I looked at the postmark on the envelope. It was earlier that morning. I asked Chappell: "Well, what are you going to do?"

He swallowed and said: "I'll give them every cent I've got if it will bring Louise home safe."

At half past eleven o'clock that night Chappell left his house with another five thousand dollars. When he returned the first thing he said was: "The money I took last night is really gone."

This night was much like the previous one except that he had less hopes of seeing Mrs Chappell in the morning. Nobody said so, but all of us expected another letter in the morning asking for still another five thousand dollars.

Another special-delivery letter did come, but it read:

> MARTIN CHAPPELL
> *DEAR SIR*
> *WE WARNED YOU TO KEEP THE POLICE OUT OF IT AND YOU DISOBEYED. TAKE YOUR POLICE TO APT 313 AT 895 POST ST. AND YOU WILL FIND THE CORPSE WE PROMISED YOU IF YOU DISOBEYED.*
> *DEATH & CO.*

Callahan cursed and jumped for the telephone.

I put an arm around Chappell as he swayed, but he shook himself together and turned fiercely on me.

"You've killed her!" he cried.

"Hell with that," Muir barked. "Let's get going."

Muir, Chappell, and I went out to Chappell's car, which had stood two nights in front of the house. Callahan ran out to join us as we were moving away.

The Post Street address was only a ten-minute ride from Chappell's house the way we did it. It took a couple of more minutes to find the manager of the apartment house and to take her keys away from her. Then we went up and entered apartment 313.

A tall slender woman with curly red hair lay dead on the living-room floor. There was no question of her being dead: she had been dead long enough for discoloration to have got well under way. She was lying on her back. The tan flannel bathrobe—apparently a man's—she had on had fallen open to show pinkish lingerie. She had on stockings and one slipper. The other slipper lay near her.

Her face and throat and what was visible of her body were covered with bruises. Her eyes were wide open and bulging, her tongue out: she had been beaten and then throttled.

More police detectives joined us and some policemen in uniform. We went into our routine.

The manager of the house told us the apartment had been occupied by a man named Harrison M. Rockfield. She described him: about thirty-five years old, six feet tall, blond hair, gray or blue eyes, slender, perhaps a hundred and sixty pounds, very agreeable personality, dressed well. She said he had been living there alone for three months. She knew nothing about his friends, she said, and had not seen Mrs Chappell before. She had not seen Rockfield for two or three days but had thought nothing of it as she often went a week or so without seeing some tenants.

We found a plentiful supply of clothing in the apartment, some of which the manager positively identified as Rockfield's. The police department experts found a lot of masculine fingerprints that we hoped were his.

We couldn't find anybody in adjoining apartments who had heard the racket that must have been made by the murder.

We decided that Mrs Chappell had probably been killed as soon as she was brought to the apartment—no later than the night of her disappearance, anyhow;

"But why?" Chappell demanded dumb-foundedly.

"Playing safe. You wouldn't know till after you'd come across. She wasn't feeble. It would be hard to keep her quiet in a place like this."

A detective came in with the package of hundred-dollar bills Chappell had placed under the brick-pile the previous night.

I went down to headquarters with Callahan to question the men stationed at a nearby apartment window to watch the vacant lot. They swore up and down that nobody—"not as much as a rat"—could have approached the brick-pile without being seen by them. Callahan's answer to that was a bellowed "The Hell they couldn't—they did!"

I was called to the telephone. Chappell was on the wire. His voice was hoarse.

"The telephone was ringing when I got home," he said, "and it was him."

"Who?"

"Death and Co., he said. That's what he said, and he told me that it was my turn next. That's all he said. 'This is Death and Co., and it's your turn next.' "

"I'll be right out," I said. "Wait for me."

I told Callahan and the others what Chappell had told me.

Callahan scowled. "—," He said, "I guess we're up against another of those—damned nuts!"

Chappell was in a bad way when I arrived at his house. He was shivering as if with a chill and his eyes were almost idiotic in their fright.

"It's—it's not only that—that I'm afraid," he tried to explain. "I am—but it's—I'm not that afraid—but—but with Louise—and—it's the shock and all. I—"

"I know," I soothed him. "I know. And you haven't slept for a couple of days. Who's your doctor? I'm going to phone him."

He protested feebly, but finally gave me his doctor's name.

The telephone rang as I was going towards it. The call was for me, from Callahan.

"We've pegged the finger-prints," he said triumphantly. "They're Dick Moley's. Know him?"

"Sure," I said, "as well as you do."

Moley was a gambler, gunman, and grifter-in-general with a police record as long as his arm.

Callahan was saying cheerfully: "That's going to mean a fight when we find him, because you know how tough that—is. And he'll laugh while he's being tough."

"I know," I said.

I told Chappell what Callahan had told me. Rage came into his face and voice when he heard the name of the man accused of killing his wife.

"Ever hear of him?" I asked.

He shook his head and went on cursing Moley in a choked, husky voice.

I said: "Stop that. That's no good. I know where to find Moley."

His eyes opened wide. "Where?" he gasped.

"Want to go with me?"

"Do I?" he shouted. Weariness and sickness had dropped from him.

"Get your hat," I said, "and we'll go."

He ran upstairs for his hat and down with it.

He had a lot of questions as we went out and got into his car. I answered most of them with: "Wait, you'll see."

But in the car he went suddenly limp and slid down in his seat.

"What's the matter?" I asked.

"I can't," he mumbled. "I've got to—help me into the house—the doctor."

"Right," I said, and practically carried him into the house.

I spread him on a sofa, had a maid bring him water, and called his doctor's number. The doctor was not in.

When I asked him if there was any other particular doctor he wanted he said weakly: "No, I'm all right. Go after that—that man."

"All right," I said.

I went outside, got a taxicab, and sat in it.

Twenty minutes later a man went up Chappell's front steps and rang the bell. The man was Dick Moley, alias Harrison M. Rockfield.

He took me by surprise. I had been expecting Chappell to come out, not anyone to go in. He had vanished indoors and the door was shut by the time I got there.

I rang the bell savagely.

A heavy pistol roared inside, twice.

I smashed the glass out of the door with my gun and put my left hand in, feeling for the latch.

The heavy pistol roared again and a bullet hurled splinters of glass into my cheek, but I found the latch and worked it.

I kicked the door back and fired once straight ahead at random. Something moved in the dark hallway then and without waiting to see what it was I fired again, and when something fell I fired at the sound.

A voice said: "Cut it out. That's enough. I've lost my gun."

It wasn't Chappell's voice. I was disappointed.

Near the foot of the stairs I found a light-switch and turned it on. Dick Moley was sitting on the floor at the other end of the hallway holding one leg.

"That damned fool maid got scared and locked this door," he complained, "or I'd've made it out back."

I went nearer and picked up his gun. "Get you anywhere but the leg?" I asked.

"No. I'd've been all right if I hadn't dropped the gun when it upset me."

"You've got a lot of ifs," I said. "I'll give you another one. You've got nothing to worry about but that bullet-hole if you didn't kill Chappell."

He laughed. "If he's not dead he must feel funny with those two .44s in his head."

"That was—damned dumb of you," I growled.

He didn't believe me. He said: "It was the best job I ever pulled."

"Yeah? Well, suppose I told you that I was only waiting for another move of his to pinch him for killing his wife?"

He opened his eyes at that.

"Yeah," I said, "and you have to walk in and mess things up. I hope to—they hang you for it." I knelt down beside him and began to slit his pants-leg with my pocket-knife.

"What'd you do? Go in hiding after you found her dead in your rooms because you knew a guy with your record would be out of luck, and then lose your head when you saw in the extras this afternoon what kind of a job he'd put up on you?"

"Yes," he said slowly, "though I'm not sure I lost my head. I've got a hunch I came pretty near giving the what he deserved."

"That's a swell hunch," I told him. "We were ready to grab him. The whole thing had looked phoney. Nobody had come for the money the first night, but it wasn't there the next day, so he said. Well, we only had his word for it that he had actually put it there and hadn't found it the next night. The next night, after he had been told the place was watched he left the money there, and then he wrote the note saying Death & Company knew he'd gone to the police. That wasn't public news, either. And then her being killed before anybody knew she was kidnapped. And then tying it to you when it was too dizzy—no, you are dizzy, or you wouldn't have pulled this one. Anyhow we had enough to figure he was wrong, and if you'd let him alone we'd have pulled him, put it in the papers, and waited for you to come forth and give us what we needed to clear you and swing him." I was twisting my necktie around his leg above the bullet-hole. "But that's too sensible for you. How long you been playing around with her?"

"A couple of months," he said, "only I wasn't playing. I meant it."

"How'd he happen to catch her there alone?"

He shook his head. "He must've followed her there that afternoon when she was supposed to be going to the theater. Maybe he waited outside until he saw me go out. I had to go downtown, but I wasn't gone an hour. She was already cold when I came back." He frowned. "I don't think she'd've answered the doorbell, though maybe—or maybe he'd had a duplicate made of the key she had."

Some policemen came in: the frightened maid had had sense enough to use the telephone.

"Do you think he planned it that way from the beginning?" Moley asked.

I didn't. I thought he had killed his wife in a jealous rage and later thought of the Death and & business.

Bonus: The Unfinished Op

"THREE DIMES"

I

McKay & Maclean had a stationery store in San Francisco's Market Street. They had cash registers and a normally honest sales force, but, like most retailers, they didn't trust these two things blindly. Twice a year they got the agency to check up the sales force. About once a year we would catch somebody beating the damper. The thief would be called into the partners' office and worked on. Usually he confessed, gave a more or less modest estimate of how much his stealing added up to in all, made that amount good, or promised to, and was fired. The sums were never large, and McKay & MacLean never worried the police with this petty larceny.

Dinky little jobs of that sort are not much fun for the operatives working on them, but detective agencies depend on them for bread and butter money: there are always plenty of them on tap, while murders, big swindles, kidnappings, and the rest of the showy crimes, are comparatively rare.

This time we nailed a boy of sixteen named Richard Allan. He was a tall stringy lad with wavy red hair, long-lashed blue eyes, girlish skin, and a pretty face that didn't show any character, good or bad. I hung a thirty-cent hold-out on him.

I had bought a box of writing paper for a dollar and a quarter, receiving my cash register receipt with it. Then I picked up a thirty-cent memoranda book from the counter rack, said, "I'll take this too," handed him three dimes, put the book in my pocket, and walked out. That was the routine.

He had no change to make, nothing to wrap up, and I was gone, leaving him a clear field in which to do whatever he wanted to do with the thirty cents. The catch in it was that I had a receipt for a dollar and a quarter, with his letter on it, and that the cash register tape was similarly stamped. If the partners, after getting my report, didn't find his letter with a thirty-cent sale on the tape immediately after the dollar and a quarter one, they had him cold. If he pocketed the thirty cents, the only thing that could save him would be that the next sale he rang up happened also to be a thirty cent one.

Well, he did pocket my thirty cents, and no coincidences came to his rescue.

He was the only employee we trapped this time. I had landed him. It was my job to break him down, to make him confess he had been stealing regularly, and to try to find out how much.

The boy was selling a fountain pen to a girl when I went into the store a couple of mornings after my purchase. I went through to the rear of the store and climbed steps to the partners' office on the mezzanine.

McKay's bony face was solemn and full of righteousness. There was a grim glint in his never warm gray eyes. He had put on a black necktie. Plump MacLean, ten years younger than his partner, was nervous, uncomfortable, and very plainly on hand only because McKay had insisted that it was his duty to be on hand. I had heard them argue about it before.

"Shall we have the young man up now?" McKay asked after we had good-morninged each other. His voice had already taken on the tone in which he always made for-your-own-good-and-let-it-be-a-lesson-to-you speeches to his victims on these occasions.

I nodded. MacLean wet his lips and said wearily:

"Let's get it over with."

"Miss Carter," McKay told the stenographer, "will you ask Mr Allan to come up?"

The girl went out of the office, and, when she returned, said that the boy would be up as soon as he had finished with a customer.

Ten minutes went by. McKay stared at a calendar with the look of a man thinking about what he was going to say. MacLean smoked cigarettes, fidgeted, and drew lopsided houses on his desk blotter.

McKay cleared his throat sternly and looked at the clock on the wall. Miss Carter stopped clattering her typewriter and went out. Presently she was back, frowning.

"Richard has gone out," she said. "Mr Marrow says he went out as soon as the customer left, without his hat. He called to him, asking where he was going, but Richard didn't say anything, just went on out."

MacLean's face brightened, and he began drawing a girl's head on the blotter.

McKay said angrily that it was nonsense. The boy couldn't have gone out like that. His employees didn't go out without saying where they were going. He got up from his chair and marched out of the office.

MacLean grinned happily at me and said:

"Scared him away. A good job, too. Him and his undertaker's tie—going around looking like a cartoon of a Prohibitionist."

McKay was all steamed up when he returned from downstairs. The boy had skipped. McKay wanted me to gallop after him, catch him, and drag him back.

MacLean protested:

"Aw, let the kid alone, John. What do you want to hound him for?"

McKay didn't like the word *hound*. It made him indignant. The boy should be brought back, confronted with the proof of his crime, and made to realize its seriousness, all for his own good. It was the clear duty of both partners to do their utmost to turn the youth's feet from the pathway of crime, and both would be morally responsible for any further missteps he might make if, through weak sentimentality, they failed to do their duty toward him. McKay unloaded on us the sermon he had meant for the boy. MacLean maliciously stuck to the word *hound*, but he was no match for his partner. He hadn't McKay's stubborn certainty that what he thought right was right.

McKay gave me the Allan boy's address. He lived in a Sacramento Street apartment with his sister. I went up there. It was a smallish building across the street from the Pacific Union Club. I pushed the button beside *408 Allan* in the vestibule directory. When I didn't get any answer I pushed one of the other buttons and the street door buzzed open. I went in, rode up to the fourth floor, found that 408 was the right-hand front apartment, tried its bell with no luck, and went downstairs again and out of the building. Huntington Square sits beside the Pacific Union Club grounds. I went over into the square, found a bench from which I could see both the street door of the apartment house and the windows of the Allans' apartment, and settled there. I spent the afternoon there. It was a pleasant enough afternoon except that too many children stumbled over my feet whenever I forgot to keep them tucked under the bench. I didn't see Richard Allan.

II

At six-fifteen, the Allans' window blinds were drawn down—I couldn't see who did it—and a moment later lights were turned on behind them. I hadn't seen Richard Allan go in. I had seen half a dozen men, enter the building since five o'clock and three or four young women, anyone of whom could have been the boy's sister.

By ten minutes after seven, when the Allans' lights went off, it was fairly dark.

Five minutes later one of the young women I had seen came out. She was a slender girl not a long way past twenty. Her green clothes were good and she knew how to wear them. She walked down the hill to Powell Street and boarded a cable car going downtown. That's what I did. The boy hadn't come home. The chances were now that he wouldn't come home till late. Or, if he was badly frightened, he might not be coming home at all. He might have phoned his sister. She might be going to meet him. What I hoped was that she was going to dinner. I hoped she hadn't grabbed a bite during the hour she had been inside. Sitting in the park, smoking cigarettes and meditating had given me an appetite.

HAMMETT'S NOTES, UNDATED
THREE DIMES

Boy working in store suspected of knocking back. Op makes test on him with 30¢ buy and secures dope. Boy becomes panic striken when being shaken down, beats it, goes in hiding, is helped and used by gang of crooks who are staging big crime, Op being drawn into it through his pursuit of boy.

McKay & Maclean's Stationery Store. Richard Allan. Celia Allan. Big Frank Stutz. Sterno Riley. The Indian Kid. Tommy Poole. Black Kate.

Op goes to store, checks boy, catches him with 30¢ purchase. Other Op's fail. Op returns two days later to grill boy. Boy recognizes him and, when proprietor sends for him, beats it. Next day proprietor phones agency that Celia had called up boy missing. Op sets out to find him.

Allan goes to Big Frank Stutz, who had been pointed out to him as con man, and asks him to help him. Big Frank pumps kid and frames a plan to use him.

Section Four: The Continental Op Novels

Red Harvest and *The Dain Curse*

CONTENTS

Red Harvest

1. The Cleansing of Poisonville 323
2. Crime Wanted—Male or Female 381
3. Dynamite 431
4. The 19th Murder 472

The Dain Curse

1. Black Lives 530
2. The Hollow Temple 583
3. Black Honeymoon 637
4. Black Riddle 687

1

THE CLEANSING OF POISONVILLE

BLACK MASK, NOVEMBER 1927

In recent years there have been too many examples where civic politics has degenerated into a business for profit. This story is the first, complete, episode in a series dealing with a city whose administrators have gone mad with power and lust of wealth. It is, also, to our minds, the ideal detective story—the new type of detective fiction which Black Mask is seeking to develop. You go along with the detective, meeting action with him, watching the development as the plot is unfolded, finding the clues as he finds them; and you have the feeling that you are living through the tense, exciting scenes rather than just reading a story. Poisonville is written by a master of his craft.

I first heard Personville called Poisonville in 1920, in the Big Ship in Butte, by a red-haired mucke named Hickey Dewey. But he also called his shirt a shoit, so I didn't think anything of what he had done to the city's name. Later, when I heard men who could manage their r's give it the same twist, I still didn't see anything in it but the meaningless sort of humor that used to make richardsnary the thieves' word for dictionary. In 1927 I went to Personville and learned better.

Using one of the phones in the station, I called the *Herald*, asked for Donald Willsson, and told him I had arrived.

"Will you come out to my house at ten this evening?" He had a pleasantly crisp voice. "It's 2101 Mountain Boulevard. Take a Broadway car, get off at Laurel Avenue, and walk two blocks west."

I promised to do that. Then I went up to the Great Western Hotel, dumped my bags, and went out to look at the city.

It wasn't pretty. Most of its builders had gone in for gaudiness. Maybe they had been successful at first. But since then the smelters, whose brick stacks stuck up tall against a gloomy mountain to the south, had yellow-smoked everything into a uniform dinginess. The result was an ugly city of 40,000 people, set in an ugly notch between two ugly mountains that had been all dirtied up by mining. Spread over this was a grimy sky that looked as if it had come out of the smelters' stacks.

The first policeman I saw needed a shave. The second had a couple of buttons off his shabby uniform. The third stood in the middle of Personville's main intersection—Broadway and Union Street—directing traffic with a cigar in one corner of his mouth. After that I stopped checking them up.

At nine-thirty I caught a Broadway car and followed the directions Donald Willsson had given me. His house was set in a hedged grassplot on the corner. The maid who opened the door told me he wasn't home. While I was explaining that I had an appointment a slender blonde woman of something less than thirty, in green crepe, came to the door. When she smiled her blue eyes didn't lose their stoniness. I repeated my tale to her.

"My husband isn't in now." A barely noticeable accent slurred her s's. "But if he's expecting you he'll probably be home shortly."

She took me upstairs to a room on the Laurel Avenue side of the house, a square room with a lot of books in it. We sat in leather chairs, half facing each other, half facing a burning coalgrate, and she set about learning my business with her husband.

"Do you live in Personville?" she asked first.

"No—San Francisco."

"But this isn't your first visit?"

"Yes."

"Really? How do you like our city?"

"I haven't seen enough of it to know." That was a lie. I had. "I just got in this afternoon."

Her shiny eyes stopped prying while she said: "I'm afraid you'll find it a dreary place." She shrugged and returned to her digging with: "I suppose all mining towns are like this. Are you engaged in mining?"

"Not just now."

She looked at the clock over the fire and said:

"It's inconsiderate of Donald to bring you out here and then keep you waiting, at this time of night, long after business hours."

I said that was all right.

"Though perhaps it isn't a business matter," she suggested.

I didn't say anything. She laughed—a brief laugh with something sharp in it.

"I'm ordinarily not curious about other people's affairs, really," she said gaily. "But you're so excessively secretive that you goad me on. You aren't a bootlegger, are you? Donald changes them so often."

I let her get whatever she could out of a grin. Downstairs a telephone bell rang. Mrs Willsson stretched her green-slippered feet out toward the burning coal and pretended she hadn't heard the bell. I didn't know why she thought that necessary.

She began: "I'm afraid I'll ha—"and stopped to look at the maid in the doorway. The maid said Mrs Willsson was wanted at the phone. She excused herself and followed the maid out. She didn't go downstairs, but spoke over an extension within earshot of my seat.

I heard: "Mrs Willsson speaking... Yes... I beg your pardon?... Who?... Can't you speak a little louder?... *What?*... Yes... Yes... Who is this?... Hello! Hello!" The telephone hook rattled. Then her quick steps sounded down the hallway.

I set fire to a cigarette and stared at it until I heard her going downstairs. Then I went to a window, lifted the edge of the blind, and looked out at Laurel Avenue and at the small white garage that stood in the rear of the house on that side. Presently a slender woman in dark coat and hat came into sight, hurrying from house to garage. She drove away in a Buick coupé. It was Mrs Willsson. I went back to my chair and waited.

Three quarters of an hour went by. At five minutes past eleven automobile brakes screeched outside. Two minutes later Mrs Willsson came into the room. She had taken off hat and coat. Her face was white, her eyes almost black.

"I'm awfully sorry." Her little tight-lipped mouth moved jerkily. "You've had all this waiting for nothing. My husband won't be home tonight."

I said I would get in touch with him at the *Herald* in the morning and went away—wondering why the green toe of her left slipper was dark and damp with something that could have been blood.

II

I walked over to Broadway and got into a street car. Three blocks north of my hotel I got off to see what the crowd was doing around a side entrance of the City Hall. Thirty or forty men and a sprinkling of women stood on the sidewalk looking at a door marked *Police Department*—a mixed crowd—men from mines and smelters still in their working clothes, gaudy boys from poolrooms and dance-halls, sleek men with cunning pale faces, men with the dull look of respectable fathers of families, a few just as respectable and dull women, and some ladies of the night.

On the edge of this congregation I stopped beside a square-set man in rumpled gray clothes. His face was grayish, too, even to the thick lips, though he didn't look much more than thirty—a broad, thick-featured face with intelligence in it. For color he depended on a red Windsor tie that blossomed over his gray flannel shirt.

"What's the rumpus?" I asked this fellow.

He looked at me carefully before he answered, as if to make sure that the information was going into safe hands. His eyes were as gray as his shirt, but not so soft.

"Don Willsson's gone to sit on the right hand of God—if God don't mind looking at the bullet holes in him."

"Who put them there?"

The gray man scratched the side of his neck and said: "Somebody with a gun."

I would have tried to find a less witty informant in the crowd if the red tie hadn't interested me.

"Sure. I'm a stranger in town," I said. "Hang the Punch and Judy on me—That's what strangers are for."

"Mr Donald Willsson, publisher of the *Morning* and *Evening Heralds*, son of the well-known Mr Elihu Willsson," he recited in a rapid sing-song, "was found lying in Hurricane Street a little while ago, very dead, having been shot several places. Does that keep your feelings from being hurt?"

"Yeah. Thanks." I put out a finger and touched a loose end of his tie. "Mean anything? Or just wearing it?"

"I'm Bill Quint."

"The hell you are!" I exclaimed, trying to place the name. "By gad, I'm glad to meet you!"

I dug out my card case and ran through the collection of credentials I had picked up here and there by one means or another. The red card was the one I wanted. It identified me as Henry F. Brannan (a lie), member in good standing of Industrial Workers of the World, Seaman's No.—. I passed it to Bill Quint. He read it carefully, front and back, returned it to me, and looked me over from hat to shoes—not trustfully.

"He's not going to die again," he said. "Which way are you going?"

"Any."

We walked down the street together, turned a corner, strolled along—aimlessly so far as I knew.

"What brought you in here, if you're a sailor?" he asked casually.

"Where'd you get that idea?"

"There's the card."

"Yeah. I got another that proves I'm a timberbeast. If you want me to be a miner I'll get one for that tomorrow."

"No, you won't. I run 'em here."

"Suppose you got a wire from Chi?" I asked.

"To hell with Chi. I run 'em here. Drink?"

"Only when I can get it."

We went through a restaurant, up a flight of stairs, and into a narrow room with a long bar and a row of tables. Bill Quint nodded and said, "Hello," to some of the boys and girls at tables and bar and guided me into one of the booths that lined the opposite wall. We spent the next two hours drinking whiskey and talking.

The gray man didn't think I was a good Wobbly, didn't think I had any right to the red card I had shown him and the other one I had mentioned. As chief muckademuck of the I.W.W. in Personville he considered it his duty to find out how-come, and not to let himself be pumped about radical affairs while he was doing it. That was all right with me. I was more interested in Personville affairs. He didn't mind discussing them. They were something he could hide behind between casual pokings into my business with the red cards, my radical status.

What I got out of him amounted to this:

For forty years old Elihu Willsson had owned Personville heart, skin, guts and soul. He was president and majority stockholder of the Personville Mining Corporation, ditto of the First National Bank, owner of the *Morning Herald* and the *Evening Herald*, the city's only newspapers, and at least part owner of nearly every other enterprise of any importance in the city. Along with this other property he owned a United States Senator, a couple of Representatives and most of the State Legislature. Elihu Willsson was Personville, and he was almost the whole state.

Back in the war days, when the I.W.W. was blooming, they had lined up a lot of the Personville Mining Corporation's help. The help hadn't been pampered, and they used their new strength to demand the things they wanted. Old Elihu gave in to them and bided his time. In 1919 it came. Business was slack. He didn't care whether he had to shut down for a while or not. He cut wages, lengthened hours, generally kicked the help back into their old place.

Of course the help had yelled for action. Bill Quint had been sent out from Chicago to give it to them. He had been against a strike—a walkout. What he advised was the old sabotage racket, staying on the job and gumming things up from the inside. But the Personville crew wouldn't listen to him. They wanted to put themselves on the map, make labor history. So they struck.

The strike lasted eight months. Both sides bled plenty. The Wobblies had to do their own bleeding. Old Elihu could hire strike-breakers, gunmen, National Guardsmen and even parts of the regular army to do his. When the last skull had been cracked, the last rib kicked in, organized labor in Personville was a used firecracker.

But, said Bill Quint, old Elihu didn't know his Machiavelli. He had won the strike, but he had lost his hold on city and state affairs. To beat the Wobblies he had had to let his lieutenants run wild. When the fight was over he couldn't shake them off. Personville looked good to them and they took it over. Elihu was an enfeebled czar. He had given his city to his hired thugs, and now he wasn't strong enough to take it away from them. They had won his strike for him and now they took his city for their spoils. He couldn't openly break with them because he was responsible for all they had done during the strike. They had too much on him.

"They?" I asked. "Have they got names?"

"Uh-huh." Quint emptied his glass and pushed his hair out of his eyes. We were both fairly mellow by the time we had got this far. "The strongest of 'em is probably Pete the Finn. Then there's Lew Yard. He's got a loan joint down on Parker Street, does a lot of bail business, maybe handles hot stuff, and is pretty thick with Noonan, the chief of police. This kid Max Thaler has got a lot of friends, too. Little, slick dark guy with something wrong with his throat—a gambler. They call him Whisper because he does, which is a pretty good reason. Those three about help Elihu run his city, help him more than he wants. But he has to play with them or else."

"This fellow who was knocked off tonight—Elihu's son—where did he stand?"

"Where Papa put him, and he's where Papa put him now."

"You mean his old man had him—?"

"Maybe, at that, but it's not my guess. This Don just came home and began running the papers for the old man. It wasn't like old Elihu, even if he is getting along in years, to let anybody take his city away from him. But he had to be cagey. He brought the boy and his French wife home from Paris and used him as his monkey—a nice fatherly trick. Don starts a clean-up campaign in his papers—clear the city of vice and corruption, which means clear it of Pete and Lew and Max, if it goes far enough. See? The old man's using the boy to pry 'em loose. Well, I guess they got tired of being pried."

"I could find things wrong with that guess," I said.

"Uh-huh, you could find things wrong with everything in Poisonville. Had enough of this gut-paint?"

I said I had and we went down to the street. Bill Quint walked as far as my hotel with me. In front of it a beefy man with a look of a copper in civvies stood on the curb talking to a man in a Stutz touring car.

"That's Whisper in the car," Quint told me.

I looked past the beefy man and saw Thaler's profile, young, dark, small, with features as regular as if they had been cut with a die—pretty features.

"He's cute," I said.

"Uh-huh," the gray man agreed. "So's dynamite."

III

The *Morning Herald* gave two pages to Donald Willsson and his death. His picture showed a pleasant, intelligent face with curly hair, smiling eyes and mouth, a cleft chin and a striped necktie. The story of his death was simple. At ten-thirty-five the previous night he had been shot four times with .32 pistol bullets in stomach, chest and back, in the eleven-hundred block of Hurricane Street and had been dead before anyone reached him.

Residents of the neighborhood who had looked out their windows after hearing the shooting had seen him lying on the sidewalk with a man and a woman bending over him. But the street was too dark for anyone to see anything or anybody clearly. The man and woman had disappeared before any of the neighbors had reached the street, and nobody knew exactly how or in what direction they had gone.

The police found that six shots had been fired at Willsson. The two that had missed him had hit a vacant house in front of which he had been shot. Tracing the course of the bullets from those two shots, the police had learned that the shooting had been done from a narrow alley across the street. Outside of that nobody knew anything.

Editorially, the *Morning Herald* gave a brief summary of the dead man's short career as a civic reformer and expressed its belief that he had been removed by some of the people who didn't want Personville cleaned up. The *Herald* said that the chief of police could best show his own innocence by speedily catching the murderer. The editorial was both blunt and bitter.

I finished it with my breakfast coffee, jumped a Broadway car, dropped off at Laurel Avenue, and turned down toward the dead man's house. I was half a block from it when something changed my mind.

A smallish young man in three shades of brown crossed the street ahead of me, showing a dark profile that was pretty—Max Thaler, alias Whisper. I reached the corner of Mountain Boulevard in time to catch the flash of his brown-covered rear leg vanishing into the late Donald Willsson's vestibule.

I went back to Broadway, found a drug store with a phone booth in it, searched the directory for Elihu Willsson's residence number, called it, told somebody who claimed to be Elihu's secretary that I had been brought from San Francisco by Donald Willsson, that I knew something about his death, and that I wanted to see his father. When I made it emphatic enough I got an invitation to present myself.

The czar of Poisonville was propped up in bed when his secretary—a noiseless, slim, sharp-eyed man of forty—brought me into the bedroom.

The old man's head was small and almost perfectly round under its thick crop of closecut white hair. His ears were too small and plastered too close to his head to spoil the spherical effect. His nose also was small, carrying down the curve of his bony forehead. Mouth and chin were straight lines chopping the sphere off. Below them a short thick neck ran down into white pajamas between square, meaty shoulders. One of his arms was outside the covers—a short, compact arm that ended in a thick-fingered, blunt, pink hand. His eyes were round, blue, small, and watery. But they looked as if they were hiding behind the watery film and under the bushy white eyebrows only until the time came to jump out and grab something. He wasn't the sort of man whose pocket you'd try to pick unless you had a lot of confidence in your fingers.

He ordered me into a bed-side chair with a two-inch jerk of his round head, chased the secretary away with another, and said:

"Now what is this about my son?" His voice was harsh. His chest had too much and his mouth not enough to do with his words for them to be very clear.

"I'm with the Continental Detective Agency's San Francisco branch," I told him. "We got a five hundred dollar check from your son and a letter asking that a man be sent over to do some work for him. I'm the man. I called him up when I got in yesterday afternoon. He told me to come to his house last night. I went there. He didn't show up. When I got downtown I learned he had been killed."

Elihu Willsson regarded me suspiciously and asked:

"Well, what of it?"

"While I was waiting your daughter-in-law got a phone message, went out, came back with what looked like blood on her shoe, and told me it was no use waiting, her husband wouldn't be home."

He sat straight up in bed and called Mrs Willsson a flock of things. When he ran out of words of that sort he still had some breath left, so he used it to shout at me:

"Is she in jail?"

I said I didn't think so.

"What the hell are you waiting for, damn you?" was his response to that.

When a man, who is too old or too sick to be smacked, curses you, you can either curse back or laugh. I laughed and said:

"Evidence."

"Evidence! What do you want? You—"

"Don't be such a chump," I interrupted his bawling. "Why should she have killed him?"

"Because she's a French hussy! Because—"

The noiseless secretary's frightened face appeared at the door.

"Get out o' here!" the old man roared at it, and the face went.

"She jealous?" I asked before he could go on with his ranting. "And if you don't yell maybe I'll be able to hear you anyway. My deafness is a lot better since I've been eating yeast."

He put a fist on top of each hump his thighs made in the covers and pushed his square chin at me.

"Old as I am and sick as I am," he said very deliberately, "I've a mind to get up and kick you down the stairs—"

I paid no attention to that and repeated:

"Was she jealous?"

"She was," he said, not shouting now, "and she's domineering, and spoiled, and suspicious, and greedy, and mean, and unscrupulous, and deceitful, and selfish, and damned bad—altogether damned bad."

"Any reason for her jealousy?"

"I hope so," he said bitterly. "I'd hate to think a son of mine would be faithful to *her*. Though likely enough he was. He'd do things like that."

"But you don't know any reason why she should have killed him?"

"Don't know any?" He was bellowing again. "Haven't I just been telling you that—"

"Yeah. But none of that means anything. It's kind of childish."

The old man flung the covers back from his legs and started to get out of bed. Then he thought better of it, raised his red face, and roared:

"Stanley!"

The door slid open to let the secretary pop silently in.

"Throw this—out!" his master ordered, waving a fist at me.

The secretary turned to me. I shook my head and suggested: "Better get help."

He frowned. We were about the same age. He was weedy, nearly a head taller than I, but fifty pounds lighter. Some of my hundred and ninety pounds were fat, but not all of them. The secretary fidgeted, smiled apologetically, and ran out to follow my advice.

"What I was about to say," I told the old man. "I intended talking to your son's wife again this morning, but I saw Thaler go in there, so I put off my call."

Elihu Willsson carefully pulled the covers up over his legs again, leaned his head back on the pillows, screwed his eyes up at the ceiling, and said:

"Hm-m-m, so that's the way it is, is it?"

"Mean anything?"

"She killed him," he said emphatically. "That's what it means."

Feet made noises in the hall, huskier feet than the secretary's. I waited until they were just outside the door and then started a sentence:

"You were using your son to dig up dirt on—"

"Get out o' here!" the old man yelled at those in the doorway. "And keep that damned door closed!"

"Now what was I using my son for?" he demanded when we were alone again.

"To knife Thaler, Yard and the Finn."

"That's a lie. I gave the boy the papers. He did what he liked with them."

"You ought to explain that to the gang. They'd believe you—oh, yeah!"

"Whatever they believe, what I'm telling you is so."

"Well, what of it? Your son won't come back to life just because he was killed by mistake—if he was."

"That woman killed him!"

"Maybe."

"Damn you and your maybes! She did! If you're going to fool around with any other numbskull ideas you might just as well go back to Frisco now. You and your damned—"

"I'll go back to San Francisco when I'm ready," I said unpleasantly. "And it won't be just now. I'm at the Great Western Hotel. Don't bother me unless you want to talk sense for a change."

His curses followed me down the stairs. The secretary hovered around the bottom step, smiling apologetically.

"A fine old rowdy," I growled.

"A remarkably vital personality," the secretary murmured.

IV

From the old man's house I went down to the *Herald* and hunted up the murdered man's secretary. She was a small girl of nineteen or twenty with wide chestnut eyes, light brown hair and a pale pretty face. Her name was Lewis.

She said she hadn't known about the check and letter that had brought me from San Francisco.

"But then," she explained, "Mr Willsson always liked to keep everything to himself as long as he could. It was—I—I don't think he trusted anybody here—completely."

"Not you?"

She flushed and said: "No. But of course he didn't know any of us very well. He had been here only such a short time."

"There must have been more to it than that," I protested.

"Well," she bit her lip and made a row of forefinger-printss down the polished edge of the dead man's desk top, "his father wasn't—wasn't in sympathy with what he was doing, and his father really owned the papers, so I guess it was natural for Mr Donald to think some of the employes might be more loyal to Mr Elihu than to him."

"The old man wasn't in favor of the clean-up campaign? Then why did he stand for it, if the papers were his?"

She bent her head to study the finger-prints she had made, and her voice was so low that I had to lean closer to catch the words.

"It's—it's not easy to understand unless you know—The last time Mr Elihu was taken sick he sent for Donald—Mr Donald. Mr Donald had lived in Europe most of his life, you know. Dr Pride had told Mr Elihu that he'd have to turn all his business affairs over to someone else, so he cabled his son to come home. But when he got here Mr Elihu couldn't make up his mind to let go of everything. But he wanted Mr Donald to stay, so he made him publisher of the papers. Mr Donald liked that because he had been interested in journalism in Paris, and when he found out how terrible everything was here—in civic affairs and so on—he started that reform campaign. He didn't know—he had been away since he was a boy—and he didn't know—he didn't—"

"He didn't know his father was in it as deep as anybody else," I helped her along.

She squirmed a little over her examination of the fingerprints on the desk, nodded reluctantly, and went on:

"Mr Elihu and he had a quarrel. Mr Elihu told him to stop stirring things up, but Mr Donald wouldn't. Maybe he would have if he had known—all there was to know. But I don't suppose it would ever have occurred to him that his father could have been really—deep in it. And Mr Elihu wouldn't tell him. I guess it would be hard for a father to tell a son a thing like that. He threatened to take the papers away from him. But Mr Donald said he'd start one of his own, and he said then he'd know his father had reasons for not wanting the light turned on Personville. He got terribly angry. I don't think Mr Elihu was going to do anything, but he got sick again, and things went along like they did."

"Donald Willsson didn't confide in you?" "No." It was almost a whisper.

"Then you learned all this—where?"

"I'm trying—trying to help you find the murderers," she said earnestly, looking at me with chestnut eyes that had pleas in them. "You've no right to—"

"Just now you'll help me most by telling me where you got this dope."

She stared at the desk again, chewing her lower lip. I waited. Presently she said:

"My father is Mr Elihu's secretary." "Thanks."

"But you mustn't think that we—"

"It's nothing to me," I assured her. "What was Willsson doing in Hurricane Street last night at a time when he had a date with me at his house?"

She said she didn't know. I asked her if she had been with him when he told me, over the phone, to come to his house at ten o'clock. She had.

"What did he do after that? Try to remember every least thing that was said and done from then until you left at the end of the day."

She leaned back in her chair, shut her eyes and wrinkled her forehead.

"You called up—if it was you he told to come to his house—around two o'clock. Mr Donald dictated some letters after that—one to a paper mill, one to Senator Keefer about some changes in post office regulations and—Oh, yes! He went out for about twenty minutes, a little before three o'clock. But just before he went he wrote out a check."

"For whom?"

"I don't know, but I saw him writing it."

"Where's his check book? Carry it with him?"

"No, it's here." She jumped up, went around to the front of his desk and tried the center drawer. "Locked."

I joined her in front of the drawer, straightened out a wire clip, and with that and a blade of my knife fiddled the drawer open. The girl took out a thin flat First National Bank check book. The last used stub was marked $5,000. Nothing else. No name. No explanation.

"He went out with this check," I said, "and was gone twenty minutes. Long enough to get to the bank and back?"

"It wouldn't take him more than five minutes to get there."

"What else happened just before he wrote the check? Did he get any mail, any messages, any phone calls?"

"Let's see." She shut her eyes again. "He was dictating a letter and—Oh, how stupid of me! He did have a phone call, and he said, 'Yes, I can be there at ten, but I shall have to hurry away to keep an engagement.' Then again he said, 'Very well, at ten.' That was all he said except, 'Yes, yes,' several times."

"Man or woman he was talking to?"

"I don't know."

"Think. There'd be a difference in his tone."

She thought and said: "Then it was a woman."

"Did Willsson leave before you did in the evening?"

"No. He—I told you my father is Mr Elihu's secretary. He and Mr Donald had an engagement for that evening—something about the papers' finances. My father came in a little after five. They were going to dinner together after they left here, I think."

That's all the Lewis girl could give me. The rest of my pumping brought up nothing. We frisked the dead man's desk—nothing. I went up against the girl at the switchboard—nothing. I put in half an hour working on city editors and the like—nothing.

I went away from the *Herald* tickling my brains with the information I had got from the girl. Not a bad haul—if a fair share of it happened to be true.

V

In the First National Bank I got hold of an assistant cashier named Albury, a nice-looking blond youngster of twenty-five or so.

"I certified the check for Willsson," he said after I had unloaded my story. "It was drawn to the order of Dinah Brand—$5,000."

"Dinah Brand—know who she is?"

"Oh yes, I know her."

"Mind telling me what you know about her?"

"Not at all. I'd be glad to, but I'm already eight minutes overdue at a meeting with—"

"Suppose you had dinner with me this evening?"

"Glad to," he said.

"Seven, at the Great Western?"

"Righto."

"I'll run along then," I said, "but tell me, has she an account here?"

"Yes, and she deposited the check this morning. The police have it now."

"And where does she live?"

"1232 Hurricane Street."

I said, "Well, well!" and, "See you tonight," and went away.

My next stop was in the office of the chief of police in the City Hall. Noonan, the chief, was a fat man with twinkling greenish eyes set in a round, red, jovial face. When I told him what I was doing in his city he seemed glad of it, and gave me a hand-shake, a cigar and a comfortable chair.

"Now," he said when we were settled, "tell me who killed the man."

"His secret's safe with me."

"You and me both," the chief said cheerfully through smoke. "But what do you guess?"

"You know more about it than I do. Tell me what you know and I'll tell you what I guess."

"Fair enough. 'T won't take long to tell. Willsson got a $5,000 check in Dinah Brand's name certified yesterday afternoon. Last night he was shot and killed by bullets from a .32 pistol less than a block from her house. People that heard the shooting saw a man and a woman bending over the remains. Bright and early this morning the said Dinah Brand deposits the said check in the bank. Well?"

"Who is this Dinah Brand?"

The chief dumped the ash off his cigar in the center of his desk, flourished the cigar in his fat hand, and said:

"A soiled dove, as the fellow says, a de luxe hustler, a big-league gold-digger."

"Gone up against her yet?"

"Nope. There's a couple of angles to be gathered in. So we're just keeping an eye on this baby and waiting. This I've told you is under the hat."

"Yeah. Now listen to this." And I told him what I had seen and heard while waiting in Donald Willsson's house the previous night.

When I had finished the chief bunched his fat mouth, whistled softly, and exclaimed:

"Man, that's an interesting thing you've been telling me. So it was blood on her slipper, was it? And she said her husband wouldn't be home, did she?"

"That's what I took it for," I replied to the first question, and, "Yeah," to the second.

"And have you talked to her since then?" he asked.

"No. I was up that way this morning, but a young fellow named Thaler went into the house ahead of me, so I put off my visit."

"Grease us twice! Are you telling me the Whisper was there?" His greenish eyes glittered happily.

"Yeah."

He threw his cigar on the floor, stood up, planted his fat hands on the desk top and leaned over them toward me, oozing delight from every pore.

"Man, man, you've done something!" he purred. "Dinah Brand is this Whisper's woman! Let's me and you just go out and kind of talk to the widow."

VI

We climbed out of a police department touring car in front of Mrs Willsson's. The chief stopped for a second with one foot on the bottom step to look at the black crepe hanging over the bell. Then he said: "Well, what's got to be done has got to be done," and we went up the steps.

Mrs Willsson wasn't anxious to see us, but people usually see the chief of police if he insists. This one did. We were taken upstairs to where our lady sat in the library. She was dressed in black. Her blue eyes had frost in them.

Noonan and I took turns mumbling condolences, and then he began:

"We just wanted to ask you a couple of questions. For instance, like where'd you go last night?"

She looked disagreeably at me, then back to the chief, frowned, and spoke haughtily:

"May I ask why I am being questioned in this manner?"

I wondered how many times I had heard that question asked while the chief, disregarding it, went on amiably:

"And then there was something about one of your shoes being stained. The right one, or maybe the left. Anyway it was one or the other."

A muscle began to twitch in her upper lip.

"Was that all?" the chief asked me. Before I could reply he made a clucking noise with his tongue and turned his genial face to the woman again. "I almost forgot—there was a matter of how you knew your husband wouldn't be home."

She rose a little unsteadily, holding the back of her chair with one hand.

"Under the circumstances, I'm sure you'll excuse—"

"'S all right." The chief made a big-hearted gesture with one beefy paw. "We don't want to bother you. Just where you went, and about the shoe, and how you knew he wouldn't be home. And, come to think of it, there's another—what Thaler wanted here this afternoon."

The woman sat down again, very rigidly. The chief looked at her—a tender smile making funny curves and lines in his fat face. After a little while her shoulders began to relax, her chin went lower, a curve came into her back. I moved a chair over to face her and sat in it.

"You'll have to tell us, Mrs Willsson," I said, making it as gravely sympathetic as I could. "It's all hopelessly muddled without these things explained."

Her body jerked stiff and straight in the chair again, and if her eyes were half so hard as they looked you could have cut diamonds with them.

"Do you think I have anything to conceal?" She turned each word out very precisely, except that the slight foreign accent slurred the "s" sound. "I did go out. The stain was blood. I knew my husband was dead. Thaler came to see me about my husband's death. Are your questions answered now?"

"Not fully." I shook my head. "We knew all that. Please, Mrs Willsson, this is as distasteful to us as to you. Won't you help us get it over with?"

"Very well!" Her blue eyes looked cold defiance into mine. She took a deep breath and spat out words like rain pattering on a tin roof. "While we were waiting for Donald I had a phone call. It was a man who wouldn't give his name. He said Donald had gone to the house of a woman named Dinah Brand with a five-thousand-dollar check. He gave me her address. I drove out there and waited down the street in the machine until Donald came out.

"While I was waiting I saw Thaler, whom I knew by sight. He went to that woman's house, but did not go in. He went away. Then Donald came out and walked down the street. I intended to drive home before he could get there. I had just started the engine when I heard the shots, and I saw Donald fall. I ran over to him. He was dead. I was frantic. Then Thaler came. He said if I was found there they would say I had killed him. He made me hurry back to the car and drive home. Is that enough?"

"Practically," Noonan assured her. "What did Thaler say this afternoon?"

"He urged me not to say anything." Her voice had suddenly become very small and flat. "He said either of us would be suspected if anyone knew we were there, because Donald had been killed coming from that woman's house after giving her money."

"Where did the shots come from?"

"I don't know. I saw nothing—except when I looked up—Donald falling."

"Did Thaler fire them?"

"No," she said quickly, and then mouth and eyes spread. She put a hand to her breast. "I don't know. I didn't think so, and he said he didn't. I don't know where he was. I don't know why I thought he hadn't."

"What do you think now?"

"He—he may have."

The chief winked at me, an athletic sort of wink in which all his facial muscles took part, and cast back a little farther:

"And you don't know who called you up?"

"He wouldn't give his name."

"Didn't recognize his voice?"

"No."

"What kind of voice was it?"

"He spoke in an undertone, as if afraid of being overheard. I had trouble understanding him."

"He whispered?" The chief's mouth hung open as the last sound had left it, and his greenish eyes sparkled greedily between their pads of fat.

"Yes—a hoarse whisper."

The chief shut his mouth with a click, opened it again to say persuasively:

"You've heard Thaler talk..."

She raised her head and looked at the chief.

"It was he!" she cried. "It was he!"

Noonan turned his broad back on her and beckoned me over to a window.

"We'll take her down to the Hall and have her go over it again with the Prosecuting Attorney and a stenog," he muttered triumphantly.

"All right." I looked at my watch. "But I've got a date for seven. I'm going to run along. I'll see you in the morning, or you can get me at the Great Western if anything turns up."

"Well, be good," he said.

VII

The assistant cashier, young Albury, was sitting in the lobby when I reached the hotel. We went up to my room, had some ice-water brought, used its ice to put chill in Scotch, lemon-juice and grenadine, and then went down to the dining-room.

"Now tell me about the lady," I said when we were working on the soup.

"Have you seen her yet?" he asked.

"Not yet."

"But you've heard something about her?"

"Only that she's an expert in her line."

"She is," he agreed. "You'll go see her, of course. You'll be disappointed at first. Then, without being able to say how or when it happened, you'll find you've forgotten your disappointment, and the first thing you know you'll be telling her your life's history, and all your troubles and hopes." He laughed with boyish ruefulness. "And then you're caught—absolutely caught."

"Thanks for the warning. How'd you come by the information?" He grinned shamefacedly across his suspended soup spoon and confessed:

"Bought it."

"Then I suppose you paid plenty. I hear the lady likes dinero."

"She's money-mad, all right, but somehow you don't mind it. She's so thoroughly mercenary, so frankly greedy, that there's nothing disagreeable about it. You'll understand what I mean when you get to know her."

"Maybe. Mind telling me how you came to part with her?"

"No, I don't mind. I spent it all, that's how."

"Cold-blooded like that?"

His face flushed a little. He nodded.

"You seemed to have taken it well, anyway," I said.

"There's nothing else to do." The flush in his pleasant young face deepened and he spoke hesitantly. "And it happens I owe her a lot for it. She—I'm going to tell you this—I want you to see this side of her. I had a little money. After that was gone—you must remember I'm not very old and I was head over heels—there was the bank's money. I had—You don't care whether I had actually done anything or just thinking about it. Anyhow, she found it out. I never could hide anything from her. And that was the end."

"She gave you the air?"

"Yes, she did. So if it hadn't been for her you might have been hunting for me now. I owe her that!" He wrinkled his forehead earnestly. "You won't say anything about this—you know what I mean. I just wanted you to know that she had her good side, too."

"Maybe she has. Or maybe it was that she didn't think she'd get enough to pay for the chance of being caught in a jam."

He turned that over in his mind for a minute and shook his head.

"How about Dan Rolff?" he objected.

"Who's he?"

"A down-and-outer—t. b. He's supposed to be her brother, or half-brother, or something of the sort. He lives there. She keeps him. She's not in love with him or anything of the sort. She just found him somewhere and took him in."

"Mark up one for her. Any more?"

"There was that radical chap she used to play with. It's a cinch she never got much money out of him."

"What radical chap was this?"

"The chap who came here in 1919 to run the strike—Quint."

"So he's *still* on her list?"

"That's supposed to be the reason he stayed after the strike was over."

"So he's *still* on her list?"

"No. She told me she was afraid of him—he had threatened to kill her."

"Has she had everybody in town on her string at one time or another?" I asked.

"Everybody she wanted," he said, and he said it seriously.

"Well, what about her and Donald Willsson?"

"I don't know a thing about that—absolutely nothing. He had never issued any cheeks to her before, that I know of."

"Then he was probably recent?"

"Probably—but why did he have the check certified?"

I didn't know. I could have made some guesses, but none that I wanted to put into words. During the rest of the dinner we talked back and forth over the ground we had already covered, and I picked up nothing else of any value. At eight-thirty young Albury ran off to keep a date.

Bill Quint had told me he was living in the Miners' Hotel in Forest Street. I walked down that way and was lucky enough to run into him in the street half a block or so from the hotel.

"Hello," I hailed him, "I was just coming down to see you."

He stopped in front of me, looked me up and down, growled, "So you're a lousy gumshoe," pursed his gray lips, and by forcing breath out through them made a noise like a rag tearing.

"That's the bunk!" I complained. "I come all the way down here to rope you and you're smarted up!"

"What'd you want to know this time?" he demanded.

"I'll save my breath. You'd only lie to me. So long."

I walked back to Broadway, found a taxi, and told the driver to take me to 1232 Hurricane Street.

VIII

My destination was a gray frame cottage with an iron picket fence around it. When I rang the bell the door was opened by a very thin man with a very tired face that had no color in it except a red spot the size of a half-dollar high on each cheek. This, I thought, is the lunger, Dan Rolff.

"I'd like to see Miss Brand," I told him.

"What name shall I tell her?" His voice was a sick man's voice, also an educated man's.

"It wouldn't mean anything to her. I want to see her about Willsson's death."

He looked at me with level, tired, dark eyes and said: "Yes?"

"I'm from the San Francisco office of the Continental Detective Agency. We're interested in the murder."

"That's nice of you," he said ironically. "Come in."

I went in—into a ground-floor room where a young woman sat at a table with a lot of papers on it. The room was disorderly, cluttered up. There were too many pieces of furniture in it, and none of them seemed to be in its proper place.

"Dinah," the lunger introduced me, "this gentleman has come from San Francisco to inquire into the late Mr Willsson's demise on behalf of the Continental Detective Agency."

The young woman got up from the table, kicked a couple of newspapers out of her way, and came toward me with one hand out.

She was a couple of inches taller than I, which would make her about five feet eight, with a broad-shouldered, full-breasted, round-hipped body and big muscular legs. The hand she gave me was soft, warm, strong. Her face was the face of a girl of twenty-five, already beginning to show signs of wear. Little lines ran across the corners of her big ripe mouth. Other lines made nets around her thick-lashed eyes. They were large eyes, blue, and a bit blood-shot. Her coarse brown hair needed trimming and was parted crookedly. Her upper lip had been rouged higher on one side than the other. She wore a dress of a particularly unbecoming wine color, and it gaped here and there down one side, where she had neglected to snap the fasteners, or they had popped open. There was a run in the front of her left stocking.

This was Dinah Brand, Poisonville's Cleopatra, if there was any truth in what I had been told.

"His father sent for you, of course," she said as she moved a pair of lizard-skin slippers and a cup and saucer off a chair to make room for me. Her voice was soft, lazy.

I told her the truth:

"Donald Willsson sent for me. I was waiting to see him when he was out being killed."

"Don't go away, Dan," she called to Rolff. He came back into the room. She returned to her place at the table. He sat on the opposite side, leaning his thin face on a thinner hand, staring at me without interest. She drew her brows together, making two creases between them, and asked: "You mean he knew someone was going to try to kill him?"

"I don't know," I admitted. "He didn't say what he wanted—maybe just help in the cleanup."

"But do you—?"

I made a complaint:

"It's no fun being a sleuth when somebody steals your stuff—does all the asking."

"I like to find out what's going on," she said, with a little laugh gurgling down in her throat.

"I'm that way, too," I replied. "For instance, I'd like to know why you made him have the check certified."

Very casually, Dan Rolff shifted in his chair, leaning back, lowering his thin hands out of sight below the table's edge.

"So you found out about that?" She crossed left leg over right and looked down. Her eyes focused on the run in her stocking. "I'm going to stop wearing 'em! I paid five bucks for these socks yesterday. Now look at the damned things! Every day—runs! Runs! Runs!"

"It's no secret," I said. "I mean the check, not the runs. Noonan's got it."

She looked at Rolff, who stopped watching me long enough to nod once.

"If you talked my language," she drawled, looking at me through narrowed lashes, "maybe I could give you some help."

"Maybe I could talk it if I knew what it was."

"Money," she explained. "The more the better. I like it."

I got proverbial:

"Money saved is money earned. I can save you trouble and dough."

"I can save my own. What I need is more."

"Giving it to lawyers isn't saving it."

"That doesn't mean anything to me," she said.

"The police haven't told or asked you anything about the check?"

She shook her head no.

"I thought not," I said. "Noonan's figuring on hanging the rap on you as well as Whisper."

"Don't scare me," she lisped, "I'm only a child."

"Noonan knows that Thaler knew Willsson brought the check here, that Thaler came while he was here but didn't get in, that Thaler was hanging around the neighborhood when Willsson was shot, and that Thaler and a woman were seen bending over the dead man."

The girl picked a pencil up from the table and thoughtfully scratched her cheek with it. It made little black lines over the rouge. Rolff's eyes had suddenly lost their weariness. They were bright, feverish, fixed on mine. He leaned forward, but kept his hands out of sight below the table.

"Those things," he said softly, "concern Thaler, not Miss Brand."

"Thaler and Miss Brand are not strangers," I pointed out. "Willsson brought a five-thousand-dollar check here and was killed leaving. That way, Miss Brand might have had trouble cashing it—if Willsson hadn't been thoughtful enough to have it certified."

"Say!" the girl objected, "If I'd been going to kill him I'd have done it in here where nobody could have seen it! Or waited till he got out of sight of the house! What kind of dumb onion do you take me for?"

"I'm not altogether satisfied you killed him," I assured her. "I'm just telling you the fat chief means to hang it on you."

"What *are you* trying to do?"

"Learn who killed him—not who might have or could have—who did."

"I could give you some help," she said, "but there'd have to be something in it for me."

"Safety," I reminded her, but she shook her head.

"I mean it would have to get me something in a financial way," she went into details. "It'd be worth something to you, and you ought to pay, even if not a lot."

"Can't be done." I grinned at her. "Forget your bank-roll for once and go in for charity. Pretend I'm Bill Quint."

Dan Rolff started up from his chair, his lips white as the rest of his face, his eyes burning. He sat down again when the girl laughed, a lazy, good-natured laugh.

"He thinks I didn't make any profit out of Bill, Dan!" She leaned forward and put a hand on my knee. "Listen, old timer. Suppose you knew far enough ahead that a company's employees were going to strike, and when, and then far enough ahead when they were going to call the strike off. Could you take that information and some capital to the stock market and do yourself some good playing with the company's stock? You bet you could!" she wound up triumphantly. "So don't go round thinking Billy boy didn't pay his way."

"Well, you've been spoiled. I'm not going to make you worse."

"What's the use of being so tight?" she demanded. "It's not like it had to come out of your own pocket. You've got an expense account to charge it to, haven't you?"

I said nothing. She frowned at me, at the run in her stocking, and at Rolff. Then she said to him:

"Maybe he'd loosen up if he had a drink."

The thin man got up and went out of the room.

IX

Dinah Brand pouted at me, prodded my shin with her toe, and explained:

"It's not so much the money. It's the principle of the thing. If a girl's got something that's worth something to somebody, she's a boob if she doesn't collect."

I grinned.

"Why don't you be a good guy?" she coaxed.

Dan Rolff came in with a siphon, a bottle of gin, some lemons, and a bowl of cracked ice. We had a drink apiece. The lunger went away. The girl and I wrangled over the money question while we had more drinks. I kept trying to bring the talk around to Thaler and Willsson. She kept bringing it back to the money she deserved. It went on like that until the gin-bottle was empty. My watch said it was a quarter after one.

She chewed a piece of lemon peel and said for the thirtieth or fortieth time:

"It won't come out of *your* pocket. What do you care?"

"It's not the money," I assured her. "It's the principle of the thing."

She made a face at me and set her glass where she thought the table was. She was eight inches wrong. I don't remember whether the glass broke when it hit the floor, or what happened to it. But I do remember that I took her missing the table for my cue to launch another attack.

"Another thing," I opened up, "I'm not dead sure I really need what you can tell me. I'd like to have it, but maybe I can get along without it."

"It'll be nice if you can," she replied, "but don't forget I'm the last person who saw him alive, besides the murderers."

Neither of us was talking as clear as it looks here.

"You're mistaken, my dear," I said. "His wife saw him come out, walk away and get shot."

"His wife?"

"Yeah. She was sitting in a machine across the street."

"How did she know he was here?"

"She says Thaler phoned her that Willsson was coming here—or had come—with a five-thousand-dollar check."

"You're trying to kid me. Max couldn't have known it!"

"I'm telling you what she told Noonan and me."

The girl spit what was left of the lemon peel out on the floor, further disarranged her hair by running her fingers through it, wiped her mouth on the back of her hand, and then slapped the table.

"All right, Mr Knowitall, I'm going to play with you! You can think it's not going to cost you anything, but I'll get mine before we're through. You think I won't?" she challenged me, peering at me as if I were a block distant.

This was no time to start an argument, so I said, "I hope you do." I think I said it three or four times, very earnestly.

"I will. Now listen to me. You're drunk and I'm drunk, and I'm just drunk enough to tell the truth. I'll tell you anything you want to know. That's the kind of girl I am. If I like a person I'll tell 'em anything they want to know. Just ask me! Go ahead, ask me!"

I did: "What did Willsson give you five thousand dollars for?"

"For fun!" She leaned back and laughed heartily. Then: "Listen to this, old darling, it's a humdinger and I want you to get it the first time. Donald was hunting for scandal on the home talent. I had some stuff stuck away, some affidavits and things that I thought might be good for some jack some day. I'm a girl that likes to pick up a piece of change when she can. So I put these affidavits and things away in the old sock.

"So when this Donald began putting the boys on the pan for hunching, I let him know that I had some dirt on them, and it was for sale. He came to bargain and I gave him enough of a look at some of them to let him know they were good. And they *were* good! Then we talked how much. He wasn't as tight as you—nobody ever was—but he was a little bit close. So the deal hung fire, till yesterday.

"Then I gave him the rush—phoned him and told him I had another customer for the stuff, and that if he wanted it he could have it by showing up at ten that night with five thousand smacks—either cash or a certified check. That was hooey, but he fell for it. He was a nice boy in his way, but he didn't know much. You want to know why it had to be cash or a certified check, huh? All right, I'll tell you. I'll tell you anything you want to know. That's the kind of girl I am. Always was."

She went on for five or more minutes telling me in detail just exactly what and which sort of girl she was and always had been, and why. I finally cut in:

"I knew you were regular as soon as I saw you. A good girl, I told myself, a good girl. Now why did it have to be cash or a certified check?"

She shut one eye, waggled a forefinger at me, and said:

"So he couldn't stop payment. Because he couldn't use the stuff I sold him. It would have put his old man in jail along with the rest of 'em." She thumped my knee and laughed hilariously—"A good one, huh? The stuff I sold him would have nailed old Elihu tighter than anybody else!"

I laughed with her while I fought to keep my head above the gin I had guzzled.

"Who else would it nail?"

"The whole damned gang of 'em." She waved a hand in the air. "Max and Lew Yard and Noonan and Pete the Finn and old Elihu—the whole blooming crew!"

"Did Max know what you were doing?"

"Of course not—nobody knew but Willsson and me."

"Sure of that?"

"Sure I'm sure. You don't think I was going to brag about it ahead of time, do you?"

"Who do you think knows about it now?"

"I don't care," she said. "It was only a joke on him. That's all I meant it for."

"Yeah. But the gents whose secrets you sold won't see anything funny in it. Noonan's trying to hang the killing on you and Thaler. That means he found the stuff in Willsson's pocket. The rest of the gang already thought that old Elihu was using his son to chase them out of the city with that clean-up campaign, didn't they?"

"Yes, sir!" she said. "And I'm another one that thinks it!"

"You're probably wrong, but that doesn't matter. Now if Noonan found your stuff in young Willsson's pocket, and found out about the check, why shouldn't he add 'em up to mean that you and Thaler had gone over to old Elihu's side. See? That's why he's pointing the rap at you and Thaler."

"I don't care what he thinks," she said obstinately. "It was only a joke. That's all I meant it for. Willsson would have found out he couldn't use the stuff without hurting the old man. It was only a joke—that's all it was."

"That's good. You can go to the gallows with a clear conscience. Just what was this stuff you sold him?"

But she had gone stubborn on me.

"I've told you enough," she said. "I've told you too much."

"Haven't you seen Thaler since the murder?"

"No. But Max didn't kill him, even if he was around."

"Why?"

"Lots of reasons. First place, Max wouldn't have done it himself. He'd have had somebody else do it, and he'd have been off some place else with an alibi nobody could shake. Second place, Max packs a .38, and anybody he sent on the job would have had that much gun or more. What kind of a gunman would use a .32?"

"Then who did kill him?"

"I've told you all I know. And remember, it's going to cost you something before you're through. I'm going to cash in somewhere."

"I hope you do," I said as I stood up. "You deserve it. You've practically cleaned up the job for me."

"You mean you know who killed him?"

"Yes, thanks, though there are a couple of things I'll have to cover before I make the pinch."

"Who? Who?" She stood up, suddenly almost sober, tugging at my lapels. "Who did it? Tell me!"

"No, I won't do that."

She let go my lapels, put her hands behind her, and laughed in my face.

"All right. Try to figure out which part of what I've told you is true."

I thought Albury had been right when he said that after you had been with this girl a while you forgot to be disappointed in her. I said:

"Thanks for the part that is, anyway. Don't let Noonan job you, and if Max means anything to you you ought to pass him the tip. And thanks for the gin."

X

It must have been close to two o'clock of a crisp morning when I said, "Goodnight," to Dinah Brand at her door and started to foot it downtown to my hotel. The first half a block of the distance went very nicely. Then somebody shot at me—twice.

I dived into a dark doorway.

I wasn't exactly sober, but my head was clear enough for me to know that it was close to my present location that Donald Willsson had died the previous night, and that the present shooter had a heavier gun than a .32.

I wasn't exactly drunk, but I had too much gin in me for effective gun-fighting in the dark with somebody I couldn't see.

I crowded myself back into a corner of my dark vestibule and wondered what I ought to do about it. My foot upset a milk-bottle. A window was lifted squeakily down the street. The two things clicked together in my mind.

I picked up the milk-bottle, swung it underhand, let it go at the front of the house across the street. It smashed through the glass of a second-storey window. That was capital!

I put a hand around the front of my crouching-place, found a bell-button, pushed it. Behind me the bell made a jangling clamor in the house.

I made a megaphone of my hands, pointed it at the street, and bellowed:

"Help! Help! Police! Help! Help!"

Windows began to go up along the street. In the house whose doorway I occupied a man's voice, shrill with fright, whined: "Go away from there! Go away, or I'll call the police!"

I thought that a swell idea.

"Do that," I encouraged him, "and the fire department and the public health service."

The whining voice made no reply. On hands and knees I peeped out into the street. The occupants of most of the houses seemed to be looking out, up and down the street, hunting for a repetition of last night's murder. That was fine! I didn't think anybody wanted my life badly enough to assassinate me in front of all these witnesses.

I jumped up, trotted down the front steps, waved my hand gratefully at the audience, and went away from the neighborhood. I turned most of the corners I came to, making sure that nobody turned them after me. Presently I got lost, but I kept on turning corners. After a while I found myself down in Union Street, four or five blocks from my hotel. I got back to it without anything happening to me.

With my key the night clerk gave me a memorandum that asked me to call Poplar 605. I knew the number, had called it earlier, it was Elihu Willsson's.

"How long has it been here?" I asked.

"Since a little after one o'clock."

That sounded urgent. I went back to a booth and put in the call. The secretary answered, and told me the old man desired my company at once. I promised to hustle, asked the night clerk to get me a taxi, and went up to my room for a couple of shots of Scotch. I would rather have been cold sober. But I wasn't, and if the night held more work for me I didn't want it to catch me in the raggedy condition that sobering-up brings. Two snifters revived me a lot. I poured more of the King George into a flask, pocketed it, and went down to the taxi.

Elihu Willsson's house was lighted from top to bottom. The secretary opened the door before I could get my finger on the button. His thin body was shivering in pale blue pajamas and dark blue bathrobe. His face was full of excitement.

"Hurry!" he begged. "Mr Willsson is waiting." His dark eyes had something horrified in them. "And please, will you try to persuade him to let us remove the body!"

I nodded and followed him up to the old man's bedroom. He was in bed as before, but now a black automatic pistol lay on the covers under one of his hands.

As soon as I appeared he took his head off the pillows, leaned forward, and barked at me:

"Have you got as much guts as you've got gall?"

His face was an unhealthy dark red. The film was gone from his eyes. They were hard and hot.

I let his question wait while I looked at the corpse on the floor between door and bed. A short thick-set man in brown, half on his side, half on his back, with dead eyes staring at the ceiling from under the visor of a gray cap. A piece of his jaw had been knocked off. His chin was tilted to show where another bullet had gone through tie and collar to make a hole in his neck. One hand was bent under him. The other still held a blackjack as big as a milk bottle. There was a lot of blood.

I looked up from this mess at the old man again. His grin was both vicious and idiotic.

"You're a great talker," he said. "I know that. A two-fisted, you-be-damned man with your words! But have you got anything else? Have you got the guts to match your gall? Or is it just the gab you've got?"

There was no use trying to get along with the old boy. I scow led and reminded him:

"Didn't I tell you not to bother me unless you wanted to talk sense for a change?"

"You did, my boy!" There was a foolish sort of triumph in his sneer. "And I'll talk you your sense. I want a man to clean this pig-sty of a Personville for me, to smoke out the big rats and the little ones. It's a man's job. Are you a man?"

"What's the use of getting poetic about it?" I growled. "If you've got an honest job to be done, and want to pay an honest price for it, maybe I'll take it. But a lot of howling about smoking rats and pig-pens doesn't mean anything."

"All right. I want Personville emptied of crooks and grafters. Is that plain enough language for you?"

"You didn't want that last week," I said. "Why do you want it this week?"

"Nobody that ever lived can tell Elihu Willsson where he's got to get on and where he's got to get off," he blustered at the top of his voice. "That's why!" He turned loose a cloud of profanity. "While they keep their places I let 'em alone. But when they begin to think Personville belongs to them, and that they can tell me what I've got to do, then it's time to show them, the—, who Personville does belong to. I built this city with my own hands, and I'll keep it or I'll wipe it off the side of the mountain." More cursing. "I'll show them what they'll get out of their threats!" He pointed at the dead body on the floor. "I'll show 'em there's still a sting in the old man!"

I wished I was sober. The old man's clowning puzzled me. I couldn't put my finger on the something under it.

"Was he from your friends?" I asked, nodding at the corpse.

"I only talked to him with this," he boasted, patting the gun on the bed, "but I reckon he was."

"How did it happen?"

"It happened simple enough. I heard the door opening, and I switched on the light, and there he was, and I shot him, and there he is."

"What time?"

"It was about one o'clock."

"And you've let him lie there all this time?"

"Yes, that I have!" The old man laughed savagely and began blustering again: "Does the sight of a dead man turn your stomach? Or is it his ghost you're afraid of?"

I looked at him and laughed. I had it. The old boy was scared—scared stiff. That's why he blustered. That's why he hadn't let them take the corpse away. He wanted it there to look at, to keep panic away—visible proof of his ability to defend himself. Now I knew where I stood.

"You really want the burg cleaned up?" I asked.

"I said I did and I do."

"I'll have to have an absolutely free hand—no favors to anybody—handle the job as I please. And I'll have to have a ten-thousand-dollar retainer to cover expenses and service charges."

"Ten-thousand-dollar retainer! Why in hell should I pay that much money to a man I don't know from Adam, a man who's done nothing I know of but talk?"

"Be serious. When I say, 'Me,' I mean the Continental Detective Agency."

"You do, do you? Well, if I know your Continental Detective Agency, then they ought to know me, and they ought to know I'm good for—"

"That's not the idea! These people you want taken to the cleaners were your friends last week. Maybe they will be again next week. I don't care about that. But we're not going to play politics for you. We're not starting a job and having it blow up on us. If you really want the burg ventilated you'll plank down enough cash to pay for a complete job. Any that's left over will be returned. That's the way it'll have to be. Take it or leave it."

"I'll damned well leave it," he bawled.

He let me get half-way down the stairs before he yelled for me. I went back.

"I'm an old man," he grumbled. "If I was ten years younger, I'd—"

He glared at me and worked his lips together. "I'll give you your damned check."

"And a free hand?"

"And a free hand."

"We'll get it done now. Where's your secretary?"

Willsson pushed a button on his bedside table and the secretary silently appeared from wherever he had been hiding. I told him:

"Mr Willsson wants to draw a ten-thousand-dollar check to the order of the Continental Detective Agency. Also he wants to write a letter to them, saying that the ten thousand dollars are to be used in investigating crime and so forth in Personville, and giving the agency full power to conduct the investigation as they see fit."

The secretary looked questioningly at the old man, who scowled and nodded his round white head.

"But first," I told the secretary as he moved to the door, "you'd better phone the police that we've a dead burglar here. And call Mr Willsson's doctor."

The old man flared up:

"I don't want any damned doctors!"

"You're going to have a nice shot in the arm so you can sleep," I promised him, stepping over the corpse to take the black gun from the bed.

He said he wouldn't, making a long and profane story of it. He was still going strong when the secretary returned with the check and a typed letter. The old man gave up his cursing long enough to put a shaky signature on each. I had them folded in my pocket when the police arrived.

XI

The first copper into the room was the chief himself, fat Noonan. He nodded amiably at Willsson, shook hands with me, and looked at the dead man with twinkling green eyes.

"Well, well," he said. "It's a good job he did, whoever did it—Yakima Shorty. And will you look at the sap he's toting?" He kicked the big blackjack out of the dead man's hand. "Big enough to sink a battleship. You drop him?" he asked me.

"No, Mr Willsson."

"Well, that certainly is fine," he congratulated the old man. "You saved a lot of people a lot of troubles, including me. Pack him out, boys," he said to the four men behind him.

The two in uniform picked Yakima Shorty's remains up by legs and armpits and went away with him, while one of the others gathered up the blackjack and a flashlight that had been under the body.

"If everybody did that to their prowlers, it would certainly be fine," the chief babbled on. He produced three cigars, stuck one at me, threw one over on old Elihu's bed, and put the other in his own mouth. "I was just wondering where I could get hold of you," he told me as we lighted up. "I got a little job ahead that I thought maybe you'd like to be in on." He put his mouth close to my ear and whispered: "Going to pick up Whisper. Want to go along?"

"I do."

"I thought you would. Hello, Doc!" He shook hands with a man the secretary had just ushered in—a little plump man with a tired round face and eyes that still had sleep in them.

The doctor went over to the bed, where one of Noonan's men was asking Willsson all about the shooting. I followed the secretary out into the hallway and asked him:

"Any men in the house besides you?"

"Yes—a chauffeur, the gardener, and the Chinese cook."

"Let one of 'em stay in the old man's room tonight. I don't think you'll have any more excitement, but no matter what happens don't leave the old man alone. And don't leave him alone with Noonan or any of Noonan's men."

The secretary's mouth and eyes popped wide.

"What time did you leave Donald Willsson the night he was killed?" I asked.

"At precisely ten minutes after nine." He seemed to have been expecting the question.

"You were with him from five o'clock till then?"

"From about a quarter after five. We went over some financial statements and that sort of thing in his office until seven o'clock. Then we went to Bayard's and finished our business over our dinners. He left at ten minutes after nine, saying he had an engagement."

"What else did he say about this engagement?"

"Not a thing."

"Didn't give you any hint of where he was going, who he was going to meet?"

"He only said he had an engagement."

"And you didn't know anything about it?"

"No. Why? Did you think I did?"

"I thought he might have said something." I switched back to tonight's doings: "What visitors did Willsson have today—not counting the one he shot?"

"You'll have to pardon me." The secretary shifted his feet, smiling apologetically. "I can't tell you that without Mr Willsson's permission. I'm sorry."

"Weren't some of the local powers here—say, Lew Yard, Pete the Finn, and—?"

The secretary shook his head, repeating: "I'm sorry."

I gave it up, said, "We won't fight about it," and started back toward the bedroom door. The doctor came trotting out, buttoning his overcoat.

"He will sleep now," he said hurriedly. "Someone should stay with him. I shall be in early in the morning." And he ran down the stairs.

I went into the bedroom. The chief and the man who had questioned Willsson were standing beside his bed. The chief grinned as if he were glad to see me. The other man scowled. Willsson was lying on his back, staring at the ceiling.

"That's about all there is here," Noonan said cheerfully. "What say we mosey along?"

I agreed and said, "Goodnight," to the old man. He said, "Goodnight," without looking at me. The secretary came in with a tall sunburned young man who looked like a chauffeur. The chief, the other sleuth and I went downstairs and out to a black touring car at the curb. The other man—Noonan called him McGraw—drove. The chief and I sat in the back seat.

"We'll make the pinch along about daylight," the chief explained to me as we rode. "Whisper's got a joint over on King Street. He generally leaves there about daylight. We could crash the place, but that'd mean gun-play, and it's just as well to take it easy. So we'll pick him up when he leaves."

I wondered if he meant to pick him up or pick him off. I asked:

"You've got enough on him to make the rap stick?"

"Enough?" He laughed good-naturedly. "If what the Willsson dame gave us ain't enough to swing him I'm a pickpocket."

I thought of a couple of wise-crack answers to that, but kept them to myself.

Our ride lasted half an hour. The chief didn't ask any questions about my progress, about what I had done since I left him with Mrs Willsson. That was clumsy. He had told me he was keeping an eye on Dinah Brand. I had been shot at leaving her house. My guess was that I had been shot at by one of Noonan's bulls. Otherwise, how come none of the men he had watching the house had come to my rescue? The chief's silence now made my guess look better—just as too many questions would have made it look better. I wondered why he was getting careless.

While I was wondering our machine came to rest under a line of trees in a dark street. We got out and walked down to the corner. A burly man in a gray overcoat, with a gray hat pulled far down over his eyes, came to meet us.

"Whisper phoned Donohoe that he's in his joint and going to stay there," the burly man told the chief. "If you think you can pull him out, he says, try it."

Noonan chuckled, scratched an earlobe, and asked pleasantly:

"How many would you say was in there with him?"

"Fifty, anyhow."

"Aw, now! There wouldn't be that many this time of morning."

"The hell there wouldn't!" the burly man snarled. "They've been drifting in since midnight."

"Is that so? A leak somewhere. Maybe you oughtn't to have let 'em in."

"Maybe I oughtn't!" The burly man was mad. "But I did what you told me. You said to let anybody go in or out that wants to, but when Whisper showed to—"

"To arrest him," the chief said.

"Well, yes," the burly man agreed, and looked savagely at me.

More men joined us and we held a talk-fest. Everybody was in bad humor except the chief. He seemed to enjoy it all. I didn't know why.

Whisper's joint was a three-storey brick building in the middle of the block, between two two-storey buildings. The ground floor of his joint was occupied by a cigar store that served as entrance and cover for the gambling establishment upstairs. Inside, if the burly man's information was to be depended on, Whisper had collected half a hundred friends, presumably loaded for a fight. Outside, Noonan's force was spread around the building, in the street in front, in the alley in back, and on adjoining roofs.

"Well, boys," the chief said amiably after the talk had gone around in circles for a while, "I don't reckon Whisper wants trouble any more than we do, or he'd have tried to shoot his way out before this, if he's got *that* many with him, though I don't mind saying I don't think he has—not *that* many."

The burly man said: "The hell he ain't!"

"So if he don't want trouble," Noonan went on, "maybe talking might do some good. You run over, Nick, and see if you can't argue him into being peaceable."

The burly man said: "The hell I will!" "Phone him then," the chief suggested.

The burly Nick growled, "That's more like it," and went away. When he came back he looked completely satisfied with his message.

"He says," he reported, "'Go to hell!' "

"Get the rest of the boys down here," Noonan said cheerfully. "We'll knock it over as soon as it gets light."

XII

The burly Nick and I went around with the chief while he placed his men. I didn't think much of them—a shabby, shifty-eyed lot with no enthusiasm for the job ahead of them.

The sky became a faded gray. The chief, Nick and I had stopped in a plumber's doorway diagonally across the street from our target. Whisper's joint was dark, blank, with the cigar store blinds down over window and door, all upper windows curtained.

"I hate to start this without giving Whisper a chance," Noonan said. "He's not a bad kid. But there's no use o' me trying to talk to him. He never did like me much."

He looked at me. I said nothing.

"You wouldn't want to make a stab at it?" he asked.

"I'll try it."

"That's fine of you! I'll appreciate that, if you will. You just see if you can't talk him into coming along peaceable. You know what to say—for his own good and all that—like it is."

"Yeah," I said, and started across the street toward the cigar store, taking pains to let my hands be seen swinging empty at my sides.

Day was still a little way off. The street was the color of smoke. My feet seemed to be making a lot of noise on the paving. I stopped in front of the door and knocked the glass with a knuckle, not heavily. The green blind down inside the door made a mirror of the glass. In it I saw two men moving up the other side of the street.

No sound came from inside. I knocked louder, then slid my hand down to rattle the knob.

Advice came from indoors:

"Get away from there while you're able."

It was a muffled voice, but probably not Thaler's because it wasn't a whisper.

"I want to talk to Thaler," I said.

"Go talk to the fat—that sent you!"

"I'm not talking for Noonan. Is Thaler where he can hear me?"

A pause. Then the muffled voice, "Yes."

"Listen, Thaler: I'm the Continental op who tipped Dinah Brand off that the chief was framing you. I want five minutes' talk with you. I've got nothing to do with Noonan except to queer his game if I can. I'm alone. I'll drop my gun in the street if you say so. Let me in."

I waited. It depended on whether the girl had got to him with the story of my call. I waited what seemed a long time. Then the muffled voice came:

"When we open, come in quick! And no stunts!"

"All set!" I said.

The latch clicked.

I plunged in with the door.

Across the street a dozen guns emptied themselves. Glass shot from door and windows tinkled everywhere.

Somebody tripped me. As I fell I twisted around to face the door. My gun was in my hand before I hit the floor.

Fear gave me three brains and half a dozen eyes. These birds couldn't help thinking I was taking part in a trick of Noonan's.

Across the street the burly Nick had stepped out of a doorway to pump lead at us with both hands.

I steadied my gun-hand wrist on the floor. The detective's burly body showed over the front sight. I squeezed.

Nick stopped shooting. He put both hands tight to his belly and piled down on his face.

Hands on my ankles dragged me back. The floor scraped pieces off my chin. The door slammed shut. Some comedian said:

"Uh-huh, people don't like you."

"I wasn't in on that," I said earnestly through the racket.

A husky whisper came through the darkness:

"Dropping Big Nick squares you. Hank, you and Slats keep an eye on things down here. The rest of us might as well go upstairs."

We went back through another room, into a passageway, up a flight of carpeted stairs, and into a large room that held a green-topped table banked for crap-shooting. This room was lighted, and had no windows.

There were five of us. Thaler sat down and lighted a cigarette—a small, dark young man with a face that was pretty in a chorus-man way until you took another look at the thin, hard mouth. An angular blond kid of hardly more than twenty, in tweeds, sprawled on his back on a couch and blew cigarette smoke at the ceiling. Another boy, just as blond and just as young, but not so angular, was busy straightening his tie, smoothing down his yellow hair. A thin-faced man of thirty, with little or no chin under a wide, loose mouth, wandered up and down the room humming *Rosy Cheeks* and looking bored.

The gunfire had stopped.

"How long is Noonan going to keep this up?" Thaler asked. His voice was a hoarse whisper, but there was no great amount of emotion in it—just a little annoyance.

"He's after you this trip," I gave my opinion. "He means to see it through." Thaler smiled a thin, contemptuous smile.

"Maybe he thinks so now, but the longer he thinks it over the smaller his chance of hanging a one-legged rap like that on me will look."

"He's not figuring on proving anything in court."

"What, then?"

"You're to be knocked off resisting arrest or trying to escape. He won't need much of a case after that."

The thin lips twisted themselves into another contemptuous smile. This lad didn't seem to think much of the fat man's deadliness.

"He's getting tough in his old age. Any time he rubs me out I deserve rubbing. What's he got against you?"

"I'm getting to be a nuisance around town, too."

"Too bad," Thaler said. "Dinah told me you were a pretty good guy—except kind of Scotch with the roll."

"I had a nice visit. Will you tell me what you know about Donald Willsson's killing?"

"Sure," he said coolly. "His wife turned the trick."

"You saw her?"

"Saw her the next second—with the rod in her hand."

"That's no good to me, Thaler. And it's no good to you. If you've got it rigged right maybe it would work in court, but you're never going to tell it there. If Noonan takes you at all he'll take you stiff. Give me low-down. I only need your angle to clean up the job."

He leaned forward, his dark eyes seeming to draw together.

"Are you that hot?"

"With your story I'll be ready to make the pinch—if I can get out."

He dropped his cigarette on the floor, mashed it under his foot, lighted another, and studied its red end.

"Mrs Willsson said it was me that phoned her about the check?" he asked.

"She said that after Noonan had persuaded her. But she believes it now—maybe."

He put some smoke in and out of his lungs, brushed a flake or two of ash off his black suit with a hand that was very small and very manicured, nodded to himself, and said:

"A man phoned me that night. I don't know who he was. Said Willsson had gone to Dinah's with a check for five grand. What the hell did I care? But, see, it was funny that somebody I didn't know phoned me about it. So I went around. Dan stalled me away from the door. That was all right. But still it was funny that guy phoned me. I went up and took a plant in a doorway. I saw Mrs Willsson's car down the street, but didn't know it was her in it then.

"Willsson came out and walked down the street. I didn't see the shots, but I heard 'em. Then this woman jumps out of the car and runs over to him. I knew she hadn't done the shooting. I ought to have beat it. But curiosity got me. When I saw it was Mrs Willsson I went over. That was a bull, see? So I had to make an out for myself, in case something slipped. I strung the woman. That's all there was to it—on the level."

"Thanks," I said. "That's what I came for. Now the trick is to get out of here without being mowed down by Noonan's crew."

"No trick at all," Thaler assured me. "We go any time we want to."

"Well, I'm ready now; And if I were you, I'd go, too. You don't think much of Noonan, but he might pull something. And if you'll take a sneak and hide out till noon his frame-up will be a wash-out."

"Yeah?"

"Yeah."

Thaler put a hand in his pants pocket and dragged out a fat roll of bills. He counted off a hundred or two, some fifties, twenties, tens, and held them out to the chinless man.

"Buy us a getaway, Jerry," he ordered. "And you don't have to give anybody any more dough than they're used to."

Jerry took the sheaf of bills, picked up a hat from the table, and strolled out. Half an hour later he strolled in again and returned part of the sheaf to Thaler, saying casually:

"We wait in the kitchen until we get the office."

We went down to the kitchen. It was dark there. More men joined us.

Presently something hit the door.

Jerry opened it and we went down three steps into the back yard. It was almost full daylight. There were ten of us in the party.

"This all?" I asked Thaler.

He nodded.

"Nick said there were fifty of you."

"Fifty to stand off that crummy force?" he asked scornfully.

A copper in uniform held the back gate open for us, muttering nervously:

"Hurry it up a little, boys, please!"

I was willing to oblige him, but everybody else ignored the request. We crossed the alley, were beckoned through another gate by a beefy man in brown, passed through a house, out into the next street, and climbed into a touring car that stood at the curb.

One of the blond boys drove. He knew what speed was.

"I want to be dropped off near the Great Western," I said.

The blond driver looked at Whisper, who nodded. We turned the next corner, and five minutes later I got out in front of my hotel.

"See you later," Thaler said, and the car slid away. The last I saw of it was its police department license plate vanishing around a corner.

XIII

It was half-past five. I went up Broadway to where an unlighted electric sign said Hotel Windom, mounted a flight of steps to the second floor office, left a call for ten o'clock, was shown into a shabby room, moved some of the Scotch from my flask to my stomach, and took Elihu Willsson's ten-thousand-dollar check and my gun to bed with me.

When my call roused me I dressed, went up to the First National Bank, found young Albury, and asked him to certify the old man's check for me. He kept me waiting a while, so I supposed he phoned Willsson's residence to find out if the check was on the up-and-up. Finally he brought it back to me, properly scribbled on.

I sponged an envelope, put Willsson's letter and check in it, addressed it to the agency in San Francisco, stuck a stamp on it and went out to drop it in the mail-box on the corner.

Then I returned to the bank and said to the boy:

"Now, sonny, tell me why you killed him."

"Cock Robin or President Lincoln?" he asked, smiling.

"You're not going to admit off-hand that you killed Willsson?"

"I don't want to be disagreeable," he laughed, "but I'd rather not."

"That makes it bad," I complained. "We can't stand here and talk very long without being interrupted. Who's the stout party with the cheaters coming this way?"

The boy's face pinkened, and he said: "Mr Dutton, the cashier."

"Introduce me."

The boy looked uncomfortable, but he called the cashier's name. Dutton—a large man with a smooth pink face, a fringe of white hair around an almost totally bald pink head, and rimless nose-glasses—came over to us. The assistant cashier mumbled the introduction. I shook Dutton's hand without losing sight of the boy.

"I was just saying," I addressed Dutton, "that we ought to have a more private place for our talk. He probably won't confess till I've worked on him a while, and I don't want everybody in the bank to hear me yelling at him."

"Confess?" The cashier's tongue showed between his lips.

"Sure." I kept my voice and manner bland, mimicking Noonan. "Didn't you know that Albury is the fellow who killed Donald Willsson?"

A polite smile at what he thought a foolish joke started in back of the cashier's glasses—changed to puzzlement when he looked at his assistant. The boy was rouge-red and the grin he was forcing his mouth into was a terrible thing.

Dutton cleared his throat and said heartily: "It's a splendid morning. Splendid weather."

"But isn't there a private room where we can talk?" I insisted.

Dutton jumped nervously and questioned the boy:

"What—what is this?"

Young Albury mumbled something unintelligible.

"If there isn't," I said, "I'll have to take him down to the City Hall."

Dutton caught his glasses as they slid down his nose, jammed them back in place, sputtered:

"Come back here!"

We followed him down the length of the lobby, through a gate, and into an office whose door was marked *President*. Old Elihu's office. Nobody was there. I motioned Albury into one chair and picked another for myself. The cashier fidgeted with his back against the desk, facing us.

"Now, sir, will you explain this," he said, but his words weren't as impressive as they were meant to be.

"We'll get around to that, I hope," I told him and turned to Albury. "You're the only person I've run across who knew Dinah Brand inti-mately, and who knew about the check in time to phone Mrs Willsson and Thaler. You were in love with

Dinah and were given the gate. Willsson was shot with a .32. Banks like that caliber. I'm going to have a gun-sharp compare the bank's guns with the bullets taken out of Willsson. Maybe the gun you used wasn't a bank gun. I think it was. Maybe you didn't put it back. Then there'll be one missing, but I think you returned it to its place next morning."

The boy had his control back. He looked boldly at me and said nothing. That wouldn't do.

"I know you were nuts about this girl," I said, "because you confessed to me that it was only because she refused to be tangled up in it that you didn't help yourself to—"

"Don't! Please don't!" The boy's face was sick white. My murderer didn't like being labeled *Thief* in front of his boss.

I looked at the boy, making myself sneer until his eyes went down. Then I let him have the other barrel:

"You know you killed him. You know if you used a bank gun—and if you put it back. If you did, you're nailed right now, without an out. An expert with a microscope and a micrometer can prove absolutely that a certain bullet was fired from a certain gun. And an expert is going to look at the bank guns. If you didn't use a bank gun, I'm going to nail you anyhow. If you did, you're nailed *now!*

"All right. I don't have to tell you whether you've got a chance or not. *You know!* But here's something. Noonan is framing Thaler for the job. He can't convict him, but the frame-up is strong enough that if Thaler is killed resisting arrest, the chief will be in the clear. That's what he means to do. Thaler stood off the whole force all night in his King Street joint. He's standing them off now, unless they've got to him. The first copper that gets to him—exit Thaler. If you figure you've got a chance to beat your rap—and you want to let Thaler be killed for you—that's your business. But if you know you haven't got a chance—and you haven't if the gun can be found—and God's sake give Thaler one by clearing him!"

"I'd like—" Albury didn't look up and his voice was as an old man's. "You'll find the gun in Harper's cage. I didn't—" He looked up, saw Dutton, and stopped.

I scowled at the cashier and asked him:

"Will you get the gun?"

He ran out as if he was glad to go.

"I didn't mean to kill him," the boy said. "I don't think I did—though I took the gun with me. I *was*—what did you say?—nuts about Dinah. It was worse some days than others. The day Willsson came in with the check was one of the bad ones. All I could think about was that I lost her because I had no more money, and he was taking five thousand dollars to her. I watched her house that night and saw him go in. I had the gun in my pocket and was afraid of what I might do.

"Believe me when I say I didn't want to do anything. But it was one of the bad days, and I couldn't think straight—couldn't think of anything except that I had lost her because my money was gone, and he had taken five thousand dollars to her. And there was the bank gun in my pocket, and I was afraid of what I might do.

"I knew Willsson's wife was jealous—everybody knew that. I thought if I called her up and told her—I don't know what I thought then, but I went and called her up. And then I called Thaler. I didn't know whether he was—I only knew I had heard that he and Dinah—were—you know—so I called him up. Then I went back and watched her house again. I saw Mrs Willsson come, and then Thaler, and saw them both stay watching the house. I was glad of that.

"Then Willsson came out and walked down the street. I looked up at where Mrs Willsson and Thaler were. Neither did anything, and he was walking away. I knew then why I had wanted them there. I had thought that maybe they would do something, and I wouldn't have to. But they didn't do anything. And he was walking down the street—away. Maybe if one of them had gone over and said something to him, or even followed him, I wouldn't have done anything. But they didn't. I remember taking the gun out of my pocket. I don't remember anything else until I was running up the alley. When I got home I found the gun was empty—all the cartridges had been fired. I cleaned it and reloaded it and put it back in the paying teller's cage the next morning."

"Well," I said, "you're certainly a swell actor. Nobody would have guessed you were still in love with the girl from the way you talked to me about her."

He winced.

"That wasn't acting," he said slowly. "After—after I was in danger—facing the gallows—she—she didn't seem so—so important. I couldn't understand why I had—you know—and that spoiled the whole thing—made it—and me—cheap."

XIV

I took Albury and the gun down to the City Hall in a taxicab. In the chief's office we found one of the men who had been along on the storming party last night—a red-faced lieutenant named Biddle. He goggled at me with fishy blue eyes, but asked no questions about my part in last night's doings.

Biddle called in the Prosecuting Attorney. The boy was repeating his story to these officials when the chief of police arrived, looking as if he had just crawled out of bed.

"Well, it certainly is fine to see you!" Noonan pumped my hand up and down while patting my back jovially with his other hand. "You had a narrow one last night—the rats! I was sure they'd got you till we kicked in the doors and found the place empty. Tell me how those son-of-a-guns got out of there!"

"One of your men let them out the back door and sent them away in a department car. They took me along so I couldn't tip you off."

"One of my men did that?" He didn't seem very surprised. "Well, well! If I line 'em up in front of you, will you pick him out for me?"

"Sure."

"Fine! Now what's all this?" nodding his fat face at Albury, the Prosecuting Attorney and Biddle.

I told him briefly. He chuckled and said:

"Well, well, I did Whisper an injustice. I'll have to hunt him up and square myself. So you landed the boy? That certainly is fine! Congratulations and thanks!" He grabbed my hand and pumped it up and down again. "You'll not be leaving our city now, will you?"

"Not for a while."

"That's fine!" he assured me.

I hung around the office a little longer and then went out for breakfast-and-lunch. After that I treated myself to a shave and a hair-cut, hunted up a telegraph office, wired the agency to send Dick Foley and Mickey Linehan to join me, and then went over to my hotel.

There was another telephone memorandum in my box. Elihu Willsson's number. I called it and was invited out by the secretary.

The old man, wrapped in blankets, was sitting in an armchair at a sunny window. He held out his stubby hand to me and thanked me for catching his son's murderer. I made some more or less appropriate reply.

"The check I gave you last night," he said, "is only fair pay for the work you've done."

"Your son's check more than covered that," I protested.

"Then call mine a reward or bonus."

"We've got a rule against taking rewards or bonuses."

His face began to redden.

"Well, damn it—"

"You haven't forgotten that your check was to cover the expense of investigating crime and corruption in Personville, have you?"

"That was damned nonsense!" he snorted. "We were excited last night. That's off."

"Not with me."

He exploded. First a string of profanity. Then:

"It's my money and I won't have it used for any such damned silliness. If you won't take it for what you've done, give it back to me! I'll stop payment on—"

"Stop yelling at me. You can't stop payment, because it's been certified. We made a bargain. You and your playmates each thought the other was trying to double-cross them. I suppose as soon as the word got out that your son had been killed by Albury you made peace again—deciding that there hadn't been any double-crossing. I expected something like that. That's why I got you sewed up. And you are sewed up.

"I've got ten thousand dollars of your money to work with and I'm going to use it to open Personville up from Adam's Apple to ankles. Your fat chief of police tried to assassinate me twice last night. That's at least once too many. Now I'm going to have my fun. I'll see that my reports are mailed to you regularly. I hope you enjoy reading them."

And I went out of the house with his curses sizzling around my head.

CRIME WANTED—MALE OR FEMALE, relates the further adventures of the Continental detective in THE CLEANSING OF POISON-VILLE, by Dashiell Hammett.

CRIME WANTED is packed with action and is told as only Mr Hammett can tell a story.

It will appear in the next issue of BLACK MASK—the DECEMBER number.

2

CRIME WANTED—MALE OR FEMALE

BLACK MASK, DECEMBER *1927*

The grim adventures of the Continental detective in The Cleansing of Poisonville.

I had just decided in favor of a pounded rumps steak with mushrooms when I heard myself being paged. The boy took me to one of the lobby booths. Dinah Brand's lazy voice came out of the receiver:

"Max wants to see you. Can you run up tonight?"

"Your place?"

"Yes."

I promised to be there in an hour, and went back to the hotel dining-room and my meal. When that was through I went up to my room—front, fifth floor. I unlocked the door and went in, snapping on the light.

A bullet kissed a hole in the door-frame close to my noodle. The report sounded outside. I moved across the floor, out of line with the window. There were more reports. More bullets made more holes in door, door-frame and wall.

In a safe and far corner I took off a shoe. The shooter had to be on the roof of a four-storey office building across the street, I knew—a roof a little above the level of my window. The roof would be dark. My light was on. I chucked my shoe at it. The globe popped apart, giving me darkness. But the shooting had already stopped.

Pieces of the broken globe and of the bullet-punctured window-panes bit into my shoeless foot as I crept over to the window. I knelt with one eye in one of its lower corners. The roof across the street was dark and too high for me to see beyond its rim. Ten minutes of this one-eyed peeping got me nothing except a kink in my neck.

I went to the phone and asked the girl to send up the house copper. I waited for him in the bathroom, sitting on the side of the tub, picking fragments of glass out of my stocking-sole.

The hotel detective was a portly, white-mustached man with the round, undeveloped forehead of a child. He wore a too-small hat on the back of his head to show the forehead. His name was Keever. He got too excited over the shooting.

The hotel manager came in, a plump man with carefully controlled face, voice and manner. He didn't get excited at all. He struck the this-is-unheard-of-but-not-really-serious-of-course attitude of a street fakir whose mechanical dingus flops during a demonstration.

We risked light, getting a new globe for the bedroom socket, and added up the bullet-holes. There were ten of them. Policemen under Detective Sergeant McGraw—a flat-faced, big man I had met before—came, went, and returned to report no luck in picking up any traces of my gunman. Noonan, chief of police, phoned. He talked to McGraw and then to me.

"I just this minute heard of the shooting," he told me. "Now who do you reckon would be after you like that?"

"I couldn't guess," I lied.

"None of 'em touched you?"

"None."

"Well, that certainly is fine!" he said heartily. "And we'll nail that baby, whoever he is, you can bet your life on that! Would you like me to leave a couple of the boys with you—just to see nothing else happens?"

"No, thanks."

"You can have 'em if you want 'em," he insisted.

"No, thanks."

He made me promise to come over to the City Hall the next day to see him, told me the Personville police department was at my disposal, gave me to understand that if anything happened to me his whole life would be spoiled, and I finally got rid of him.

The police detail went away. I had my stuff moved into another room—one that bullets couldn't be so easily funneled into. The manager pretended he wasn't disappointed in my not leaving his hotel.

Then I changed clothes and set out for Hurricane Street, to keep my date with the whispering gambler and his gold-greedy ladylove.

II

Dinah Brand opened the door for me. Her big ripe mouth was rouged evenly this night, but her brown hair still needed trimming, was parted haphazardly, and there were spots down the front of her orange silk dress.

"So you're still alive," she said. "Well, I suppose nothing can be done about it. Come on in."

We went into her cluttered-up living-room. Dan Rolff and Max Thaler were playing pinocle there. Rolff nodded to me. The fever-spots were bright on the cheek-bones of his thin, tired, sickman's face. Thaler stood up to shake my hand—a small, dapper young man with hard, narrow lips that kept his dark face from being merely pretty.

His hoarse, whispering voice said:

"I hear you've declared war on Poisonville."

"Don't blame me. I've got a client who wants the burg cleaned up."

"Wanted—not wants," he corrected me as we sat down. "Why don't you chuck it?"

I made a speech:

"No. I don't like the way Poisonville's treated me, I got my chance now and I'm going to even up. If you people had let me alone while I was clearing up Donald Willsson's murder, I'd have been riding back to San Francisco now. But you didn't—especially that fat chief of police, Noonan, didn't. He's tried for my scalp three times in two days, and I'm disagreeable when I'm picked on. So when I got old Elihu Willsson in a corner—scared stiff that the rest of you were going to wipe him out—I tied him up with a contract to clean house, and got a ten-grand certified check out of him.

"Now that he knows his son was bumped off by one of Miss Brand's boy friends and that the rest of you weren't double-crossing him, he wants to call the deal off. Well, he can't! Now that your little family of Poisonville bosses is reunited—everybody trusting everybody else like they used to before Donald Willsson was killed and you all began suspecting each other of backcarving—you want me to go away and let you alone. Well, I won't!

"Yesterday I was the one who wanted to be let alone. All I was interested in was finding young Willsson's murderer. Did you let me alone? Like hell! You were afraid I'd turn up things you didn't want turned up—so you tried your best to run me ragged. Now it's my turn. I've got ten thousand dollars of old Elihu's money to spend and I'm going to spend it turning up the things you don't want turned up. It's my turn to run somebody ragged, and that's what I'm going to do. Poisonville's ripe for the cleaners. It's a job I like and I'm going to it!"

"While you last," the gambler added.

"Yeah," I agreed. "I was reading in the paper this morning about a fellow choking to death eating a chocolate eclair in bed."

"That sounds good," Dinah Brand said, "but it wasn't in this morning's paper."

She had sprawled her big body down in an armchair. She lighted a cigarette and threw the match out of sight under the Chesterfield. The sick man had gathered up the cards and was shuffling them over and over, aimlessly. Thaler frowned at me and said:

"But Willsson's willing for you to keep the ten grand. Why don't you let it go at that?"

"I've got a mean disposition. Being shot at makes me mad."

"That won't get you anything—except a box. I'm for you. You kept Noonan from framing me. That's why I'm telling you—forget it and go back to Frisco."

"I'm for you," I said. "That's why I'm telling you—split with the gang. They tried to double-cross you once. Now you're back with 'em. But it'll happen again. Anyway, they're slated for the chute. Break with 'em, Thaler."

He shook his head and replied:

"I'm sitting too pretty. Both my joints are taking in plenty. I'm able to look out for myself."

"Maybe, but you know the racket's too good to last long. You've had your pickings. Now it's get-away day. If ever a burg was ripe for a shake up this one is."

"I don't know where you get that stuff," he objected. "Just because some bright light nicknames Personville Poisonville don't mean anything. It's a swift town, maybe, but there are tougher ones."

"But no crookeder ones."

"You've got a lot of words," he said, "but what of it? Suppose it is the kind of camp you think? Suppose you're set on cracking it? And suppose you live long enough to make your play? Just where are you figuring on getting the dope you need to bust it open?"

"Honest to Gawd," Dinah Brand complained, yawning, "you sound like a couple of school-kids arguing over who's got the biggest father! He's going to advertise in the *Herald—Crime Wanted—Male or Female.* Isn't there anything to drink in the dump, Dan?"

The lunger got up from the table and went out. Thaler said:

"You can't buck the game. I'd like to see you do it. If I thought you could, I'd be with you. You know how I stand with Noonan—the rat! But you can't make it. Chuck it!"

"No—he's had three tries at me in two days. Now I'm going to have mine."

"You're wrong. Law of averages against you. He's chief of police. He can have you shot at from now till Prohibition. Don't make any difference how bad the shooting is—one of 'em will get into you some time. Law of averages."

"Maybe. But you can still lose. The Continental's got more ops."

"That'll do you a lot of good. Chuck it!"

"No."

"I told you he was too damned pig-headed to listen to reason," the girl said.

"All right." Thaler shrugged. "You're supposed to know what you're doing. Going to the fights tomorrow night?"

I said I thought I would. Dan Rolff came in with gin and trimmings. We had a couple of drinks apiece. We talked about the fights and nothing more was said of me versus Poisonville. Thaler apparently had washed his hands of me, but he didn't seem annoyed at my stubbornness. He even gave me a tip on the next night's main event—suggesting that any bet would be good if its maker remembered that Kid Cooper would probably knock Ike Bush out in the sixth round. He seemed to know what he was talking about, and it didn't seem to be news to the others.

I left a little after eleven, returning to the hotel by taxi, without anything happening.

III

I woke up next morning with an idea in my skull. Personville had only some 40,000 inhabitants. It shouldn't be hard to spread news. Ten o'clock found me out spreading it. I did my spreading on street-corners, in poolrooms, cigar stores, soft-drink speakeasies—wherever I found a man or two loafing. My spreading technique was something like this:

"Got a match?... Thanks... Going to the fights tonight?... I hear Ike Bush takes a dive in the sixth... It ought to be straight—I got it from Whisper... Yeah, they all are."

Folks like inside stuff, and anything that had Thaler's name to it was very inside in Poisonville. The news spread nicely. Half the men I gave it to worked as hard as I passing it on to others, just to show they knew what was what. When I started my Paul Revereing 7 to 4 was being offered that Ike Bush would win, 2 to 3 that he'd win by a knockout, in the joints where bets were taken. By two o'clock the best that any would give was even money, and by half-past three Kid Cooper was a 2 to 1 favorite.

I made my last stop a lunch-counter, where I tossed the news out to a waiter and a couple of customers while wrapping myself around a hot beef sandwich. When I went out I found a man waiting by the door for me. He had bowed legs and a long, sharp jaw, like a hog's. He nodded and walked down the street beside me, chewing a toothpick, squinting sidewise into my face. At the corner he said:

"I know for a fact that ain't so."

"What?" I asked.

"About Ike Bush flopping. I know for a fact it ain't so."

"Then it oughtn't bother you any. But the wise money's going 2 to 1 on Cooper, and he's not that good unless Bush lets him be."

The hog jaw spit out the mangled toothpick and snapped yellow teeth at me.

"He told me his own self that Cooper was a set up for him, last night, and he wouldn't do nothing like that—not to me."

"Friend of yours?"

"Not exactly, but he knows I—Hey, listen! Did Whisper tell you that? On the level?"

"On the level."

He cursed bitterly; "And I put my last thirty-five bucks in the world down on that—on his say-so. Me—that could send him over for—" He broke off and stood staring down the street.

"Could send him over for what?" I asked.

"Plenty," he said. "Nothing."

I had a suggestion.

"If you've got something on him, maybe we ought to talk it over. I wouldn't mind seeing Bush win, myself. If what you've got on him is any good, what's the matter with putting it up to him?"

He looked at me, at the sidewalk, fumbled in his vest pocket for a toothpick that had a second hand look, put it in his mouth, and mumbled:

"Who are you?"

I gave him a name—something like Hunter or Hunt or Huntington—and asked him his. He said it was MacSwain—and I could ask anybody in town if it wasn't right. I said I believed him and asked:

"What do you say? Will we put the squeeze to Bush?"

Little hard lights came into his mud-colored eyes and died.

"No," he gulped. "I ain't that kind of fellow. I never—"

"You never did anything but let people gyp you," I finished for him. "You don't have to go up against him. Give me the dope and I'll make the play—if it's any good."

He thought that over, licking his lips, letting the toothpick fall down to stick on his coat-front.

"If I give it to you, you won't let on about me having any part in it?" he asked. "I belong here and I wouldn't stand a chance if it got out. And you won't turn him up? You'll just use it to make him fight?"

"Right."

He grabbed my hand excitedly and demanded: "Honest to Gawd?"

"Honest to God."

"Mind, I'm trusting you! He was in on the Keystone Trust knock-over in Philly two years ago, when Scissors Haggerty's mob croaked two messengers. He didn't do the killing, but he was in on the caper. His real moniker is Al Kennedy. He used to scrap around Philly. The bulls got the rest of 'em, but he made the sneak. They're still looking for him. That's why he's sticking out here in the bushes. That's why he won't let 'em put his mug on any cards or in any papers. That's why he's a pork-and-beaner when he's as good as any of 'em. See? This Ike Bush is Al Kennedy that the Philly bulls want for the Keystone trick. See? He was in on—"

"I see, I see," I stopped the merry-go-round. "The next thing is to get to see him. How will we do that?"

"He flops at the Maxwell, on Union Street. I guess maybe he'd be there now, resting up for the mill."

"Resting for what? He don't know he's going to fight yet. We'll give it a try, though."

"We! We! Where do you get that *we* at? You swore you'd keep me covered!"

"Yea, I remember that now. What kind of looking bird is he?"

"A black-headed kid, kind of slim, with one tin ear and eyebrows that run straight across. I don't know that you can make him like it."

"Leave that to me. Where'll I see you afterward?"

"I'll be hanging around Murry's. Mind you don't drag me in it—you promised."

IV

The Maxwell was one of the dozens of hotels along Union Street with narrow front doors between stores and shabby flights of steps leading up to second-storey offices. The office was a wide place in the hall, with a key and mail rack behind a wooden counter that needed paint just as badly. A brass bell and a dirty day-book register were on the counter. Nobody was there.

I had to run back eight pages in the book before I found *Ike Bush, Salt Lake City, 214*. The pigeon-hole that had that number was empty. I climbed another flight of stairs and knocked on a door that had it. Nothing came of that. I tried it two or three times more and then turned back to the stairs. Somebody was coming up.

I stood at the top waiting for a look at him. There was just light enough to see by. He was a slim, muscular lad in army shirt, blue suit, gray cap. Black eyebrows made a straight line over his eyes.

I nodded at him and said, "Hello!"

He nodded without stopping or saying anything.

"Win tonight?" I asked.

"Hope so," he said shortly, passing me.

I let him go a couple of steps more toward his room and then told him:

"So do I. I'd hate to have to ship you back to Philly, Al."

He took another step, turned around very slowly, rested one shoulder against the wall, let his eyes get sleepy, and grunted: "Huh?"

"If you were smacked down in the sixth or any other round by a palooka like Kid Cooper it'd make me peevish," I said. "Don't do it, Al. You don't want to go back to Philly."

The youngster put his chin down in his neck and came back to me. When he was within an arm's length he stopped, letting his left side turn a bit to the front. His hands were hanging loose. Mine were in my overcoat pockets.

He said "Huh?" again.

I said: "Try to remember that—if Ike Bush don't turn in a win tonight, Al Kennedy will bending East in the morning."

He lifted his left shoulder an inch or two. I moved the gun around in my overcoat pocket, enough. He grumbled:

"Where do you get that stuff about me not winning?"

"Just something I heard. I didn't think there was anything in it—except maybe a ducat back to Philly."

"I ought to bust your jaw, you fat crook!"

"Now's the time to do it. Because if you win tonight you're not likely to see me again. If you lose you'll see me all right, but your wrists won't be loose."

I found MacSwain in Murry's, a poolroom in Broadway.

"Did you get to him?" he asked.

"I think it's fixed—if he don't blow town, or say something to his backers, or just pay no attention to me, or—"

MacSwain developed a lot of nervousness.

"You better damn sight be careful," he warned me hurriedly. "They might try to put you out the way. He—I got to see a fellow down the street," and he deserted me.

Personville's prize-fighting was done in a big wooden ex-casino in what had once been an amusement park on the edge of town. When I got there at eight-thirty most of the population seemed to be on hand, packed tight in close rows of folding chairs on the main floor, packed still tighter on benches in two dinky balconies. Smoke. Stink. Noise. Heat.

My seat was in the third row, ringside. Moving down to it, I discovered Dan Rolff sitting in an aisle seat not far away, with Dinah Brand beside him. She had had her hair trimmed at last, and marcelled, and looked like a lot of money in a big gray fur coat.

"Get down on Cooper?" she asked after we had swapped hellos.

"No. You playing him heavy?"

"Not as heavy as I'd have liked to. We held off', thinking the odds would get better, but they went to hell."

"Yeah," I said. "Everybody in town seems to know Bush is going to dive. I saw a hundred berries put on Cooper at four to one a couple of minutes ago." I leaned past Rolff and put my mouth close to where the gray fur collar hid the girl's ear. "The dive is off. Better copper your bets while there's time."

Her big bloodshot eyes went wide and dark with curiosity, anxiety, greed, suspicion.

"You mean it?" she asked huskily.

"Yeah."

She chewed her reddened lips, frowned, asked: "Where'd you get it?"

I wouldn't say. She chewed her mouth some more, asked: "Is Max on?"

"I haven't seen him since I left your place. Is he here?"

"I suppose so," she said absent-mindedly, a distant look in her eyes. Her lips moved as if she was counting to herself.

I said: "Take it or leave it, but it's a gut."

She opened her bag and dragged out a roll of bills the size of a coffee-can. Part of the roll she pushed at Rolff.

"Here, Dan, slap it on Bush. You've got an hour anyway to look for the best odds."

Rolff took the money and went off on his errand. I took his seat. She put a hand on my forearm and said:

"God help you if you've made me drop that dough!"

I pretended the idea was ridiculous, pretended I was absolutely sure Bush was going to win. The preliminary bouts got going—four-round affairs between assorted hams. I kept an eye out for Thaler, but didn't spot him. The girl fidgeted beside me, paying little attention to the preliminaries, dividing her time between asking me where I had got my information and threatening me with hell-fire and damnation if it turned out to be a bust.

The semi-final was on when Rolff came back and gave the girl a handful of tickets. She was straining her eyes over them when I left for my own seat. Without looking up she called after me: "Wait outside for us when it's over."

Kid Cooper climbed into the ring while I was squeezing through to my seat. He was a ruddy, straw-haired, solid-built boy with a dented face and too much meat around the top of his lavender trunks. Ike Bush, alias Al Kennedy, came through the ropes in the opposite corner. His body looked better—slim, nicely ridged, snaky—but his face was pale and worried.

They were introduced, went into the center of the ring with referee and seconds for the usual instructions, returned to their corners shedding bathrobes, stretched on the ropes, the gong rang, and the scrap was on.

Cooper was a clumsy bum. He had nothing but a pair of wide swings that might have hurt if they landed—but anybody with two feet could have kept away from them. Bush had class—nimble legs, a smooth, fast left hand, and a right that got away quick. It would have been murder to put Cooper in the ring with him, if he had been trying. But he wasn't. That is, he wasn't trying to win. He had a sweet job on his hands trying not to.

Cooper waddled flat-footed around the ring throwing his wide swings at everything from the lights to the corner posts. His system was simply to turn 'em loose and let 'em take their chances. Bush moved in and out, putting a glove on the ruddy boy whenever he wanted to, but not putting anything behind the glove.

The customers were booing before the first round was over. The second round was just as bad. I didn't feel so good, myself. Bush didn't seem to have been much influenced by our little conversation. Out of the corner of my eye I could see Dinah Brand trying to catch my attention. She looked hot. I took care not to have my attention caught.

The room-mate act in the ring was continued in the third round, to the tune of yelled Throw-'em-outs, Why-don't-you-kiss-hims and Make-'em-fights from the seats. The pugs' waltz brought them around to the corner nearest me just as the booing broke off for a moment. I made a megaphone of my hands and bawled:

"Back to Philly, Al!"

Bush's back was to me. He wrestled Cooper around, shoving him into the ropes, so he—Bush—faced my way.

From somewhere far back in another part of the house another voice yelled: "Back to Philly, Al!" MacSwain, I supposed. A drunk down the line raised a puffy face and bawled the same thing, laughing as if it were a swell joke. A couple of other birds took up the cry for no reason at all.

Bush's eyes jerked from side to side under the black bar of his eyebrows. One of Cooper's wild mitts clouted the slim boy on the side of the jaw and piled him at the referee's feet.

The referee counted five in two seconds, but the gong cut him off. I looked over at Dinah Brand and laughed. What else was there to do? She looked at me and didn't laugh. Her face was sick as Dan Rolff's, but madder.

Bush's handlers had dragged him to his stool and were rubbing him up, not working very hard at it. He opened his eyes and watched his feet. The gong was tapped.

Cooper paddled out hitching up his trunks. Bush waited until the bum was in the middle of the ring, and then came to him, fast. Bush's left glove went down, out—practically out of sight in Cooper's belly.

Cooper said, "Ugh!" and backed away, folding up. Bush straightened him with a right hand poke in the chin, and sank the left again. Cooper said, "Ugh" again and had trouble with his knees. Bush cuffed him once on each side of his head, cocked his right, carefully pushed Cooper's face into position with a long left, and threw his right hand straight from under his jaw to Cooper's.

Everybody in the house felt the punch. Cooper hit the floor, bounced, and settled there. It took the referee half a minute to count ten seconds. It would have been just the same if he had taken half an hour. Kid Cooper was out.

When the referee had finally stalled through the count he raised Bush's hand. Neither of them looked happy.

A twinkle of light, high up, caught my eye. A short silvery streak slanted down from one of the small balconies. A woman shrieked. The silvery streak ended its flashing slant in the ring—with a sound that was partly a snap, partly a thud.

Ike Bush took his arm out of the referee's hand and pitched down on top of Kid Cooper. A black knife-handle stuck out of the nape of Bush's neck.

V

Half an hour later, when I left the building, Dinah Brand was sitting at the wheel of a pale blue little Marmon, talking to Max Thaler, who stood in the road. The girl's square chin was tilted up. Her big red mouth was brutal around the words it shaped, and the lines that crossed its ends were deep, hard. Her eyes were heavily lashed dark slits. The gambler looked as unpleasant as she. His pretty face was yellow and tough as oak, and when it was his turn to talk his lips curled paper-thin. It seemed to be a nice family party. I wouldn't have joined it if the girl hadn't seen me and called:

"My Gawd, I thought you were never coming!"

I went over to the car. Thaler looked across the hood at me with no friendliness at all.

"Last night I advised you to get out of town." His whisper was harsher than anybody's shout could have been. "Now I'm telling you."

"Thanks, just the same," I said.

The girl swung the door open and I got in beside her. While she was stirring up the engine Thaler said to her:

"This isn't the first time you've sold me out. It's the last."

As we slid away she turned her head back over her shoulder and sang:

"To hell, my love, with you!"

We rode into town rapidly.

"Is Bush dead?" she asked as she twisted the car into Broadway.

"Decidedly. When they turned him over the point of the knife was sticking out in front."

"He ought to have known better than to double-cross them. Let's get something to eat. I'm almost eleven hundred ahead on the night's doings, so if the boy friend doesn't like it, it's just too bad. How'd you come out?"

"Didn't bet. So your Max didn't like it?"

"Didn't bet?" she cried, stopping the car violently in front of a Chinese restaurant. "What kind of an ass are you, anyway? Who ever heard of anybody not betting when they had a thing like that sewed up?"

"I wasn't very sure it was sewed up. So Max didn't like the way things came out?"

"You guessed it! He must have dropped a couple of thousand. And then he got sore with me because I had sense enough to switch over and get in on the pickings. Well, to hell with him, the little tin-horn runt!"

Her eyes were shiny—because they were wet. She jabbed them with a wadded handkerchief as we got out of the car.

"My Gawd I'm hungry!" she said, dragging me across the sidewalk to the restaurant door. "Will you buy me a ton of *chow mein?*"

She didn't eat a ton of it, but she did pretty well, putting away a heaping dish of her own and half of mine. Then we got back into the Marmon and rode out to her house.

Dan Rolff was in the dining-room. A brown bottle with no label and a water glass stood on the table in front of him. He sat straight up in a chair, staring at the bottle with eye-pupils the size of pin-heads. The room smelled of laudanum.

Dinah Brand slid her fur coat off, letting it fall half on a chair, half on the floor, and snapped her fingers at Rolff, saying impatiently:

"Did you collect?"

Without looking up from the bottle, he took a wad of paper money out of his inside coat pocket and dropped it on the table. The girl grabbed it, counted the bills twice, smacked her lips, and stuffed the money in her bag.

She went out to the kitchen and began chopping ice. I sat down and lighted a cigarette. Rolff stared at his bottle. He and I never seemed to have much to say to one another. Presently the girl brought in some gin, lemon-juice, seltzer and ice. We drank and she told the sick man:

"Max is sore as hell. He heard you'd been running around putting last-minute money on Bush, and the little monkey thinks I double-crossed him. What did I have to do with it? All I did was what any sensible person would have done—get in on the win. I didn't have any more to do with it than a baby, did I?" she asked me.

"No."

"Of course not. What's the matter with Max is he's afraid his gang will think he was in on it too—that Dan was putting down his dough as well as mine. Well, that's his trouble. He can go climb trees for all I care, the lousy little runt! Another little drink would be all right."

She poured another for herself and me. Rolff hadn't touched his first one. He said, still staring at the brown bottle:

"You can hardly expect him to be hilarious over it."

The girl scowled and said disagreeably:

"I can expect anything I want. And he's got no right to talk to me the way he did. He doesn't own me! Maybe he thinks he does. But I'll show him he doesn't!" She emptied her glass, banged it down on the table, and twisted around in her chair to face me. "Is that on the level about you having ten grands from Elihu Willsson to clean up Personville?"

"Yeah."

Her bloodshot eyes glistened hungrily.

"And if I help you will I get some of the ten—"

"You can't do that, Dinah!" Rolff's voice was thick, but gently firm, as if he were talking to a child. "That would be utterly filthy."

The girl turned her face slowly around toward him, and her mouth began to take on the look it had worn while she talked to Thaler.

"I *am* going to do it," she said. "That makes me utterly filthy, does it?"

He didn't say anything, didn't look up from the bottle. Her face got red, hard, cruel, her voice soft, cooing:

"It's just too bad that a gentleman of your purity, even if he is a little bit consumptive, has to associate with a filthy bum like me."

"That can be remedied," he said slowly, getting up. He was laudanumed to the scalp.

Dinah Brand jumped out of her chair and ran around the table. He watched her with no expression in his thin face—only weariness. She put her face close to his and demanded:

"So I'm too utterly filthy for you now, am I?"

He said evenly:

"I said to betray your friends to this chap would be utterly filthy, and it would."

She seized one of his thin wrists and twisted it until he was on his knees. Her other hand, open, beat his hollow cheeks, half a dozen times on each side, rocking his head from side to side. He could have put up his free arm to cover his face, but didn't. She let go his wrist, turned her back on him and reached for gin and seltzer. She was smiling to herself. I didn't like the smile.

He got up on his feet, blinking. His wrist was dark where she had gripped it, his face bruised. He steadied himself and looked at me with dull eyes.

Without any change in face or eyes he put a hand under his coat, brought out a black automatic and fired at me. But he was too shaky for either speed or accuracy. I had time to toss my glass at him. The glass hit his shoulder. His bullet went somewhere overhead. Before he got the next one out I had jumped—was close to him—close enough to knock the gun down. The second slug went into the floor. I socked him in the jaw. He fell away from me and lay still where he fell.

I turned around. Dinah Brand was getting ready to bat me over the head with the seltzer bottle—a heavy glass siphon that would have made pulp of my skull.

"Don't!" I yelped.

"You didn't have to bust him like that!" she snarled.

"Well, it's done. You'd better get him straightened out."

She put down the siphon and I helped her carry him up to his bed-room. When he began moving his eyes I left her to finish the work and went down to the dining-room again. She joined me there fifteen or twenty minutes later.

"He's all right," she said. "But you could have handled him without that."

"I know, but I did it for him. You know why he took the shot at me?"

"So I'd have nobody to sell Max out to?"

"No. Because I'd seen you maul him around."

"That doesn't make sense to me," she said. "I was the one that did it."

"Sure, but he's probably in love with you, and besides, this isn't the first time you've done it—he acted like he knew there was no use matching muscle with you. But you can't expect him to enjoy having another man see you slap his face."

"I used to think I knew men," she complained, "but, by Gawd, I don't! They're lunatics, all of 'em!"

"So I poked him to give him back some of his self-respect. You know—treated him like a he-man instead of a down-and-outer who could be spanked by girls."

"Anything you say," she sighed. "I give it up. We ought to have a drink."

VI

We had the drink and I said:

"Before the excitement broke loose you were saying you'd work with me if there was a share of the Willsson money in it for you. There is."

"How much?"

"Whatever you earn. Whatever what you do is worth."

"That's kind of uncertain."

"So's your help, so far as I know."

"Is it? I can give you the stuff, loads of it, brother, and don't think I can't. I'm a girl who knows her Poisonville." She looked down at her gray-stockinged knees, waved one leg at me, and exclaimed indignantly: "Look at that! Another run! Did you ever see anything to beat it? Honest to Gawd, I'm going barefooted!"

"Your legs are too big," I told her. "They put too much strain on the material."

"That'll do out of you! What's your idea of how to go about purifying our village?"

"You weren't far off yesterday when you said I was going to advertise—*Crime Wanted—Male or Female.* If I haven't been lied to, Thaler, Pete the Finn Lew Yard and Noonan are the four men who've made Poisonville the sweet mess it is. Old Eihu Willsson comes in for his share of the blame, too, but it's not all his fault. He has to play with the others whether he wants to or not and, besides, he's my client—even if he doesn't want to be now—so I'd like to go easy on him. Well, my scheme is simply to dig up anything that looks like it might implicate one or more of those four and run it out. If they're as crooked as I think they are, sooner or later I'll land 'em."

"Is that what you were up to when you uncooked the fight?"

"That was only an experiment—just to see what would happen."

"So that's the way you scientific detectives work! Good Gawd! For a fat, middle-aged, hard-boiled, pig-headed guy, you've got the vaguest way of doing things I ever heard of!"

"Plans are all right sometimes," I said. "And sometimes just stirring things up is all right—if you're tough enough to survive, and keep your eyes open so you'll see what you want when it comes to the top."

"That ought to be good for another drink," she said.

We had it. She put her glass down, licked her lips and said:

"If stirring things up is your system, I've got a swell spoon for you, old darling. Did you ever hear of Noonan's brother Tim—the one that committed suicide out at Mock Lake a couple of years ago?"

"No."

"You wouldn't have heard much good. Anyway, he didn't commit suicide. Max killed him."

"Yeah?"

"Yeah. For Gawd's sake, wake up! This I'm giving you is real. Noonan was like a father to the kid. He'll be after Max like nobody's business if you take the proof to him. That's what you want, isn't it—split 'em?"

"We've got proof, have we?"

"There are two people that got to Tim before he died, and he told 'em Max had done it. They're both in town, though one of 'em isn't going to live a lot longer. How's that?"

She looked as if she was telling the truth, though with women—especially blue-eyed women—that doesn't always mean anything.

"Sounds all right so far," I said. "Let's listen to the rest of it. I like details and things."

"You'll get 'em. You ever been out to Mock Lake? Well, it's our summer resort, thirty miles up the canyon road. It's a dump, but it's cool in summer, so it gets a good play. This was summer a year ago—the last week-end in August. I was out there with a fellow named Holly. He's back in England now, but you don't care about that, because he hasn't anything to do with it. He was a funny sort of an old woman—used to wear white silk socks inside out so the loose threads wouldn't hurt his feet. I got a letter from him last week. It's around here somewhere, but that doesn't make any difference.

"We were up there, and Max was up there with a girl he used to play around with. She's in the hospital now—City Hospital—dying of Bright's disease or something. She's all swelled up now, but she was a classy-looking kid then—a slender blonde. I liked her, except that she got too gay when she had a few drinks. Tim Noonan was crazy about her, but she couldn't see anybody but Max that summer. Tim wouldn't let her alone. He was a big, good-looking Irishman, but a sap and a cheap crook that only got by because his brother was chief of police. Wherever Myrtle went, he'd pop up sooner or later. She didn't like to say anything to Max about it—not wanting Max to get in wrong with Noonan—the chief.

"So Tim showed up at Mock Lake this Saturday. Myrtle and Max were just by themselves. Holly and I were with a crowd, but I saw Myrtle to talk to and she told me she had got a note from Tim, asking her to meet him for fifteen minutes that night in one of the little arbor things on the hotel grounds. He said if she didn't he was going to kill himself. That was a laugh for us—the big false alarm! I tried to talk her out of meeting him, but she said she was going to give him a mouthful.

"That night we were all dancing in the hotel. Max was there for a while and then I didn't see him any more. Myrtle was dancing with a fellow named Rutgers—a lawyer here in town. After a while she left him and passed me, going out one of the side doors. She winked when she passed, so I knew she was going out to meet Tim. She'd just got out when I heard the shot. Nobody else paid any attention to it, if they heard it. I suppose I wouldn't have either if it hadn't been that I knew about Myrtle and Tim and the note.

"I told Holly I wanted to see Myrtle, and went out after her. I must have been at least five minutes behind her. When I got outside there were lights down by one of the arbors, and people. I went down there and—This talking is thirsty work!"

I poured a couple of shots of gin. She went into the kitchen for another siphon and more ice. We mixed them up, wet our mouths, and she settled down to her tale again.

"Well, there was Tim Noonan, dead, with a hole in his temple and his gun laying beside him. There were, say, a dozen people standing around—hotel people, guests, one of Noonan's bulls—a dick named MacSwain. As soon as Myrtle saw me she grabbed me and took me away from the crowd, back in the dark.

"'Max killed him!' she said. 'What'll I do?'

"I asked her all about it, and she told me she had seen the flash of the gun and she thought Tim had killed himself after all. But when she ran down to him he was rolling around, moaning. 'He didn't have to kill me over her. I'd have—' She couldn't make out the rest of it. He was pitching and rolling around, bleeding from the head. Myrtle was afraid right way that Max had done it, but she had to know for sure. So she knelt down and tried to pick up Tim's head, asking, 'Who did it, Tim?'

"He was almost gone, but before he passed out he got strength enough to tell her, 'Max!'

"She kept asking me, 'What'll I do?' I asked her if anybody else had heard him, and she said the dick had. He had come running up while she was trying to lift Tim's head. She didn't think anybody else had been close enough to hear, but the dick had.

"I didn't want Max to get in a jam over killing a mutt like Tim Noonan. Max didn't mean anything to me then, but

I liked him, and I didn't like any of the Noonans. I knew the dick—MacSwain. He had been a pretty good guy—was straight as ace, deuce, trey, four, five till he got on the force. Then he went the way of the rest of 'em. Graft and booze. I knew his wife. She stood as much of it as she could and then left him. So, knowing this dick, I told Myrtle I thought we could fix things. A little jack would ruin MacSwain's memory, or if he didn't like that Max could have him bumped off. She had Tim's note threatening suicide. If the dick would play along, the hole in Tim's temple from his own gun and the note would smooth everything over pretty.

"I left Myrtle in the bushes and went out to look for Max. He wasn't around. There weren't very many people there, and I could hear the hotel orchestra still playing dance music. There were even people strolling along the slope between the hotel and the arbors, not knowing anything had happened. I couldn't find Max, so I went back to Myrtle. She was all worked up over another idea. She didn't want Max to know that she knew he had killed Tim. She was afraid of him. She was afraid that if she and Max ever broke off he'd put her out of the way if he knew she had enough on him to swing him. I know how she felt. I got the same notion later, and kept just as quiet as she did. So we figured that if it could be fixed without his knowing about it—so much the better.

"I didn't want to be in it either. So Myrtle went back alone to the crowd around Tim and got hold of MacSwain. She took him off a littleway and made the deal with him. She had some dough on her. She gave him two hundred smacks and a diamond ring that had cost a thousand. I thought he'd come back for more, later. But he didn't. He shot square with her. With the help of the letter he put over the suicide. Noonan knew there was something fishy about the layout, and I think he suspected Max of being tied up in it. But Max had an air-tight alibi—trust the boy for that—and I think even Noonan finally gave up that notion, but he never believed it all happened the way it was made to look. He broke MacSwain—kicked him off the force.

"Max and Myrtle slid apart a little while after that—no row or anything—they just slid apart. I don't think she ever felt easy around him again, though so far as I know he never suspected her of knowing anything. She's got Bright's disease or something now, I told you, and hasn't got long to live. I think she'd not so much mind telling the truth if she was asked. MacSwain's still hanging around town. I don't suppose he'd mind talking either if there was something in it for him. Anyway, those two have got the stuff on Max—and wouldn't Noonan eat it up! Is that good enough to give your stirring-up a start? Let's have a little drink."

VII

We had the drink, and I asked:

"Couldn't it have been suicide? With Tim Noonan getting a last-minute bright idea to stick it on Max?"

"That four-flusher shoot himself! Not a chance! Besides, he was right-handed and was shot in the side of his left temple—an awkward place to shoot himself. That's what made Noonan leery. But if Tim had wanted to go in for acrobatics he could have plugged himself there, so they had to let it go at that."

"How about Myrtle? Could she have shot him?"

"Noonan didn't overlook that one, either. But she couldn't have been a third the distance down the slope when the shot was fired. Tim had powder marks on his forehead, and he hadn't been shot and rolled down. Myrtle's out. Max."

"But he had an alibi?"

"Sure. He was in the hotel bar, on the other side of the building, all the time. He had four men who said so. As I remember, they said it openly and often, long before anybody asked them. It happens there were other men in the bar who didn't remember his being there, but these four remembered all right—they'd remember anything Max wanted remembered."

Her eyes got large and then narrowed to two black-fringed slits. She leaned toward me, upsetting her glass with an elbow.

"Here's something that might help," she exclaimed. "Peak Murry was one of the four. He and Max are on the outs now. Peak might tell it straight. He's got a pool-room on Broadway."

"This MacSwain—does he happen to be named Bob? A bow-legged man with a long jaw like a hog's?"

"Yes—you know him?"

"By sight. What does he do now?"

"A small-time grifter. What do you think of the stack-up?"

"Not bad. Maybe I can do something with it."

"Then let's talk scratch."

I grinned at the greed in her eyes, and said:

"Not just yet, sister. We'll have to wait and see how it works out before we start scattering pennies around."

She called me a damned nickel-nurser and reached for the gin.

"No more for me," I told her, looking at my watch. "It's getting along toward five A.M. and I'm in for a busy day scouting up these people you've been telling me about."

She decided she was hungry again. It took her half an hour or more to get waffles, ham and coffee off the stove. It took us another while to move them from table to stomachs and to smoke some cigarettes over extra cups of the coffee. It was after six when I left.

"If you don't mind," I said, "I'll leave by the back door. What with Noonan and Thaler not liking me, and the number of times I've already had to dodge lead in this burg, I'd like to be as little conspicuous as possible."

"Get a taxi."

"Too showy. And I need air and exercise now that there's no chance of getting any sleep."

She let me out the back door. Everything was quiet in the morning light. I went through her yard, into the alley, down it for a couple of blocks, over into one of the streets paralleling Broadway, down it, and over to my hotel and a tub of cold water.

The cold water braced me up, and I had needed it. At forty I could get along without sleep, but not comfortably. After I had dressed I sat down and composed a document:

> Just before he died Tim Noonan told me he had been shot by Max Thaler. Detective Bob MacSwain heard him tell me. I gave MacSwain $200 and a diamond ring worth $1000 to keep quiet and make it look like suicide.

With this document in my pocket I went downstairs, had another breakfast that was chiefly coffee, and went up to the City Hospital. Visiting hours were in the afternoon, but by flourishing my Continental Detective Agency credentials and giving everybody to understand that an hour's delay might cause hundreds of deaths, or words to that effect, I got to see Myrtle Jennison.

She was in a ward on the third floor, alone. The other four beds were empty. She could have been a girl of twenty-five or a woman of fifty-five. Her face was a bloated, spotty mask. Lifeless yellow hair was gathered in two stringy braids that lay on the pillow beside her. I waited until the nurse who had brought me in was gone. Then I held my document out to the invalid and said:

"Will you sign this, please, Miss Jennison?"

She looked at me with unpleasant eyes that were shaded into no particular color by the pads of flesh around them, then at the document, and finally brought a shapeless, fat white hand from under the covers to take it. She pretended it took her nearly five minutes to read the forty-one words I had written. She let it fall down on the covers and asked:

"Where'd you get that?" Her voice was tinny, irritable.

"Dinah Brand told me."

She licked her swollen lips and asked eagerly:

"Has she broken off with Max?"

"Not that I know of," I lied. "I imagine she just wants to have this on hand in case it should come in handy."

"And get her fool throat slit. Give me a pencil."

I gave her my fountain pen and held my notebook under the document to stiffen it while she scribbled her signature at the bottom, and to have it in my hands as soon as she had finished. While I fanned the paper dry she said:

"If that's what she wants it's all right with me. What do I care what anybody does any more? I'm done. Hell with 'em all!" She sniggered evilly.

"Thanks very much for this, Miss Jennison." "That's all right. It's nothing to me any more. Only"—her puffy chin quivered—"it's hell to die ugly as this."

VIII

I went out to hunt for MacSwain. Neither city directory nor telephone book told me anything. I did the pool-rooms, cigar stores, speak-easies, looking around first, then asking cautious questions. That got me nothing. I walked the streets, looking for bowed legs. That got me nothing. I decided to go back to my hotel, take a nap, and resume the hunt that night.

In a far corner of the lobby a man stopped hiding behind a newspaper and came out to meet me. He had bowed legs, a hog jaw, and was MacSwain. I nodded carelessly at him and walked on to the elevator. He followed me, mumbling:

"Hey, you got a minute?"

"Yeah." I stopped, pretending indifference.

"Let's get out of sight then."

I took him up to my room. He straddled a chair and put a match in his mouth. I sat on the side of the bed and waited for him to say something. He chewed his match a while and began:

"I'm going to come clean with you, brother, I'm—"

"You are?" I asked. "You mean you're going to tell me you knew who I was when you braced me yesterday? And you weren't a friend of Bush's? And you didn't have any money down on him then? And you knew who he was because you used to be a bull? And you thought if you could get me to put it to him you could clean up a little dough playing him?"

"I'll be damned if I was going to come through with that much," he said, "but you've got it about right, so I'll put a yes to it."

"Did you clean up?"

"I win myself six hundred iron men." He pushed his hat back and scratched his forehead with the chewed end of his match. "And then I lose myself six hundred and forty iron men in a crap game. What do you think of that? I pick up six hundred berries like shooting fish—and have to bum four bits for breakfast!"

I said it was a tough break but that was the kind of world we lived in.

He said "Uh-huh," put the match back in his mouth, ground it some more, and added: "That's why I thought I'd come and see you. I used to be in the racket myself, and—"

"What did Noonan put the skids under you for?"

"Skids? What skids? I quit! I come into a piece of change when my wife got killed in an automobile accident—insurance—ten grand—and I quit."

"I heard he kicked you off the force the time his brother shot himself."

"You heard wrong. It was just after that—maybe a week—but I quit, and you can ask him if I didn't."

"It's not that much to me. Go on telling me why you came to see me."

"I'm busted—flat. I know you're a Continental op and I got a pretty good idea what you're up to here. I'm pretty close to a lot that's going on in this burg. There's things I could do for you, knowing the ropes both ways, being a ex-dick myself."

"You want to stool-pigeon for me."

He looked me straight in the eye and said evenly:

"There's no sense in a man picking out the worst name he can find for everything."

"All right, MacSwain. I'll give you something to do." I took out Myrtle Jennison's document and passed it to him. "Tell me about that."

He read it through carefully, his lips framing the words, the match jumping up and down in his mouth. He got up, put the paper on the bed beside me, and scowled down at it.

"There's something I'll have to find out first," he said, very seriously. "I'll be back in a little while and give you the whole story."

I laughed.

"Don't be silly," I told him. "You know I'm not going to let you walk out on me."

"I don't know that." He shook his head, still very serious. "Neither do you. All you know is whether you're going to try to stop me."

"The answer's yeah," I said while I considered that he was fairly hard and strong, six or seven years younger than I, twenty or thirty pounds lighter.

He stood at the foot of the bed and looked at me with solemn eyes. I sat on the side of the bed and looked at him with whatever sort of eyes I had at the time. We did this for nearly three minutes. I used part of the time measuring the distance between us, figuring out how, by throwing my body back on the bed and turning on my hip, I could get my heels in his face if he jumped me. He was too close for me to pull the gat. I had just finished this mental map-making when he spoke:

"That lousy ring wasn't worth no grand. I did swell to get two centuries for it."

"Sit down," I suggested, "and tell me about it."

He wouldn't. He shook his head and stood where he was, within reach of me.

"Then tell me about it without sitting down."

He shook his head again and said:

"First I want to know what you're going to do about it.

"Cop Whisper."

"I don't mean that. I mean with me."

"You'll have to go over to the Hall with me."

"Won't!"

"Why not? You're only a witness."

"That's right. I'm only a witness that Noonan can hang a bribe-taking rap and a perjury rap, or both, on. And he'll be tickled simple to have the chance, damn him!"

The jaw-wagging didn't seem to be getting us anywhere. I said:

"That's too bad. But you're going to see him just the same."

"Try and take me."

I sat up straighter and slid my right hand back to my hip. He grabbed at me. I threw my body back on the bed, did the hip-swing, swung my feet at him. It was a good trick, only it didn't work. In his hurry to get at me he bumped the bed aside just enough to spill me off on the floor. I landed all sprawled out on my back. I kept dragging at my gun while I tried to roll under the bed. Missing me, his lunge carried him over the low footboard, over the side of the bed. He came down beside me, on the back of his neck, his body somersaulting over. I put the muzzle of my gun in his left eye and said:

"You're making a swell pair of clowns out of us! Be still while I get up or I'll make an opening in your head for brains to leak in."

I got up, found and pocketed my document, and let him get up.

"Knock the dents out of your hat and put your necktie back in front," I ordered after I had run a hand over his clothes and found nothing that felt like a weapon, "so you won't disgrace me going through the street. And you can suit yourself about whether you want to remember this gat is in my overcoat pocket, with a hand on it."

He straightened his hat and tie and said:

"Hey, listen! I'm in this, I guess, and cutting up won't get me nothing. Suppose I come clean when we get up there? Could you forget about the tussle? See—maybe it'd be smoother for me if they thought I come along without being dragged."

"O.K."

"Thanks, brother."

IX

We went over to the City Hall. Noonan was out eating. We had to wait half an hour for him. When he came in he greeted me with the usual hearty *How are you? That certainly is fine!* and the rest of it. Then his fat face and greenish eyes lost their geniality for sourness as he looked at MacSwain.

"Let's go inside," I said, and the chief led the way back to his private office. He pulled a chair over to his desk for me and then sat in his own, ignoring the ex-dick.

I gave Noonan the document. He gave it one glance, bounced out of his chair, and smashed a fist the size of a cantaloup into MacSwain's face.

The punch carried MacSwain across the room until a wall stopped him. The wall creaked under the strain, and a framed photograph of Noonan and some other city dignitaries welcoming somebody in spats dropped down to the floor with the hit man. The fat chief waddled over, picked up the picture and beat it into splinters on MacSwain's head and shoulders.

Noonan came back to his desk, puffing, smiling, saying cheerfully to me: "That fellow's a rat if there ever was one."

MacSwain sat up and looked around, bleeding from nose, mouth and head.

Noonan roared at him: "Come here, you—!"

MacSwain said, "Yes, chief!" scrambled up and ran over to the desk.

Noonan said: "Come through or I'll kill you!"

MacSwain said: "Yes, chief! It was like she says in the letter, only that rock wasn't worth no grand. But she give me it and the two centuries to keep my mouth shut, because I got there just when she asks him, 'Who did it, Tim?' and he says, 'Max!' He says it kind of loud and sharp, like he wanted to get it out before he died, because he died right then, almost before he'd got it out. That's the way it was, chief, only that rock wasn't worth no—"

"Damn the rock!" Noonan barked. "And stop bleeding on my rug!"

MacSwain fumbled in his pocket for a dirty handkerchief, mopped his nose and mouth with it, and jabbered on:

"And that's the way it was, chief. Everything else was like I said at the time, only I didn't say anything about hearing him say Max done it. I know I hadn't ought to—"

"Shut up!" Noonan yelled, and pressed one of the buttons on his desk. A uniformed copper came in. The chief jerked a thumb at MacSwain and said: "Take this—down cellar and let the wrecking crew work a while on him before you lock him up."

MacSwain started a desperate plea, "Aw, chief!" but the copper took him away before he could get any further.

Noonan stuck a cigar at me, tapped the document with another and asked:

"Where is this broad?"

"In the pogy—dying. You'll have the cuter get a stiff out of her? That's not so good, legally—I framed it for effect. Another thing: I hear that Peak Murry and Whisper aren't playmates any more. Wasn't Murry one of his alibis? How about going up against him?"

The chief nodded, picked up one of his phones, said "McGraw" and then: "Get hold of Peak Murry. Have him come in. And have Tony Agosti picked up. That knife-throwing."

He put the phone down, stood up, made a lot of cigar smoke, and spoke through it:

"I haven't always been on the up-and-up with you." I thought that was putting it mildly, but I didn't say anything, while he went on: "You know your way around. You know what these jobs are. There's this one and that one that's got to be listened to. Just because a man's chief of police don't mean he's chief. Maybe you're a lot of trouble to somebody that can be a lot of trouble to me. Don't make any difference if I think you're a good guy. I got to play with them that play with me. See what I mean?"

I wagged my head to show that I did.

"That's the way it was," he said. "But no more. This is something else—a new deal. When the old woman kicked off, Tim was just a lad. There was only the two of us, and the old woman said to me, 'Take care of him, John.' And I said I would. And then Whisper murders him on account of that tramp!" He reached down and took my hand. "See what I'm getting at? That's a year and a half ago, and you give me my first chance to hang it on him. I'm telling you there's no man in Personville with a voice big enough to talk you down—not after today."

That made me happy, and I said so. We held a mutual admiration meeting until a lanky man with an extremely upturned nose in the middle of a round and freckled face was ushered in. It was Peak Murry.

"We were just wondering about the time when Tim died," the chief said when Murry had been given a chair and a cigar, "where Whisper was. You were out to the Lake that night, weren't you?"

"Yep!" Murry said, and the end of his nose seemed to get sharper and higher.

"With Whisper?"

"I wasn't with him all the time."

"Were you with him at the time of the shooting?"

"Nope."

The chief's greenish eyes got smaller and brighter. He asked softly:

"Know where he was?"

"Nope."

The chief sighed in a thoroughly satisfied way and leaned back in his chair.

"Damn it, Peak, you said before that you were with him in the bar!"

"Yep, I did," the lanky man admitted. "But that don't mean nothing except that he asked me to and I didn't mind helping out a friend."

"Meaning you don't mind standing a perjury rap?"

"Don't kid me!" Murry spit emphatically at the cuspidor. "I didn't say nothing in no court rooms."

"How about Jerry and George Kelly and O'Brien?" the chief asked. "Did they say they were with him just because he asked 'em to?"

"O'Brien did. I don't know nothing about the others. I was going out of the bar when I run into Whisper, Jerry and Kelly, and went back to have a snifter with them. Kelly told me Tim had been knocked off. Then Whisper says, 'It never hurts anybody to have an alibi. We were here all the time, weren't we?' and he looks at O'Brien, who's behind the bar. O'Brien says, 'Sure you was!' and when Whisper looks at me I say the same thing. That was then. But I don't know no reason why I've got to cover him up nowadays."

"And Kelly said Tim had been knocked off? Didn't say he'd been found dead?"

"Nope. Knocked off was the words he used."

The chief said: "Thanks, Peak. You oughtn't to have done like you did, but what's done is done. How are the kids?"

Peak said they were doing fine, only the baby wasn't quite as fat as he would have liked to have him. Noonan had an assistant prosecuting attorney—a young fellow-named Dart—come in with a stenographer. Peak repeated his story to them, waited until it had been typed, swore to it and signed it. Then he went away.

The rest of them set out for the City Hospital to get Myrtle Jennison's statement. I didn't go along. I saw another chance to get the nap MacSwain had robbed me of. So I told the chief I'd see him later, and went over to the hotel.

X

I had my vest unbuttoned when the phone rang.

It was Dinah Brand, complaining that she had been trying to get me since ten o'clock.

"Have you done anything on what I told you about?" she asked.

"I've been looking the ground over. It looks pretty good. I think maybe I'll crack it this afternoon."

"No! Hold off till I see you! Can you come up now?"

I looked at the vacant white bed, and said "Yes" without much enthusiasm.

Another tub of cold water did me so little good that I nearly fell asleep in it. Dan Rolff let me in when I rang the girl's bell. He looked and acted as if nothing out of the ordinary had happened the night before. Dinah Brand came into the hall to help me off with my overcoat. She had on a tan woolen dress with a two-inch tear in one shoulder seam.

She and I went into the living-room. She sat on the Chesterfield beside me and said:

"I'm going to ask you to do something for me. You like me enough, don't you?"

I admitted it. She counted the knuckles of my left hand with a warm forefinger and explained:

"I want you to not do anything more about what I told you last night. Now wait a minute! Wait till I get through! Dan was right. I oughtn't sell Max out like that—it *would* be utterly filthy. Besides, it's Noonan you chiefly want, isn't it? Well, if you'll be a nice darling and lay off Max this time I'll give you enough on Noonan to swing him. You'd like that better, wouldn't you? And you like me too much to take advantage of me by using the information I gave you when I was mad at what Max had said, don't you?"

"What is this dirt on Noonan?" I asked.

She kneaded my biceps, and murmured: "You promise?"

"Not yet."

She pouted at me and said:

"I'm off Max for life—on the level. You've got no right to make me turn rat."

"What about Noonan?"

"Promise first."

"No."

She dug her fingers into my arm and asked sharply:

"You've already gone to Noonan?"

"Yeah."

She let go my arm, frowned, shrugged and said gloomily: "Well, how can I help it?"

I stood up, and a voice said: "Sit down!"

It was a hoarse, whispering voice. I knew it belonged to Thaler before I turned to see him standing in the dining-room doorway, a big rod in one of his little hands. A red-faced man with a scarred cheek stood behind him. The other doorway—opening to the hall—filled up as I sat down. An almost chinless man with a wide, loose mouth in a thin, pimply face came a step through it. He had a couple of guns. An angular blond kid looked over his shoulder. I had met this pair before, in Whisper's King Street joint. The chinless one was called Jerry—probably the Jerry of the alibi party.

Dinah Brand got up from the Chesterfield, put her back to Thaler and addressed me. Her voice was husky with rage.

"This is none of my doing. He came here by himself, said he was sorry for what he said last night, and showed me how he and I could make ourselves a lot of money by turning Noonan up for you. Now I know it was a plant. He was to wait upstairs while I put it to you. I didn't know anything about these others."

Jerry's casual voice drawled:

"If I shoot a pin from under her she'll sure sit down and maybe shut up. O.K.?"

I couldn't see Whisper. The girl was between us. He said: "Not now. Where's Dan?"

The blond kid said: "Up on the bathroom floor. I had to sap him."

Dinah Brand turned around to face Thaler. Stocking seams made s's up the ample backs of her legs. She said:

"Max Thaler, you're a lousy little—"

He whispered, very deliberately: "Shut... up... and... get... out... of... the... way."

She surprised me by doing both, and she kept quiet while he spoke to me:

"So you and Noonan are trying to paste his brother's death on me?"

"It don't need pasting. It's a natural."

He curved his thin lips at me and said: "You're as crooked as he is."

I said: "You know better. When he tried to frame you for Donald Willsson's killing I played your side. This time he's got you copped to rights."

Dinah Brand flared up again, waving her arms in the middle of the room, storming:

"Get out of here, the whole lot of you! Why should I give a damn about your troubles? Get out!"

The blond kid who had sapped Rolff squeezed past Jerry and came grinning into the room. He caught one of the girl's flourished arms and bent it behind her. She twisted toward him, socked him in the belly with her other fist. It was a very respectable wallop—man-size. It broke his grip on her arm, sent him back a couple of long steps.

The kid gulped in a wide mouthful of air, whisked a blackjack from his hip, and stepped in again. His grin was gone. Jerry laughed what little chin he had out of sight. Thaler whispered harshly: "Lay off!" The kid didn't hear him. He was snarling things at the girl. She watched him with a face hard as a silver dollar. She was standing one-legged, her weight on her left foot. I guessed blondy was going to stop a kick when he closed in.

The kid feinted a grab with his empty left hand—started the blackjack at her face. Thaler whispered "Lay off!" again, and fired.

The bullet smacked blondy under the right eye, spun him around and dropped him backwards into Dinah Brand's arms.

This looked like the time, if there was to be any. In the excitement I had got a hand on my hip. I dragged the gun out and snapped a cap at Thaler, trying for his shoulder. That was wrong. If I'd tried for a bull's-eye I'd have winged him. Chinless Jerry hadn't laughed himself blind. He beat me to the shot. His bullet burnt my wrist, throwing me off the target. But, missing Thaler, my slug crumpled the red-faced man behind him.

I didn't know how bad my wrist was nicked, so I shifted the gun to my left hand. Jerry took another try at me.

The girl spoiled it by heaving the corpse at him. The dead yellow head banged into his knees. I jumped for him while he was off balance.

The jump took me out of the way of Thaler's bullet. It also tumbled Jerry out into the hall. I was all tangled up with him. He wasn't very tough to handle. But I had to work quick. There was Thaler to consider.

I socked Jerry twice, kicked him a couple of times, butted him once and was hunting for a place to bite when he went limp under me. I poked him again where his chin should have been—just to make sure he wasn't faking—and went away on hands and knees—down the hall a bit, out of line with the door.

Then I sat on my heels against the wall, held my gun level at Thaler's part of the premises, and waited. I couldn't hear anything for the moment except the blood singing in my head.

Dinah Brand stepped out of the door I had tumbled through, looked at Jerry, at me, smiled with her tongue between her teeth, beckoned with a jerk of her head, and returned to the living-room.

I followed her in, cautiously.

Whisper stood in the center of the floor. His hands were empty and so was his face. Except for his vicious little mouth, he looked like something displaying suits in a clothing-store window. Dan Rolff stood behind him with a gun-muzzle tilted to the little gambler's left kidney. Rolff's face was mostly blood. A piece of his scalp dangled over his forehead. The blond kid had sapped him plenty.

I grinned at Thaler and said: "Well, this is nice," before I saw that Rolff had another gun—centered on my chubby middle. That wasn't so nice. But my own gun was reasonably level, so I didn't have much worse than an even break.

Rolff said: "Drop your pistol!"

I looked at Dinah—looked puzzled, I suppose. She shrugged and told me:

"It seems to be Dan's party."

"Yeah. Well, somebody ought to tell him that I don't like to play this way."

Rolff repeated: "Drop your pistol!"

"I'll be damned if I will! I've shed twenty pounds trying to nab this baby. I got twenty more I'm willing to spend doing the same thing."

Rolff said: "I'm not interested in what is between you two, and I have no intention of giving either of you into the other's hands. You shall—"

Dinah Brand had wandered across the room. When she was behind Rolff I interrupted his speech by telling her:

"If you upset him now you're sure of making two friends—Noonan and me. You can't trust Whisper any more, no matter what happens, so there's no use helping *him*."

She laughed and said:

"Talk money, darling."

"Dinah!" Rolff protested. He was caught. She was behind him and he knew she was strong enough to handle him. He couldn't look away from me unless he shot me first, and even then, unless he wanted to shoot her, too, he'd still be at her mercy.

"A hundred dollars," I bid.

"My Gawd!" she exclaimed, "I've actually got a cash offer out of you at last! But you ought to do a little better than that."

"Two hundred."

"You're getting positively reckless. But I still can't hear you."

"Try," I said. "It's worth that to me not to have to try to shoot Rolff's gat out of his hand, but no more than that."

"You've got a good start. Don't weaken. One more bid."

"Two hundred dollars and ten cents, and that's all."

"You big bum!" she said. "I won't do it."

"Fair enough!" I made a face at Thaler and told him: "When what happens happens be damned sure you keep still."

Dinah cried:

"Wait! Are you really going to start something?"

"I'm going to take Thaler out with me—regardless."

"Two hundred and a dime?"

"Yeah."

"Dinah!" Rolff called again. "You won't—"

But she laughed, came close to his back and wound her strong arms around him. I shoved the gambler aside, kept him covered while I used my wounded right hand to yank Rolff's weapons away. Dinah turned Rolff loose.

He took two steps toward the dining-room door, said calmly, "There is no—" and collapsed on the floor.

Dinah gave a cry and ran to him. I pushed Thaler out into the hall, past the still sleeping Jerry, and to the alcove beneath the front stairs, where I had seen a phone. I called Noonan, told him I had Thaler, and where.

"Grease us twice!" he said. "Don't kill him till I get there!"

XI

The news of Whisper's capture spread quickly. When Noonan, the half a dozen coppers he had brought along, and I took the gambler and the now conscious Jerry out of the police car and into the City Hall there were at least a hundred men standing around watching us. All of them didn't look pleased. Noonan's coppers—not a good lot at best—moved around with whitish, drawn faces. But Noonan was the most triumphant guy west of the Mississippi.

Even the bad luck he had trying to third-degree Whisper couldn't spoil his happiness. Whisper stood up under everything they gave him. He would talk to his lawyer, he said, and not to anybody else, and he stuck to it. As much as Noonan hated him, I noticed that here was a prisoner he didn't give the works—didn't turn him over to the wrecking crew. Whisper had killed the chief's brother, and the chief hated his guts, but Whisper was still somebody in Personville, and not a tramp like MacSwain.

Noonan finally got tired of playing with his prisoner and sent him up—the prison was on the top floor of the City Hall—to be stowed away till morning.

I lighted another of Noonan's cigars and glanced through the detailed statement he had got from the woman in the hospital. There was nothing in it that I hadn't heard from Dinah or MacSwain. The chief wanted me to come out to his house to dinner, but I lied out of it, pretending that my wrist—now bandaged—was bothering me. It was really nothing more than a bruise and a burn.

While we were talking about that a couple of plainclothes men came in with the red-faced bird who had been hit by the slug I had missed Whisper with. It had broken a rib for him, and he had taken a back-door sneak while the rest of us were busy. Noonan's men had picked him up in a doctor's office. The chief failed to get any information out of him, and sent him off to the hospital.

I got up and prepared to leave, saying: "It was the Brand girl who gave me the tip-off on this. That's why I asked you to keep her and Rolff out of it."

The chief grabbed my left hand for the fifth or sixth time in the past couple of hours.

"If you want her taken care of that's enough for me," he assured me. "But if she had a hand in turning that up, you can tell her any time she wants anything from me all she's got to do is name it."

I said I'd tell her that, and went over to my hotel, thinking about that neat white bed again. But it was nearly eight o'clock, and my stomach needed attention. I went into the dining-room and had that fixed. A leather chair tempted me into stopping in the lobby while I burnt up a cigar. That led to conversation with a traveling railroad auditor from Denver who knew a man I knew in St. Louis. Then there was a lot of shooting in the street.

We went to the door and decided the fire-works were up near the City Hall. I shook the auditor and moved up that way. I had done two-thirds of the distance when an automobile came down the street toward me, coming like a bat out of hell, leaking gunfire from the rear.

I backed into an alley entrance and slid my own gun loose. An arc-light brightened two faces in the front of the car. The driver's meant nothing to me. The upper part of the other's was hidden by a pulled-down hat. The lower part was Whisper's.

Across the street was the entrance to another block of alley, lighted at the far end. Between me and the light somebody moved just as Whisper's car roared past. The somebody had dodged from behind one shadow that might have been an ash can to another. What took my eyes away from Whisper, and kept me from taking a shot at him, was that the legs of the somebody in the alley had a bowed look.

A load of coppers buzzed past, throwing lead at the first car. I skipped across the street and into the section of the alley which held a man who might have bowed legs. It was a fair bet he wasn't heeled if he was my man. I played it that way, moving straight up the slimy middle of the alley, looking into shadows with eyes, ears and nose.

Three-quarters of a block of it—and a shadow broke away from another shadow—a man going hell-bent away from me.

"Stop!" I bawled, pounding my feet after him. "Stop, or I'll plug you, MacSwain!"

He ran half a dozen strides farther and stopped, turning.

"Oh, it's you," he said, as if it made any difference who took him back to the hoosegow.

"Yeah," I confessed. "What are all you people doing wandering around outside?"

"I don't know. Somebody dynamited the floor out of the can. I dropped down through the hole with the rest of 'em. There was some mugs standing off the bulls. I made the back-trotters with one bunch, and then we split, and I was figuring on cutting across and making the hills. I didn't have nothing to do with it. I just went along when she blew open."

"Whisper was pinched this afternoon," I told him.

"Hell, then that's it! Noonan had ought to know he'd never keep that guy screwed up—not in this burg."

We were still standing where MacSwain had stopped running, in the alley.

"You know what he was pinched for?" I asked.

"Uh-huh—for killing Tim."

"You know who killed Tim."

"Huh? Sure he did!"

"You did."

"Huh? What's the matter? You simple?"

"There's a gun in my left hand," I cautioned him.

"But look here—didn't he tell the broad that Whisper done it? What's the matter with you?"

"He didn't say *Whisper*. I've heard women call Thaler *Max*, but I've never heard a man here call him anything but *Whisper*. Tim didn't say *Max*. He said *MacS*—the first part of *MacSwain*—and died before he could finish it. Don't forget about the gun."

"What would I have killed him for? He was after Whisper's—"

"I haven't got around to the motive yet," I admitted, "but let's see. You and your wife had busted up. Tim seems to have been a ladies' man. Maybe there's something there. I'll have to look it up. What started me thinking was that you never tried to get any more dough out of the girl. I reckon you had sense enough to know what luck you'd played in and to let it alone."

"Cut it out!" he begged. "You know there ain't no sense to it. What would I have hung around afterwards for? I'd have been out getting an alibi, like Whisper!"

"Why? You were a bull then—close by was the place for you—to see the job was handled right."

"You know damned well it don't hang together—don't make no sense. Cut it out, for God's sake!"

"I don't mind how goofy it is," I said. "It's something to put to Noonan when we go back. He's likely all broken up over Whisper's crush-out. This'll take his mind off it."

MacSwain got down on his knees in the muddy alley and cried: "Oh, God, no! He'd croak me with his hands!"

"Get up and stop yelling!" I growled. "Now will you give it to me straight?"

He whined: "He'd croak me with his hands!"

"All right. Suit yourself. If you won't talk, I will—to Noonan. If you'll come clean with me I'll give you my word that I'll do what I can to keep it to myself while you're where Noonan can get at you."

"You mean it?" he asked eagerly, and then started sniveling again: "How do I know you'll do what you say?"

I risked a little truth on him:

"You said you had some idea of what I was doing in Personville. Then you can see that it's my play to keep Noonan and Whisper split. Letting Noonan think Whisper croaked Tim will keep 'em split. But suit yourself. If you don't want to play with me, come on, we'll play with Noonan."

He spent a few more minutes hemming and hawing, but he was too afraid of the chief to hold out on me, and the story finally came out:

"I don't know how much you know, but it was like you said. My wife fell for Tim. That's what made a bum out of me. You can ask anybody if I wasn't a good guy before that. It got me in a bad way, see? I couldn't stop being in love with her, and I wanted her to do whatever she wanted to do, even if it wasn't what I wanted. Can you understand that? And mostly what she wanted was tough on me. But I couldn't do anything else, see? So I had to let her move out and put in divorce papers, so she could marry him, thinking he meant to.

"Pretty soon I begin hearing that he's chasing this Myrtle Jennison. I couldn't go that. I had given him his chance with Helen, fair and square. She wanted him and I didn't stand in the way. Now he was giving her the air for this Myrtle. I wasn't going to stand for that. He had to keep his bargain with Helen. She wasn't no trollop. It was accidental, though, running into him at the Lake that Saturday. I kept my eye on him till I seen him go down by them summer houses. Then I went after him. That looked like a good quiet place to have it out with him.

"I guess maybe we'd both had a little too much hooch. Anyway, we had it hot and heavy. When it got too hot for him he pulled the gun. He was yellow! I grabbed it, and in the tussle it went off. I swear to God I didn't shoot him, excepting like that. It went off while the both of us had hold of it. I ran away, back in some bushes. I had seen the hole it knocked in his head and I knew he was croaked. But when I got in the bushes I could hear him still moaning and talking. There was people coming—especially a broad running down from the hotel—that Myrtle Jennison.

"I wanted to go back and hear what he said, so I'd know where I stood, but I was afraid to be the first one there. So I had to wait till the girl got to him, listening all the time to his moaning and talking, but too far away to make it out. When she got to him I ran over and got there just as he died trying to say my name. I didn't think about that being Whisper's name till she came and propositioned me with the suicide letter and the two centuries and the rock. I'd just been stalling around, pretending to get the job lined up—being on the force then—and trying to find out how I stood. Then she makes that play and I know I'm sitting pretty. And that's the way it went till you started digging it up again."

He slopped his feet up and down in the mud and added: "Next week my wife was killed—an accident. Uh-huh, accident. She drove the Ford square in front of Number 6 where it comes down the long grade from Tanner and stopped it there. But what the hell do you or anybody else care about that?"

"Keep your mouth shut when we get up to the Hall," I said, "and I'll keep my promise."

He went back meekly—three blocks of walking without either of us saying anything. Noonan was trotting up and down his office floor, cursing the half-dozen bulls who stood around wishing they were somewhere else.

"I found this walking around loose," I said, pushing MacSwain forward.

Noonan knocked MacSwain down, kicked him, and told one of the coppers to take him away. I slipped out without saying good-night and walked back to the hotel.

Off to the north some guns popped. A group of three men passed me, shifty-eyed, walking-pigeon-toed. Down the street a little farther another man moved all the way over to the curb to give me plenty of room. I didn't know him and don't suppose he knew me. A lone shot sounded not far away. As I reached the hotel a battered black touring car went down the street, crammed to the curtains with men, hitting fifty at least.

I grinned after it. Poisonville was beginning to boil out under the lid. And I felt so much like a native that even the memory of my part in the boiling—of the frame-up I had engineered—didn't keep me from getting twelve solid hours of sleep.

THE CLEANSING OF POISONVILLE

is not a serial, but in reality is a series of adventures of the Continental detective who is drawn into a fight for life with the crooked bosses of a city, who have gone mad with the power of their own corruption. Outside of their gripping interest, these stories are remarkable if only for the fact that their manner of telling points the way to a new type of detective fiction, which in BLACK MASK is coming to take the place of the old, worn-out formula sort of gruesome-murder-and-clever-solution detective story. The first of these adventures appeared in November BLACK MASK. Any reader who missed that number may have it by sending ten cents with his name and address to the Editor, 578 Madison Avenue, New York City.

DYNAMITE, the third adventure in The Cleansing of Poisonville, by Dashiell Hammett, is probably one of the most exciting detective action tales ever told. It appears in JANUARY BLACK MASK.

3

DYNAMITE

BLACK MASK, JANUARY 1928

The Cleansing of Poisonville.

Mickey Linehan used the telephone to wake me at noon.

"We're here," he told me. "Where's the reception committee?"

"Probably stopped to get a rope. Check your bags and come up to the hotel. Room 537. Don't advertise your visit."

I was dressed when they arrived.

Mickey Linehan was a big slob with sagging shoulders and a shapeless body that seemed to be coming apart at all its joints. His ears stuck out like red wings, and his round red face usually wore the meaningless smirk of a half-wit. Dick Foley was a boy-sized Canadian with a sharp, irritable face. He wore high heels to increase his height, perfumed his handkerchiefs, and saved all the words he could. They were both good operatives.

"What did the Old Man tell you about the job?" I asked when we had settled into seats.

"He didn't seem to know much," Mickey said. "Said you'd wired for help, and that he hadn't got any reports from you for a couple of days."

"The chances are he won't for a couple more. Know anything about this Personville?"

Dick shook his head. Mickey said:

"Only that people call it Poisonville as if they meant it."

"Here's the way it stacks up," I said. "Old Elihu Willsson owns the Personville Mining Corporation, the First National Bank, the newspapers—practically the whole city and a fair slice of the state. He used to run it as well as own it—by himself. Now he's got help—more than he wants. A few years back, when he had a strike and other troubles on his hands, he needed help. Now his helpers have got him by the neek. He has to play along with them whether he likes it or not.

"There seem to be four of these helpers who count. Pete the Finn, who is Poisonville's bootleg king; Lew Yard; Max Thaler, alias Whisper, who runs a couple of gambling joints; and Noonan, chief of police. I'm told Lew Yard is head man and fence for the burg's grifters. I don't know much about him or Pete the Finn. I've been too busy to look 'em over.

"Elihu Willsson is old and sick. His doctor told him he'd have to give up handling his affairs. So Elihu brought his son Donald home from Paris. But when the son gets here the old man can't make up his mind to pass everything over to him. He compromised by giving the boy the newspapers to play with. Donald seems to have been a pretty nice boy, but he wasn't a wise head. It didn't take him long to find out that Personville wasn't exactly a paradise of righteousness, but he didn't tumble to the fact that his old man was in the mud as deep as the rest.

"The youngster starts a reform campaign in his—or really his father's—papers. Papa tries to reason with him, but he doesn't want to admit that he's tied up with the town's choicest thugs. So he doesn't make much headway. Papa's confederates—

knowing he'd shake 'em off if he could—begin to think he's using Donald to do it. I don't think he was—but he might have been at that. Anyway, everybody suspects everybody else all around.

"That's the way it stood last week when we got a check from Donald and a letter asking that an op be sent here to do some work for him. I was the op. I got here Monday. Donald was shot and killed before I saw him. He was killed right after buying some graft evidence from a Dinah Brand, who was Max Thaler's girl. It comes out afterwards that he couldn't have used what she sold him—or so she thought. She was gypping him. But—with everybody watching everybody else—Lew Yard, Pete the Finn and Noonan got the idea that Thaler and old Elihu were double-crossing them. They hit back by trying to frame Thaler for the killing, and trying to knock off Elihu.

"That was none of my business, then. All I wanted was to nail Donald's murderer. But these people wouldn't let me alone. They were afraid I'd dig up stuff they didn't want dug up. See, they thought the boy's killing was part of the double-crossing. They ran me ragged for a couple of days, until this thing of being shot at by coppers got on my nerves. Elihu, scared stiff that his ex-friends were going to wipe him out, sent for me. He wanted *them* wiped out. I was sore enough by then to be glad of the chance.

"I took advantage of his fright to get a certified check out of him, and a letter that was as good as a contract, so he couldn't call the job off if he and the others patched up their quarrel. It was a good thing I did. When I landed Donald's murderer—a boy named Albury, ex-boy friend of Dinah Brand's—everybody found out that the killing had nothing to do with politics, was just the result of crazy jealousy.

"Elihu, Thaler, Yard, Pete and Noonan immediately fell on each other's necks and kissed their differences away. Elihu tried to call me off. But I had him sewed up too tight for that. He couldn't block me without raising more stink than he wanted. Since then it's been me versus Poisonville. I had—"

The telephone bell interrupted me. Dinah Brand's lazy voice:

"Hello! How's the wrist?"

"Only a scratch. What do you think of the crush-out?"

"It's not my fault," she said. "I did my part. If Noonan couldn't hold him, it's just too bad. I'm coming downtown to buy a hat this afternoon. I thought I'd drop in and see you for a couple of minutes if you're going to be there."

"What time?"

"Oh, around three."

"Right. I'll expect you, and I'll have that two hundred berries and a dime I owe you."

"Do," she said. "That's what I'm coming in for. Cheerio!"

I went back to my seat on the bed and my story:

"I had kept Thaler from being framed for Donald's murder. That gave me a good stand-in with him. But I had to blow it. This girl of his—Dinah Brand, that was her on the phone—is a money-hungry baby with some local knowledge I could use. So I tried my hand at splitting her and Thaler. He had a fight fixed Thursday night. A pug who called himself Ike Bush was to lay down to another named Kid Cooper.

"With the help of an ex-bull named MacSwain I unfixed it, making Bush win, letting the girl in on it in time to switch her bets. It stirred things up plenty. Bush won but got a knife through his neck before he could get out of the ring. Thaler accused the girl of selling him out. She got mad and tipped me off to where I could dig up proof that Thaler killed Noonan's brother a year and a half ago.

"That was what I wanted—something to set the boys against one another. I took the dope to Noonan. Later, the girl helped me turn Thaler in to him. That's where I got this bandaged wrist—we fireworked each other. Last night Thaler's friends dynamited him out of the hoosegow. I don't know whether Noonan has caught him again or not. I haven't been out yet today. I hope he hasn't. I imagine Lew Yard and Pete the Finn will try to make the chief lay off of Thaler. I don't know what he'll do. He's shifty as hell and he does want his revenge for brother Tim's bump-off.

"The tricky part of it is that Thaler didn't kill Noonan's brother. The ex-copper MacSwain, who helped me uncook the fight, did it. He's in the can now, held as a witness or something. He got away during the crush-out last night. I caught him. He came through to me on the murder. I took him back to jail, but promised him I wouldn't crack the rap on him while he was in Noonan's hands. The chief would kill him in a second. With a fair trial I think MacSwain will beat his case—self-defense. That, gents, is what's what and who's who in Poisonville today."

Mickey Linehan whistled, said:

"Maybe the Old Man wouldn't crucify you if he knew what you've been doing! No wonder you're afraid to send in reports!"

"If it works out the way I want it, there'll be no reason for reporting all the details," I said. "It's all right for our Continental Detective Agency to have its rules and regulations, but when you're out on a job you do it the best way you can. The work's got to be done. And anybody that brings any ethics to Poisonville is going to get 'em rusty. But a report is no place for the dirty details. Don't you birds be sending any to San Francisco without letting me see them first."

"Fair enough," Mickey agreed. "What kind of crimes have you got for us to pull?"

"I want you to go after Pete the Finn. Dick will take Lew Yard. You'll both have to play it the way I've played. Do what you can when you can. I could buy more dope on them from Dinah Brand. But the way it stands now there's no use taking anybody into court no matter what you've got on 'em. They own the courts. Evidence won't do. What we've got to have is dynamite. If we can smash things up enough—break the combination—they'll have their knives in each other's backs, doing our work for us. The break between Noonan and Thaler is a starter. I'm afraid it'll sag on us if we don't help it along."

"How about your client, old Elihu?" Mickey asked. "What are you going to do with him?"

"Maybe ruin him. Maybe club him into backing us up. I don't care. You'd better stay at the Hotel Person, Mickey, and Dick can go to the National. Keep apart and for God's sake burn the job up before the Old Man gets hep! Make notes of these, so you'll know 'em when and if you run across 'em."

I gave them names, descriptions and addresses—when I had them—of Elihu Willsson; Stanley Lewis, his secretary; Dinah Brand; Dan Rolff, her tubercular boy friend; Chief of Police Noonan; Max Thaler, alias Whisper; and his right-hand man, the chinless Jerry.

"Now go to it," I said. "And don't kid yourselves that there's any law in Poisonville except what you make for yourself."

Mickey said:

"You'd be surprised how many laws I can get along without."

Dick said: "So long."

They departed. I went down to the cafe for breakfast, then over to the City Hall to see the fat chief of police.

II

His greenish eyes were bleary—as if they hadn't been sleeping—and his fleshy face had lost some of its color. But he pumped my hand up and down as enthusiastically as ever, and the usual cordiality was in his voice and manner.

"Any line on Whisper?" I asked when we had finished the glad-handing.

"I think I've got something." He looked at the dock on the wall and then at his phone. "I'm expecting a word any minute now. Sit down."

"Who else got away?"

"Jerry Hooper and Tony Agosti are the only others still out. We picked up all the rest. Jerry is Whisper's right bower, and the wop's one of the mob, too. He's the bozo that put the knife in Ike Bush the night of the fights."

"Any more of Whisper's mob in?"

"No—we just had the three of 'em. Except Buck Wallace, the fellow you potted. He's in the hospital."

Noonan looked at the wall-clock again, then at his watch. It was exactly two o'clock. He turned to the phone. It rang. He grabbed it, said:

"Noonan speaking... Yes... Yes... Yes... Right."

He pushed the phone back and played a tune on the row of pearl buttons on his desk. The office filled up with coppers.

"Cedar Hill Inn," he said. "You follow me out with your detail, Bates. Terry, you shoot out Broadway and hit the dump from behind. Pick up the boys on traffic duty as you go along. It's likely we'll need everybody we can get. Duffy, take yours out Union Street and around by the old mine road. McGraw will hold headquarters down. Get hold of everybody you can and send 'em after us. Jump!"

He grabbed his hat and went after them, calling over his shoulder to me:

"Come on, man! This is the kill!"

I followed him down to the department garage, where the engines of half a dozen police cars were roaring. The chief sat beside his driver. I sat in the rear of his car with four of his bulls.

Men climbed into other cars. Machine-guns were unwrapped. Armloads of rifles, riot-guns were distributed. Packages of ammunition were dumped into cars.

We got away first—off with a jump that clicked our teeth together. We missed the garage doorway by half an inch, chased a couple of pedestrians diagonally across the sidewalk, bounced off the curb into the roadway, missed a truck as narrowly as we had missed the door, and dashed out King Street with our siren wide open. Panicky automobiles darted right and left—regardless of traffic rules—to let us through. It was a lot of fun.

I looked back, saw another police car following us, another turning into Broadway; Noonan chewed a cold cigar and told the driver:

"Give her a bit more, Pat."

Pat twisted us around a frightened woman's coupé, put us through a slot between street car and laundry wagon—a slot too narrow for us to slide through if our car hadn't been so smoothly enameled—and said:

"All right, but the brakes ain't good."

"That's nice!" the gray-mustached dick on my left said. He didn't sound sincere.

Out of the center of the city there wasn't so much traffic to bother us, but the streets were rougher. It was a nice half-hour's ride, with everybody getting a chance to sit on everybody else's lap. The last ten minutes of it was over an uneven road that had hills enough to keep us from forgetting what Pat had said about the brakes.

We wound up at a gate topped by a shabby electric sign that had said *Cedar Hill Inn* before it lost its globes. The roadhouse—twenty feet behind the gate—was a squat wooden building painted a moldy green and chiefly surrounded by rubbish. Front door and windows were closed, blank.

We followed Noonan out of the car. The machine that had been trailing us came into sight around a bend in the road, slid to rest beside ours, unloaded its cargo of men and artillery.

Noonan ordered this and that.

A couple of coppers went around each side of the building. A couple more, including a machine-gunner, remained at the gate. The rest of us walked through tin cans, bottles and ancient newspaper to the front of the house.

The gray-mustached detective who had sat beside me in the car carried a red axe. We stepped up on the porch.

Noise and a slice of fire came out from under a window-sill.

The gray-mustached detective fell down, hiding the axe under his corpse.

The rest of us ran away.

I ran with Noonan. We hid in the ditch on the Inn side of the road. It was deep enough, and banked high enough, to let us stand almost erect without being targets.

The chief was excited.

"What luck!" he said happily. "He's here! By God, he's here!"

"That shot came from *under* the sill," I said. "A machine-gun ought to be able to spoil that trick."

"Spoil it?" he asked cheerfully. "We'll sieve the dump! Duffy ought to be pulling up on the other road by now, and Terry Shane won't be more than a minute or two behind him. Hey, Donner!" he called to a man who was peeping around a boulder. "Swing around back and tell Duffy and Shane to start closing in as soon as they come, letting fly with all they got. Where's Kimble?"

The peeper jerked a thumb toward a tree on his far side. We could see only the upper part of it from our ditch.

"Tell him to set up his mill and start popping," Noonan ordered. "Low, across the front ought to do it like cutting cheese."

The peeper disappeared. Noonan went up and down the ditch, risking his noodle over the top now and then for a look around, once in a while gesturing or calling to his men. He came back, sat on his heels beside me, gave me a cigar and lighted one for himself.

"It'll do," he said complacently. "Whisper won't have a chance in the world."

The machine-gun by the tree fired, haltingly, experimentally, half a dozen shots. Noonan grinned and let a ring of cigar smoke drift out of his fat mouth.

The machine-gun got down to business, grinding out metal like the busy little death-factory it was. Noonan blew another smoke ring and said:

"That's exactly what'll do it."

Farther away another machine-gun began, then others. Irregularly, rifles, pistols, shotguns joined in. Noonan nodded approvingly and said:

"Five minutes of that ought to do things."

I agreed that it ought. We leaned against the clay bank and smoked until the five minutes were up. I suggested a look at the remains, if any. I gave him a boost up the bank and climbed up after him. The roadhouse was as bleak and empty-looking as at first, but more battered. No shots came from it. Plenty were going into it.

"What do you think?" Noonan asked.

"If there's a cellar, there might be a mouse alive in it."

"Well, we could finish him afterward."

He took a whistle out of his pocket and made a lot of noise. He waved his fat arms and the gunfire began to dwindle. We had to wait a while for the word to go all the way around.

Then we crashed the door.

The first floor was ankle-deep with booze that was still gurgling from bullet holes in the stacked-up cases and barrels that filled most of the house. Dizzy from the fumes of spilled hooch, we waded around until we found four dead bodies and no live ones. The four were swarthy, foreign-looking men in laborers' clothes. Two of them were practically shot to pieces.

Noonan said: "Leave 'em here and get out."

His voice was cheerful, but in a flashlight's glow his greenish eyes showed white-ringed with fear.

We went out gladly, though I did hesitate long enough to pocket an unbroken bottle labeled *Dewar.*

At the gate a khaki-dressed copper was tumbling off a motorcycle. He yelled at us:

"The First National Bank has been stuck up!"

Noonan cursed savagely, bawled:

"He's foxed us, damn him! Back to town, everybody!"

Everybody except us who had ridden with the chief beat it for the machines. Two of them carried the dead dectective with them.

Noonan looked at me out of his eye-corners and said:

"This is a tough one, no fooling."

I said, "Well," shrugged, and sauntered out to his automobile, where the driver was sitting at the wheel. I stood with my back to the house, talking to Pat. I don't remember what we talked about. Presently Noonan and the other detectives joined us.

Only a little flame showed through the open roadhouse door before we had passed out of sight around the bend in the road.

III

There was a mob around the First National Bank. We pushed through it to the door, where we found McGraw, a raw-boned, sour police captain.

"Was six of 'em, masked," he reported to the chief as we went inside. "They hit it about two-thirty. Five of 'em got away clean with the jack. The watchman here dropped one of 'em—Jerry Hooper. He's over on the bench—cold. We got the roads blocked, and I wired around, if it ain't too late. Last seen of 'em was when they made the turn into King Street—in a black Lincoln."

We went over for a look at dead Jerry, lying on one of the lobby benches with a shabby robe over him.

The bullet had gone in under his left shoulder-blade.

The bank watchman, a harmless looking old duffer, pushed up his chest and told us all about it:

"There wasn't no chance to do nothing at first. They was in 'fore anybody knew anything. And maybe they didn't work fast! Right down the line, scooping it up. No chance to do anything then. But I says to myself, 'All right, young fellows, you've got it all your way now', but wait till you try to leave!' And I was as good as my word, you bet! I runs right to the door after 'em and cuts loose with the old firearm. I got that fellow just as he was stepping in the car. I bet you I would have got more of 'em if I had more bullets, because it's kind of hard shooting like that, standing in the door, and I bet you—"

Noonan stopped the monologue by patting the old boy's back hard enough to empty his lungs, telling him, "That certainly was fine of you."

McGraw drew the blanket over the dead man again and growled:

"No identifications. But if Jerry was there it's a cinch it was Whisper's caper."

The chief nodded happily and said:

"Well, I'll leave it in your hands, Mac. Going to poke around here or down to the Hall with me?" he asked me.

"Neither. I've got a date and I want to get into dry shoes."

Dinah Brand's blue little Marmon was standing in front of the hotel. I didn't see her. I went up to my room, leaving the door unlocked. I had got my hat and overcoat off when she came in without knocking.

"My Gawd, you keep a boozy smelling room," she said.

"It's my shoes. Noonan took me wading in rum."

She crossed to the window, opened it, sat on the sill and asked:

"What was that for?"

"He thought he was going to find your Max out in a dump called Cedar Hill Inn. So we went out, shot the joint silly, murdered some dagoes, spilled gallons of liquor, and left the place burning."

"Cedar Hill Inn? I thought it had been closed up for a year or more?"

"It looked it, but it was somebody's warehouse."

"But you didn't find Max there?" she asked.

"While we were there he seems to have been knocking over Elihu Willsson's First National Bank."

"I saw that!" she said. "I had just come out of Bengren's—the store two doors away. I had just got in my car when I saw a big guy backing out of the bank, carrying a sack and a gun, and with a black swipe over his face."

"Was Max with them?"

"No—he wouldn't be. He'd send Jerry and the boys. That's what he has them for. Jerry was there. I knew him as soon as he stepped out, in spite of the rag. Four of 'em came out of the bank, running down to the car at the curb. Jerry and another fellow were in the car. When the four came across the sidewalk Jerry jumped out and went to meet them. That's when the shooting started and Jerry dropped. The others jumped in the car and beat it. How about that dough you owe me?"

I counted out ten twenty-dollar bills and a dime. She left the window to come for the money.

"That's for pulling Dan off so you could cop Max," she said when she had stowed it in the bottom of her bag. "Now how about what I was to get for showing you where you could get the dope on him for killing Tim?"

"You'll have to wait till he's indicted. How do I know the dope's any good?"

She frowned and said:

"What do you do with all the money you don't spend?" Her face brightened. "You know where Max is now?"

"No."

"What's it worth to know?"

"Not much."

"I'll tell you for five hundred bucks."

"I wouldn't want to take advantage of you that way."

"I'll tell you for three hundred bucks."

I shook my head.

"A hundred and fifty," she said.

"I don't want him. I don't care where he is."

"A hundred."

"Why don't you peddle the news to Noonan?" I asked.

"Yes—and try to collect. Do you only perfume yourself with hooch, or is there any for drinking purposes?"

"Here's a bottle of Dewar that I picked up at Cedar Hill this afternoon. There's a bottle of King George in my bag. What's your choice?"

She voted for King George. We had a drink apiece, straight, and I said:

"Sit down and play with it while I get into clean clothes."

When I came out of the bathroom twenty-five minutes later she was sitting at the secretary, smoking a cigarette and studying a memoranda book that had been in the side pocket of my Gladstone bag.

"I guess these are the expenses you've charged up on some other cases," she said without looking up. "I'm damned if I can see why you can't be a little bit liberal with me, then! Look. Here's a six-hundred-dollar item marked *Inf.* That's information bought from somebody, isn't it? And here's a hundred and fifty below it—*Top*—whatever that is. And here's another day when you spent nearly a thousand dollars."

"They must be telephone numbers," I said, taking the book from her. "Where were you raised? Fanning my baggage!"

"I was raised in a convent," she told me. "I won the good behavior medal every year I was there. I thought little girls who put extra spoons of sugar in their chocolate went to hell for gluttony. I didn't even know there was such a thing as profanity till I was eighteen. The first time I heard any I damned near fainted." She spit on the rug in front of her, tilted back in the chair, put her feet on my bed, and asked: "And what do you think of that?"

I pushed her feet off the bed and said:

"I was raised in a waterfront saloon. Keep your saliva off my floor or I'll toss you out on your neck."

"Let's have another drink first. Listen. What'll you give me for the inside story of how the boys got themselves a quarter of a million building the city hall three years ago?"

"That doesn't click with me. Try another."

"Then how about why the first Mrs Lew Yard was sent to the insane asylum?"

"No."

"King, our district attorney, eight thousand dollars in debt four years ago, now the owner of a couple of downtown blocks. I can't give you the whole thing, but I can show you where to start digging—say, a hundred dollars' worth?"

"Keep trying," I encouraged her.

"No. You don't want to buy anything. You're just hoping you'll pick up something for nothing. This isn't bad Scotch. Where'd you get it?"

"Brought it from San Francisco with me."

"Well, what's the idea of not wanting any of this information I offered? Think you can get it cheaper?"

"Uh-uh! Information's not much good to me now. I need dynamite—something to blow 'em apart."

She laughed and jumped up, her big eyes hot.

"I've got one of Lew Yard's cards. Suppose we sent the bottle of Dewar you copped to Pete with the cards. Wouldn't he take that as a declaration of war? Think Noonan had pulled it under orders from Lew?"

I considered it and said:

"No, I don't think it would fool him. Besides, I'd rather have him and Lew both against the chief just now."

She pouted and said:

"You're just hard to get along with. You think you know it all. Take me out tonight? I've got a new dress and hat that will knock 'em all cockeyed."

"Yeah."

"Come up for me around eight." She patted my cheek with a warm soft hand, said "Ta-Ta," and went out as the telephone began jingling.

IV

"The chief wants to know if you can drop in and see him for a little minute," said a bass voice.

"Tell him I'm on my way."

"I'll do that."

I stalled a few minutes, giving Dinah Brand time to get away from the hotel, and then went up to the City Hall. A pock-marked sergeant, one of the three men in the chief's outer office, told me Noonan was in the Identification Bureau on the second floor.

"He sent for me," I said. "Shall I wait here or go up?"

The sergeant said:

"If he sent for you, maybe you'd—"

The door of the chief's private office came over and smashed the sergeant.

Blasting red heat quivered out of the doorway. The building rocked. Things flew around. Noise paralyzed eardrums, giving the effect of total silence.

I sat cross-legged in a corner, with a shoe in my lap. It wasn't my shoe. It was high, black and police-size. It was empty but fully laced. I put it aside and stood up, moving slowly, taking stock of myself. My back was sore. My hands were smeared with dirt and blood. A warm trickle itched on one of my cheeks. There didn't seem anything seriously the matter with me.

The air was thick with dust, smoke, and the stink of burnt chemicals. Fragments of metal, wood, plaster, clothing and glass were all over everything. None of the windows had any glass in it.

I lifted the door off the pock-marked sergeant, and was sorry I had. He hadn't any face.

The chief's secretary was huddled behind the desk, arms over head. I pulled him out flat on the floor. He was battered a lot on one side and quite still, but not dead.

Across the room the third man was stirring, on his back, taking his feet out of his chair-seat. One of his feet was in a white stocking, with no shoe. I went back to where I had dropped the shoe, picked it up, and had carried it to him before I realized what a damned silly thing that was to do.

There were a lot of men in the room and they did a lot of talking and moving around. None of it meant much to me yet.

I went to the door of the chief's private office. His room looked as if the wrath of God had hit it. The center of the floor was gone—a hole a horse could have fallen through. Around the edge of the hole the rug smouldered. The mahogany desk was a lot of splinters scattered around. The iron swivel of the chief's chair was imbedded in the plaster high up in a wall. Part of a man was lying where the bookcase had been. His hips and legs weren't there. The wickerwork waste basket had tilted on its side but was otherwise unharmed.

"Who's that?" I asked, pointing at the mangled man.

"Biddle. For God's sake, what happened?"

I was conscious enough now to recognize McGraw's voice, and Noonan's big face when he came puffing in.

"Well, well," the chief exclaimed good-naturedly, "somebody's certainly been doing something to us!"

"Did you have anybody phone me to come over?" I asked him.

"No, sir!"

"Somebody did."

"They did, did they?" He smacked his fat lips apart, shut one eye, said, "Uh-huh! And I reckon it was that same baby. I was up in Identification. Somebody gets me on the phone and asks me to hold the line. I'm holding it when I hear this racket. See it? They send you over. Then they call me up, thinking that if I answer the phone it shows I'm in my office—see? They got us together where a bomb chucked through my window will do a lot of good. They pull it fast, so we won't have much time for thinking after you find I didn't phone you. The window's too high for 'em to see in. Get it?"

I said I did. I suggested we try to do something about it. Noonan gave McGraw a flock of orders, then asked me:

"You all right?"

"Except that my back's sore and I've a damned rotten headache."

"Well, I certainly am glad it's no worse than that," he assured me, patting my shoulder. "We'll go back in—"

I moved away from his patting hand and said:

"I'm going over to my room to lie down a while."

"Better let the doc have a look at you."

"No, rest is all I need."

I went back to the hotel. One of my eyes was swollen. There were metal slivers in my left cheek. They weren't hard to get out. Cold water made my face feel human again. A bellhop fetched ammonia for my headache. I spread myself on the bed.

I was feeling a lot spryer half an hour later, when Mickey Linehan phoned.

"My bird and Dick's were together at your client's house this afternoon," he said. "Mine's been generally busy as hell, though I don't know what it's all about yet. Anything new?"

"No. Things are breaking pretty good, though."

I sprawled on the bed again until seven-thirty. Then I dressed, loaded my pockets with my gun and a pint flask of Scotch, and went up to Dinah Brand's house in Hurricane Street.

V

"Now what have you been up to?" she asked when she got a look at my face.

"Up to City Hall. Somebody tossed a package of dynamite in Noonan's window."

"Kill the big sap?" she asked hopefully.

I said it hadn't and gave her the details. She wrinkled her forehead and suggested:

"Sounds a little like something he rigged himself."

"Yeah, I noticed that, too."

"That's more than you've done to my new dress," she complained, backing off and revolving. "Do you like it?"

I said I did. She explained that the color was rose beige, and that the dinguses on the side were something or other, winding up:

"And you really think I look good in it?"

"You always look charming. Lew Yard and Pete the Finn went calling on Elihu this afternoon."

She made a face at me and said:

"You don't give a damn about my dress. What did they do there?"

"A pow-wow, I suppose."

She looked at me through her lashes and asked:

"Don't you really know where Max is?"

Then I did. There was no use admitting I hadn't known before. I said:

"At Willsson's, probably, but I haven't been interested enough to make sure."

"That's goofy of you. He's got reasons for not liking you and me. Take mama's advice and nail him quick—if you like living and like having mama live, too."

I laughed and said:

"You don't know the worst of it. Max didn't kill Noonan's brother. Tim didn't say *Max*. He tried to say *MacSwain* and died before he could finish."

She grabbed my shoulders and tried to shake my hundred and ninety pounds. She was nearly strong enough to do it.

"Damn you!" Her breath was hot in my face. Her face was white as her teeth. Rouge stood out sharply like red labels pasted on her mouth and cheeks. "If you've framed him and made me frame him you've got to kill him—now! You've—"

I don't like being manhandled, even by young women who look like something out of mythology when they're steamed up. I took her hands off my shoulders and said:

"Stop bellyaching. You're still alive."

"Yes—still. But I know Max better than you do. And I know how much chance anybody that frames him has of staying alive. It would be bad enough if we had got him right, but—"

"Don't make such a fuss over it. I've framed my millions and nothing's happened to me. Get your hat and coat and we'll feed. You'll feel better then."

"You're crazy if you think I'm going out. Not with that—"

"Stop it, sister! If he's that bad he's just as likely to get you here as any place else. So what difference does it make?"

"It makes a—You know what you're going to do? You're going to stay here till Max is put out of the way. It's your fault and you've got to look out for me. Dan's still in the hospital. You've got to stay here!"

"I can't," I said. "I've got work to do. You're all burnt up over nothing. He's probably forgotten all about you by now. Get your hat and coat. I'm hungry."

She put her face close to mine again and her eyes looked as if they had found something horrible in mine.

"Oh, you're rotten!" she said. "You don't give a damn what happens to me! You're using me as you used the others—that dynamite you wanted! I trusted you!"

"You're dynamite, all right," I agreed, "but the rest of it's kind of foolish. You look a lot better when you're happy. Your features are heavy. Anger makes 'em downright brutal. I'm hungry, sister."

"Well, you'll eat right here," she said emphatically. "You're not going to get me outside after dark."

She meant it. She swapped the rose beige dress for an apron and took inventory of the icebox. There were potatoes, lettuce, canned soup and half a fruit cake. I went out and got a couple of steaks, rolls, asparagus and tomatoes.

When I came back she was mixing gin, vermouth and orange bitters in a quart shaker—not leaving a whole lot of space for them to move around in.

"Did you see anything?" she asked.

I sneered at her in a friendly way. We carried the cocktails into the dining-room and played bottoms-up while the meal cooked. The drinks cheered her a lot. By the time we sat down to the food she had almost forgotten her fright. She wasn't a very good cook, but we ate as if she were.

We put a couple of gin-and-seltzers in on top the dinner. She decided she wanted to go places and do things. No lousy little runt could keep her cooped up, because she had been as square with him as anybody could until he got nasty over nothing, and if he didn't like it he could go climb trees, and we'd go out to the Silver Arrow where she had meant to take me, because she had promised Reno she'd show up at his party, and anybody who thought she wouldn't was crazy as a pet cuckoo, and what did I think of that?

"Who's Reno?" I asked while she tied herself tighter in the apron by pulling the strings the wrong way.

"Reno Starkey. You'll like him. He's a right guy. I promised him I'd come to his celebration, and that's just what I'll do."

"What's he celebrating?"

"What the hell's the matter with this apron? Sprung this afternoon."

"Turn around and I'll unwind you. What was he in for? Stand still."

"Blowing a safe six or seven months ago—Aigren's, the jeweler. Reno, Put Collings, Blackie Whalen, Hank O'Marra, and a little lame guy called Step-and-a-half. They had plenty of cover—Lew Yard—but the jewelers' association dicks tied the job to 'em last week. So Noonan had to go through the motions. Doesn't mean anything. They got out on bail at five o'clock this afternoon, and that's the last anybody will hear about it. Reno's used to it. He was already out on bail for three or four other capers. Suppose you mix another little drink while I'm inserting myself in my dress."

VI

The Silver Arrow was half-way between Personville and Mock Lake. "It's not a bad dump," Dinah Brand told me as her little Marmon carried us toward it. "Polly de Voto is a good scout and anything she sells you is good, except maybe the Bourbon. You'll like her. She's a good scout. Anything you do out there's all right so long as you don't get noisy. She won't stand for a racket—not that kind. There it is. See the red and blue lights through the trees."

We rode out of the woods into full view of the roadhouse—a very electric-lighted imitation castle set close to the road.

"What do you mean she doesn't like noise?" I asked, listening to the chorus of pistols singing *Bang-bang-bang.*

"Something up," the girl muttered, stopping the car.

Two men dragging a woman between them ran out the roadhouse's front door, ran away into the darkness. A man sprinted out a side door, away. The guns were still talking. I didn't see any flashes.

Another man came out and disappeared around the back.

A man leaned far out a front second-storey window, a black gun in his hand. Dinah Brand blew her breath out sharply.

From a hedge by the road a flash pointed briefly up at the man in the window; his gun flashed downward. He leaned farther out. No second flash came from the hedge.

The man in the window put a leg over the sill—bent—hung by his hands—dropped. Our car jerked forward.

The man who had dropped from the window was gathering himself up slowly on hands and knees. Dinah Brand put her face in front of mine and screamed:

"Reno!"

The man jumped up, his face to us. He made the road in three leaps—as we got to him.

Dinah had the Marmon wide open before Reno's feet were on the running-board beside me. I wrapped my arms around him and damn near dislocated them holding him on. He made it as tough as he could for me by leaning out to try for a shot at the guns that were tossing lead all around us.

Then it was all over. We were out of range, sight and sound of the Silver Arrow, speeding away from Personville.

Reno turned around and did his own holding on. I took my arms in and found that all the joints still worked. Dinah was busy with the car.

Reno said: "Thanks, kid. I needed pulling-out."

"That's all right," she told him. "So this is the kind of party you throw?"

"We had guests that wasn't invited. You know the Tanner road?"

"Yes."

"Take it. It'll put us over to Mountain Boulevard and we can get back to town thataway."

The girl nodded, slowed up a little, and asked:

"Who were the uninvited guests?"

"Some guerrillas that don't know enough to lay off o' me."

"Do I know them?" she asked, too casually, as she turned the car into a narrower and rougher road.

"Let it alone, kid," Reno said. "Better get as much out of the heap as it's got."

She prodded another fifteen miles an hour out of the Marmon. She had plenty to do now holding the car on the road, and Reno had plenty holding himself on the car. Neither of them made any more conversation until the road brought us into one that had more and better paving. Then he asked:

"So you paid Whisper off?"

"Um-hmm."

"They're saying you turned rat on him."

"They would. What do you think?"

"Ditching him was all right. But throwing in with a dick and cracking the works to him is kind of sour. Damned sour, if you ask me."

He looked at me while he said it. He was a man of thirty-four or five, fairly tall, broad and heavy without fat. His eyes were large, brown, dull and set far apart in a long, slightly sallow horse-face. It was a humorless face, stolid but somehow not unpleasant. I looked at him and said nothing.

The girl said:

"If that's the way you—"

"Look out!" he barked.

We had rounded a curve. A long black car was drawn straight across the road in front of us—a barricade.

Bullets flew around us. Reno and I threw bullets around while the girl made a polo pony of the little Marmon.

She twisted it over to the left of the road, let the left wheels ride the bank high, crossed the road again with Reno's and my weight on the inside, got the right bank under the left wheels just as our side of the car began to lift in spite of our weight, slid us down in the road with our backs to the enemy, and took us out of the neighborhood by the time we had emptied our guns.

A lot of people had done a lot of shooting, but so far as we could tell nobody's bullets had hurt anybody.

Reno, holding to the door with his elbows while he pushed another clip into his automatic, said:

"Nice work, kid. You handle the bus like you meant it."

Dinah asked, "Where now?"

"Far away first. Just follow the road. We'll have to figure it out. Looks like they got the burg closed up on us. Keep your foot on it."

We put ten or twelve more miles between Personville and us. We passed a few cars, saw nothing to show we were being chased.

A short bridge rumbled under us. Reno said,

"Take the right-hand branch at the top of the hill."

We took it, a dirt road that wound between trees down the side of a rock-ridged hill. Here ten miles an hour was fast going. After five minutes of this creeping Reno ordered a halt. We heard nothing, saw nothing during the half-hour we sat in the darkness. Then Reno said:

"There's an empty shack a mile or two down the way. We'll camp there, huh? There's no use trying to crash the city line again tonight."

Dinah said she would rather do anything than be shot at again. I said it was all right with me, though I'd rather have found some way back to Personville.

We followed the dirt track cautiously until our headlights settled on a small clapboard building that badly needed the paint it had never got.

"Is this it?" Dinah asked.

"Uh-huh. Stay here till I look it over," Reno said, leaving us.

He appeared in the beam of our lights at the shack door. He fumbled with keys at the padlock, got it off, opened the door, went in. Presently he came to the door and called:

"All right. Come in and make yourselves to home."

Dinah switched off the engine and got out.

"Is there a flashlight in the car?" I asked.

She said, "Yes," gave it to me, yawned, "My Gawd, I'm tired! I hope you haven't lost that flask."

The shack was a one-room affair that held an army cot covered with brown blankets, a deal table with a deck of cards and some poker chips on it, a brown iron stove, four chairs, an oil lamp, dishes, pots and pans, three shelves with canned food on them, a pile of firewood and a wheelbarrow.

Reno was lighting the lamp when we came in. He said:

"Not so lousy. I'll hide the heap and then we'll be all set till daylight."

Dinah went over to the cot, turned back the blankets, reported:

"Maybe there's things in it, but anyway it's not alive with them. Now give me that drink."

I took the top off the flask and passed it to her while Reno went outside to hide the car. When she had finished with the flask I took a shot at it. The purr of the Marmon's engine grew fainter. I opened the door and looked out. Down-hill, through trees and bushes, I could see broken flashes of white light going away. When I lost them for good I returned indoors and asked the girl:

"Have you ever had to walk back before?"

"What?"

"Reno has gone with the car."

"The dirty tramp! Thank God he left me where there's a bed, anyway!"

"That'll get you nothing."

"No?"

"No. Reno had the key to this dump. Ten to one the birds after him know about it. That's why he ditched us here. We're supposed to argue with them—hold them off his trail a while."

She got up wearily from the cot, cursed Reno, me, all men from Adam down, said disagreeably :

"You know everything. What do we do next?"

"Find a comfortable spot not too near, not too far, and wait to see what happens."

"I'm going to take the blankets."

"Maybe one won't be missed, but if you take more than that you'll tip our mitts."

"Damn your mitts," she grumbled, but she took only one blanket.

I blew out the lamp, padlocked the door behind us, and with the help of the flashlight picked a way through the undergrowth.

On the hillside above the shack we found a little hollow from which road and shack could be not too dimly seen through foliage thick enough to hide us unless we showed a light.

I spread the blanket there and we settled down. The girl leaned against my shoulder and complained that the ground was damp, that she was cold in spite of her fur coat, that she had a cramp in her leg, that she wanted a cigarette. I gave her another drink from the flask. That bought me ten minutes of peace. Then she said:

"I'm catching cold. By the time anybody comes, if they do, I'll be sneezing and coughing loud enough to be heard in the city."

"Just once," I told her. "Then you'll be strangled."

"There's a mouse or something crawling under the blanket."

"Probably only a snake."

"Are you married?"

"Aw, don't start that!"

"Then you are?"

"No."

"I'll bet your wife's glad of it."

I was trying to find a comeback for that wisecrack when a distant light gleamed up the road. It vanished as I sh-h-hed the girl.

"What is it?" she asked.

"A light. It's gone now; Our visitors have left their car and are finishing the trip afoot."

A lot of time went by. The girl shivered with her cheek warm against mine. We heard footsteps, saw dark figures moving on the road and around the shack, without being sure whether we did or didn't.

A flashlight ended our doubt by putting a bright circle on the shack's door.

A heavy voice said:

"We'll let the broad come out."

There was a half-minute of silence while they waited for a reply from indoors. Then the same heavy voice demanded: "Coming?" More silence.

Gunfire—a familiar sound tonight—broke the silence. Something hammered boards.

"Come on!" I whispered to the girl. "We'll have a try at their car while they're making their noise."

"No, let them alone," she said, pulling my arm down as I started up. "I've had enough of it for one night. We're all right here."

"Come on!" I insisted.

She said, "I won't," and she wouldn't, and presently, while we argued, it was too late. The boys below had kicked in the door, found the joint empty, and were bellowing for their car. It came, took six or eight men aboard, and followed Reno's track down-hill.

"We might as well move in again," I said. "It's not likely they'll be back this way again tonight."

"I hope to Gawd there's still some Scotch left," she said as I helped her to her feet.

VII

The shack's supply of canned goods didn't include any solids that tempted us for breakfast. We made a meal off of coffee made with very stale water from a galvanized bucket.

A mile of walking brought us to a farm house where there was a kid who didn't mind earning a few dollars by driving us to town in the family Ford. He had a lot of questions, to which we gave him phony answers or none. He set us down in front of a little restaurant in upper King Street, where we ate quantities of waffles and fried ham.

A taxicab put us at Dinah's door a little before nine o'clock. I searched the place for her, from roof to cellar, and found neither visitors nor signs of visitors.

"When will you be back?" she asked as she went to the door with me.

"I'll try to pop in between now and midnight, if only for a few minutes. Where does Lew Yard live?"'

"1622 Painter Street. Painter's three blocks over. 1622's four blocks up. What are you going to do there?" Before I could answer she put her hands on my arm and begged: "Get Max, will you! Honest to Gawd, I'm afraid of him!"

"Maybe I'll sic Noonan on him a little later. It depends on how things work out."

She called me a damned rotten double-crossing something or other who didn't care what happened to her so long as his dirty work got done.

I went over to Painter Street. 1622 was a red brick house with a garage under the front porch. A block up the street I found Dick Foley sitting in a hired drive-yourself Buick. I got in beside him, asking:

"What's doing?"

The little Canadian said:

"Spot four—office to Willsson's—Mickey—five—home—busy—kept plant—off three-seven—Lewis maybe eight-thirty—still there."

That was supposed to inform me that he had started shadowing Lew Yard at four the previous afternoon, had tailed him to Willsson's house, where Mickey had gone behind Pete the Finn, had tailed him away at five, to his home, had seen people going in and out of the house but had not shadowed any of them, had watched the house until three in the morning, had returned to the job at seven, had seen a man who answered Stanley Lewis' description go into Yard's house at eight-thirty, and had not seen him come out.

"We'll wait for a look at him," I said. "Then you'll have to drop Yard and take a plant on Willsson's. I hear Thaler is staying there."

While we waited I told Dick what had happened to me since I last saw him.

It made him talkative.

"You asked for dynamite," he said, almost smiling. "Nice burg."

"Yeah. There they are!" Two men, hatted and over-coated, were coming down Yard's porch steps. One of them was a slim man of forty. "That's Willsson's secretary, right enough," I said. "The other's Yard?"

"Yes."

At that distance all I could make out was that he was tall, gaunt, and had white hair. He unlocked the garage door, opened it, and Lewis followed him in.

"We might as well see where they go before we drop them," I decided.

Dick put the Buick's engine in motion.

The bottom of Lew Yard's house blew apart, sifting bricks and mortar all over the street.

"More dynamite," Dick said.

I jumped out of the car and told him:

"Beat it! Go up and keep your eye on Willsson's."

The neighbors were all out by then. The dynamited house was half-hidden by a cloud of dust. A policeman was running up the street toward it. Other people were following his example.

The dust cleared a little. The upper part of the house toppled forward, sprawled down lazily over the blasted garage, burying it.

I hung around the fringes of the gathering crowd until a squad of coppers, a couple of loads of firemen arrived, failed to find anybody alive in the ruins, and began digging for corpses. Then I went down to my hotel.

There was a letter from the Old Man:

> "Send by return mail full explanation of present operation and of circumstances under which you accepted it, with your daily reports to date."

I put the letter in my pocket and hoped things would keep breaking fast. To send him the information he wanted at that time would have been the same as handing in my resignation. I bent a fresh collar around my neck and trotted over to the City Hall.

The chief of police had moved across the corridor from the dynamited office, to one that had no windows for anybody to chuck things through.

"Hullo," he said. "I was hoping you'd show up. Tried to get you at your hotel, but they said you hadn't been in. How's the head? And the back? That certainly is fine!"

He didn't look well this morning, but under his glad-handing he seemed, for a change, genuinely glad to see me.

"Been out to view Lew Yard's remains?" I asked.

"No. To tell the truth, I'm getting sick of this killing. It—it's getting to me, on my nerves, I mean. Was Lew there?"

"Yeah," I said, surprised, "and Stanley Lewis, Willsson's secretary."

"Sure of that?" he asked, not looking at me.

"I saw them come out of the house, go into the garage—then the blow-up. Didn't they find them?"

"Not yet. Mrs Yard and the servant girl were found, both dead, but the last I heard they hadn't got to the bottom of the ruins yet, so I thought maybe there was a chance that Lew hadn't been home. Was the explosion in the garage?"

"Yeah. My guess is that a bundle of dynamite was hooked up to his starter. Think it's the same party that had a try at us yesterday?"

"God knows," he said wearily. "It's so damned easy to get hold of a fistful of dynamite in these mining towns that everybody starts tossing it around as soon as trouble breaks."

"Who do you think tossed yesterday's batch? Pete the Finn—because we shot up his ware-house?"

Noonan winced and said:

"God knows!"

I considered his low spirits and asked:

"Anybody knocked off in the battle at the Silver Arrow last night?"

"Three."

"Who are they?"

"A pair of yeggs—Blackie Whalen and Put Collings—that only got out on bail around five yesterday evening, and Dutch Jake, gunman."

"What was it all about?"

"Just a roughhouse, I guess. It seems Blackie and Put and the others that got out with them were celebrating with a lot of friends, and it wound up in smoke."

"All of 'em Lew Yard's men?"

"I don't know anything about that yet."

I got up, said, "Oh, all right," and started for the door.

"Hey, wait," he called. "Don't run off like that. I guess they were."

I came back to my chair. Noonan watched the top of his desk. His face was gray, flabby, damp—like fresh putty.

"Thaler's staying at Willsson's," I told him.

He jerked his head up. His eyes darkened. Then his mouth twitched, and he let his head sag again. His eyes faded.

"I can't go through with it," he mumbled. "I'm sick of this killing. I can't stand any more of this."

"Sick enough to give up the idea of evening the score for Tim's killing—if it'll make peace?" I asked.

"I am."

"That's what started it," I said. "If you're willing to call that off, it ought to be possible to stop it all."

He raised his face and looked at me with eyes that were almost childishly hopeful.

"Tell the others how you feel about it," I went on. "They ought to be as sick of it as you are. Have a get-together with 'em and make peace."

"They'd think I was up to some kind of trick," he objected.

"Have your meeting at Willsson's. Thaler's there now. You'd be the one who risked tricks going there. Are you afraid of that?"

He frowned and asked:

"Will you go with me?"

"Sure, if you want me."

"Thanks," he said. "I—I'll try."

VIII

All the other delegates to the peace conference were on hand when Noonan and I arrived at Elihu Willsson's home at the appointed time, nine o'clock that night. Everybody nodded to us, but the greetings didn't go any farther than that.

Pete the Finn was the only one I hadn't met before. The bootleg king was a big-boned man of fifty, with a completely bald head. His forehead was small, his jaws enormous—wide, heavy, bulging with muscles.

We sat around Willsson's library table.

Old Elihu sat at the head. The short-clipped hair on his round, pink skull was like silver in the light. His round blue eyes were hard, domineering, under their tangled white brows. Mouth and chin were horizontal lines.

On his right sat Pete the Finn, watching everything with tiny black eyes that never moved. Reno Starkey sat next to the bootlegger. Reno's sallow horseface was as stolidly dull as his eyes.

Max Thaler was tilted back in a chair on Willsson's left. The little gambler's carefully pressed pants-legs were crossed carelessly. A cigarette hung from one corner of the thin, tight-lipped mouth that kept his delicately molded dark face from being the face of a wax-model. I sat next to Thaler. Noonan sat on my other side.

Elihu Willsson opened the meeting.

He said things couldn't go on the way they were going. We were all sensible men, reasonable men, grown men, who had been in the world long enough to know that no matter who a man was he couldn't have everything his own way all the time. Compromises were things everybody had to make sometimes. To get what he wanted a man had to give up something that somebody else wanted. He said he was sure that what we all wanted most just now was to stop this senseless killing. He said he was sure that everything could be frankly discussed and settled in an hour without turning Personville into a slaughterhouse.

It wasn't a bad speech.

When it was over there was a moment of silence. Thaler looked at Noonan, as if he expected something of him. The rest of us did the same. Noonan's face turned red and he spoke huskily:

"Whisper, I'll forget you killed Tim!" He stood up and held out a beefy hand. "Here's my hand on it."

Thaler's thin lip-corners curved scornfully.

"Your—of a brother needed killing, but I didn't kill him," he whispered coldly.

Red became purple in the chief's face. I said loudly:

"Wait, Noonan! We're doing this wrong. We're not going to get anywhere unless everybody comes clean. Be on the up-and-up or we'll be worse off than if we hadn't got together. MacSwain killed Tim." I added a lie for the final touch: "And you know it!"

He stared at me with astonished eyes. He gaped. He couldn't understand what I had done to him.

I looked at the others, tried to look virtuous as hell, asked:

"That's settled, isn't it? Let's get the rest of the kicks squared." I addressed Pete the Finn: "How do you feel about yesterday's accident to your warehouse? And the four men?"

"One hell of an accident!" he growled.

I explained:

"Noonan didn't know you were using the joint. He went there thinking it empty, just to clear the way for a job in town. Your men shot first and he really thought he had run into Thaler's hiding place. Then when he found he'd been stepping in your puddle he lost his head and touched the place off."

Thaler was watching me with a hard little smile around eyes and mouth. Reno Starkey was all dull stolidity. Elihu Willsson was leaning toward me, his old eyes sharp and wary. I couldn't afford to look at Noonan. I was in a good spot if I played my hand right, but it was easy to go wrong.

"The men, they get paid for taking chances," Pete the Finn rumbled. "For the other—twenty-five grand will make it right."

"All right, Pete. Twenty-five thousand. All right," Noonan agreed. "I'll give you the check tomorrow."

I had to fight to keep from laughing at the quickness and eagerness with which he surrendered. He was licked now, I knew, broken, willing to do anything to save his fat neck. I could look at him safely. He wouldn't look at me. He sat down and looked at nobody. He was busy trying to look as if he didn't expect to be murdered before he got away from these enemies to whom I had betrayed him. In a way it was pitiful. But a pitiful fat brute is more disgusting than pitiful. I went back to my work, turning to Elihu Willsson.

"Do you want to squawk about your bank being knocked over, or do you like it?"

Before he could answer, Max Thaler touched my arm and suggested:

"We could tell better who's entitled to squawk if you'd spill the story first, maybe."

I was glad to.

"Noonan wanted to nail you, Thaler, but he either got word or expected it from Lew Yard and Willsson to let you alone. So he thought if he had the bank stuck up, framing you for it, your backers would ditch you. Yard, I understand, was supposed to put his O.K. on all the capers in town. You'd be going over into his territory, and gypping Willsson. That was supposed to make them mad enough that they'd help him cop you. He didn't know you were staying there.

"Reno and his mob were in jail. Reno was Yard's pup, but he didn't mind crossing his headman. He already had an idea that he was about ready to take the city away from Lew. Noonan fakes a tip that you're at Cedar Hill, and takes all the bulls he can't trust out there with him, even cleaning the traffic cops out of Broadway, so Reno would have no interference. McGraw and the bulls that are in it with Noonan let Reno and his mob sneak out of the can, pull the job, and duck back in. Nice alibi. Then they get sprung on bail a couple of hours later.

"It looks as if Lew tumbled to the trick. He sent Dutch Jake and some other boys out to the Silver Arrow to teach Reno and his mob not to take things in their own hands like that. But Reno got clear, got back to the city. It was either him or Lew then, so he made sure who it would be by prying himself into Lew's garage, attaching some dynamite to Lew's car. Reno seems to have had the dope, because I notice that right now he's holding down a seat that would have been Lew's if Lew hadn't been blown to hell."

Everybody was sitting very still, as if to call attention to the fact that they weren't doing anything. Nobody had any friends. It was no time for careless motions.

Thaler whispered very softly:

"Didn't you skip some of it?"

"You mean about Jerry?" I went on being the life of the party: "I was coming back to that. I don't know why he didn't escape when you did, how Noonan came to recapture him; but he did catch him. I don't know whether Jerry went along willingly on the stick-up or not. But he was dropped and left in front of the bank because he was your pal and his being killed there was supposed to tie the job to you. He was kept in the car until the get-away was on. Then he was put out, and was shot in the back. He was facing the bank, with his back to the car. Dinah Brand saw it."

Thaler nodded to me, looked at Reno Star-key, whispered: "Well?"

Reno looked with dull eyes at Thaler and asked calmly: "What of it?"

Thaler stood up, said to Willsson and Pete the Finn: "Deal me out." To me: "Thanks." He walked to the door.

Pete the Finn stood up, leaning on the table with bony hands, speaking from deep in his chest:

"Whisper!" And when Thaler had stopped and turned to face him: "I'm telling you this. 'That damned gun-work is out. All of you understand it. You've got no brains to know what is best for yourselves. So I'll tell you. This busting the town open is no good for business. I won't have it. You'll be nice boys or I'll show you what playing with guns and dynamite is. I've got me an army of young fellows that know what to do on either end of the gun. I got to have 'em in my racket. If I got to use 'em on you I'll use 'em on you. Be good. If you think any of you or all of you can get together mobs that'll stop my young fellows—just don't pay attention to what I tell you. That's all—if you're going to fight I'll give you something to fight."

Pete the Finn sat down. Thaler looked thoughtful for a moment and went out without saying or showing what he had thought.

His going made the others impatient. None wanted to remain until some earlier departer had time to accumulate a few guns in the neighborhood.

In a very few minutes Elihu Willsson and I were the only occupants of his library.

IX

We sat and looked at one another. Presently he said:

"How would you like to be chief of police?"

"Not at all. I'm a rotten errand boy."

"I don't mean with this bunch—after we clean them out."

"And get another just like 'em?"

"Damn you," he snarled, "it wouldn't hurt to take a nicer tone to a man old enough to be your father!"

"Who curses me and hides behind his age," I added.

Anger brought a vein out blue in his forehead. Then he laughed.

"You're a damned nasty talking lad," he said, "but I can't say you haven't done what I paid you to do."

"A swell lot of help I got out of you!"

"Did you need wet-nursing? I gave you the money and turned you loose. What more do you want?"

"You old pirate," I said, "I blackmailed you into it! And you played against me all the way, until tonight, when even you can see they're hell-bent on blasting each other out of the game. Now you're talking about what you did for me!"

"Pirate!" he repeated. "Son, if I hadn't been a pirate I'd be working for the Anaconda Copper Company today—straw boss—and there'd be no Personville Mining Corporation. You're a damned little woolly lamb, yourself, I suppose. I believe that after what you've done to Personville, what you did to this friendly gathering just now.

"I was had, son, where the hair was short. There were things I didn't like, worse things that I didn't know about until this night. But I was caught, and what could I do but bide my time? And don't think I wasn't doing that. Why since that damned Whisper Thaler has been here I've been a prisoner in my own home—understand—a damned hostage!"

"Tough! Where do you stand now?" I demanded. "Are you behind me?"

"If you win."

I got up and said: "I hope to God you get caught with them!"

He said: "I reckon you do, but I won't." He squinted his eyes merrily at me. "I'm financing you. Doesn't that show I mean well? Don't be too hard on me, son, I kind of— "

I said: "Go to hell!" and walked out.

Dick Foley in his hired Buick was at the next corner. I had him drive me over to within a block of Dinah Brand's house and walked the rest of the way.

"You look tired," she said when I followed her into the living-room. "Been working?"

"Yeah. Attending a peace conference out of which at least a dozen murders ought to grow."

The phone rang. She answered it and called me.

Reno Starkey's voice:

"I thought maybe you'd like to hear about Noonan being shot to hell and gone in front of his house tonight just as he was getting out of his heap. You never saw anybody that was deader. Must have had thirty bullets in him."

"Thanks."

Dinah's big blue eyes asked questions.

"First fruits of the peace conference, plucked by Whisper Thaler," I told her. "Where's the gin?"

THE 19TH MURDER

BY DASHIELL HAMMETT

A Complete Novelette

The fourth and concluding adventure of the Continental detective in "The Cleansing of Poisonville," a dramatic and intensely exciting climax to one of the greatest stories of politics and crime ever written.

IN FEBRUARY BLACK MASK.

4

THE 19TH MURDER

BLACK MASK, FEBRUARY 1928

The Continental detective cleans up.

"Reno Starkey, wasn't it?" Dinah Brand asked as I put the phone down.

"Yeah. He thought I'd like to hear about Poisonville being all out of police chiefs."

"You mean—?"

"Noonan was knocked off in front of his house tonight, according to Reno. Haven't you got any gin, or do you just like making me beg for it?"

"You know where it is. He owes his death to one of your cute little tricks!"

I went back into her kitchen, opened the top of the refrigerator and attacked the ice with an ice pick that had a six-inch awl-sharp blade set in a round blue and white handle. The girl stood in the doorway and asked questions. I didn't answer them while I put ice, gin, lemon juice and seltzer together in a couple of glasses.

"I hope to God the gin improves your disposition," she said as we carried the drinks into her dining-room. "What have you been doing? You look ghastly!"

I put my glass on the table, sat down in front of it, and complained:

"This damned town's getting me. If I don't get back to San Francisco soon I'll be going blood-simple like the natives. There's been what? Eighteen murders since I've been here. Donald Willsson, Ike Bush, the four wops and the dick out at Cedar Hill; Jerry Hooper, the pockmarked sergeant and Biddle when the chief's office was dynamited; Lew Yard, his wife and servant, and Stanley Lewis when Yard's joint was blown up; Dutch Jake, Blackie Whalen and Put Collings at the Silver Arrow last night, and now Noonan. An even dozen and a half of 'em, not counting the more or less necessary killings, like the blond kid Whisper got here, the prowler old Elihu got, and Big Nick, the bull I potted. A dozen and a half of 'em in a week, and more coming up!"

She frowned, said sharply:

"Don't look like that!"

I laughed and said:

"I've arranged a death or two in my time, when it was necessary. But this is the first time I've ever had the killing fever. It started right enough. When old Elihu Willsson ran out on me after hiring me to clean town, there was nothing I could do but set the boys against each other and have 'em wipe themselves out for me. Without Elihu's backing I couldn't have got anywhere fooling with courts and legal evidence. I had to do the job the best way I could, which meant stacking things so everybody—Pete the Finn, Whisper Thaler, Lew Yard and Noonan, especially—would think everybody else was double-crossing them. That couldn't lead anywhere but to a lot of killings. How in hell could I help it? The job couldn't be swung any other way without Elihu's support."

"Well, you couldn't help it, so what's the use of making a fuss over it?" The girl's eyes were uneasy. "Drink your drink."

I drank half of it and felt the urge to talk some more.

"Play with enough murder, and it gets you one of two ways. It makes you sick, or you get to like it. It got Noonan the first way. I saw him this afternoon—after Yard was killed. He was green around the gills, all the stomach gone out of him, willing to do anything to make peace in Poisonville. I took him in, suggesting that he and the other survivors get together and patch up their differences. He fell for it after I'd promised to attend the peace conference with him.

"We had it tonight at Willsson's. Besides old Elihu, there were Pete the Finn, Whisper, Reno Starkey—who's making a play for the vacancy left by Yard—Noonan and me. It was a nice party. Pretending to try to clear away everybody's misunderstanding by coming clean all around, I stripped Noonan naked and threw him to the wolves—him and Reno. I published the news that they had pulled the First National Bank stick-up, killing Jerry Hooper to pin the job on his friend Whisper.

"That broke up the peace conference. Whisper got up and declared himself out. Before he left Pete the Finn made a speech at everybody, telling them where they stood. Pete said the quarreling was hurting his bootleg business and he wasn't going to stand for any more of it. He said anybody that started anything from then on could expect to have his army of booze guards turned loose on them. Whisper didn't look impressed."

"He wouldn't," the girl agreed.

"Whisper was the first man out, and he seems to have had time to collect some rods in front of Noonan's house by the time the chief reached home. The chief was shot down. Pete the Finn looks like a man who means what he says. Then he'll be out after Whisper. Reno was as much to blame as Noonan for Jerry Hooper's murder, so Whisper will be gunning for him.

And, knowing it, Reno will be out to get Whisper first. Besides that, Reno will have a job on his hands standing off those of the late Lew Yard's underlings who don't happen to want Reno for a boss. Any trouble Reno makes will bring Pete the Finn's beer-mob down on him, too. All in all, one swell dish."

Dinah Brand reached across the table, patted my hand, said:

"It's not your fault, darling. You say yourself there was nothing else you could do. Finish your drink and we'll have another."

"There was plenty else I could do," I contradicted her. "Old Elihu ran out on me at first simply because these birds had too much on him for him to risk a break with them unless he was sure he could wipe them out. He couldn't see how I was going to win, so he played with them. But he's not their brand of cut-throat, and besides, he thinks Personville is his own property, and doesn't take kindly to having them run it for him.

"I could have gone to him this afternoon and showed him how I had them sewed up, had enough on them to ruin the whole lot. He'd have listened to reason. He'd have come over to my side, have given me the backing I needed to swing the play legally. I could have done that. But it's easier to have 'em killed off—easier and surer and—now that I'm feeling this way—more satisfying.

"Listen: I sat at Willsson's table tonight and played 'em like you play trout and got just as much fun out of it. Understand? I looked at Noonan and knew he couldn't live another day because of what I was doing to him, and I laughed and felt warm and happy inside. That's what this damned burg has done to me!"

She smiled too indulgently and spoke too softly:

"You exaggerate so, honey! They deserve all they get. I wish you wouldn't look like that. You make me feel creepy."

I laughed, picked up the glasses and went out into the kitchen for more gin. When I came back she frowned at me over anxious dark eyes and asked:

"What in the name of God did you bring the ice pick in for?"

"To show you how my mind's running. Yesterday, if I thought about it at all, it was as a good tool to pry off hunks of ice." I ran a finger down its half-foot of round steel blade to the needle point. "Not a bad thing to pin a man to his clothes with. That's the way I'm getting, on the level. There's a piece of copper wire lying out in the gutter in front of the house—thin and soft and just long enough to twist around a neck with enough ends to hold good. I had one hell of a time to keep from picking it up and putting it in my pocket, just in case—"

"You're crazy!"

"I told you I was going blood-simple."

"I don't like it. Put that thing back in the kitchen and sit down and be sensible."

I obeyed at least two-thirds of the order.

"The trouble with you is," she scolded, "your nerves are shot to hell. You've been through too much excitement the last few days. Keep it up and you're going to have a nervous breakdown—the heebie-jeebies for fair."

I held up a hand with spread fingers. It was steady enough. She looked at it and said:

"That doesn't mean anything. It's inside you. Why don't you sneak off for a couple of days—rest? You've got things stirred up here enough to run themselves. Let's go down to Salt Lake. It'll do you good."

"Can't, sister. Somebody's got to stay here to count the dead. Besides, the whole program is arranged for the present combination of people and things. Our going out of town would change that. The chances are I'd have to do the job all over again."

"Nobody would have to know you were gone, and *I've* got nothing to do with it."

"Since when?"

She leaned forward, made her eyes small, asked:

"Now what are you getting at?"

"Nothing. Just wondering how you got to be a disinterested bystander all of a sudden. Forgotten that it was because of you Donald Willsson was killed and the whole thing started? Forgotten that the dope you gave me on Whisper after you broke with him kept the job from petering out in the middle?"

"You know just as well as I do that none of that was my fault," she said hotly. "It's all past anyhow. You're just dragging it up because you're in a hell of a frame of mind tonight and want to argue."

"It wasn't past last night, when you were scared stiff Whisper was going to kill you."

"Will you stop talking about killing!"

"Young Albury once told me that Bill Quint had threatened to kill you," I said.

"Stop it!"

"You seem to have a gift for arousing murderous notions in your boy friends. There's Albury waiting trial now for killing Donald Willsson because of you. There's Whisper, who's got you shivering in corners. I've got a private idea that Dan Rolff's going to have a try at you

some day."

"Dan? You're crazy! Why, I—"

"Yeah. He was a lunger and down and out and you took him in. You gave him a home and all the laudanum he needed. You use him for errand boy. You've slapped his face in front of me and I've seen you knock him around in front of others. He's in love with you. One of these days you're going to wake up and find he's whittled your neck away."

"I'm glad one of us knows what you're talking about, if you do," she said as she carried our empty glasses through the kitchen door.

I lighted a cigarette and wondered why I felt the way I did, wondered if there was anything to this presentiment business or if my nerves were just ragged.

"The next best thing for you to do," the girl advised me when she returned with the full glasses, "is to get plastered and forget everything for a few hours. I put a double slug of gin in yours. You need it."

"It's not me," I said. "It's you. Every time I mention killing you jump on me. You're a woman. You think if nothing's said about it, none of the God knows how many people in town who might want to kill you will. That's silly. Nothing we say is going to make Whisper, for instance—"

"Please, please stop!" she begged, so softly that I had to watch her lips to make out the words. "I am silly. I am afraid of the words. I'm afraid of him. I—Oh, why didn't you put him out of the way when I asked you?"

"Sorry," I said, meaning it.

"Do you think he'll—?"

"I don't know," I told her, "and, as you say, there's no use talking about it. The thing to do is to drink—though there doesn't seem to be much authority to this gin."

"That's you, not the gin. Do you want an honest to God rear?"

"I'd drink nitroglycerine tonight."

"That's just about what you're going to get," she promised me.

She rattled bottles in the kitchen and brought me in a glass of what looked like the stuff we had been drinking. I sniffed at it and said:

"Some of Dan's laudanum, huh? He still in the hospital?"

"Yes. There's your nitroglycerine, mister, if that's what you want."

I put the doped gin down my throat. Presently I felt more comfortable. Time went by as we drank and talked in a world that was rosy, cheerful and full of friendship and peace on earth.

She stuck to gin. I tried that for a while, too, then had another gin and laudanum. It finished me up nicely. For a while I played a game, trying to hold my eyes open as if I were awake, even though I couldn't see a damned thing out of them. When the trick wouldn't fool her any more I gave it up.

The last I remembered was her helping me in to the living-room Chesterfield.

II

I dreamed I was sitting on a bench, facing the tumbling fountain in Harlem Park, Baltimore, beside a woman who wore a veil. I had come there with her. She was some one I knew well. But now I had suddenly forgotten who she was. I couldn't see her face because of the long black veil. I thought if I said something to her I would recognize her voice when she answered. But I was very embarrassed and it took me a long time to find anything to say. Finally I asked her if she knew a man named Carroll T. Harris. She spoke, but the roar and swish of the tumbling fountain drowned her voice, and I could hear nothing.

Fire engines went out Edmondson Avenue. She left me to run after them. As she ran she cried, "Fire! Fire!" I recognized her voice then, knew who she was—some one important to me. I ran after her, but it was too late. She and the fire engines were gone. I walked streets hunting for her—half the streets in the United States—Gay Street, Mount Royal Avenue in Baltimore, Colfax Avenue in Denver, Aetna Road, St. Clair Avenue in Cleveland, McKinney Avenue in Dallas, Lamartine, Cornell, Amory Streets in Boston, Berry Boulevard in Louisville, Lexington Avenue in New York—until I came to Victoria Street in Jacksonville, where I heard her voice again, though I still could not see her.

She was calling a name, not mine, one strange to me. I could hear her calling but no matter how fast I walked or in what direction, I could get no nearer the voice. It was the same distance from me in the street that runs past the Federal Building in El Paso as in Detroit's Grand Circus Park. Then the voice stopped. Discouraged, tired, I went into the lobby of the hotel that faces the railroad station in Rocky Mount, North Carolina, to rest. While I sat there a train came in. She got off it and came into the lobby, over to me, and began kissing me. I was very uncomfortable because everybody stood around looking at us and laughing.

That dream ended there.

I dreamed I was in a strange city, hunting for a man I hated. I had an open knife in my coat pocket and meant to kill him with it when found him. It was Sunday morning. Church bells were ringing, crowds of people were in the streets, going to and from church. I walked almost as far as in the first dream, but always in this same strange city.

Then the man I was after yelled at me, and I saw him. He was a small brown man who wore an immense sombrero. He was standing on the steps of a tall building on the far side of a wide plaza, laughing at me. Between us the plaza was crowded with people, packed shoulder to shoulder. Keeping one hand on the open knife in my pocket, I ran toward the little brown man, running on the heads and shoulders of the people in the plaza. It was difficult running. I slipped and floundered. The heads and shoulders were of unequal heights and not evenly spaced.

The little brown man stood on the steps and laughed until I had almost reached him. Then he ran into the tall building. I chased him up miles of spiral stairway, always just an inch more than a hand's reach behind him. We came to the roof. He ran straight across to the edge and jumped just as one of my hands touched him. His shoulder slid out of my hand. My hand knocked his sombrero off. My fingers closed on his head, wrapping themselves around it. It was a smooth, hard, round head, no larger than a large egg.

Gripping his head with one hand, I tried to bring my knife out of my pocket with the other—and realized that I had gone off the edge of the roof with him. We dropped giddily down toward the millions of upturned faces in the plaza below—miles down...

I opened my eyes in the dull light of morning sun filtered through drawn blinds. I was lying face down on the dining-room floor, my head resting on my left forearm. My right arm was stretched straight out. My right hand held the round blue-and-white handle of Dinah Brand's ice pick. The pick's six-inch needle-shaped blade was buried in the left side of Dinah Brand's bosom.

She was lying on her back—dead. Her long muscular legs were stretched out toward the kitchen door. There was, I noticed, a run in the front of her right stocking.

Very slowly and gently, as if I were afraid of awakening her, I let go the ice pick, withdrew my arm, and got up.

My eyes burned. My throat and mouth were hot, woolly. I went into the kitchen, found a bottle of gin, tilted it to my mouth, and kept it there until I had to breathe. The kitchen clock said 7:41.

With the gin in my belly, I returned to the dining-room, switched on the lights, and looked at the dead girl.

Not much blood was in sight—a spot the size of a silver dollar around the hole the ice pick made in her blue silk dress. There was a bruise on her right cheek, just under the cheek bone. Another bruise, finger-made, was on her right wrist. Her hands were empty. I moved her enough to look under her body. Nothing was there.

I examined the room. If anything had been changed in it since we sat drinking there the previous night I couldn't find it. I went back to the kitchen and found no recognizable changes.

The back door was locked, with no marks to show it had been tampered with. I went to the front door, failed to find any marks on it. I went through the house from roof to cellar, and learned nothing. The girl's jewelry—on her dressing-table—and four or five hundred dollars in paper money—in her handbag, on a bedroom chair—were undisturbed. The windows were all right.

In the dining-room again, I knelt beside the dead girl and used my handkerchief to wipe the ice pick handle clean of any prints my fingers might have left on it. I did the same to glasses, bottles, doors, light buttons, and the pieces of furniture I had touched, or was likely to have touched. Then I washed my hands, couldn't find any blood on my clothes, made sure I was leaving none of my property behind, and went to the front door. I opened it, wiped the inner knob, closed it behind me, wiped the outer knob, and went away.

III

From a drug store in upper Broadway I telephoned Dick Foley, at the National Hotel, and asked him to come over to my room in the Great Western. He arrived a few minutes after I had got there.

"Dinah Brand was killed in her house last night or early this morning," I told him, "stabbed with an ice pick. The police don't know it yet. I've told you enough about her for you to know there are any number of people who might have reasons for getting her. There are three I want looked up first. A red named Bill Quint, who threatened to kill her when she gave him the air some time ago, Whisper Thaler, and the lunger, Dan Rolff.

"Quint lives at the Miner's Hotel in Forest Street. He's a square-built man of thirty, broad, thick face, kind of grayish, even to the mouth. He goes in for flowing, red ties. You already have Whisper's and Rolff's descriptions. Rolff is, or was, in the hospital, getting over the effects of being blackjacked. I don't know which hospital, but try the City first. Get hold of Mickey Linehan. He's still keeping his eye on Pete the Finn. Tell him to lay off that and give you a hand on this. Run those three down. See if you can learn where they were last night. And time means something."

The little Canadian operative had been watching me curiously while I talked. Now he started to say something, changed his mind, grunted "Righto," and departed.

I went out to look for Reno Starkey. After an hour of searching I located him, by telephone, in a Ronney Street rooming-house.

"By yourself?" he asked when I had said I wanted to see him.

"Yeah."

He said I could come out, and told me how to get there. I took a taxi. It was a dingy two-storey house near the edge of town. A couple of men loitered in front of a grocer's on the corner above. Another pair sat on the low wooden steps of the house down at the other corner. None of the four was conspicuously refined in appearance.

When I rang the bell at the address Reno had given me, two men opened the door. They weren't so mild-looking either.

I was taken upstairs to a shabby room where Reno, collarless and in shirt-sleeves and vest, sat tilted back in a chair, with his feet on the window-sill.

He nodded his sallow horse face and said:

"Pull a chair over."

The men who had brought me up went away, closing the door. I sat down and said:

"I want an alibi. Dinah Brand was killed last night, after I left her. There's no chance of my being copped for it, but, with Noonan dead, I don't know how I'm hitched up with the police department. I don't want to give 'em any openings to even try to hang anything on me. If I've got to, I can prove where I was last night, but you can save me a hell of a lot of trouble if you will."

Reno looked at me with dull brown eyes and asked:

"Why pick on me?"

"You phoned me there. You're the only person who knows I was there the first part of the night. I'd have to fix it with you even if I got the alibi somewhere else, wouldn't I?"

He asked:

"You didn't croak her, did you?"

I said, "No," casually.

He stared out of the window for a little while before he spoke:

"You was at the Tanner House in Tanner. That's a little burg twenty-thirty miles up the hill. You went up there after the meeting bust, and stayed till morning. A guy named Ricker that hangs around Murry's with a hire heap drove you up and back. You ought to know what you was doing up there. Give me your sig and I'll have it put on the register."

"Thanks," I said as I unscrewed my fountain pen.

"Don't say 'em. I'm doing this because I need all the friends I can get. When the time comes that you sit in between me and Whisper and Pete I don't expect the sour end of it."

"You won't get it," I promised. "Who's going to be chief of police now?"

"McGraw's acting chief. He'll likely cinch it."

"How'll he play?"

"With Pete. Rough stuff will hurt his grift just like it does Pete's beer racket. It'll have to be hurt some. I'd be a swell palooka to sit still with a guy like Whisper on the loose. It's me or him. Think he croaked the broad?"

"He had reasons enough," I said as I gave him the slip of paper on which I had scribbled my name. "She double-crossed him, sold him out plenty."

"You and her was kind of—"

Somebody in the street whistled a bar from *I Left My Sugar Standing in the Rain.*

Reno dropped his feet to the floor and stood on them. He put his back to the wall beside the window; twisting his head over his shoulder so he could look down into the street without showing himself.

Through the window came the hum of big automobile engines tuned to the last fraction.

I got up and went to the other window, imitating Reno's position. It gave me a good view of the edge of the sidewalk in front just as a long black car that looked like a 1912 Pierce-Arrow halted there. The nose of another snuggled up behind it.

Men got out—not hiding their guns.

I looked at Reno. He was stolid as ever. Friends, I thought.

Reno stretched an arm across the window, high, and let it fall.

From the door and windows of a house that faced ours, across the street, a lot of guns were fired. More guns made more noise downstairs in our building. Some of the men who had got out of the cars below got back in them. The cars slid away from the curb, straightened themselves out, and roared off down the street with slugs sprinkling around them.

The shooting stopped.

I let Reno be first to put his head out the window. Nothing happened to it. I risked mine. Five men were lying on our sidewalk. Only two of them were squirming.

We pulled our heads in as the door of our room opened. A long-legged youngster of twenty-two or three, with a thin freckled face around reckless eyes, was shoving a .45 into a shoulder-holster as he came into the room.

"Whisper wasn't there?" Reno said.

"Nope. Just like you said—that little—wouldn't walk into the trap. He'd send the boys."

"We'll slide along." Reno picked up a coat and hat from a chair and followed the long-legged boy to the door, telling me, "You might as well go along with me and Hank."

I went along. Three other men joined us as we climbed, by way of chair and table, through a trap door to the roof. We crossed that roof and half a dozen others that were between the rooming-house and the lower cross street. We walked three roofs down the side street, and went through another trap door into a storeroom in one corner of a garage's second storey.

We waited in the storeroom until long-legged Hank—I took him to be the Hank O'Marra who had been in on the First National stick-up with Reno—went out, staid ten minutes, and returned. Then we went downstairs one at a time and got into one of the dozen or more cars on the ground floor. There were only a couple of garage men in sight. They kept their backs to us while we were there.

"Where do you want to be dropped?" Reno asked me as we drove out of the garage.

"Any car line that'll take me downtown will do," I said, and asked him where I could reach him if I needed to.

"Know Peak Murry?" he asked.

"I've met him." He ran a pool room in Broadway, and was on the outs with Whisper.

"Anything you give him will get to me. That Tanner lay is all set."

"Thanks," I said.

IV

Downtown, I went first to police headquarters. I found McGraw holding down the chief's desk. His blond-lashed eyes looked at me suspiciously and the lines in his leathery face were even deeper and sourer than usual.

"When'd you see Dinah Brand last?" he asked before the door was closed behind me. His voice rasped disagreeably through his bony nose.

"Ten-forty o'clock last night, or thereabout," I said. "Why?"

"Where?"

"1232 Hurricane Street—her house."

"How long were you there?"

"Five minutes, maybe ten."

"Why?"

"Why what?"

"Why didn't you stay any longer than that?"

"What," I asked, sitting down in the chair he hadn't offered me, "makes it any of your business?"

He glared at me while he filled his lungs so he could yell, "Murder!" in my face.

I laughed and said:

"You don't think *she* had anything to do with Noonan's killing!"

I wanted a cigarette, but cigarettes were too well known as first aids to the nervous for me to take a chance on one just then. McGraw was trying to look through my eyes. I let him look, having all sorts of confidence in my belief that, like a lot of people, I looked most honest when I was lying.

Presently he gave up the gimlet-eye posturing and asked:

"Why not?"

That was weak.

I said: "All right, why not?" indifferently, offered him a cigarette and took one myself. Then I added: "My guess is that Whisper did it."

"Was he there?" For once McGraw cheated his nose, snapping the words off his teeth.

"Was he where?"

"At Brand's!"

"No," I said, wrinkling my forehead. "Why should he have been there if he was off killing Noonan?"

"Damn Noonan!" the acting chief exclaimed irritably. "What do you keep dragging him in for?"

I tried to look at him as if I thought he was crazy. He said: "Dinah Brand was murdered last night."

I said: "Yeh?"

"Now will you answer my questions?"

"Of course. I was at Willsson's with Noonan and the others. After I left there, around ten-thirty, I dropped in at her house to tell her I had to go up to Tanner. I had half a date with her. I staid there about ten minutes—just long enough to have a drink. There was nobody else there, unless they were hiding. When was she killed? And how?"

McGraw told me he had sent a pair of his detectives—Shepp and Vanaman—to see the girl that morning, to see how much help she'd give the department in copping Whisper for Noonan's murder. The dicks got there at nine-thirty. The front door was ajar. Nobody answered their ringing. They went in and found the girl lying on her back in the dining-room, dead from a stab wound in her left breast.

The doctors said she had been stabbed at close to three o'clock that morning, with a pointed, round blade about half a foot long. Bureaus, closets, trunks, and so on showed signs of having been skilfully and thoroughly searched. There was no money in the girl's handbag and none elsewhere in the house. The jewel case on her dressing-table was empty, though two diamond rings had been left on her fingers. The weapon with which she had been killed was not found. The finger-print experts hadn't turned up anything they could use. Neither doors nor windows seemed to have been forced. The kitchen looked as if the girl had been drinking with a guest or guests.

"Half a foot long, round, pointed," I repeated the weapon's description. "That sounds like her ice pick."

McGraw reached for the telephone and told somebody to send Shepp and Vanaman in. McGraw introduced us and asked them about the ice pick. They were positive it hadn't been there. They wouldn't have missed an article of that sort.

"Was it there last night?" McGraw asked me.

"Yeah. I stood beside her while she chipped off pieces of ice with it."

I described it. McGraw told the dicks to search the house again, and then to try to find the pick in the neighborhood.

"You knew her. What's your slant on it?" he asked me when the sleuths had gone.

"Too new for me to have one," I dodged the question. "Give me a couple of hours to chew it over. What do you think?"

He fell back into sourness, growling, "How the hell can I tell?"

But the fact that he let me go away without further questioning told me he had already made up his mind that Whisper was the murderer. I wondered if the little gambler was guilty—or if this was another of the wrong raps that Personville police chiefs liked to hang on him. It didn't seem to make much difference now. It was a gut he had—personally or by deputy—put Noonan down, and they could only hang him once anyway. That would be enough.

There were a lot of men in the corridors. Some of them were very young, quite a few were foreigners, most of them were every bit as tough-looking as any man should be. On my way to the street door I met Donner, a bow-legged bull who had been on a couple of expeditions with the dead chief and me.

"Hello," I greeted him. "What's the mob? Emptying the can to make room for more?"

"Them's our new specials," he told me as if he didn't think much of them. "We're going to have a argumented force."

"Congratulations," I said and went on out.

I found Peak Murry sitting at his desk, behind the cigar-counter, in his pool room, talking to three men. I sat down on the other side of the room and watched a couple of kids knock the balls around. In a little while the lanky proprietor came over to me.

"If you see Reno sometime," I told him, "you might let him know that Pete the Finn's having his mob sworn in as special coppers."

"I might," Murry promised.

V

Mickey Linehan was sitting in the lobby when I got back to my hotel. He followed me up to my room and reported:

"Your Dan Rolff pulled a sneak from the pogy somewhere after midnight last night. The croaker are kind of steamed up about it. Seems they were figuring on cutting a lot of little pieces of bone out of his brain this morning. But him and his duds were gone. We've got nothing on Whisper yet. Dick's out trying to place Bill Quint now. I hear there was some caps snapped down Ronney Street today."

"Yeah. It oughtn't—"

The telephone hell rang.

A man's voice, carefully oratorical, spoke my name with a question mark after it.

I said: "Yes."

The voice said:

"Mr Charles Proctor Dawn is speaking. I think you will find it well worth your while to appear at my office immediately."

"Yeah? Who are you?"

"Mr Charles Proctor Dawn, attorney-at-law. My suite is in the Rutledge Block, 310 Green Street. I think you will find it well—"

"Mind telling me what it's all about?" I asked.

"There are affairs best not discussed over the telephone. I think you will find—"

"All right," I interrupted him again. "I'll be around to see you this afternoon if I'm not too busy."

"You will find it very, very advisable," he assured me.

I hung up on that. Mickey Linehan said:

"You were going to tell me about this morning's shooting."

I said:

"I wasn't. I started to say it oughtn't be hard to trace Rolff, running around with a fractured skull and probably a lot of bandages. Suppose you try it. I'd play Hurricane Street first, if I were you."

Mickey grinned all the way across his red comedian's face, said, "Don't tell me anything of what's going on—I'm only working with you," picked up his hat and left me.

I spread myself across the bed, smoked cigarettes end to end, and thought about last night, my frame of mind, my passing out, my dreams, and the situation into which I woke. The thinking was unpleasant enough to make me glad when it was interrupted.

Fingernails scratched on the outside of my door. I opened the door.

A man stood there, a stranger to me. He was young, thin, gaudily dressed, with heavy eyebrows and a small mustache that were coal-black against a very pale, nervous but not timid, face.

"I'm Ted Wright," he said, holding out a hand as if I were glad to meet him. "I guess you've heard Whisper talk about me."

I gave him my hand, let him in, closed the door, and asked:

"You're a friend of Whisper's?"

"You bet!" He held up two thin fingers pressed tightly together. "Me and him are just like that."

I didn't say anything. He looked around the room, smiling nervously, crossed to the open bathroom door, peeped in, came back to me, rubbed his lips with his tongue, and made his proposition:

"I'll knock him off for you for half a grand."

"Whisper?"

"Uh-huh. And it's dirt-cheap."

"Why do I want him killed?" I asked.

"He carved you all out of girls."

"Yeah?"

"You ain't dumb as that," Wright said.

A notion began crawling around in my noodle. To give it time I said:

"Sit down. This needs talking over."

"It don't need nothing," he said, looking at me sharply, not moving toward either chair. "You either want him knocked off or you don't."

"Then I don't."

He said something I couldn't catch—down in his throat—and turned toward the door. I got between him and it. He stood still, his eyes fidgeting. I said:

"So Whisper's dead?"

He stepped back and put a hand behind him.

I poked his jaw;

He got his legs crossed and went down.

I pulled him up by his wrists, yanked his face close to mine, growled:

"Come through. What's the racket?"

"I ain't done nothing to you."

"Let me catch you. Who got Whisper?"

"I don't know nothing a—"

I let go one of his wrists, slapped his face with an open hand, caught his wrist again, and tried my luck at crunching both of them while I repeated:

"Who got Whisper?"

"Dan Rolff," he whined. "He walked right up to him and stuck him with the same skewer Whisper used on the twist. That's right!"

"How do you know it was the one Whisper killed the girl with?"

"Dan said so."

"What did Whisper say?"

"Nothing. He looked funny as all hell, standing there with the butt of the sticker sticking out his side. Then he flashes the rod and puts two slugs in Dan just like one, and the both of 'em go down together, cracking heads. Dan's all bloody through the bandages."

"Then?"

"Then I roll 'em over, and they're a pair of stiffs. Every word I'm telling you is right."

"Who else was there?"

"Nobody. Whisper was hiding out, with only me to go between him and the mob. He killed Noonan hisself, and he didn't want to trust nobody for a couple of days, nobody but me."

"So you, being a smart boy, thought you could go around to his enemies and pick up a piece or two of jack for killing him after he was dead?"

"I was clean, and this won't be no place for Whisper's friends after the news gets out he's croaked," Wright whined. "I had to raise a getaway stake."

"How'd you make out?"

"I got a century from Pete, and a century and a half from Peak Murry—for Reno—with a promise of more from both after I turned the trick," he said, the whine changing into boasting as he talked. "I bet you I could collect from McGraw, too—and I thought you'd kick in with something."

"They must be high in the air to put out dough on a game like that."

"I don't know," he said. "It ain't such a lousy one." He got humble again. "Give me a chance, brother. Don't gum it on me. I'll give you fifty bucks now and a split of whatever I get from McGraw if you'll keep your clam shut till I put it over and grab a rattler out."

"Nobody knows where Whisper is but you?"

"Nobody else, excepting Dan that's as dead as he is."

"Where are they?"

"It's the old Redman warehouse down on Porter Street. In the back, upstairs, Whisper had a room fixed up with a bed and stove and some grub. Give me a chance. Fifty bucks now and a cut on the rest."

I let go his arms and said:

"I don't want the dough, but go ahead. I'll lay off for a couple of hours, anyway. That ought to be long enough."

"Thanks, thanks, thanks!" And he hurried away from me.

I put on my hat and coat, went out, found Green Street and the Rutledge Block.

It was a wooden building a long while past any prime it might ever have had. Mr Charles Proctor Dawn's establishment was on the second floor. There was no elevator. I climbed a worn and rickety flight of wooden stairs.

The lawyer had two rooms—both dingy, smelly and poorly lighted. I waited in the outer one while a clerk, who went well with the rooms, carried my name in to the lawyer. Half a minute later the clerk opened the door and beckoned me in.

Mr Charles Proctor Dawn was a little fat man of fifty-something. He had prying triangular eyes of a very light color, a short, fleshy nose, and a fleshier mouth whose greediness was only partly hidden between a ragged gray mustache and a ragged gray Vandyke beard. His clothes were dark and unclean looking without actually being dirty.

He didn't get up from his desk, and throughout my visit he kept his right hand on the edge of a desk drawer that was some six inches open.

He said:

"Ah! my dear sir, I am extremely glad that you had the good judgment to follow my counsel."

His voice was even more oratorical than it had been over the wire.

I didn't say anything. He nodded his whiskers as if my not saying anything was another exhibition of good judgment. He said:

"I may say, in all justice, that you will find it the invariable part of sound judgment to follow the dictates of my counsel."

He knew a lot of sentences like that, and he didn't mind using them on me. Finally he got along to:

"Thus, that conduct which in a minor practitioner might seem irregular, becomes, when he who exercises it occupies such indisputable prominence in his community, simply that greater ethic which scorns the pettier conventionalities when confronted with an opportunity to serve mankind through one of its individual representatives. Therefore, my dear sir, I have not hesitated to summon you, to brush aside scornfully all trivial considerations of accepted precedent, to say to you frankly and candidly, my dear, sir, that your interests will best be served by retaining me as your legal representative."

I asked:

"What'll it cost?"

"That," he said loftily, "is of but secondary importance. However, it is a detail that has its place in our relationship, and must be arranged. We shall say, a thousand dollars now. Later, perhaps—" he ruffled his beard and didn't finish the sentence.

I said I hadn't, of course, that much money with me.

"Naturally, my dear sir! Naturally! But that is of no importance—none whatever. Any time will do for that—any time up to ten o'clock tomorrow morning."

"At ten tomorrow," I agreed. "Now I'd like to know why I need a legal representative."

He made an indignant face.

"My dear sir, it is no matter for jesting, I assure you!"

I explained that I hadn't been joking, that I really was puzzled.

He cleared his throat, frowned more or less majestically; said:

"It may well be, my dear sir, that you do not fully comprehend your peril, but it is indubitably preposterous that you should expect me to suppose that you are without any inkling of the difficulties—the legal difficulties, my dear sir—with which you are confronted. However, there is no time to go into that matter now. I have a pressing appointment with Judge Leffner. Tomorrow morning I shall be glad to go more thoroughly into every least ramification of the affair with you. Tomorrow at ten."

From this joker's office I went to Peak Murry's pool room, bought a bottle of Scotch, returned to my hotel for dinner, and went up to my room. I spent the evening drinking unpleasant Scotch, thinking unpleasant thoughts and waiting for reports that didn't come from Dick Foley and Mickey Linehan.

I went to sleep at midnight.

VI

I was half dressed at eight-thirty the next morning when Dick Foley came in. The little Canadian reported, in his word-saving manner, that Bill Quint had checked out of his hotel at noon the previous day, leaving no forwarding address. A train left for Ogden at twelve-fifty-five. Dick had wired the Continental's Salt Lake branch to send a man up there to trace Quint.

"I don't think we want Quint," I gave my opinion, "but we can't pass up any leads. My guess about him is that when he heard she had been killed he decided to duck—being a discarded lover who had threatened her. She gave him the air long ago. If he'd been going to do anything about it, he'd have gone into action before this."

Dick nodded and said:

"Gun-play out road last night—hijacking—four trucks of hooch nailed, burned."

That sounded like Reno Starkey's answer to the news that the big bootlegger's beer mob had been sworn in as special coppers.

As I finished dressing, Mickey Linehan arrived.

"Rolff was at the girl's house, all right," he reported. "The Greek grocer on the corner saw him come out around nine yesterday morning. The Greek thought he was drunk. He went down the street wobbling and talking to himself."

"How come the Greek didn't tell the coppers? Or did he?"

"Wasn't asked. A swell force this burg's got! Well, do we find him for 'em and turn him in with the job all sewed up?"

"Unless he left and came back for the ice pick later," I said, "Rolff didn't turn the trick. She was cut down at three in the morning. He wasn't there at eight-thirty, and the pick was still in her. It was—"

Dick Foley left his chair, stood in front of me, asked:

"How do you know?"

I didn't like the way he looked nor the way he spoke. I said:

"You know because I'm telling you."

Dick didn't say anything. Mickey, grinning his half-wit's grin, asked:

"What do we do next? Let's get the thing polished off."

"I've got a date for ten," I told them. "Hang around the hotel until I get back. Whisper and Rolff are dead, probably, so we won't have to hunt for them." I scowled at Dick and added: "I was told that. I didn't kill either of them."

The little Canadian nodded without lowering his steady eyes from mine.

I ate breakfast alone and set out for the lawyer's office.

Turning off King Street, I saw Hank O'Marra's freckled face in an automobile that was going up Green Street. He was sitting beside a man I didn't know. The long-legged youngster waved an arm at me and stopped the car. I went over to him. He said:

"Reno wants to see you."

"Where'll I find him?"

"Jump in."

"I can't go now," I explained. "Maybe not till late this afternoon."

"See Peak when you're ready."

I said I would.

O'Marra and his companion drove on up Green Street. I walked half a block south to the Rutledge Block.

With a foot on the first of the rickety steps that led up to the lawyer's floor, I stopped to look at something.

It was barely visible back in a dim corner of the first floor. It was a shoe. It was lying in a position that empty shoes don't lie in.

I took my foot off the step and went toward the shoe. Now I could see an ankle and the cuff of a black pants-leg above the shoe-top.

That prepared me for what I found.

I found Mr Charles Proctor Dawn huddled among two brooms, a mop and a couple of buckets in a little alcove formed by the back of the stairs and a corner of the wall. His Vandyke beard was red with blood from a cut that ran diagonally across his forehead. His head was twisted sidewise and backward at an angle that was impossible without a broken neck.

I did what seemed necessary. Gingerly pulling one side of the dead man's coat out of the way, I emptied the inside pocket, transferring a black book and a sheaf of papers to my own coat. I couldn't get at any of his other pockets without moving him, so I passed them up.

Five minutes later I was going through a side door into my hotel. To avoid Dick and Mickey in the lobby I walked up to the mezzanine and took the elevator there.

In my room I sat down and examined my loot.

I took the book first—a small, imitation-leather-covered memoranda book of the sort that sells for not much money in any stationery store.

It held some fragmentary notes that meant nothing to me, and thirty or forty names and addresses that meant as little—with one exception:

Helen Albury
    1229A Hurricane Street

That was interesting because, (1) a young man named Robert Albury was in jail, having confessed that he shot and killed Donald Willsson, my client's son, because he thought young Willsson had taken his place as Dinah Brand's lover, and (2) Dinah Brand had lived and had been murdered at 1232 Hurricane Street, across the street from 1229A.

I didn't find my name in the book. I put it aside and began unfolding and reading the papers I had taken from Dawn's pocket. Here, too, I had to wade through a lot that meant nothing to find anything that meant something.

This find was a group of four letters held together by a rubber band. The letters were in slitted envelopes that had postmarks dated a week apart, roughly. The latest was some six months old. The letters were addressed to Dinah Brand. The first wasn't so bad, for a love letter. The second was a bit goofier. The third and fourth were swell examples of how silly an ardent and unsuccessful wooer can be, especially if he's getting along in years. The letters were signed by Elihu Willsson.

I had found nothing to show definitely why Mr Charles Proctor Dawn had thought he could blackmail me out of a thousand dollars, but I had found plenty to think about. I encouraged my brain with two Fatimas and then went down to join the two operatives in the lobby.

"Go out and see what you can dig up on a lawyer named Charles Proctor Dawn," I told Mickey. "He's got offices in Green Street. Stay away from them. Don't put in a lot of time on him. I just want a rough line."

I told Dick to give me five minutes start and then follow me out to the neighborhood of 1229A Hurricane Street.

I went out there. It was a two-storey building almost directly opposite Dinah Brand's, divided into an upstairs and a downstairs flat, with a private entrance for each. 1229A was the upper flat. I rang the bell.

The door was opened by a thin girl of eighteen or nineteen, with dark eyes set close together in a shiny yellowish face under shortcut brown hair that looked damp.

She opened the door, made a choked, frightened sound in her throat, and backed away, holding both hands to her open mouth.

"You are Miss Helen Albury?" I asked.

She shook her head violently from side to side. There was no truthfulness in it. Her eyes were crazy.

I said:

"I'd like to come in and talk to you a few minutes," going in as I spoke, closing the door behind me.

She didn't say anything. She went up the stairs in front of me, her head bent over her shoulder so she could watch me with scary eyes.

We went into a scantily furnished living-room. Dinah Brand's house could be seen from the window's.

The girl stood in the middle of the room, her hands still to her mouth. I wasted time and words trying to convince her that I was harmless. It was no good. Everything I said seemed to increase her panic. It was a damned nuisance. I quit trying and got down to business.

"You are Robert Albury's sister."

No reply—nothing but the senseless look of utter fear. I said:

"After he was arrested for killing Willsson, you took this flat so you could watch her. What for?"

Not a word from her. I had to supply my own answer:

"Revenge. You blamed her for your brother's trouble. You watched for your chance. It came night before last. You sneaked into her house, found her drunk, stabbed her with the ice pick."

She didn't say anything. There was no change in the blankness of her frightened face. I said:

"Dawn helped you—engineered it for you. He wanted Elihu Willsson's letters. Who was the man he sent to do the actual killing? Who was he?"

No answer. No change in her expression. I thought I'd like to spank her. I said:

"I've given you your chance to talk. I'm willing to listen to your side of the story. But suit yourself."

She suited herself by keeping quiet. I went out of the flat not sure that she had understood a single word I had said.

At the corner I told Dick Foley:

"There's a girl in there—Helen Albury. She's about eighteen, five feet six, skinny, not more than a hundred, if that, eyes close together, yellowish skin, brown bobbed hair, straight, got on a gray suit now. Tail her. If she cuts up on you throw her in the can. Watch her—she's crazy as a pet cuckoo."

VII

I set out for Peak Murry's place to see what Reno wanted. Half a block from my destination I stepped into an office building doorway to look the situation over.

A police patrol wagon stood in front of Murry's pool room. Men were being led, dragged, carried from pool room to wagon. The leaders, draggers and carriers didn't look like regular policemen. They were Pete the Finn's boys, now special coppers, I supposed. Pete, with McGraw's help, evidently was making good on his threat to give Whisper and Reno all the war they wanted.

While I watched an ambulance arrived, was loaded, departed. I couldn't recognize anybody—or any bodies—from my post. When the height of the excitement was over I circled a couple of blocks and returned to my hotel.

Mickey Linehan was there, with information about Charles Proctor Dawn:

"He's the guy that the joke was wrote about: 'Is he a criminal lawyer?' 'Yes, very.' This fellow Albury that you nailed for the killing—some of his family hired Dawn to defend him. Albury wouldn't talk to him when he came to see him. This three-named shyster nearly went over himself last year on a blackmail rap—something about a parson named Hill—but managed to wriggle out of it. Got some property out Ledbury Street, wherever that is. Want me to keep digging?"

"That's enough. We'll stick around till we hear from Dick."

Mickey yawned and said he was satisfied with that, never being one that had to run around a lot to keep his blood circulating, and asked if I knew we were getting nationally famous.

I asked him what he meant by that, if anything.

"I just saw Tommy Robins," he said. "The Consolidated Press sent him here to cover the doings. He tells me some of the other press associations and a big-city paper or two are sending in special correspondents—beginning to play our troubles up."

I was making one of my favorite complaints—that newspapers were good for nothing except to hash things up so nobody could unhash them—when I heard a boy chanting my name. For a dime he told me I was wanted on the phone. Dick Foley:

"She showed right away—to 310 Green Street—full of coppers—mouthpiece named Dawn killed—coppers took her to headquarters."

"Still there?"

"Yes. Chief's office."

"Stick and get anything you learn to me quick."

I went back to Mickey Linehan, gave him my room key and instructions:

"Camp in my room. Take anything that comes for me and pass it on. I'll be at the Shannon around the corner, registered J. W. Clark. Tell Dick and nobody."

Mickey asked, "What the hell?" got no answer, and moved his loose-jointed bulk toward the elevators.

I went around to the Shannon Hotel, registered my alias, paid my day's rent, and was taken to room 321.

An hour went by slowly before the phone bell rang.

Dick Foley said he was coming up to see me.

He arrived within five minutes. His sharp, worried face wasn't friendly. Neither was his voice. He said:

"Warrants out for you. Murder. Two counts—Brand and Dawn. I phoned. Mickey said he'd stick. Told me you were here. Police got him. Grilling him now."

"Yeah—I expected that."

"So did I!" he snapped.

I said, making myself drawl the words:

"You think I killed 'em, don't you, Dick?"

"If you didn't it's a good time to say so."

"Going to put the finger on me?" I asked.

He pulled his lips back over his teeth, his face white. I said:

"Go back to San Francisco, Dick. I've got enough to do without having to keep an eye on you."

He put his hat on very carefully and very carefully closed the door behind him when he went out.

At four o'clock I had some luncheon, cigarettes, and an *Evening Herald* brought up to me.

Dinah Brand's murder and the newer murder of Charles Proctor Dawn divided the newspaper's front page, with Helen Albury connecting them.

She was, I read, Robert Albury's sister, and she was, in spite of his confession, thoroughly convinced that her brother was not guilty of murder but the victim of a plot. She had retained Charles Proctor Dawn to defend him. (I could guess that the late Charles Proctor had hunted her up, and not she him.) The brother refused to have Dawn or any other lawyer or to repudiate his confession, but the girl (properly encouraged by Dawn, no doubt) hadn't given up the fight.

Finding a flat vacant across the street from Dinah Brand's house, Helen Albury had rented it and installed herself therein with a pair of field-glasses and one idea—to prove that Dinah and her associates were guilty of Donald Willsson's murder. It seems that I was one of the "associates." The paper called me "a man supposed to be a private detective from San Francisco, who has been in this city for several days, apparently on intimate terms with Max ('Whisper') Thaler, Daniel Rolff, Oliver ('Reno') Starkey and Dinah Brand." We were the plotters who had framed Robert Albury.

The night that Dinah Brand had been killed, Helen Albury, peeping through her window, had seen things that were very, very significant, according to the *Herald*, when considered in connection with the subsequent finding of Dinah's dead body. As soon as the girl heard of the murder, she took her important news to Charles Proctor Dawn. He, the police learned from his clerks, had immediately sent for me, and had been closeted with me that afternoon, and had told his clerks that I was to return the next morning at ten.

This morning I had not appeared to keep my appointment. At twenty-five minutes past ten the janitor of the Rutledge Block had found Charles Proctor Dawn's body in a corner behind the staircase, murdered. Valuable papers were gone from the dead man's pocket.

At the very minute that the body was being found I, it seems, was in Helen Albury's flat, having forced an entrance and was threatening her. After she succeeded in throwing me out, she hurried to Dawn's office, arriving while the police were there, telling them her story. Police sent to my hotel and had not found me there, but in my room they had found one Michael Linehan, who also represented himself to be a San Francisco private detective. Michael Linehan was being questioned by the police. Whisper, Reno, Rolff and I were being hunted by the police—on murder charges. Important developments were expected.

The whole thing was designed to tell the world that we "associates" were the poison in Poisonville, and the rest of the citizens angels.

Page two held an interesting half-column. Detectives Shepp and Vanaman, the discoverers of Dinah Brand's corpse, had mysteriously vanished. Foul play on the part of us "associates" was feared.

There was nothing in the paper about last night's hijacking, nothing about the raid on Peak Murry's.

After dark I went out.

VIII

I wanted to get in touch with Reno. From a drug store I telephoned Peak Murry's pool room.

"Is Peak there?" I asked.

"This is Peak," said a voice that didn't sound the least bit like his. "Who's talking?"

I said disgustedly, "This is Lillian Gish," hung up the receiver, and removed myself from the neighborhood.

I gave up the idea of finding Reno and decided to go calling on my client, old Elihu Willsson and try to blackjack him into good behavior with the love letters he had written Dinah Brand and I had stolen from Dawn's remains.

I walked, keeping to the darker side of the darkest streets. It was a fairly long walk for a man who sneers at exercise. By the time I reached Willsson's block I was in bad enough humor to be in good shape for the sort of interviews he and I usually had. But I wasn't to see him for another while.

I was two pavements from my destination when somebody "s-s-s-sed" at me.

I probably didn't jump twenty feet.

"'S all right," a voice whispered.

It was dark. Peeping out under my bush—I was on one hand and my knee in somebody's front yard—I could make out the form of a man crouching close to a hedge, on my side of it.

My gun was in my hand. There was no special reason why I shouldn't take his word for it that it was all right.

I got up off my knees and went to him. When I got close enough I recognized him as one of the men who had let me into the Ronney Street rooming house the day before.

I sat on my heels beside him and asked:

"Where'll I find Reno? Hank O'Marra said he wants to see me."

"He does. Know where Kid McLeod's place is at?"

"No."

"It's on Martin Street above King—corner the alley. Ask for the Kid. Go back thataway three blocks and then down. You can't miss it."

I said I'd try not to, and left him crouching behind his hedge, waiting, I imagined, for a shot at Pete the Finn, Whisper, or any of Reno's other enemies that happened to come calling on old Elihu.

Following directions, I came to a soft drink and rummy establishment with red and yellow paint all over it. Inside I asked for Kid McLeod. I was taken into a back room, where a fat man with a dirty collar, a lot of gold teeth and only one ear admitted he was McLeod.

"Reno sent for me," I said. "Where'll I find him?"

"And who does that make you?" he asked.

I told him who I was. He went away without saying anything. I waited ten minutes. He brought a boy back with him, a kid of fifteen or so with a vacant expression on a pimply red face.

"Go with Sonny," Kid McLeod told me.

I followed the boy out a side door, down two blocks of a back street, across a sandy lot, through a ragged back gate and up to the back door of a frame house.

The boy knocked on the door and was asked who he was.

"Sonny with a guy the Kid sent," he replied.

The door was opened. Sonny went away. I went into a kitchen where Reno Starkey and four other men—one of them was O'Marra—sat around a table that had a lot of beer on it. I noticed that two automatics hung on nails over the top of the doorframe through which I had come. They'd be handy if anybody in the house opened the door, found an enemy with a gun there, and was told to stick up his hands.

Reno gave me a glass of beer and led me through the dining-room into a front room. A man lay on his belly there, with one eye to the crack between the drawn blind and the bottom of the window.

"Go back and get some beer," Reno told him. He got up and went. We made ourselves comfortable in adjoining chairs.

"When I fixed up that Tanner alibi for you," Reno said, "I told you I was doing it because I needed all the friends I could get."

"You got one."

"Crack the alibi yet?" he asked.

"Not yet."

"It'll hold," he assured me, "unless they got too damned much on you. Think they have?" he asked with a grin.

I thought so. I said:

"No. McGraw's just feeling playful. That'll take care of itself. How's your end holding up?"

He emptied his glass, wiped his mouth on the back of his hand, and said:

"I'll make out. But that's what I wanted to see you for. Here's how she stacks up, see—Pete's throwed in with McGraw; That lines bulls and the beer mob up against me and Whisper. But hell! Me and Whisper are busier trying to put the chive in each other than bucking the combine. That's a sour racket. While we're tangling, them bums will eat us up!"

I said I had been thinking the same thing. He went on:

"Whisper'll listen to you. Find him, will you? Put it up to him. Here's the proposish: He means to get me for knocking off Jerry Hooper. I mean to get him first. Let's forget that for a day or two. Nobody won't have to trust nobody else. He don't ever show in any of his jobs anyway. He just sends the boys. I'll do the same this time. We'll just put the mobs together to swing the job. We run 'em together, wipe out that damned Finn, and then after that we'll have plenty of time to go gunning for each other in peace.

"Put it to him cold. I don't want him to get any idea that I'm leery of him or any other guy. Tell him I say if we get Pete out the way we'll have more space to do our own scrapping in. Pete's holed-up down in Whiskeytown. I ain't got enough men to go down there and pull him out. Neither has Whisper. The two of us together have. Put it to him."

"Whisper," I said, "is dead."

Reno said, "Is that so?" as if he didn't exactly believe me.

"Dan Rolff killed him yesterday morning down in the old Redman warehouse; stuck him with the ice pick Whisper used on Dinah."

Reno asked:

"You *know* this? You're not just running off at the head, are you?"

"I know it," I exaggerated.

"Damned funny none of his mob act like he was gone," he said, but he was beginning to believe me.

"They don't know it. He was hiding out, with Ted Wright the only one that knew where. led knew it. He cashed in on it. He told me he got a hundred and fifty from you—from Peak Murry."

"I'd have given the big sap twice that much for the straight dope," Reno growled. He rubbed his chin, said, "Well, that settles the Whisper end."

I said: "No."

"What do you mean, no?"

"If his mob don't know where he is, let's tell 'em. They blasted him out of the can when Noonan copped him before. Think they'd try it again if the news got around that McGraw had picked him up?"

"Keep talking," Reno said.

"If his mob try to crack the hoosegow they'll give the department—including Pete's specials—something to do. While they're doing it, you could try your luck in Whiskey town."

"Maybe," he said slowly, "maybe we'll try just that thing."

"It ought to work," I said, standing. "I'll see you—"

"Stick around. This is as good a spot for you as any while the bulls are out for you. And we'll need a good guy like you on this party."

I didn't like that. I knew enough not to say so. I sat down again.

Reno got busy arranging the rumor. The telephone was worked overtime. The kitchen door was worked just as hard, letting men in and out. More men came in than went out. The house filled up with men, smoke and excitement.

IX

At half-past one Reno turned from answering a phone call and said:

"Let's take a ride."

He went upstairs. When he came down he carried a black valise. Most of the men had disappeared through the kitchen door by then. Reno gave me the valise, saying:

"Don't wrastle it around too much."

It was heavy.

The seven of us left in the house went out the front door and got into a curtained black touring car that had just pulled up to the curb. O'Marra was at the wheel. Reno sat beside him. I was squeezed in between men in the back seat, with the valise squeezed between my legs.

Another car came out of the first cross street and ran on ahead of us. A third followed us. Our speed hung around forty—fast enough to get us somewhere, not fast enough to get us a lot of attention. We had nearly finished the trip before we were bothered.

The action started in a block of one-storey houses of the shack type, down in the southern part of the city. A man put his head out of a door, put his fingers in his mouth and whistled noisily.

Somebody in the car behind us shot him down.

At the next corner we ran through a volley of pistol bullets.

Reno turned around to tell me:

"If they pop the bag we'll all of us hit the moon. Get it open. We got to work fast when we get there."

I had the clasps loose by the time we came to rest at the curb in front of a dark three-storey brick building.

The car in front had gone on to the next corner, passing out of sight around it. I looked back. The rear car was planted up the street, trading-shots with the neighborhood.

Men crawled all over me, opening the valise, helping themselves to its contents—bombs made out of short sections of two-inch pipe, packed in sawdust in the bag. Bullets bit chunks out of the car's black curtains.

Reno reached back for one of the bombs, hopped out to the sidewalk, heaved the stuffed pipe at the brick building's door.

A sheet of flame, deafening noise, hunks of things pelting us while we tried to keep from being knocked over by the concussion—and there was no door to keep us out of the brick building.

A man ran forward, swung his arm, let a pipeful of hell go through the doorway. The shutters came off the downstairs windows, fire and glass flying behind them.

O'Marra, out in the middle of the street, bent far over, tossed a bomb to the roof. It didn't go off. O'Marra put one foot high in the air, clawed at his throat, fell solidly backward.

Gunfire sounded behind the brick building—a lot of it.

Another of our party went down under the slugs that were cutting at us from a frame house next to the brick one.

Reno cursed stolidly and said:

"Burn 'em out, Fat."

Fat spit on a bomb, ran around the back of our car, swung his arm. We picked ourselves up off the sidewalk, dodged flying things, and the frame house was all out of whack, with flames climbing up its torn edges.

"Any left?" Reno asked as we looked around, enjoying the feeling of not being shot at.

"Here's the last one," Fat said, holding out a bomb.

Fire was dancing inside the upper windows of the brick house. Reno nodded at it, took the bomb from Fat and ordered:

"Back up. They'll be coming out."

We moved away from the front of the house.

A heavy voice indoors yelled:

"Reno!"

Reno slipped into the shadow of our car before he called back:

"Well?"

"We're done. We're coming out. Don't shoot."

Reno asked:

"Who's we're?"

"This is Pete," the heavy voice said. "There's four of us left."

"You come first," Reno ordered, "with your mitts on the top of your head. The others come out one at a time, same way, after you. And half a minute apart is close enough. Come on."

Pete the Finn appeared in the blasted doorway, his hands holding the bald top of his head. In the glare from the burning next-door house we could see that his face was cut, his clothes torn.

Stepping over wreckage, the bootlegger came down the steps to the sidewalk.

Reno called him a lousy fish-eater and shot him four times in face and body.

Pete went down. A man behind me laughed. Reno hurled the remaining bomb through the doorway. We scrambled into our car. Reno took the wheel. The engine was dead—a bullet had got to it.

Reno worked the horn while the rest of us jumped out.

The machine that had stopped at the corner behind came for us. I looked up and down the street that was bright with the glow from two burning buildings. There were faces at windows, but whoever besides us was in the street had taken to cover. Not far away fire-bells sounded.

The other machine slowed down for us to climb in. It was already full. We packed it in layers, with the overflow hanging to the running boards.

We bumped over dead O'Marra's legs and headed for home. We covered one block with safety if not comfort. After that we had neither.

A limousine turned into the street ahead of us, came halfway to us, put its side to us and stopped. Out of the side—gunfire.

Another car came around the limousine and charged us. Out of it—gunfire.

We did our best, but we were too amalgamated for good fighting. You can't shoot straight holding a man in your lap, another hanging on your shoulder, while a third does his shooting from an inch or two behind your ear.

Our other car—which had been around at the rear of the brick building—came up and gave us a hand. But by then two more cars had joined the opposition. Thaler's mob's attack on the jail was over, one way or the other, apparently, and Pete's army—sent to help there—had returned in time to spoil our getaway. It looked like a sweet mess.

I leaned over a burning gun and yelled in Reno's ear:

"This is the bunk! Let's us extras get out and do our fighting in the street.

He thought it a good idea and gave orders:

"Pile out, some of you birds, and take 'em from the pavements!"

I was the first man down, with my eye on a dark alley entrance.

Fat followed me to it. In my shelter I turned on him and growled:

"Pick your own hole. There's a cellarway that looks good."

He agreeably trotted off toward it and was shot down at his third step.

I explored my alley. It was only twenty feet long and ended against a high board fence with a locked gate. A garbage can helped me over the gate into a brick-paved yard. The side fence of that yard led me into another, and from there I got into another, where a fox terrier raised hell at me. I kicked it out of the way, made the opposite fence, untangled myself from some clothesline, crossed two more yards, got yelled at from a window, had a bottle thrown at me and dropped into a cobblestoned back street.

The shooting was behind me, but not far enough. I did all I could to remedy that. I must have walked as many streets as I did in my dreams the night Dinah was killed.

My watch said it was 3:30 A.M. when I looked at it on Elihu Willsson's front steps.

X

I had to push my client's doorbell a lot before I got any play on it.

Finally the door was opened by the tall, sunburned chauffeur. He was dressed in undershirt and pants, and had a piece of billiard cue in one fist.

"What do you want?" he demanded, and then, when he got another look at me: "Oh, it's you! Well, what do you want?"

"I want to see Mr Willsson."

"At four o'clock in the morning! Go on with you!" and he started to close the door.

I put a foot against it. He looked from my foot to my face, hefted the piece of billiard cue and asked:

"You after getting your kneecap cracked?"

"I'm not playing," I insisted. "I've got to see the old man. Tell him."

"I don't have to tell him. He told me no later than this afternoon that if you came around he didn't want to see you."

"Yeah?" I took the four love letters out of my pocket, found the first and least idiotic of them, held it out to the chauffeur, and said: "Give him that and tell him I'm sitting on the steps with the rest of 'em. Tell him I'll sit here five minutes and then carry 'em to Tommy Robins of the Consolidated Press."

The chauffeur scowled at the letter, said: "To hell with Tommy Robins and his blind aunt!" took the letter and closed the door. Four minutes later he opened the door and said: "Come in, you!"

I followed him upstairs to old Elihu's bedroom. My client sat up in bed with his love letter crushed in one round, pink fist, its envelope in the other. His short white hair bristled all over the top of his round head. His round eyes were as much red as blue. The parallel lines of mouth and chin almost touched. He was in a lovely humor. As soon as he saw me he shouted:

"So after all your brave talking you had to come back to the old pirate to have your neck saved, did you?"

I said I didn't anything of the sort. I said if he was going to talk like a sap he ought to lower his voice so the people in Los Angeles wouldn't learn what a sap he was.

The old boy let his voice out another notch, bellowing:

"Because you've stolen a letter or two that don't belong to you, you needn't—"

I put fingers in my ears. It didn't shut out the noise, but it insulted him into cutting the bellows short. I took the fingers out and said:

"Send the flunkey away so we can talk. You won't need him. I'm not going to hurt you."

He said, "Get out!" to the chauffeur. The chauffeur, looking at me without fondness, left us, closing the door behind him.

Old Elihu gave me the rush act, demanding that I surrender the rest of the letters immediately, wanting to know loudly and profanely where I got them, what I was doing with them, threatening me with this, that and the other, but mostly cursing me.

I didn't give them to him. I said:

"I took 'em from the man you hired to recover 'em. Tough on you that he had to kill the girl."

Enough red went out of the old man's face to leave it normally pink. He worked his lips over his teeth, screwed his eyes up at me, said:

"Is that the way you're playing it?"

His voice came comparatively quiet from his chest. He had settled down to fight.

I pulled a chair over by the bed, sat, put as much amusement as I could in a grin, and said:

"That's one way."

He watched me, worked his lips, said nothing. I said:

"You're the damndest client I ever had! What do you do? You hire me to clean town, change your mind and run out on me, work against me until I begin to look like a winner, then get on the fence, and now when you think I'm licked you don't even want to let me in the house. Lucky for me I happened to pick up those letters!"

He said: "Blackmail."

I laughed and said:

"Listen who's naming it! All right, call it that." I leaned forward to tap the edge of the bed with a forefinger. "I'm not licked, old top. I've won. You came crying to me that four naughty men had taken your little city away from you and were playing with it as they damned pleased. Pete the Finn, Lew Yard, Whisper Thaler and Noonan. Where are they now?

"Yard died Tuesday morning, Noonan Tuesday night, Whisper Wednesday morning, and the Finn a little while ago. I'm giving your city back to you whether you want it or not. If that's blackmail—O.K. Now here's what you're going to do. You're going to get hold of your mayor—I suppose the lousy burg's got one—and you and he are going to get the governor on the phone—Keep quiet till I get through!

"You're going to have the governor turn out the national guard—martial law for Poisonville. I've been told that the governor and the mayor are both pieces of your property, and will do what you tell 'em. That's what you're going to tell 'em! I don't know how various ruckuses around town came out tonight, but I know the big leaders are dead. The ones that had too much on you for you to talk back to 'em. There are plenty of substitutes working like hell to get into the dead men's shoes. The more the better. They'll make it easier for the white-collar soldiers to take hold while everything's disorganized. And none of the substitutes are likely to know enough about you to do much damage.

"There it is. It can be done. It's got to be done. Then you'll have your city back, all nice and clean and ready to go to the dogs again. If you don't do it, I'm going to turn these love letters of yours over to the newspaper buzzards—not to your *Herald* crew, but to the special men from the press associations. I got the letters from Dawn. You'll have a lot of fun proving you didn't hire him to recover them, and that he didn't have to kill the girl to get 'em. But the fun you'll have is nothing to the fun people will have reading them. They're hot! I haven't laughed so much over anything since the hogs ate my kid brother!"

I stopped talking.

He was shaking, but not from fear. His face was purple again. He opened his mouth and roared:

"Publish them and be damned!"

I took them out of my pocket, dropped them on his bed, got up from my chair, put on my hat, and said:

"I'd give my right leg to be able to believe that the girl was killed by somebody you sent to get the letters. By God, I'd like to top off the clean-up by sending you to the gallows!"

He didn't touch the letters. He said:

"You told me the truth about Thaler and Pete?"

"Yeah. But what difference does it make? You'll only be pushed around by somebody else instead of them."

He threw the bed clothes aside and swung his stocky, pajamaed legs and bare pink feet over the edge of the bed.

"Have you got the guts," he barked, "to take the chief of police job I offered you before?"

"No. I lost my guts out fighting your fights while you were hiding in bed thinking up new ways of disowning me. Find some other wet nurse."

He glared at me. Then shrewd wrinkles came around his eyes. He said:

"You're afraid to take the job. You *did* kill the girl."

I left him as I had left him the last time, saying, "Go to hell!" and walking out.

The tall chauffeur, still toting his billiard cue, still regarding me without fondness, met me on the ground floor and took me to the door, looking as if he hoped I'd start something. I didn't. He slammed the door after me.

XI

The street was gray with the beginning of daylight. Up the street a black coupé stood under some trees. I couldn't see if any one was in it. I played safe by walking in the opposite direction. The coupé moved after me.

There's nothing in running down streets with automobiles in pursuit. I stopped, facing this one. It came on. I took my hand away from my side when I saw Mickey Linehan's red face through the windshield. He swung the door open for me to get in beside him.

"I thought you might come up here," he said as I got in, "but I was a second or two too late. I was too far away to get your eye when you went in."

"How'd you make out with the police?" I asked. "Better keep driving while we talk."

"I didn't know anything, couldn't guess anything, didn't have any idea what you were working on, just happened to hit town and meet you. Old friends—that line. They were still trying to get more out of me when the riot broke. They had me in one of the little offices across from the assembly room. When the circus cut loose I back-doored 'em."

"How'd the circus wind up?"

"The coppers shot hell out of 'em. They'd got the tip-off half an hour before and had the whole neighborhood packed with specials. Seems to have been a juicy row while it lasted—no duck soup for the bulls at that. Whisper's mob, I hear."

"Yeah. Reno and Pete the Finn tangled tonight. Hear anything about it?"

"Only that they'd tangled."

"Reno killed Pete and ran into an ambush in the get away. I don't know what happened after that. Seen Dick?"

"I went up to his hotel and was told he'd checked out to catch the evening train."

"I told him to go back to San Francisco," I explained. "He seemed to think I'd killed Dinah Brand. He was getting on my nerves with it."

"Well?"

"You mean, did I kill her? I don't know. I'm trying to find out. Want to follow Dick back to the coast, or you want to keep riding with me?"

Mickey said:

"Don't get so swelled up over one lousy murder. That's likely to happen to anybody. But what the hell? You didn't lift her dough and pretties!"

"Neither did the killer. They were still there after eight, when I left. Dan Rolff was in and out between then and nine. He wouldn't have taken them. The—I've got it! The coppers that found the body—Shepp and Vanaman—got there at nine-thirty. Besides the jewelry and the money, some letters old Willsson had written the girl were—must have been—taken. I found them later in Dawn's pocket. The two coppers disappeared just about then. See it?

"When they found the girl dead they looted the joint before turning in the alarm. Old Willsson being wealthy, the letters looked good to them, so they took them along with the other valuables and turned the letters over to the shyster to peddle back to Elihu for them. Dawn was killed before he had done anything on that end. I took the letters. Shepp and Vanaman—whether they did or didn't know the letters weren't found in the dead man's possession—got cold feet. They were afraid the letters would be traced to them. They had the money and jewelry. They beat it."

"Sounds fair enough," Mickey agreed, "but it doesn't seem to put any fingers on any murderers."

"It clears things up some. We'll try to clear up another point. See if you can find Porter Street and an old warehouse called Redman. The way I got it—Rolff killed Whisper there—walked up to him and stabbed him with the ice pick he'd found in the girl's corpse. If he did it that way, then Whisper didn't kill her, or he'd have been expecting something of the sort, and would have dropped Rolff before the lunger got to him. I'd like to look at Whisper's remains and check up on it."

"Porter's over beyond King," Mickey said. "We'll try the southern end first. It's nearer and more likely to have warehouses. Where do you set this Rolff guy?"

"Out. My notion is that he left the hospital, spent the night God knows where, showed up at the girl's house in the morning, after I'd left, let himself in with his key—he lived there, you know—found her, decided Whisper had killed her, took the sticker out of her and went hunting Whisper. She had bruises on her cheek and arm. He wasn't strong enough to manhandle her, even without his fractured skull."

"So? And where do you get the idea that you might have—"

"Stop it!" I growled as we turned into Porter Street, "And let's find the warehouse."

We rode down the street, jerking our eyes around, hunting for buildings that looked like deserted warehouses. It was light enough now to see well.

Presently I spotted a big, square, rusty-red building set in the middle of a weedy lot. Disuse stuck out all over building and lot. It was a likely candidate.

"Pull up at the next corner," I said. "That looks like the dump. You stick with the heap while I scout it."

I walked two extra blocks so I could come into the lot behind the building. I crossed the lot carefully, not sneaking, but not making any noises I could avoid.

I tried the back door cautiously. It was locked, of course. I moved around to a window, tried to look in, couldn't because of gloom and dirt, tried the window, couldn't budge it.

I went to the next window—with the same luck. I rounded the corner of the building and began working my way along the north side. The first window had me beaten. The second went up slowly with my push—and didn't make much noise doing it.

Across the inside of the window frame, from top to bottom, boards were nailed. They looked solid and strong from where I stood.

I cursed them and remembered hopefully that the window hadn't made much noise when

I raised it. I climbed up on the sill, put a hand against the boards, tried them gently.

They gave.

I put more weight behind my hand. The boards went away from the left side of the frame, showing me a row of shiny nail points. I pushed them back farther, looked past them, saw nothing but darkness, heard nothing.

With my gun in my right fist, I stepped over the sill, down into the building. Another step to the left put me out of the window's gray light. I switched my gun to my left hand while I used my right to push the boards back over the window.

A full minute of breathless listening got me nothing. Holding my gun-arm tight to my side I began exploring the joint. Nothing but the floor came under my feet as I inch-by-inched them forward. My groping left hand felt nothing until it touched a rough wall. I seemed to have crossed a room that was empty.

I moved along the wall, hunting for a door. Half a dozen of my undersized steps brought me to one. I leaned an ear against it. No sound.

I found the knob, turned it softly, eased the door back.

Something swished.

I did four things at the same time: let go the knob, jumped, pulled trigger, and had my left arm hit with something as hard and heavy as a tombstone.

The flare of my gun showed me nothing. (Most of the things people see in the dark by gunfire are imaginary.) Not knowing what else to do, I fired again, and once more.

An old man's voice pleaded:

"Don't do that, partner! You don't have to do that!"

I said:

"Strike a light."

A match spluttered on the floor, kindled, put flickering yellow light on a time-battered face. It was the useless, characterless sort of old face that goes well with a park bench. He was sitting on the floor, his stringy legs sprawled far apart. He didn't seem hurt anywhere. A table-leg lay beside him.

"Get up and make a light," I ordered, "and keep matches burning till you've done it."

"What are you doing here?" I asked when a candle was burning.

I didn't need his answer. One end of the room was filled with wooden cases piled six-high, branded *Perfection Maple Syrup*. While the old man explained that as God was his keeper he didn't know nothing about it, that all he knew was that a man named Keeler had two days ago hired him as night watchman, and if anything was wrong he was as innocent as innocence. I pulled part of the top off one case. The bottles inside had Canadian Club labels that looked like they had been printed with rubber stamps.

I left the cases, drove the old man with his candle in front of me, and searched the building. As I expected, I found nothing to show that this was the warehouse Whisper had occupied.

By the time we returned to the room that held the liquor my left arm was strong enough to lift a bottle. I put it in my pocket and advised the old man:

"Better clear out. You were hired to take the place of some of the guards that Pete the Finn turned into special coppers. Pete's dead. His racket's gone blooey."

When I climbed out the window the old man was standing in front of the cases, looking at them with greedy eyes while he counted on his fingers.

XII

"Well?" Mickey asked when I returned to him and his hired coupé.

I took out the bottle of anything but Canadian Club, pulled the cork, passed it to him, and then put a shot into my own system.

He asked, "Well?" again.

I said:

"Let's try to find the old Redman warehouse."

He said:

"You're going to ruin yourself some time telling people too much," and urged the car down the street.

Three blocks farther on we saw a faded sign—*Redman & Co.* The building under it was long, low, narrow, with corrugated iron roof and few windows.

"We'll leave the boat around the corner," I said. "And you'll go with me. I didn't have a lot of fun by myself last time."

When we climbed out of the coupé, an alley ahead promised a path to the warehouse's rear. We took it. A few people were wandering around the streets, but it was still too early for the factories that filled most of this part of town to have come to life.

At the rear of the warehouse we found something interesting. The back door was closed. Its edge, and the edge of the frame, close to the knob, were scarred. Somebody had worked there with a jimmy.

Mickey tried the door. It was unlocked. Six inches at a time, with pauses between, he pushed it far enough back to let us squeeze in.

When it was open that far we could hear a voice inside. We couldn't hear what it said. All we could hear was the faint rumble of a distant man's voice—with a suggestion of quarrelsomeness in it.

Mickey pointed a thumb at the door's scar and whispered:

"Not coppers."

I went in, keeping my weight on my rubber heels. Mickey followed, his breath hot down the back of my neck.

Ted Wright had told me Whisper's hiding place was in the back, upstairs. I twisted my face around to Mickey and asked:

"Flashlight?"

He put it in my left hand. I put my gun in my right. We crept forward.

The door, still a foot open, let in enough light to show us the way across the room to a doorless doorway. The other side of the doorway was dark. I flicked the light across darkness, found a door, shut off the light and went forward. The next squirt of light showed us steps leading up.

We went up them as if we were afraid the) would break under our feet. The rumbling voice had stopped. There was something else in the air. I didn't know what. Maybe a voice not quite loud enough to be heard—if that means anything.

I had counted nine steps when a voice spoke clearly above us:

It said:

"Sure, I killed her, the—!"

A gun said something—the same thing four times—roaring like a 16-inch rifle under the iron roof.

The first voice said: "All right."

By that time Mickey and I had put the rest of the steps behind us, had shoved a door out of the way, and were trying to pull Reno Starkey's hands away from Whisper's throat.

It was a tough job and a useless one. Whisper was dead.

Reno recognized me and let his hands relax. His eyes were as dull, his sallow face as stolid as ever.

Mickey spread the dead gambler on a cot that stood in one end of the room. The room, apparently once an office, had two windows. In their light I could see a body stowed under the cot—Dan Rolff. A Colt's service automatic lay in the center of the floor.

Reno bent his shoulders, swaying.

"Hurt?" I asked.

"He put all four in me," he said calmly, bending to press both forearms against his lower body.

"Get a doc!" I told Mickey.

"No good," Reno said. "I got no more belly left than Peter Collins."

I pulled a folding-chair over and sat him down on it as Mickey ran out, so he could lean forward and hold himself together.

"Did you know he wasn't croaked?" he asked, nodding at Whisper.

"No. I gave it to you the way I got it from Ted Wright."

"Ted left too soon," he said. "I was leery of something like that—came to make sure. He trapped me pretty—played dead on me till I was under the gun. Game at that, damn him! Dead but wouldn't lay down—bandaging self—waiting all by hisself." He smiled, the first smile I'd ever seen him use. "But he's just meat now, and not much of it."

His voice was thickening. A little red puddle had formed under the edge of the chair. I was afraid to touch him. Only his arms and his bent-forward position were holding him together.

He stared at the puddle and asked:

"How the hell did you figure out that you didn't croak the girl?"

"I didn't know whether I killed her or not," I said, "till just now. The best I could do was hope I hadn't. I had you pegged for it, but couldn't be sure. I was all laudanumed up that night. I had a couple of dreams, with bells ringing, and voices calling and me trying to find people. I got an idea that they mightn't have been straight dreams so much as hop-head nightmares stirred up by things that were happening around me at the time.

"When I woke up and found her dead, the lights were out. I couldn't have turned 'em out if I had killed her and kept my fist on the ice pick. You knew I was there the first part of the night. When I went to you for the alibi, you gave it to me right off the reel, without any bargaining or questions. That got me thinking. Then Dawn tried to blackmail me after he had heard Helen Albury's story. The police, after hearing her story, tied you, Whisper, Rolff and me together. I found Dawn killed after meeting O'Marra half a block away. It looked like the shyster had tried the same game on you as on me. That—and the police tying us all together—started me suspecting that the Albury girl had as much on the rest of you as on me. What she had on me, of course, was that she'd seen me go in or out or both. There were good reasons for counting Whisper and Rolff out. That left you the best prospect. But the why's still got me puzzled."

"I bet you," he said, watching the red puddle grow on the floor. He spoke slower, turned out his words more deliberately, as talking became more difficult. He meant to die as he had lived—inside the same hard-boiled, stolid shell. Talking could be torture, but he wouldn't bat an eye, wouldn't stop talking on that account. "It was her own damned fault. She calls me up—tells me Whisper's coming to see her—says if I get there first I can bushwhack him. I'd like that—I go over there—stick around—he don't show.

"I get tired of waiting—hit her door—ask how come. She takes me in—tells me there's nobody there. I get leery—she swears she's alone—we go back in kitchen. Knowing what she is—I'm getting the idea that me and not Whisper is the one being trapped."

Reno stopped as Mickey came in. Mickey said he had phoned for an ambulance.

Reno continued his story:

"Later I find out Whisper did phone her he was coming—got there before me—you were hopped—she was afraid to let him in—he went away. She don't tell me that—afraid I'd go—she's scared—you're hopped—she wants protection if he comes back. I don't know none of that. I'm leery I've walked into something. Think I'll take hold of her—slap the truth out of her. Try it. She grabs the ice pick—screams. When she screams, I hear man's feet hitting floor. The trap's sprung, I think. I don't mean to be the only one hurt. Twist pick out of her hand—stick it in her. You gallop out of the dark living-room—coked to the edges—charging at the whole world with both eyes shut.

"She tumbles into you. You go down—roll round till your hand hits the butt of the pick. You go to sleep there—peaceful as she is. I see it then—what I've done. But hell, she's croaked! Nothing to do about it. I switch off the lights and go home. When you come—"

A tired-looking ambulance crew—Personville gave them plenty of work those days—brought a litter into the room, cutting off the story.

I took Mickey over into a corner and muttered in his ear:

"The job's yours. I'm going to duck. I ought to be in the clear now, but I know my Poisonville too well to take chances. I'll drive the coupé to some way station where I can catch a train for Ogden. I'll be at the Roosevelt, registered as P. F. King. Stay with the job and let me know when it's best to either take my own name again or buy a ticket to Honduras."

I spent most of my two-day wait in Ogden fixing up my reports so they wouldn't sound as if I had broken as many laws, rules and bones as I had.

On the third night Mickey arrived. He told me that Reno was dead, that I was no longer officially a criminal, and that Poisonville, under martial law, was developing into a sweet-smelling and thornless bed of roses.

We went back to San Francisco. The trouble I'd taken to make my reports read harmlessly didn't keep the Old Man from giving me merry hell.

5

BLACK LIVES

BLACK MASK, OCTOBER 1928

Author of "The Cleansing of Poisonville" and other stories of the "Continental" detective.

I

It was a diamond, all right, sparkling in the grass half a dozen feet from the blue brick walk. It was small—not more than a quarter of a carat—and unmounted. I put it in my pocket and began examining the lawn as thoroughly as I could without going at it on hands and knees.

I had covered a couple of square yards of sod when the Leggetts' front door opened. A woman stepped out on the broad stone top step and looked down at me with good-natured curiosity.

She was a woman of about my age—forty—with darkish blonde hair, a pleasant, plump face, and dimpled pink cheeks. She had on a lavender-flowered white house dress.

I called off my search for the time and went up to her, asking: "Is Mr Leggett in?"

"Yes." Her voice was as pleasant and placid as her face. She smiled from me to the lawn. "You're another detective, aren't you?"

I admitted it. She led me up to a green, orange and chocolate room on the second floor, put me in a brocaded chair, and told me she would call her husband from his laboratory.

While I waited for him I looked around the room, deciding that the dull orange rug under my feet was probably both genuinely Oriental and genuinely ancient, that the carved walnut furniture hadn't been ground out by machinery, and that the Japanese prints on the walls hadn't been selected by a puritan.

Edgar Leggett came in, saying:

"I'm sorry to have kept you waiting, but I was at a point at which I couldn't stop. Have you learned something?"

His voice was unexpectedly harsh, metallic, though friendly enough. He was a dark-skinned, erect man of forty-five or so, medium in height, muscularly slender. He would have been handsome if his brown face hadn't been so deeply marked with lines of pain or of bitterness—sharp, hard lines across his forehead, from his nostrils down across his mouth-corners. Dark hair, worn rather long, curled above and around his broad grooved forehead. Red-brown eyes of abnormal brightness looked out through horn-rimmed spectacles. His nose was long, thin and high-bridged. His lips were thin, sharp and nimble over a small but bony chin. Black and white clothes, carefully made, carefully pressed and laundered, carefully worn, finished the picture.

He was as unusual, and as striking, in appearance as his wife—who had followed him into the room—was wholesomely normal.

"Not yet," I answered his question. "I'm not a police detective—Continental Agency, for the insurance company, and I've just started."

"The insurance company?" he repeated, surprised.

"Yes—North American Surety. Did—"

"Surely," he said quickly, smiling, stopping my words with a flourish of one of his hands. It was a long, thin, dark hand with over-developed finger-tips, ugly as most highly trained hands are. "Surely, they would have been insured. I hadn't thought of that. The diamonds did not belong to me, you know. They were Halstead & Beauchamp's."

"I didn't know that. The insurance company gave us no details. You had them from Halstead & Beauchamp on approval?"

"No. I was using them for experimental purposes. Last year I devised a method by which color could be introduced into glass after its manufacture. Halstead became interested in the possibility of the same method being adapted to precious stones, especially in improving the color of off-shade diamonds, removing yellowish and brownish tints, emphasizing blues. He asked me to attempt it, and supplied me with the stones on which to work. These are the diamonds the burglar got."

"How long had you had them, and how many were there?"

"Five weeks, I think, and there were eight of them, none especially valuable. The largest weighed only a trifle more than half a carat, the smallest only a quarter, and all but two were of poor color."

"Then you hadn't succeeded?"

"Not yet," he admitted readily. "This was a much more delicate matter than staining glass, and on more obdurate material. I had, frankly, made not the slightest progress."

"Where were the diamonds kept?"

"They were locked up last night, though quite often I had left them lying out in the open, considering them as subjects for my experiments rather than as valuables. But last night they were locked in a cabinet drawer in the laboratory. I put them there several days ago, after my last unsuccessful experiment."

"Who knew about your experiments?"

"Anyone, everyone—there was no necessity for secrecy."

"Now, about the burglary?" I said.

"We heard nothing last night. This morning we found our front door open, the cabinet drawer forced, and the diamonds gone. The police found marks on the kitchen door, and say he came in that way and left by the front door."

"The front door was ajar when I came downstairs this morning, at half-past seven," said Mrs Leggett. She was sitting beside her husband, her hands folded in her lap. "I went upstairs again and awakened Edgar, and we searched the house and found the diamonds gone."

"What else was taken?"

"Nothing else seems to have been touched."

"How about your servants?"

"We've only one," she said, "Minnie Hershey, a negress. She doesn't sleep here, and I'm sure she had nothing to do with it. She has been with us for two years, and I'm sure of her honesty."

I said I'd like to talk to Minnie, and Mrs Leggett called her in. The servant was a small, wiry mulatto of twenty-something, with the straight black hair and the brown features of an Indian. She was very polite and very insistent that she had nothing to do with the theft of the diamonds, and had known nothing about it until she arrived at the house at eight-thirty this morning. She gave me her home address, a Geary Street number.

"The police questioned her this morning," Mrs Leggett told me after the girl had gone out. "They don't think she had anything to do with it. They think it was the man I saw—the one Gabrielle saw three nights ago."

I asked for more details.

"When I opened the bedroom windows last night, about midnight, just before going to bed, I saw a man standing up on the corner. I can't say, even now, that there was anything very suspicious-looking about him. He was simply standing there as if waiting for someone, and, though he was looking down this way, there was nothing about him to make me think he might have been watching this house or any other. He was a man past forty, I should say, rather short and broad, somewhat of your build. But he had a bristly brown mustache and was pale. And he wore a brown soft hat and a brown—or dark—overcoat."

"Somebody else had seen him three nights before?" I asked.

"Yes, Gabrielle, my daughter. Coming home late one night, he passed her a pavement or two up the street. She was in an automobile and he was walking. She thought she had seen him come from our steps, but she wasn't sure, and she thought nothing more of it until after the burglary."

"Is she home now? I'd like to talk to her."

Mrs Leggett went out to get her. I asked Leggett:

"Were the diamonds loose?"

"They were unset, of course, and in small manila envelopes—Halstead & Beauchamp's—each in its own, with a number and the weight of the stone written on it in pencil. The envelopes were taken, too."

Mrs Leggett returned with her daughter, a girl of twenty or less, in a sleeveless white silk dress; a girl of medium height who looked slenderer than she really was. I stood up to be introduced to her and then asked her about the man she had seen coming from the house the other night.

"I'm not positive that he came from the house," she replied, "or from the lawn." Her manner was a bit petulant, as if being questioned was distasteful. "I thought he might have, but I only saw him walking up the street."

"This was Saturday night?"

"Yes—that is, Sunday morning."

"What time?" I asked, studying her as we talked. Her hair was as curly as, and no longer than, her father's, but of a much lighter brown. Of her features, only her green-brown eyes were large, forehead, mouth and teeth were unusually small.

There was a barely noticeable hollowness at cheeks and eyes. She had a pointed chin and extremely white, smooth skin. Her expression was sullen: I couldn't tell whether it was habitual or simply in resentment of my prying.

"Three o'clock or after," she said impatiently.

"Were you alone?"

"Hardly. Eric Collinson brought me home."

I asked her where I could find Eric Collinson. She frowned, hesitated, and said that he was employed by Spear, Hoover & Camp, stock brokers, that she had a putrid headache, and that she hoped I would excuse her now as she knew I couldn't have any more questions to ask.

Without waiting for my answer, she turned and went out of the room. Her ears, I noticed, were without lobes and peculiarly pointed at the tops.

Leggett and his wife took me up to the laboratory, a large room that occupied most of the third story. Charts were hung here and there between the windows on the white-washed walls. The wooden floor was uncovered. An X-ray machine—or something similar—four or five smaller machines, a small forge, a large sink, a large zinc table, some smaller porcelain ones, stands, racks of glassware, siphon-shaped metal tanks—that sort of stuff filled the room.

The cabinet from which the diamonds had been taken was a green-painted steel affair of six drawers, all locking together. The second drawer from the top—the one the diamonds had been in—was open. Its edge was dented where a jimmy or chisel had been forced between it and the frame. The other drawers were still locked.

From the laboratory we went downstairs, through a room where the mulatto girl was walking around behind a vacuum cleaner, and into the kitchen. The back door and its frame were marked much as the cabinet had been, the same tool apparently having been used on it.

When I had finished looking at the door I took the diamond I had found out of my pocket and showed it to the Leggetts, asking:

"Is this one of them?"

Leggett picked it up with forefinger and thumb, held it up to the light, turned it from side to side, and said:

"Yes. It has that cloudy spot down at the culet. Where did you get it?"

"Out front, in the grass. I saw it when I came up the walk."

"Ah, where our burglar dropped it in his hurried departure."

I said I doubted it.

Leggett pulled his brows together, looked at me with smaller eyes, asking harshly:

"What do you mean?"

"I think it was planted there," I explained. "Your burglar knew exactly which drawer to go to, and he didn't waste any time on anything else. Somebody who—"

Mrs Leggett put a hand on my forearm and said earnestly:

"No, no. You're thinking of Minnie. You are mistaken, I assure you. She—"

Minnie came to the door, still holding the vacuum cleaner, and began to cry that she was an honest girl, and nobody had any right to accuse her of anything, and they could search her and her room if they wanted to, and just because she was a colored girl was no reason, and so on and so on. Not all of it could be made out, because the vacuum cleaner was still humming in her hand and she sobbed while she talked. Tears ran down her cheeks.

Mrs Leggett went to her, patted her shoulder, saying: "There, there, don't cry. I know you hadn't anything to do with it. Nobody thinks you had. There, there." Presently she got the girl's tears turned off and sent her upstairs.

Leggett sat on a corner of the kitchen table and asked: "You suspect someone in this house?"

"Somebody who's been in it."

"Whom?"

"Nobody yet."

"That"—he smiled, showing white teeth almost as small as his daughter's—"means everybody—all of us."

"Let's go out and look at the lawn," I suggested. "If we find any more diamonds I'll admit I'm mistaken about this one being planted."

Half-way through the house, as we went toward the front door, we met Minnie Hershey, in a tan coat and violet hat, coming to say "Goodbye" to her mistress.

She wouldn't, she said tearfully, work anywhere where anybody thought she had stolen anything. She was just as honest as anybody else, and more than some, and just as much entitled to respect, and if she couldn't get it in one place she could in another, because she knew places where people wouldn't accuse her of being a thief after she had worked for them for two long years without ever taking so much as a slice of bread.

Mrs Leggett pleaded with her, reasoned with her, scolded her, and commanded her, but none of it was any good. The brown girl's mind was made-up. She went away. Mrs Leggett looked at me as severely as her pleasant face would let her, and said reprovingly: "Now see what you've done."

I said I was sorry, and Leggett and I went out to search the lawn. We didn't find any more diamonds.

II

Leaving Leggett's, I put in a couple of hours canvassing the neighborhood, trying to place the man Mrs and Miss Leggett had seen. I didn't have any luck on him, but I picked up news of another suspicious character.

A Mrs Priestly—a pale semi-invalid who lived three doors below the Leggetts—gave me the first news of him. She often sat at a front window in the dark at night, when she couldn't sleep, looking into the street. On two nights she had seen this man.

The first time had been a week ago. He had passed up and down the other side of the street five or six times, at intervals of fifteen or twenty minutes, with his face turned as if he was watching something on Mrs Priestly's—and the Leggetts'—side of the street. She thought it was between eleven and twelve o'clock when she had seen him the first time, and perhaps one o'clock the last. Several nights later—Saturday night—she had seen him again, not walking, this time, but standing on the corner below, looking up the street, at a little after midnight. He went away after she had watched him for half an hour, down the street, and she had not seen him again.

She said he was a fairly tall man of medium build, young, she thought, and he walked with his head thrust out in front. The street was too dark for her to describe his clothes.

Mrs Priestly knew all the Leggetts by sight, but said she knew very little about them, except that the daughter was supposed to be a trifle wild. They seemed to be nice people, but kept to themselves. He had moved into the house in 1921, alone except for the housekeeper, a Mrs Begg, who, Mrs Priestly understood, was now keeping house for a family named Freemander in Berkeley. Mrs Leggett and Gabrielle had not come to live with Leggett until 1923.

Mrs Priestly said she had not been at her window the previous night, and she had not seen the man Mrs Leggett and her daughter had seen.

A man named Warren Darley, who lived on the opposite side of the street from the Leggetts, but down near the corner on which Mrs Priestly had seen her man, had, when locking up the house one night, surprised a man—apparently the same one Mrs Priestly had seen—in his vestibule. Darley was not at home when I called, but Mrs Darley, after telling me this much, got her husband on the phone for me.

Darley said the man had been standing in the vestibule, either hiding from or watching someone in the street. As soon as Darley opened the door the man ran away, paying no attention to Darley's "What are you doing there?" Darley said he was a man of thirty-five or six, fairly well dressed in dark clothes, and with a very long, thin and sharp nose.

That was all I could get out of the neighbors. I went downtown, to the Montgomery Street offices of Spear, Hoover & Camp, and asked for Eric Collinson.

He was young, blond, tall, broad, sunburned and immaculate, with the good-looking dumb face of one who would know everything about polo, or shooting, or flying, or stocks and bonds, or whatever interested him, and nothing about anything else. We sat on a broad leather seat in the customers' room, now, after market hours, empty except for a weedy boy juggling numbers on the board. I told Collinson about the burglary and asked him about the man he and Miss Leggett had seen Saturday night.

"Ordinary looking chap—short, chunky. You think he took them?"

"Was he coming from the Leggetts' house?"

"From the lawn, yes. Jumpy looking chap. I thought he'd been snooping around. That's why I suggested going after him. Gaby wouldn't have it. Probably a friend of papa's. He goes in for odd eggs."

"Wasn't that late for a visitor to be leaving? What time was it?"

"Midnight, I dare say," but he didn't look at me while he said it.

"Midnight?" I asked sharply.

"That's the word. Time when the graves give up their dead and ghosts walk."

"Miss Leggett said it was after three o'clock."

"You see how it is?" he asked, blandly triumphant, as if he had just demonstrated something we had been arguing about. "Half blind and won't wear glasses for fear of losing beauty. Always doing things like that. Plays abominable bridge—takes deuces for aces. Probably a quarter after twelve. Looks at the clock and gets the hands mixed."

I said, "That's too bad. Thanks," and went around the corner to see Archie Little, junior partner of the Brenderman-Little Company, investment bankers.

I asked Archie what he knew about Collinson. He said there was nothing to know about him, except that his old man was the lumber Collinson and Eric was Princeton and stocks and bonds, a nice boy.

"Maybe he is," I agreed, "but he just lied to me."

"Ts, ts, ts!" Archie shook his sleek head, grinning. "Isn't that like a sleuth? You must have had the wrong fellow. Somebody's impersonating him. The Chevalier Bayard doesn't lie, and, besides, lying requires imagination. You've—Wait! Was there a woman involved in your question?"

I nodded.

"You're correct, then," Archie assured me. "I apologize. The Chevalier Bayard always lies when there's a woman involved, even if it's unnecessary and puts her to a lot of trouble. It's one of the conventions of Bayardism—something to do with guarding her honor and the like. Is she young? Do I know her? I make a point of knowing all the women people lie about."

I thanked him instead of answering his questions and went up to the Geary Street jewelry store of Halstead & Beauchamp.

Halstead was a suave, pale, bald, fat man with vague eyes and a too-tight collar. I told him what I was doing and asked him if he knew Leggett very well.

"I know him as an occasional customer, and by reputation as a scientist. Why do you ask?"

"The burglary looks phoney."

"Preposterous! That is, it's preposterous if you think a man of his caliber would have anything to do with it. A servant, of course, that is possible, but not Leggett. He is a scientist, and he is, unless our credit department has been misinformed, which I think unlikely, if not wealthy, at least of sufficient means to prevent suspicion falling on him. I happen to know that he has at present with the Seamen's National Bank a balance in excess of ten thousand dollars."

"What were the diamonds worth?"

"Not more than fifteen hundred dollars at retail."

"That would be seven hundred at cost?"

"Well," smiling, "eight-fifty would be closer."

"How did you come to give him the diamonds?"

"I knew him as a customer, and then, when Fitzstephan told me of his work with glass, it occurred to me that the same sort of treatment applied to diamonds might be of great value. So I persuaded Leggett to try it."

"What Fitzstephan?" I asked.

"Owen, the novelist."

"I've met him," I said, "but I didn't know he was on the Coast. Have you his address?"

Halstead gave it to me—a Nob Hill apartment building.

From the jeweler's I went out to the vicinity of the Geary Street address Minnie Hershey had given me. It was a negro neighborhood, which made the getting of reasonably accurate information even more difficult than it always is.

What I got added up to this: The girl had lived in San Francisco for four or five years, coming from Winchester, Virginia. For the last half-year she had been living in a flat at her present address, with a negro called Rhino Tingley. One informant told me Tingley's first name was Ed, another Bill, but both descriptions agreed; he was young, big, black, and could readily be recognized by his scarred chin and his tie pin, pearls grouped to make a cluster of grapes; he was rather shiftless, depending for his living on Minnie and pool, but not bad except when he got mad—then he was a holy terror.

I was told that I could get a look at him the early part of almost any evening in either Bunny Mack's barber shop or Bigfoot Gerber's cigar store. I learned where these establishments were located, and then went downtown again, to the police detective bureau in the Hall of Justice.

Nobody was in the Pawnshop Detail office. I crossed the corridor and asked Lieutenant Duff whether any one had been assigned to the Leggett job.

"See O'Gar," he said.

I went into the assembly room, looking for O'Gar and wondering what he—a detective-sergeant attached to the Homicide Detail—had to do with it. Neither O'Gar nor his partner, Pat Reddy, was in. I smoked a cigarette, worried about homicide men being mixed up in my job, and decided to phone Leggett and see if anything had happened out there.

"Have any of the police detectives been in to see you since I left?" I asked when Leggett's harsh voice was in my ear.

"No, but the police called up a little while ago and asked my wife and daughter to come to a house in Golden Gate Avenue to see if they could identify a man who had been killed there. They left a few minutes ago. I didn't accompany them, since I hadn't seen the supposed burglar."

"What was the address?"

He didn't remember the exact number, but he knew the block, one near Van Ness Avenue. I thanked him and went out there.

A uniformed policeman standing in the doorway of a small apartment house guided me to my goal when I reached the designated block. I asked him if O'Gar was there, and where.

"Three-ten," he said.

I went up in a rickety elevator. When I got out of it on the third floor I came face to face with Mrs Leggett and her daughter, leaving.

"Now I hope you're satisfied that Minnie had nothing to do with it," Mrs Leggett said chidingly.

"Was he the man you saw?"

"Yes. And the envelopes the diamonds were in are there."

I turned to Gabrielle Leggett and said:

"Eric Collinson insists that it was only midnight, or a few minutes after, that you got home, and saw the man, Saturday night."

"Eric," she said irritably, walking past me to enter the elevator, "is an ass."

Her mother, following her into the elevator, reprimanded her amiably: "Now, dear!"

I closed the door for them and walked down the hall to a doorway where Pat Reddy stood talking to a couple of reporters, said "Hello" to them, squeezed past them into a short passageway, and went through that to a shabbily furnished room where a dead man lay on a wall bed.

Phels of the Identification Bureau looked up from his magnifying glass to nod at me, and then went on examining the edge of a mission table that stood against one wall. O'Gar pulled his head and shoulders in the open window and growled:

"So we got to put up with you again?"

He was a burly hard-faced, stolid man of fifty who wore wide-brimmed soft black hats of the movie village-constable sort. There were a lot of shrewd ideas in his grizzled bullet head and he was comfortable to work with.

I looked at the corpse—a man of forty or so, with a heavy face, short hair touched with gray, a scrubby dark mustache, thick shoulders and stocky arms and legs. There was a bullet-hole just above his navel, and another high in the left side of his chest.

"It's a man," O'Gar informed me as I put the blanket over him again. "He's dead."

"What else did somebody tell you?" I asked.

"Looks like him and another bimbo nicked Leggett for the ice and then the other bimbo decided to take a one-way split. The envelopes are here"—O'Gar took them out of his pocket and ruffled them with his thumb—"but the stuff ain't. Neither is the gun the two slugs came out of. It went down the fire-escape with Mr X a little while back. People saw him go down, but they lost him when he cut through the alley. Tall guy with a long nose. This one"—O'Gar pointed at the bed with the envelopes—"has been here a week. Name of Louis Upton. New York labels. We don't know him. Nobody in the dump's ever seen him with anybody else. Nobody will say they know Mr X."

Pat Reddy, a big, jovial youngster, with almost enough brains to make up for his lack of experience, came in. I told him and O'Gar what I had turned up on the diamond job so far.

"Long-nose and this bird taking turns watching Leggett's," Reddy suggested when I was through.

"Maybe," I admitted, "but there was an inside angle to the job."

"How about the yellow girl?"

"I'm going out for a look at her man tonight. You people are trying New York on this Upton?"

"Practically," O'Gar said.

III

At the Nob Hill address that Halstead had given me I told the boy at the switchboard my name, wondering if Fitzstephan would remember it. I had run into him five years ago, in New York City, where I had been digging dirt on a chain of fake mediums who had taken a coal-and-ice dealer's widow for a hundred thousand dollars. Fitzstephan was combing the same field for literary material, and, becoming acquainted, we had pooled forces. He knew the ghost racket inside and out. With his help I had cleaned up my job in a week or two. We kept up a fairly intimate friendship for a couple of months after that, until I left New York for the West.

At that time he had been in his early thirties—a long, lean, sorrel-haired man with sleepy gray eyes, a wide, humorous mouth, and carelessly worn clothes. He pretended to be lazier than he was, would rather talk than do anything else, and had a lot of what seemed to be accurate information and original ideas on any subject that happened to come up, so long as it was out of the ordinary.

"Mr Fitzstephan says to come right up, sir," the boy said.

His apartment was on the sixth floor. He was standing at its door when I got out of the elevator.

"By God!" he said, holding out a lean hand, "It is you."

"None other."

We went into a room where half a dozen bookcases and four tables left little room for anything else. Magazines and books in various languages, papers, clippings, proof sheets, were scattered everywhere—all exactly as it had been in his New York rooms.

We sat down, found places for our feet between table-legs, and accounted, more or less roughly, for our lives since we had last seen one another. He had been in San Francisco a little less than a year. He liked the city, he said, but he wouldn't oppose any movement to give the West back to the Indians.

"How's the literary grift go?" I asked.

He looked at me sharply, demanded:

"You haven't been reading me?"

"No. Where'd you get that idea?"

"There was something in your tone, something proprietary, as in the voice of one who had bought an author for two dollars and a half. I haven't met it often enough to be used to it. Good God! Remember once I offered to give you a set of my books?"

"You were drunk," I said.

"On sherry—Elsa Donne's sherry. Remember Elsa? She showed us a picture she had just finished and you said it was pretty. Whoops, wasn't she furious! You said it so vapidly, and sincerely. Remember? She put us out, but I had already got tight on her sherry, and so had you. But you weren't plastered enough to accept the books."

"I was afraid I'd read them and understand them," I explained, "and then you'd have felt insulted."

A Chinese boy brought us cold white wine. Fitzstephan said:

"It's queer we should have been in the same city for a year without running into one another. How did you finally come across me?"

"Watt Halstead gave me your address, after he'd told me you knew Edgar Leggett."

A gleam pushed through the sleepiness in the novelist's gray eyes.

"Leggett's been up to something?" he drawled, sitting a little higher in his chair.

"Why do you say that?"

"I didn't say it." He sank back lazily in his chair, but the gleam was still in his eyes. "I asked it. Come—out with it. I'm a novelist. My business is with souls and what goes on in them. What's Leggett been up to?"

"We don't do it that way. We trade information. How long have you known him?"

"Nearly a year. I met him soon after I came here, I think at Marquard's—the sculptor, not the restaurant. He interested me. There's something obscure in him, something dark and inviting. Physically ascetic—neither smoking nor drinking—

eating meagerly, a vegetarian, sleeping only four hours a night, I'm told. Mentally sensual—does that mean anything?—to the point of decadence. You think I like the fantastic—you should know him. His friends—he hasn't any. His choice in companions are those who have the most outlandish ideas to offer—the wildest, most maniac, brutal, degenerate, abnormal. Marquard, with his insane figures that are not figures but boundaries of the portions of space which are the real figures; Denbar Curt, with his algebraism; crazy Laura Joines; Farnham—"

"And you," I put in, "with your explanations and descriptions that explain and describe nothing. I hope you don't suppose that what you've said so far means anything to me."

"I remember you now; you were always like that." He grinned at me, running long fingers through his sorrel hair. "Tell me what's up while I try to find one-syllable words to use on you."

I told him about the diamonds, and about the dead man. He looked very disappointed.

"That's trivial, sordid," he complained. "I've been thinking of Leggett in terms of Dumas, and you bring me a piece of gimcrackery out of O. Henry. You've let me down—you and your shabby diamonds. But"—his eyes brightened again—"they may lead to something. Leggett may or may not be a criminal, but there's more to him than a two-penny insurance swindle."

"You mean," I asked sarcastically, "that he's one of these master minds? So you've been reading newspapers? What do you think he is? King of the bootleggers? Chief of an international crime syndicate? A white slave magnate? Head of a dope ring? Or maybe queen of the counterfeiters in disguise?"

"Don't be an idiot. He's got brains, that man, and there's something black in him. There's something he doesn't want to think about. I've told you that he revels in all that's dizziest in thought, yet he's intellectually as cold as a fish, but with a bitter-dry coldness. He's neurotic, yet he doesn't even smoke. He keeps his body sensitive and fit and ready—for what?—while he drugs his mind against memory with the wildest of intellectual lunacies, with ideas that belong to the mad. Yet the man is cold and sane.

"There's only one explanation: there's darkness in his past that he wants to forget. But why shouldn't he anesthetize his mind through his body, by sensuality if not by drugs? There's still only one explanation; the darkness in his past is not dead, and he must keep himself fit to cope with it should it come into the present."

"All right. What is it?"

"If I don't know—and I don't—it isn't because I haven't tried to learn; but try getting information out of Leggett some time. I don't believe that's his name."

"No?"

"No," Fitzstephan said, "he's French. I'd risk anything on it. He told me once that he came from Atlanta, but he's French in outlook, in quality of mind, in everything but admission."

"What of the rest of the family? The daughter's cuckoo, isn't she?"

"I wonder." Fitzstephan looked queerly at me. "Are you saying that carelessly, or do you really think she's off?"

"I don't know, but she's odd. She's got animal ears and almost no forehead, and her eyes change from green to brown. An uncomfortable sort of person."

"If you're cataloging her physical peculiarities you can add that her upper thumb joints—between metacarpal bones and first phalanx—don't work."

"I'm not. In your snooping around have you been able to pry into any of her affairs?"

"Are you—who make your living snooping and prying—sneering at my curiosity about people and my attempts to satisfy it?"

"We're different," I said. "I do mine with the object of putting people in jail, and I get paid for it, though not as much as I should."

"That's not different," he said. "I do mine with the object of putting people in books, and I get paid for it, and not as much as I should. Gabrielle hates her father. He worships her."

"How come the hate?"

Fitzstephan shrugged his lean shoulders; said:

"I don't know. Perhaps because he worships her."

"There's no sense to that," I growled. "You're just being literary. How about Mrs Leggett?"

"You've never eaten one of her meals, I suppose? You'd have no doubts about her if you had. None but a serene sane soul ever achieved such cooking. I've often wondered what she thinks of the weird pair that is her husband and daughter, or if she simply accepts them as they are without being aware of their weirdness. I rather suppose she does."

"All this is well enough in its way," I said, "but you still haven't told me anything definite about them. Come on, loosen up."

"I've told you," he insisted, "everything I know. And that's the thing, my son. You know what a—in your words—a snooper and prier—I am. Well, if, after a year of it, I know no more about a man who interests me than I do about Leggett, isn't that the most conclusive sort of evidence that he's hiding something, and that he is a hider of no mean sort?"

"Is it? I don't know. But I know I've wasted enough time here learning nothing that anybody can be jailed for."

It was a little after five o'clock when I left Fitzstephan's apartment. I stopped at a restaurant for some food, and then went out for a look at Minnie Hershey's man, Rhino Tingley.

I found him in Big-foot Gerber's cigar store, rolling a fat cigar around in his mouth, telling something to the other negroes—four of them in the place.

"... says to him, 'Nigger, you talking yourself out of skin,' and I reaches out my hand for him, and, 'fore Gawd, there wasn't none of him there excepting his footprints in the cement pavement, eight feet apart and leading home."

Buying a package of cigarettes, I weighed him in while he talked. He was a chocolate man of not more than thirty years, close to six feet tall, and weighing two hundred pounds plus, with big yellow-balled pop eyes, a broad nose, a big mouth, and a ragged black scar running from his lower lip down behind his blue and white striped collar. His clothes were new enough to look new, and he wore them sportily. His voice was a heavy bass, and when he laughed with his audience after he had finished his story the glass of the show cases shook.

I went out of the store while they were laughing, heard his laughter stop short behind me, resisted the temptation to look back, and moved down in the direction of the building where he and Minnie lived. He came abreast of me when I was half a block from the flats.

I said nothing while we took seven steps. Then he said:

"You the man that been inquiring around about me?"

The sour odor of Italian red wine came thick enough to be seen.

I considered and replied:

"Yeah."

"What you got to do with me?" he asked, not disagreeably, but as if he wanted to know.

On the other side of the street, Gabrielle Leggett, in brown coat, brown and yellow hat, came out of Minnie's building and walked up the street, not turning her head toward us. She walked swiftly and her lower lip was between her teeth.

I looked at the negro. He was looking at me. There was nothing in his face to show that he had seen Gabrielle Leggett or that the sight of her meant anything to him. I said:

"You've got nothing to hide, have you? What do you care who asks about you?"

"All the same, I'm the party to come to if he wants to know about me. You the man that got Minnie fired?"

"She wasn't fired. She quit."

"Minnie don't have to take nobody's lip. She—"

"Let's go over and talk to her," I suggested, leading the way across the street. At the door he went ahead, up a flight of steps, down a dark hall to a door that he opened with one of the twenty or more keys on his ring.

Minnie Hershey, in a pink kimono trimmed with yellow ostrich feathers that looked like little dead ferns, came out of the bedroom to meet us in the living-room. Her eyes got big when she saw me.

Rhino Tingley said: "You know this gentleman, Minnie?"

Minnie said: "Yes."

I said: "You shouldn't have left Leggetts' that way. Nobody thinks you had anything to do with the diamonds. What did Miss Leggett want here?"

"There been no Miss Leggetts here," she told me. "I don't know what you talking about."

"She came out just as we were coming in."

"Oh, *Miss* Leggett! I thought you said *Mrs* Leggett. I beg your pardon. Yes, sir. Miss Gabrielle was sure enough here. She wanted to know if I wouldn't come back. She thinks a powerful lot of me, Miss Gabrielle does."

That, I thought, is a lie.

"That," I said, "is what you ought to do. It was foolish—leaving like that." Rhino Tingley took the cigar out of his mouth and pointed it at the girl. "You away from them," he boomed, "and you stay away from them. You don't have to take nothing from nobody." He put a hand in his pants pocket, lugged out a thick bundle of paper money, thumped it down on the table, and rumbled: "What for you have to work for folks?"

He was talking to the girl, but looking at me, grinning, gold teeth shining. The bundle of money was on the table close to me. I picked it up, counted it—eleven hundred and sixty-five dollars—and dropped it on the table again. Rhino, still grinning, returned it to his pocket.

The girl looked at the man, said scornfully, "Lead him around, vino," and turned to me again, her small face tense, anxious to be believed, saying:

"Rhino got that money in a crap-game, mister. Hope to die if he didn't."

I assured her that I believed every word she said, again advised her to go back to the Leggetts, and departed.

Downtown, in an Owl drug store, I looked in the Berkeley section of the telephone directory, found only one Freemander listed, and called it. Mrs Begg was there, and she told me she could see me if I came over right away. I caught the next ferry. The Freemander house was set off a road that wound uphill toward the University of California.

Mrs Begg was a scrawny, big-boned woman with not much gray hair packed close around a bony skull, hard gray eyes, and hard, capable hands. She was sour and severe, but plain-spoken enough to let us talk turkey without a lot of hemming and hawing.

I told her about the theft of the diamonds and my belief that the burglar had been helped, at least with information, by someone who knew the Leggett household, and added:

"Mrs Priestly told me you had been Leggett's housekeeper a few years ago, and thought you could help me."

Mrs Begg said she doubted if she could tell me anything that would help me, but she was willing to do all she could, being an honest woman and having nothing to conceal from anybody. Once she started, she told me a great deal, damned near talking me earless. Throwing out the stuff that didn't interest me, I came away with the following information:

In the spring of 1921 Mrs Begg had been hired by Leggett, through an agency, as housekeeper. At first she had a girl to help her, but there wasn't work enough for both, so, at her suggestion, the girl was let go. Leggett was a man of simple tastes, and spent most of his time on the top floor, where he had his laboratory and bedroom. He seldom used the rest of the house except when he had friends in for an evening. Mrs Begg didn't like his friends, though she could tell me nothing much about them except that "the way they talked was a shame and a disgrace."

Edgar Leggett was as nice a man as a person could want to know, she said, only so secretive that he made a person nervous. She was never allowed to go up on the top floor, and the doors were kept locked. Once a month he would have a Jap in to clean up under his supervision. Well, she supposed he had a lot of scientific secrets, and maybe dangerous chemicals, that he didn't want people poking into, but just the same it made a person uneasy.

She didn't know anything about her employer, and knew her place better than to ask him. In August, 1923—it was a rainy morning, she remembered—a woman and a girl of fifteen with a lot of suitcases arrived at the house. She let them in and the woman asked for Mr Leggett. Mrs Begg went up to the laboratory and told him, and he came down. Never in all her born days had she seen such a surprised man as he was when he saw them. He turned absolutely white and she thought he was going to fall down, he shook so bad.

She didn't know what Leggett said to the woman and girl, because they all jabbered in some foreign language, though the lot of them could talk as good English as anybody else, and better than most. She went about her work. Pretty soon Leggett came out to the kitchen and told her the visitors were a Mrs Dain, his sister-in-law, and her daughter Gabrielle, neither of whom he had seen for ten years, and that they were going to stay with him. Mrs Dain later told the housekeeper that they were English but had been living in New York for several years. Mrs Begg said she liked Mrs Dain, who was a sensible woman and a real housewife, but Gabrielle was a tartar.

With Mrs Dain's arrival, and with her ability as a housekeeper, there was no longer any place in the household for Mrs Begg. They had been very liberal with her, she said, helping her find a new place and giving her a generous bonus when she left. She had seen none of them since, but in the *Examiner* a week later—she was the sort of woman who keeps a careful watch on marriages, deaths and births—she saw that a marriage license had been issued to Edgar Leggett and Alice Dain.

IV

When I arrived at the agency at nine the next morning, Eric Collinson was sitting in the outer office. His sunburned face was dingy without pinkness, and he had neglected to put stick-em on his hair.

"Do you know anything about Miss Leggett?" he asked, jumping up and striding toward me as soon as I appeared in the doorway. "She wasn't home last night, and she's not home yet. Her father wouldn't say he didn't know where she was, but I'm sure he didn't. He told me not to worry, but how can I help worrying? Do you know anything about it?"

I said I didn't, told him I had seen her leaving Minnie Hershey's, gave him the mulatto's address, and suggested that he see if he could learn anything from her. He jammed his hat on his head and hurried out of the office.

Getting O'Gar on the phone, I asked if he had heard from New York.

"Uh-huh. Upton—that's his right name—was once a private detective, till '23, when him and a fellow named Harry Ruppert were sent over to Sing Sing for fixing a jury. They were sprung last month. How'd you make out with the dinges?"

"Her man—a big smoke called Rhino Tingley—is toting an eleven-hundred-buck roll. He says he won it in a crap-game. It's more than he could have got for the diamonds, but maybe the diamonds aren't the big item in this job. Suppose you have Rhino looked up."

O'Gar said he would and hung up.

I wired our New York branch for additional dope on Upton and Ruppert, and then trotted up to the County Clerk's office, in the City Hall, and dug into the August and September, 1923, marriage licenses. I found the applications I wanted, dated August 26. Edgar Leggett had stated that he was born in Atlanta, Georgia, on March 6, 1883, and that this was his second marriage. Alice Dain had given London as her birthplace, October 22, 1888, as the date, and had stated that she had never been married before.

That clicked with my opinion that Gabrielle, if not the daughter of both, was more likely the man's than the woman's.

When I got back to the agency, Eric Collinson, his yellow hair still further disarranged, confronted me again.

"I saw Minnie," he said excitedly, "and she wouldn't tell me anything. She said Gaby was there last night to ask her to come back to work, but that's all she knows about her. But she—she was wearing an emerald ring which I'm positive is Gaby's."

"Did you ask her about it?"

"Who? Minnie? No. How could I? It would have been—you know."

"That's right," I agreed, "we must always be polite. Why did you lie to me about the time you and Miss Leggett got home the other night?"

His face got stupider than ever with embarrassment.

"That was silly of me," he stammered, "but I didn't—I was afraid you'd—I thought that—"

He wasn't getting anywhere. I suggested:

"You thought that was too late for her to be out and didn't want me to get wrong notions about her?"

"Yes, that's it."

I thought of Little's *Chevalier Bayard,* hid my grin, and shooed Collinson out.

In the operatives' room Mickey Linehan—big, loose-hung, red-faced—and Al Mason—slim, dark, sleek—were swapping lies about the times they had been shot at, each pretending to have been more frightened than the other. I told them who was who in my diamond job, and sent Al out to keep an eye on the Leggetts, Mickey to see how Minnie and Rhino were behaving.

Mrs Leggett, a worried shadow on her pleasant face, opened the door when I rang her bell an hour later. We went up to the green, orange and chocolate room, where we were joined by her husband.

I passed on to them the information about Upton that O'Gar had got from New York, and told them I had wired for additional information on Harry Ruppert.

"Some of your neighbors saw a man who was not Upton loitering around, and the same man was seen running down the fire-escape from Upton's room. There's no reason why he couldn't have been Ruppert."

Nothing changed in the scientist's too bright red-brown eyes. They held interest and nothing else. No muscle flickered in his face.

I asked "Is Miss Leggett in?"

"No," he replied.

"When will she be?"

"Probably not for several days."

"Where can I find her?" I asked, turning to Mrs Leggett. "I've some questions to ask her."

Mrs Leggett avoided my gaze, looking at her husband. His metallic voice answered my question:

"We don't know, exactly. Friends of hers, a Mr and Mrs Harper, drove up from Los Angeles and asked her to go with them on their trip up in the mountains. I don't know which route they are taking, and doubt if they had any definite plans."

I didn't believe that. I asked questions about the Harpers. Edgar Leggett admitted knowing very little about them. Mrs Harper's given name was Carmel, he said, and everybody called the man Bud, but he, Leggett, didn't know either his first name or his initials. Nor did he know their Los Angeles address. He thought they had a house somewhere near Pasadena, but he wasn't sure.

While he told me all this nonsense, his wife sat staring at the floor, lifting her blue eyes now and then to look swiftly, pleadingly, at her husband.

"Don't you know more about them than that?" I asked her.

"N-no," she said weakly, darting a timid look at her husband's face, while he, paying no attention to her, stared levelly at me.

"When did they leave?" I asked.

"Early this morning," Leggett told me. "They were staying at one of the hotels—I don't know which—and Gabrielle spent the night with them, so they could make an early start."

I had enough of the Harpers.

"Did any of you have any dealings with Upton before this affair?" I asked.

"No."

There were other questions to which I would have liked answers, but the sort of replies he gave me answered nothing. I was tempted to tell him what I thought of him, but there was no profit in that. I stood up.

He got on his feet, smiled apologetically, and said:

"I'm sorry to have caused the insurance company all this trouble and expense. After all, the diamonds were probably lost because of my carelessness in not safeguarding them. I should like your opinion; do you really think I should accept the responsibility for the loss and make it good?"

"I think you should," I replied, "but it won't stop the investigation."

Mrs Leggett put her handkerchief to her mouth quickly. Leggett said calmly:

"Thanks. I'll have to think it over."

On my way back to the agency I dropped in on Owen Fitzstephan for a half-hour visit. He was writing, he told me, an article for the *Psychopathological Review,* or something of the sort, condemning the hypothesis of an unconscious or subconscious mind as a snare and delusion, a pitfail for the unwary and a set of false whiskers for the charlatan, a gap in psychology's roof that made it impossible, or nearly, for the sound scientist to smoke out such faddists as, for example, the psychoanalyst and the behaviorist. He went on like that for ten minutes or more before he came back to the United States with:

"How are you getting along with the problem of the elusive diamonds?"

"This way and that way," I said, and told him all I had done and learned so far.

"You've certainly," he complimented me when I had finished, "got it all as tangled and confused as possible."

"It'll be worse before it's better," I predicted. "I'd like to have ten minutes alone with Mrs Leggett. Away from her husband, I imagine things could be got out of her. Could you do anything with her?"

"I'll try. Suppose I go out there tomorrow afternoon, to borrow a book—Waite's *Rosy Cross* will do it. They know I'm interested in that sort of stuff. He will be working in the laboratory and I'll insist on not disturbing him, and perhaps I can get something from her, though it'll have to be in a casual, off-hand way."

I thanked him, returned to the agency, and spent most of the afternoon putting my findings on paper and trying to fit them together in some sort of order. Eric Collinson phoned twice to ask if I had found his Gabrielle. Neither Mickey Linehan nor Al Mason sent in any report. At six o'clock I called it a day.

V

The following day brought happenings.

Early in the morning there was a telegram from our New York branch. Decoded, it read:

> *Louis Upton formerly proprietor detective agency here* stop *arrested September first one nine two three for bribing two jurors in Sexton murder trial* stop *Upton attempted to save self by implicating Harry Ruppert operative in his employ* stop *Upton and Ruppert convicted and sent to Sing Sing* stop *released February six this year* stop *Ruppert in New York following week hunting for Upton* stop *threatened to kill him for framing him on bribery charge* stop *Ruppert thirty two years five feet eleven inches one hundred fifty pounds brown hair and eyes sallow complexion thin face long sharp nose walks with slight stoop and chin out* stop *mailing photographs.*

That placed Harry Ruppert; he was undoubtedly the man Mrs Priestly and Darley had seen, and the man who had been seen leaving Upton's room.

My phone rang. Detective-sergeant O'Gar:

"That nigger Rhino Tingley of yours was picked up last night in a hock shop, trying to unload some jewelry, pretty good junk. We haven't been able to crack him yet—just got him identified this morning. I sent the stuff out to Leggett's, thinking maybe they'd know something about it, but they didn't."

"Try Halstead & Beauchamp," I suggested. "Tell them you think the stuff is Gabrielle Leggett's, but don't tell them the Leggetts have said 'no.' "

Half an hour later O'Gar phoned me from the jeweler's, telling me that Halstead had positively identified two pieces—a string of pearls and a topaz brooch—as articles Leggett had purchased there, gifts for his daughter.

"Fine!" I said. "Now will you do this? Go out to Rhino's house and put the screws on his woman, Minnie Hershey. Frisk the joint, rough her up, the more you scare her the better, but don't stay too long, and then beat it, leaving her alone. I've got her covered. I'll give you all the explanations later."

"I'll turn her white," O'Gar promised.

Dick Foley was in the operatives' room, writing a report on a warehouse robbery that had kept him up all night. I chased him out to help Mickey Linehan with Minnie.

"Both of you tail her if she leaves her joint after the police are through," I instructed him, "and as soon as you put her anywhere, one of you get to a phone and let me know."

I went back to my cubbyhole and burned cigarettes. I was destroying the third one when Eric Collinson called up to ask if I had learned anything yet.

"Nothing definite, but I've got prospects. If you aren't busy you might come over here and wait with me."

He said, very eagerly, that he would do that.

Five minutes later Mickey Linehan phoned:

"The high yellow's in the Primrose Hotel on Mason Street."

The phone rang again by the time I had put it down.

"This is Watt Halstead," a voice said. "Can you come down?"

"Not right now. Perhaps not for several hours. Is it—?"

"It's about Edgar Leggett, and it's quite puzzling. The police brought in some jewelry this morning, asking if we could tell whether it belonged to Gabrielle Leggett. I recognized a string of pearls and a brooch which her father bought from us last year—the brooch in the spring, the pearls at Christmas. After the police had gone I, quite naturally, phoned Leggett, and he took the most peculiar attitude. He waited until I had told him all about it, then said, 'I thank you very much for your interference in my affairs,' and hung up. What do you suppose is the matter with him?"

"God knows. Thanks. I've got to run now, but I'll be in as soon as I can."

Eric Collinson had arrived while I was listening to the jeweler's story.

"Just a minute," I told the blond youngster, "and we'll dash out on what might not be a false alarm."

I called Information, got Fitzstephan's number, had it rung, and heard his drawled "Hello."

"You'd better get going with your book-borrowing, if any good's to come of it," I advised him.

"Why? Are things taking place?"

"Things are."

"Such as?"

"This and that, but it's no time for anybody who wants to poke into the Great Leggett Mystery to be dilly-dallying with pieces about unconscious minds."

"Come on," I told Collinson, putting the phone down and leading the way to the elevators.

He had a Chrysler roadster around the corner. We got in it and bucked traffic and traffic signals for the ten blocks that lay between our starting point and the Primrose Hotel, a gaudy establishment of the fly-by-night variety, run by an ex-tent-showman named Felix Weber.

I made Collinson drive past the hotel to the next corner, where Mickey Linehan was leaning his lopsided bulk against a garage door. He came to us when we stopped at the curb.

"The shine left ten minutes ago," he reported, "with Dick behind her. Nobody else has been out that looks like any of the birds you told us about."

"You camp in the car and watch the door," I told him. "We're going in. Let me do the talking," I instructed Collinson as we walked back to the Primrose, "and try not breathing so hard. Everything will come out O.K."

At the desk I asked for Weber and was directed to a frosted glass door marked *Manager's Office.* Weber, a little fat blond man with round blue childish eyes and no conscience, looked up from his desk when we came in, and then jumped up to shake my hand enthusiastically. We were old friends. Ten years back I had just barely missed putting him in the West Virginia bighouse for a swindle, and wouldn't have missed if he hadn't had too much money to spend on witnesses. In the same affair he had just barely missed putting a .45 slug in my body, and wouldn't have missed if he hadn't had too much white mule in him.

I introduced Collinson and said:

"We're looking for a girl who probably came here night before last. Her name is Leggett, no matter what one she's using. A girl of twenty, medium height and build, with a small face, pointed chin, white skin. Maybe she was wearing a brown coat and a brown and yellow hat. She here?"

"I'll see," he said, starting for the door.

"Never mind seeing. If she owes you anything we'll pay it, so you won't have to find out if she does, and collect it, before you let us have her."

He came back from the door, smiling good-naturedly, saying:

"She's in 416, registered as Geraldine Long. What do you want her for?"

"We're going up to see her. The chances are she'll leave with us, so have the bill, if any, ready when we come down."

Outside the manager's door, Collinson put a hand on my arm and mumbled:

"I don't know whether I—whether we ought to do this. She won't—"

"Suit yourself," I growled, "but I'm going up. Maybe she won't like it, but neither do I like people running away and hiding when I want to ask them about diamonds."

He frowned, chewed his lip, and made uncomfortable faces, but he went along with me. We found room 416, and I tapped the door with the backs of my fingers. There was no answer. I knocked again, louder.

Behind the door a voice spoke. It might have been anybody's voice, though probably a woman's, but it was too faint for identification, too smothered for us to know what it was saying.

I poked Collinson with my elbow and ordered:

"Call her."

He pulled at his collar with a forefinger and called hoarsely:

"Gaby, it's Eric."

That didn't bring any answer.

I thumped the door again and called: "Open the door." The voice said something that was nothing to me. I repeated my thumping and calling. Down the corridor a door opened and a pasty-faced boy with patent-leather hair stuck his head out to ask: "What's the matter?"

I said, "None of your damned business," and pounded 416 again.

The voice inside rose strong enough now for us to know that it was complaining, though no words could be made out.

Then a bed creaked. Feet rustled on carpet. Presently the key rattled on the other side of the lock.

When the lock clicked, I turned the knob and pushed the door open.

"Good God!" Eric Collinson exclaimed chokingly.

Gabrielle Leggett stood there, swaying a little. Her face was white as paper. Her eyes were all brown, dull, focused on nothing, and her tiny forehead was wrinkled, as if she knew there was something in front of her and was trying to decide what it was.

She had on one yellow stocking, a brown velvet skirt that was wrinkled as if it had been slept in, and a yellow chemise. Scattered around the room were a pair of brown slippers, the other stocking, a brown and gold blouse, a brown coat and a brown and yellow hat.

I pushed Collinson into the room, followed him, and closed the door, turning the key. He stood gaping at the girl, his jaw sagging, his eyes as vacant as hers, though more horrified. She leaned unsteadily against the wall beside the door and stared at nothing with her dark, blank eyes and ghastly, puzzled face.

I put an arm around her and led her to the bed, telling Collinson:

"Gather up the clothes." I had to tell him twice before he came out of his trance.

The girl went docilely across the room with me—if I had let go of her she would have stopped still where I left her—and let me set her down on the edge of the rumpled bed.

Collinson had finished gathering up her clothes when fingers drummed on the door.

"Well?" I called.

Weber's voice, full of curiosity:

"Everything all right?"

"Swell! Will you send a boy down to the corner and tell the man in the Chrysler roadster to drive up to the door and wait. The boy can't miss him—a big man with ears like a pair of red wings and a wide, red face."

With disappointment in his voice, Weber promised to send, and went away from the door. I began dressing the girl.

Collinson dug his fingers in my shoulder and protested in a tone that would have been appropriate if I had been robbing an altar:

"No! You can't—"

I pushed his hand away, growling:

"What the hell? You can have the job if you want it."

He was sweating. He gulped and stuttered:

"No. No. It—I couldn't—" He broke off and walked to the window.

"She told me you were an ass," I said to his back, and discovered that I was putting the brown and gold blouse on backward.

She gave me no more assistance than if she had been a wax figure, but at least she didn't struggle when I pushed her around and she stayed in whatever position I shoved her. Putting on her stockings, I found another physical peculiarity to add to the list Fitzstephan and I had made. There were only four toes on her foot, three small ones—instead of the normal four—beside the big toe. I felt her other foot through its stocking and found it the same.

By the time I had got her into hat and coat, Collinson had come away from the window and was spluttering questions at me. What was the matter with her? Oughtn't we get a doctor? Was it safe to take her out? And when I stood up he took her away from me, supporting her with his long, muscular arms, babbling "It's Eric, Gaby. Don't you know me? Speak to me. What's the matter, dear?"

"There's nothing wrong with her except a skinful of dope," I said. "Don't try to bring her out of it now. Wait till we get her home. You take that arm and I'll take this. She can walk, and there's no use putting on a show for the public. Let's go."

We got her downstairs and into the roadster without attracting any crowds. I sent Mickey up to her room to see what he could find; Collinson and I wedged the girl between us on the seat, and he put the car in motion.

We rode three blocks and he asked:

"Are you sure home is the best place for her?"

I said I was. He didn't say anything more for another five blocks and then repeated his question, adding something about a hospital.

"Why not a newspaper office?" I sneered.

Three blocks of silence, and he started again: "I know a doctor who—"

"I've got work to do," I informed him, "and Miss Leggett, home now, in the shape she's in now, will help me do it. So she goes home."

He scowled at me, accusing me angrily:

"You'd humiliate her, disgrace her, endanger her life for the sake of—"

"Her life's in no more danger than yours or mine. She's simply got a little more hop in her than she can stand up under. And she took it. I didn't give it to her."

The subject of our argument was alive and breathing between us—even sitting up with her eyes open—but knowing no more of what was going on than if she had been in Finland.

We should have turned to the right at the next corner. Collinson held the car straight, and stepped it up to forty-five miles an hour, staring ahead, his face hard and lumpy.

"Take the next turn," I commanded.

"No," he said, and the speedometer showed a 50. People on the sidewalks began looking at us as we whizzed past.

"Well?" I asked, wriggling an arm loose from the girl's side.

"We're going down the peninsular," he announced firmly. "She's not going home in that condition."

I grunted, "So?" and flashed my free arm at the controls. He knocked my hand aside, holding the wheel with one hand, stretching the other out to block me if I should try to kill the engine again.

"Don't do that," he cautioned me, increasing our speed another half-dozen miles. "You know what will happen to us all if you—"

I cursed him, bitterly, fairly thoroughly, and from the heart.

His face jerked around to me, full of righteous indignation, because, I suppose, my language wasn't the kind one should use in a lady's presence.

And that brought it about.

A blue sedan came out of a cross street a split second before we got there.

Collinson got his eyes and attention back to his driving in time to twist the roadster away from the sedan, but not in time to make a neat job of it.

We missed the sedan by a couple of inches, but as we passed behind it our rear wheels started sliding out of line. Collinson did what he could, giving the roadster its head, going with the skid, but the corner curb wouldn't cooperate. It stood stiff and hard where it was.

We hit the curb sidewise and rolled over on the lamp-post behind it. The lamp-post snapped, crashed down to the sidewalk. The roadster, over on its side, slipped us out on the lamp-post. Gas from the broken pipe roared up at our feet.

Collinson, most of the skin off one side of his face, crawled on all fours to the roadster and turned off the motor. I sat up, raising the girl, who was on my chest, with me. My right shoulder and arm were out of whack—dead. The girl was making whimpering noises in her chest, but I couldn't see any marks on her except a shallow scratch on one cheek. I had been her cushion, had taken the bump for her. The soreness of my chest and belly told me how much I had saved her.

People helped us up. Collinson stood with his arms around the girl, begging her to say she wasn't dead, and so on. The smash-up had shaken her into semi-consciousness, but she was still too full of narcotics to know whether there had been an accident or a wedding.

I went over and helped Collinson hold her up—though neither needed help—saying earnestly to the gathering crowd: "We've got to get her home. Who can—?"

A pudgy man in plus fours offered his and his car's services. Collinson and I sat in the back with the girl, and I gave the pudgy man her address. He said something about a hospital, but I insisted that home was the place for her. Collinson was too rattled over the girl's various troubles to say anything.

Twenty minutes later we were taking the girl out of the car in front of her house. I thanked the pudgy man profusely, giving him no opportunity to follow us indoors, and Collinson and I led the girl up the blue brick walk and up the front steps.

VI

The girl was now nearly enough awake to answer "No" when I asked her if she had a key. I rang the bell. The door was opened, after a little delay, by Owen Fitzstephan. There was no sleepiness left in his gray eyes; they were hot and bright, as they always got when he found life interesting. Knowing the sort of things that interested him, I wondered what had happened.

"What have you been doing?" he asked, looking at our clothes, at Collinson's scraped face, and at the girl's scratched cheek.

"Automobile accident," I explained. "Nothing serious. Where's everybody?"

"Everybody," he said, stressing the word, "is up in the laboratory. Come here."

He took me across the reception hall to the foot of the stairs, leaving Collinson and the girl standing together by the door, put his mouth to my ear, and whispered:

"Leggett's committed suicide."

"Where is he?" I was more annoyed than surprised.

"In the laboratory. Mrs Leggett and the police are up there, too. It happened not more than half an hour ago."

"We'll all go up," I decided.

"Isn't that," he protested, "rather unnecessarily brutal—taking the girl there?"

"Maybe," I said irritably, "but it can't be helped. Anyway, she's coked up and better able to stand the shock than she will be later, when the stuffs dying out in her." I turned to Collinson. "Come on, we'll all go up to the laboratory."

I went ahead, letting Fitzstephan help Collinson with the girl.

There were six people in the laboratory: a uniformed policeman, a big man with a red mustache, standing beside the open door; Mrs Leggett, sitting on a wooden chair in the farther end of the room, her body bent forward, her hands holding a handkerchief to her face, sobbing quietly; O'Gar and Reddy, standing by one of the windows, close together, reading a sheaf of papers that the bullet-headed sergeant held in his thick fists; a gray-faced, dandified man in dark clothes, standing beside the zinc table, twiddling eyeglasses on a black ribbon in his hand; and Edgar Leggett, seated on a chair at the table, his head and upper body resting on the table, his arms sprawled out.

O'Gar and Reddy looked up from their reading as I came in. Passing the table, to join them at the window, I saw blood, a small black automatic pistol lying close to one of Leggett's hands, and seven unset diamonds grouped close to his head.

O'Gar said, "Take a look," and handed me part of his sheaf—four sheets of stiff white paper covered with very small, precise and plain handwriting in black ink. I was getting interested in what was written when Fitzstephan and Collinson came to the door with the girl.

Collinson saw what had happened in a glance. His face went white, and he put his big body between the girl and her dead father.

"Come in," I said.

"This is no place for Miss Leggett, in her condition," he replied hotly, turning to take her away.

"We ought to have everybody in here," I told O'Gar. He nodded his bullet head at the policeman, who put a hand on Collinson's shoulder and said: "You'll have to come in, the both of you."

Fitzstephan placed a chair by one of the end windows for the girl. She sat in it and looked around the room—at the dead man, at Mrs Leggett, who had not looked up, at all of us—with eyes that were dull, but no longer completely blank. Collinson stood beside her chair, looking belligerently at me.

I addressed O'Gar loudly enough for the rest to hear:

"Let's read Leggett's letter out loud."

He screwed up his eyes, hesitated, then thrust the rest of the sheets at me, saying:

"Fair enough. You read it."

Not wanting the job, I passed it on to Owen Fitzstephan. Standing beside me, he read:

> My name is Maurice Pierre de Mayenne. I was born in Fécamp, department of Seine-Inférieure, in France, on March 6, 1883, and was educated chiefly in England. In 1903 I went to Paris to study art, and there, four years later, I met Alice and Lily Dain, orphan daughters of a British naval officer. The following year I married Lily Dain, and in 1909 our daughter Gabrielle was born.
>
> Shortly after my marriage I had discovered that I had made a terrible mistake, that it was really Alice, and not Lily, whom I loved. I kept this discovery to myself until the child was past the more difficult baby years, that is, until she was nearly five. Then I told my wife, and asked her to divorce me so I could marry Alice. She refused.
>
> On June 6, 1913, I shot and killed Lily, and fled with Alice and Gabrielle to London, where I was soon arrested and returned to Paris. There I was tried, found guilty, and sentenced to life imprisonment on Devil's

Island. Alice, who had no part in the murder, and who had been horrified by it, and had gone to London with me only through her love for the child, was also tried, but, justly, acquitted.

If there is any humanity or human likeness left in me, it is not the fault of those who have made Devil's Island the almost perfect hell it is. In 1918 I escaped with a fellow convict named Jacques Labaud on a flimsy raft. Neither of us knew how long we were adrift in the ocean, nor, toward the last, how long we had been without food and water. A week, perhaps, but every hour was a new eternity. Then Labaud died. He died of exposure and starvation. I did not kill him. No living creature could have been feeble enough for me to kill. But when Labaud was dead there was enough food for one, and I lived until I was washed ashore in the Golfo Trieste.

Ghanging my name to Armand Bacot, I secured employment with a British copper mining company at Aroa, and within a few months became private secretary to Philip Howart, the resident manager. Shortly after that I was approached by a cockney named John Edge, who described to me a plan by which we could defraud the company. When I refused to take part in it, Edge told me he knew who I was, and threatened to expose me. That Venezuela had no extradition treaty with France would not save me, Edge said, since Labaud's body had been cast ashore, undecomposed enough to show what had happened to him, and I could not prove that I had not killed him in Venezuelan waters to keep from starving.

I still refused to take part in Edge's plan and made up my mind to go away. But before I could start, Edge killed Howart and robbed the company safe. He urged me to flee with him, arguing that I could not face the sort of investigation the police would make. That was true, and so I agreed. Two months later, in Mexico City, it became apparent to me why Edge had asked me to accompany him. He had a firm hold on me and expected to use me in crimes that were beyond his abilities. I was determined, no matter what happened, no matter what became necessary, I would never go back to Devil's Island, or to any prison, but neither did I intend becoming a professional criminal. I attempted to desert Edge, he found me, and we fought. I killed him, but it was in self-defense. He struck me first.

In 1920 I came to the United States, to San Francisco, changed my name once more, to Edgar Leggett, and began making a new career for myself, developing some experiments I had made with colors when I was a young artist. In 1923, believing that Edgar Leggett could never now be connected with Maurice de Mayenne, I sent for Alice and Gabrielle, who were then living in New York, and Alice and I were married.

But the past was not dead. Alice, not hearing from me after my escape, not knowing what had happened to me, employed a private detective to find me—a Louis Upton. He sent a man named Harry-Ruppert to South America. Ruppert succeeded in tracing me step by step from my landing in the Golfo Trieste up to, but no farther than, my departure from Mexico City. In doing this he of course learned of the deaths of Labaud, Howart and Edge—three deaths of which I was innocent, but of which I most certainly should be convicted if tried.

I do not know how Upton found me here. Possibly he traced Alice and Gabrielle to me. Late last Saturday night he called on me and demanded money. Having no money available at the time, I put him off until

Tuesday, when I gave him the diamonds as part payment of his demands. But I was desperate, and I knew what being at Upton's mercy would mean, so I determined to kill him. I decided to pretend a burglar had taken the diamonds, notifying the police. Upton, I was sure, would immediately communicate with me then, and I would make an appointment with him and shoot him down in cold blood. The diamonds would be found in his possession. It would not be difficult for me to fix up a story that would make me seem justified in killing this man whom the police would suppose was the burglar.

But Harry Ruppert—hunting for Upton, with a grudge against him—saved me that killing, himself shooting Upton. Ruppert, the man who had traced me through Venezuela and Mexico for Upton, had also—either by following Upton here or making Upton talk before killing him—learned my identity. With the police after him for Upton's murder, he came here, demanding that I shelter him from them, returning the incriminating diamonds to me, and demanding money in their stead.

I killed him. His body is in the cellar. Out front, a detective is watching my house. Other detectives are busy elsewhere inquiring into my life. I have not been able to satisfactorily explain certain of my acts, nor to avoid contradictions, and, now that I am suspected, there is no chance of keeping the past a secret. I have always known that this would sooner or later happen. I am not going back to prison again.

MAURICE DE MAYENNE.

Nobody said anything for a long moment after Fitzstephan had finished his reading. Mrs Leggett had taken the handkerchief from her face, listening, sobbing now and then. Gabrielle Leggett was looking jerkily around the room light fighting cloudiness in her eyes, her lips writhing together as if she were trying to get words out but couldn't.

I went to the table, bent over the dead man, felt his clothes. The inside coat pocket was stuffed. I reached under his arm, unbuttoned and opened the coat, took a brown wallet out of the pocket. The wallet was thick with paper money—fifteen thousand dollars, when we counted it afterward.

Showing the wallet's contents to the others, I asked:

"He leave any message besides the one that's been read?"

"None that's been found," O'Gar replied. "Why?"

"He didn't commit suicide," I said. "He was murdered."

Gabrielle Leggett screamed piercingly and sprang out of her chair, pointing a sharp white finger at Mrs Leggett.

"She killed him," the girl shrieked. "She said, 'Come back here,' and held the kitchen door open with one hand, and picked up the butcher-knife from the drainboard with the other, and when he went past her she pushed it in his back, I saw her do it. I wasn't dressed, and when I heard them coming, I hid in the pantry."

Mrs Leggett got to her feet, her face washed empty by amazement and grief. She staggered and would have fallen if Fitzstephan hadn't gone over to steady her.

The gray-faced, dandified man by the table—a Doctor Riese, learned later—said in a cold, crisp voice:

"There is no stab wound. He was shot through the temple by a bullet from this pistol, held close, slanting up. Clearly suicide, I should say."

Collinson forced the girl down in her chair again, trying to calm her.

I disagreed with the doctor's last statement, and said so, while my brains were busy with another matter:

"Murder. His letter is the letter of a man who is still fighting. There's plenty of determination in it, but no despair. When he wrote it he meant to go away. If he had intended to kill himself he would have left some word for his wife and daughter. How was he found?"

"I heard," Mrs Leggett sobbed, "I heard the shot, and ran up here, and he—he was like that. And I went down to the telephone, and the bell—the doorbell—rang—and it was Mr Fitzstephan, and I told him. It couldn't—there was nobody else in the house to—to kill him."

"You killed him," I said to her. "He was going away. He wrote this statement, taking the blame for your crimes. You killed Ruppert down in the kitchen. That's what the girl was talking about. Your husband's statement sounded enough like a suicide letter to pass for one, you thought, so you murdered him—murdered him believing that his death and confession would close up the whole business, stop us from poking into it any more."

Her face didn't tell me anything. It was distorted, but in a way that might mean almost anything. I filled my lungs and went on, not exactly bellowing, but making plenty of noise:

"There are a half-dozen lies in your husband's statement—a half-dozen that I know of now. He didn't send for you and his daughter. Mrs Begg said he was the most surprised man she had ever seen when you arrived from New York. He wouldn't have given Upton the diamonds and then called in the police. He'd have given him money or he would have killed him without giving him anything. Upton didn't come to Leggett with his demands; he came to you. You were the one he knew. His agency had traced Leggett here for you—not only to Mexico City—all the way here, but he and Ruppert had been jailed before they could bleed you. When he got out, he came here and made his play. You got the diamonds for him, and you didn't tell your husband anything about the burglary being a fake. Why? You didn't want him to know that you knew about his South American and Mexican murders. Why? A good additional hold on him, if you needed it? Anyway, *you* dealt with Upton.

"Maybe Ruppert had got in touch with you, and you had him kill Upton for you—a job he'd be glad to do on his own hook. Probably, because Ruppert *did* kill Upton, and he *did* come to see *you* afterward, and you thought it necessary to put the knife in him down in the kitchen. You didn't know that the girl, concealed in the pantry, saw it. Horrified, having known all along that her father had killed her mother, seeing you now kill a man, she got dressed and ran away from this slaughter-house, taking her jewelry to Minnie to sell, drugging herself into forgetfulness.

"You didn't know she had seen you kill Ruppert, but you *did* know you had got out of your depth. You *did* know that your chances of disposing of the body were slim—your house was too much in the spotlight. So you played your only part; you told your husband the whole thing, got him to shoulder it for you, and then handed him his—here at the table.

"He shielded you. He had always shielded you. *You*," I thundered, my voice in fine form by now, "killed your sister Lily, his first wife, and let him take the fall for you. *You* went to London with him afterward. Would you have gone with your sister's murderer if you were innocent? *You* had him traced here, and *you* came here after him, and *you* married him. *You* were the one who decided that he had married the wrong sister—and *you* killed her."

"She did, she did!" cried Gabrielle Leggett, trying to get up from the chair in which Collinson held her. "She—"

Mrs Leggett drew herself up straight, and smiled, showing white teeth set edge to edge, and came two steps toward the center of the room. One hand was on her hip, the other hanging at her side. The housewife—Fitzstephan's "serene, sane soul"—was gone; this was a wild animal in the form of a blonde woman—except the eyes, which were the animal's own.

Even her body seemed now not rounded with the plumpness of well-cared-for early middle age; it was rounded as a tiger's or panther's is, with cushioned, soft-sheathed muscles.

I picked the gun up from the table and put it in my pocket.

"You wish to know who killed my sister?" she asked softly, speaking to me, her teeth clicking together between words, her lips smiling, her eyes burning. "She—the dope fiend—Gabrielle—she killed her mother. She is the one he shielded."

The girl cried out something unintelligible.

"Nonsense," I said. "She was a baby."

"Oh, but it is not nonsense," the woman insisted. "She was nearly five, a child of five playing with a pistol she had taken from a drawer while her mother slept. The pistol went off, and Lily died. An accident, of course, but Maurice, a sensitive soul, could not bear that the child should grow up knowing that her hand had sent her mother out of this world. Besides, it was likely that Maurice would have been convicted in any event. He and I had been intimate, you know. But that was a slight matter to him. His one thought was to erase from the child's mind all memory of the accident, so she might never remember what she had done, so that her life might not be darkened by the knowledge that she had, even though accidentally, killed her mother."

It wouldn't have been so bad if she hadn't been smiling so coolly as she talked, selecting her words so carefully, almost fastidiously, and mouthing them so daintily. She went on:

"Gabrielle was always, even before she began using drugs, a child of, one might say, limited mentality, so by the time the London police found us we had succeeded in quite emptying her mind of the last trace of memory, that is, of that particular memory. This is, I assure you, the truth of the whole affair. She killed her mother, and her father—to use your quaint expression—'took the fall for her.' "

"Fairly plausible," I said, "but weak in spots. You're trying to hurt her because she witnessed *your* latest murder."

She pulled her lips back from her teeth and started toward me, her eyes flaring, then checked herself, laughed sharply, and began talking again, rapidly, with a hysterical swing or cadence to her words, almost as if she were singing:

"Am I? Then I must tell you this, which I should not tell unless it were true. I taught her to kill her mother. Do you understand? I taught her, trained her, drilled her. Do you understand that? Lily and I were true sisters, inseparable, hating one another poisonously. Maurice—he wished to marry *neither* of us, though he was intimate enough with *both*. You are to understand that literally. But we were poor and he was not, and because he was not, Lily wanted to marry him. And because Lily wanted to, I wanted to. We were like that in all things. But she got him—first—*trapped* him into matrimony.

"Gabrielle was born six or seven months later. I lived with them. What a happy little family we were! From the first Gabrielle loved me more than her mother. I saw to that; there was nothing Aunt Alice wouldn't do for her niece, because her preferring me infuriated Lily. It infuriated Lily, not because she herself loved the child, but because we had always hated one another, had always each tried to take everything from the other. When Gabrielle was no more than a year old I planned what I would some day do.

"When she was nearly five I did it. I taught her a little amusing game. Maurice's pistol, a small one, was kept in a locked drawer high in a chiffonier. I unlocked the drawer, unloaded the pistol, and lay on Lily's bed, pretending I was asleep. The child pushed a chair over to the chiffonier, climbed on it, took the pistol from the drawer, crept across to the bed, put the muzzle of the pistol to my head, and pressed the trigger. When she did well, making little or no noise, holding the pistol correctly in both of her tiny hands, I rewarded her with candy, cautioning her to say nothing about the game to anyone else, as we were going to surprise her mother with it.

"We did; we surprised her completely, one afternoon when Lily, having taken aspirin for a headache, was sleeping in her bed. I unlocked the drawer, but did not unload the pistol. Then I told the child she might play the game with her mother, and I went down to visit friends on the floor below, so no one would think I had anything to do with my dear sister's death. I thought Maurice would be out all afternoon, and intended, as soon as we heard the shot, to rush upstairs with my friends and find that the child playing with the pistol had killed her mother.

"I had little fear of the child's talking afterward. Of, as I have said, no brilliant mentality, loving and trusting me as she did, and in my hands both before and during the official inquiry into her mother's death, it would have been very easy for me to control her, to be sure she said nothing that would reveal my part in the—ah—enterprise. But Maurice, coming home unexpectedly, came to the bedroom door just as Gabrielle pressed the trigger, the tiniest fraction of a second too late to save his wife's life. His subsequent desire to wipe all memory of the deed from the child's mind made any further effort, or anxiety, on my part unnecessary. I did follow him here, and I used Gabrielle's love for me and her hatred of him—which I had carefully cultivated by deliberately clumsy attempts to make her forgive him for killing her mother—to persuade him to marry me, so that Gabrielle, whom he loved, could be kept close to him. *The day he married Lily I swore I would take him away from her—and I did—and I hope my dear sister in hell knows it!*"

Her face had changed as she talked—or chanted—her eyes growing wilder, the wildness spreading down from them, making her face less and less human. By now the last trace of sanity was gone from voice and features. She spun to face the girl across the room, flung an arm out toward her, screamed shrilly:

"You're her daughter, and you're cursed with the same rotten soul and black blood that she and I and all the Dains have had; you're cursed with your mother's death on your hands before you were five; you're cursed with the warped mind and the need for drugs that I've given you in pay for your silly love since you were a baby. Your life will be black as Lily's and mine were black; the lives of those you touch will be black as Maurice's was black; and the—"

"Stop!" Collinson gasped brokenly. "Make her stop!"

Gabrielle Leggett, both hands to her ears, her face twisted with terror, shrieked once—horribly—and fell forward out of her chair.

Reddy was young at the game, but O'Gar and I should have known better than to lose sight of Mrs Leggett, even for a half-second, no matter how strongly Collinson's gasp and the girl's shriek drew our attention. But we did look at them—if for less than a half-second—and that was long enough.

When we looked at Mrs Leggett again, she had a gun in her hand, and she had taken a step toward the door.

Nobody was between her and the door. Nobody was behind her, because her back was to the door and by turning she had brought Fitz-stephan into her field of vision.

She glared savagely over the black gun, crazy eyes darting from one to another of us, taking another step backward, snarling:

"Don't you move!"

Pat Reddy shifted his weight to the balls of his feet. I frowned at him, shaking my head. The hall or stairs were better places in which to take her alive. In here somebody would die.

She went over the sill, blew her breath between her teeth with a hissing, spitting sound, and was gone down the hall.

Owen Fitzstephan was first through the door after her. The policeman got in my way, but I was second out. The woman had reached the head of the stairs, at the other end of the dim hall, with Fitzstephan, not far behind, rapidly overtaking her.

He caught her on the mid-floor landing just as I reached the top of the stairs. He had one of her arms pinned to her body, but the hand holding the gun was free. He grabbed at it and missed.

She twisted the muzzle in to his body as I—with my head bent to miss the edge of the floor—leaped down at them.

I landed on them just in time, crashing into them, smashing them into the corner of the wall, sending her bullet, meant for the sorrel-haired man, ripping into a step.

None of us was standing up. I caught with both hands at the flash of her gun, missed, and had her by the waist. Close to my chin, the novelist's lean fingers closed around her gun-hand wrist.

She twisted her body against my right arm, which, benumbed in the automobile accident, wouldn't hold. Her thick body heaved up, turning over on me.

Gunfire roared in my ear, burnt my cheek. The woman's body went limp. When O'Gar and Reddy pulled us apart she lay still. The last bullet had torn through her throat.

I went up to the laboratory. Gabrielle Leggett, with Collinson and the doctor kneeling beside her, was lying on the floor. I told the doctor:

"Mrs Leggett's dead, I think, but you'd better see if there's any chance. She's on the stairs."

The doctor went out. Collinson, chafing the unconscious girl's hands, looked at me as if I were something he didn't like, and said:

"I hope now you're satisfied with the manner in which your work got done."

"I'm not particularly satisfied with the manner," I told him, "but"—stubbornly—"it got done."

Collinson returned his attention to the girl, who had moved an arm.

I walked down the hall toward the stairs, repeating my last three words—*It got done.* I didn't think I was soft-headed enough to have been impressed by Mrs Leggett's curse, yet I didn't feel that everything was done here. I hadn't the sort of satisfaction you feel when you've completely and finally wound up a job. The diamonds had been recovered; their going had been explained; and everybody who might have been jailed over their going was dead. There were no loose ends that I knew of. Nevertheless... I gave it up, telling myself as I went downstairs:

"Well, if more comes, it'll come."

I was, it turned out, right about that.

THE HOLLOW TEMPLE, BY DASHIELL HAMMETT

A further incident in the "black life" of Gabrielle Leggett

IN DECEMBER BLACK MASK

6

THE HOLLOW TEMPLE

BLACK MASK, DECEMBER 1928

Eric Collinson came into my office. There was too much pink in his eyes and not any in his skin. He sat down and said:

"She can't go. They can't let her go. You've got to go with her."

His voice, like his face, was dull and tired and hopeless and bewildered.

"Miss Leggett?" I asked, though I didn't need to; and then: "How is she now?"

"You've killed her."

He spoke bitterly, but without heat, not looking at me; staring at my inkwell, with a beaten look in his eyes.

I ignored the accusation, saying:

"Where is it that she can't go, and that I've got to go with her?"

He replied, still staring at the inkwell, that Madison Andrews was crazy, and so was Dr Riese, and so would he—Collinson—be if this thing kept on.

"I thought they were just about as cool and level-headed a pair as you could find."

"But good God!" he exclaimed, "they want to let her go to this Joseph."

"Who is he?"

Instead of answering my question he began complaining that it was all my fault; that if it hadn't been for me, her father and step-mother would still be alive, Gabrielle would know nothing of their "horrible past," nothing of the crime that she herself had committed as the five-year-old tool of her step-mother, and, most important of all, she would not have been made to believe that she was accursed—bound to live in blackness herself and to bring blackness into the lives of all who came in contact with her.

"She's better off now than she's ever been," I argued. "I know that, in the shape she was in when it all broke, she was upset a lot by the melodramatic curse her step-mother put on her, or said was on her. But I can't see that she's as bad off as when she was under her step-mother's influence."

He lifted his haggard young face to look at me, and he spoke as if his throat hurt him:

"I'm going to tell you: I didn't think anybody could be as brutal as you were to her."

"Is that," I asked irritably, "why you're here now telling me I've got to go somewhere with her?"

"But what else can I do?" he demanded, puckering his brows, his lower lip drooping down from his teeth. "They're going to let her go. They're crazy, I tell you. And she can't go alone like that—with only Minnie."

"Go with her yourself. You think *you*—"

"But I can't." Face, voice, and the slant of his wide shoulders were advertisements of hopelessness. "Good God! Don't you think I would? But she won't even let me see her. She's afraid of the curse settling on me. I—I haven't seen her for a week. She wouldn't let me. You've got to go. There's nobody else that's—"

"That's brutal enough?" I suggested.

"You know her, and you know the whole story, and you're already in it. You can take care of her." He took hold of my wrist with a big sunburned hand and pushed his face over the desk toward me. "You've got to go. And you've got to see that nothing happens to her."

I took my wrist out of his hand and growled:

"I haven't got to do anything. I'm not likely to do anything that I know as little about as I do about this. What is it? Where is she going?"

"I told you," he said wearily. "She's going to Joseph's. They're going to let her go. It's Dr Riese's doing, though Andrews ought to know better. They're crazy. You've got to—"

"Who is Joseph?" I asked.

"That's it. Who is he? What do they know about him? Or about what will happen to Gaby in his Temple? For a man like Andrews to agree to such a thing!"

He put his elbows on my desk, his face between his hands, and stared at the desk-top with dull bloodshot eyes.

"How long since you've slept?" I asked.

"Tuesday," he muttered without looking up, "or maybe Sunday. What difference does it make? You'll go with her?"

"I don't know. Maybe you think you've given me the whole story, but you haven't. You haven't told me anything. Try again? Start with Joseph."

"Another cult," he said impatiently. "He calls his place the Temple of the Holy Grail. I don't know where Gabrielle ran into them, but she's known them for a month or so. I suppose it's the fashionable cult just now. You know how they come and go in California. This Joseph came to see her after her trouble, and now she wants to go to the Temple and stay for a while. They do that—retreats—like the Catholics.

"Dr Riese—God knows why—said he thought it would be good for her. Andrews said, 'No,' at Erst, but they persuaded him. He said he had had the cult investigated and it seemed all right. I suppose he meant by that that there was no proof that anybody had ever been murdered there. It's idiotic! What if Mrs Payson Laurence and Mrs Ralph Coleman are members? Their social positions won't keep them from being made fools of like anybody else. And Mrs Livingston Rodman's being a resident of the Temple now doesn't have to mean anything except that she too can be deceived. But Andrews seems to think that because the cult's dupes are beyond suspicion, so must it be. So the old ass has agreed to let Gabrielle go there.

"I don't want her to go, but what can I do? She won't even see me. But I'm damned if she's going there with nobody but her maid, even if Dr Riese will see her every day. There's got to be somebody there to see that nothing happens to her. You've got to go. I meant what I said about your being brutal, but I know—I know you—she will be safe with you there. You will go, won't you?"

I thought it over without enthusiasm. It wasn't my idea of an inviting job, but the Continental Detective Agency was in business to make money, and I couldn't very well turn down any honest and profitable employment in our line.

Collinson took his face from between his hands and said:

"I don't know what else you may have on hand, but—the money end of it—any amount you charge for your services will be quite all right."

"Andrews is in charge of the girl's affairs," I stalled. "I'll have to see him first."

Collinson said eagerly that that was all right. He had spoken to both Andrews and Riese about engaging me, and they had not only consented, but thought it an excellent idea. Collinson used my telephone to call Andrews and tell him I would be over at his office in a few minutes.

Collinson didn't go to the lawyer's office with me. He said gloomily that if he did he would get into another argument with Andrews, and after a solid week of trying to change the old man's mind he had given it up as a futile business. Leaving me, Collinson gripped my hand violently, asking me to promise all sorts of things concerning the carefulness with which I would guard Gabrielle Leggett. I advised him to get some sleep.

Madison Andrews was a tall, gaunt man of sixty, with ragged white hair, eyebrows and mustache that exaggerated the ruddiness of his face—a bony, hard-muscled face. He wore his clothes loose, chewed tobacco, and had twice in the past ten years been named correspondent in divorce suits.

"I dare say," he told me, "young Collinson has babbled all sorts of nonsense to you. He seems to think I'm in my second childhood—as good as told me so."

"He doesn't think you ought to let her go."

"He has spared no pains in making that known to me," the lawyer said. "But even though he is her fiancé, I am responsible for her care; and I prefer to follow Dr Riese's advice in this. He is her physician. He insists that letting her go to the Temple for a week or two of seclusion from the world will do more to restore her sanity than anything else that can be done. Can I disregard that?

"Joseph may be—probably is—a charlatan, but he certainly is the only person to whom Gabrielle has willingly talked, and in whose company she has been at peace, since her parents' deaths. Dr Riese tells me that to cross her in her desire to go to the Temple will be to send her mind deeper into its illness. Am I to snap my fingers at Riese's opinion because young Collinson doesn't like it?"

I said: "No."

"I have learned something of the members of this sect. I know decent, responsible, even prominent people, who are members. Mrs Livingston Rodman is living there now. I have no illusions concerning the sect: it is probably as full of quackery as any other. But I am not interested in it as religion—rather as therapeutics—as a cure for Gabrielle's mental illness vouched for by her physician. The character of the cult's membership is such that I will consider Gabrielle safe there. Even if I were not quite sure of that, I still should think that no other consideration should be allowed to interfere with her recovery. That, as I see it, comes first."

I nodded my agreement and asked:

"When is she proposing to go?"

"Tomorrow morning. You can go then?"

"Yeah. What is the layout?"

"I'll notify Joseph that you are coming. You are supposed to be a male nurse, and will be given a room close to Gabrielle's. They know of her mental trouble, so your presence there will be quite all right, whether they believe you to be a nurse or not. You needn't go with her. Perhaps it would be best if you were there when she arrives, at, say, eleven o'clock. There is no need of my giving you instructions. It is simply a matter of taking every precaution, seeing that nothing happens to her. Dr Riese and I have every confidence in your ability to handle it. Gabrielle's maid, Minnie, will be with her, and Dr Riese will call every day. Ask for Aaronia Haldorn when you arrive. She is Joseph's wife, I think, and manages the material end of the cult."

"Does Gabrielle Leggett know I'm going?"

"No," Andrews said, "and I don't think we need say anything to her about it. You'll make your watch over her as unobtrusive as possible, of course, and, while she knows you, I don't think that, in her present condition, she will pay enough attention to your presence to resent it. If she does—well, we'll see."

II

From the street, the following morning, the Temple of the Holy Grail looked like what it had originally been—a six-storey yellow brick apartment building. There was nothing about its exterior to show that it wasn't one still. I rang the door bell.

The door was opened immediately by a broad-shouldered meaty woman of some year close to fifty. She was a good three inches taller than my five feet six. Flesh hung in little bags on her face, but there was neither softness nor looseness in eyes and mouth. Her long upper lip had been shaved. She was dressed in black.

I told her I wanted to see Mrs Haldorn. She took me into a small, dimly lighted reception room to one side of the lobby, told me to wait there—her voice was a heavy bass—and went away.

I put my Gladstone bag on a chair, my hat on top of it, and sat down. Drawn blinds let in too little light for me to make out much of the room, but the carpet was soft and thick and what I could see of the furniture leaned more toward luxury than severity.

No sound came from anywhere in the building. I looked at the open doorway and discovered that I was being looked over. A small boy of twelve or thirteen stood there staring at me with big dark eyes that seemed to have lights of their own in the semi-darkness. I said:

"Hello, son."

The boy said nothing, looked at me a minute longer with the cold, unblinking, embarrassing stare that only children can manage, turned his back on me, and walked away, making no more noise than he had made coming.

Looks like I'm going to have a swell time here, I thought, if the two I've seen are fair samples of the joint's occupants—besides Gabrielle Leggett, who's still worse.

A woman, walking silently on the thick carpet, appeared in the doorway, came through it. She was tall, graceful, and her dark eyes had lights of their own, like the boy's. That's all I could see then.

I stood up and asked:

"Mrs Haldorn?"

"Yes." Her voice, saying that one word, was the most beautiful I had ever heard. It wasn't a voice, it was pure music.

"Madison Andrews told you I was coming?" I said, hoping she would speak more than one syllable this time.

"Oh, you are Miss Leggett's attendant?" The slightest of pauses before the last word told me that she didn't believe in the male nurse pretext. Her voice was all that the first *Yes* had made me think it. "*Yes*, he told me."

She walked past me to raise a blind, letting in a fat rectangle of morning sun. While I blinked at her in the sudden brightness, she sat down and motioned me back to my chair.

I saw her eyes first. They were enormous, black, soft, glowing, heavily fringed with black lashes. They were the only live, human, things in her face. There was warmth and there was beauty in her oval, olive-skinned face; but, except for the eyes, it was unnatural—almost weird—warmth and beauty. It was as if her face were not a face, but a mask that she had worn until it had almost become a face. Even the curving red mouth looked not so much like flesh as like an almost perfect imitation of flesh—softer, redder, maybe warmer, than genuine flesh, but not genuine. Above this face—or mask—uncut black hair was bound close to her head, parted in the middle, drawn down across temples and upper ears to meet in a knot on the nape of her neck. Her neck was long, strong, slender; her body tall, fully fleshed, supple; her clothes dark, silky, part of her body.

She offered me Russian cigarettes in a white jade case. I apologized for sticking to my Fatimas, and struck a match on the smoking stand she pushed out between us.

When our cigarettes were burning she said:

"We shall try to make you as comfortable as possible. We are neither barbarians nor fanatics. I explain this because so many people are surprised to find us neither. This is a Temple, but none of us supposes that happiness, comfort, or any of the ordinary matters of civilized living, will desecrate it. You are not one of us. Perhaps—I hope—you will become one of us. However—do not squirm—you won't, I assure you, be annoyed. You may attend our services or not, as you choose, and you may come and go as you wish. You will show us, I am sure, the same consideration we show you, and I am equally sure that you will not interfere in any way with anything you see—no matter how peculiar you may think it—unless it definitely and disagreeably affects your—ah—patient, Miss Leggett."

"Of course not," I promised.

She smiled, as if to thank me, rubbed her cigarette's end into the ash tray, and stood up, saying:

"I'll show you your room."

Picking up my hat and bag, I followed her out into the lobby, where we entered an automatic elevator. She took me to a room on the fifth floor. Everything in the room, as in the connecting bathroom, was white: white papered walls and painted ceiling; white enameled chairs, bed, table, dresser, fixtures and woodwork; white felt on the floor. None of the furniture was hospital furniture, but the solid whiteness of everything gave it that appearance. There were two windows in the bedroom, looking out over roofs, and one in the bathroom. The only doors were those connecting bathroom and bedroom, bedroom and corridor. Neither had a lock.

I left my hat and bag there and went with the woman to see the room Gabrielle Leggett would occupy. Its door faced mine across a six-foot corridor's purple carpet. The interior was a duplicate of my room's, except that, on the opposite side from the bathroom, there was a small square dressing-room without windows.

"Her maid?" I asked.

"She will sleep in one of the servant's rooms on the top floor. Shall we go downstairs now?"

She took me down to the second floor and pushed back half of a pair of sliding doors, showing me a room dark with walnut paneling and furniture.

"Our dining-room," she said, as she slid the door shut again and moved on along the corridor. "Breakfast and luncheon are usually served in our rooms, but for dinner—at seven—you may either come here or have it in your room, as you prefer. This is the library."

We were at the doorway of a large square room where tan burlaped walls ran up high behind glass-fronted bookcases.

A man turned from one of the cases toward us. He was a tall man, built like a statue, in a black silk robe. His thick hair, rather long, and his thick beard, trimmed round, were white and glossy.

Aaronia Haldorn introduced me to him, calling him Joseph. He came forward to give me a white and even-toothed smile and a warm strong hand. His face was healthily pink and without line or wrinkle. It was a tranquil face, especially the clear brown eyes, somehow making you feel at peace with the world. The same soothing quality was in his baritone voice as he said:

"We are happy to have you here."

The words were merely polite, meaningless; yet, as he said them, I believed that for some reason he was happy. I understood now Gabrielle Leggett's desire to come to this place. I said that I, too, was happy to be there, and at the time I actually thought I was.

We went on, the woman showing me various other rooms, and finally leading me to a small iron door on the ground floor. She opened it and said:

"Our services are held here."

The floor was of white marble, pentagonal tiles. The walls were white, smooth, unbroken except for this door and another exactly like it on the other side. These four straight, whitewashed, undecorated walls rose straight up for six storeys—to the sky. There was no ceiling, no roof. In the other end of the room—of what had been a room until it had been cut through to the sky—a gray tarpaulin covered something that was shaped like an upright piano, but several times larger than any piano.

"The altar," Aaronia Haldorn explained.

Behind us a soft buzzing sounded.

"That is probably Miss Leggett," the woman said, and we went back through the iron door.

At the elevator I left her, going up to my room. Presently I heard the rustle of people moving in the corridor, going into Gabrielle Leggett's room. I didn't hear her voice, but I did hear Minnie Hershey, her mulatto maid, answering some question Aaronia Haldorn had asked, and I heard the bass rumble of the woman who had let me into the house.

A few minutes later a small frosted globe fixed to the white telephone on my bedside table glowed, and I was asked what I wanted for luncheon. "Anything and coffee will do," I said, and agreed that cold sliced meat and artichoke salad sounded appetizing, declined dessert, and then went into the bathroom to wash.

A maid in black and white brought the meal in to me on a white tray. She was somewhere in her middle twenties, a hearty, pink and plump blonde, with blue eyes that looked curiously at me and had jokes in them.

I said something about the food on the tray looking good. She said, "Oh, yes, sir," without seriousness, put the tray on the table, looked at me out of the corners of twinkling eyes, and went out.

After I had eaten I dug a bottle of King George scotch out of my bag, put it on the table beside the tray, and went into conference with it and a deck of cigarettes. Sounds drifted up through the open windows, but none came from inside the building until, an hour or so later, the blonde maid returned for the tray.

She pretended she didn't see the bottle. I asked:

"Can I be shot at sunrise for having that here?"

She put up her tawny eyebrows and said:

"I really can't say," gathering up the tray.

"Ever use it yourself?"

"What?" The skin around her eyes twitched. "A shot at sunrise?"

"Yeah. Or now."

She carried the tray toward the door, smiling, saying:

"I couldn't—now; The Village Blacksmith would break my neck if she smelled it on me."

The Village Blacksmith, I guessed, was the big woman with the bass voice.

"Later? When you're through for the day?"

She said, "Maybe," over her plump shoulder as she went through the door.

I spent the afternoon in my room. Dr Riese came in to see me a little before five o'clock, after visiting Gabrielle Leggett's room. He was a gray-faced, slender, dandified man with a crisp, precise way of turning out his words, usually emphasizing them by making gestures with the black-ribboned nose-glasses that I had never seen on his nose. I had learned that I stood high in his estimation because I had discovered that Edgar Leggett had been murdered, immediately after he—Riese—had pronounced him a suicide.

He told me the girl was in a better frame of mind than she had been since her parents' deaths, and cautioned me against making my surveillance of her too thorough.

"The less she is reminded that she is being guarded, the better for her," he said. "I am glad you are here, but, after all, it is not likely that you will find anything to do."

I promised to manage things so that the girl would see as little of me as possible, and the doctor went away, saying he would be in again in the morning.

I went down to the dining-room for dinner. There were eight of us at the table: Mrs Livingston Rodman, a tall, frail woman with transparent skin, faded, tired eyes, and a voice that never rose above a semi-whisper; a man named Fleming, who was young, dark, very thin, with a dark mustache and the detached air of one who had a lot of things on his mind; a Miss Hillen, sharp of chin and voice, scrawny, forty, with an eager, intense manner; a Mrs Pavlow, who was quite young, with a high-cheek-boned dark face and dark eyes that avoided everybody's gaze; Aaronia Haldorn; and her son, Manuel, the boy who had looked at me from the reception room doorway. Neither Joseph nor Gabrielle Leggett appeared.

The food, served by two Filipino boys, was good. There was little conversation—except that which Miss Hillen made—and none of it religious. She tried to prod Fleming into conversation with questions about Aztec customs. He replied evasively, busy with his own thoughts. Getting nothing from him, Miss Hillen turned to Manuel Haldorn, asking him what he intended being when he grew up, a question any boy hears often enough to be bored by. He smiled at her with a shyness that didn't seem sincere to me—remembering the stare he had given me—and replied that he didn't know—whatever Mama decided was best—and turned his eyes to his plate again.

Miss Hillen's gaze switched to Mrs Pavlow, whose face suddenly went panicky with embarrassment. Aaronia Haldorn saved her from the sharp-chinned woman's curiosity by asking:

"How are your roses, Miss Hillen?"

Miss Hillen talked roses through dessert and coffee.

III

At nine o'clock I got hold of Gabrielle Leggett's maid—Minnie Hershey—as she was leaving her mistress' room. The mulatto girl's eyes jerked wide when she saw me standing in the doorway of my room.

"Come in," I said. "Didn't Dr Riese tell you I was here?"

"No, sir. Are—are you—You're not wanting anything with Miss Gabrielle, sir?"

"Just looking out for her, to see that nothing happens. So you and I are really working together. And if you'll keep me wised up, let me know everything she does and says, and what others do and say, and so on, you'll be helping me, and helping her, because then I won't have to bother her."

The girl said, "Yes, sir," readily enough; but, so far as I could make out from examining her dark face, my cooperative idea wasn't getting over any too well.

"How is she this evening?" I asked.

"She's right cheerful this evening, sir. She likes this place."

"How did she spend the afternoon and evening?"

"She—I don't know, sir. She just kind of spent it—quiet like."

No news there. I said:

"Dr Riese thinks she'll be better off not knowing I'm here, so don't say anything about me to her."

"No, sir, I sure won't," she promised but it sounded more polite than sincere.

At ten-thirty the plump blonde maid who had brought up my luncheon came in to have some scotch and some cigarettes with me. She insisted that we would have to be very quiet, so the Village Blacksmith wouldn't learn that she was there; but I wasn't a lot impressed by her insistence; I knew that as likely as not the girl had been sent up to me.

Her name was Mildred. She was careless, pleasant, a bit tough, and shrewd without being intelligent. She told me she had been working in the establishment for six months, since the present Temple had been opened. It had been donated to the cult by Mrs Rodman. Mildred's attitude toward her employers' religion was one of tolerant indifference. They were decent enough people, she said. There were no wild parties of the sort that got other cults into the newspapers; and she supposed they had as good a religion as any, but she herself was a Methodist, and that was good enough for her.

She told me that there were half a dozen converts staying there in addition to the ones I had seen at dinner; and that at times there had been as many as twenty or twenty-five of them, all, she added, "real society people." When she asked me what I was doing there, I told her the truth, except that I didn't mention my detective agency connection.

"Is she really cracked?" she asked.

"No, but she's too close to it to be left alone. You've seen her before?"

"She's been here for services, but this is the first time she has even stayed."

"Here often?"

"I've seen her twice."

"See her today?"

"I took her dinner in, but I didn't get a good look at her. It was nearly dark, the lights weren't on, and she was lying on the bed."

Mildred went off at eleven-thirty. A few minutes later I crossed the corridor to put my ear against Gabrielle Leggett's door, keeping it there until my neck got tired—and that's all the good it did me.

I returned to my room, smoked a cigarette, put a flashlight in my pocket, and went for a stroll through the building. The thick carpets that were everywhere made silent walking easy.

Lights burned dimly in the corridors. I wandered around for nearly an hour, seeing nobody, hearing breathing through a few bedroom doors, but nothing else. I didn't do any prying, but confined myself to the corridors and more public rooms, like dining-room, library, reception rooms and so on. The iron doors leading to the hollow core of the building where services were held were locked. I tried both of them.

Ten minutes more of listening at the girl's door brought me nothing. I went to bed. At four-something I got up again, put on slippers and bathrobe, and went for another stroll. It was no more profitable than the first.

Dr Riese visited my room at ten the next morning, apparently quite pleased with the progress his patient was making.

I caught Minnie Hershey in the corridor a little later, tried to get some information out of her, and got nothing but a lot of polite *Yes, sirs*.

When Mildred brought my luncheon in at noon she told me that services would be held at nine o'clock that evening.

In the library, after luncheon, I found Fleming busy making notes from a stack of books. He didn't seem to feel like talking, so I wandered out. The Village Blacksmith passed me in the corridor, paying no attention to me until I spoke, then barely nodding. Aaronia Haldorn came to my room later that afternoon to smoke a cigarette and ask if anything could be done to make me more comfortable. Joseph was in Gabrielle Leggett's room for an hour. I could hear his voice, but, no matter how tight I clamped my ear to her door, I couldn't catch his words.

Before dinner I went out for half an hour's walk in the streets, stocking up with cigarettes, magazines and newspapers.

The shy Mrs Pavlow didn't appear for dinner. Neither did Gabrielle Leggett, but Joseph was there, and a man and woman I had not seen before. He was a well-tailored, carefully mannered man, stout, bald, and sallow, a Major Jeffries. The woman was his wife, a pleasant sort of person in spite of a kittenish way that was thirty years too young for her.

Joseph, at the head of the table, eating no more than half a dozen good bites, speaking not many more than that number of words, seemed to have the same sort of soothing effect on everyone as he had on me. Even the sharp-chinned Hillen woman prodded nobody with questions. Presently, however, I discovered that there was one at the table who seemed to have escaped this influence—the boy Manuel. I caught him—once, and only for a split second—glancing at his father almost furtively through long lashes; and what I saw in the boy's eyes was either contempt or hatred. I had only his eyes to go by; his face remained angelic. It was only a quick flash that I got of the eyes, but one of those things was in them. I watched the boy surreptitiously through the rest of the meal, but he never looked at Joseph again. He looked often at his mother—somewhat furtively too—but when his eyes were on her there was adoration in them.

I attended the services in the Temple's hollow core that night. The altar, uncovered by tarpaulin now, was a glistening, dazzling, affair of white and crystal in a beam of blue-white light that slanted down from an edge of the roof. The beam was so strong that the altar seemed to quiver in it, to expand and contract. The glare hurt my eyes, tired them, but held them. When I wanted to look around at the congregation I had to fight with my eyes to get them away from the altar.

There were between thirty and forty people there, sitting on white enameled benches. Only ten of them, including me, were men. Men and women sat stiffly on their benches, staring at the dazzling altar with peculiarly fixed, unblinking gazes. Faces seemed white and unreal in the reflected glare, pupils of wide eyes were shrunken.

I saw Gabrielle Leggett on the other side of the room, but she was sitting in the front row, and I couldn't see her face. Minnie Hershey was beside her.

Joseph, in a white robe, moved to and fro in front of the altar, going through some ritual. I didn't know enough about religious ceremony to tell how this one differed from others. It was rather impressive, in a very dignified way. The strained, rigid, attention of the people on the benches gave a tense, expectant, air to it all, as if something tremendous, or violent, or exciting, was about to happen. Nothing of the sort did happen. There was some chanting in which everybody took part. The whole thing lasted an hour and ten minutes.

The congregation went out slowly, not talking much, most of them looking tired and worn, as if they had been through some sort of emotional struggle. I, who knew nothing about whatever spiritual significance the service may have had, felt somewhat the same way myself, probably from staring so long at the dazzling white altar.

I went slowly toward one of the little iron doors, waiting for a closer look at Gabrielle Leggett. Close to the door she passed me, not looking at me. She was thinner than when I had last seen her—ten days before—and what had been barely a suggestion of hollowness around her eyes and in her cheeks then was now a pronounced hollowness. Her small mouth was drawn tight, the lips colorless. She was no paler than usual, because she had always been white-cheeked, but now her whiteness seemed less healthy. Her green-brown eyes were more brown than green, enlarged, blank. She walked as in her sleep, with Minnie beside her.

I tried to catch the mulatto's eyes, but she too was walking blank-faced and dazed.

Those of the congregation who were not staying in the building went away. The others vanished into their rooms. Mildred came into my room for more drinks and smokes. I got no information out of her, nor she out of me.

The house quieted for the night. I left my bed three times at odd hours to prowl through the building. I saw nothing, heard nothing, that was meat to my grinder.

The next day Dr Riese reported still further improvement in his patient. I wondered what sort of shape she had been in before—if she was better now, as I had seen her last night. I laid in wait for Minnie in the corridor. Her face was not yet clear of last night's daze. I could get nothing out of her.

I had a brief conversation with the boy Manuel that day. I strolled into the library and found him snuggled into a big chair, reading a book entitled *Candide.*

"Morning," I said. "What's exciting in your young life today?"

"Morning," he replied calmly. "What's your opinion of Mildred now? Rather nice legs—hasn't she?—if you like them a bit fat."

I laughed at that one and asked:

"What do you know about it—a young sprout of your age?"

He stared at me coldly for a moment and then returned his big-eyed gaze to the book. Fleming came into the room. I exchanged *Good mornings* with him and went away.

Three more days went by.

On each of them Dr Riese expressed increasing satisfaction with Gabrielle Leggett's condition. I saw her four or five times in those three days and she didn't look any better to me, but I wasn't a doctor. I gave up trying to get anything out of Minnie. She had gone into a trance; the last time I tried to question her I had to call her three times before she even heard me. I spoke to Dr Riese about her, but he didn't think it was important.

"Probably just the worry and strain of nursing her mistress," he said. "You know how devoted she is to Miss Leggett."

I said that didn't sound like an explanation to me.

I continued to roam the corridors at night, profitlessly, chiefly because that was about the only thing I could do to earn my pay. New faces came and went. I attended services again—a carbon copy of the first ceremony.

Occasionally I saw and exchanged a few words with Aaronia Haldorn and Joseph. He spent a lot of time with Gabrielle

Leggett. Once I asked for his opinion of her condition. He said something about her passing through a spiritual crisis. I felt reassured by his words at the time, but, later, away from him, I thought them over and found that they really hadn't meant anything at all—not anything I could understand.

The plump blonde Mildred came in every evening for an hour or so. We had both given up trying to pump the other, it was now simple a sociable hour or two over whiskey and cigarettes. I went down to the agency one afternoon. There were nine telephone messages and a letter from Eric Collinson on my desk—all demanding assurance that all was well with Gabrielle Leggett. I phoned him that it was.

On the fourth morning, Dr Riese seemed less sure that the girl was improving; and by the next day he was noticeably worried, though I couldn't get any details out of him. He told me he would be in again to see her at seven that evening.

IV

I spent most of the day fidgeting in and out of my room. The general vagueness of my job in this Temple hadn't bothered me much before—I had had plenty of even more aimless operations in my twenty years of sleuthing—but now that Dr Riese had found something to worry about—even though it was probably a medical worry and out of my field—I began to get restless, uneasy, irritable.

Dr Riese did not show up that evening as he had promised. I supposed that one of the emergencies that are a regular part of a doctor's life had held him elsewhere, but his not coming annoyed me.

I sat in my room from half past six on, with my door open, looking at Gabrielle Leggett's door. Mildred took a tray into the girl's room at a few minutes past seven. When she brought me mine I asked her how Gabrielle Leggett seemed to be.

"She's all right, I suppose," she said. "I don't think there's much the matter with her but showing off."

"What was she doing?"

"Sitting at the window, looking out, posing, if you ask me. How is it you're not going down to the dining-room tonight?"

"Tired of eating in the graveyard atmosphere," I said.

At half-past seven Minnie Hershey left her mistress' room, looking with startled eyes through my open door at me, but going on without saying anything. She returned at a little after eight, a few minutes before Mildred came up for my tray.

At nine o'clock Joseph appeared, spoke a few words about nothing in particular, smilingly refused the chair I offered him, and went into the girl's room, opening the door without knocking. I cursed him and myself, because he had, for the time he was in my room, chased away my restlessness and uneasiness.

Half an hour later he left the girl's room, nodded at me, said, "Good night," and went down the corridor toward the rear. A couple of the house's inmates passed my door between then and ten o'clock, apparently on their way to their rooms.

At a quarter to eleven Mildred appeared. I asked her not to close the door when she started to. She looked sharply at me, saying:

"I can't stay, then."

"If you knew what a bad humor I'm in you wouldn't want to stay."

She hesitated, lingering for a moment with her hand on the knob, bit her lip, and said:

"Oh, well, I'll come back some time when you're over your grouch," and went away.

At eleven o'clock Minnie Hershey left the girl's room again. I was tempted to stop her and try some questions on her, but didn't. My last several attempts in that line had got me nothing, and I was in too disagreeable a mood for diplomacy. By this time I had given up all hope of seeing Dr Riese before morning.

Turning off my lights, I sat in the dark, looking at the girl's door and grumbling to myself, cursing the world. At a quarter to twelve Minnie Hershey, in hat and coat, as if she had come in from the street, went into the girl's room once more. She remained inside until nearly one o'clock; and when she came out she closed the door very softly, walking tiptoe, an altogether unnecessary precaution on the thick carpet.

Because it was unnecessary it made me nervous. I went to my door and called softly:

"Minnie."

She tiptoed on down the corridor as if she hadn't heard me. That increased my jumpiness. I went after her, quickly, and stopped her by taking hold of one of her thin wrists.

Her Indian features were expressionless.

"How is she?" I asked.

"Miss Gabrielle's all right, sir. You just leave her alone," she mumbled.

"She's not all right," I growled, "and you know it. What's she doing now?"

"Sleeping."

"Doped?"

She raised angry dark eyes and let them drop again, saying nothing.

"She sent you out to get dope?" I demanded, tightening my grip on her wrist.

"She sent me out to get her some—some medicine, yes, sir."

"And she took some and went to sleep?"

"Y-yes, sir."

"We're going back and have a look at her," I said.

The girl took a quick step away and tried to yank her wrist free. I held it. She said:

"You leave me alone, Mister, or else I'll yell."

"I'll leave you alone after we've had our look, maybe," I said, turning her around with my other hand on her shoulder. "So if you're going to yell, you might as well get started now."

She wasn't at all willing to go back, but she didn't make me drag her.

Gabrielle Leggett's door, like mine and all the guest-room doors, had no lock.

She was lying on her side in bed, sleeping quietly, the bedclothes stirring gently with her breathing. Her small white face, at rest, with her curly brown hair tumbled over the little forehead, looked like a sick child's.

I turned Minnie loose and went back to my room. Sitting there in the dark I understood why people bit their fingernails.

I sat there for an hour or more and then went for a cruise through the building, drawing the usual blank. In my dark room again, I took off my shoes, sat in the most comfortable chair, put my feet in another, hung a blanket over me, and went to sleep facing Gabrielle Leggett's door, through my open doorway.

Later I opened my eyes for a moment, drowsily, decided that I had only dozed off for a moment, that it was too soon for another trip; closed my eyes, drifted back toward slumber, and then roused sluggishly again.

Something wasn't right.

I wrestled my eyes open, then closed them. Whatever was wrong had to do with that. Blackness was before them when they were open, and when they were closed. That was reasonable enough, it was a dark, starless night, and my windows were out of the street lights' range. That was reasonable enough—damned if it was!

My door was open, and the corridor lights burned all night. I opened my eyes again. No pale rectangle of light was in front of them, no dim shape of Gabrielle Leggett's door.

I was too much awake now to jump up suddenly. I held my breath and listened, hearing nothing but the ticking of the watch on my wrist. Cautiously moving my hand, I looked at the luminous dial: 3:17. I had been asleep longer than I had thought—and the corridor light had been put out.

My head was numb, my whole body heavy, stiff, and there was a bad taste in my mouth. I got out from under my blanket, and out of my chairs, moving clumsily, my muscles stubborn, and crept on stocking feet to the door—bumped into the door. It had been closed. When I opened it, the corridor light was on as usual. The air coming through the door seemed surprisingly fresh, pure.

I turned, facing into my room, and sniffed. There was an odor of flowers, faint, a bit stuffy, more the odor of a closed place in which flowers had died than of flowers themselves. Lilies-of-the-valley, moonflowers, perhaps another one or two. I had a vague memory of having dreamed of a funeral. Trying to remember what I had dreamed, I leaned against the door-frame and nodded sleepily.

The jerking up of my neck muscles when my head had sunk too low awakened me. I wrestled my eyes open again, standing there on legs that didn't seem part of me, stupidly wondering what it was all about and whether it wouldn't be just as well to go to bed and sleep. While I drowsed over the thought I put out an arm against the wall, to take some of the strain off my tired legs. The hand—no more a part of me than the legs—touched the light button. I had enough sense to push it.

The light scorched my eyes. Squinting, I could once more see a world that was real to me, and I could remember that I had work to do. I made for the bathroom and doused my face and head in cold water. The water left me still stupid, muddled, but at least partly conscious.

Turning off my lights, I crossed to Gabrielle Leggett's door, listened, and heard nothing. I opened the door quickly, stepped inside, and closed it.

My flashlight showed me an empty bed with covers thrown down across the foot. I put a hand on the hollow her body had made in the bed—cold. There was nobody in bathroom or dressing alcove. There were no signs of a fight. Under the edge of the bed lay a pair of slippers, and a green kimono, or something of the sort, was hung on the back of a chair. There was nothing to indicate that she had dressed before she left the room.

I went back to my own room for my shoes, and then walked down the front stairs to the ground floor, intending to go through the house from top to bottom, silently first. If I ran across nothing—as was probable—then I would start kicking in doors, turning people out of beds, and raising hell until I turned up the girl. I wanted to find her as soon as possible, but she had too long a start on me for a few minutes to make much difference. So if I didn't waste any time getting down the stairs, neither did I run.

I was half-way between the second and first floor when I saw something move—or rather I saw the movement of something without seeing it. It moved from the direction of the street door toward the interior of the house. I was looking at the elevator door at the time, as I descended. The banister shut out my view of the street door. What I saw was a flash of movement through half a dozen of the spaces between the banister's uprights. By the time I had brought my eyes into focus on it, there was nothing to see. I thought I had seen a face, but I knew that's what anybody would have thought they had seen under the circumstances, and I knew that all I had actually seen was the movement of something pale.

The lobby, and what I could see of corridors, were vacant when I reached the ground floor. I moved in the direction that I imagined the moving thing I had seen must have taken—and stopped.

I heard—for the first time since I had awakened—a noise that I had not made. A shoe-sole had scuffed on the stone steps on the other side of the front door.

I walked to the front door, got one hand on the bolt, the other on the key, snapped them back together; and yanked the door open with my left hand, letting my right hand hang within a twist of my gun.

Eric Collinson stood on the top step.

"What the hell are you doing here?" I asked sourly.

It was a long story, and he was too excited to make it a clear one. As nearly as I could untangle his words, he had been in the habit of phoning Dr Riese for daily reports on Gabrielle Leggett. Today—or rather yesterday—and last night he had been unable to get the doctor on the phone. He had called up as late as two o'clock this morning. Dr Riese was not at home, he had been told, and none of his household knew where he was or why he was not at home. Collinson had immediately come to the neighborhood of the Temple, on the chance that he might see me, get some word of the girl. He hadn't intended coming to the door—until he had seen me looking out.

"Until you did what?" I asked.

"Saw you."

"When?"

"A minute ago, when you looked out."

"You didn't see me," I said. "What did you see?"

"Someone looking out—peeping out. I thought it was you."

"You mean you hoped and persuaded yourself it was. It wasn't. Who was it? What did he look like?"

"I don't know. I thought it was you, and came up from the corner where I was sitting in the car. Is Gabrielle all right?"

"Sure," I said. There was no use telling him I was hunting for her, and have him blow up on me. "Don't talk so loud. Riese's people don't know where he is?"

"No, and they seem worried. But that's all right if Gabrielle is all right." His haggard young face became pleading. "Could—could I see her? Just for a second? I won't say anything. She needn't know I'm here. Can't you arrange it somehow, please?"

This bird was young, tall, broad, strong, and perfectly willing to have himself broken all up for Gabrielle Leggett's sake. I knew something was wrong, but I didn't know what; neither did I know what I was going to have to do to make it right, how much help I was going to need. I couldn't afford to turn him away; on the other hand I couldn't give him the low down on the racket; that would have turned him into a wild man.

"Come in," I said. "I'm on one of my inspection tours. You can go along if you keep quiet and behave, and afterwards we'll see what we can do."

He came in acting and looking as if I had been St. Peter letting him into Heaven.

I closed the door and led him through the lobby, down the main corridor. So far as I could tell, we had the joint to ourselves.

And then we didn't.

V

Around a corner just ahead of us came Gabrielle Leggett, barefooted and in a yellow silk nightgown that was splashed with dark stains.

In both hands, held out in front of her as she walked, she carried a large dagger, almost a small sword. It was red and wet. Her hands and bare forearms were red and wet. There was a dab of blood on one of her cheeks. Her eyes were clear, bright, calm. Her small forehead was smooth, her mouth and chin firmly set.

She walked up to me, her untroubled gaze holding my troubled one, thrust the dagger toward me, and said evenly, just as if she had expected to find me there, had come there to see me:

"Take it. It is evidence. I killed him."

I said: "Huh?"

Still looking straight into my eyes, she said:

"You are a detective. Take me to where they will hang me."

It was easier to move my hand than my tongue. I took the bloody dagger from her. It was a broad, thick-bladed weapon, double-edged, with a bronze hilt like a cross.

Eric Collinson thrust himself past me, babbling words that nobody could have made out, going for the girl with shaking outstretched hands. She shrank over against the wall, away from him, fear in her face.

"Don't let him touch me," she begged.

"Gabrielle!" he cried, reaching for her.

"No! No!" she gasped.

I walked into his arms, my body between him and her, facing him, pressing him back with a hand on his chest, growling at him:

"Be still, you."

He put his big lean hands on my shoulders and began pushing me out of the way. I got ready to rap him on the chin with the dagger hilt. Looking past me at the girl, he seemed to forget his intention of forcing me out of his road. I leaned on the hand that was against his chest, moving him back until the wall stopped him.

"Be still till we see what's happened," I ordered.

His hands had gone loose on my shoulders. I stepped back from him, and a little to one side, so that I could see both him and her, facing each other from opposite walls.

"What's happened?" I asked, pointing the dagger at the girl.

She had recovered her calmness.

"Come," she said, "I'll show you. Don't let Eric come, please."

"He won't bother you," I promised.

She nodded at that, gravely, and led the way back down the corridor, around the corner, and to the little iron door that opened into the place where the altar was. The door was standing open. She went first through the door. I followed her, Collinson me. It was dark there under a dark sky. Walking unhurriedly on bare feet that must have found the marble floor chilly, she led us straight toward the altar, a vague dark shape without its tarpaulin.

I got my flashlight out as we walked. When she halted in front of the altar and said, "There," I clicked on the light.

On the first of the three altar steps, Dr Riese lay dead on his back.

His face was composed, as if he were sleeping. His arms straight down at his sides. His clothes were not rumpled, though his coat and vest were unbuttoned in front. His shirt front was all blood. There were four holes in his shirt front, all alike, all the shape and size that the weapon the girl had given me would have made.

No blood was coming from his wounds now, but when I put a hand on his head I found it not quite cold. There was blood on the altar steps, and on the floor below, where his nose glasses, unbroken, on the end of their black ribbon, lay.

I straightened up and swung the beam of my flashlight directly into the girl's face. She blinked and squinted in the light, but her face showed nothing except that physical discomfort.

"You killed him?" I asked.

Young Collinson came out of his trance to bawl:

"No!"

"Shut up," I snarled at him, stepping closer to the girl, so he couldn't wedge himself in between us. "Did you?" I asked her again.

"Are you surprised?" she asked quietly. "You were present when my step-mother told of the curse of the Dain blood in me, of how I had murdered my mother before I was five, of my warped mind, of the blackness that would be in my life and in the lives of all that I touched. Is this," she pointed almost carelessly at the dead man, "anything that should not be expected by those who come in contact with me?"

"Don't talk nonsense," I said while I tried to figure out her calmness. I knew she was a hophead, had seen her coked to the ears before, but this wasn't that. I didn't know what it was. "Why did you kill him?"

Collinson grabbed my near arm and yanked me around to face him. He was all on fire.

"We can't stand here talking," he exclaimed. "We've got to get her out of here, away from here. We've got to hide the body, or put it some place where they'll think somebody else did it. You know how those things are done. I'll take her home. You fix it."

He had nice ideas.

"Yeah?" I asked. "What'll I do? Frame it on one of the Filipino boys, so they'll hang him instead of her?"

"Yes, that's it. You know how to—"

"Like hell that's it," I said. "Not with me."

His face got redder. He stammered:

"I—I didn't mean so they'll hang anybody, really. I wouldn't want you to do that. But couldn't it be fixed for him to get away? I—I'd make it worth his while—any amount. He could—"

"Turn it off," I growled. "You're talking out of my territory."

"But you've got to," he insisted. "You came here to see that nothing happened to Gabrielle, and you've got to go through with this."

"Yeah? You're full of funny ideas, son."

"I know it's a lot to ask, but I'll pay you—"

"Stop it. You've wasted enough time for us." I took my arm out of his hands and turned to the girl, again, asking: "Who else was here when it happened?"

"No one."

I played my light around the place again, even up the walls, on corpse and altar, and discovered nothing I hadn't already seen. I put the dagger beside the body, snapped off the light, and told Collinson:

"We'll take Miss Leggett up to her room."

"For God's sake, let's get her out of this house now, while there's time," he urged.

I said she would look swell running through the streets in bare feet, with nothing on but a blood-spattered nightie.

He jerked his arms out of his overcoat, saying, "I've got the car just down the street; I can carry her to it," and started toward her with the coat held out.

She ran around to the other side of me, moaning:

"Oh, don't let him touch me!"

I put out an arm to stop this. It wasn't strong enough. The girl got behind me. Collinson pursued her and she came around in front. I felt like the center of a merry-go-round, and didn't like the feel of it.

When Collinson appeared in front again, I drove my shoulder into his side, sending him staggering over against the side of the altar. Following him, I planted myself in front of the big sap and blew off steam:

"Let her alone. Let me alone. The next break you make, I'm going to sock your jaw with the flat of a gun. If you want it now, say so."

He got his legs straight under him and began:

"But, good God, you can't—"

I had heard enough of that. I cut in with:

"Stop it. If you want to play with us you've got to stop bellyaching, do what you're told, and let her alone. Yes or no?"

He muttered: "All right."

I turned around and saw the girl—a gray shadow running toward the open iron door, her bare feet making little noise on the marble floor. My shoes seemed to make an ungodly racket as I went after her.

Just inside the door I caught her with an arm around her waist. The next moment my arm was jerked away, and I was flung aside, crashing into the wall, slipping down to one knee.

Collinson, looking eight feet tall in the darkness, stood close to me, storming down at me, but all I could pick out of his many words was a "damn you."

I was in a swell frame of mind when I got up from my knee. It took all my twenty years of the-job-comes-first training to keep my hand off my gun. Bending his face with it would have been sweet.

"There's one coming to you, boy," I promised him, "but it'll wait. We can't spend the whole morning clowning here."

I don't know what his reply was; he mumbled it to my back while I was going over to where the girl was watching us from the doorway.

"We'll go up to your room," I told her.

"Not Eric," she objected.

"He won't bother you," I promised again. "Go ahead."

She hesitated, and then went through the doorway. Collinson looking partly sheepish, partly savage, and altogether dissatisfied, followed me through. I closed the door, asking the girl if she had the key.

"No," she said, as if she hadn't known there was one.

We rode up to the fifth floor in the elevator, the girl keeping me always between her and her fiancé. He stared fixedly at nothing. I studied the girl's face, still trying to dope her out, to decide whether she had been shocked into sanity or deeper into insanity. Looking at her, the first guess seemed most likely, but I had a hunch that it wasn't. At that, I thought sourly, she's no goofier than her boy friend, the big simpleton.

We saw nobody in the corridor between the elevator and her room. I switched on her lights and we went in; I closed the door and put my back to it.

Collinson put his overcoat and hat on a chair and stood beside them, folding his arms. The girl sat on the side of her bed, looking at my feet.

"Tell us the whole thing, quick," I commanded her.

She raised her eyes and said:

"I should like to go to sleep now."

That settled the question of her sanity so far as I was concerned: she hadn't any at all. But now I had another thing to worry about. This room was not exactly as it had been before. Something had been changed since I had been in it not many minutes ago. I shut my eyes, trying to shake up my memory for a picture of it as it had been then; I opened them, looking at it as it was now.

"Can't I?" she asked.

I let her wait for a reply while I put my gaze around the room, checking it up item by item, as far as I could. The only change I could put my finger on was Collinson's coat and hat on the chair. There was no mystery to their being there, and the chair, I decided, was what had bothered me. It still did. I went to it and picked up the coat. There was nothing under it. Then I knew what was wrong; a green kimono, or something of the sort, had been there, and was not there now. I didn't see it elsewhere in the room, and I didn't have enough confidence in its being there to make a complete search.

I wondered what its absence meant while I told the girl:

"Not now; Go in the bathroom, wash the blood off your hands and arms, and get dressed for the street. Take the clothes in there with you. When you come out, give your nightgown to Collinson." I turned to him: "Put it in your pocket and keep it there. Don't go out of this room and don't let anybody come in. I won't be gone long. Got a gun?"

"No," he said, "but I—"

The girl got up from the bed, came over to stand close to me, and interrupted him:

"You cannot leave him here with me. I won't have it. Isn't it enough for you that I have killed one man tonight? Don't make me murder another." She spoke earnestly, but without great excitement, almost as if she were declining an invitation that someone was pressing on her.

"I've got to go out for a while," I said, "and you can't stay alone. Do what I tell you."

"You don't realize what you're doing," she protested in a thin, tired voice. "You know there's a curse on me, and on all who touch me. You know what happened to Dr Riese, whose only crime was that he was my physician." Her back was to Eric Collinson. She lifted her face so that I could see rather than hear the nearly soundless words on her lips shaped: "I love Eric. Let him go."

I felt sweat in my armpits. A little more of this and she would have had me ready for the cell next to hers: I was actually tempted to let her have her way. I jerked my thumb at the bathroom and said:

"You can stay in there, if you like, but he'll have to stay here."

She nodded her small, suddenly hopeless, face once, gently, and went into the dressing alcove. When she crossed from there to the bathroom, carrying some clothes in her hands, a tear was shiny below each eye.

I gave my gun to Collinson. The brown hand in which he took it was tense and shaky. He was making a lot of noise with his breathing. I told him:

"She's trying to save you from the family curse. She says she loves you. Now don't be a sap. Give me some help this once instead of trouble."

He tried to say something, couldn't, grabbed my nearest hand, did his best to disable it. I took it away from him, and went down to the scene of Dr Riese's murder.

I had some difficulty in getting there. The iron door through which we had passed a few minutes ago was locked now; I went around to the other one. It too was locked. The lock seemed simple enough. I went at it with the fancy attachments on my pocket knife, and presently had it open.

I didn't find the green kimono inside. Dr Riese's body was gone from the altar steps, was nowhere in sight. The dagger was gone, and every trace of blood—except where the pool on the marble floor had left a yellow stain—had been mopped up.

Somebody had been tidying up.

I put my flashlight back in my pocket and headed for an alcove off the lobby, where I had seen a telephone. The phone was there, but it was dead. I put it down and set out for Minnie Hershey's room on the sixth floor. I hadn't been able to do much with her, but I knew she was devoted to Gabrielle Leggett, and perhaps I could send her out to do my phoning.

I opened her door—lockless as the others—and went in, closing the door behind me. Holding one hand over the front of my flashlight, I snapped it on. Enough light leaked out to show me the mulatto girl in her bed, sleeping. The windows were closed, the atmosphere heavy, with a faint odor that was familiar—the odor of a closed place where flowers had died, the odor I had smelled in my own room earlier in the night.

I looked at the girl again. She was lying on her back, breathing through open mouth, her face more an Indian's than ever with the peace of heavy sleep on it. Looking at her, I felt drowsy myself. It seemed a shame to rouse her. Perhaps she was dreaming of—I shook my head, trying to clear it of the muddle settling there. Lilies-of-the-valley, moonflowers... that had died... death was restful... so was sleep... little death, somebody called it... it was restful... sleep... sleep... the flashlight was heavy in my hand... too heavy... hell with it... I let it drop... it fell on my foot... puzzling me... who touched my foot? somebody...

Gabrielle Leggett... asking to be saved... Gabrielle Leggett... a job... Gabrielle I.eggett... the job comes first... work to do...

I tried to shake my head again, tried desperately. It weighed a ton, and would barely creep from side to side. I felt myself swaying, put out a foot to steady myself. The foot and leg were weak, limp, dough. I had to take another step or fall; took it; forced my head up, my eyes open, to find a place to fall, and saw the window six inches ahead of me.

I swayed forward until the window sill caught my thighs, steadying me. My hands rested on the sill. I tried to find the handles on the bottom of the window, wasn't sure whether I had them or not, put everything I had into an attempt to raise the window.

It didn't budge.

I think I sobbed then, and holding the sill with my right hand, I beat the glass out of the center of the pane with my open left.

Air that stung like ammonia came through the opening. I put my face to it, hanging to the sill with both hands, sucking it in through mouth, nose, eyes, ears, and pores; laughing, with water from my eyes trickling down into my mouth.

I hung there drinking air only until I was reasonably sure of my legs under me again, and of my eyesight; until I was able to think and move again, though neither speedily nor surely. I couldn't afford to wait longer. I put a handkerchief over my face and nose and turned away from the window.

Not more than three feet away, there in the black room, a pale bright thing like a body, but not like flesh, stood writhing before me.

VI

It was tall, yet not so tall as it seemed, because it did not stand on the floor, but hovered with its feet a foot or more above the floor. Its feet—it had feet, but I don't know what their shape was. They had no shape—just as its legs and torso, arms and hands, head and face were without shape—without fixed form. They writhed, swelling and contracting, stretching and shrinking, not greatly, but without pause. An arm would drift into the body, be swallowed by it, come out again as if poured out. The nose would stretch down over the gaping shapeless mouth, shrink back up, into the face until it was flush with the cheeks, grow out again. The eyes would spread across the face until they were one enormous eye that had blotted out all the upper face, then contract until there was no eye, then three, then two again. The legs became one thick leg, like a pedestal, then three, then two again. And no feature or member ever stopped its quivering and writhing until its contours could be determined, its shape recognized.

It, or he, was a thing like a man, who floated above the floor; with a horrible grimacing greenish face and pale flesh that was not flesh, that was visible in the darkness, and that was as fluid, and as unresting, and as transparent, as tidal water.

I knew that I was ninety percent unbalanced, mentally and physically, from breathing the dead-flower stuff. But I couldn't—though I tried to—tell myself that I didn't see this thing.

It was there, within reach of my hand if I had leaned forward, shivering, writhing, between me and the door. I didn't believe in the supernatural—but what of that? Here was a thing that was not a natural thing, and it was not, I knew, a man with a sheet over him, or a trick of luminous paint.

I gave it up. I stood there with my handkerchief jammed to my nose and mouth; not breathing, not stirring—for all I know, my blood may have stopped running. I could say I was waiting to see what happened next; but I wasn't conscious of any intentions at all at the time.

I was there, and the thing was there, and I stayed where I was.

The thing spoke, though I could not have said whether I heard the words or simple became somehow conscious of them:

"Down, enemy of the Lord God; down on your knees!"

I stirred then, to lick my lips with a tongue drier than they were.

"Down, accursed of the Lord God, before the blow falls!"

I moved my handkerchief enough to say.

"Go to hell."

It sounded silly, especially in the croaking voice I had.

The thing's horrible body twisted convulsively, swayed, bent toward me.

I dropped my handkerchief and reached for it with both hands.

I got hold of the thing—and I didn't. My hands were in it to the wrists—into the center of it—were shut on it. And there was nothing in my hands but dampness that was without temperature, was neither warm nor cold.

That same dampness came into my face as the thing's face floated into mine.

I bit at its face—yes—and my teeth closed on nothing, though I could see and feel that my face was *in* its face.

And in my hands, on my arms, against my body, in my face, the thing writhed and squirmed, shuddered and quivered, swirling wildly now, breaking apart, reuniting madly in the black air.

Through the thing's flesh I could see my hands, clenched in the center of its damp body. I opened them, struck up and down inside it with stiff crooked fingers, trying to gouge it open—could see it being torn apart by my fingers, could see it going together again after my clawing fingers had passed—but I could feel nothing but dampness.

Now another feeling came to me, growing quickly once it had started—of suffocation and of an immense weight bearing me down.

This thing that had no solidity had weight, weight that was pressing me down, smothering me. My knees were going soft.

I tore my right hand free of its body and struck up at its face—felt nothing but its dampness brushing my fist.

I clawed at its insides again with my left hand, tearing at this substance that was so plainly seen, so faintly felt. Then on my left hand I saw something else—blood, dark, thick and real, covering the hand, running out between the fingers, dripping from it.

I laughed, got enough strength to straighten my back against the monstrous weight on me, and wrenched at the thing's insides again, croaking:

"I'll gut you plenty."

More blood washed my left hand.

I tried to laugh again, couldn't, choked instead. The thing's weight on me was twice what it had been. I staggered back, sagged against the wall, turning to lie against it.

Pure air from the broken pane, bitter, cold, stung my nostrils, told me—by its difference from the air I had been breathing—that it was not the thing's weight, but the poisonous flower-smelling stuff that was the weight on me.

The thing's pale dampness squirmed over my face and body.

Coughing, I stumbled through it, to the door, got the door open, and tumbled down into the corridor that was now as black as the room I had just left.

As I tumbled, somebody fell over me.

This was no indescribable thing. It was human. The knees that hit my back were human, sharp. The grunt that blew hot breath in my ear was human, surprised. The arm my fingers caught was human, thin.

I thanked God for its thinness. The corridor air was doing me a lot of good, but I was in no shape to battle with an athlete.

I put what strength I had into my hold on the thin arm, dragging it under me as I rolled over on the body it belonged to. My other hand, flung out across the man's thin body as I rolled over, struck something hard and metallic on the floor. Twisting my wrist, I got my fingers on it and knew what it was. It had been in my hand too recently for me to have forgotten the feel of it—the over-sized dagger with which Dr Riese had been killed.

The man on whom I was rolling had, I guessed, stood beside the door of Minnie's room, with the dagger in his hand, waiting to stick it into me when I came out. My tumble through the door had saved me, making him miss my body with that blade; and in missing he had gone off-balance, tripping over me.

Now he was kicking, jabbing, butting up at me from his face-down position on the floor, with my hundred and ninety pounds draped over his back, anchoring him down.

Holding on to the dagger with my left hand, I took my right hand away from his arm, found the back of his head in the dark, spread my hand on it, and began grinding his face into the floor, taking it easy, waiting for more of the strength that was coming back to me with each breath. A minute more and I would be ready to pick this baby up and get words out of him.

But I had to move before that.

Something hard pounded my right shoulder, then my back, then struck the carpet close to my noodle. Somebody was swinging a club on me.

I rolled off the thin man, thumping his skull with the heavy bronze dagger hilt as I left him. The club-swinger's feet stopped my rolling. I looped my right arm above the feet, took another rap on the back, missed the legs with my circling arm, and felt skirts against my hand.

Surprised, I pulled my hand back. Another blow from the club, on my side, reminded me that this was no place for gallantry. I made a fist of my hand and struck back at the skirt. It folded around my fist: a solid, meaty shin stopped my fist.

The shin's owner snarled in pain above me, and backed off before I could hit out again.

Scrambling up on hands and knees, I bumped my head into wood—a door. A hand on the knob helped me stand up. Not far away the club swished in the darkness again. The knob turned in my hand. I stepped back with the door, into a room, softly closing the door.

Behind me in the room a voice said:

"Go right out of here or I'll shoot you."

It was plump Mildred's voice, frightened. I turned, bending low, in case she did shoot. Enough of the dull grayness of approaching daylight came into this room to outline a thick body sitting up in bed holding something small and dark in one outstretched hand.

"It's me, your little playmate," I told her.

"Oh, you!" she exclaimed, as if in relief, but she did not lower the thing in her hand.

"You in on the racket?" I asked, risking a slow step toward her.

"I do what I'm told, and I keep my mouth shut, but I'm not going in for any strong-arm work, not for the money they're paying me."

"Swell," I said, taking more and quicker steps toward her. "Could I get down through this window to the one on the floor below if I tied a couple of sheets or blankets together, do you think?"

"I don't know—Ouch! Stop!"

I had her gun—a .32 automatic—in my right hand, her wrist in my left, twisting.

"Let go of it," I ordered, and she did.

Dropping her wrist, I stepped away from the bed again, picking up the dagger I had dropped on the foot of the bed. I tiptoed to the door and listened. I heard nothing. I opened the door, and heard nothing; saw nothing in the faint grayness that went through into the corridor.

Minnie Hershey's door was open. The thing I had fought with was not there. I crossed the corridor and went into her room, switching on the lights.

The mulatto was lying as she had lain before, sleeping heavily. I pocketed my gun, pulled down the covers, picked Minnie up, and carried her over into Mildred's room.

"See if you can bring her to life," I told Mildred, dumping the sleeping girl on the bed beside her.

"She'll come around in a few minutes. They always do."

I said, "Yeah?" and went out, down to the floor below, to Gabrielle Leggett's room.

The room was empty.

Collinson's hat and overcoat were gone; so were the clothes she had taken into the bathroom; and so was her nightgown.

I cursed the pair of them bitterly, snapped off the lights, and ran down the stairs to the first floor, feeling as bloodthirsty and violent as I must have looked—battered and torn and bruised, with a bloody dagger in my bloody left hand, a gun in my right.

Going down the stairs, I heard nothing, but when I reached the foot of them, a noise like small thunder suddenly broke out. I stopped until I had identified it as somebody's knocking on the front door. Then I went to the door, unlocked and opened it.

There was Eric Collinson, wild-eyed, whitefaced and frantic.

"Where's Gaby?" he panted.

"Damn you," I said, and hit him in the face with the gun.

He drooped, folding forward, stopped himself with his hands on the vestibule walls, hung there a moment, and slowly pulled himself upright again. Blood leaked from a corner of his mouth.

"Where's Gaby?" he repeated, doggedly.

"Where'd you leave her?"

"Here. I was taking her away. She asked me to. She sent me out first to see if anybody was in the street. Then the door shut."

"When?"

"Not a minute ago. Where is she?"

"She tricked you," I grumbled, "still trying to save you from the curse. If you had done what I told—But come on; we'll have to find her."

The reception rooms off the lobby were empty. We left the lights burning in them and hurried down the main corridor.

A small figure in white pajamas sprang out of a doorway and fastened itself on me, tangling itself up with my legs, nearly upsetting me.

Unintelligible words came from it. I pulled it loose and saw that it was the boy Manuel. Tears wet his panic-stricken face; sobs mangled the words he was trying to say.

"Take it easy, son," I said. "I can't understand a thing you're saying."

"Don't let him kill her," I understood.

"Who kill who? And take your time."

He didn't take his time, but out of his sobbing my ears fastened on "father" and "mother."

"Your father's going to kill your mother?" I asked, not greatly surprised.

His head went up and down.

"Where?"

He fluttered a hand at the iron door ahead.

I started toward it, and stopped.

"Listen, son," I bargained. "I'd like to save your mother, but I've got to find Miss Leggett first. Do you know where she is?"

"She's in there with them," he cried. "Oh, hurry! hurry!"

"Right. Come on, Collinson," and we raced for the iron door.

Beyond it, another door opened in the corridor, and the big woman I knew as the Village Blacksmith ran out, toward us, limping as she ran—from the crack I'd given her shin upstairs—and firing a heavy automatic pistol. The reports were deafening in the corridor. Her aim was terrible, playing hell with the ceiling.

I fired twice.

She dropped as I yanked the iron door open.

The white altar was dazzling, almost blinding, again in the beam of white light from the roof-edge. At one end of the altar Gabrielle Leggett crouched, her face turned up into the light-beam. The light on her face was too glaring for her expression to be made out.

Aaronia Haldorn lay on the altar step where Riese had lain. There was a dark bruise on her forehead. Her hands and feet were tied. Most of her clothes had been torn off. Her eyes, glaring at Joseph, held enough hatred to stock hell; her mask-like face was twisted into a fitting setting for the eyes.

Joseph, white-robed, stood in front of the altar, and of his wife. He stood with both arms held high and widespread, his back and neck bent so that his bearded face was lifted to the sky.

In his right hand he held an ordinary horn-handled carving knife, with a long curved blade; in his left a horn-handled, two-pronged fork.

He was talking to the sky, but his back was to Collinson and me, and we couldn't hear his words.

As we ran forward, he lowered his arms and bent over his wife. I was still a good thirty feet from him, Collinson at my side. I bellowed:

"Joseph!"

He straightened again, turning, and when the knife and fork came into view I saw that they were still clean, shiny.

I halted ten feet from the man in white, Collinson stopping beside me.

"Who calls Joseph, a name that is no more?" the priest asked, and I'd be a liar if I didn't admit that, standing there, looking at him, listening to him, I didn't begin to feel that there was nothing so very wrong with anything here or elsewhere in the world. "There is no Joseph," he went on, not waiting for an answer to his question. "You may know now, as all the world shall know, that he who went among you as Joseph was not Joseph, but God Himself. Now that you know, go!"

To any other man I would have said, "Bunk!" and jumped him. To this one I couldn't. I said:

"I'll have to take Miss Leggett and Mrs Haldorn with me," and said it weakly, indecisively.

He drew himself up taller, and his white-bearded face became stern.

"Go!" he commanded, his voice deep and vibrant. "Go from me before your defiance leads to destruction."

Aaronia Haldorn spoke to me from where she lay tied on the altar steps:

"Shoot. Shoot now—quick. Shoot."

I said to the man:

"You can be Joseph, or God, or Barney Google, but you're going along to police headquarters. Now put down the knives and things."

"You have blasphemed," he thundered, and took a step toward me. "You must die."

"Stop!" I barked.

He wouldn't stop. I was afraid. I fired.

The bullet hit his cheek. I saw the hole it made.

No muscle twitched in his face; he did not even blink an eye.

He walked deliberately, unhurriedly, toward me.

I worked the trigger, pumping seven more bullets into his face and body. I saw the holes they made.

He came on, deliberately, unhurriedly, no muscle twitching, no sign that he had felt the bullets.

His eyes and face were calm, stern. When he was close to me, the knife in his hand went up high above his head.

He was not fighting; he was bringing retribution to me; and he paid as little attention to my attempts to stop him as a father would to the struggles of a small boy he was punishing.

I was fighting.

The knife glistened up high, and started down.

I went in under it, bending my right forearm against his knife arm, driving the dagger in my left hand at his throat.

I drove the heavy blade into his throat, all the way in till the hilt's cross stopped it. Then I knew I could do nothing more...

I didn't know I had closed my eyes until I opened them. The first thing I saw was Eric Collinson kneeling beside Gabrielle Leggett, turning her face from the glaring light, trying to rouse her. Next I saw Aaronia Haldorn, still lying bound on the altar steps, but unconscious now. Then I discovered that I was standing with my legs apart, and that Joseph was on the floor between my feet, dead, with the dagger through his neck.

"Thank God he wasn't really God," I mumbled to myself.

A brown body in white brushed past me, and Minnie Hershey was throwing herself down in front of Gabrielle Leggett, crying:

"Oh, Miss Gabrielle, I thought that Satan had come alive and was after you again!"

I went over and took the mulatto by the shoulders, lifting her up, turning her to face me.

"How could he?" I asked. "Didn't you kill him dead?"

"Yes, sir, but—"

"But he might have come back in some other shape than Dr Riese?"

"Yes, sir, I thought he was—" She stopped and worked her lips together.

"Me?" I asked.

She nodded, not looking at me.

VII

I was waiting in Madison Andrews' reception room when he arrived at ten-thirty that morning. He looked anxiously into my face and at my bandaged left hand, and as soon as we were in his private office he asked:

"What is it? Anything gone wrong?"

"Plenty did, but most of it's all right now—except that Dr Riese is dead."

Andrews looked sharply at my face and bandaged hand again, sat down at his desk, motioned me to a chair, cut off a piece of tobacco, put it in his mouth, pushed a box of cigars at me, and said:

"I'm listening."

"These Temple of the Holy Grail people—Aaronia and Joseph Haldorn—were actors originally. I'm giving it to you as I got it from her and some of the other survivors. As actors they were pretty good—not getting on as well as they wanted to. This religious cult racket had been getting a lot of publicity, and they decided to give it a whirl. They rigged up a cult that was supposed to be a revival of an old Gaelic church back in the days of King Arthur. They brought it to California because our state's known to be a green meadow for anything in that line, and picked San Francisco instead of Los Angeles because the competition was less.

"With them they brought a little fellow named Tom Fink, who had taken care of the mechanical end of things for most of the well-known stage magicians and illusionists at one time or another; and Fink's wife, a big village blacksmith of a woman. They didn't want a lot of converts; they wanted few but wealthy ones. The racket went slow at first, until they landed Mrs Rodman. She fell plenty, and they worked her for one of her apartment buildings. She also footed the remodeling bill. The stage mechanic Fink had a lot to do with the remodeling, and did a good job.

"They didn't need the kitchens that each apartment in the building had, but Fink found that part of the kitchen space could be used for concealed rooms and cabinets, and that the gas and water pipes and the electric wires that were in them could be adapted to his hocus-pocus with little trouble. I can't give you all the mechanical details now—not until we've had time to take the joint apart. It's going to be interesting.

"I saw some of their work in action—a ghost that was made by an arrangement of lights thrown up on a body of steam rising from a padded pipe which had been pushed into a dark room from a concealed opening in the wainscoting under the bed. The part of the steam that wasn't lighted was invisible in the darkness, showing only a man-shape that quivered and writhed, and that was damp and real without any solidity to the touch. You'd be surprised how weird a trick like that can be, especially when you've been filled with that stuff they pump into the room before they start the vision going. I don't know whether it was ether or chloroform or something else; its odor was nicely disguised with some sort of flower perfume. This ghost—I fought with it—on the level—and even thought I had it bleeding, not knowing that I had cut my hand breaking a window to let in fresh air. It made a few minutes seem like a lot of hours to me.

"There wasn't until the very last—when he went off his base—anything crude about the Haldorns' work. Their services were as dignified and orderly as any could be. The hocus-pocus was all worked in the privacy of the victim's room. First the perfumed gas was pumped in, to get him groggy. Then the lighted steam vision was shown him, with a voice coming out of the same pipe to give him his orders, or whatever he was to be given. The gas kept him from being too sharp-eyed and suspicious, and also weakened his will so that he would be more likely to do what he was told. It was slick enough. The victim could talk about it afterward or not, just as he wished, but its happening in his own room, and the way it was handled, gave it a lot of authority. I imagine they squeezed a lot of pennies out of the customers that way.

"Some friends of Gabrielle Leggett's ran her into the Temple a little while back, and she went there a couple of times. She had enough money—or her parents did then—to make her eligible. When her trouble came and she broke up, the Haldorns decided it was time to play her, and Joseph went to see her. Have you ever seen Joseph?"

"No," the lawyer said.

"Well, he had what he needed. He looked at you and spoke to you, and things happened inside you. I'm not the easiest guy in the world to flimflam, but he had me going. I came damned near thinking he was God at the last. He was young, but he had grown a beard and had had the coloring killed in its hairs as well as in the hairs of his head. His wife tells me that she used to hypnotize him before he went into action, and that most of his effect on people was a result of that. Later he got so that he could get himself in the same condition of his own accord, and toward the last it became permanent.

"Aaronia Haldorn didn't know her husband had fallen for Gabrielle until after she came to the Temple. Until then she thought that he looked on the girl simply as another customer. But he had fallen in love with her, or wanted her, anyway. I don't know how far he had gone in working on her, using his hocus-pocus and her fear of her curse to sew her up, but Dr Riese finally discovered that everything wasn't going well with her. That was yesterday morning. He told me he was coming back later to see her, and he did come back, but he didn't see her, and I didn't see him—not then.

"He went in to see Joseph before he came upstairs, and overheard Joseph giving instructions to the Finks. He was foolish enough to let Joseph know he had overheard him. Joseph locked him up—a prisoner. They had sent one of the maids up to try to pump me when I first arrived, but after that they let me alone. It was wiser to let me see nothing funny than to try to stir me up with their supernatural stuff. But they had cut loose on Minnie Hershey from the first.

"She was a mulatto, and her negro blood made her susceptible to that sort of thing, and she was devoted to Gabrielle Leggett. They chucked visions and voices at the poor girl until she was dizzy. I had told Dr Riese that she was going queer, but he refused to take it seriously. Now they decided to make her kill Riese. They drugged him and put him on the altar. They ghosted her into believing that he was Satan, come up from hell to carry her mistress down there so she couldn't become a saint. Minnie was ripe for it—poor girl—and when the spirit told her that she had been selected to save her mistress, that she'd find the anointed weapon on her table, she followed the instructions the spirit gave her. She got out of bed, picked up the dagger that had been put on her table, went down to the altar, and killed Riese.

"That was the first time they did anything to me. I used to wander around the joint at night. To play safe, they pumped some gas into my room to keep me out of the way—slumbering—while Minnie was doing her stuff. But I was nervous, jumpy, and was sleeping in a chair in the center of the room instead of on the bed, close to the gas-pipe, so I came out of the dope before the night was over.

"By this time Aaronia Haldorn had discovered two things. First, that her husband's interest in the girl wasn't altogether financial. Second, that he had gone off center, was a dangerous maniac. Going around hypnotized all the time, what mind he had—not a whole lot, his wife says—had gone under completely. His success in flimflamming his followers had gone to his head. He thought he could do anything, get away with anything. He had dreams, she says, of the entire world deluded into belief in his divinity, he didn't see that that was any—or much—more difficult than fooling the handful that he had fooled.

"Aaronia Haldorn didn't like either of these things, but the first of them seemed the easiest remedied. She decided that if Gabrielle were sent down to find the murdered doctor, she would probably be shocked into complete insanity, and would be put out of Joseph's reach, in an asylum. She turned a vision and a voice loose on the girl and sent her down to the altar. The shock did upset Gabrielle still further, and worked out, for the time, even better than Aaronia had expected. The curse was never out of Gabrielle's thoughts. Now she took it for granted that this curse was responsible for Riese's death, because of his contact with her. Collinson and I met her in the hall saying she had killed him and should be hanged for it.

"I suspected then that she hadn't really killed him, from the way she talked of the curse; and when I saw him I was sure of it. He was lying in an orderly position. It was plain that he had been drugged before he was stabbed. The door leading to the altar—always kept locked—was unlocked, and she knew nothing about its key. There was a chance that she had been somebody's tool in the murder, but I doubted that.

"Haldorn and his wife both heard Gabrielle's confession that she had killed Riese. The place was scientifically equipped for eavesdropping. Haldorn didn't like that confession. His wife did. He decided that if the body were removed, and I were killed, Collinson would be the only sane witness to the whole thing—except the Haldorns and their allies—and he had heard

Collinson trying to persuade me to hush it up. He could count on Collinson's silence.

"Aaronia, planning to spoil her hubby's scheme, went up to Gabrielle's room, got her kimono, wrapped the bloody dagger in it, and stuck it in a corner where the police could easily find it. Meanwhile her husband and the Finks, having removed Riese's remains and cleaned up the place, started to work on Minnie again, to make her kill me. Aaronia crossed them up again, turning on the flower-smelling stuff so strong that it knocked the maid out—put her so soundly asleep that a dozen voices and visions couldn't have stirred her into action.

"Haldorn discovered then what his wife was doing, and he found the dagger wrapped in the kimono. I crashed into Minnie's room just about then, intending to wake her, and Haldorn—or the Finks—turned their ghost loose on me. It gave me hell, and when I finally tottered out of the room, I was jumped by the Finks. I beat them off, got a gun, and went downstairs.

"Meanwhile, Haldorn, up to his neck in a killing spree, condemned his wife to death for her treachery. He had got himself into a fine muddle by this time, and I suppose the only way out that he could see was through continued killing. He still had enough belief in his divinity-shield to take his wife down to the altar before he carved her. She was tied up there when Collinson and I, steered by their son, arrived. I killed Haldorn, but I almost didn't. I put eight bullets in him. Steel-jacketed .32's go in clean, without much of a thump, true enough. But I put eight of them in him—in his face and body—standing close to him and firing point-blank—and he didn't even know it. That's how completely hypnotized he had himself. I finally got him down by driving the dagger through his neck, cutting the spinal cord. God! it was—That's the story."

"And Gabrielle?" Andrews asked.

"The last I heard of her, Collinson was bearing her off to Reno, for marriage, not wanting to wait the three days the California law calls for."

The old lawyer's eyes burned at me from under his ragged brows.

"You'd no right to let them go," he roared. "You know she's in no condition to know what she's doing."

"She's not," I agreed. "But I didn't let them go. I was busy, and the first I knew of it was when I got Collinson's note, saying they had gone, two hours later."

Andrews pulled at a mustache corner and glowered at me.

"What about the police? The inquest?" he said. "You know they've got to be here for that."

"Sure you and I know it, but what do they care?"

"I care," he said, "and I engaged you, and I had a right to expect you to protect my interests."

"Yeah. Well, you're her guardian, or whatever you are, and you're a lawyer, so you ought to be able to do something about it—besides yelling."

He glowered at me for another moment and then his face slowly cleared.

"I'm sorry," he said. "I don't like it though, not a damned bit. But it may work out all right, may take her mind off that curse foolishness."

"I hope so," I replied, "but I doubt it. I don't think we're through with the curse yet."

His gaunt body jerked upright in his chair.

"What?" he demanded. "You haven't started believing in—?"

"I haven't started believing anything," I growled, standing up, "except that whatever it is that's hanging over Miss Leggett hasn't been smoked out yet, and that it'll probably be good for a lot more trouble before it is. And I don't believe in curses either—unless they have arms and legs and the rest of the things that make up a human being."

He leaned forward to ask, "Who?"
I shook my head. I didn't know.
He sat back in his chair, smiling.
"Preposterous," he said, and waved me out of his office.

THE BLACK HONEYMOON, BY DASHIELL HAMMETT

The third adventure of the Continental Detective in

"THE DAIN CURSE"

In JANUARY BLACK MASK

Black Lives, the first of the Dain Curse adventures, appeared in the November issue. Until exhausted, copies will be furnished on request at the regular news stand price.

7

BLACK HONEYMOON

BLACK MASK, JANUARY 1929

I

Eric Collinson wired me from Quesada:

> Come Immediately Meet Me Sunset Hotel Do Not Communicate Gabrielle Must Not Know Hurry Need You

The telegram came to me early Friday morning. I couldn't leave San Francisco immediately. Tommy the Rags was being tried for the California Steel and Iron payroll stick-up, and I had to go on the witness stand that day. I was still on it when court adjourned till Monday.

Then I had a date with an ex-wife of Phil Leach. We wanted him for a bank swindle in Des Moines. She had offered to sell us a photograph of him. I made the deal with her, but it was then after six, too late for a train that would put me in Quesada that night.

I ate dinner, packed a bag, got my car from the garage, and drove down.

Quesada was a one-hotel town pasted on the rocky side of a young mountain that sloped down into the Pacific Ocean some eighty miles from San Francisco. Quesada's beach was too abrupt, hard, jagged, for bathing, so Quesada had never got into the summer resort money, but for a while it had been a hustling rum-running port. That racket was dead now—bootleggers had learned there was more profit and safety, less worry and confusion, in handling domestic hooch than imported—and Quesada had gone back to sleep.

I got there at eleven-something that night, garaged my car, and crossed the street to the Sunset Hotel. It was a low sprawled-out yellow building. There was nobody in the lobby except the night clerk. He was a small effeminate man well past sixty who went to a lot of trouble to let me see that his fingernails were rosy and shiny.

When I had registered he gave me a sealed envelope—hotel stationery. My name was on it in Eric Collinson's handwriting. I tore it open and read:

Do not leave the hotel until I have seen you.
Eric Collinson.

"How long has this been here?" I asked.

"Since about eight o'clock. He was here waiting for you for about an hour, until after the last stage got in from the railroad."

"Isn't he staying here?"

"Oh, dear, no. He and his bride got the Tooker place, down in the cove."

"How do you get there?" Collinson was too muddle-brained for me to pay much attention to his instructions.

"You'd never be able to find it at night," the clerk assured me, "unless you went all the way around by the East road, and not then unless you knew the country."

"Yeah? How do you get there in the daytime?"

"You go down this street to the end, take the fork of the road on the ocean side, and follow that up along the cliff. It isn't really a road, more of a path. It's about three miles, a brown house, shingled all over, on a little hill. It's easy enough to find in the daytime if you remember to keep to the right, to the ocean side, all the way down."

I thanked the clerk, let him guide me to a room, told him to call me at five, and was asleep by midnight.

The morning was dull, ugly, foggy and cold when I climbed out of bed to say, "All right, thanks," into the telephone. It hadn't improved much by the time I had put on my clothes and gone downstairs. The clerk told me there was no chance of getting anything to eat in Quesada before seven o'clock.

I went out of the hotel, down the street until it became a dirt road, kept along the road until it forked, and turned into the branch that bent toward the ocean. This branch was never a road from its very beginning, and soon it was nothing but a rocky path climbing sidewise along a rocky ledge that kept pushing closer to the water's edge.

The side of the ledge became steeper and steeper, until the path was simply an irregular shelf on the face of a cliff, six or eight feet wide in places, no more than three in others. Above and behind the path, the cliff rose sixty or seventy feet; below and in front, it slanted down a hundred feet or more to ravel out into the ocean. A breeze from the general direction of China was pushing fog over the top of the cliff, making noisy lather of sea-water at its rocky base.

Rounding a corner where the cliff was steepest—was, in fact, for a hundred yards or so, straight up and down—I stopped to look at a small ragged hole in the path's outer rim. The hole was perhaps six inches across, with fresh loose earth piled in a little semicircle mound on one side of it, scattered on the other side. It wasn't an exciting sight, but it said plainly to even such a city man as I was: *Here, not long ago, a bush was torn up by its roots.*

There was no torn-up bush in sight. I chucked my cigarette away and got down on hands and knees, putting my head over the path's rim, looking down. Twenty feet below I saw it. It was perched on the top of a stunted tree that grew almost parallel to the cliff, fresh brown dirt sticking to its roots.

The next thing that caught my eye was also brown—a soft hat lying upside down between two jagged gray rocks, fifty feet below me, halfway to the water.

I looked down at the bottom of the cliff and saw the feet and legs.

They were a man's feet and legs, in tan shoes and dark trousers. The feet lay on the top of a smooth, water-rounded boulder, lay on their sides, perhaps six inches apart, both pointing to the left. From the feet, the dark-trousered legs slanted down into the water, disappearing beneath the surface a few inches above the knees. That was all I could see from the path.

I went down the cliff, but not at that point. It was a lot too steep there to be tackled by a middle-aged fat man. A couple of hundred yards back, the path had crossed a crooked ravine that creased the cliff diagonally from top to bottom. I returned to the ravine and went down it, stumbling, sliding, sweating and swearing, but reaching the bottom all in one piece, with nothing more serious the matter with me than torn fingers, dirty clothes, and ruined shoes.

The fringe of rock that lay between cliff and ocean wasn't meant to be walked on, but I managed to travel over it most of the way, having to wade only once or twice, and then not up to my knees.

When I came to where the feet and legs lay I had to go waist-deep in the Pacific to lift the body, which rested on its back on the worn slanting side of the boulder, covered from thighs up by frothing water. I got my hands under its armpits, found solid spots for my feet, and lifted.

It was Eric Collinson's body—horribly crushed. There was no back to his head. The water had washed away all blood.

I lugged him out of the water, put him on his back on dry rocks. I couldn't find any marks on him that hadn't apparently been made by the fall. His dripping pockets told me nothing; they held a hundred and fifty-some dollars, a watch, a knife, a gold pen and pencil, papers, letters, and a memoranda book that held nothing informative. There was nothing anywhere in sight to tell me more about his death than the uprooted bush, the hat caught between rocks, and his body had told me.

I left him on the dry rocks, going back to the ravine, panting and heaving myself up it to the path, returning to where the bush had grown. The path was chiefly rough stone. I couldn't find anything on it in the way of significant marks, footprints or the like. I went on.

Presently the cliff began to bend away from the ocean, lowering the path along its side. After another mile there was no cliff at all, merely a brush grown ridge at whose foot the path ran. There was no sun yet. My pants stuck disagreeably to my chilly legs. Water squunched in my torn shoes. I hadn't had any breakfast. I discovered that my cigarettes had got wet. My left knee ached from a twist I had given it sliding down the ravine. I cursed the detective business and slopped on along the path.

It took me away from the sea for a while, across the neck of a wooded point that pushed the ocean back, down into a little valley, up the side of a low hill, and then I saw the house the night clerk had described.

It was a fairly large two-storey building, roof and walls brown-shingled, set on a hump in the ground close to where the ocean came in to take a quarter-mile U-shaped bite out of the coast. The house faced the water. I was behind it. There was nobody in sight. The ground-floor windows were closed, with drawn blinds. The second-storey windows were open. Off to one side were some smaller buildings and a shed.

I went around to the front of the house. Wicker chairs and a table were on the screened front porch. The screened porch-door was hooked on the inside. I rattled it noisily. I rattled it off and on for at least five minutes, and got no response. Then I went around to the rear and knocked on the back door.

My knocking knuckles pushed the door open half a foot. Inside was a dark kitchen and silence. I opened the door wider, knocking on it again, loudly. I called:

"Mrs Collinson."

I knew the girl. When no answer came, I went through the kitchen and a darker dining-room, found a flight of stairs, climbed them, and began poking my head into rooms.

There was nobody in the house. Two bedrooms, bathroom, and a cross between a library and a sitting room made up this floor.

In the bathroom—in the tub—was a large bath-towel stained with blood and mud, both still damp.

In one bedroom a .38 automatic pistol lay in the center of the floor. There was an empty shell close to it, another under a chair across the room, and a faint odor of burnt gunpowder in the air. In one corner of the ceiling was a hole that a .38 bullet could have made; under it, on the floor, a few crumbs of plaster. The bedclothes were smooth and undisturbed. Clothes in the closet, things on the dressing table and in the bureau drawers, told me this was Eric Collinson's bedroom.

Next to it was his wife's, according to the same sort of evidence. Lying on the floor of her clothes closet were a black satin dress, a oncc-white handkerchief, and a pair of black suede slippers, all wet with mud, the handkerchief also wet with blood. Her bed had not been slept in.

On her dressing table was a small piece of thick white paper that had been folded. White powder clung to one crease. I put the end of my tongue to it—morphine.

II

Quesada was awake when I got back there, a little after nine that morning. My pants were very nearly dry. I changed shoes and socks, got a quick breakfast and a dry supply of cigarettes, and asked the clerk—a dapper boy, this one—who was responsible for law and order in Quesada.

"The marshal's Dick Cotton," he told me, "but he went up to the city last night. Ben Roily's deputy sheriff. You can likely find him over at his old man's office."

"Where is that?"

"Just two doors down."

I found it, a one-storey red brick building with wide glass windows labeled *J. King Roily, Real Estate, Employment Agency, Mortgages, Loans, stocks and Bonds, Insurance, Notes, Notary Public, Moving and Storage,* and a lot more that I've forgotten.

Two men were inside, sitting with their feet on a battered desk behind a battered counter. One was a man of fifty plus, with hair, eyes and skin of an indefinite washed-out tan color—an amiable, aimless looking man in shabby clothes. The other was twenty years younger, and in twenty years would look just like the first.

"I'm hunting," I said, "for the deputy sheriff."

"Me," the younger man said, easing his feet from desk to floor. He didn't get up. Instead he put a foot out, hooked a chair by its rounds, pulled it out from the wall, and returned his feet to the desk-top. "Set down. This is Pa," wiggling a thumb at the older man. "You don't have to mind him."

"Know Eric Collinson?" I asked.

"The young fellow honeymooning down at the Tooker place—I didn't know his front name was Eric.

"Eric H. G. Collinson," the older man said. "That's the way I made out the rent receipt for him."

"He's dead," I told them. "He fell off the cliff path last night or this morning—fell or was pushed."

The father looked at the son with round tan eyes. The son looked at me with questioning tan eyes and said:

"Tch.Tch.Tch."

I gave him my card. He read it carefully, turned it over to see that there was nothing on the back, and passed it to his father.

"Go down and take a look at him?" I suggested.

"I guess I ought to," the deputy sheriff agreed, getting up from his chair. He was a larger man than I had supposed, as big as the dead Collinson boy, and, in spite of its slouchiness, his body was full-muscled and trim.

I followed him out to a dusty car in front of the office. Roily senior didn't go with us.

"Somebody told you about it?" the deputy asked when we were riding.

"I stumbled over it. Know who the Collinsons are?"

"Uh-uh. Are they anybody special?"

"Hear about a Dr Riese's murder in San Francisco three weeks ago?"

"I read the paper."

"Mrs Collinson was the Gabrielle Leggett mixed up in that."

"Tch. Tch. Tch," he said.

"And whose father was killed by her stepmother a couple of weeks before that."

"Tch. Tch. Tch," he repeated. "What's the matter with them?"

"A family curse."

"Sure enough?" I didn't know how seriously he meant that. I hadn't got a line on him yet. But, clown or not, he was the deputy sheriff stationed at Quesada, and this was his party.

I gave him the spread-out while we bumped over the lumpy road.

"Mrs Collinson's father was a French artist named Mayenne. In Paris in 1908 he married a British girl named Lily Dain. She had a sister Alice who wanted him. When Lily's and Mayenne's daughter—the present Mrs Collinson—was five her Aunt Alice taught her to play a little game with a pistol, which ended in the child shooting and killing her mother. That's what Aunt Alice had wanted, but the outcome wasn't what she wanted: Mayenne was convicted of the murder and shipped to Devil's Island.

"In 1918 he escaped, roamed South America, Central America and Mexico, having to kill a couple of men, according to his story, to keep from being returned to prison, and finally landed in San Francisco, where he took the name Edgar Leggett and made himself a comfortable fortune with some inventions. Alice Dain and his daughter joined him there, and he and Alice married. He didn't know anything about her part in his first wife's—her sister's—death, and the child had forgotten it all long ago.

"In San Francisco things went along smoothly until a couple of blackmailers showed up, a pair of ex-convict-ex-private-detectives who knew about Leggett's past. Alice Dain—Mrs Leggett then—bought one of them off with some diamonds that didn't belong to her, and the works began to come to light. That's where I first got into it, for the company that had insured the diamonds. Blackmailer number two bumped off number one. When the game got too hot for her, Mrs Leggett killed blackmailer number two, and then her husband, trying to shove all the blame on him. I spoiled that, and she tried to gun her way out of the house, shooting and killing herself in the ensuing tussle.

"Before she passed out of the picture, she did her best to fix things all wrong for the girl; telling her about her part in her mother's death; telling her she was cursed with the bad blood, black soul, and so on, that all the Dains had had; predicting that her life would be black and so would the lives of all who came in contact with her. This youngster Gabrielle is way off in the head. Her step-mother had made her that way—maybe there was something in the Dain inheritance to build on—and had kept her that way; and she fell for the curse stuff. She was engaged to Collinson then, but she wouldn't see him after that—afraid of ruining his life.

"Joseph Haldorn and his wife—running that Temple of the Holy Grail where Riese was murdered later—had the girl on their come-on list; and after her parents were wiped out Haldorn persuaded her to come to the Temple for a week or two. Riese, her physician, seemed to think that letting her go was about the only chance of keeping her from going completely nuts—she was damned close to it, and still is. He—Riese—persuaded Madison Andrews, who's her guardian, or who's handling her affairs anyhow, to O.K. it. She went there and ran into more trouble.

"Haldorn fell in love with her. He already had a wife, but his success in hocus-pocussing his converts had made him think he could get away with anything. Dr Riese came to the Temple every day to see the girl, and presently he discovered that things were being done to her, that she was in danger there. He was foolish enough to let Haldorn know what he had discovered. Haldorn drugged him, put him on the altar, and worked on Gabrielle's mulatto maid—Minnie Hershey—with visions and voices until the dinge went down and slaughtered Riese, under the impression that he was Satan.

"The Holy Grail racket blew up then. I killed Haldorn in the blow-up. His wife, the maid, and one of the Haldorns' assistants—Tom Fink—are in prison now, waiting trial for Riese's murder. Collinson took advantage of the excitement to grab the girl, smother her objections, and carry her off to Reno, where they were married. They had to come back to San Francisco for the inquest, and the girl was in no shape—mentally or physically—for much traveling, so they came down here to honeymoon."

I took Collinson's telegram and note out of my pocket, held them where the deputy could read them without taking his hands from the wheel, and told him what I had done and seen since my arrival in Quesada.

He nodded woodenly, saying:

"Tch. Tch. Tch. He might of been pushed off, all right, but what made you say you thought he had?"

I hadn't said so, but I let it go at that.

"He sent for me. Something was wrong. Outside of that, too many things have happened around the girl for me to believe in accidents."

"There's the curse, though," he reminded me.

"Yeah," I agreed, studying his vague face, still unable to decide whether he was serious. "But the trouble with it is it's worked out too well so far. It's the first one I've ever run across that did."

He frowned over that for a couple of minutes, and then stopped the car, saying, "We'll have to leave the car here. The road ain't so good the rest of the way." None of it had been. "Still and all, you do hear of them working out. There's things that happen that make a fellow think there's things in life—in the world—that he don't know much about." He frowned again as we set off afoot, and found a word he liked. "It's inscrutable," he said.

I let that go at that.

He led the way up the cliff path, stopping of his own accord where the bush had been uprooted. I hadn't said anything about that detail. I didn't say anything while he stared down at Collinson's body at the foot of the cliff, looked searchingly up and down the cliff face, and then went up and down the path, bent far down, his tan eyes examining the ground.

He wandered around that way for ten minutes or more, then straightened up and said:

"There don't seem to be nothing here. Let's go down."

I started to go back to the ravine, but he said there was a better way ahead. There was. We went down it to the dead man.

Rolly looked from the corpse up at the path-edge and complained:

"I don't hardly see how he could have landed just that away."

"He didn't. I pulled him out of the water," I explained, showing the deputy exactly how the body had been placed.

"That's more like it." He went around almost on hands and knees, looking at, touching, moving, rocks, pebbles and sand. I sat on a boulder, smoked, and watched him. He didn't seem to have any luck.

When he had finished, we climbed to the path again and went on to the Collinsons' house. I showed him the stained towel, handkerchief, dress and slippers; the paper that had held morphine, on the girl's dressing table; the gun on Collinson's floor, the bullet-hole in the ceiling, and the two empty shells on the floor.

"The shell under the chair is where it was," I said, "but that one over in the corner was here, close to the gun when I left."

"What good would moving it over there do anybody?" he objected.

"None that I know of, but it's been moved."

That didn't interest him. He was looking at the ceiling. He said:

"Two shots and one hole. I wonder. Maybe out the window."

He went back to Gabrielle Collinson's bedroom and examined the mud-stained dress. There were some torn places down near the bottom, but no bullet holes. He put the dress back on the closet floor and picked up the morphine paper from her dressing table.

"What do you suppose this is doing here?"

"She uses it," I said. "It's one of the things her step-mother did for her."

"Tch. Tch. Tch. Kind of looks like she might of done it."

"Yeah?"

"You know it does. She's a dope fiend, ain't she? They had had trouble, and he sent for you, and—" He broke off, pursed his lips, then asked: "What time you reckon he was killed?"

"I don't know. Probably last night, on his way back from waiting for me."

"You was in the hotel all night?"

"From eleven-something till a little after five this morning. Of course I could have sneaked out long enough to pull a murder between those times."

"I didn't mean nothing like that," he said. "I was just wondering. What kind of looking woman is this Mrs Collinson. I never saw her."

"She's about twenty; five feet tall; looks thinner than she really is; light brown hair, short and curly, big eyes that are sometimes green and sometimes brown; very white skin; hardly any forehead; small mouth and teeth; pointed chin; no lobes on her ears, and they're pointed at the top; only four toes on each foot; been sick for a couple of months and looks it."

"Oughtn't to be hard to pick her out," he said, and began poking into drawers, closets, trunks, and so on. I had poked into them during my first visit to the house, and hadn't found anything either.

"Don't look like she did any packing, or took much with her," he decided when he came back to where I was standing by the dressing table. He pointed a thick finger at the monogrammed silver toilet set on the table. "What's the G. D. L. for?"

"Her name was Gabrielle Something Leggett before she was married."

"Oh, yes," he said. "Went away in the car, I reckon. Huh?"

"Did he have one down here?"

"He used to come to town in a Chrysler roadster when he didn't walk. She could only of took it out by the East road. We'll go out that away and see."

Outside, I waited while he made some circles around the house, finding nothing. In front of the shed where a car had been kept, Roily examined the ground and gave his verdict: "Drove out this morning." I took his word for it.

We walked along a dirt road to a gravel one, and along the gravel road perhaps a mile to a gray house that stood among a group of red farm buildings. A small-boned, high-shouldered man with a slight limp was oiling a pump behind the house. Roily called him Debro.

"Sure, Ben," he replied to Roily's questions, "she went by here about seven this morning, going like a bat out of hell. There wasn't anybody else in the car."

"How was she dressed?" I asked.

"She didn't have on any hat and a tan coat."

I asked him what he knew about the Collinsons; he was their nearest neighbor. He didn't know anything about them. He had talked to Collinson two or three times, and thought him a nice enough young fellow. Once he had taken the missus over to call on Mrs Collinson, but Collinson had told them she was lying down, not feeling well. None of the Debros had ever seen her except at a distance, walking or driving with her husband.

"I don't suppose there's anybody around here that's talked to her," he wound up, "except of course Mary Nunez."

"Mary working for them?" the deputy asked.

"Yes. What's the matter, Ben? Something the matter over there?"

"He fell off the cliff last night, and she's gone away without saying anything to anybody."

Debro whistled. Roily went into the house to use Debro's phone, reporting to the sheriff at the county seat. I remained outside with Debro, trying to get more—if only his opinions—out of him. All I got were expressions of amazement.

"We'll go over and see Mary Nunez," the deputy said when he had finished reporting, and then, when we had left Debro, crossed the road, and were walking through a field toward a cluster of trees: "Funny she wasn't there."

"Who is she?"

"A Alex. Lives down in the hollow with the flock of them. Her man, Pedro, is doing a life-stretch in San Quentin for killing a bootlegger named Dunne in a hijacking two-three years back."

"Local?"

"Uh-huh. Down in that cove in front of the Collinsons' place."

We went through the trees and down a slope to where half a dozen shacks—shaped, sized and red-leaded to resemble box cars—lined the side of a stream, with vegetable gardens spread out behind them.

In front of one of the shacks a shapeless Mexican woman in a pink-checkered dress sat on an empty canned-soup box, smoking a corncob pipe and nursing a brown baby. Ragged and dirty children played between the buildings, with ragged and dirty mongrels helping them make noise. In one of the gardens a brown man in overalls that had once been blue was barely moving a hoe.

The children stopped playing to watch Roily and me cross the stream on conveniently placed stones. The dogs came yapping down to meet us, snarling and snapping around us until chased by one of the boys. We stopped in front of the woman. The deputy grinned down at the baby at her breast and said:

"Well, ain't he getting to be the husky son-of-a-gun?"

The woman removed the pipe from her mouth long enough to complain stolidly:

"Colic all the time."

"Tch. Tch. Tch. Where's Mary Nunez?"

The pipe-stem was pointed at the next shack.

"I thought she was working for them people at the looker place," he said.

"Sometimes," she replied indifferently.

We went to the shack. An old woman in a gray wrapper had come to the door, watching us while stirring something in a yellow bowl.

"Where's Mary?" the deputy asked her.

She spoke over her shoulder into the shack's dark interior, and moved aside to let another woman take her place in the doorway. This other woman was short and solidly built, somewhere in her early thirties, with intelligent dark eyes in a wide flat face. She held a dark blanket together around her throat. The blanket hung to the floor all around her.

"Howdy, Mary," the deputy greeted her. "Why ain't you over to Collinson's today?"

"I'm sick, Mr Roily." She spoke without accent. "Chills—so I stayed home."

"Tch. Tch. Tch. That's too bad. Have you had the doc?"

She said she hadn't. Roily said she ought to. She said she didn't need him; she often had chills. Roily said that might be so, but it was best to play safe and have them kind of things looked into. She said yes, but doctors took so much money, and it was bad enough being sick without having to pay for it. He said in the long run it was likely to cost folks more not having a doctor than having him. I began to think they were going to keep it up all day, but presently he brought the talk around to the Collinsons, asking the woman about her work there.

She told us Collinson had hired her two weeks ago, when he took the house. She went there each morning at nine o'clock—they never got up before ten—cooked their meals, did the housework, and left after washing the dinner dishes, usually somewhere around half-past seven.

She seemed surprised enough at the news that Collinson had been killed and his wife had gone away, but there was no way of telling whether she was as surprised as she looked. Collinson had gone out by himself, for a walk he said, after dinner last night. That was at about half-past six; dinner, for no especial reason, had been a little early.

She couldn't—or wouldn't—tell us anything that would help us guess why Collinson had sent for me. She knew very little about them, except that Mrs Collinson didn't seem happy. She—Mary Nunez—had it all figured out: Mrs Collinson loved someone else, but her parents had made her marry Collinson, and so, of course, Collinson had been killed by the other man, with whom his widow had then run off.

I got her away from this romance and asked her about the Collinsons' visitors. She said she had never seen any. Roily asked her if the Collinsons ever quarreled. She said they did, often, and were never on very good terms: Mrs Collinson didn't like to have him near her and several times had told him that if he didn't go away from her and stay away she would kill him. I tried to pin the woman down to details, asking what had led up to these threats, how they had been worded; but she wouldn't be pinned down. All she remembered positively, she said, was that Mrs Collinson had threatened to kill her husband if he didn't go away from her.

"That pretty well settles that," Roily said contentedly when we had forded the stream again and were climbing the slope toward Debro's.

"What settles what?"

"That his wife killed him."

"Think she did?"

"So do you."

I said: "No."

Roily stopped walking and looked at me with vaguely worried eyes.

"How can you say that?" he remonstrated. "Ain't she a dope fiend, and crazy in the bargain, according to your own way of telling it? Didn't she run away? Wasn't them things she left behind torn and dirty and bloody? Didn't she threaten to kill him so much that he sent for you?"

"Mary didn't hear threats. They were warnings—about the curse. Gabrielle really believes in it, and she thought enough of him to try to save him from it. I've been through that before with her. That's why she wouldn't have married him if he hadn't have carried her off while she was more rattled than usual—and she was afraid on that account afterwards."

"But who's going to believe—?"

"I'm not asking anybody to believe anything," I growled, walking on again. "I'm just telling you what I believe. And one of the things I believe is that Mary's a liar when she says she didn't go there this morning. Maybe she didn't have anything to do with Collinson's death. Maybe she simply went there, found her employers gone, saw the bloody things and the gun, kicked that empty shell across the room in her excitement, without noticing it, or not bothering about it if she did notice it; then beat it and fixed up that chills story just to keep out of the whole affair, having had enough of that sort of thing when her husband was sent over. Maybe not. Anyway, I want some proof before I start believing that her chills just happened to hit her this special morning."

"Well," the deputy sheriff said, "if she didn't have nothing to do with his death, what difference does all that make anyway?"

All the answers I could think up to that were both profane and insulting. So I kept them to myself.

At Debro's again, we borrowed a loose-jointed touring car of at least three different makes, and ran on down the East road, trying to trace the girl in the Chrysler. Our first stop was at the farmhouse of a man named Claude Baker. He was a lanky, sallow man with an angular face three or fours days behind the razor. His wife was probably younger than he, but looked older—a tired and faded thin woman who might have been pretty at one time. The oldest of their six children was a bow-legged, freckled girl of ten. The youngest was a fat and noisy infant in its first year. Some of the in-betweens were boys, some girls, but they all had colds in their heads. The whole Baker family came out on the unpainted front porch to receive us. They hadn't seen anything, they said; they were never out of bed as early as seven o'clock. They knew the Collinsons by sight, but knew nothing about them. The Bakers asked lots of questions.

Shortly beyond the Baker house, the road changed from gravel to asphalt. Up to that point the Chrysler's tire-marks had told us that it was the last car to travel this road.

Two miles from Baker's we stopped in front of a small bright green house surrounded by rose bushes. Roily bawled:

"Harvel! Hey, Harvel!"

A big-boned man of thirty-five or so came to the door and said, "Hullo, Ben," and came down the walk to us. His features, like his voice, were heavy; he moved and spoke deliberately. His name was Whidden. Roily asked him if he had seen the Chrysler.

"They went past, hitting it up, around a quarter after seven this morning," he said. "Yes, I saw them."

"They?" I asked, while Roily asked: "Them?"

"There was a man and a woman—maybe a girl. I didn't get a good look at them—just saw them whizz past. She was driving—a kind of small girl or woman, with brown hair. The man was maybe forty, and didn't look like he was so damned tall. Pinkish face, he had, and gray coat and hat."

"Ever see Mrs Collinson?" I asked.

"The bride living down the cove? No. I seen him, but not her. Was that her?"

I said we thought it was.

"The man wasn't him. He was somebody I never seen before."

"Know him if you saw him again?"

"I reckon I would if I saw him going past like that."

Four miles beyond Whidden's house we found the Chrysler.

It was a foot or two off the road, on the left-hand side, standing on all fours with its radiator jammed into a eucalyptus tree. All its glass was shattered, and the front third of its metal was pretty well crumpled. It was empty. There was no blood in it. The deputy and I seemed to be the only people in the vicinity.

We walked up and down and around in circles, straining our eyes at the ground, and when we got through we knew what we had known when we started—the Chrysler had run into a eucalyptus tree.

There were tire-marks on the road, and marks that could have been footprints on the ground by the car; but it was possible to find the same sort of marks almost anywhere along the road; and these didn't tell us anything. We got back in our borrowed car and drove on, asking questions wherever we found someone to ask; and all the answers were no.

"What about this fellow Baker?" I asked Roily as we turned around to go back. "Debro saw her alone in the car. There was a man with her by the time she got to Whidden's. The Bakers saw nothing and it was in their territory that the man would have had to join her."

The deputy scratched his chin and said:

"Well, that could of happened, couldn't it?"

"Yeah, but it might be just as well to go back and talk to them some more."

"If you want to," he said without enthusiasm. "But don't be dragging me into any arguments. He's my wife's brother."

That made it different.

"What sort of man is he?" I asked.

"Mort's kind of shiftless all right. Like the old man says, he don't raise nothing much but kids on that place of his, but I never heard tell that he did anybody any harm."

"If you say he's all right," I lied, "that's enough for me. We won't bother him."

III

Sheriff Feeney—fat and florid, with a lot of brown mustache—and Prosecuting Attorney Vernon—sharp-featured, aggressive, and hungry for fame—came over from the county seat. They listened to our stories, looked the ground over, and agreed with Roily that Gabrielle Collinson killed her husband. When Marshal Dick Cotton—a pompous, unintelligent man in his forties—returned from San Francisco, he added his vote to theirs. The coroner and his jury were of the same opinion, though officially they limited themselves to the well known "person or persons unknown" with recommendations involving the girl.

Little that was new came out at the inquest. The pistol found in Collinson's room was identified as his. No finger-prints had been found on it. There was a suspicion in a few official minds that I had perhaps seen to that, but nobody said anything definite about it.

The time of Collinson's death was placed between eight and nine o'clock Friday night; the cause, his fall. No marks not apparently caused by it had been found on or in him.

Mary Nunez stuck to her story of being kept home by chills. She produced a flock of Mexican witnesses to back it up. I couldn't find any to knock holes in it.

The marshal's wife—a frail young woman with a weak pretty face and nice shy manner, who worked in the telegraph office—said Collinson had come in early Friday morning to wire me. He was pale and shaky, with dark-rimmed, bloodshot eyes. She had supposed he was drunk, though she had smelled no alcohol.

Collinson's father and brother came down from San Francisco. Hubert Collinson was a big calm man who had taken three or four millions out of Pacific Coast timber and looked capable of taking as many more as he wanted. Laurence Collinson was a year or two older than his dead brother, and much like him in looks. Both Collinsons were careful to say nothing which would suggest that they thought Gabrielle had been responsible for Eric's death, but there was little doubt that they did think so.

The senior Collinson's instructions to me were simply:

"Go ahead. Get to the bottom of it."

Madison Andrews—Gabrielle's guardian—also had come down from San Francisco. He and I had a talk in my room in the hotel. He sat on a chair by the window, cut a cube of tobacco off a yellowish plug, put it in his mouth, ruffled his ragged white mustache, and decided that Collinson had committed suicide.

I sat on the side of the bed, set fire to a Fatima, and contradicted him:

"He wouldn't have torn up a bush as he went over if he was going willingly."

"Then it was an accident. He missed his footing in the dark."

"I've stopped believing in accidents where Gabrielle's concerned," I said. "And he had sent me an S.O.S."

His gaunt body leaned forward in his chair. His eyes were hard and watchful. He was a lawyer cross-examining a witness.

"You think she was responsible?"

I wasn't ready to go that far. I said:

"He was murdered. He was murdered by—I told you three weeks ago that we weren't through with that damned curse."

"Yes. I remember." He didn't quite sneer. "You advanced a theory that the curse was a person, but, as I recall it, your theory didn't include his or her name or motive. Don't you think that deficiency has a tendency to make your theory a little—uh—vaporous?"

"No. Her father, step-mother, physician, and husband are killed, one after the other, inside of two months. I haven't got enough faith in chance to think that just happened to happen, with no connection between the murders."

"Preposterous," he said, irritable now. "We know about her parents' deaths, and about Riese's, and we know there was no connection between them. We know that those responsible for Riese's death are now either dead or in prison, waiting trial. There's no use saying there has to be a connection between them when we know there isn't."

"We don't know anything of the sort," I insisted. "All we know is that we haven't found any connection. Who profits by keeping the girl in trouble?"

"Not a single person, so far as I know."

"Suppose she died? Who would get her money?"

"I don't know. I dare say there are distant relatives in France or England."

"That doesn't get us very far," I growled. "Anyway, nobody's tried to kill her so far. It's her friends who get the knock-off."

The lawyer reminded me that there was no way of knowing whether anybody had tried to kill her—or had succeeded—until we found her. I couldn't argue with him about that.

Her trail still ended where the eucalyptus tree had stopped the Chrysler. Andrews had offered a thousand dollars reward for information that would enable us to find her. Hubert Collinson had added another thousand, with an additional twenty-five hundred for the arrest and conviction of his son's murderer. Half the population of the county had turned bloodhound. Anywhere you went within ten miles of Quesada you could find men walking, or even crawling, around searching fields, paths, hills and valleys for clues; and in the woods you were likely to find more amateur sleuths than trees.

Her latest photographs had been copied and distributed widely. The San Francisco newspapers gave the whole thing a big play; this was the third affair of the sort that she had figured in very recently, and the "curse" was eggs-in-the-coffee for feature writers. I had all the San Francisco Continental operatives who could be pulled off other jobs—six—searching the exits from Quesada, hunting, questioning, and finding nothing. Radio broadcasting stations helped. The Continental's branches in other cities, the police everywhere, had been called on for assistance.

And all this effort had brought us nothing.

I had to return to San Francisco Monday morning for Tommy the Rags' trial. That kept me until noon, by which time I had finished my share in sending him back to Folsom. From the court I went down to the agency. There was a memorandum on my desk:

Phone Owen Fitzstephan, Prospect 2888.

Fitzstephan was a lanky, sorrel-haired novelist who had given me a lot of help on a fake medium job in New York some years before. I had run into him again in San Francisco when I was working on the job in which Gabrielle's father and step-mother had been killed. He had known them, and had given me more help in swinging that job. So now I didn't waste any time getting him on the wire.

"I've a puzzle for you, or perhaps the solution to a puzzle," he said; "and if you can come up now I'll supplement it with luncheon. Is that enough to bring you?"

I said it was, rode up Nob Hill on a cable car, and within fifteen minutes was going into his apartment.

"All right, spring the puzzle," I said as we sat down in his paper-magazine - and book-littered living-room.

"Any trace of Gabrielle yet?" he asked.

"No. Spring the puzzle," I repeated. "Please don't be literary with me. Don't start with an introduction, and lead up to your climax step by step, creating a lot of suspense and the like. I'm too crude to be impressed that way—it'll only give me a bellyache."

"Oh, very well, then," he said, trying to make his sleepy gray eyes and wide humorous mouth register disappointment combined with disgust. "You'll always be what you are. Have it your own way. At twenty minutes past one Saturday morning—mark my accuracy—my phone rang. A man's voice asked: 'Is this Fitzstephan?' I said, 'Yes,' and then the voice said, 'Well, I've killed him.'

"I'm sure of those words, though they weren't very clear. There was a lot of noise on the line and his voice seemed very distant. I asked, 'Killed who? Who is this?' but I couldn't understand any of his answer except something about money. He repeated 'money' several times. There were some people here—the Marquards, Laura Joines, Curt, and some girl he had brought—and we had been in the middle of a wild argument over the value of immediacy in art. I was anxious to get back to it, and I couldn't make out what the voice on the phone was talking about; so I decided it was a drunken joker, or something of the sort, and hung up.

"Yesterday morning, when I read about Collinson's death in the *Chronicle*, I began to wonder if the phone conversation had anything to do with it. I was at Pebble Beach, having gone down Saturday afternoon for a week-end with the Colemans. I came back last night, intending to tell you about it. This was in my mail this morning."

He picked up an envelope from the table and tossed it over to me. It was a cheap and shiny white envelope of the kind you can buy anywhere. Its corners were dark and curled, as if it had been carried in a pocket for a week or so before being used. Fitzstephan's name and address had been printed on it, with a hard pencil, by someone who was a rotten printer, or who wanted to give that impression. It was postmarked San Francisco, nine o'clock Saturday morning.

Inside was a soiled and crookedly torn piece of brown wrapping paper with one sentence—as poorly printed with pencil as the envelope—on it.

Anybody that wants Mrs Cullison can have same by paying $10,000.

There was no salutation, no signature.

"She was seen driving away from the house as late as seven-something that morning," I said. "This was mailed here, eighty miles away, in time to be taken from the box in the first morning collection. Funny it should have been sent to you instead of Andrews, who is in charge of her affairs, or old man Collinson, whose daughter-in-law she was, and who's got the most money."

"It is funny and it isn't." The sleepiness had gone out of the novelist's eyes. His lean face was eager. "There may be a point of light there. I've probably told you that I spent two months in Quesada last spring, finishing *The Wall of Ashdod.* I lived in a little two-room house a mile or two from the town, up in this direction though, on the shore. I knew about the Tooker place being vacant, and when Collinson, after their return from Reno, told me he wanted a quiet place to take Gabrielle, I suggested that he go there—if it was still unoccupied—and gave him a letter to a real estate dealer named Roily who had the renting of it.

"Now look at this letter. My name is correctly spelled on the envelope, but Collinson is spelled C-u-l-l-i-s-o-n, the way it is pronounced. The letter was sent to me, but starts off, *Any body that,* as if I were to pass the information on to whoever was interested. Does all that mean anything?"

I nodded, saying:

"It might mean that the sender was a native of Quesada who knew you better than he knew the Collinsons, who knew you had sent them down there, who knew your address but didn't know how to reach any of the girl's connections direct."

"Or it might mean," the novelist warned me, "that the sender wanted us to think those things."

"Not likely," I decided. "Except for the wooziness of the printing, which booze, excitement, or both, could have been responsible for, the whole thing looks genuine. It's simple. When your crook gets subtle he usually overdoes it. I'm willing to string along with our first guess. We'll check up your acquaintances down there. J. King Roily would be the first suspect, but he doesn't look like a murderer and abductor to me, and he knew how Collinson was spelled. However, he's the one man we're sure knew you had sent Collinson down there, so he'll have to be pried into. Who next?"

Fitzstephan made a hopeless gesture with his thin hands. "I knew everybody."

"Which of them knew your address here?"

"None that I know of, but my name's in the phone book."

"Who did you know there," I tried again, "that might be capable of this sort of trick?"

That brought me a long discourse in which it was proven that every man who ever lived was a potential criminal, needing only the right set of circumstances to make him an actual one; that character was a thing which didn't exist, since all men had every trait that any man had, the difference in people being only a matter of which attitude they happened to strike; and that therefore any man in Quesada, or out of it, was, given the necessary circumstances, capable of this sort of trick.

I listened while working on my share of the cocktails, chicken-liver omelette, salad, rolls and coffee that Fitzstephan's Chinese boy had put between us.

"That's nice," I grumbled when the novelist had finished his speech, "and for all I know there may even be some sense in it, but it doesn't help find the girl, and it doesn't help put anybody in jail, so what good is it to me?"

He accused me of having the brains of a detective, and said:

"I haven't said anything to anybody about the phone call and letter—except that I mentioned the call to the people who were here when it came, but that was before I took it seriously. I saved it for you. Should I go to the police now? Or will you take care of that? Would it do any good if I went to Quesada?"

"It might. I'd like to have you down there to go over the ground with me. You know the place, and you're not a bad hand at snooping except when you're being literary. Can you go down for a day?"

"Surely. I was angling for an invitation. We'll drive down the first thing in the morning?"

I thought I had to get back on the job that night. Fitzstephan had a date he couldn't break. He promised to meet me in the Sunset Hotel in the morning.

IV

I went back to the office and put in a Quesada call. I couldn't get hold of Vernon Roily, or the sheriff. I talked to Cotton, giving him the information I had got from Fitzstephan, promising to produce the novelist for questioning the next morning. The marshal said the search for the girl was still going on, and still without results.

Reports had come in that the girl had been seen—practically simultaneously—in Los Angeles, Eureka, Carson City, Portland, Tijuana, Sacramento, Ogden, San Jose, Denver, and Vancouver. All except the absolutely ridiculous ones were being run out.

The telephone company could tell me that Owen Fitzstephan's phone call had not been a long distance call, and that nobody in Quesada had called San Francisco either Friday night or early Saturday morning.

I went over to Madison Andrews' office, telling him about the Fitzstephan angle, giving him our explanation of how the novelist had been brought into the affair. He nodded his bony, white-thatched head and said:

"And whether that's the true explanation or not, the county authorities will now have to give up their absurd theory that Gabrielle killed Eric."

I shook my head sideways.

"What?" he asked explosively.

"They're going to think that this was cooked up to clear her," I predicted.

"Is that what you think?" His jaws got lumpy in front of his ears, and his white eyebrows came down over his narrowed eyes.

"I hope you didn't, because if it's a trick it's a damned childish one."

"How could it be?" he blustered. "Don't talk nonsense. None of us knew anything then. The body hadn't been found when—"

"Yeah," I agreed, "and that's why, if it turns out to have been a trick, it'll hang Gabrielle."

"I don't understand you," he said disagreeably. "One minute you're talking about somebody persecuting the girl, and the next minute you're acting as if you thought she was the murderer. Just what do you think?"

"Both can be true," I replied no less disagreeably. "And what difference docs it make what I think? It'll be up to the jury when she's found. The question now is, what are you going to do about that ten-thousand-dollar demand, if it's on the level?"

"There's nothing I can do. The letter doesn't say anything."

"Except that you're to get ten thousand dollars ready. Will you?"

"What I'm going to do," he said stubbornly, "is increase the reward for finding her, with an additional reward for the arrest of her abductor."

"That's the wrong play," I assured him. "Enough reward money has been posted. The only way to handle a kidnapping is to come across. I don't like that any more than you do, but it's the only way. Uncertainty, disappointment, fear, nervousness, can turn even a mild kidnapper into a maniac. Buy the girl free, and then do your fighting; but pay what's asked when it's asked."

He tugged at his ragged mustache, his jaw set obstinately, his eyes worried. But the jaw won out.

"I'm damned if I'll submit," he said.

"That's your business." I got up and reached for my hat. "Mine's finding Collinson's murderer, and having Gabrielle killed is more likely to help me than not."

He didn't say anything.

I went down to Hubert Collinson's offices. He wasn't in. I told Laurence Collinson my story and asked him to urge his father to put up the ten thousand dollars.

"That's hardly necessary," he said immediately. "Of course we shall pay whatever is required to secure her safe return."

I caught the 5:25 train south. It put me in Poston, a dusty town twice Quesada's size, at 7:30, and a rattletrap stage, in which I was the only passenger, got me to my destination half an hour later, as a light rain began trickling down.

Jack Santos, a reporter on the San Francisco *Bulletin,* came out of the telegraph office while I was leaving the stage.

"Hello," he said. "Anything new?"

"Maybe, but I'll have to give it to Vernon first. He still here?"

"Up in his room, or he was ten minutes ago. You don't mean the kidnap letter that somebody got?"

"Yeah. He's already given it out?"

"Cotton started to, but Vernon headed him off, told us to let it alone."

"Why?"

"No reason at all except that Cotton was giving it to us." Santos pulled the corners of his thin mouth down. "It's gotten down to a contest between Vernon, Feeney and Cotton, to see who can get his picture and name printed most."

"They been doing anything besides that?"

"How can they?" he asked disgustedly. "They spend ten hours a day trying to make the front page, ten more trying to keep the others from making it, and they've got to sleep some time."

In the hotel I gave "nothing new" to a couple of more reporters, registered, left my bag in my room, and went down the hall to 204.

Vernon opened the door when I knocked. He was alone, and apparently had been reading the newspapers that made a pink, green and white pile on the bed. The room was blue-gray with cigar smoke.

This prosecuting attorney was a thirty-year-old dark-eyed man who carried his chin up and out so that it was more prominent than nature had intended, bared all his teeth when he spoke, and was very conscious of being a go-getter.

He shook my hand briskly and said:

"I'm glad you're back. Come in. Sit down. Are there any new developments?"

"Cotton pass you the dope I gave him?"

"Yes." He posed in front of me, hands in pockets, feet far apart. "What importance do you attach to it?"

"I advised Andrews to get the money ready. He wouldn't. The Collinsons will."

"They will," he said, as if confirming a guess I had made. "And?" He held his lips back so that his teeth remained exposed.

"Here's the letter." I took it out of my pocket and handed it to him. "Fitzstephan will be down in the morning."

He nodded emphatically, carried the letter closer to the light, and examined it and its envelope minutely. When he had finished he tossed it contemptuously to the table.

"Obviously a fraud," he said. "Now what, precisely, is this Fitzstephans's—is that the name?—story?"

I told him, word for word. When I had finished, he clicked his teeth together, turned to the telephone, and told someone to tell Feeney that he—Mr Vernon, the prosecuting attorney—wished to see him immediately.

Ten minutes later the sheriff came in wiping rain off his big brown mustache.

Vernon jerked a thumb at me, and ordered:

"Tell him."

I repeated what Fitzstephan had told me. The sheriff listened with an attentiveness that turned his florid face almost purple and had him panting. When I had finished, the prosecuting attorney snapped his fingers and said:

"Very well. He claims there were people in his apartment when the phone call came. Make a note of their names. He claims to have been at Pebble Beach over the week-end, with the—who were they? Colemans? Very well. Sheriff, see that those things are checked up at once. We'll see how much of his story is true."

I didn't argue with them, but gave the sheriff the names Fitzstephan had given me. Feeney wrote them down on the back of a laundry list and puffed out to get the county's crime detecting machinery going on them.

Vernon hadn't anything to tell me. I left him to his newspapers and went downstairs. The effeminate night clerk beckoned me over to the desk and said:

"Mr Santos asked me to tell you that services are being held in his room tonight."

I thanked the clerk and went up to Santos' room. He, three other newshounds and a photographer were there. The game was stud. I was sixteen dollars ahead at half-past twelve, when I was called to the phone to listen to the prosecuting attorney's aggressive voice:

"Can you come to my room immediately?"

"Yeah." I gathered up my hat and coat, telling Santos, "Cash me in. Important call. I always manage to have them when I get a little ahead of the game."

"Vernon?" he asked as he counted my chips.

"Yeah."

"It can't be much," he sneered, "or he'd have sent for Red, too," nodding at the photographer, "so tomorrow's readers could see him holding it in his hand."

V

Cotton, Feeney and Roily were with the prosecuting attorney. Cotton—a medium-sized man with a round dull face dimpled in the chin—was dressed in wet and muddy black rubber hat, slicker and boots. He stood in the middle of the floor, and his round eyes looked very proud of their owner.

Feeney, straddling a chair, was playing with his mustache. His florid face was sulky. Roily stood beside him rolling a cigarette, looking vaguely amiable as usual.

Vernon closed the door behind me and said irritably:

"Cotton thinks he's discovered something. He thinks—"

Cotton came forward, chest first, interrupting:

"I don't think nothing. I know durned well—"

Vernon snapped his fingers sharply between the marshal and me, saying just as snappishly:

"Never mind that. We'll go out there and see."

I stopped at my room for raincoat, gun and flashlight. We went downstairs and climbed into a muddy car. Cotton drove. Vernon sat beside him. The rest of us sat in back. Rain beat on the top and curtains, and leaked through cracks.

"A hell of a night to be chasing pipe dreams," the sheriff grumbled, trying to dodge a leak.

"Flick'd do a lot better to mind his own business," Roily agreed. "What's he got to do with anything outside of Quesada?"

"If he'd mind his business there better he wouldn't have to worry so much about what happens down the shore," Feeney said, and he and his deputy sniggered together.

Whatever point there was to this conversation was over my head. I asked:

"What does he think he is up to?"

"Nothing," the sheriff told me. "You'll see that it's nothing, and, by God, I'm going to give him a piece of my mind. I don't know what's the matter with Vernon, paying any attention to him at all."

That didn't mean anything to me. I peeped out between the curtains. Rain and darkness kept me from seeing any scenery, but I had an idea that we were headed for some point on the East road. It was a rotten ride—wet, noisy, and bumpy.

It ended in as dark, wet, and muddy a spot as any we had gone through. Cotton switched off the lights and got out, the rest of us following, slipping and slopping in wet clay up to our ankles.

"This is too damned much," the sheriff complained.

Vernon started to say something, but the marshal was walking away, down the road. We plodded after him, keeping together more by the sound of our feet squashing in the mud than by sight. It was black.

Presently we left the road, struggled over a high wire fence, and went on with less mud under our feet, but slippery grass. We climbed a hill. Wind blew rain down it into our faces. The sheriff was panting. I was sweating. We reached the top of the hill, and went down the other side, with the rustle of sea-water on rocks ahead of us. Rocks began crowding grass out of our path as the descent got steeper.

Once Cotton slipped to his knees, tripping Vernon, who saved himself from a fall by grabbing me. The sheriff's panting was almost a sobbing. We turned to the left, going along in single file, with the surf close beside us. We turned to the left again, climbed a slope, and halted under a low shed without walls—a wooden roof propped on a dozen posts. Ahead of us a larger building made a black blot against an almost black sky.

Cotton whispered: "Wait till I see if his car's here."

He went away leaving us to wait.

The sheriff blew out his breath and grunted:

"Damn such an expedition."

Roily sighed.

The marshal returned, jubilant.

"It ain't there, so he ain't here. Come on, it'll get us out of the rain, anyways."

We followed him up a muddy path to the black house, up on what seemed to be its back porch. We stood there while he got a window open, clambered through it, and unlocked the door.

Our flashlights, which we used for the first time now, showed us a small, neat kitchen. We went in, muddying its floor.

Cotton was the only member of the party who showed any enthusiasm. His face, from dimpled chin to forehead, was the face of a master-of-ceremonies who is about to spring what he is sure is going to be a delightful surprise. Vernon regarded him skeptically, Feeney disgustedly, Roily indifferently. I didn't know what we were there for, so I suppose I regarded him curiously.

It turned out that we were there to search the house.

We did it, or at least Cotton did it while the rest of us pretended to help him. It was a small house. There was only one room besides the kitchen on the ground floor, and only one—a half-storey bedroom—above. A grocer's bill and a tax receipt in a table drawer told me whose house we were in—Harvey Whidden's. He was the bigboned deliberate man who had told Roily and me of seeing a man in the car with Gabrielle.

We finished the ground floor with a blank score and went up to the bedroom.

There after ten minutes of poking around we found something. Roily pulled it out from between bed-slats and mattress. It was a small flat bundle wrapped in a white towel.

Cotton dropped the mattress which he had been holding up for the deputy to peep under and helped the rest of us crowd around Roily's package. Vernon took it from the deputy and unrolled it on the bed.

Inside the towel there were a package of hair pins, a lace-edged white handkerchief, a silver hair brush and comb engraved G. D. L. and a pair of black kid gloves small and feminine.

I was more surprised than anybody else seemed to be.

"G. D. L.," I said to be saying something, "could be Gabrielle Something Leggett—Mrs Collinson's name before she was married."

Cotton said triumphantly: "You bet it could."

A harsh voice said from the door:

"Have you got a search warrant? You know what it is if you ain't. Burglary, and you know it. Where's your warrant?"

It was Harvey Whidden. His big body in a yellow slicker filled the doorway. His heavy face was dark with anger.

Vernon began:

"Whidden, I—"

The marshal screamed: "It's him!" and pulled a gun from under his coat.

I pushed his arm as he fired at the man in the doorway.

The bullet went into a wall.

Whidden yelled something that the noise of the shot drowned. There was more astonishment than anger in his face now. He jumped out of the doorway and ran downstairs.

Cotton, partly upset by my push, straightened himself up, cursed me, and ran out after Whidden.

Vernon, Feeney and Roily stood staring after him.

I said:

"This is a lot of fun, but it makes no sense to me. What's it all about?"

Nobody told me. I said:

"This comb and brush were on Mrs Collinson's dressing table when we searched her house, Roily."

The deputy nodded uncertainly, still staring at the door. No sound came through it now;

I looked at Feeney and asked:

"Would there be any reason for Cotton planting them on Whidden?"

The sheriff said:

"They ain't good friends." (I had noticed that.) "What do you think, Vern?"

The prosecuting attorney took his gaze from the door, rolled the things in their towel again, and stuffed it in his pocket.

"Come on," he snapped, and strode downstairs.

The front door was open. We saw, heard nothing of Cotton or Whidden. A Ford—Whidden's—stood at the front gate soaking up rain. We got in it. Vernon took the wheel, and drove to the house the Collinsons had occupied. We hammered on the door until it was opened by an old man in gray underwear, put there as caretaker by the sheriff.

The old man told us that Cotton had been there at eight o'clock that night, just, he said, to look the place over again. He, the caretaker, didn't know no reason why the marshal had to be watched, so he hadn't bothered him, letting him do what he wanted; and, so far as he knew, the marshal hadn't disturbed anything, though he might of.

Vernon and Feeney gave the old man hell, and we went back to Quesada. Roily and I were together on the rear seat.

"Who is this Whidden?" I asked. "Why should Cotton pick on him?"

"Well, for one thing, because Harve's got kind of a bad name, from being in trouble a couple of times back when a little booze used to be run through here."

"Yeah? And for another thing?"

Roily hesitated, frowning, hunting for words, and before he could find them we had stopped in front of a vine-hung cottage on a dark street corner. The prosecuting attorney led the way to its front porch, and rang the bell.

After a little while a woman's voice called from overhead:

"Who's there? What do you want?"

We had to retreat to the porch steps to see her—Mrs Cotton at a second-storey window.

"Dick got home yet?" Vernon asked.

"No, Mr Vernon, he hasn't," she said. "I was getting worried. Wait a minute, I'll come down."

"Don't bother. We won't wait for him. I'll see him in the morning."

"No. Wait," she said urgently, and vanished from the window.

A moment later she opened the door. Her blue eyes were dark and excited. She had on a rose dressing gown, in which her frail body looked like a child's.

"You needn't have bothered," Vernon said. "There was nothing special. We got separated from Dick an hour or so ago, and just wanted to know if he had got back. He's all right."

"Was—" Her hands worked folds of her dressing gown over her thin breasts. "Was he after—after Harvey—Harvey Whidden?"

Vernon didn't look at her when he said, "Yes"; and he said it without showing all his teeth. Feeney and Roily looked even more uncomfortable than Vernon.

Mrs Cotton's face got very pink. Her lower lip trembled blurring her words:

"Don't believe him Mr Vernon. D-don't believe a word he tells you. Harve didn't have anything to do with the Collinsons, with either one of them. Don't let Dick tell you he did. He didn't."

Vernon looked at his feet and didn't say anything. Roily and Feeney were looking intently out through the open door—we were standing just inside it—at the rain. The sheriffs face was red and miserable. Nobody seemed to have any intention of speaking.

I said, "No?" putting more doubt in my voice than I really felt.

"No, he didn't," she cried, jerking her face around to me. "He couldn't—He couldn't have done it." The pink went out of her face, leaving it pale and desperate. "He—he was here that night—all night—from before seven until day-light."

"And your husband?"

"Was up in the city, at his mother's."

"Where does his mother live?"

She gave me the address, in Noe Street.

"Did anybody—"

"Aw, come on," the sheriff protested, still staring at the rain. "Ain't that enough?"

Mrs Cotton turned from me to the prosecuting attorney again, grabbing one of his arms.

"Don't tell it on me, please, Mr Vernon," she begged. "I don't know what I'd do if it came out. But I had to tell you. I couldn't let him put it on Harve. Please, you won't tell anybody else?"

The prosecuting attorney swore that under no circumstances would he, or any of us, say a word about it to anybody; and the sheriff and his deputy agreed with vigorous red-faced nods.

But when we were in the Ford, away from her, they forgot their embarrassment and became man-hunters again. Within ten minutes they had decided that Cotton, instead of going to San Francisco to his mother's, had remained in Quesada or vicinity till after dark; had killed Collinson; had gone to the city to phone Fitzstephan and mail the letter; and then had returned to Quesada in time to kidnap the girl; planning to use his official position to frame Whidden, with whom he had long been on bad terms, suspecting what everybody else knew—that Whidden and Mrs Cotton were intimate.

The sheriff—he whose chivalry had prevented my thoroughly questioning the woman a few minutes ago—laughed his belly up and down.

"That's rich," he gurgled. "Him out framing Harve, and Harve getting himself a alibi in his bed. Dick's face is going to be a picture for Puck when we spring it on him. Let's find him tonight."

"Better wait," I advised. "It won't hurt to check up his San Francisco trip. I can have that done early in the morning. All we've got on him so far is that he's tried to frame Whidden. If he killed Collinson and kidnapped Mrs Collinson, he seems to have done a lot of unnecessary and goofy things."

Feeney scowled at me and defended their theory:

"Maybe he was more interested in framing Harve than anything else."

"Maybe," I agreed, "but why not give him a little more rope and see what he does with it?"

Feeney was against that. He wanted to grab the marshal pronto. But Vernon reluctantly backed me up. We dropped Roily at his house and the rest of us returned to the hotel.

In my room, I put in a phone call for the agency in San Francisco. While I was waiting for the connection, knuckles tapped my door. I opened it and let in Jack Santos, pajamaed, bath-robed and slippered.

"Have a nice ride?" he asked, yawning.

"Swell."

"Anything break?"

"Not for publication yet," I said, "but—under the hat—the new angle is that our marshal is trying to hang the job on his wife's boy friend, with homemade evidence. The other big officials think Cotton turned the trick himself."

"That ought to get all of them on the front page." Santos sat on the foot of my bed and lit a cigarette. "Ever happen to hear that Feeney was Cotton's rival for the telegraphing hand of the present Mrs Cotton, until she picked the marshal—the triumph of dimples over mustachios?"

"No. What of it?"

"How do I know. I just happened to pick it up. A fellow in the garage told me."

"How long ago?"

"That they were rivals? Less than a couple of years."

The phone rang, my call. I told Field, the agency night man, to have somebody check up the marshal's Noe Street visit the first thing in the morning. Santos yawned and went out while I was talking. I yawned and went to bed when I had finished.

VI

At a little before ten o'clock the telephone roused me—Mickey Linehan talking from San Francisco. Cotton had arrived at his mother's house between seven and seven-thirty Saturday morning, had slept for five or six hours—telling his mother he had been up all night laying for a burglar—and had left for home at six that evening.

Cotton was in the lobby when I went down there. He was red-eyed and tired, but still determined.

"Catch Whidden?" I asked.

"No, durn him, but I will. Say, I'm glad you jiggled my arm, even if it did let him get away. I—well, sometimes a fellow's enthusiasm gets the best of his judgment."

"Yeah. We stopped at your house on our way back early this morning, to see how you'd made out."

"I ain't been home yet," he said. "I put in the whole durned night hunting that fellow."

"Better get some sleep," I suggested. "Vernon and Feeney are probably still pounding their ears. I'll ring you if anything turns up."

He set off for home. I went into the cafe for breakfast. While I was eating, Vernon came in and joined me. He had telegrams from Pebble Beach and San Francisco, confirming Fitzstephan's story of having had company in his apartment Friday night, of having spent the week-end with Mr and Mrs Ralph Coleman at Pebble Beach.

"I got my report on Cotton," I said. "He arrived at his mother's between seven and halfpast Saturday morning, and left at six that evening."

"Seven and half-past." Vernon didn't like that. If the marshal had been in San Francisco at that time, he couldn't have been abducting the girl. "Are you sure?"

"No, but that's the report I got. Excuse me a moment."

Looking through the cafe door, I had seen Owen Fitzstephan's lanky back at the hotel desk. I went over, hailed Fitzstephan, brought him back to the table with me, and introduced him to Vernon. The prosecuting attorney stood up to shake his hand, but was too busy with thoughts of Cotton to be very interested in anything the novelist could have told him.

Fitzstephan ordered a cup of coffee, saying he had had breakfast before leaving the city. I was called to the phone.

Cotton's voice, but excited almost beyond recognition:

"For God's sake get Vernon and Feeney and come up here. Something terrible's happened."

"What?" I asked.

"Hurry, hurry!" he cried, and hung up.

I went back to the table and told Vernon about it. He jumped up, upsetting Fitzstephan's coffee. Fitzstephan got up too, but hesitated, looking at me.

"Come on," I invited him, "maybe this'll be something you'll like."

Fitzstephan's car was in front of the hotel. The marshal's house was only seven blocks away. Its front door was open. Vernon knocked on the open door as we went in, but we did not wait for an answer.

Cotton met us in the hall. His eyes were wide and blood-shot in a face as hard-white as marble.

He tried to say something, couldn't get the words past his tight-set teeth, and gestured toward the door behind him with a fist that was clenched on a piece of brown paper.

Through the doorway we saw Mrs Cotton. She was lying on the blue-carpeted floor. She had on a pale blue house dress. Her throat was covered with dark bruises. Her lips and tongue—the tongue, swollen, hung out—were darker, more purplish, than the bruises. Her eyes were wide open, bulging, upturned, and dead. Her hand, when I touched it, was still warm.

Cotton, following us into the room, held out the brown paper in his hand when we turned to him. It was an irregularly torn piece of wrapping paper, covered on both sides with writing—nervously, unevenly, hastily scribbled in pencil.

I was closer to Cotton than Vernon. I took the paper and read it aloud:

> Harvey Whidden came here last night—said my husband was trying frame him for Collinson murder—they were after him. I hid him in garret. He said only way to save him was for me to say he was here that night. He was not here that night—but was some other nights when my husband was away. I did not want to

> say that—he said if I did not my husband would have him hung—I could tell Mr Vernon and ask him to tell nobody else. I said no—but when Mr Vernon and men came Harve said he would kill me and self if I did not. So I did. I did not know Harve was guilty then. He told me afterwards. He tried kidnap Mrs C. Thursday night, but C. nearly caught him. He was afraid C. recognized him. He came in telegraph office Friday right after C. gave me telegram and he read it. I did not know that then. He followed C. that night—pushed him off cliff. Then he drove to San Francisco. He had whiskey and drank it. Then decided to kidnap Mrs C. anyway. He knew of some man who knew her, and called him up to try to find out who he could get money from—but he was too drunk to talk good. So he wrote him letter and came back here. Met Mrs C. on road, took her in his car, rubbed out marks where he turned around, and took her some hiding place he has. Below Dull Point. He goes there in boat. That is all I know. When he told me this I told him I would not have anything more to do with him. I am locked in garret now while he is downstairs getting food. I am afraid he will kill me. He is a murderer and I will not help him even if he does.
>
> Daisy Cotton.

The sheriff and Roily had arrived while I was reading it. Feeney's face was as white and as set as Cotton's.

Vernon bared his teeth at the marshal, snapping:

"You wrote that."

Feeney grabbed it from my hands, looked at it, shook his head and said hoarsely:

"No, that's her writing, all right."

Cotton was babbling:

"No, before God, I didn't, Vern. I planted that stuff on him, I admit that, but that was all. I came home and found her like that, and found this. I swear to God!"

"Where were you Friday night?" the prosecuting attorney demanded.

"Here, watching the house. I thought—I thought they might—But he wasn't here that night, like she said. I watched till daybreak and then went to the city. I didn't—"

The sheriff interrupted, waving the letter, bellowing:

"Below Dull Point! What are we waiting for?"

He plunged out of the house, the rest of us after him. Cotton and Roily rode down to the waterfront in the deputy's car. Vernon, the sheriff and I rode with Fitzstephan. The sheriff cried throughout the short trip, tears splashing on the automatic he held in his lap.

At the waterfront we changed from the cars to a green and white motor boat run by a pink-cheeked, tow-headed young man called Tim. Tim said he didn't know anything about any hiding places below Dull Point, but if there was one there he could find it.

In his hands the boat produced a lot of speed, but not enough for Feeney and Cotton. They stood together in the bow, guns in their fists, dividing their time between straining forward and yelling back at Tim for more speed.

Half an hour from the dock we rounded a blunt promontory that the others called Dull Point; and Tim cut down our speed, putting the boat's nose in closer to the rocks that jumped up high and sharp at the water's edge.

We were all eyes—eyes that soon ached from staring under the noon sun, but kept on staring. Twice we saw clefts in the rock-walled coast, pushed hopefully in to them, saw that they were blind, leading nowhere, opening into no hiding places.

The third was even more hopeless looking at first sight, but, now that Dull Point was some distance behind us, we couldn't pass up anything. We slid in toward the cleft, got close enough to decide that it was, as we had suspected, another blind one, gave it up, and told Tim to go on.

We were washed another couple of feet nearer before the tow-headed boy could bring the boat around.

Cotton, in the bow, bent forward from the waist and yelled:

"Here it is."

He pointed his gun at one side of the cleft.

Tim let the boat drift in another foot or so. Craning our necks, we could see that what we had taken for the shore line on that side was really a high, thin, saw-toothed ledge of rock separated from the cliff on this end by twenty feet of water.

"Put her in," Feeney ordered.

Tim frowned at the water, hesitated, said:

"She can't make it."

The boat backed him up by shuddering suddenly under our feet with an unpleasant rasping noise.

"That be damned!" the sheriff bawled. "Put her in."

The gun in his hand was leveled at Tim's belly, and the sheriff's eyes weren't sane.

Tim put her in.

The boat shuddered under our feet again, more violently, and now there was a tearing noise in the rasping; but we went through the opening and turned down behind the saw-tooth ledge.

We were in a V-shaped pocket, twenty feet wide where we had come in, eighty feet long, high-walled, inaccessible by land, accessible by sea only as we had come. The water that floated us—and was now leaking in to sink us—ran a third of the way down the pocket. White sand paved the other two-thirds.

A small green motor boat was resting its nose on the edge of the sand. It was empty.

"Harve's," Tim said.

Nobody was in sight. There didn't seem to be any place for anybody to hide. There were footprints, large and small, in the sand, empty tin cans, and the remains of a fire.

Our boat grounded. We jumped, splashed ashore—Cotton ahead, the rest of us spread out behind him.

Suddenly, as if he had sprung out of the air, Whidden appeared in the far end of the V, standing on the sand, a rifle in his hands.

Anger and utter astonishment were in his heavy face, and in his voice when he yelled:

"You damned, double-crossing—"

The noise his gun made blotted out the rest of his words.

Cotton threw himself down sideways.

The rifle bullet missed him by inches, clipped the brim of Fitzstephan's hat and splattered on the rocks behind us.

Four of our guns went off together, some of them more than once.

Whidden went over backward, his feet flying in the air.

He was dead when we got to him—three bullets in his chest, one in his head.

We found Gabrielle Collinson lying on blankets that had been spread over a pile of dry seaweed in a narrow cave that carried the V ten or twelve feet farther back into the cliff. There was some canned food and a lantern there.

I helped the girl sit up. Her small face was flushed with fever, and she had to whisper because of a cold in her chest; but her mind was clear enough to recognize me and to answer my questions.

She was in no shape for a grilling, but there were things I had to know quick.

She told me she had known nothing about Whidden's first attempt to kidnap her, nor that Eric had sent for me. She sat up all Friday night waiting for him to come back from his walk, and at daylight, frantic, had gone to hunt for him. She had found him—as I had. She had gone back to the house and tried to commit suicide—to put an end to the curse.

"I tried twice," she whispered, "but it was no use. I'm a coward. I couldn't keep the pistol pointing at myself while I did it. It would jerk away just before I fired. The second time, I tried to shoot myself in the breast, but only hurt my arm a little." She raised her bandaged left arm for me to see. "And then I hadn't even courage to try any more."

She had changed her clothes—muddy and torn from her search along the rocks—had put a rough bandage on her arm and had driven away from the house. She didn't say where she had intended going. I don't suppose she had any destination; she was just going away from the place where the curse had settled on the man she was married to.

She hadn't gone far when she saw a car coming toward her driven by the man who had brought her here. He had turned his car across the road in front of her, blocking the road. Trying to avoid him, she had run into a tree—and knew nothing else until she regained consciousness here. The man had left her here alone most of the time. She had neither the strength nor the courage to try to escape by swimming, and there was no other way.

"Was he the only man ever here?" I asked, remembering Whidden's last words. "Wasn't there more than one?"

"No, just he—the one who went out with the rifle when he heard you come."

"How long had he been here this time?"

"Since before daylight," she whispered. "The sound of his boat woke me."

"Sure of that?"

"Yes."

I had been sitting on my heels in front of her. I stood up and turned to face the marshal, close to him.

"You killed your wife," I said.

He goggled at me. His gun was in his hand, hanging down at his side. I stood too close for him to raise it between us. He stammered:

"Wh—what's that?"

"You killed your wife. She was afraid Whidden meant to, but he's been here since daylight, and she was warm when we found her—after eleven. You found the letter, found that what you had suspected—her intimacy with him—was true, and you strangled her, counting on the letter to hang it on him."

"That's a lie," he cried. "There ain't a word of truth in it."

He pushed back against the others, trying to get far enough from me to bring his gun up. I moved after him, keeping close, getting one hand on his gun, the other on the wrist above it.

He snarled and hit at me with his other fist. The sheriff caught that arm, wrenched it back, growling:

"That'll do."

I twisted the marshal's gun out of his hand.

Feeney and Roily took him out of the cave.

Vernon stuck his chin up and spoke over it in a satisfied voice, carefully baring his teeth around each word:

"Just as I suspected. We can congratulate ourselves on having brought an extremely difficult affair to a decidedly neat ending."

I was glad somebody liked it. I didn't. Here, for the third time in a very few weeks, the girl had been the center around which crime and death revolved; and for the third time we had discovered everything except what connection there was between the first, second and third times. And, not having discovered that connection, I didn't believe we had brought anything to any kind of an ending.

Whatever or whoever the Curse was—it or he was still loose.

I put all the hypocrisy I had into my voice as I turned back to the girl.

"Well," I said amiably, "let's get back to Quesada."

8

BLACK RIDDLE

BLACK MASK, FEBRUARY 1929

I

"It doesn't make sense," I said. "It's dizzy. When we grab our man—or woman—we're going to find he's a goof, and Napa will get him instead of the gallows."

"That," Owen Fitzstephan said, "is characteristic of you. You're stumped, bewildered, flabbergasted. Do you admit you've met your master, have run into a criminal too wily for you? Not you. He's outwitted you; therefore he's an idiot. Now really. Of course there's a certain modesty to that attitude."

"But he's got to be goofy," I insisted. "Look: Mayenne marries—"

"Are you," he asked wearily, "going to recite that catalogue again?"

"I am. Mayenne marries Lily Dain in Paris in 1908, and their daughter Gabrielle is born. Lily's sister Alice wants Mayenne. When Gabrielle is five, Alice teaches her a game with a pistol, and it winds up as Alice planned, by the youngster killing her mother. But Mayenne is convicted of the murder and sent to Devil's Island. He escapes after some years and comes to San

Francisco, where he settles as Edgar Leggett. In 1923 Alice and Gabrielle join him, and he and Alice marry. Call that the prelude if you want."

"I might have called it that yesterday," Fitzstephan complained, "but after hearing it gone over a dozen times today I can't call it anything but damned tiresome."

"You've a flighty mind. That's no good in this business. You can't catch murderers by amusing yourself with interesting thoughts. You've got to sit down to all the facts you can get and turn them over and over till they click. There's—"

"Stop," he said. "If it must be one or the other, I'd rather hear you discuss your mystery—even for the thirteenth time—than your technic."

"If that's the case, the Leggetts then have five years of peace, until a pair of ex-sleuths who know the family history show up. One of them—Upton—shakes Alice down for a handful of diamonds. The other kills Upton, either on his own account or Alice's, and goes to her for money and concealment. By this time Alice is in a hole, and she tries to pull it in after her by killing the second ex-sleuth—Ruppert. Gabrielle sees the murder. Half-cracked or more, she beats it. Her going gums things for Alice, even though she doesn't know the girl saw the murder; because I, trying to trace the diamonds, have begun to find things wrong with the Leggetts and am hunting for Gabrielle.

"Whatever Leggett knows up to this point, Alice has to go to him now with the works and ask him to take the fall for her. He's got to powder out anyhow, if he doesn't want to be shipped back to the Island, and there's enough chalked up against him that a little more won't hurt. So he comes through with a written confession that he killed Ruppert, that he's to blame for everything. Alice reads his statement, figures it sounds as much like a pre-suicide document as anything else, thinks that's the safest way to play it, and knocks him off—like that. When the trick goes sour on her, she tries to shoot her way out of the house, and, when you and I grab her, succeeds in shooting herself. All that may be part of the prelude too, though it doesn't have to be."

"In any event," the novelist murmured, "it gets you halfway through. Continue, my son, have it over with."

"The shock of all this raises hell with Gabrielle's mind, which wasn't any too strong in the first place, and makes her easy pickings for the Haldorns and their Temple of the Holy Grail cult. They've been working on her for some time, and now they persuade her to come to the Temple for a stay. She wants to go, and Dr Riese thinks that letting her go is about the only thing that will keep her from going completely cuckoo. They persuade Madison Andrews, who is in charge of her affairs since her parents' death, to agree—over the objections of Eric Collinson, to whom she's engaged.

"Joseph Haldorn's got a wife, Aaronia, who helps him run the cult racket, but that doesn't keep Joseph from getting a yen for Gabrielle. His success in flimflamming his converts makes him think he can get away with anything. Dr Riese, coming to see Gabrielle every day, soon discovers that something's wrong, but he hasn't got sense enough to keep it to himself. He lets Haldorn know what he's discovered, and Haldorn has him killed. Then, when Aaronia interferes, Haldorn tries to carve her. I kill Haldorn and one of his associates, Mrs Fink, and the Holy Grail trick falls apart, landing the survivors—Aaronia Haldorn, Tom Fink, and Gabrielle's maid Minnie—in jail, where they staid till yesterday."

"Till yesterday?" Fitzstephan's sleepy gray eyes woke up. "They've been released?"

"Aaronia and Fink have. Minnie will probably have to stand trial but I don't think any jury will tie Riese's murder on her. She was too plainly spooked into it by Haldorn. There's no chance of hanging it on Fink or Aaronia. They were accomplices in the Temple racket, but there's no proof that they had anything to do with his going crazy and murdering people. They may have—but there's no proof."

"You're watching them, of course?"

"That's what we sprung them for. Well, when the Temple blew up, Eric Collinson grabbed Gabrielle, carried her off to Reno, and married her. They came back to San Francisco for the inquest, and then down here to Quesada, to the house in the cove, a quiet place where she can recover health and sanity. Last Friday Eric wires me, *Come immediately*. I can't get down till late that night. Eric waits here at the hotel for me till after the last train bus is in, and then starts back to his house, but is killed en route—pushed off the cliff by Harvey Whidden, a native with a rum-running record.

"After killing Collinson, Whidden sends messages through you—whose address he knows—demanding ten thousand dollars ransom for Gabrielle's return, and then, after sending the messages, kidnaps her. That same Friday night, Cotton, the marshal here, suspecting what everybody else knows—that his wife and Whidden are chummy—has pretended he was going to San Francisco, but has hidden where he can watch his house, to see if Whidden visits it. Whidden doesn't. When the Collinson murder and kidnapping break, Cotton tries to frame Whidden for it. Whidden, running away, hides in the marshal's house, and makes the marshal's wife tell us that he—Whidden—had been with her the night of the murder.

"When Mrs Cotton learns what Whidden has done she—so she says—refuses to have anything more to do with him, and is afraid he will kill her to keep her quiet. So she writes a statement giving the whole thing away. Cotton, coming home after Whidden has left, finds the statement. It verifies his suspicion of his wife's unfaithfulness. He strangles her, calls us in, and her written statement seems to be proof enough that Whidden had killed her. Following the statement's directions, we go to Whidden's hiding place and find him there with Gabrielle. He throws up his rifle, yells, 'You double-crossing something-or-other,' and fires. Cotton ducks in time to let the bullet go elsewhere, and we have to kill Whidden. Gabrielle gives Whidden an alibi for Mrs Cotton's murder by saying he had been with her since daybreak—and the woman had been killed at close to eleven that morning, was warm when we saw her. That means, apparently, that Cotton killed her. He's in the county jail now, insisting on his innocence. Whidden's last words are still unexplained. Gabrielle saw or heard of nobody except Whidden throughout the abduction. They're the facts, brother, as we've got them. Do they make sense?"

Fitzstephan ran long fingers through his sorrel hair and asked:

"Why not? Cotton persuaded Whidden to kidnap Gabrielle. Collinson stumbled on to the plan and had to be killed. According to the plan, Cotton was supposed to see that the other officials didn't get anywhere while Whidden did the actual work. What Cotton did was to make his wife write that statement—I don't know how it hit you, but it didn't read to me like the sort of thing she would have written of her own accord—kill her, and then lead us to Whidden. He was the first man ashore when we reached Whidden's hiding place—to make sure that Whidden was killed resisting arrest before he got a chance to say much. Jealousy would give Cotton sufficient motive for that, surely?"

I shook my head, saying:

"It doesn't click for me, though Vernon and Feeney are figuring it that way. Whidden wouldn't have put himself in Cotton's hands like that. Besides, where would that fit in with the Temple merry-go-round, and the passing out of the Leggetts?"

"I don't know," the novelist admitted, "but are you sure you're right in thinking there must be a connection?"

"Yeah. Gabrielle's father, stepmother, physician and husband have been killed, and her maid jailed, in less than a handful of weeks—all the people closest to her. That's enough to tie it all together for me, but if you want more links you can have them. Upton and Ruppert were the apparent instigators of the first trouble, and got killed. Haldorn of the second, and got killed. Whidden of the third, and got killed. Mrs Leggett killed her husband, Cotton killed his wife, and Haldorn would have killed his if I hadn't blocked him. Gabrielle as a child was made to kill her mother, and Gabrielle's maid was made to kill Riese, and nearly me. Gabrielle's father left behind him a long statement explaining—not altogether satisfactorily—everything, and was killed. So did and was Mrs Cotton. Doesn't that look like some one person who's got a system he likes, and sticks to it?"

Fitzstephan nodded slowly, agreeing:

"As you tell it, it sounds like the work of one mind."

"And a goofy one."

"Be obstinate about it," he said. "But even your goof must have a motive of some sort."

"Why?"

"Damn your sort of mind," he said with good-natured impatience. "If he had no motive connected with Gabrielle, why should his crimes be connected with her?"

"We don't know that all of them are. We only know of the ones that are."

Fitzstephan grinned and said:

"You'll go any distance to disagree, won't you?"

I said:

"Then again, maybe his crimes are connected with her because he is."

The novelist let his eyes get sleepy over that, pursing his mouth, looking at the closed door between my room and Gabrielle's.

"All right," he said, looking at me again. "Who's your maniac close to Gabrielle?"

"The closest and goofiest person to Gabrielle is Gabrielle herself."

Fitzstephan got up and crossed the hotel room—I was sitting on the edge of the bed—to shake my hand with solemn enthusiasm.

"You're wonderful," he said. "You amaze me. liver have night sweats? Put out your tongue and say, 'Ah.' "

"Suppose," I began, but was interrupted by a feeble tapping on the corridor door.

I went to the door and opened it. A thin man of my own age and height in wrinkled black clothes stood in the corridor. He breathed heavily through a red-veined nose, and his small brown eyes were timid.

"You know me," he said apologetically.

"Yeah. Come in." I introduced him to the novelist: "Fitzstephan, this is the Tom Fink who was one of Haldorn's helpers in the Temple."

Fink looked reproachfully at me, then dragged his crumpled hat off his head and crossed the room to shake Fitzstephan's hand. That done, he returned to me and said, almost whispering:

"I come down to tell you something."

"Yeah?"

He fidgeted, turning his hat around in his hands. I winked at Fitzstephan, said, "Will you excuse us for a moment?" and went out with Fink. In the corridor I closed the door and stopped, saying:

"Let's have it."

Fink rubbed his lips with his tongue and then with the back of one scrawny hand. He said in his half-whisper:

"I come down to tell you something I thought you ought to know."

"Yeah?"

"It's about that fellow Harvey Whidden."

"Yeah?"

"He was my step-son."

"You—?"

Floor, walls and ceiling danced under, around and over us. The door to my room roared open, wriggling, a yellow crack curving down it from top to bottom. Tom Fink was carried away from me, backward. I had sense enough to throw myself down as I was flung in the other direction, and got nothing worse out of it than a bruised shoulder when I hit the wall. A door-frame stopped Fink, wickedly, its edge catching the back of his head. He came forward again, folding over to lie face-down on the floor, still except for blood running from his head.

I got up and made for my room. Fitzstephan was a mangled pile of flesh and clothing in the center of the floor. My bed was burning. There was no glass in the window: I checked up these things mechanically while staggering toward Gabrielle's room. The connecting door was open—had been blown open, perhaps.

She was crouching on all fours in bed, facing the foot of the bed, her bare feet on the pillows. Her night dress was torn at one shoulder. Her green-brown eyes—glittering under the brown curls that had tumbled down to hide what little forehead she had—were the eyes of an animal gone trap-crazy. Saliva glistened on her pointed chin. There was nobody else in the room.

"Where's the nurse?" My voice was husky.

The girl said nothing. Her eyes kept their crazy terror focused on me.

"Get under the covers," I ordered. "You're sick enough without getting pneumonia."

She didn't move. I walked around to the side of the bed, lifting an end of the covers with one hand, reaching the other out to help her, saying:

"Come on, get under the covers."

She made a queer noise in her throat, dropped her head, and put her sharp teeth into the back of my hand. It hurt. I put her under the covers, went back to my room, and was pushing my burning mattress through the window when people began to arrive.

"Get a doctor," I called to the first of them, "and stay out of here."

I had got rid of the mattress by the time Mickey Linehan pushed through the crowd that was now packing the corridor. Mickey blinked at what was left of Fitzstephan, at me, and asked:

"What the hell?"

His big loose mouth sagged at the ends, looking like a grin turned upside-down.

I licked burnt finger-tips and asked, not pleasantly:

"What the hell does it look like?"

The grin turned right-side-up on his red face. He scratched one of his ears—they stood out like loving cup handles—and said:

"More trouble, of course. Of course—you're here."

Deputy sheriff Ben Roily came in—a tall, big-built, slouchy youngish man with hair, eyes and skin of indefinite tan shades.

"Tch, tch, tch," he said, looking around. "What do you suppose happened?"

"Bomb."

"Tch, tch, tch."

Dr George came in and knelt beside the wreck of Fitzstephan. George had been looking after Gabrielle since we had rescued her from Whidden the previous day. He was a short, chunky, middle-aged man with a lot of black hair everywhere except on his lips, cheeks and chin. His hairy hands moved over Fitzstephan.

"Damn my soul," the doctor exclaimed. "The man's not dead."

I didn't believe him. Fitzstephan's right arm was gone, and most of his right leg. His body was too twisted to see how much of it was left, but there was only one side to his face. I said: "There's another one out in the hall, with his head knocked in."

"Oh, he'll pull through all right," the doctor muttered without looking up. "But this one—well, damn my soul."

He scrambled up to his feet and began ordering this and that. He was highly excited. A couple of men came in from the corridor. The woman who had been nursing Gabrielle—Mrs Herman—joined them, and another man, with a blanket. They took Fitzstephan away.

"What's Fink been doing?" I asked Mickey.

"Hardly anything. I got on his tail when they sprung him yesterday at noon. He went from the can to a hotel on Kearny Street and got himself a room. Then he went up to the Public Library and hunted up everything the newspapers have printed about the girl's troubles from beginning to date. Then he went to a lunch-room for some grub, ambled back to his hotel, and camped in his room. He might have back-doored me. His room was dark at midnight, when I knocked off. I got on the job again at six A.M. He showed at seven-something, grabbed breakfast, and a train to Poston, got the stage for here, and came straight into the hotel, asking for you. That's the crop."

"That the fellow out in the hall?" Roily asked.

"Yeah." I told him what Fink had told me, adding: "The chances are he hadn't given me all he had when the blow-up came. We'll find out when he comes to."

"So Harve was his step-son," the deputy said. "Tch, tch, tch. What about Harve's mother?"

"I killed her in the Temple," I said. "It was her or me."

"Tch, tch, tch. You think this Fink meant the bomb for you, because you'd killed his wife?"

"No. He was standing outside, talking to me, when it popped. I wonder if it was meant for him, to keep him from telling me what he had come down to tell?"

Mickey said: "Nobody followed him down from the city, excepting me. I reckon I'd better go see what they're doing with him." He went out.

"The window was closed," I told Roily. "There was no noise, as if something had been thrown through the window, just before the explosion, and there's no broken window-glass inside the room now. It wasn't chucked in that way."

Roily nodded vaguely, looking at the connecting doorway.

"Fink and I were in the corridor. I ran straight through here into her room. Nobody could have got out of her room without my seeing or hearing them, even if they could have sneaked in there without raising an alarm. The heavy screen I had nailed over her window is O.K."

"Wasn't Mrs Herman in there?" Roily asked.

"She was supposed to be, but was out at the time. We'll find out about that. There's no use of thinking the girl—Mrs Collinson—chucked it. She's been in there, in bed, since we brought her back yesterday. I picked that room out. She couldn't have had a bomb planted there even if she had any reasons for wanting one. Nobody's been in there except the doctor, the nurse, you, Feeney, Vernon and me."

"I didn't say she had anything to do with it," the deputy mumbled, looking vaguer than ever. "What does she say?"

"We can talk to her now, if you want, but I doubt if it'll get us much."

It didn't. Gabrielle lay in the middle of the bed, the covers gathered close to her chin as if she was preparing to duck down under them at the first alarm, and shook her head, "No," to everything we asked her, whether the answer fitted or didn't.

The nurse came in, a big-hearted, red-haired woman of forty-something with a face that looked honest because it was homely, blue-eyed and freckled. She swore by the Gideon Bible that she had been out of the room for only five minutes, just to go downstairs for some stationery, intending to write a letter to her nephew in Vallejo while her patient was sleeping; and that was the only time she had been out of the room all day. She had met nobody in the corridor, she said.

"You left the door unlocked?" I asked.

"Yes, so I wouldn't be so likely to wake her up when I came back."

"Where's the writing paper you got?"

"I didn't get it. I heard the explosion, and ran back upstairs." Fear came into her face, turning the freckles into ghastly spots. "You don't think—!"

"Better look after Mrs Collinson," I said irritably.

II

Roily and I went back to my room, closing the connecting door.

He said:

"Tch, tch, tch. I'd of thought Mrs Herman was the last person in the world to—"

"You ought to've," I grumbled. "You recommended her. Who is she?"

"She's Tod Herman's wife. He's got the garage here. She used to be a trained nurse. I thought she was all right."

"She got a nephew in Vallejo?"

"Uh-huh, that would be the Schultz kid that works at Mare Island. How do you suppose she got mixed up in—"

"Probably didn't, or she would have had the writing paper she went after. Let's lock this place up till we can borrow a San Francisco bomb expert to go over it."

Mickey Linehan was in the lobby when we got down there.

"Fink's got a cracked skull. He's on his way over to the county hospital with the other wreck."

"Fitzstephan died yet?" I asked.

"Nope, and the doc seems to think that if they get him over to where they got the right kind of tools they can keep him alive. God knows what for, the shape he's in. But you know croakers—that's just the kind of stuff they think is a lot of fun."

"Who's shadowing Aaronia Haldorn?"

"Al Mason."

"Phone the agency and see if you can get a report on her. Tell the Old Man what's happened while you're at it, and see if they've found Andrews."

"Andrews?" Roily asked as Mickey headed for the telephone. "What's the matter with him?"

"Nothing that I know of—only we haven't been able to find him to tell him Mrs Collinson is safe. His office—he's a lawyer—hasn't seen him since the day before yesterday, and nobody there will say they know where he is. I saw him that same day, and he didn't say anything about going anywhere."

"Is there any special reason for wanting him?"

"Well," I said sourly, "I don't want to have her on my hands the rest of my life. He's in charge of her affairs; he's responsible for her; I want to turn her over to him."

Roily nodded vaguely. We went outside and asked all the people we could find all the questions we could think of. None of the answers led anywhere, except to assure us that the bomb hadn't been chucked through the window. We found six people who had been in sight of that side of the hotel at the time of the explosion, and none of them had seen anything that could be twisted into having any bearing on the bomb-throwing.

Mickey came away from the telephone with the information that Aaronia Haldorn, when released from the city prison, had gone to the home of a family named Jeffries—former members of her cult—in San Mateo, and had remained there ever since;

and that Dick Foley, hunting for Madison Andrews, had hopes of locating him in Sausalito.

Prosecuting attorney Vernon and sheriff Feeney, with a horde of reporters and photographers close behind them, arrived from the county seat. They went through a lot of detecting motions that got them nowhere except on the front pages of all the San Francisco papers—which was the place they liked best.

I had Gabrielle Collinson moved into another room, and left Mickey Linehan next door, with the connecting door ajar. She talked now—to Vernon, Feeney, Roily and me—but what she told us didn't help much. She had been asleep, she said; had been awakened by the noise, and then I had come in. That was all she knew.

Late in the afternoon, McCracken, a San Francisco police department explosive expert, arrived; and, after examining all the fragments of this and that which he could find in the blasted room, gave us a preliminary report that the bomb had been a small one, of aluminum, filled with a low-grade nitroglycerine, and exploded by a crude friction device.

"Amateur or professional job?" I asked.

McCracken spit loose shreds of tobacco out—he's one of these birds who chew the ends of their cigarettes—and said:

"I'd say it was made by a guy that knew his stuff, all right, but had to work with what material he could get. I'll tell you more after I've worked this junk over in the lab."

Dr George returned from the county hospital with the news that what was left of Fitzstephan still breathed. The doctor was tickled pink. I had to yell at him to make him hear my questions about Fink and Gabrielle. Then he told me Fink's life was in no danger, and the girl's cold was enough better that she could get out of bed if she wished. I asked him about her nervous condition, but he was in too much of a hurry to get back to Fitzstephan to pay much attention to that.

"Hm-m-m, yes, certainly," he muttered, edging past me toward his car.

"Quiet, rest, freedom from anxiety," and he was gone.

I ate dinner with Vernon and Feeney in the hotel dining-room. They didn't think I had told them all I knew about the explosion, and kept me on the witness stand all through the meal, though neither of them accused me point-blank of holding out.

After dinner I went up to my new room. The door between it and Gabrielle's was closed. Mickey Linehan was sprawled on the bed reading a newspaper.

"Go feed yourself," I said. "How's our baby?"

"She's up. How do you figure her—only fifty cards to her deck?"

"Why?" I asked. "What's she been doing?"

"Nothing. I was just thinking."

"That's from having an empty stomach. Better go eat."

"Aye, aye, master mind," he said and went out.

The next room was quiet. I listened at the door and then tapped it. Mrs Herman's voice said: "Come in."

She was sitting beside the bed making gaudy butterflies on a piece of yellowish cloth stretched on hoops. Gabrielle Collinson sat in a rocking chair on the other side of the room, frowning at hands clasped in her lap—clasped hard enough to whiten the knuckles and spread the finger-ends. She had on the tweed clothes in which she had been abducted. They were still rumpled but had been brushed clean. She didn't look up when I came in. The nurse did, pushing her freckles together in an uneasy smile.

"Good evening," I said, trying to make a cheerful entrance. "Looks like we're running out of invalids."

That got no response from the girl, too much from the nurse.

"Yes, indeed," she exclaimed, with too much enthusiasm. "We can't call Mrs Collinson an invalid now—now that she's up and about—and I'm almost sorry that she is—he, he—because I certainly never did have such a nice patient; but that's what we girls used to say in training—the nicer the patient was, the shorter the time we'd have him, while you take a disagreeable one, and she'd live—I mean, be there—forever, it seems like. I remember once when—"

I made a face at her and jerked my head at the door. She let the rest of her words drop inside her open mouth. Her face turned red, then white. She dropped her embroidery and got up, saying idiotically: "Yes, yes, that's the way it is. Well, I've got to go see about that—you know—what do you call 'em. Excuse me for a few minutes, please." She went out quickly, sideways, as if afraid I would sneak up behind her and kick her.

When the door had closed, Gabrielle looked up from her hands and said:

"Owen is dead."

She didn't ask, she said it, but there was no way of handling it except as a question.

"No." I sat down in the nurse's chair and fished out cigarettes. "It doesn't seem possible, but he's still alive."

"If he lives"—her voice was husky from the tail-end of her cold—"will he—?" She left the question unfinished, but her husky voice was impersonal enough.

"He'll be pretty badly maimed."

She spoke more to herself than to me:

"That should be even more satisfactory."

I grinned. If I was as good an actor as I thought, there was nothing in my grin but good-natured amusement.

"Laugh," she said gravely. "I wish you could laugh it away. But you can't. It's there. It will always be there." She looked down at her clasped hands and whispered: "Cursed."

Spoken in any other tone, that word would have been—or would have sounded—ridiculous, melodramatic, stagey. But she said it without any feeling, mechanically, as if saying it were a habit. I saw her lying in bed in the dark, whispering it to herself; whispering it to her body when she put on her clothes; to her face when she saw it reflected in mirrors—day after day.

I squirmed in my chair and growled:

"Stop it. Just because a bad-tempered woman works off her hatred and anger in a ten-twenty-thirty speech about—"

"No, no, my step-mother only put in words what I have always known. I didn't know that she and my mother were cursed too—that it was in the Dain blood—but I knew it was in mine. I knew it from the time I was old enough to compare myself with other children. How could I help knowing? Hadn't I all the physical signs of degeneracy?" She came across the room to stand in front of me, turning her head sidewise, pushing back brown curls with both hands. "Look at my ears—without lobes, pointed at the top. People don't have ears like that. Animals do." She twisted her face to me again, still holding back the curls. "Look at my forehead—its smallness, its shape—animal. My teeth." She bared them—white, small, pointed. "The shape of my face." Her hands left her hair to slide down her cheeks and come together under her oddly pointed small chin. "Look at my hands." She held them out to me. "The thumbs, with those useless joints—hardly different from fingers. I've only four toes on each foot. I've—"

"I'm disappointed in that," I said. "I thought you'd have cloven hoofs. Suppose these things were all as peculiar as you seem to think them? What of it? Your step-mother was a Dain, and God knows she was poison—but where were her 'physical marks of degeneracy'? Wasn't she as normal, as wholesome a looking woman as you're likely to find?"

"But that's no answer." She shook her head impatiently. "She didn't have the physical marks. I have—and the mental ones too. I—" She sat down on the side of the bed close to me, elbows on knees, tortured white face between hands. "I've not ever been able to think clearly, as other people do, even the simplest thoughts. Everything is always a muddle in my mind. No matter what I try to think about, there's a fog between me and my thought, and other thoughts get in the way, and I barely catch a glimpse of the thought I want before I lose it, and have to hunt through the fog and at last find it, only to have the same thing happen again and again and again. Can you understand how horrible that can be? Going through life—year after year—knowing you are and always will be like that—or worse?"

"I can't," I said. "It sounds normal as hell to me. Nobody thinks clearly, no matter what they pretend. People either don't think at all or they go about it exactly as you do. Thinking's a dizzy business—a matter of catching as many of those foggy glimpses as you can and fitting them together the best you can. That's why people hang on so tight to their beliefs and opinions; because, compared to the haphazard way in which they're arrived at, even the goofiest opinion seems wonderfully clear, sane, and self-evident. And if you let it get away from you, then you have to dive back into that foggy muddle to wangle yourself out another to take its place."

She took her face out of her hands and smiled shyly at me, saying:

"It's funny I didn't like you before." Her face became serious again. "But—"

"But nothing. You're old enough to know that everybody except very crazy people and very stupid people suspect themselves now and then—or whenever they happen to think of it—of being not exactly sane. Evidence of goofiness is easily found—the more you dig into yourself the more you turn up. Nobody's mind could pass the sort of examination you've been giving yours—going around trying to prove yourself cuckoo!—it's a wonder you haven't driven yourself nuts."

"Perhaps I have."

"No. Take my word for it, you're sane. Or don't take my word for it. Look. You got a hell of a start in life. You got into bad hands at the very beginning. You were brought up by a stepmother who was plain poison, and who did her best to make a complete ruin of you, and who in the end succeeded in convincing you that you were cursed with some very special family curse. In the past couple of months—the time I've known you—all the calamities known to man have been piled on you—and your belief in your curse has made you hold yourself responsible for ex cry item in the pile.

"All right. How's it affected you? You've been dazed part of the time, hysterical now and then, and when your husband was killed you tried to commit suicide but weren't unbalanced enough to face the shock of the bullet in your flesh. Well, good God, woman, I'm only a hired man with only a hired man's interest in your troubles, and some of them have had me groggy. Didn't I try to bite a ghost back in that Temple? And I'm supposed to be old and toughened to crime. This morning—after all you've gone through—somebody touches off a package of nitroglycerine almost beside your bed. Here you are this evening—up and dressed—arguing about your sanity with me.

"If you aren't normal, it's because you're tougher, cooler, saner, than normal. Stop thinking about your Dain blood and think a little of the Mayenne blood in you. You're more like your father than your mother—judging by her sister. You've got more of his blood in you, if appearance is a guide, and owe it more. It's his toughness that has carried you through this far—and will carry you the rest of the way."

She seemed to like that. Her eyes were almost happy. But I had talked myself out of words for the moment, and while I was hunting for more behind a cigarette the shine went out of her eyes.

"I'm glad—I'm grateful to you for what you've said, if you meant it." Hopelessness was in her tone again, and her face was back between her hands. "But, whatever I am, she—my stepmother—was right. You cannot say she was not. Surely my life has been cursed, blackened—and the lives of everyone who has come in contact with me."

"I'm one answer to that," I said. "I've been around a lot recently, and nothing's happened to me that a night's sleep wouldn't fix up." I shut my mouth in time to avoid dragging Madison Andrews in as another answer. Until we found him we couldn't be sure that nothing had happened to him.

"But in a different way," she protested slowly, wrinkling her forehead. "There's no personal relationship with you. It's simply your work. That makes the difference."

I laughed and said:

"That won't do. There's Fitzstephan. He was a friend of your family, of course, but his presence here was through me—on my account. He was helping me. Why then—a step further away from you than I—should he have got the bomb? I was closer to you than he. Why shouldn't I have gone down first? Maybe the bomb was meant for me? It's reasonable. But that brings us to a human mind behind the whole thing—one capable of making mistakes—and not your infallible and airtight curse."

"You are mistaken," she said, staring at her knees. "Owen loved me."

I decided not to appear surprised. I said:

"Had you—?"

"No, please, please don't ask me to talk about it. Not now—after this morning." She jerked her shoulders up high and straight, said briskly: "A moment ago you said something about an infallible curse. I don't know whether you've misunderstood me, or are pretending to, to make it look more foolish. But I don't believe in your infallible curse—one coming from God or the devil, like Job's, say." She was earnest now, no longer talking to change the conversation. "But can't there be—aren't there people who are so thoroughly—fundamentally—evil that they poison, or bring out the worst in everybody they touch? And can't that—?"

"Maybe there are people who can," I half agreed, "if they want to."

"No, no! Whether they want to or not. When they desperately don't want to. It is so. It is. I loved Eric because he was clean and fine. You knew him well enough to know he was. I loved him that way, wanted him that way. And then, when we were married—" She shuddered and gave me both of her hands. The palms were dry and hot, the ends of the fingers cold. I had to hold them tight to keep the nails out of my flesh.

I said:

"You're being silly. He was too young, too much in love with you, maybe too inexperienced, to keep from being clumsy. You can't make anything horrible out of that."

"But it wasn't only Eric. Every man I've known—Don't think I'm conceited. I know I'm not beautiful. But I don't want to be evil. I don't. Why do men—why have all the men I've known—?"

"Are you," I asked, "talking about me?"

"No—you know I'm not. Don't make fun of me, please."

"Then there are exceptions? Any others? Madison Andrews, for instance?"

"If you knew him very well, or had heard much about him, you wouldn't ask that?"

"No," I agreed. "But with him it's a habit. You can't blame the curse. Was he very bad?"

"He was very funny," she said bitterly.

"How long ago was that?"

"Oh, possibly a year and a half. I didn't say anything to my father or step-mother. I was—I was ashamed that men were like that to me—and afraid—"

"How do you know," I grumbled, "that most men aren't like that to most women? What makes you think your case is so damned unique? If your ears were sharp enough you could probably hear thousands of women in San Francisco making the same complaint at this moment, and—God knows—maybe half of them would be thinking they were sincere."

She took her hands away from me and sat up straight on the bed-edge. Some pink came into her face.

"Now you *have* made me feel silly," she said.

"No sillier than I do. I'm supposed to be a detective. I've been riding a blooming merry-go-round since this job began—going around and around the same distance behind your curse, suspecting what it'd look like if I came face to face with it, but never catching up with it. Well, I've got it now. Can you stand another week or two?"

"You mean—?"

"I'm going to earn my wages," I promised her, "and show you that your curse is a lot of hooey. It may take a week or two, though."

She was white-faced and trembling, wanting to believe me, afraid to.

"That's settled," I said. "What are you going to do now?"

"I—I don't know. Do you mean what you've said?"

"Yeah. Could you go back to the house in the cove for a while? It might help things along, and I think you'll be safe enough now. We could take Mrs Herman and maybe an op or two from the agency with us."

"I'll go," she said.

I looked at my watch and stood up, saying:

"Better get back to bed. We'll move tomorrow. Good night."

She chewed her lower lip, wanting to say something, not wanting to say it, finally blurting it out:

"I'll have to have morphine down there."

"Sure. What's your day's ration?"

"Five—ten grains."

"That's mild enough," I said, and then, casually: "Do you like using the stuff?"

"I'm afraid it's too late for my liking it or not liking it to make any difference now."

"You've been reading Sunday papers," I said. "If you want to break off, and we've a few days to spare down there, we'll use them weaning you. It's not so tough."

She laughed shakily, with a queer twitching of her lips.

"Go away," she cried. "Don't give me any more assurances, promises, please. I can't stand any more tonight. I'm drunk on them now. Please."

"All right. Night."

"Good night—and thanks."

I went into my room. Mickey was unscrewing the top of a flask. His knees were dusty. He turned his half-wit's grin on me and said:

"What a swell dish you are. What are you trying to do? Win yourself a home?"

"Sh-h-h. Anything new?"

"The big officials have gone back to the county seat. The redhead nurse was getting a load at the keyhole when I came back from eating. I chased her."

"And took her place?" I asked, nodding at his dusty knees.

You couldn't embarrass Mickey. He said:

"Hell, no. She was at the other door, in the hall."

III

I got Fitzstephan's car from the garage and drove Gabrielle and Mrs Herman down to the house in the cove late the next morning. The girl was in low spirits. She made a poor job of smiling when spoken to, and had nothing to say on her own account. I thought it might be because she was returning to the house where her honeymoon had been ended by Collinson's murder; but when we got there she went in with no appearance of reluctance, and there was nothing to show that the place depressed her any further.

After luncheon—Mrs Herman turned out to be a good cook—Gabrielle decided she wanted to go outdoors, so she and I walked over to the little Mexican settlement on the creek to see Mary Nunez, the Mexican woman who had done her housework before. Mary promised to show up for work the next day. She seemed quite fond of Gabrielle, but not of me.

We returned to the house by way of the shore, picking our way between, over, and around pebbles, sand, boulders, and young mountains. We walked slowly. The girl's forehead was puckered between the eyebrows. Neither of us said anything from the time we left the Mexican settlement until we were within a quarter of a mile of home. Then Gabrielle sat down on the rounded top of a rock that was warm in the sun.

"Can you remember what you told me last night?" she asked, running her words together in her hurry to get them out. She looked frightened.

"Yeah."

"Tell me again," she begged, moving over to one side of the rock. "Sit down and tell me again—all of it."

I did—spending nearly three-quarters of an hour at it. I didn't make such a lousy job of it, either. The fear went out of her eyes as I talked. Toward the last she was smiling to herself. When I had finished she jumped up, laughing, working her fingers together.

"Thank you. Thank you," she babbled. "Please don't let me ever stop believing you. Make me believe you—even if—No. It is true. Make me believe it always. Come on. Let's walk some more."

She almost ran me the rest of the way. Mickey Linehan was on the front porch. I stopped with him while the girl went indoors.

"Tch, tch, tch, as Mr Roily says." He shook his grinning face at me. "I ought to tell her what happened to that poor girl up in Poisonville who got to thinking she could trust you."

"Bring any news down from the village with you?" I asked.

"Madison Andrews's found. He was at the Jeffries place in San Mateo, where Aaronia Haldorn's staying. She's still there. Andrews went there Tuesday afternoon and stayed till last night. Al Mason was watching the place; saw him go in, but didn't tumble to who it was till he left. The Jeffries are away—San Diego. Dick Foley's tailing Andrews now; Al says the Haldorn woman hasn't been off the place. Roily tells me that Fink's awake, but don't know anything about the bomb; and Fitzstephan's still hanging on to life."

"I think I'll run over and talk to Fink this afternoon," I said. "Stick around here. And—oh, yeah—you'll have to act more respectful to me when Mrs Collinson's around. It's important that she keep on thinking I'm hot stuff."

"For God's sake bring back some booze—I can't do it sober."

Fink was propped up in bed when I got to him, looking out under bandages. He insisted that he knew nothing about the bomb, that all he had come down for was to tell me about Harvey Whidden being his step-son.

"Well, what of that?" I asked.

"I don't know what of it," he said. "After they let me out, I read in the papers what had happened down here, and I thought I ought to come down and tell you that."

"How much can you tell me about Whidden?"

"Not anything much. Me and him wasn't too friendly. He was at the Temple for a couple of weeks, working for the Haldorns, but they couldn't get along with him, so they let him go."

"You know Madison Andrews?" I asked.

"No. I read about him in the papers. Ain't he that Leggett girl's guardian or something?"

"You don't know him? Aaronia Haldorn does."

"Maybe she does, mister, but I don't. I just worked for the Haldorns. It wasn't anything to me but a job."

The nurse who was fluttering around had become a nuisance by this time, so I left the hospital for the court house and the prosecuting attorney's office.

Vernon pushed aside a stack of papers with a the-world-can-wait gesture, and said, "Glad to see you; sit down," nodding vigorously, showing me all his teeth.

I sat down and said:

"Been talking to Fink. I couldn't get anything out of him, but he's our meat. The bomb couldn't have got in there except by him."

Vernon looked thoughtful for a moment, then shook his chin at me and snapped:

"What's his motive? And you were there. You say you were looking at him all the time he was in the room. You say you saw nothing."

"What of it?" I asked. "He could outsmart me there. It's his game. The Haldorns hired him because he was an expert at that sort of stuff—had been in charge of the mechanical end of all the best known stage magicians' acts at one time or another. He'd know how to make a bomb, and how to put it down in front of me. We don't know what Fitzstephan saw. Let's hang on to this Fink till Fitzstephan can talk. They tell me he'll pull through."

Vernon clicked his teeth together and said: "Very well, we'll hold him."

I found the local telephone office and put in a call for Vic Dallas' drug store in San Francisco's Mission.

"I want," I told Vic, "about fifty grains of M. and eight of those calomel-atropine-cascara-ipecacstrychnine shots. I'll have somebody pick up the package tonight or in the morning. Right?"

"If you say so, but if you kill anybody, don't tell them where you got the stuff."

I promised not to and put in a call for the agency, talking to the Old Man. He said there were no new reports on Aaronia Haldorn and Madison Andrews, and he agreed to send me another op, MacMan, and to tell him to get a package from Dallas.

I drove back to the house in the cove. We had company. Three strange cars were parked in the driveway, and half a dozen newshounds were sitting and standing around Mickey on the porch. They turned their questions on me.

"Mrs Collinson's here for a rest," I told them. "Let her alone. If any news breaks here I'll see that you get it, those who let her alone. The only thing I can tell you now is that Fink will be held for the bombing."

"What did Andrews come down for?" Jack Santos of the *Bulletin* asked.

That wasn't a surprise to me, of course: I had expected him to show up now that he was out of hiding.

"Ask him," I suggested. "He's administering Mrs Collinson's estate. You can't make a mystery out of his seeing her."

"Is it true that they're on bad terms?"

"No."

"Then why didn't he show up before this—yesterday or the day before?"

"Ask him."

"Is it true that he's up to his tonsils in debt—or was before the estate came into his hands?"

"Ask him."

Santos smiled with thinned lips and said:

"We don't have to. We asked his creditors. Is there anything to the story that Mrs Collinson and her husband quarrelled over her being too friendly with Whidden, a couple of days before her husband was killed?"

"Anything but the truth. Tough. You could do a lot with a story like that."

"Is it true that Mrs Haldorn and Thomas Fink were released to keep them quiet, because they had threatened to tell all they know if they were held for trial?"

"Now you're kidding me, Jack," I said. "Is Andrews still here?"

"Yes."

I went indoors and called Mickey in.

"Seen Dick?" I asked.

"He drove past a couple of minutes after Andrews got here."

"Sneak away and find him. Tell him not to let the newspaper gang make him, even if he has to risk losing Andrews for a while. They'd go crazy all over the front of their sheets if they learned we were shadowing Andrews."

Mrs Herman was coming down the stairs. I asked her where Andrews was.

"In the front room."

I went up there. Gabrielle, in a low-cut black velvet gown, was sitting stiff and straight on the edge of a leather rocker. Her face was white and sullen. She was looking at a handkerchief stretched between her hands. When I came in she turned to me as if glad to see me.

Madison Andrews stood with his back to the fireplace. His white hair, eyebrows and mustache stood out every which way from his bony pink face. He shifted his scowl from the girl to me, and didn't seem at all glad to see me.

I said, "Hello," and found a table corner to lean against.

He said: "I've come to take Mrs Collinson back to San Francisco."

Gabrielle didn't say anything. I said:

"Yeah? Not to San Mateo?"

"What do you mean by that?" The white tangle of his brows came down to hide the upper halves of his blue eyes.

"God knows. Maybe my mind's been corrupted by the questions the newspapers have been asking me."

He didn't quite wince. He said, slowly, deliberately:

"Mrs Haldorn requested my assistance, as an attorney. I went to see her to explain how, in the circumstances, I could not advise or represent her."

"That's all right with me," I said. "And if it took you thirty hours to explain that to her, it's nobody's business."

"Exactly."

"But—I'd be careful how I told that to the half a dozen reporters waiting out front for you. You know how suspicious they are—for no reason at all."

He turned to the girl, speaking quietly but with some impatience:

"Well, Gabrielle, are you going with me?"

"Should I?" she asked me.

"Not unless you especially want to."

"I don't."

"Then that's settled," I said.

Andrews nodded and went forward to take her hand, saying:

"I must get back to the city, my dear. You should have a phone put in, so you can reach me in case of need."

He declined her invitation to stay to dinner, said, "Good evening," not unpleasantly to me, and went out. Through the window I could see him presently getting into his car, paying as little attention as he could to the newspaper men clustering around him.

Gabrielle was frowning at me when I turned from the window.

"What did you mean by what you said about San Mateo?" she asked.

"How friendly are he and Aaronia Haldorn?" I asked.

"I don't know. I know they're acquainted, of course, but nothing beyond that. Why? Why did you talk to him as you did?"

"Detective business. For one thing, there's a rumor that getting control of your father's estate may have helped him to keep his own head above water. Maybe there's nothing in it. Anyway, it won't hurt to give him a little scare, so he'll get busy straightening things out—if he has done any juggling—between now and clean-up day. No use of you losing money along with your other troubles."

"Then he—?" she began, spreading her eyes at me.

"He's got a week—several days at least—to unjuggle in. That ought to be enough."

"But—"

Mrs Herman, calling us to dinner, ended the conversation.

Gabrielle ate very little. She and I had to do most of the talking until I got Mickey started telling about a job he had been on up in Eureka, where he had posed as a foreigner who knew no English. Since English was the only language he did know, and Eureka normally contains at least one specimen of all the nationalities there are, he'd had a hell of a time keeping people from finding out just what he was supposed to be. He made a long and funny story of it. Maybe some of it was the truth.

After dinner he and I strolled around the grounds while the summer night darkened them.

I told him MacMan was coming down and asked him if Foley had had any news.

"No, he said Andrews came straight here from his home."

The front door opened, throwing yellow light across the porch. Gabrielle, a dark cape over her gown, came into the yellow light, closed the door, and came down to the gravel walk.

"You'll be doing the watch-dog from bedtime till morning," I told Mickey. "Take a nap now if you want. I'll call you."

"You're a darb." He laughed in the dark. "By God, you're a darb." The grass swished against his shoes as he walked away.

I moved toward the gravel walk, meeting the girl.

"Isn't it a lovely night?" she said.

"Yeah. But you can't go roaming around alone in the dark, even if your troubles are practically over."

"I didn't intend to." She took my arm, suddenly let it go. "Or have you something else—?"

"No."

"Practically over," she repeated when we had reached the road. "What does that mean?"

"That there are a few details still to be taken care of. The morphine, for instance."

She shivered and said: "I've only enough left to last me tonight. You promised to—"

"Fifty grains will be down in the morning."

She kept quiet, as if waiting for me to say something more. I didn't say anything. Her fingers wriggled on my sleeve.

"You said it wouldn't be hard to cure me." She spoke half questioningly, as if expecting me to deny that I had said anything of the sort.

"It wouldn't."

"You said perhaps..." the rest of it faded off.

"We'd do it while we were here?"

"Yes."

"Want to?" I asked. "It's no go if you don't."

"Do I want to?" She stood still in the road, facing me. "I'd give—" A sob ended that sentence. Her voice came again, high-pitched, thin: "Are you being honest with me? Are you? Is what you've told me—all that you said last night and this afternoon—as true as you've made it sound? Do I believe in you because you are sincere? Or because you've learned how—as a trick of your business—to make people believe in you?"

This girl might be crazy, but she wasn't any too stupid. I gave her the answer that seemed best at the time:

"Your belief in me is built on mine in you. If mine's unjustified, so is yours. So let me ask you a question first; were you lying when you said, 'I don't want to be evil'?"

"Oh, I don't. I don't."

"Well then," I said with an air of finality, as if that settled it. "Now if you want to get off the junk, off you get."

"How—how long will it take?"

"Say a week. Maybe less, but we'll say a week to be safe."

"Do you mean that? No longer than that?"

"That's all for the part that counts. You'll have to take care of yourself for some time afterward, till your system's in shape again, but you'll be off the junk."

"Will I suffer—much?"

"A couple of bad days, but they won't be as bad as you'll think they are, and you've got enough of your father's toughness to stand them."

"If," she said slowly, "I should find out in the middle of it that I can't go through with it, will you—?"

"There'll be nothing you can do about it," I promised cheerfully. "You'll stay in till you come out the other end."

She shivered again and asked:

"When shall we start?"

"Day after tomorrow. Take your usual allowance tomorrow, but don't try to stock up. And don't worry about it. It'll be tougher on me than on you—I'll have to put up with you."

"And you'll make allowances—you'll understand—if I'm not always nice while going through it? Even if I'm nasty sometimes?"

"I don't know." I didn't want to encourage her to cut up on me. "I don't think much of niceness that can be turned into nastiness by a little grief."

"Oh, but—" She stopped, wrinkled her forehead, said: "Can't we send Mrs Herman away? I don't want to—I don't want her looking at me."

"I'll get rid of her tomorrow."

"And if I'm—you won't let anybody else see me—if I'm not—if I'm too terrible?"

"No," I promised. "But look here: apparently you're preparing to put on a circus for me. Stop thinking about that end. You're going to behave. I don't want too much monkey business out of you."

She laughed suddenly, asking:

"Will you beat me if I'm bad?"

I said she might still be young enough for a spanking to do her good.

IV

Mary Nunez came to work at half-past seven the following morning. A little later Mickey Linehan, in our borrowed car, drove Mrs Herman in to Quesada, returning with MacMan, a bottle of gin, and a load of groceries.

MacMan was a square-built, stiff-backed man. Ten years of soldiering on the islands had baked his tight-mouthed, solid-jawed, rather grim, face a dark oak. He was the perfect soldier; he went where you sent him, stayed where you put him, and had no ideas of his own to keep him from doing exactly what you told him.

He gave me the druggist's package. I opened it and took ten grains of morphine up to Gabrielle. She was sitting in bed, eating breakfast. Her eyes were watery, her face damp and grayish. When she saw the bindles in my hand she pushed her tray aside and held her hands out eagerly, wriggling her shoulders.

"Come back in five minutes?" she asked.

"You can take your shot in front of me. I'll try not to blush."

"But I would," she said, and did.

I went out, closed the door, and leaned against it, hearing the rustle of paper and the clink of the water glass touching a spoon. Presently she called:

"All right."

I went in again. A crumpled ball of white paper in the tray was all that was left of one bindle. The others weren't in sight. She was leaning back against her pillows, eyes half-closed, comfortable as a cat full of goldfish. She smiled lazily at me and said:

"You're a dear. Know what I'd like to do today? Take some lunch and go out on the water—spend the whole day simply floating in the sun."

"That ought to be good for you," I agreed. "Take either Linehan or MacMan with you, though. You're not to go anywhere alone."

"What are you going to do?" she asked.

"Ride up to Quesada, over to the county seat, maybe as far as the city."

"Mayn't I go with you?"

I shook my head, saying:

"No. I've got work to do, and, besides, you're supposed to rest."

She said, "Oh," and reached for her coffee. I turned to the door. "The rest of the morphine?" She spoke over the edge of the cup. "You've put it in a safe place? Where nobody will find it?"

"Yeah," I said, grinning at her, patting my coat pocket.

In Quesada I spent half an hour talking to Roily and reading the San Francisco papers. They were beginning to poke at Andrews with hints and questions that stopped just short of libel. That was so much to the good. The deputy sheriff hadn't anything to tell me. I went over to the county seat. Vernon was in court. Twenty minutes of the sheriffs conversation didn't add to my knowledge. I phoned the agency and talked to the Old

Man without learning anything. At the hospital they told me Fitzstephan was certainly going to live.

I drove up to San Francisco, had dinner at the St. Germain, stopped at my room to collect another suit and a bagful of clean shirts and the like, and got back to the house in the cove a little before midnight. MacMan came out of the darkness while I was tucking the car under the shed. He said nothing had happened during my absence. We went into the house together. Mickey was in the kitchen, yawning and mixing himself a drink preparatory to relieving MacMan on sentry duty.

"Mrs Collinson gone to bed?" I asked.

"I don't know. She's been in her room all day, and the light's still on."

MacMan and I had a drink with Mickey and then went upstairs. I knocked at the girl's door.

"Who is it?" she asked. I told her. She said: "Yes?"

"No breakfast in the morning," I said.

"Really?" Then, as if it were something she had almost forgotten. "Oh, I've decided not to put you to all the trouble of curing me." She opened the door and stood in the opening, smiling too pleasantly at me, a finger holding her place in a book. "Did you have a nice ride?"

"All right," I said, taking the rest of the morphine from my pocket and holding it out to her. "There's no use of my carrying this around."

She didn't take it. She laughed in my face and said:

"You are a brute, aren't you?"

I said:

"Well, it's your cure, not mine," stuffing the stuff back in my pocket. "If you—" I broke off to listen. A board had creaked down the hall. Now there was a soft sound, as of a bare foot dragging across the floor.

"That's Mary Nunez watching over me," Gabrielle whispered gaily. "She made herself a bed in the attic and refused to go home. She doesn't think I'm safe with you Continentals. She warned me against you—said you were—what was it?—oh, yes—wolves. Are you?"

I said: "Absolutely."

The next afternoon I gave Gabrielle the first dose of Vic Dallas' mixture, and three more at two-hour intervals afterward. She spent the day in her room. That was Saturday.

On Sunday she had ten grains of morphine and was in high spirits all day, considering herself already practically cured.

On Monday she had the rest of Vic's concoction, and the day was pretty much like Saturday. Mickey Linehan returned from a visit to the county seat with the news that Fitzstephan was conscious, but too weak and bandaged to have talked even if the doctors would have let him; that Andrews had been to San Mateo to see Aaronia Haldorn again; and that she had been to the hospital to see Fink, but had been refused permission by the sheriff's office.

Tuesday was a more exciting day.

Gabrielle was up and dressed when I carried her orange-juice breakfast in. She was bright-eyed, restless, talkative, and laughed easily until I mentioned—off-hand—that she was to have no more morphine.

"Ever, you mean?" Her face and voice were panicky. "No, you don't mean that?"

"Yeah."

"But I'll die." Tears filled her eyes, ran down her little white face, and she wrung her hands. It was childishly pathetic. I had to remind myself that tears were one of the regular symptoms of morphine withdrawal. "You know that's not the way. I don't expect as much as usual. I know I'll get less and less each day. But you can't stop it like that. You're joking. That would kill me." She cried some more at the thought of being killed.

I made myself laugh as if I were sympathetic but amused.

"Nonsense," I said cheerfully. "The chief trouble you're going to have is being too full of life. A couple of days of that—then you'll be all set."

She bit her lower lip, finally managed a smile, holding out both hands to me.

"I'm going to believe you," she said. "I do believe you. I'm going to believe you no matter what you tell me."

Her hands were clammy. I squeezed them and said:

"Fine. Now back to bed. I'll look in every now and then, and if you want anything in between, sing out."

"You're not going away today?"

"No," I promised.

She stood the gaff pretty well all afternoon. Of course there wasn't much heartiness in the way she laughed at herself between attacks when the sneezing and yawning set in; but the thing was that she tried to laugh.

Madison Andrews came at half-past five. Having seen him drive in, I met him on the porch. The ruddiness of his face had washed out to a weak orange.

"Good afternoon," he said agreeably enough. "I wish to see Mrs Collinson."

"I'll deliver any message to her," I offered.

He pulled his eyebrows down and some of his normal ruddiness came back.

"I wish to see her." It was a command.

"But she doesn't wish to see you. Is there any message?"

All of his ruddiness was back now. His eyes were hot. I was standing between him and the door. He couldn't go in while I stood there. For a moment he seemed about to push me out of the way. That didn't worry me. He was carrying a handicap of twenty-some years and twenty-some pounds.

He pulled his jaw into his neck and spoke in the voice of authority:

"Mrs Collinson must return to San Francisco with me. She cannot stay here. This is a preposterous arrangement."

"She's not going to San Francisco," I said. "If necessary, the prosecuting attorney will hold her here as a material witness. Try upsetting that with any of your court orders, and we'll give you something else to worry about. We'll prove that she might be in danger from you. How do we know that you haven't monkeyed with her money? That you don't mean to take undue advantage of her unfortunate condition to shield yourself now? Why, man, you might even be planning to send her to an insane asylum so the estate will stay in your hands forever."

He was sick behind his eyes, but the rest of him stood up gamely under this broadside. When he had got his breath he swallowed and demanded:

"Does Gabrielle believe this?" His face was purple.

"Who said anybody believed it?" I asked. "I'm just telling you what we'll go into court with. You're a lawyer. You know what we can do with the local court—and the newspapers."

The sickness spread from behind his eyes, pushing the color out of his face, the stiffness out of his bones, but he held himself tall and found a level voice.

"You may tell Mrs Collinson that I shall return my letters testamentary to the court this week, with an accounting of the estate and a request that I be relieved."

"That'll be swell," I said; but I felt sorry for the old scoundrel shuffling down to his car, climbing slowly into it.

I didn't tell Gabrielle he had been there.

She was whining a little now between her yawning and sneezing, and her eyes were running water. Face, body and hands were damp with sweat. She could not eat. I kept her full of orange juice. Noises and odors—no matter how faint or how pleasant—were beginning to bother her too sensitive nerves, and she was twitching and jerking around continually in her bed.

"Will it get much worse than this?" she asked.

"Not very much. There'll be nothing you can't stand."

Mickey Linehan was waiting for me when I got downstairs.

"The spick's got herself a chive," he said pleasantly.

"Yeah?"

"It's the one I've been halving lemons with to take the stink out of that gin. It's a paring knife—four or five inches of stainless steel blade—so you won't get rust marks on your undershirt when she sticks it in your back. I couldn't find it, and asked her about it, and she didn't look like I was a well-poisoner when she said she didn't know anything about it, and that's the first time she ever looked like that at me, so I knew she had taken it."

"You're a smart boy," I said. "Keep an eye on her—she's gone on record as saying we're a flock of wolves."

"I'm to do that?" Mickey grinned. "My idea would be that everybody looked out for himself, seeing that you're the lad she dog-eyes most, and it's most likely you that'll get whittled on. What'd you ever do to her? You haven't been dumb enough to trifle with a Mex lady's affections, have you?"

I didn't think he was funny, though he may have been.

Aaronia Haldorn arrived just before dark, in a Lincoln limousine driven by a negro who turned the siren loose when he brought the car into the drive. I was in Gabrielle's room when the thing howled. She all but jumped out of bed, utterly terrorized by this racket that must have been pretty bad in her too sensitive ears.

"What was that? What was it?" she cried between rattling teeth, her body shaking the bed.

"S-h-h," I soothed her. I was acquiring a fair bedside manner. "Just an automobile horn. Visitors. I'll go down and head them off."

"You won't let anybody see me?" she begged.

"No. Now be a good girl till I get back."

Aaronia Haldorn was standing beside the limousine talking to MacMan when I came out. In the dim light her oval face—between black hat and black fur coat—looked more than ever like an olive-tinted, red-mouthed mask. But her enormous black eyes were real enough.

"How do you do?" she said, holding out a hand. Her voice was a thing to make warm waves run up your back. "I'm glad for Mrs Collinson's sake that you are watching over her. She and I have already had excellent proof of your ability in that direction—both of us owing our lives to it."

That was all right, but it had been said before. I made a gesture that was supposed to indicate modest distaste for the subject, and beat her to the first tap with:

"I'm sorry she can't see you. She isn't well."

"Oh, but I should so much like to see her, if only for a moment. Don't you think it might be good for her?"

I said I was sorry. She seemed to accept that as final, though she said: "I came all the way from the city to see her."

I tried that opening with:

"Didn't Mr Andrews tell you...?" letting the sentence ravel out at the end.

She didn't say whether he had or not. She turned beside me and began walking slowly across the grass. There was nothing for me to do but go along with her. Full darkness was only a few minutes away. Presently, when we had gone thirty or forty feet from the car, she said:

"Mr Andrews thinks you suspect him."

"He's right."

"Of what do you suspect him?"

"Juggling the estate."

"Really?"

"Really," I said, "and of nothing else."

"Oh, I should suppose that would be enough."

"It's enough for me," I said, "but I didn't think it was enough for you." I piled up what facts I had, put some guesses on them, and then took a jump into space from the top of the heap: "When you got out of prison, you sent for Andrews, pumped him for all he knew, and then, when you learned he had been playing with the girl's pennies, you saw a chance to confuse things by throwing suspicion on him. The old boy's woman-crazy; he was duck-soup for a woman like you. I don't know what you're planning to do with him, but you seem to have got him started—and to have got the newspapers started after him. I take it you gave them the tip-off on his high-financing? It's no good, Mrs Haldorn. Chuck it. It won't work. You could stir him up, all right, make him do something criminal, get him into a swell jam. He's desperate enough now that people are poking at him. But it'll do you no good. Whatever he does now won't confuse what somebody else did in the past. He's promised to get the estate in order and hand it over. Let him alone."

She didn't say anything while we took another dozen steps. A path came under our feet. I said:

"This is the path that runs up the cliff—the one Eric Collinson was pushed off of. Did you know him?"

She drew in her breath sharply—with almost a sob in her throat—but her voice was steady, quiet, musical when she replied:

"You know I did. Why should you ask?"

"Detectives like questions they already know the answers to. Why did you come down here, Mrs Haldorn?"

"Is that another whose answer you know?"

"I know that you came for one or both of two reasons. First, to learn how close we had got to the answer of our riddle. Right?"

"I've my share of curiosity, naturally," she said.

"I don't mind making that part of your trip a success. We know the answer."

She stood still in the path, facing me, her eyes phosphorescent in the dim light. She put one hand on my shoulder. The other was in her coat pocket. She put her face closer to mine. She spoke very slowly, as if taking great pains to be understood:

"Tell me truthfully. Don't pretend. This is important. I don't want to do an unnecessary wrong. Wait, wait—think before you speak—and believe me when I say that to lie—to bluff—now will be to commit the most dangerous sort of folly. Now tell me—do you know the answer?"

"Yeah."

She smiled faintly, took her hand from my shoulder, saying: "Then there's no use of our fencing."

I plunged into her. If she had fired from the pocket she might have plugged me. But she tried to get the gun out. By then I had a hand on her wrist. The bullet went into the ground between us. The nails of her free hand put three red ribbons down the side of my face. I tucked my head under her chin, turned my hip to her before her knee came up, brought her body hard against mine with one arm around her, and bent her gun-hand behind her.

She dropped the gun as we fell. I was on top. I remained there until I had found the gun. I was getting up when MacMan arrived.

"Everything's oke," I told him, having trouble with my voice. "See that the chauffeur's behaving."

MacMan nodded and went away. The woman sat on the ground with her legs tucked under her and rubbed her wrist. I said:

"That was the second reason for your coming—though I thought you meant it for the girl. Since we've gone this far, it won't do you any harm and it might do some good to talk."

"I don't think anything will help me now." She got up. I didn't help her because I didn't want her to know how shaky I was. "You say you know." She shrugged. "Then lies are worthless, and only lies would help." She set her hat straight. "Well, what now?"

"Nothing—if you'll promise to remember that the time for being desperate is past. This kind of thing splits up in three parts—being caught, being convicted, and being punished. Admit it's too late to do anything about the first, and—well, you know what California juries, judges and prison boards are."

She looked curiously at me and asked: "Why do you tell me this?"

The answer was, of course, because I was a damned fool; but I said:

"Because being shot at's no treat to me, and because when a job's done I like to get it over with. I'm not interested in trying to convict you of any part in this game, and it's a nuisance having you horning in at the last, trying to muddy things up. Go home and keep yourself quiet."

Neither of us said anything more until we had walked back to her car. Then she turned, held her hand out to me, and said:

"I think—I don't know yet—but I think I've even more to thank you for now."

"I didn't say anything, and I didn't take her hand. She asked:

"May I have my pistol?"

"No."

"Will you give my best wishes to Mrs Collinson, and tell her I'm so sorry I couldn't see her?"

"Yeah."

She said, "Goodbye," and got into the car; I took off my hat and she rode away.

V

Mickey Linehan opened the front door for me. He looked at my scratched face and laughed:

"You do have one hell of a time with your women. Why don't you try getting along with them?" He jerked a thumb at the ceiling. "Better go up and negotiate with that one. She's been raising hell."

I went up to Gabrielle's room. She was sitting in the middle of the wallowed-up bed. Her fingers were in her hair, tugging at it. Her face—wet with tears and sweat—was thirty-five years old. She was making hurt-animal noises in her throat.

I grinned at her from the door and said:

"It's a fight, huh?"

She took her fingers out of her hair.

"I won't die?" The question was a whimper between teeth set edge to edge.

"Not a chance."

She sobbed and lay down. I straightened the covers over her. She complained that there was a lump in her throat, that her jaws and the hollows behind her knees ached.

"Regular symptoms," I assured her. "They won't bother you much, and you won't have cramps."

She remembered the visitor then, and asked me who it had been, asked me about the shot she had heard, and about my scratched face.

"It was Aaronia Haldorn, and she lost her head for a moment. No harm done. She's gone."

"She came here to kill me," the girl said, not excitedly, but as if she knew it positively.

"May be. She wouldn't admit anything."

It was a long bad night. I spent most of it in the girl's room, in a leather rocker dragged in from the front room. She got perhaps an hour and a half of sleep, in three instalments. Nightmares brought her screaming out of all three. I dozed when she let me. Off and on through the night I heard stealthy sounds in the hall—Mary Nunez watching over her mistress, I supposed.

Wednesday was a longer and worse day. By noon my jaws were as sore as Gabrielle's, from going around holding my back teeth together.

She was getting the works now. Light was positive, active, pain to her eyes, sound to her ears, odor to her nostrils. The weight of her silk nightgown, the touch of sheets under and over her, tortured her skin. Every nerve she had yanked at every muscle she had, continually. Promises that she wasn't going to die did no good now: Life wasn't nice enough.

"Stop fighting it, if you want," I said. "Let yourself go. I'll take care of you."

She took me at my word, and I had a maniac on my hands. Once her shrieks brought Mary Nunez to the door, snarling and spitting at me in Mex-Spanish. I was holding Gabrielle in bed by the shoulders at the time, sweating as much as she was.

"Get out of here," I snarled back at the Mexican woman.

She put a brown hand into the bosom of her dress and came a step into the room. Mickey Linehan came up behind her, pulled her back into the hall, and shut the door.

Roily came down from Quesada that afternoon with word that Fitzstephan had come sufficiently alive to be questioned by the prosecuting attorney. Fitzstephan had told Vernon that he had not seen the bomb, had seen nothing to show where it had come from; but that he had an indistinct memory of hearing a noise just after Fink and I had left the room—a tinkling and a thud on the floor close to him.

I told Roily I'd try to get to the county seat next day, and to tell Vernon to hang on to Fink, that he was our meat.

Gabrielle spent the rest of the afternoon shrieking, begging, and crying for morphine. That evening she made a complete confession:

"I told you I didn't want to be evil. That was a lie. I've always wanted to, always have been. I wanted to do to you what I did to the others, but now I don't want you. I want morphine. They won't hang me—I know that. And I don't care what else they do to me—if I can only get some morphine."

She laughed viciously, wadding the bedclothes in feverish hands, and went on:

"You were right when you said I could bring out the worst in men because I wanted to. I did want to, and I did—except, I failed with Dr Riese and with Eric. I don't know what was the matter with them. And with both of them I went too far, let them know too much about me. And that's why they were killed. Joseph drugged Dr Riese and I killed him myself, and then we made Minnie think she had done it. And I persuaded Joseph to kill Aaronia, and he would have done it—he would have done anything I asked—if you hadn't interfered. I got Harvey Whidden to kill Eric for me. I was tied to Eric, legally—tied to a good man who wanted to make me a good woman."

She laughed again, licking her lips.

"Harvey and I needed money, so we pretended he had kidnapped me, hoping to get it that way. He was a glorious beast; it's a shame they killed him. I had that bomb—had had it for months. I had stolen it from father's laboratory when he was making some experiments for a motion picture company. I always carried it with me—it wasn't large. I meant it for you in the hotel room. I was feverish, and I was sure when I heard two men going out of the room, that you were the one who had remained. I didn't see that it was Owen till after I had opened the door a little way and thrown the bomb. Now you've got what you wanted from me. Give me morphine. Have what I've told you written out, and I'll sign it. You can't pretend now that I'm worth curing, worth saving. Give me morphine."

I laughed at her and her confession, reminding her that she'd forgotten to include the kidnapping of Charlie Ross and the blowing up of the *Maine*.

We had some more hell—a solid hour of it, before she succeeded in exhausting herself again. The night dragged through. She got a little more than two hours' sleep, a half-hour improvement over the previous night. I dozed in a chair when I could.

Sometime before daylight I woke to the feel of a hand in my pocket. Keeping my breathing regular, I pushed my eyelids apart till I could squint through the lashes. We had a very dim light in the room, but I thought Gabrielle was in bed. My head was tilted back on the chairback. I couldn't see the hand that was exploring my inside coat pocket, nor the arm that came down over my shoulder, but they smelled of the kitchen, so I knew they belonged to Mary Nunez. She was standing behind me. Mickey had told me she had a knife. Good judgment told me to let her alone. I did that, closing my eyes again. Paper rustled between her fingers, and then her hand left my pocket.

I moved my head sleepily and changed a foot's position. I heard the door close quietly behind me. I sat up and looked around. Gabrielle was asleep. I counted the bindles in my pocket and found that eight had been taken.

Presently Gabrielle opened her eyes. This was the first time since the cure started that she hadn't been awakened by a nightmare. Her face was haggard, but not wild-eyed. She looked at the window and asked:

"Isn't day coming yet?"

"It's getting light." I gave her some orange juice. "We'll get solid food into you today."

"I don't want food. I want morphine."

"You'll get food. You won't get morphine. Today won't be like yesterday. You may have a couple of bad spots, but you're over the hump, and the rest of it's downhill going. It's silly to ask for morphine now. What do you want to do? Have nothing to show for all the hell you've been through. You've got it licked—stay with it."

"Have I—have I really got it licked?"

"Yeah. All you've got to buck now is nervousness—and the memory of how nice it felt to have a skinful of hop."

"I can do it," she said. "I can do it because you say I can."

She got along fine until late in the morning, when she blew up for an hour or two. I discovered that cursing her helped, so I finally got her straightened out. When Mary brought her luncheon up I left them together and went downstairs for my own.

When I came back Gabrielle, in a rose dressing gown, was sitting in the leather rocker that had been my bed for two nights. She had brushed her hair and powdered her face. Her eyes were mostly green, with a lift to the lower lids, as if she was hiding a joke. She said with mock solemnity:

"Sit down; I want to talk seriously to you."

I sat down.

"Why did you go through all this with—for me?" She was really serious now. "You didn't have to, and it couldn't have been pleasant. I was—I don't know how bad I was." She turned red from forehead to chest. "I know it must have been disgusting, revolting. I know how I must seem to you now. Why—why did you do it?"

I said:

"I'm twice your age, Gabrielle, an old man. I'm damned if I'll make a chump of myself by telling you why I did it, why it was neither revolting nor disgusting, why I'd do it again and be glad of the chance."

She jumped out of the chair, her eyes wide and dark, her mouth trembling.

"You mean—?"

"I don't mean anything that I'll admit," I said, "and if you parade around with that gown hanging open you're going to catch yourself some bronchitis. As an ex-hophead, you've got to be careful about catching cold."

She sat down on the bed, put her hands over her face, and began crying. I let her cry. Presently she giggled through tears and fingers and asked:

"Will you go out and let me be alone all afternoon?"

"Yeah, if you'll keep warm."

I drove over to the county seat, went to the hospital, and argued with people until they let me into Fitzstephan's room.

He was mostly bandages, with one eye and one side of his mouth peeping out. The eye and mouth-half smiled out of linen at me, and a voice came out:

"Don't ever invite me to any more of your hotel rooms." It wasn't a clear voice, because it had to come out sideways and the novelist couldn't move his jaw; but there was plenty of vitality in it. There was no doubt about its being the voice of a man who was going to live a while.

I grinned at him and said:

"No hotel rooms this time. I'm inviting you to San Quentin. Strong enough to stand up under a third-degree now, or shall I wait a day or two?"

"I ought to be at my best now—facial expressions will hardly give me away."

"Good. Now here's the point: Fink handed that bomb to you when he shook hands with you. That's the only way it could have got in without my seeing it. His back was to me then. You didn't know what he was handing you, of course, but you had to take it—just as you have to deny it now—because otherwise you'd tip us off that you were tied up with Fink and the Holy Grail people, and that he had reasons for killing you."

Fitzstephan said: "You say the most remarkable things. No doubt you know what his reasons were?"

"You engineered Riese's murder in the Temple. Fink, Aaronia Haldorn and Joseph were accomplices. Joseph was killed. The rest of them put the blame on him—saying he went crazy. That lets them out, or ought to. But here you are killing

Collinson and planning God knows what else. Fink's got sense enough to know that if you keep on you're going to let the truth out and drag him and the others to the gallows with you. So he tries to stop you—with me as his alibi."

Fitzstephan said: "Better and better. So I had Collinson killed?"

"Yeah. Hired Whidden, and then wouldn't pay him. He kidnapped the girl, holding her for his money, knowing she was what you wanted. But you made your double-cross stick, by luck."

Fitzstephan said: "I'm running out of exclamations. So I was after her? I wondered about my motive."

"You must have been pretty rotten with her. She'd had a bad time with Andrews, even with Eric, but she didn't mind talking about them. When it came to you, she shuddered and shut up. I suppose she slammed you down hard—and you're the sort of egoist who'd be driven to anything by something like that."

Fitzstephan said: "I suppose. You've suspected me how long?"

"Well, you were standing beside Mrs Leggett back in their house when she suddenly got a gun to hold us off with, and you were struggling with her when she shot herself. So was I, but your hand was on her gun-hand. There was no proof of anything then. The morning that Fink hoisted you, you and I had gone over the whole story and decided that it was all the work of one mind. You are the one person whose connection with each episode can be traced, who has the sort of mind needed, and who has the motive. I couldn't be sure of the motive until I got my first chance at an undisturbed talk with Gabrielle—the evening after the explosion. I didn't definitely connect you with the Temple crowd until Fink and Aaronia Haldorn did it for me."

Fitzstephan said: "Ah, Aaronia helped you connect me? What has she been up to?"

"She's done her best to set us off sideways after Andrews, trying to cover you up by gumming the works, even by trying to shoot me."

"She's so impetuous," he said lightly, and turned his head on the pillow so that his uncovered eye looked at the ceiling—narrow and thoughtful. "You really think," he drawled presently, "that you've punctured the great Dain curse?"

"That's what."

"No," he said. "I am a Dain—on my mother's side. She and Gabrielle's maternal grandfather were brother and sister. I insist on the curse. It's going to help save my very dear neck." He squirmed in bed, and his one eye and the one visible side of his mouth smiled together at me—a twisted fraction of humorous triumph.

"You're going to see a most remarkable defense, my son," he went on; "one that will make the papers go into happy convulsions. I promise you that. I'm a Dain, with that cursed blood in me; and the crimes of Cousin Alice and Cousin Lily and Second-cousin Gabrielle, and of the Lord knows how many other criminal Dains, will be evidence in my behalf. The very number of my own crimes will be all to my advantage—nobody but a lunatic could have committed so many and they shall be many. I'll produce crimes and crimes, starting as soon after the date of my birth as will seem reasonable.

"Then there are my books. Didn't most reviewers agree that *The Pale Egyptian* was clearly the work of a sub-Mongolian; and didn't at least one critic insist that the author of *Eighteen Inches* showed every sign of degeneracy? Evidence, my son, to save my sweet neck. And then I shall wave my mangled body at them—an arm gone, a leg gone, part of my torso and of my face—a ruin whose crimes—or perhaps high Heaven—has surely brought sufficient punishment upon him. And the shock, perhaps, has cured me of my criminal tendencies. Perhaps I'll become religious. It'll be splendid. I may wind up with a statue erected to me in Golden Gate Park. Perhaps not—but my neck shall be saved."

"You'll probably make a go of it," I said. "I'm satisfied. You've paid something—and legally you're entitled to beat the jump if anybody ever was."

"Legally entitled?" he repeated, mirth going out of his gray eye. He looked away, and then back to me. "Tell me the truth—am I?"

I nodded.

"But damn it," he complained, fighting to recover his usual lazy, amused manner, and not making such a bad job of it, "that spoils it. It's no fun if I'm really cracked."

When I got back to the house in the cove, Mickey and MacMan were sprawled on the front steps, smoking. They looked more comfortable than they had been for several days, so I imagined Gabrielle had had a good afternoon.

"Bring any fresh woman-scars back with you?" Mickey asked. "Your little playmate's been asking for you."

Gabrielle was propped up on pillows in her bed, her face still—or again—powdered, her eyes shining happily.

"I didn't mean you were to go away forever," she scolded. "It was a nasty thing to do. I've got a surprise for you and I've nearly burst waiting. Shut your eyes."

I shut them.

"Open your eyes."

I opened them. She was holding out to me the eight bindles Mary had stolen from my pocket.

"I've had them since noon," she said proudly, "and they've got fingermarks and tearmarks on them, but not one has been opened. It—honestly—it wasn't so hard not to."

"I knew it wouldn't be—for you," I said. "That's why I didn't take them away from Mary."

"You knew? You trusted me that much—to go away and leave me with them?"

It would have been idiotic to have confessed that for two days the folded papers had held powdered sugar instead of the original morphine, so I only nodded.

"You're the nicest man in the world." She caught one of my hands and rubbed her cheek into it; then dropped it quickly, frowned her face all out of shape, and said: "Except! You sat there this noon and deliberately tried to make me think you were in love with me."

"Well?" I asked, trying to keep my face straight.

She laughed at me and said:

"You hypocrite. You deceiver of young girls. It would serve you right if I made you marry me, or sued you for breach of promise. I honestly believed you all afternoon—and it did help me. I believed you till you came in just now, and then I saw—" She stopped.

"Saw what?"

"A monster—a nice one, the sort to have around when you're in trouble—but an inhuman monster, just the same, without any foolishness like love in him."

I said:

"Don't be silly. I'd change places with Fitzstephan now—if Aaronia Haldorn was part of the bargain."

VI

Two days later the newspapers blossomed out with Owen Fitzstephan's confession. He had made a high, wide and handsome job of it. Throwing out the decorations, the fictitious parts, and those that didn't have anything to do with us, something like this remained:

He had organized the Haldorns' cult and had come to San Francisco with them. Joseph Haldorn was only a puppet—in the Haldorn family as well as in the Temple. Fitzstephan's connection with them was kept secret, everybody who knew him knew he was a skeptic, and for him to have openly shown his connection would have been to advertise the cult as a fake. Aaronia was Fitzstephan's mistress. He knew his cousin Alice—Gabrielle's step-mother—was in San Francisco, and he had heard through family channels some of the Leggett history. He located her and became intimate with the family, though neither he nor Alice said anything about their relationship. He claimed that Alice became his mistress, too, but that might have been untrue.

He tried his luck with Gabrielle, and the sort of turn-down she gave him made him doubly determined to land her. He was that sort. He managed to get the Haldorns introduced to the Leggetts and had them work on her. When Upton and Ruppert tried to shake Alice down for blackmail, she took her troubles to Fitzstephan and asked his advice. Whether through spite against Gabrielle—a desire to hurt her—or through a desire to turn the Leggett affairs inside out and learn all that he did not yet know, or through pure malice—being a Dain—Fitzstephan deliberately misled Alice, giving her advice that was sure to ruin her and all the family—as it did. He had to kill her in the end; she would have turned against him when she saw what he had done.

Fitzstephan's success there encouraged him to go on with his plans to get the girl, and made them seem more likely to be successful. The Haldorns now had no difficulty in getting her to come to the Temple. They thought his interest in her was purely financial. They didn't know what he had done to the Leggetts. But Dr Riese stumbled on the truth of his connection with the Temple. That was dangerous for Fitzstephan—it might lead to the truth about the Leggett trouble. Fitzstephan had had a taste of successful murder. He had two easily handled tools—Joseph and Minnie. He had Riese killed. Then Aaronia woke up—discovered that Fitzstephan's interest in Gabrielle wasn't purely financial. Aaronia could and would either make him give up the girl or ruin him. He persuaded her husband that *his* life also depended on Aaronia's death. I had spoiled that, killing Haldorn, and that had seemed to save Fitzstephan for the time—Aaronia and Fink had to keep quiet to save themselves.

By this time, Fitzstephan looked on Gabrielle as his property, bought and paid for by the killing he had done. Each death had increased her value to him, in his eyes. When Eric Collinson had married her, Fitzstephan hadn't hesitated. Collinson must be removed, and he knew who he could hire to do it. He had offered Whidden a thousand dollars. Whidden refused at first, but he wasn't nimble-witted and Fitzstephan was eloquent enough. Whidden had fortified himself with whiskey for the job; and when he had finally done it, he called Fitzstephan on the phone and boasted: "Well, I killed him easy enough and dead enough. Where's my money?"

Fitzstephan's phone came through the apartment house switchboard. He didn't know who might have heard Whidden. He pretended he didn't know who was talking, what was being said, or what it was all about. Thinking he has been double-crossed, and knowing what Fitzstephan wanted, Whidden wrote him a note saying he was taking the girl and holding her for ten thousand dollars. Then he went back to Quesada and got the girl. He had enough drunken cunning to disguise his handwriting, not to sign his name, and to word the note so that Fitzstephan could not tell the police who had sent it without explaining how he knew who had sent it.

Fitzstephan wasn't sitting any too pretty. As soon as he had angled an excuse for coming to Quesada out of me, he came down—some hours ahead of time—and went to the marshal's house to ask Mrs Cotton—Whidden's mistress—if she knew where Whidden was. Whidden was there at the time. Fitzstephan talked him into something again, explaining everything to Whidden's satisfaction, and assuring him that now everything could be handled so Whidden would get his ten thousand dollars in safety. Whidden went back to his hiding place at daylight. Fitzstephan remained with Mrs Cotton. She knew too much, and she didn't like what she knew. She was doomed. He had murdered people before, to keep them quiet, and he knew it always worked. If he could get her to leave a signed statement behind, that would help a lot. He got her to do it, but it took him till late in the morning—she suspected what he was up to. His description of how he finally got it wasn't pleasant, but he got it, and then strangled her, barely finishing the job when her husband came home.

Fitzstephan escaped by the back door and joined me and the others at the hotel. He went with us to Whidden's hiding place. He knew Whidden, knew how Whidden would react to this second double-crossing, knew that the sheriff would welcome an excuse to shoot Whidden, and so would Cotton. If neither of them did, he had decided to jump out of the boat with a pistol in his hand, stumble, and shoot Whidden accidentally. He might have been blamed for that—but hardly convicted. Luck was with him. Whidden, seeing him with us, had gone crazy, tried to shoot him, and we had had to kill Whidden.

Fink's bomb had been a small cubical one wrapped in white paper. Fitzstephan had thought it something Aaronia had sent to him, something important enough to risk that sort of sending. He couldn't have refused to take it without opening my eyes, anyway, so he had concealed it until Fink and I left the room. Then he had unwrapped it—and knew nothing else till he came to in the hospital.

Owen Fitzstephan put on the promised show in the court room, and the newspapers went into the happy convulsions he had predicted, and he saved his dear neck. Afterward, Aaronia Haldorn took him away—up in the mountains, I've heard.

Gabrielle topped off her cure with a couple of months in a sanatorium. I've seen her now and then since, usually with a big-shouldered youngster fresh from somebody's college not more than a foot or two from her. Whatever kind of an effect she has on him they both seem to like it.

A fan of Sherlock Holmes?
Then meet Solar Pons

The original fan fiction from the great August Derleth—the Sherlock Holmes of Praed Street.

"the best substitutes for Sherlock Holmes known."
– Vincent Starrett

"an excellent series of adventures in detection in their own right." – *The Chicago Tribune*

For more details and a full list of titles:
visit https://www.hachetteindia.com/home/yellowbacks

Yellowback range available...

1. The Old Man in the Corner by Orczy, Baroness Emma
2. The Complete Max Carrados Vol 1 by Bramah, Ernest
3. The Complete Max Carrados Vol 2 by Bramah, Ernest

THE ARSÈNE LUPIN SERIES BY LEBLANC, MAURICE:

4. Arsène Lupin 1: The Extraordinary Adventures of Arsène Lupin - Gentleman Burglar
5. Arsène Lupin 2: Arsène Lupin vs. Herlock Sholmes
6. Arsène Lupin 3. The Hollow Needle
7. Arsène Lupin 4: 813
8. Arsène Lupin 5: The Crystal Stopper
9. Arsène Lupin 6: The Confessions of Arsène Lupin
10. Arsène Lupin 7: The Teeth of the Tiger
11. Arsène Lupin 8: The Shell Shard (aka The Woman of Mystery)
12. Arsène Lupin 9: The Return of Arsène Lupin (aka The Golden Triangle)
13. Arsène Lupin 10: The secret of Sarek (aka Island of Thirty Coffins)
14. Arsène Lupin 11: The Eight Strokes of the Clock
15. Arsène Lupin 12: The Secret Tomb
16. Arsène Lupin 13: The Countess of Cagliostro (aka Memoirs of Arsène Lupin)
17. Arsène Lupin (bonus book): Arsène Lupin (novelised by Edgar Jepson from LeBlanc's original play)

18. The Complete Raffles by Hornung, E. W.
19. The Mysterious Mickey Finn by Paul, Eliott
20. You Play the Black and the Red Comes Up by Hallas, Richard
21. The Mr. Moto Omnibus Vol 1 by Marquand, John P.
22. The Mr. Moto Omnibus Vol 2 by Marquand, John P.
23. The Complete Father Brown Vol 1 (with original illustrations) by Chesterton, G. K.
24. The Complete Father Brown Vol 2 (with original illustrations) by Chesterton, G. K.
25. A Peter Wimsey omnibus: Murder Must Advertise & The Nine Tailors by Sayers, Dorothy L.
26. Was it Murder? by Hilton, James
27. The Complete Just Men Volume 1 by Wallace, Edgar
28. The Complete Just Men Volume 2 by Wallace, Edgar
29. Carnacki by Hodgson, William Hope
30. Grey Mask by Wentworth, Patricia
31. The Case With Nine Solutions by Connington, J. J.
32. Murder by Matchlight by Lorac, E. C. R.
33. The Crossword Mystery by Punshon, E. R.
34. The Cask by Crofts, Freeman Wills
35. The Bells of Old Bailey by Bowers, Dorothy
36. Crime Unlimited by Hume, David
37. The A. A. Milne Mystery Omnibus (contains: The Red house and Four days' wonder) by Milne, A. A.
38. She Faded into Air by White, Ethel Lina
39. The Wheel Spins by White, Ethel Lina
40. The Spiral Staircase by White, Ethel Lina
41. Murder of a Lady by Wynne, Anthony
42. Thirteen Guests by Farjeon, J. Jefferson
43. The Daughter of Time by Tey, Josephine
44. The Man in the Queue by Tey, Josephine
45. A Shilling for Candles by Tey, Josephine
46. The Franchise Affair by Tey, Josephine
47. Tragedy at Law by Hare, Cyril
48. The Moonstone by Collins, Wilkie
49. The Woman in White by Collins, Wilkie
50. The Circular Staircase by Rinehart, Mary Roberts
51. The Benson Murder Case by Van Dine, S. S.
52. The Philip Marlowe Omnibus by Chandler, Raymond
53. Monsieur Lecoq by Gaboriau, Emile
54. Aurora Floyd by Braddon, Mary Elizabeth
55. The Big Bow Mystery by Zangwill, Israel
56. Dossier 113 (aka The Blackmailers) by Gaboriau, Emile
57. The Mystery of a Hansom Cab by Hume, Fergus
58. The W Plan by Seton, Graham
59. Inspector French's Greatest Case by Crofts, Freeman Wills

60. Mr Bowling Buys a Newspaper by Henderson, Donald
61. A Voice Like Velvet by Henderson, Donald
62. The Deductions of Colonel Gore by Brock, Lynn
63. The Rogue's Syndicate by Froest, Frank
64. The Middle Temple Murder by Fletcher, J. S.
65. The Millionaire Mystery by Hume, Fergus
66. Below the Clock by Turner, J. V.
67. The Rouletabille Omnibus: The Mystery of the Yellow Room and The Perfume of the Lady in Black by Leroux, Gaston
68. The Complete Dupin by Poe, Edgar Allan
69. The Complete Thinking Machine Vol 1 by Futrelle, Jacques
70. The Complete Thinking Machine Vol 2 by Futrelle, Jacques
71. The Complete Thinking Machine Vol 3 by Futrelle, Jacques
72. The Complete Montague Egg by Sayers, Dorothy L.
73. The Complete J. G. Reeder by Wallace, Edgar
74. The Complete Charlie Chan Vol 1 by Biggers, Earl der
75. The Complete Charlie Chan Vol 2 by Biggers, Earl der
76. The Dr Nikola Omnibus Vol 1 by Boothby, Guy
77. The Dr Nikola Omnibus Vol 2 by Boothby, Guy
78. A Prince of Swindlers: The Simon Carne collection by Boothby, Guy
79. The Slim Callaghan Omnibus by Cheyney, Peter
80. The Fu Manchu Omnibus by Rohmer, Sax
81. The Bulldog Drummond Omnibus: The Complete Peterson Rounds by Sapper
82. The Avenging Ray by Seamark
83. The Richard Chandos Omnibus by Yates, Dornford
84. The Alan Quatermain Omnibus: King Solomon's Mines & Allan Quatermain by Haggard, H. Rider
85. The 39 steps by Buchan, John
86. At The Villa Rose by Mason, A.E.W.
87. The Eye of Osiris by Freeman, R. Austin
88. The Weapons of Mystery by Hocking, Joseph
89. The House of Dr. Edwardes by Beeding, Francis
90. The Seven Secrets by Le Queux, William
91. Call Mr Fortune by Bailey, H. C.
92. The Three Taps by Knox, Ronald
93. The Girl at Central by Bonner, Geraldine
94. The Experiences of Loveday Brooke, Lady Detective by Pirkis, Catherine Louisa
95. Mary Louise by Baum, L. Frank
96. That Affair Next Door by Green, Anna Katherine
97. Dead Letter by Regester, Seeley
98. The Tragedy of Pudd'nhead Wilson by Twain, Mark
99. The Big Clock by Fearing, Kenneth
100. The Woman in the Window by Wallis, J. H.
101. The Sexton Blake Collection Vol 1 by Hal Meredeth (or many?)
102. The Complete Simon Iff Stories by Crowley, Aleister
103. The Castle of Otranto by Walpole, Horace
104. The Adventures of the Infallible Godahl by Anderson, Frederick Irving

THE COMPLETE SHERLOCK HOLMES

105. A Study In Scarlet
106. The Sign Of Four
107. The Adventures Of Sherlock Holmes
108. The Memoirs Of Sherlock Holmes
109. The Hound Of The Baskervilles
110. The Return Of Sherlock Holmes
111. His Last Bow
112. The Valley Of Fear
113. The Case-Book Of Sherlock Holmes

114. Graustark: The Story of a Love Behind a Throne by George Barr McCutcheon
115. Beverly of Graustark by George Barr McCutcheon
116. Truxton King: A Story of Graustark by George Barr McCutcheon
117. The Prince of Graustark by George Barr McCutcheon
118. The Complete Zenda Omnibus by Anthony Hope
119. The Mad king by Burroughs, Edgar Rice
120. The Fantomas Omnibus by Souvestre, Pierre

121. The Problemist by Clinton H. Stagg
122. The Dorrington Deed-Box by Morrison, Arthur
123. The Lone Wolf by Vance, L. J.
124. The Complete Martin Hewitt Collection Vol 1: Martin Hewitt, Investigator & Chronicles of Martin Hewitt by Morrison, Arthur
125. The Complete Martin Hewitt Collection Vol 2: Adventures of Martin Hewitt & The Red Triangle: Further Chronicles of Martin Hewitt by Morrison, Arthur
126. Seven Keys to Baldpate by Earl Derr Biggers
127. No Pockets in a Shroud by McCoy, Horace
128. The John Silence Collection by Blackwood, Algernon
129. Lady Molly Of Scotland Yard by Orczy, Baroness Emma
130. Skin O' My Tooth by Orczy, Baroness Emma
131. The Wrong Box by Stevenson, R. L. and Lloyd Osbourne
132. Tutt and Mr Tutt by Train, Arthur C.
133. The Clue by Wells, Carolyn
134. The Complete Trent Case Book by Bentley, E. C.
135. The Luck of the Vails by Benson, E. F.
136. The Rome Express by Griffiths, Arthur
137. The Complete Curious Mr Tarrant by C. Daly King
138. Rope and Gaslight (2-in-1 text) by Hamilton, Patrick
139. Prince Zaleski and Cumming's King Monk by Shiel, M. P.
140. The Assassination Bureau Ltd. by London, Jack
141. Introducing Clubfoot by Williams, Valentine
142. Master of Mysteries: The complete Uncle Abner collection by Post, Melville Davisson
143. The Red Redmaynes by Phillpotts, Eden
144. Thrilling Stories of the Railway by Whitechurch, Victor L.
145. The Grey Wig: Stories and Novelettes by Zangwill, Israel
146. The Lodger by Lowndes, Marie Belloc
147. The Man from Manchester by Donovan, Dick (Joyce Emerson Preston Muddock)
148. Mr. Meeson's Will by H. Rider Haggard by Haggard, H. Rider
149. Devlin the Barber by Farjeon, B. L.
150. Checkmate by Joseph Sheridan Le Fanu
151. Recollections of a Detective Police-Officer by Waters
152. The Widow Lerouge by Gaboriau, Emile
153. The Expressman and the Detective by Pinkerton, Allan
154. Zadig and Vathek by Voltaire
155. The Stillwater Tragedy by Aldrich, Thomas Bailey
156. The Memoirs of Constantine Dix by Pain, Barry
157. Ashes to Ashes by Ostrander, Isabel
158. The Jewel of Seven Stars by Stoker, Bram
159. The Thomas Love Peacock Collection by Peacock, Thomas Love

THE COMPLETE DERLETH SOLAR PONS

160. In Re: Sherlock Holmes - The Adventures of Solar Pons
161. The Memoirs of Solar Pons
162. The Return of Solar Pons
163. The Reminiscences of Solar Pons
164. The Casebook of Solar Pons
165. The Novels of Solar Pons: Terror over London and Mr. Fairlie's Final Journey
166. The Chronicles of Solar Pons
167. The Apocrypha of Solar Pons

168. The Triumphs of Eugene Valmont
169. The Female Detective by Forrester, Andrew
170. Cain's Jawbone by Torquemada
171. The Great Impersonation by Oppenheim, E. Phillips

THE DASHIELL HAMMETT COLLECTION

172. The Complete Sam Spade
173. The Complete Thin Man
174. The Complete Continental Op Vol 1
175. The Complete Continental Op Vol 2